THE BEST OF JAMES VAN PELT

FAIRWOOD PRESS
Bonney Lake, WA

THE BEST OF JAMES VAN PELT

A Fairwood Press Book

August 2022

Copyright © 2020 James Van Pelt

Fairwood Press

21528 104th Street Court East

Bonney Lake, WA 98391

www.fairwoodpress.com

Cover image © Gabriel Gajdoš

Cover and book design by Patrick Swenson

The stories in this book have been arranged in their original publication order,
with just a few exceptions. In addition to original publications and reprints
(see Publication History), these stories (except for those previously uncollected)
were published in the following James Van Pelt collections:

Strangers and Beggars (2002)

The Last of the O-Forms (2005)

The Radio Magician (2009)

Flying in the Heart of the Lafayette Escadrille (2012)

The Experience Arcade (2017)

ISBN: 978-1-933846-21-7

First Fairwood Press Edition: November 2020

First Fairwood Press trade paperback: August 2022

Printed in the United States of America

Praise for James Van Pelt &
THE BEST OF JAMES VAN PELT

"Van Pelt showcases his mastery of short-form fiction in these 62 stories, all published between 1993 and 2018 and ranging from apocalyptic fiction to subtle daylight horror, Lovecraftian riffs, and speculation about future social policy initiatives. . . .Van Pelt's superior combination of imaginative concepts with recognizable human emotions makes him a talent deserving of a wide readership."

—*Publishers Weekly*, starred review

"Nobody does aspiration better than Van Pelt. His characters are fighters: to make a human connection, to go to the stars as a space cadet, to understand a high school plagued by nineteenth-century gunslingers, to conquer loneliness. These stories are rich in diverse settings—suburbia, a plant nursery with horrific vegetation, the trenches of Verdun, an automotive hell (literally). In all places and times, with all characters, Van Pelt superbly illuminates the best that is in us."

—Nancy Kress, author of *Sea Change*

"In a genre like science fiction, when nearly every story is filled with incredible worlds, amazing science, and mind-blowing ideas, what does it take to stand out? It takes one of the hardest things to find in real life, too: heart. More than just those worlds and ideas and science, that's what James Van Pelt excels at: his characters, whether human or not, are people who live and die, love and cry, in ways that remind us of ourselves."

—Trevor Quachri, editor of *Analog Magazine*

"James Van Pelt is an astute observer of the human condition. He can skillfully and compassionately evoke the extraordinary in seemingly ordinary situations. James convinces us to care deeply about the fate of his compelling characters—whether they are mutated creatures, ice cream salesmen, or classroom teachers."

—Sheila Williams, editor of *Asimov's Magazine*

"What a delicious treat! James Van Pelt is a terrific storyteller. Buy this book. Read. Enjoy."

—David Gerrold, author of *Hella*

"Jim Van Pelt is one of those rare writers who swoop effortlessly across the landscape of the fantastic. I read him with admiration and envy."

—James Patrick Kelly, Hugo, Nebula & Locus Winner

"James Van Pelt is a master of the short story . . . Whether writing science fiction, fantasy, horror, or stories that fall between the categories, he can take the most commonplace topics—running, tourism, family life—and make them profound. If Van Pelt's stories don't move you, you have no heart."

—Carrie Vaughn, author of *Bannerless*

THE BEST OF JAMES VAN PELT

Also by James Van Pelt

*To every writing teacher who understood enough
to use student work as examples in class.*

TABLE OF CONTENTS

HUMANITY SERVED UP IN A BUFFET OF STORY

by

KEN SCHOLES

O NE OF MY FAVORITE PARTS ABOUT BEING A WRITER IS THE OTHER WRITERS I've met along that path, and one of the highest honors I'm ever paid is when I'm asked to introduce a writer's work to the world. So imagine my delight when Jim asked me if I would introduce *The Best of James Van Pelt*, bringing together the very best of nearly three decades of his published work.

Now, I see these books scattered throughout my popular library of around 6,000 volumes. Most are second-hand hardcover Science Fiction Book Club editions. Best ofs bringing together around 20 or so of the very best of all those giants we all read growing up in the genre. I was pretty excited to see what this book by my friend would look like and I was ambushed by it in the best of ways. This is no slender volume of a few of his best, lifted from his six collections. No, my first file for this showed it coming in at around 800 pages. This is a big chewy book full of wonder and life in motion and I am pleased to introduce it—and its author—to you.

I'm going to talk a bit about the writer and then I'll talk a bit about his work.

Jim Van Pelt will tell you he's essentially lazy.

Because of this fact, he says, he's written 200 words per day, every day, without exception, since September 1999. (I've reached out to Merriam-Webster to suggest updating their definition of lazy.) At about a page a day, every day, that will lead to a lot of pages and still leave plenty of time for a career in education, teaching high school students how to tell stories of their own.

I first became aware of him and his stories back in 1997 or 1998. I was reading through contributor copies while submitting my own short stories in the mail and ran across some of his earliest sales. He was one of the writers I was reading and learning from as I made my path. I remember running across "Plant Life" and "Miss Hathaway's Spider" before making my first sale in 1999 and being impressed enough to send him a note. When my first short story came out in *Talebones'* Winter 2000 issue, we shared our first of many tables of contents. Then, in 2001, when my story about the walking bear came out, Jim dropped me a note, and we became more regular correspondents. He was one of the first pro writers I looked to—and became friends with—on my own journey into print. In 2006, when his first novel *Summer of the Apocalypse* came out alongside my first standalone project, *Last Flight of the Goddess*, we finally met in real life and signed books together for Fairwood Press. Later, in 2008 when I had finally sold enough short stories of my own to merit a Fairwood Press collection, Jim did me the honor of introducing my work to the world. Being asked now to write this is a wonderful closing to a beautiful circle in my professional life.

Over the years, I've watched Jim's work roll down from Colorado, a steady river of story. I have no idea what his first decade yielded before laziness required a change, but at 200 words a day, 365 days per year, for twenty one years . . . that is a lot of story. All written about a page at a time while working as a school teacher, filling young minds with the words that sparked his own. You're holding quite a bucket full—the best so far—and I can tell you that it springs from just three ingredients: one portion of Hard and Constant Work, one portion of that Curiosity Driven Wonderment Lens through which artists Bend Their Lives into Story, and one part Living a Life Out In The World Open Enough to see Story Unfolding Everywhere in Everything and Everyone Around You.

You'll see how well Jim did in these pages. As I wandered through, I saw slices of humanity served up in a buffet of story, seasoned with honesty and hope. I saw hard questions raised from the dead matter of our darker impulses, and I saw language unfolding—well chosen and lovely words that march to the cadence of life.

When I traced my trail back to those earliest stories I remembered, I was pleased to discover the same chills showing up in the two I mentioned earlier. Jim's career spent in the classroom yielded quite an imaginative crop of stories beyond that spider no one wanted to deal with: a cascade of stories only an educator caught up in the U.S. education system and twisted slightly in a speculative manner could conceive. He shows us human desperation in "The Last of the O-Forms" and human invention in "Of Late I Dreamt Of Venus," both in language reminiscent of our patron saint, Bradbury. The best of thirty or so years harvesting stories from his imagination.

Along the way, the work has picked up the nods one would expect from Jim's steady pace of production. Collections of short stories garnering awards like the ALA's Best Book for Young Adults and The Colorado Book Award. Individual stories picked up like gems for our industry's Year's Best anthologies or listed as honorable mentions. Again, at 200 words a day, along with the will to write, you land a good bit of practice.

One of the big connecting points for Jim and me is that we both share the same inspiration in Ray Bradbury, who we both cite as our largest influence in bringing us to writing. Bradbury played at his work with great delight, and a sense of wonder deeply grounded in the human experience inspired so many of us. There are 24 stories in this collection inspired by Jim's Bradbury Challenge of one story per week for 52 weeks straight back in 2016. Those alone would be worth their very own collection. [And they were! In Van Pelt's *The Experience Arcade.* --ed.] So you are getting quite a bargain here, Constant Reader.

One day soon, I'll have *The Best of James Van Pelt* up on my shelf with the other "Best ofs" I've picked up during the decades of loving and collecting speculative fiction. This volume will take a place of honor and be full of places to visit from my friend Jim's heart, reminding me what it means to be human, to face fear, to find love, to solve problems, to experience . . . life.

I am over the moon with how tickled I am to introduce Jim's mightiest collection yet to you.

Ken Scholes
Cornelius Oregon
August 2020

THE BEST OF JAMES VAN PELT

PARALLEL HIGHWAYS

THE SEMI-TRAILER TRUCK'S REAR TIRES RUMBLED A YARD FROM JACK'S window. A faded sign in red, HORIZON TRANSIT, in giant letters, decorated the trailer. In the rear mirror, another eighteen-wheeler's grill loomed just off the bumper, and in the right lane a line of cars slid by, no more that a half a dozen feet between them.

White-knuckled, Jack gripped the wheel. Backwash from the semi rattled his little car, and he fought the tug that pulled him toward the tires spinning to his left. Blurred at the tip, the speedometer needle hung just beyond 80 miles per hour.

"He's coming over," said Debbie. Her voice cracked. From the corner of his eye, Jack could see she'd balled a handful of skirt into her fist. She sucked in a breath as if she were about to scream, but instead she murmured, "He's coming."

"I can see," he snapped.

The semi's trailer of ribbed aluminum, rivet-studded and coated with dust, crossed the line, narrowing the space. In the truck's mirror, dark glasses hid the driver's eyes, but he seemed to be looking right at them.

Jack whipped a glance over his shoulder. The other semi behind them had moved up, now nearly touching their bumper. No break in the line of traffic to his right, but he signaled anyway, stomped on the accelerator and slid over, hoping for a gap. Traffic behind him stretched in a domino row of glaring windshields, and he realized no one was going to let him in. They *couldn't* let him in.

Inexorably, the truck closed the distance, squeezing the lane.

"Oh, no," Debbie moaned.

"I've got it," Jack said. "I've got it."

He dumped into fourth gear, winding the car's little engine into the top of its RPMs; it jumped forward. They passed the trailer's front wheels. A woman in a beat-up station wagon on their right leaned on her horn, flipping them off, but she moved over a bit, and so did the Volkswagen in front of her.

Jack scooted close to them, crossing the lane stripes, passing the station wagon, the semi's wheels roaring in his ear. He juked the car right, bumping the Volkswagen; metal crunched, and Debbie fell against him, her chest heaving, her arm slippery with sweat.

The face in the Volkswagen contorted in anger and fear.

Better you than me, Jack thought. Although his car was small, he knew the Volkswagen didn't have any weight at all. If he had to, he could force himself into its spot in the traffic.

Now, horns all around them blared. Traffic in front of them rippled. Tail lights flashed. A pickup that had been blocking the Volkswagen cut left in front of the semi, and its air horn erupted, but now there was space to the right.

Sobbing, Jack pulled in front of the Volkswagen, clipping its bumper on the way, and another opening appeared on his right, which he took.

Two lanes separated them from the trailer-truck, now bombing along as if nothing had happened. Jack pried a hand loose from the steering wheel and wiped his mouth. His chin was slick.

He checked the mirrors. As far back as he could see, traffic. The highway faded into the blue distance. Same in front. One more lane over, a cement retainer separated them from the city, a numbing series of dirty, gray warehouses.

He took deep breaths, letting himself calm down.

"Missed us that time," he said, and he tried to laugh, but it came out tight and fake, like it felt.

Debbie sat up straight, smoothing her skirt over her legs. She looked out the side window, pressing her hand against it. Long brunette hair with just a hint of a curl at the end brushed her shoulders. Her face reflected a little in the glass. Deep, brown eyes. No makeup. A serious woman carrying despair in the lines of her frown.

Beyond, building after shadowless building rolled by. The sun stood exactly overhead, but smog or mist fuzzed away its outlines, so the sky glared hot, white and without form.

"We should have let that car in," she said.

"Which?" He knew what she was talking about. It was an old argument.

"We shouldn't have been in such a hurry."

Jack checked the mirrors again, then closed the distance between him and the next car to get the guy following him off his tail.

She said, "I don't recognize anything."

"I know."

"It could be L.A." She looked at him without moving her hand, her eyes so tired that they appeared as if they'd been punched.

"Or Pompeii."

"That's not funny."

"It's a superhighway from somewhere. Just as well could be Pompeii. Or maybe Rome, just before Nero burnt the sucker."

"Stop it."

"Do you think there was a freeway between Sodom and Gomorrah?" He laughed a little easier this time but bitter.

"Sodom and Gomorrah," she said, "L.A. What's the difference?"

If it were L.A., we might be able to get off. Merge lane," he said. Whatever the junction was, a spray-painted white hand obscured the name. "Should we take it?"

"I thought that was Anaheim we passed yesterday," she said wistfully. "I always liked Disneyland."

"I'm taking it."

Jack scanned his left, tapped the brakes and eased into a space between a Bronco with tinted windows and a guy on a motorcycle. The cyclist's head wove back and forth as if he were listening to a private symphony. Hair spilled out beneath his faded bandanna and streamed in the wind. Ahead of them, taillights blinked and cars jockeyed for position.

Traffic split, and Jack followed the curve of the road beneath an overpass. A green highway sign said, *Carmilhan—76 miles*. Within a few minutes, the warehouses disappeared, replaced by desert and twisted Joshua trees streaking by behind the concrete retainer.

Jack sighed. Highway reached before him straight to the horizon as unwavering as a knife edge. Here, the cars spaced themselves a bit. Twenty to thirty feet between them, but the asphalt still whined under the wheels at a steady 80 miles per hour. He laid his head back and stared at the ceiling for a second, then blinked hard and rubbed his hand across his eyes.

"I'm exhausted. Can you handle it for awhile?"

Debbie nodded, moving next to him, onto the emergency brake. She put a hand on the wheel and arched up as he slid underneath her, the back of her blouse wet with perspiration. Now, almost sprawled across the seat, the brake's handle digging into his back, he kept a foot on the accelerator. She stepped over his legs, careful to keep from turning the car with her hip as she dropped into his place.

"What should we do at the next junction?" she said.

Jack reached into the tiny backseat for a jacket, folded it over several times, then wedged it into the corner between the top of the seat and the doorjamb. He rested his head on it and closed his eyes. Humming wheels whipping over road whispered against his cheek. "It doesn't matter," he said. "Go where you want."

Speed varied as Debbie adjusted for the traffic. Air rushed past the window, whistling a little in some crack he'd never been able to find. After a while he drifted into a kind of false sleep, not quite dreaming, not quite aware of where he was, and he felt like he was floating. Then he said, or thought he said, or maybe even imagined he said, "How come all roads lead everywhere, but you can't get there from here?"

Debbie didn't answer, so he let the car's motion lull him further. He thought about treetops waving back and forth and a time when he rested beneath them, watching diamonds of sun coming through the leaves. All he wanted was to sleep and to wake up there—to wake up anywhere other than on the highway—not to be pounding out the miles and watching the bumper in front of him. Jack wanted to sleep and to wake up and to sleep again far away from the roads and horns. Far away from the zombie motion of driving the car.

He lurched, bouncing his forehead against the glass. No telling how long he'd been asleep. It didn't feel long. He squinted against the pain, then peeked over at Debbie. Her chin was down, eyes closed; her hands loose on the wheel.

Too late, he jolted upright, reaching for her. Concrete whizzed inches from the side window. Metal screeched. Sparks fired from the front of the car. Debbie shot up. Overcorrected.

The world keeled over and slowed as the car went sideways and rolled. Jack floated to the ceiling as it crumpled toward him. Glass shattered into the passenger compartment. His arm broke first, a wet snap above the elbow, then his shoulder. Then he hit the ceiling. And last, as the car rolled, he saw through a red veil the semi bearing down, an avalanche of metal and momentum.

Jack's consciousness surfaced in the half-death in a white flash of agony, and through the shock he thought, pain slows time. Agonizing second after second. He thought, terminal cancer victims must hear clocks in their blood slowing down. Any minute and every minute an infinite reach. Unstoppable and dispassionate. Waves lapping against the sand. Everyone like the first; none the last. All bones crushed. All flesh mangled. Pain living forever. All of it over and over again. For infinite time, his bones broke one after another, and like Prometheus, without healing and without cessation, the bones broke again. He had no way to tell, nothing to measure it against, but the crash seemed to replay for a thousand years.

I'm sorry, Jack." Debbie held the wheel in one hand and touched herself with the other. First, her face, then across her chest and onto her leg. "Oh, God, I'm sorry."

They passed under another sign, *Carmilhan—8 miles/Alice Mar—104 mile/Titanic—156 miles*. On the dunes beyond the cement retainer, isolated Joshua trees spaced themselves between long patches of bare sand. Each like a mutant sentinel, holding mutant limbs to the brilliance of the white sky.

Jack felt his own arms, stretched his back. Nothing broken. Nothing even sore. "It's inevitable," he said. "It's not your fault. We're bound to get tired."

She shook. Her hands trembled on the steering wheel. "I can't do that again. It's not fair that I should have to do that again."

Cars bunched up in front of them, closing the distances. Looking in the mirror, Debbie switched lanes, away from the congestion. In a minute, they passed a four-vehicle pile-up, two cars, a cement mixer and a bread truck. Broken glass crunched under their tires as they went by. Debbie looked away.

"Dying's the best rest I get," said Jack. "It's a silver lining."

"I don't know why we get sleepy. We don't eat. We don't go to the bathroom. The stupid car never needs gas!" Debbie said, her voice on the edge. "You know what else? I don't see enough accidents. If everybody's like us, then there ought to be accidents constantly. There are people all by themselves in half the cars. Who gives them a rest? But most of the time, traffic's moving. Why is that?"

"Well, if we're logical . . ."

"You're not a scientist anymore! I'm not a student in one of your classes. Nothing's logical about this!" Debbie's lips paled; her face was so tight.

Jack touched her arm. "It's okay. It's just conversation."

She took several shaky breaths, then relaxed. For a second, Jack saw in her face a semblance of his wife the way she was aeons ago, when they climbed in the car and left for the commute. They'd been uptight; they'd argued; they were late; it was her fault; it was his fault. He'd cut into the traffic viciously. Someone beeped at them; then they'd settled into the flow, and she'd relaxed, just for a second, like she did just now.

"Not logic, then," Jack said. "Thinking it through, though. If there are solitary drivers, and they're like us, then they ought to be crashing left and right, but they don't. So they're not like us."

"I guess we know that."

Jack peered into the car beside them, a shiny, blue Lexus. Inside, a man in a business suit stared straight ahead. Lots of commuters looked like him, focused in a kind of catatonic way. Locked on the road, frozen into position as if posing for portraits. Lost in their thoughts, he supposed.

But some of the cars that passed . . . the occupants weren't possible . . . were painful to see. He noticed that Debbie had quit looking long ago. But how often do we really see the people in the other cars on a commute? thought Jack. Maybe the highways had always been like that. Maybe I never paid enough attention. He had a theory that this is the way it had always been: traffic consisted of demons, civilians, newbies and the damned. Sometimes it was mostly civilians: drivers who got on the highway, went somewhere and got off, never knowing what drove beside them. Sometimes it was mostly the damned, like them, who died and lived and kept on driving. Sometime there were newbies: the damned before they died the first time. And then, there were demons. Jack shuddered thinking about the sunglassed face looking back at him in the semi's mirror. That driver had known they were there, but he came over anyway.

Jack said, "We have to sleep, or we'd go insane, and if we were insane, this wouldn't be so bad."

"You're assuming we're being punished."

"It's like the fate of Sisyphus. He pushed that old boulder to the top of the mountain in the Greek underworld, but it wouldn't stay there. So his curse was to walk after the thing and roll it back up. If he only had to roll it up, and he could never stop, he'd never have time to think about his sins, but the rock rolled down, and he'd go after it. The punishment was in the walk down, while he was resting. We've to sleep so we can wake up and realize again what our task is. It's our walk back to the boulder."

"So, are we wimps or heroes?" said Debbie. "Are we resisting our fate or giving in?"

"Well, I guess if this were a movie, we'd be wimps. We're not solving our problems. But in real life sometimes the most heroic thing you can do is stay even and not give up. So we're heroes."

"I don't feel like a hero. I haven't done anything."

Debbie let her hands slip to the bottom of the wheel. She was steering with the tips of her fingers barely draped. Back in the Joshua trees, a black shape moved; Jack only caught a glimpse of it. It was like a bear, but its arms were loose-fleshed, hairless and yellow. It looked up from whatever it was feeding on. Eyes glinted.

"We're not in our world," he said.

"I'm sure that was Anaheim the other day. Maybe we're there part of the time. If we could find our way back."

"One freeway to another. Merge lanes and junctions—there's never an exit."

"I remember the signs: Hermosa Beach and then Long Beach. We were going west on the 91. Maybe these are like parallel universes, except they're parallel highways. Part of the time we cross over. Do you think anybody saw us? Do you think we looked different?"

Debbie drove for three hundred miles before they switched. She rested her head and closed her eyes immediately. Ahead, a line of hills rose out of the desert, and soon he was climbing steadily. Joshua trees gave way to pinion as the road wove higher and higher. Occasionally he passed a camper or heavy truck laboring in the right lane, belching exhaust. A sign read, *Slower traffic keep right: No stopping on the shoulder*. He smirked. They'd tried stopping twice, pulling against the cement retainer, only to watch the following traffic pile into them, as if they were incapable of stopping themselves. The second time they'd burned. A thousand years in the fire.

Once he'd seen a man jump from a car; maybe he was a newbie, desperate to escape the road. The man slowed as much as the flow allowed—maybe fifty miles per hour—then opened his door and rolled out. Jack had been three cars back, and passed him as he slid and tumbled on the asphalt. Craning his head over his shoulder, Jack saw the man, amazingly, stagger to his feet just before a bus creamed him.

No stopping on the shoulder, Jack thought. No kidding.

A road sign read, *Mary Celeste—14 miles*. "That's a phantom ship," he said. Debbie turned on her seat; opened her eyes.

"What?"

"Sign said, Mary Celeste. It's a ship whose crew never made port. They found her floating around, perfectly seaworthy, but no one on board."

"I know about the Celeste," said Debbie, her eyes closed again. "We're more like Vanderdecken."

"Who?"

Debbie covered her face with one hand. Jack couldn't tell if she were crying or not. "Vanderdecken captained *The Flying Dutchman*. During a storm he swore an oath that he'd sail around the Cape of Good Hope or be damned forever."

"What does that have to do with us?" Jack said. He could feel the anger welling inside him. She's always bringing it up, he thought. She can't give it a rest.

"We should have let that car in. You shouldn't have said, 'Damned if I'll let someone cut me off this morning!' They died because of you." Her voice wasn't angry, but it was flat and tired, as if announcing news she'd accepted long ago.

His heart pounded in his ears. She won't leave it alone, he thought. It's always my fault. He remembered the morning this started, holding his own in his lane, the early commute streaming toward its destination, when he saw the mini-van coming toward him from the on-ramp. He'd measured its speed, watched it, and saw that it was going to merge in front of him. He was in a hurry. He was edgy in that special manner that driving in traffic made him. The mini-van approached. Jack would have to give way to let him in. "Damned if I'll let someone cut me off this morning," he'd said, and he smashed the accelerator. For a moment, the mini-van paralleled them, the driver leaning to his left, searching for a break in traffic.

He must not have seen the broken-down car on the shoulder. Jack didn't until the last second, just a glimpse of a jack holding up the driver's side, or a tire lay-ing on the road, of someone on his knees holding a lug wrench. Then the mini-van plowed into the parked car.

Jack pictured the crash. "I don't want to talk about it. I don't even want to think about it anymore." He heard his voice straining.

Debbie didn't say anything. Curves held Jack's attention for a moment. The road had gone to two lanes, and he had to concentrate on driving. Then the hills opened up, and the ocean spread out before them. The highway fell toward the sea. Soon they were driving a road that held close to cliff edges overlooking stony places where waves lapped dully against kelp-encrusted rock. Even through the window, he could smell the salt and rot.

Then Debbie said, "I would have done the same thing, Jack. I wouldn't have let the van in that morning."

Jack remembered the smoke from the accident. As they had driven on, a pillar of smoke had risen behind them, climbing into the sky like an angry spirit, black and red and writhing.

The memory of smoke clear in his mind, he drove on.

They stayed on the costal highway for 3,700 impossible miles before a car coming toward them crossed the lane, catching their side, driving them off the road, over the cliff, tumbling against the rocks for five hundred feet. The last thing Jack heard was water hissing against hot metal. Then the sea rushed into the car.

No one knows about pain but those who are in pain. Only the hurting know what it is. Memory of pain is not pain. Description of pain is not pain. Small hurts are not like great ones reduced. True pain lives in the ever-present moment, expecting nothing, owing to nothing, overwhelming all other thoughts. For a thousand years, Jack tried to scream. Water filled his lungs. Everything was broken, and he was always drowning.

"You were saying?" said Jack, trying to sound as if nothing had happened, as if no time passed, but Debbie didn't answer. For the longest time she kept her face to the window, so that all Jack could see was the back of her head. He turned inland and the junction to Palatine, and soon the lanes multiplied, and they were in city traffic again.

"Our driving record sucks," she said finally. "They should pull our driver's licenses." She started laughing, and it built on itself, an insane-sounding layering of laughter until Jack couldn't tell if she were laughing anymore or shrieking. It scared him. After minutes of this, she quieted down, although every once in a while, she'd chuckle, and Jack was afraid she'd start again.

She said, "You know what I'm thankful for?" She paused a half beat. "That we don't have to pay car insurance anymore. It's just a relief." The chuckle came out of the back of her throat, and she wiped tears from the bottom of her eyes.

Jack drove for twenty hours straight, 1,600 miles before switching. Mostly they passed through baking desert, their air conditioner battling vainly against the heat pouring in; the glare off windshields stabbing his eyes, but every once in a while, buildings would loom up on either side, warehouses, factories, strip malls, and he could read the signs: Aamco, Quiznos, Big O, Winchells, American Furniture Warehouse, Wal-mart. Sometimes he couldn't read the signs; they weren't in any language he recognized. But never an exit, just junctions. Highway leading to highway; concrete bridges twining over, under and around each other, filled with cars streaming end to end.

Their drivers studied the road with the peculiar dead look of the long-distance traveler. In some cases the passengers slept. In some, they read books. Jack saw kids and old folks and dogs, all closed in, all isolated in their 80-miles-per-hour fish bowls. And in some cars, he saw monsters.

Debbie covered almost nine-hundred miles before giving Jack a turn, and he went for 1,300 more. They switched a dozen times, often saying nothing for hundreds of miles; often times both awake, watching the road unreel before them.

A low set of hills shrugged up on the horizon, and soon they wound through dry, grass-covered slopes. For miles, rows of giant windmills lined the hills, their huge, high-tech blades spinning in a wind they couldn't feel in the car. Then they passed the last windmill and other highways joined theirs, adding a lane or two each time. Jack was driving when they rounded a curve and a great city sprawled in the vast valley below. Through the haze, as far as he could see, rooftops and roads, and the traffic drew them in.

Something touched his hand on the emergency brake. He looked down. Debbie's hand rested against his, and he took it, pressing his fingers between hers. They drove into the city, hand in hand.

Debbie scrutinized the buildings as Jack eased from one lane to another, always on the lookout for potential trouble. His back ached; his eyes burned with weariness.

"It's L.A. again," she whispered. "We're on the 10."

"They all look the same," Jack said, but he noticed the palms growing beyond the retaining wall and the manzanita in the median. "I haven't seen a sign."

"I think it's L.A."

"I hope it isn't. I couldn't stand it if we were this close." But he sat up more in his seat, a little less tired.

She squeezed his hand. Malls flowed by and R.V. lots. Trucks filled the road: tankers, movers and the semis. Cars darted like smelt among the shark, moving around their ponderous bulk, giving way, sliding over, clearing a path. In the distance, a series of high rises peeked out of the haze.

"I remember audiobooks," said Debbie. "If you weren't with me, I could start one in the morning and finish it on the way back. I used to think my commute was half a book long."

"I didn't know that. For me, the drive was time to get good thinking done. From Banning to San Bernardino I'd formulate the problem. From there to Pomona, I'd come up with various approaches, and by Pasadena I'd have the day planned out."

The traffic flow varied. Cars slowed and came together for miles, crawling at fifty or sixty miles an hour. Then, without any perceivable reason, they would speed up and spread out. Jack thought of it as "accordion traffic," and it took all his attention. Now he drove with both hands on the wheel, watching for the sudden cut, keeping out of others' blind spots. Drivers looked tense and focused. They snapped glances in their mirrors; kept a thumb hear their horns. Blinkers flashed. Cars vied for placement as junctions came up every mile or so.

Jack changed lanes twice to get into position for the Santa Ana junction. It was L.A. he decided. Maybe a parallel one, but L.A. just the same. He could get them to Anaheim at least. Debbie could see something familiar before they followed the road back out to alien landscapes and meaningless junctions that led them nowhere at 80 miles per hour.

He could get them to Anaheim.

Traffic flowed slightly faster in his lane. They crept up on cars, taking minutes to pass them. A semi to their right, ahead of them, blocked the signs. Jack wanted the Compton junction that would take them west on 91, but he didn't know if he needed the left or right side of the highway. A sign blinked by, and he missed what it said.

Slowly they closed the distance. The semi's wheels roared by Debbie's window, and Jack suddenly got scared. Everything felt the same as it had once before. He'd heard these tires before.

"What's that truck?" he asked, voice tight.

Debbie pushed her face to the window and read the side. "Horizon Transit. Why?"

"Jesus," said Jack. He couldn't see the driver's face, but a leather-clad arm rested on the driver's door. Only a few feet separated Jack from the car in front of them, a green lowrider with maroon tassels dangling in the rear window.

Jack tapped the top of the steering wheel. Both lanes to his left were packed solid, hardly a hand's breadth between them. No chance of cutting over and away. All he could hope for was that nothing would happen, because there was nothing he could do to protect himself.

At mid-trailer, the truck's turbulence buffeted them and pulled them over. Jack leaned on the wheel, keeping them in the center of their lane.

Debbie said, "That's the same one, isn't it?"

Howling, the trailer's front wheels passed the window in a blur of rubber and spinning metal. They were beside the cab. Jack could see the foot rest and the bottom of the door. They were by.

Closing his eyes for a second, Jack breathed easier. The lane to their right was open for a hundred yards, as if no one wanted to be in front of the semi. Keeping one eye on the truck in his mirror, Jack scanned the road ahead for junction signs. He couldn't remember how long he needed to stay on 57 before hitting 91. It seemed like years since he'd driven this stretch of road. Years of driving and driving, but never arriving.

After minutes more, they caught up to the car that was immediately ahead of the semi, now a hundred yards behind. Jack kept looking for the signs as they inched past.

"Oh," said Debbie. "That poor man."

In the car beside them, a yellow Volvo sedan with two little boys in the back seat, the driver was wide-eyed and weeping. The man rotated his head left and right, and Jack could see in his face disbelief and growing horror.

A newbie, Jack thought, and he remembered when he and Debbie realized they were trapped, how the sickening dread had welled up inside them. The traffic wouldn't let them stop; there was no place to exit, and they were trapped. They must have looked like this.

The man's face was pure anguish. He didn't even appear to see Jack and Debbie looking in at him, and in the backseat the children played, two little boys with their heads down, studying something between them. Maybe a coloring book.

What could they have done to deserve being here? The image of the children waking up in the half-death after their first inevitable crash boiled up within him. A thousand years (it seemed) of pain and death. What could they have possibly done?

Tears glistened on the man's face. He barely seemed to be paying attention to the road as he wandered from side to side.

Jack felt a fist in his throat. He couldn't take his eyes away from the man. Then the car behind Jack beeped, a short angry beep that said, "Keep up, buddy. You're slowing me down." A gap had opened in front of Jack.

He checked his rearview mirror. The driver behind beeped again, but what Jack saw was the semi closing fast. The hundred yards was now fifty. Black exhaust streamed from the truck's twin pipes above the cab, and the windshield glared like a rectangular sun. Directly in front of it, the unknowing newbie waited to be squashed. He didn't see the traffic. He didn't see anything, and his boys played on.

Debbie saw it too. She looked at Jack.

Their eyes locked, and hers brimmed with sadness.

Twenty-five yards back, the semi leapt eagerly. It growled in triumph.

Jack checked behind him. He put his hand on the emergency brake. Debbie saw, touched his hand and nodded.

He grazed the brakes. A horn blared behind him, and metal crunched, snapping Jack's head against his seat, but the Volvo scooted ahead. Their bumpers cleared, and Jack jerked the wheel to the right, pulling the emergency at the same time.

The truck was on them before they started to roll.

Pain's the dark flipside of excitement. It doesn't bore. It's always freshly minted. Blood in the wound glistens, and pain's world opens wide, all-encompassing. Jack squirmed on pain's hook, but there was no place to go, and he was all alone. Like Vanderdecken tied to the rudder off the weather-whipped coast of Africa, beating his way into the knives of wind, never arriving, never making port, and each wave a reminder of the death that had already claimed him. Like Sisyphus with his shoulder to the rock, unable to see around it, having no idea how long it would grind into his shoulder, how long his legs would quiver beneath him, begging to collapse.

Pain, as long as it lasts, is unending.

I never believe we will come back," said Debbie.

Jack stroked the wheel. If felt so good to feel anything, even the steering wheel.

"It makes me want to kiss everything around me," said Jack.

Automatically, he moved into the left lane. The sign said Compton Only, and he followed the curve around with all the other cars. Four lanes joined them on the left. The highway was congested, but moving well.

"Do you think he survived?" asked Debbie. "Do you think that it made any difference?"

"Maybe," Jack said. "At least for a moment."

They passed under a sign.

Debbie turned and grabbed his arm. "Did you see it, Jack! Did you see it?"

He was already checking his mirror and signaling. "Yeah."

The sign read, *Harbor Blvd. Disneyland exit/Left Lane, 1/2 mile.*

"It's an exit. Can we make it, Jack? Can you make the exit?"

Four lanes of solidly packed commuters moving at 80 miles per hour stood in between him and a way off the highway, the first exit they'd seen in who could guess how many years. At 80, a half mile takes only twenty seconds.

Four bumper to bumper lanes. Twenty seconds, and the Harbor Blvd. Exit into Anaheim and Disneyland.

"I think so," he said as he made the first merge. "I'm good in traffic."

MISS HATHAWAY'S SPIDER

—Knowledge—

MISS HATHAWAY FIRST NOTICED THE SPIDER ON A COOL SEPTEMBER MORNing, before the students arrived, as she dusted the chalk trays with her canary-yellow feather duster. No other teacher cleaned the chalk trays, but she knew that was a reflection of their lack of professionalism, for no one was as meticulous, as orderly, as conscientious as she. Not that she considered cleaning the chalk trays a part of her job, but the janitor never did them. She had written a memo to him once, folded it neatly into thirds and placed it in his box in the faculty mail room.

> Dear Mr. Clean,
>   I would like to commend you on the appearance of
> my classroom, but would it be possible for you to pay
> closer attention to the chalk trays? They do become
> awfully dusty. High school students are acutely aware
> of an untidy environment, don't you think?
>   Sincerely,
>   Miss Hathaway

But even after her letter, in the morning the trays were dirty, and, annoyed, she cleaned them out.

She saw the spider clinging to the underside of a web a foot above the carpet in the corner of the room farthest from the door when she bent to drop broken pieces of chalk into the trash can. She jumped back, a tidy little jump; her hands flew to her face below her wire-rim glasses and cupped her cheeks. "Oh," she said.

Miss Hathaway, who at five-foot-one and a hundred-and-two pounds and filled with the authority of her fifteen years of teaching experience, who had broken up fights between football players, who faced lunch room duty with the bravery of any soldier on Iwo Jima, who had at the beginning of this school year moved a cabinet full of books from one side of her room to the other, was afraid of spiders.

She knelt cautiously to observe it and realized that someone coming into her classroom at that moment would see her crouched in a corner at the front of the class and might think she was praying. But the presence of the remarkable spider pushed that thought from her head, and she scooted closer. Its size struck her first: at least three inches from toe-tip to toe-tip. And then its color: black and spit-shine shiny. The spider's body and the black, metallic legs reflected the fluorescent light from the ceiling in tiny star bursts.

But even a remarkable spider, she thought, had no place in a classroom. She pushed herself up from the floor, smoothed the front of her skirt, then pressed her intercom switch and asked for the unhelpful Mr. Clean.

When he arrived, she said, "Class begins in one half hour, and I do not believe the spider should be here."

He crouched down next to the web. The spider vanished into a hole in the wall. "It's a big one . . ." He poked a greasy, chewed pencil into the hole. A crumbling of rotten sheetrock drifted to the carpet. ". . . and we probably ought to call the exterminators . . ."

"Well?" Miss Hathaway crossed her arms across her chest, wrapping her fingers around her elbows. She could feel the sharp crease she had ironed into her blouse sleeves.

". . . but we're out of funding." He stood up and pushed his pencil into his shirt pocket. "You'll have to kill it yourself."

She squeezed her elbows. "But this is why I called you."

He sniffed."Our job's floors, boards and desks."

"You can't take care of the spider?"

"The exterminators are union; janitors are union, just like teachers. You wouldn't want me to scab, would you?"

"Of course not. Wouldn't dream of it. I understand our positions exactly." She picked up her feather duster, turned her back to him and began dusting an already clean chalk tray with short, brisk strokes. "Thank you for your attention."

Mr. Clean paused at the door on his way out. "I'll suck her right up, if I catch her on the carpet."

—Comprehension—

Two weeks later Miss Hathaway sat on the front three inches of a chair before Vice Principal Book's desk. The chair came from the elementary school and forced her to sit with her knees higher than her hips and her eyes level with the top of the desk.

Vice Principal Book, a large man with beefy upper arms that strained the

sleeves of his battleship-gray jacket, gazed down on her. Behind him, six certifi-
cates, their frames butting up one to the other and lined up so precisely that they
looked like one long brass and glass display, hung from the green cinder block wall.
"So, let me see if I can put this in a nutshell. You have a spider problem in your
room, and therefore you can't teach?"

"I'm sorry to bother you with this, and I wouldn't, but I talked to the janitor,
and he said it wasn't his job. I don't see how it is properly mine either." She kept her
neatly manicured hands still. Vice Principal Book made her nervous, even though he
was once only a Driver's Ed instructor.

He smiled. "Miss Hathaway, Miss Hathaway, you *are* one of our best teachers."
He consulted an open manila folder on the desk. "Spotless record. Perfect paperwork. Up to date lesson plans. Never tardy to faculty meetings. And, most important,
you don't send students up to me for discipline problems." He chuckled. "How distracting can a spider be?"

It wasn't distracting at all, at first, thought Miss Hathaway; the only reason she
didn't kill it was because the janitor should kill it; he didn't clean the trays; at least
he could get rid of the spider. Miss Hathaway thought of the web, now a yard wide,
that clouded the corner of the room, the eight inches of glistening spider that hung
there, and the mysteriously larger hole in the wall. She thought of the three times in
the last two days, while lecturing on the funnel paragraph, she had pirouetted in mid-
sentence, convinced the black spider was creeping up on her. "Maybe if you came down
and looked at it?"

"I don't think we'll need to go that far. There isn't an educational challenge that
can't be solved, if we put our heads together, right in this office, Miss Hathaway."

"This does seem to be an extraordinary situation, though." She wanted to squirm
forward on the chair because her blouse had come untucked from the back of her
skirt, but she was perched on the edge already. The thought of tucking the blouse in
with Vice Principal Book watching made her queasy.

He leaned back in his chair, squeaking the springs, and laced his fingers across
his stomach. His jacket pulled into a series of wrinkles radiating away from the
single button holding it closed. "Remember the Miracle Worker?" He continued
without waiting for her to answer. "She taught that little girl who couldn't see, hear
or talk. The Miracle Worker didn't have a beautiful classroom, did she?"

He looked at Miss Hathaway expectectantly. "Uh, no, she didn't."

"She didn't have class sets of brand new expensive Harcourt Brace Jovanovich
English texts, did she?"

"No," she answered. He was caught in his rhythm now.

"No, she didn't! She didn't have video tapes or record players or computers to
help her. Think of the primitive conditions she worked in, and think of your own sit-

uation. Why, if she had the advantages you have, she could have really done something with that little girl. So, I believe that what you need to do is to reconsider your situation. Believe in your own abilities. Do you believe, Miss Hathaway?"

"Yes," Miss Hathaway whispered. He beat the top of the desk with his fist to emphasize his words.

"Believe in the school. Believe that the principal and I are behind you all the way. Believe that the school board knows what it's doing. Believe in the goal of every child in its place. I have that dream." He lunged out of his chair and loomed above her. "Sure, you have a spider, but you have so many positives. You can stand tall in your classroom, like a pillar of fire, like a burning bush, like a tower of Babel. Can you do that?"

"Oh, yes!"

"In the teaching profession we can't dwell on the negatives; we have to accentuate the positives. Be a team player. Keep a tight lid on the boat, and your ship will come in."

He slapped her folder closed. "Be a Helen Keller for us Miss Hathaway. You can be a miracle worker like her, if you'll put your mind to it."

Momentarily engulfed in his enthusiasm, she rose. She said, "I think I can," and marched down to her classroom.

—Application—

Monday, the week after Homecoming. Melba Toast raised her hand, and Miss Hathaway thought, as she often did, of how cruel parents can be.

"There is web on my desk," Melba said. The web stretched from ceiling to floor now, and its intricate structure of thick threads anchored to points as far as ten feet from the corner of the room, including Melba's desk. Its form sprang from the corner without order, random, not a neat lattice work of geometry, but a chaotic mess of lines and darkness.

"Isn't that interesting?" Miss Hathaway said. "But I don't believe we need to consider that now. What we should think about is a topic for our next essay." Miss Hathaway felt distracted, unfocused. She knew what the next essay *should* be—the lesson plans she had used for the last fifteen years were perfectly clear—a comparison/contrast essay on abortion, but she didn't want to assign it. The whole idea of thirty essays like essays from years past exhausted her. But this attitude put her in a weird position, she realized: for the first time in her teaching career, she didn't know exactly what she was going to do next. It disturbed her. She paced the front of the classroom, her hands behind her back, avoiding the mass of web to the left of her podium. The two-foot long spider crawled along the ceiling of the room. Students under it watched warily. "Your essays on gun control were fine. Really, they were. But they lacked something: immediacy perhaps. If we wrote about a topic closer to home your writing might be livelier."

The spider paused above Jim Bag, a mediocre student with a tendency to dangle his modifiers, who turned every writing assignment into an essay on football. He clenched the edges of his desk and looked ready to bolt if the spider should make a move towards him. "Jesus Christ, that gives me the creeps," he announced.

Miss Hathaway stopped pacing. Here was something she could deal with. No one talked in her room without raising a hand. In fact, she thought, no one should ever talk. After all, this was a writing class. "While I am deciding what our next subject will be, why don't all of you take out a pen and in one paragraph write your feelings about the spider. Make sure you include a distinct thesis sentence. I'll collect them in fifteen minutes." They pulled paper out of notebooks and busied themselves at the assignment. While they were writing she studied the spider, and the distraction, the unfocusing, came back.

She thought about it being black. But it was blacker than black. Midnight black. No, blacker than that. It was black with depth. Cave black. Blind black. Not like a black mirror, but like outer space. Black like a neutron star defying color. Denying color. Fall into the pit black. A black from the back of the dream black.

And the shape, a dark, dismembered hand. Black bone fingers beating gravity. Clinging to the ceiling. Nothing that big should be able to walk above you, she thought. Each joint clearly articulated. Multiple leg knuckles, bent, full of promise. Full of threat.

And the long abdomen, packed, round. The skin taut, pulsing faintly, rising and falling, never still. At this size she could see it always moved. She envisioned her hand reaching out, stroking it.

She jerked her eyes away. Breathing hard, face flushed, she walked up and down the straight aisles between the desks, studied the students' papers and forced herself not to look up as she passed beneath the spider.

Later, at the podium, she read a sampling of the essays to the class.

"'In today's modern society, spiders are seldom thought of.'" She gazed at them in their orderly rows before her. "Can anyone make a suggestion for improving this lead-in sentence?" No one spoke. "Generally, we don't approve of ending sentences with prepositions." They looked back at her blankly. "This might be a good test question," she said, and many of them wrote down that sentences should not end with prepositions.

She read the next one. "'In the current, modern world of today, spiders are very important.' Can anyone think of a better verb than 'are' for this sentence?" No one spoke; she suggested a different verb.

Before the bell rang, she said to them, "Think about strategies to develop your paragraph on the spider into an essay. Invent ways to turn this negative into a positive." She was pleased with herself for having heeded Vice Principal Book's advice.

At the bell, they hurried to the door. "Jim!" she called. "I need to talk to you about your language."

After he left, she was alone, and the spider was with her. It moved up the wall and onto the ceiling with a cool, slow grace; and its movement made her think of a glacier creeping into an ancient civilization's valley, sliding with weighty patience inch after inch, covering roads, pushing aside viaducts, smoothing away the lines of irrigation ditches. She shook her head and realized minutes had passed. The spider had crossed the room.

—Analysis—

Before class, the day after Thanksgiving break, Vice Principal Book slapped a sheet of paper on Miss Hathaway's podium.

"We don't need to involve the principal in this now, do we?" His open jacket and tie that hung to one side exposed his belly pushing through the gaps between the buttons. "A memo like this insults my office."

Miss Hathaway had never seen Vice Principal Book in her room before, and his sudden appearance startled her into dropping her gradebook. She pushed her glasses up from where they had slid to the end of her nose so she could look at him.

"But you can see the problem," she said and waved her hand at the web-choked corner of the class where hundreds of translucent-gray, rope-thick strands originated to connect to every solid surface in the room. The ruler straight rows of desks, except for Melba's, and the podium were the only areas relatively free from sticky web. The ceiling lights filtered through and cast abstract, bizarre shadows. On the wall behind Vice Principal Book, the four-foot long spider delicately picked its way from strand to strand; its body covered a poster diagramming a keyhole essay. When she saw the spider, her attention wavered from Vice Principal Book, and it suddenly occurred to her that she hadn't been able to see the hole in the wall behind the web for weeks, and she wondered how large was it now? And where, exactly, did it lead?

"What I see," said Vice Principal Book, "is that you need to distinguish facts from fiction. The facts are that the principal runs this building with a system. The system includes a hierarchy of command. He does not deal with teachers—I deal with teachers. When you subvert the hierarchy, then the system doesn't work."

Miss Hathaway faced him. "I have to deal with this spider every day!"

Vehemently he said, "You have to deal with *me* every day. Spiders come and spiders go, but I'm here forever. You have a bad history of this kind of memo writing." Confused, Miss Hathaway looked at him. "Oh yes. I know about your memo to the janitor. Nothing is too small for me to notice, Miss Hathaway."

Early students walked into the class and put their books under their desks. The Vice Principal lowered his voice, but his tone stayed angry. "A parent complained about your essay assignment on the spider. Parents don't want their children to think—and you know this as well as I do—about things that make them uncomfortable. I don't want you drawing attention to it. As far as you and your students are concerned, it doesn't exist. No more essays. No discussions. There is no spider!" He marched out of the class, stiffly ducking his head under low strings of web that crossed from wall to wall.

Miss Hathaway grabbed a stack of essays from a shelf in the podium, crunching the first page of the top paper. They were the spider essays, each with neatly red-penned comments in the margins and a grade written in the upper right hand corner (a "happy face" drawn next to the pleasingly many "A's" and a "sad face" next to the surprisingly few "F's"). She wanted to return them today. That was what her lesson plan said: "Hand back graded essays and discuss."

She stood rigid at the podium, thinking an unthinkable thought: I will hand them back anyway. And she waited for the tardy bell to ring, but as she waited she grew less sure. He is the vice principal, after all, she thought, and the more she considered this, the sadder she became. He had never yelled at her before; hadn't he said she was "one of the best teachers?" Who would want to lose that?

She sighed, smoothed the wrinkle she had made in the top essay, placed the stack deep in the podium and opened her *Warriner's English Grammar and Composition* text to find an exercise as an alternative lesson plan.

The last few students entered the room and made their way to their desks.

And that might have been the end of it, except that when Melba Toast took her seat she did what no student, what no janitor, what Miss Hathaway herself, had not done—she brushed against a piece of the web.

"Uh oh," said Melba, and all eyes turned to her; in the spotlight of attention, she was alone. No one moved. Then the spider swarmed down from the ceiling, an avalanche of legs and dreamy black motion.

During the brief struggle, while Miss Hathaway did nothing, she suddenly realized she knew the facts, she always had. The problem was the fiction, and how was she to separate them?

*

—Synthesis—

The next day, Miss Hathaway marked her roll sheet mechanically, making tidy black checks in the exact middle of each square until she came to Melba Toast's space. Her desk was empty, but Melba herself, wrapped in a long white cocoon, hung from a net of threads coming out of the confusion of web above the class. Only her eyes peeked out, open, awake, but unfocused, as if she were seeing things beyond the walls.

After a long moment, Miss Hathaway marked Melba tardy, reasoning that although she was not in her seat when the bell rang, she was in the room.

The class labored over a fourpage worksheet on subject/verb and pronoun/antecedent agreement as Miss Hathaway finished her paperwork and began to stroll up and down the aisles; but wherever she walked, and no matter how hard she tried not to look, her eyes kept finding their way to Melba.

Someone knocked on the door, startling Miss Hathaway. It was Guidance Counselor Mitty. They talked in the hall.

"You sent for me," he said as if he had somewhere else to be that was much more important. A slight man, barely as tall as Miss Hathaway herself, he struggled to keep straight an armful of manila envelopes

"I've lost a student."

"I heard. I heard. Terrible thing. But what can we do?"

"I don't know. I thought you people had special training. It's time we did *something* though." Miss Hathaway looked back into her classroom where the students were working quietly.

"These are awful times Miss Hathaway. They always are. But we have a saying up in counseling, 'Don't lose the school, saving a whale.' Sometimes one of them slips away from us, but we can't knock ourselves out. Buck up. We win more than we lose."

"You're saying to not worry about her?"

He shrugged. "I'm doing a study. If you'll write a report on her case, I'll pull her files, and maybe we can work up a profile of what to look for next time. Keep the rest of your ducks in a row, and the sharks won't get them. But if this episode starts to bother you, come on up." He looked fatherly. "The district sponsors a support group for teachers. It's wonderful, really. I go twice a week myself, not that I need it, but I always feel refreshed after others speak about their problems."

"But what of her parents? Won't her parents want to know what happened to her?"

"Oh, we're right on top of that. Any time a student is in danger of not graduating we send a letter to the home, and, of course, failure notices come out next week, so they'll know. We are committed to communicating with parents."

Miss Hathaway opened her mouth and shut it, opened it and shut it. She raised her hands and dropped them. Guidance Counselor Mitty backed away from her. "Have you tried talking to the vice principal?" he said.

Miss Hathaway closed her eyes and thought about violent acts, of slapping his papers out of his hands, of kicking his manila folders down the hall, of tearing his reports into hundreds of pieces. She opened her eyes; he was gone.

Later, the bell rang, dismissing class. Trembling, she studied the spider high in its corner.

Each leg rested on a firm line of web, balancing the spider perfectly, leaving it poised to go in any direction, the center of stillness. She stepped towards it, and the spider elevated its two front legs as if to embrace her. She stepped back, and the legs dropped down.

She sat on the stool behind her podium and thought about Guidance Counselor Mitty, Vice Principal Book, and Mr. Clean, and she couldn't make any sense of them. And the more she thought, the angrier she became. She wrote their names on a sheet of paper and tried to sort them out. What did they want? Then she crumpled the sheet, wrote the names again, added her own name and drew lines from name to name, and then from letter to letter until the sheet was a maze of lines. Finally she stood, and then stalked around the perimeter of the room, muttering. Web touched or covered the posters, the intercom, the bulletin board, the book shelves and the blackboards.

She stopped in front of the spider and stared at it again, and she realized she was sweating. Her forehead was wet with it; hair stuck to the side of her face; she felt sweat on her back and belly. She untucked her blouse. She wanted to take it off, to throw it on the floor, to kick her shoes away from her, to unbutton the skirt and drop it, to peel off everything. Then the spider moved toward her, not quickly: slowly, barely seeming to lift its legs, placing each exactly on the next strand. Like a vision of a black tidal wave rolling up in slow motion across a gray beach, she saw it. Larger and darker, blotting out the sky, covering the sun, sweeping up the sand. Like a hand sliding under the covers, reaching closer and closer. To what? she thought. To what? And she realized a funny thing: at this size the spider didn't scare her. It was rather . . . rather . . . lovely. She stepped forward, reached out with both hands; she stroked the spider's sides between pairs of legs, drew it toward her, and the spider wrapped gently around her.

She was so warm.

*

—Evaluation—

Miss Hathaway felt as if she were a blind eye opening for the first time, like she had never been in the world before.

She floated in the spider dream, down each line of web, from wall to wall, from ceiling to floor. She connected everywhere, could move everywhere, felt air drifting, individual molecules bouncing, sounds vibrating. On the outskirts of her perception she heard Melba Toast singing a tune Miss Hathaway didn't recognize, a happy song.

Through the hole in the wall, a hole that she now knew opened beyond her classroom, a hole that was more a door than any she had ever gone through, she saw light. And beyond the door she believed waited a world she had never considered, and she could feel in herself the power to go there. Who knew how far she could go in the spider dream? But for now the spider itself delighted her. She felt its presence as a huge pillow of soft sounds, and its blackness transformed into gauzy yellow, green and blue lights with no center. No one point more interesting than any other. None of it bad or good. None of it comparable to any other thing. No degrees of complication. No head. No base. The spider was an entirety. Words were too weak. Words themselves, as soon as she thought of them, limited whatever it was. Whatever it is. She laughed. There was so much she wanted to understand, but there was no rush. She had time, she knew, she had time. A spider is nothing if it is not patient.

Then a shape moved below her and Miss Hathaway focused her eyes and realized that her body dangled from the ceiling of her own classroom. A person she had never seen before, a small angry woman in a neatly pressed blouse, hair tied tightly back in a bun, was digging into the podium, examining each piece of paper closely, then piling it on the floor in increasing exasperation. Finally, she glared up at Miss Hathaway. "Lesson plans?" she shouted. She searched through the last stack of papers. The first students came in and sat in their desks. "Where are your lesson plans?"

She was the substitute.

HAPPY ENDING

THE BULLET STIRRED FROM ITS BED OF BONE IN THE BACK OF THE SKULL, then leapt through the bloody tunnel of brain tissue behind it. Neurons closed on neurons, and severed capillaries reknit and healed as the bullet flashed through the brain, out the hole in the roof of the mouth, past shattered teeth—whose fragile fragments came home again to perfect, flawless form—and flew down the gun barrel to nest tightly in the now unexploded casing.

Against his lips, the barrel pressed heavily and tasted of oil.

Bob took the gun away from his mouth, rested it in his lap and opened his eyes. Tears crept up his cheek, as he turned his gaze away from the gun and to the window of his study where autumn leaves streamed past, their tattered glory afire in the evening sun. He couldn't see the elm or willows, just the leaves dancing by, and a fanciful thought returned to him: if you can't see the source, who can tell if leaves are falling to the ground or jumping back to the limbs? And what does it matter? The leaves are in the air. They don't know their direction. Karl was right.

I'm twenty-four, he thought, and he felt old, used up and gray. Beneath the pale, unlined skin on the top of his hand, he could sense wrinkles and liver spots. His knuckles waited to bulge, to become arthritic. I'm old, he thought. I've grown old.

Leaves tumbled across the window in shades of gold and red for a long time before he put the gun back in the desk drawer, and picked up the phone.

It droned in his ear like a death knell for a minute, then clicked. "You're no hero," unsaid Mrs. Downs in his ear. "You had a responsibility."

Bob replied, "It was just a lesson. A discussion of story theory. How could I know he identified so strongly?"

"The boy believed in you. You walked on water." Her voice stayed flat and cold. Nothing remained in it. No hope. No anger. She could have been reciting a laundry list. "He wanted to be a writer like you."

"Karl made choices. I believe if he had lived he could have done anything. Karl had great potential." Bob remembered their first days together. Karl sat in the back of the room, writing in his tight, black scribble every word Bob said. Karl *always* wrote no matter what else was going on in the room, his dark eyes occasionally looking furtively away from his legal pad. He'd shown a story to Bob after the first week of the creative writing class. It was a 1,000-word time travel piece called "Rats Live on No Evil Star."

Later, Bob gave him a copy of Hawking's *A Brief History of Time,* so he could see what modern physicists thought of time.

Karl had handed him the story reluctantly, frightened. Bob knew he'd signed up for the class because Bob had published. "Here," he'd said. "It's no good."

Mrs. Down's said, "Nothing you do today can make a difference. I know who my boy was before. I know who you are now."

Bob held the phone tightly against his ear. He could almost feel her presence. She stood in the room with him, her lips only centimeters away. "You have to blame me, I know. My name was in the note, but I didn't see it coming. It's too much . . . it's way too much to ask for forgiveness, but I hope you understand."

"Why did you call?" Mrs. Downs didn't sound surprised at all.

"Mrs. Downs, I'm Bob Wells," Bob said, his voice squeezed tight and scratchy. "Karl's teacher."

Bob dialed.

Bob put the phone down gently, fearfully and full of guilt. On the desk in front of him lay three pieces of paper: a form rejection from HarperPrism telling him his novel was being returned; a formal request from the school board for his resignation, and a note to him from Karl that had been folded into the back of the book. Hawking's book, Karl had returned to him, held down the notes.

Everywhere Bob looked within himself he could see nothing but darkness: no way out.

Gazing blankly at the letter on the floor, he thought of all the time in class lecturing from his position as a soon to be published novelist; all the conferences with students who signed up for his courses on the weight of his reputation, and it pushed upon him with the bulk of a terrible lie. He remembered looking at students' stories, his red pen in hand, marking in the margin, *Unbelievable dialogue, What's the conflict?,* or *Why should the reader care?* And as he marked, he thought about how important his words would be on their papers. This came from *the* Bob Wells, they would think. He was my Creative Writing teacher in high school.

He held his hand out, and Karl's note fluttered from the floor back to his hand. Bob's eye held to the last words that he had written on the paper—the words that he had written that ignored so much of what Karl said, that refused to read between the lines. They were, "This is an unlikely idea for a story, Karl. Trash it and work on something more believable."

Above that, Karl's note read,

Mr. Wells,

I know you don't think I can make it as a writer, but I've thought a lot about what you said about how stories are structured. I still think you are wrong about that, just as you are wrong about failing me. A story ought to work the way the universe works. According to Hawking, the universe tends toward disorder, not order. Cups don't leap off the linoleum and reassemble on table tops; they fall and shatter. Chaos is the rule, and that's the way we perceive it. So fiction that makes "order out of the chaos of life," as you put it, runs counter to the direction of the universe.

If I lived my life according to your description of stories, jumping off a cliff shouldn't kill me. The disorder of my corpse at the bottom should undo itself and I'd fly to the top alive.

I think I can prove it. I can write a story that will get an "A." Kind of a performance story. I'm a good writer. It will be a story about a cliff and how the real direction of a story should be disorder and mystery, not order and understanding.

Sincerely,
Karl Downs

Bob put the note back into the book, and returned it to his desk. He retreated to a corner of the room and sat in it, his back squeezed by the conjunction of the walls.

After a while, he stood, then backed out of the room, his head hanging, his hands like rags dangling from his arms.

Walking through the campus, he barely noticed the students passing around him. Their conversations stopped as he approached.

"That's him," Bob heard one say behind him; then the boys walked by silently, their eyes darting at Bob and switching away. Facing each other, the distance between them grew, until he saw them talking with animated pleasure.

In the principal's office, the silence lingered and vibrated like a discordant note.

"Thank you," said Bob, finally, knowing that it wasn't appropriate, but what else could he say?

"We think it best if you resigned immediately," the principal said as she closed his file.

Bob shook his head as if he were trying to wake from a dream—one of those nightmares where he knew what was going to happen but where he could do nothing to stop it. "What are you suggesting?"

"We're going to have to make a change. The Advanced Class in Creative Writing won't be offered again. It was a mistake to put you in charge of it. Karl shouldn't have been there."

"He had talent, but the boy was troubled. I didn't know," Bob said in surrender, putting hardly any voice behind the words, nearly whispering them.

The principal, a woman five years older than Bob, unfolded the photocopy of the suicide note. She appeared to mull over the lines, and Bob tried to think of anything to say. He thought, they're blaming me! And when he looked inside, he saw that they were right. The knowledge spun up to him darkly.

"The school board," she said, "has seen this. They met last night just to talk about this. It's bad, Bob. Your name is all over it, and we talked to kids in your class. They confirmed much of what Karl says here. They said you badgered him. Their words. One said you ridiculed Karl. Another said you singled him out."

Numbness dominated his face. He wanted to reach up and touch his cheeks to see if they were real. His shirt felt too tight; he could hardly breathe within it. "Karl wrote notes all the time."

"They found this from Karl," she said, holding a sheet of paper. "In his coat pocket. You know, he left his coat on the rail? It was neatly folded there. Did you know he took his shoes and socks off? Why would he do that? Fifteen years old, and he dives off a cliff, but he takes his shoes and socks off."

"I don't understand it either," Bob said. The whole conversation might as well be taking place in an echo chamber, he thought. It seemed so unreal; so much like it all was unwinding around him.

"Why did it happen, Bob?" The principal sat back in her chair. Bob could tell she'd already made up her mind.

Bob surveyed the empty class room. Marcia Binder, who loved Bob best after Karl, had left a pile of crumpled paper on her desk. He could see his own comments written on one of them; it was a feedback sheet on her last story. "Good job," it read. "With a little more work, this will really shine." She'd beamed when she'd read it the day before, and the color had risen in her cheeks when she'd thanked him after class. She has a crush on me, he'd thought, as she smiled shyly, holding her books close to her chest.

The doors opened and students backed in, pointedly not looking at Bob as they took their seats. Outside in the hall, the end of class bell rang, and the angry mutter among them rose like a muddy creek.

"It's a variation on the old Chinese blessing," Bob said desperately, aware that he'd lost them completely. "May you always have interesting material."

No one raised their hands. None of them wrote anything he was saying into their notebooks.

"There's a story about William Faulkner that he was at his father's deathbed when the old man passed on. Faulkner was supposed to have gone to a mirror and looked into his own face so that later he could write an accurate description of what a man whose father just died looked like. I'm not saying we should view Karl's death as a source for fiction, but we have gone through something here, and that something will effect us and our writing. We're more plugged into the reality of the human drama."

None of their faces offered support. Nothing is colder than high school students who think of you as the enemy, thought Bob. Marcia's lips were thin, white lines; her hands were locked firmly on top of her desk. She looked at him without blinking.

Bob realized that they couldn't get past it. Karl's empty desk vibrated like a terrible black hole, sucking all his words to it, all of his energy in, and it returned nothing.

After forty-five minutes of lecture, Bob gave up. The lesson wasn't going to work. They were more than silent; it was if they were seething in their seats.

He tried to move on, to follow his lesson plan. Yesterday had been a review of building scenes. "A scene is like a tiny story in itself," he'd said. "The beginning will be related to the end. Whatever action you start with will complete the scene; whatever emotion you provoke will be a part of its structure. It'll change the story and move it, so despair moves toward hope, or victimization to control. Everything in the scene contributes to the story, but the scene is a story too."

Today he was to discuss techniques in description. The farther he went though, the more obvious it was. They hated him.

He waited for a question. The material was abstract. Generally the students couldn't follow him when he went into fiction theory, but he'd present it anyway until someone asked him for an example. No one said a word.

He started class with "Order in a description is discovery. The reader discovers what is there in the order you present it, as if you are holding the reader's head and directing his attention. Presenting the information in a different order gives the reader a different perspective, and it can change the whole story. Order is everything."

The tardy bell rang. Facing their desks, the students backed out of the room.

Karl's death came with him into the empty class room, and the note from HarperPrism telling him that his novel ". . . does not fit our current publishing needs," still reverberated. The two seemed linked. As he prepared his lecture for the day, though, he felt the old confidence returning. In my room, I'm king, he thought. They can beat you down, but they can't kill you. Dozens of publishers rejected John Grisham.

Yesterday's ugliness could be washed away. They could start fresh. He waited almost eagerly for the students to come to class.

The radio unannounced the news of Karl's death while Bob filled his breakfast bowl, spoon after spoon.

It's probably no good either," said Bob, venom dripping from each word.

Karl handed Bob a twenty page manuscript. "Here's my semester project. I finished early." he said. "But, you won't get it, I'll bet."

Stunned, the rest of the class watched. Bob knew he was out of control, but the anger rolled up within him. The class would be so much better without this imbecile, thought Bob. This is *Advanced* Creative Writing, and they're taking it because I'm a *real* writer, not one of those lit fools that make up the rest of the department.

"You can't be a writer if you won't learn!" Bob's voice boomed in the room, overwhelming Karl finally. The boy shrank within himself, as if he suddenly understood that their battle was no mock game but a serious war. He reacted as if he just realized his teacher hated him. Karl's neck nearly disappeared as his shoulders rose to his ears.

Bob shouted, "You have a crummy attitude!"

HarperPrism's rejection buzzed around in Bob's thoughts like a malevolent horsefly. He couldn't concentrate on Karl, who glowered in the seat beside him. The arrogance of this kid, thought Bob. What does *he* know about fiction? Who does he think he is telling *me* what makes a story work?

"You told us that a reader doesn't remember a story chronologically," said Karl. "You said that the story is like a memory—that the reader has access to all of the story at once after he's read it—so it shouldn't matter what order it's told in. Time in the mind flows both ways, which is what Hawking said. *You* said that a writer revises the first word of a story knowing the last word, and that a writer writes from the end. My story does that."

Bob gave up on lecturing to the whole class. Only Karl existed. Only Karl needed to hear this. Only Karl challenged Bob's knowledge of writing. How could he? Bob thought. I'm published. I have put in the lonely hours and hours writing until my brain loosened up, and the muses came down and touched me.

"You have an 'F' on this, young man, not only because the story is three sentences long, but because it demonstrates no understanding of the order in which a story must be told. You have started with the end and moved to the beginning. The whole story, and I quote, is 'He died. He struggled. He was born.' No matter how you revise this, it will never be a story. It's backwards."

Karl scrambled through his notes. "Last week," he said, reading from his cramped handwriting on the yellow legal pad, "you told us that a story has 'profluence.' You said that was 'movement.' You also told us that stories are about reversals. 'Whatever condition begins the story must be changed by the end.' My story fulfills those requirements."

"You have purposely ignored every piece of advice I've offered about creating readable fiction. What hurts most here is that you have talent. You know your way around a sentence. There's a spark of imagination within you. But you waste it all in this tripe. Your 'story,' Karl, doesn't meet *any* of the requirements of narration."

Karl said, "It boils fiction to its essence. Stephen Hawking has told me more about the way the world works than you have. He says the arrow of time can point either way. We just perceive it the one way and not the other. The universe either moves toward the Big Bang or away from it, and that's reflected in stories."

The class giggled nervously. For a second, Bob realized he was playing to the crowd. "You don't make sense, Karl. My head aches just trying to follow your thoughts. I get twitchy thinking about it."

Karl said, "There's lots of ways of perceiving the world. Looking backwards ought to reveal themes we haven't explored the stodgy old way. I mean, for crying out loud. Plod, plod, plod. Once upon a time to they lived happily ever after. Don't you think it's more interesting to start with the result and see how it happened?"

Karl hunched forward in his seat, intense and fiery, his dark eyes lit up like Bob had never seen them.

"I know the rules," Karl said. "I've known them since Saturday morning cartoons. All of us . . ." He waved his arm to encompass the entire class. ". . . have heard a million stories."

Clenching his fists at his side, Bob said, "You can't break the rules until you know the rules."

He's mocking me, thought Bob.

"You've got to be willing to experiment," said Karl, laughing after he saw his grade. His legs sprawled out comfortably from under the desk, and he leaned back in his chair, relaxed. Bob remembered when Karl had been frightened to show him his first story. I've created a monster, thought Bob. I hinted he had talent, and now he doesn't believe he needs me anymore. Well, it's time to take Mr. Know-it-all down a notch.

All of them looked over their stories. Bob had written voluminous notes at the ends of each filled with suggestions about plot and pacing, description and conflict. He struggled with his face though. He felt sure they could read his expression and could see the HarperPrism rejection in it.

The class began innocently enough. Holding his disappointment inside like a sullen coal, Bob backed down the aisles between the desks, watching each student look over their grades eagerly, then handing their stories to him before assuming an expectant expression. Finally, he stood at the front of the class, holding their stories in a neat stack. At the bottom, because he sat in the last seat, waited Karl's story, a single page with little writing on it beside the red "F" in a big circle.

Still hungry; he hadn't eaten anything, Bob left for school.

He knew they'd rejected it by the opening salutation; "Dear Contributor."

Trembling, he folded the letter neatly, slid it back into the envelope and un-ripped it closed. This is it, he thought. They've bought the novel. They have to. The editor was so gushing in her request to see the complete manuscript after he'd sent the sample chapters.

He'd told everyone in school, casually, just dropping it in at the end of conver-sations. "Oh," he'd said, "by the way, HarperPrism has my novel now." Invariably they'd ask when it would be in the stores. He'd shrug his shoulders ruefully. "Who can guess? You know how the publishing world is." He'd wink as if they both were knowledgeable conspirators.

In the left corner, the return address said HarperPrism Publishing.

Coming out of his house, with a bounce in his step, he backed to the mailbox and put the letter in it.

Lunch is an adventure, he thought. The mail comes at lunch, and who knows what magazine has mailed an acceptance. Maybe, even, some news of the novel.

Settled comfortably into his chair now, Bob picked up Marcia Binder's story, which turned out to be a sweetly told romance between a talented high school student and her Art teacher. The ending scene took place in a subway station as the student left for college. She waits for him, hoping that he'll see her off, but he never comes. In the story, she'd not told the teacher of her love, and most of the story was of her struggling with her feelings. Bob paged back to the dream sequence in the middle—a graphically rendered fan-tasy of the student and teacher's consummation of the relationship. Taking Bob's advice to heart, she'd concentrated on senses other than sight and sound: the pressure of a fingertip, a suggestion of lemonade on the tongue, a thread of hair brushing a forehead, a hint of coppery excitement in the breath, and the rasp of a sheet sliding across skin. He wrote comments in the margin complimenting her on her use of sensory detail.

Five weeks had passed since HarperPrism asked to see the novel, and the joy of it buoyed him through the drudgery of grading, through the frustration of teaching to freshmen and the inanity of department politics. High hopes and Advanced Creative Writing pushed him through the day.

He moved on to the next student's work.

Bob neatly unwrote an "F" at the end of Karl's story, his pen tip rolling across the red line, sucking the ink back until the page was clean of any mark.

Closing his eyes, Bob thought I must have praised the boy too much. He needs to be shook up, for his own good. In the end, Karl will appreciate the lesson; he'll look back and recognize my guiding influence. Almost as good as "Bob Wells" on the cover of his own novel, Bob thought, would be the inscription inside his talented protégé's first book, "To my mentor, Bob Wells."

Bob knew he'd have to get Karl's attention some way; the grade wouldn't be enough. Why, the boy might even take the "F" as his own "Red Badge of Courage." Hadn't all the greats been misunderstood? Who recognized Poe in his lifetime? And Fitzgerald had ended his career in Hollywood scripting hack screen plays.

He tapped his forehead in disbelief. Karl's new story was only three sentences long! In a stack of students' stories, pristinely enclosed with clear, plastic covers and all ten pages or more, the single sheet of paper with Karl's name on it seemed like a joke. He read it twice.

The sun rose slowly and barely noticed in the west. Paper after paper he read until he came to Karl's.

Two weeks later, he read the first story on the stack.

The bell rang, ending class. I couldn't be happier, thought Bob. In all of their many ways, they love me.

Students nodded their heads and copied the information into their notebooks. Karl wrote furiously, and Bob could see that inspiration had overtaken him. Careful to appear casual, Bob strolled by Karl's desk and saw his first paragraph was something gruesome—something about a suicide. Bob shuddered a little. It was the only gray spot in his otherwise wonderful day. Talk of suicide hit too close to home for him. It reminded him that he too thought about swerving into oncoming traffic. It's the curse, he thought, of the overly imaginative. Suicide always seems an option, a romantic, final gesture of retribution, sacrifice or defiance.

"Remember," he said finally, "If you try an experimental technique in your semester project, like a metafiction, be sure to give your readers enough clues to figure out what's going on. They should, for example, be able to tell who's telling the story and why."

The students were busy at their desks; even Marcia Binder seemed busy now, writing. She checked her notes, then returned to her story. She had really effected him, he realized. He passed a hand over his eyebrows, depositing a thin sheen of sweat.

Thankful, Bob backed away from Marcia's desk and sat next to the next student. "So, what's your plan for your project?" Bob said. He wiped his palms against his pants.

"Umm," Bob said to Marcia, "It sounds like a challenge. I'm sure you could handle it," and that sounded stupid to him. Every word had a possible double meaning. Finally he offered, "You're a good writer. Give it a try."

Marcia looked at him, her eyes gleaming and frank. Bob forced himself not to glance down. He was sure, now, that she'd loosened a button on her blouse since he'd sat next to her.

"So what do you think?" she said.

She leaned forward, the tips of her fingers nearly touching Bob's hand.

Marcia said, "I've been exploring May-September relationships. I thought my semester project could be something that continues that theme." She sounded nervous and excited, as if she were torn between fearfulness and something else. Bob couldn't decide what it was, and with her so close to him, nearly whispering, he had a hard time thinking about it. Maybe it was love—maybe lust. He remembered the first assignment she'd handed in, an autobiographical description of a date she'd had just a month earlier where a boy had tried to kiss her. She'd confessed in the story that she'd never kissed a boy before, and the prospect had scared her, but she hadn't been able to sleep that night. In the story, she felt the ghost pressure of the kiss that never happened on her lips all the next day.

He caught a whiff of her shampoo, a soft fruity smell like peaches and cream, but under that a hint of just her. It wasn't unpleasant. Definitely warm though and animal. He wondered if she had P.E. the hour before his class.

"What will your semester project be, Marcia?" said Bob. Her hair hung across the side of her face, partially hiding her eyes.

He couldn't help but notice Marcia at the end of her row, glancing at him as he moved from student to student. She was wearing a loose peasant blouse, the top button undone, and when she leaned forward to write, he caught a glimpse of lace in the swells of shadow. As professional as he wanted to be, he couldn't help but notice, and he wondered if she *wanted* him to see. She leaned a lot when he was around, coyly, like part of her didn't know she was doing it while another part did, like her subconscious controlled her posture.

"You'll be a hero, Mr. Wells," said Karl enthusiastically as Bob unleft his desk. "It'll be cool."

Flattered, but not sure how to handle the attention, Bob said, "That might not be a good thing to do. It could be embarrassing."

"See, if I base my semester project on people I know, then I've got a better chance to get the characterization right. Like I could tell the story in first person from your point of view."

"Why would you want to do that?" Bob looked around the room.

"I've been reading Hawking, like you suggested, and he's really given me some ideas, and the stuff you just said, too. I see now that you were right. Typical time travel stories are old hat, so I'm going to write a new kind. I mean, why should the character be the only one who gets to travel in time?" said Karl. "And you'll be the protagonist."

"What will your project be?" asked Bob. Karl straightened the stack of pages on his desk, all of them apparently like the top one, filled with his crabbed, black handwriting.

Bob started class with a short lecture on metafiction. "Some stories," he said, "turn the tools of fiction upon itself. It's like Ferris Bueller talking to the audience, or *The Never Ending Story*, which makes the movie goers a part of the story at the end. Any story that reminds the readers they are reading a story is a kind of metafiction."

The class greeted him with smiles. Their eagerness to learn seemed genuine. They loved him.

"Not yet," he said.

"Any news on the novel?" someone asked.

Bending down, he placed his pencil on the floor. He stood.

The pencil undropped into his hand.

He backed to the door and opened it. The door grew smaller and smaller as he walked away.

He was unbreathing. He was unthinking. The events unrolled behind him. Life was good and getting better, and the innocence of youth waited for him.

PLANT LIFE

ERMAINE SAID, "JUST BEING AROUND GROWING YOUNG WOMEN MAKES ME feel alive." He poked a finger into the cement planter's black dirt. "That's where the excitement is, Bucko, and these are nearly ready to harvest."

Gregory looked down the long aisle through the middle of the greenhouse where rows of heavy trunked plants like the one they stood next to grew from solid, gray planters. From the top of each plant, four branches sprouted and bowed with the weight of their fruit, full sized women.

They walked to the next plant and Jermaine picked a handful of dirt out of it, felt it like an expert farmer and then let it dribble back. Even though the planter was only three feet tall, Jermaine had to reach up to replace the dirt. He was very short, almost a midget. A moody man who Gregory didn't particularly like, he had insisted they come to the flower shop when he overheard Gregory arguing with his newly "ex" girlfriend on the phone.

Jermaine said, "I hear that their secret here is meticulous care. Each gene splicing, forced mutation and pollenization is done by hand."

"I'm not sure I'm ready . . . I mean . . . a plant . . . I want to live alone," said Gregory.

"Not just a 'plant.' A designer house plant, a state of the art product! And don't give me this stuff about living alone, Bucko. Unless you think house plants think, you'll still be on your own. That's the beauty of it."

Gregory turned away from Jermaine and faced the next "fruit" dangling from an acorn-like skull cap that cupped the top half of her head. Green streaks showed faintly through her pale skin, through her eyelids.

"This one's almost ripe." Despite his three piece suit, Jermaine clambered onto the planter, grasped the "girl's" wrist and examined the hand, turning it palm up. "See, fingers separated." He pressed his thumb into the palm and the fingers closed slowly around it. "Stimulus reflexes coming along." He beckoned Gregory, "Here, touch its skin."

Shaking his head, Gregory backed away.

"Relax, Bucko, it's meant to be handled. That's what it's here for."

"I'm uncomfortable." Gregory's face flushed. "She's naked."

"Come on." Jermaine held out a hand. "It's all right."

As if afraid that someone observed his reluctance, Gregory glanced side to side then stepped up next to Jermaine.

"You said they were 'fully functioning?'"

"Fully *reflexive*. Press here." Jermaine directed Gregory's hand to the small of the woman's back; he reached around her tentatively but jerked his hand away when he touched her.

"She's warm!"

"Of course. Would you want a cold one? Hold that spot longer. Don't move your hand."

Gregory touched her again. For a few seconds the three of them stood still; fans at the far end of the greenhouse blew humid air past them, ruffling Gregory's hair, partially uncovering a bald spot. Then the plant moved. Her hips pushed against him rhythmically, and her arms moved up as if to encircle him. He stepped away. The woman's arms dropped and her torso quit moving.

"Oh, my," he exclaimed.

"That reflex will improve, naturally, when she's completely ripe, about a week after she's picked."

"Are there other . . . uh . . . models?"

"Sure. Each trunk produces three slightly different usable fruits, like sisters, but the separate plants . . . well, you can see." Jermaine gestured to the next planter where "girls" distinctly different from the one they were standing next to hung: more delicate, shorter. Gregory tried not to stare. He looked away.

"You said there were three 'fruits' per plant, but I count four." Gregory pointed to a fourth girl dangling in the shadow behind the trunk.

"Ah, you mean Rose." Jermaine sidled around the plant between the trunk and the girls. "They're a recessive gene, I understand. Quite unusable."

Gregory hopped off the planter and went around to where Jermaine was standing. His hand sunk into the wet dirt when he braced himself. Little globs of soil flew from his fingers as he shook them, and he held his hand away from his suit until Jermaine tossed him a rag to wipe it off.

Relieved to be doing something mundane, something as unembarrassing as cleaning his hands, Gregory wiped each finger meticulously. When he finished he looked at "Rose" and gasped.

"Quite striking, isn't she?"

Like the others, her toes brushed the dirt as she swayed slightly from her branch. Her hands rested against her thighs, relaxed, fingers curved as if waiting for someone to hold them, but no one would hold these hands, Gregory realized, no one would embrace this "fruit," because huge thorns, hard, wicked and sharp poked through her skin at every point. She bristled with inch long stickers so heavily that she didn't even mimic human appearance as the others did. From her forehead, her cheeks and lips, her neck and shoulders; from her breasts and belly, her hips and thighs, they curved out, translucent at the tips, needle sharp and glistening.

Gregory reached out to touch a thorn on her leg.

"Better not, Bucko. She's fully reflexive too." Jermaine lightly brushed the thorns on her belly, then pulled his hand away as her hips thrust forward. "You could get a nasty little cut from this one." He laughed. "She got me and I knew it was coming." He put the heel of his hand in his mouth.

"It's hideous."

"I don't know. Depends on how you look at her."

Gregory shuddered. "Why do they grow anything like this?"

"Like I said, a recessive gene. Completely unavoidable. Sometimes they sell one for novelty." Jermaine climbed off the planter. "Let's look at some of the others."

A half hour later, Gregory chose a "girl" that he liked and signed the contract for delivery. He felt, absurdly, like he had as a child after buying a Christmas tree.

The next day, at home, Gregory waited for the delivery. He was watering an African Violet, letting the water's weight push the leaves into the black earth, until the pot overflowed. He tapped the leave's edges to shake the drops off, then rubbed the soft fuzz on the leaf as if the plant were a mouse. The violets were Sara's, his "ex." He had expected her to pick them up after she left, but as the days passed and the leaves began to droop and shrivel, he had watered them. "You have to talk to them," she's said when she'd bought them. "Talk and TLC and they'll bloom." She'd say, "Here's water for my ducks. How are my babies?" That's ridiculous, he had thought at the time.

Pots of African Violets covered the entire counter top. She'd replaced the florescent bulb over the counter with a grow light, and as each plant flourished, she'd pinched and pruned, divided and replanted, until not a patch of the mauve linoleum counter was visible. Gregory refilled the canister and, without talking, doused the next plant.

She had loved simple things: plants, horses, sad movies, sappy poetry. For a big woman—a hint of double chin, padded shoulders and cushioned collar bones, round soft hips, broad thighs, pliant skin—she had moved over the tiny plants with a delicate grace. "Water, water everywhere and here's a drop to drink."

Finished with the violets, Gregory checked his watch, opened the front door and looked up and down the long, empty street, sat in front of the TV, staring at the blank screen. A car hummed past the house and he half got up but sat again when it didn't stop. Finally he searched his collection of DVDs for something to watch until the delivery. He paused at *The King and I,* a movie that Sara had watched over and over. He had found her slumped into the recliner one morning the week before she'd left, the remote control in hand, crying during a dance sequence. "Why?" he'd said. "Because they love each other," she'd replied.

He pushed *Little Shop of Horrors* into the player and fast forwarded to the climax. ("Feed me, Seymour! Feed me!")

He fell asleep before it ended and dreamed about Sara. He held out his hand to her, but when she took it she screamed. His palm was filled with thorns. He woke up, biting his lip.

The delivery man was scrawny and short. Gregory thought he could be a jockey if he got out of the delivery business. The heavy, blue plastic crate, like a huge Smurf coffin, stood on end in the living room. The delivery man unsnapped the buckles that held the lid closed, but he didn't open it. "You got instructions, right?" he said. Before Gregory could answer, he continued, "Keep it out of the sun. Otherwise you'll get sprouts. Wet its skin once a day. Otherwise you'll get cracks. A damp sponge'll do the trick. Unpadded manacles, whips, vibrators or anything sharp will bruise or break the skin, which will void your warranty. Keep it out of direct breezes, like a fan, air conditioner or heating duct. Store it in the carrying case when you're not using it." He paused to consult a card he held. Gregory felt like he was having his Miranda Rights read to him. "A diluted alcohol wipe will kill bug infestations. Forcing the limbs beyond normal range will void the warranty. So will the use of oil-based paints, electrical devices or abrasives, like sandpaper or nail files."

"Sandpaper?"

The man sighed. "The stories I could tell." He looked at the card again, "The case is heated, so plug it in and it'll stay at body temperature. The plant will hold heat for several hours. Sort of like a waterbed." He laughed then grabbed a pair of recessed handles in the lid and pulled it open. "Of course, it's a little green. Newly picked this morning. A couple of days, the color should be fine."

"She's wearing a robe." Gregory's voice squeaked.

"Part of the service. You can keep it. Most people don't. We'll be by in two weeks with a fresh plant."

"Two weeks?"

"Two weeks, three weeks, depends on the weather, they get soft. Like an old tomato. It's in your contract. Didn't you read it?"

Gregory had thrown the papers in his desk without looking at them. "Yes, I'm sorry. Slipped my mind."

The delivery man shut the case, looked Gregory over sagely. "Your first one, right? Nothing to it. Read the instructions. Just like when you were a kid with a model airplane."

The delivery man was in the truck and halfway down the street before Gregory realized what he meant.

During dinner, he felt the presence of the coffin-sized case in his bedroom where he had moved it, but he made himself eat slowly. Sara used to complain that he chewed his food twice as much as he needed to. She'd smiled and said, "Gregory, you're like a cow." But she stayed at the table until they were done, and on the nights they made love, they did it right after dinner.

After he cleaned the dishes and put the leftovers away, he stood in front of the case in his bedroom with the lights out a long time. When he finally opened it, the smell of grass wafted out, pasture grass after a rain.

She was, as Jermaine promised, fully reflexive.

Gregory met Jermaine the next night at a popular fern bar, The Block and Tackle. Under the dark oak sign that hung from rusted chains and illuminated by hidden lights was the Block and Tackle's slogan, "Everyone Gets Lucky."

Jermaine waited for him at a back table, far from the dim lights over the bar. Too obstinate to sit on a book or use a booster seat, his arms just cleared the edge of the table where he cradled a schooner of beer.

"So what did you think, Bucko?" asked Jermaine. Gregory flinched. He hated being called Bucko. "Was it everything I promised?" He pushed a beer toward Gregory as he sat down.

Gregory sipped from the mug for a while before answering. The beer, cool and smooth, felt good on his throat. "Different. Very different."

"Good, though, right? What did I tell you? Never a better time." Jermaine tipped his beer and swallowed a huge gulp.

"Yes." Gregory didn't know what to add to that. After he had put her on the bed, he lay beside her. The light from the window shone off her eyes, and he marveled at how lifelike, how utterly human, she appeared. He watched her breasts, perfectly formed, for a rise of breath that never came. The bedroom was utterly silent, and it made him remember Sara the last weeks before she left when she would lie beside him, awake but not speaking, aware that he was watching her, not asleep and barely breathing. Stiff, weighing down the mattress and mentally not in the room, the plant reminded him of her, so he reached across her belly and caressed her side. The plant/woman rolled into him and wrapped her arms around him, startling him so that he almost jumped from the bed, but he didn't. She was warm and felt good, her skin soft and firm; her smell, again he noticed, like wet spring grass. She pulled him tighter. For a long time he did nothing but let himself be held.

Jermaine rested his chin on the table, a posture Gregory had seen him in before but that had always unnerved him. A grown man shouldn't look comfortable that way. When Jermaine spoke, his chin anchored to the table, the top of his head bobbed up and down like a talking clam in a comic. "Give her a week. In a week she'll be at her best. Don't plan on working then, either. Stay home. She won't get any better than that."

At the bar, behind Jermaine, Gregory saw women sitting, glasses beside them. All were turned so they were looking into the tables, but shadows hid their faces. Jermaine glanced over his shoulder, then put his chin back on the table. "Beautiful, aren't they?" he said.

"Yes, they are."

"You're lucky now. Got one of your own at home."

Surprised, Gregory said, "Don't you too?"

Jermaine sighed and closed his eyes. After a few moments, Gregory thought he had gone to sleep. Then Jermaine said, "They all go rotten, you know, Bucko. All rotten." He rolled his head to the side and opened one eye. "Pick 'em while they're fresh and dump 'em before they go bad. I haven't had one in the house for six months. Before that I went through dozens, one every two weeks." He covered his face with his hands and kept talking, muffled. "I fell in love with everyone, too. I know that sounds stupid, but I did. They're dead, you know, or dying. As soon as they're plucked. It was like loving someone with a terminal illness." His breath caught, and Gregory wondered if he was crying. He wondered what he should do. Jermaine continued, "Sometimes I come here just to look, but underneath the air I smell 'em going bad. It's all bad, bad, bad." He drank deeply again.

Gregory saw a man walk down the row of girls at the bar, pause at one, look her over and then motion to the bartender who took the offered credit card and handed the man a key. He disappeared through a door at the end of the bar where Gregory supposed one of the girl's "sisters" waited. Gregory had never "gotten lucky" at the fern bar.

"If you feel that way, why don't you go out with a real woman?" Gregory asked. "I mean, Sara and I had a lot of problems, but we were together."

"Doesn't matter, Bucko. You hold them long enough, their love rots away."

"Jesus, that's depressing. So what's left if nothing lasts?"

Jermaine said, "Lots of sex. Sex, sex, sex till it hurts. And even that's a short haul, but maybe, you know, you could tie into something you can't let go of. Something that'll stick to you, and it'll either kill you then because it's so good, or you'll remember it forever when nothing else will measure up."

Sickened, Gregory looked into his beer. Because of the darkness of the bar, the liquid seemed black.

Abruptly Jermaine said, "Let me borrow your plant. I can't buy here. They're clean, but it's the smell, you know, alcohol wipe and aftershave on their skin. Just for the evening."

"Don't be ridiculous, Jermaine."

Jermaine fisted both hands as if he wanted to hit him, and Gregory pushed his chair away from the table. Gradually the fists relaxed until his finger lay flat on the table. He said, "I'm going home. Enjoy her while she's still fresh." He stood, all four-and-a-half feet of him and said, "You know what I wonder? I wonder if being plucked hurts. I wonder if it pisses them off. The beer's paid for." He left.

When Gregory got home, the smell hit him as he opened the door, a whiff of wet, old vegetables. He took a step onto the carpet and sniffed carefully, turning his head side to side, testing the air. "I'm home," he said and felt immediately stupid, and then, because he *was* alone in his own apartment and there was no one to hear him, he said it again, "I'm home, dear." He sniffed once more and rushed to the back of the house.

In the bedroom, the case leaned against the end of the bed where he'd put it in the morning. The room smelled fresh with a hint of his deodorant and shampoo. Nothing else. He put his hand on the case, snapped open the latches, but hesitated with his hand on the edge of the lid. No, he thought, it couldn't be from here. Not yet.

In the hallway he couldn't smell anything. Pictures on the wall of Sara and him horseback riding stopped him for a moment. He straightened the close-up that showed them side by side holding reins to horses that were blurry brown shapes in the background.

In the living room he caught it again, a deep, damp solid smell like packed leaves gone gray and slimy at the bottom of a barrel. He wondered how he could have missed it in the morning before leaving for work. The trash can under the coffee table was empty and dry. He moved into the kitchen where he checked the garbage can, the trash compactor, the garbage disposal and the refrigerator, all dry and odorless. Frustrated, he stood in the middle and clamped his hands on his hips to survey the room. He sniffed loudly.

"Ahhh," he said. The field of African Violets on the counter top looked suspicious. Their leaves drooped colorlessly over the edges of the pots, and when he leaned close, the source of the smell became obvious. He poked at the gummy soil at the base of several of the plants. He'd over watered, something Sara had warned him about before she left, and now the dirt was muddy and rotting the plants.

He opened the kitchen window, turned on the stove's exhaust fan and went back into the bedroom.

Later, in bed with the plant/woman, the light on, Gregory examined her skin. He pressed his finger into her upper arm, one of the few places he had discovered he could touch without triggering some kind of motion. The skin compressed exactly as if it were real, a quarter of an inch of give and then a hard resistance as if he were digging into bone. Close up, he could see nothing plant-like about her. He stroked her arm, which felt real. Even the slight whisper of his fingers moving back and forth was convincing.

He jerked his hand back and wiped it on his thigh.

An hour later, after lying beside her but not touching her, waiting, bizarrely he realized, for her to do something, he rolled away and dialed the telephone.

"Sara," he said when she answered, "The violets are dying. I over watered."

She said nothing. He listened to the wisp of static, a thread of a ghost conversation from some crossing of the lines.

"I can't talk to you now," she finally said and hung up.

The dead phone in his hand, Gregory sat on the edge of the bed. He looked at the plant lying on her back, and he couldn't detect even a thread of passion within himself. He hung the phone back up, but before he let go it rang, startling him into knocking it to the floor. He grabbed it and pressed it hard to his ear. "Sara?" he said.

"Jermaine."

"Jermaine?"

"Yes."

He squeezed the phone hard. "Jermaine?"

"I shouldn't have bothered you about borrowing your plant."

At first, Gregory couldn't figure out what Jermaine was talking about. Then he remembered. "Oh. That's okay."

"No. I mean it, Bucko. I apologize. I won't do it again."

They talked for a few minutes, and when they hung up, Gregory realized he felt more sorrow than revulsion for the little man.

In the cafeteria the next day, Gregory saw a haggard and unkempt Jermaine walk through the door, his tray in hand, and when their eyes met Jermaine looked quickly away and sat at another table. Gregory ate alone.

The African Violets weren't any livelier that evening as Gregory contemplated them. If anything, despite the open window, the smell was worse. He put a thick layer of paper towels under all the pots, using up two rolls and part of a third, reasoning that if he could blot away as much of the water as possible, he might be able to reverse the rotting. After a half hour, he replaced the soaked towels with a new layer. He called a florist who said, "If they ain't dead yet, don't water again until the dirt's like rock. Them violet's hardier than they look. Try talking."

"To the plants?" he said weakly.

"Sure. Plants got feelings too."

He turned up the heat in the apartment, figuring that the violets would dry out quicker, but he couldn't bring himself to talk to them.

Even though he had stored the plant/woman in her case, he slept that night on the couch.

Late in the night, something woke him. His neck hurt. One arm of the couch held his head higher than his pillow; the other arm forced his knees to bend a little bit so that the back of his thighs ached. He rolled to his side. What woke him? He strained his eyes in the darkened room; the DVD clock glowed a steady green, 2:17 a.m. A sound, he decided, some small sound that didn't belong. The refrigerator motor kicked on and he almost screeched. A click, maybe, a metallic sound like a briefcase unlatching. Carefully, slowly, he raised his head and listened. The refrigerator hummed. Something rumbled in the distance outside, a train, perhaps, or some industry that day noises muffled. Something thumped. He pushed himself onto one elbow. A neighbor, maybe, opening a door or dropping a book? At 2:17? But it sounded like it was in the apartment. What in his apartment could make such a noise? A latch opening and then a thud? He thought of the plant/woman's case leaning against his bed, the dead shape within, waiting only to be used.

His head raised in the dark, super aware, he listened for another minute, but heard nothing. Were these imagined sounds? Sometimes in a strange room he would hear things, creeping steps on a carpet, the tiny pop of lips separating, the crack of a knuckle or knee, and these could be like those. He began to believe he had imagined them. Then he smelled the rotting violets, but he'd been smelling them for hours and hardly noticed them now. Something else, though. He thought he smelled something else, something familiar. Cut grass. Wet, cut grass. Was she in the hallway now, hidden in the shadows, waiting for him to put his head back down? He thought, how patient is a vegetable? and he almost laughed, but he choked it back. Could her eyes really see? Jermaine didn't say that she couldn't see. Plants are light sensitive. He reached for the table lamp at the end of the couch, a lamp he couldn't see but knew was there. His arm felt naked, hairs on end, and he almost expected something to grab his wrist, a warm firm inhuman grip to stop him from turning on the light.

He turned on the light. The room was empty. The hallway was empty. He wrapped the blanket around himself, took a carving knife from the kitchen, and stalked down the hallway to the bedroom.

The top latch on the case was open. Thoughtfully, Gregory pressed it closed. The mechanism barely held. He touched it from behind and it snapped open. The sound was the same he'd heard, the one that woke him. He tested it again to make sure. It had popped open on its own, he concluded. Taking a deep breath, he unlatched the bottom one, which was firmly shut, and opened the case. She stood the way he'd left her: her head turned to one side, one arm straight and the other slightly bent so the elbow pressed against the case.

She was beautiful, but like a sculpture beautiful, like a well done photo in a men's magazine, not real, not thinking, and in an elemental way, not satisfying. A representation of human beauty. Not human. He shut the case, and pulled it into the living room. He would call the plant store in the morning and have them take it back. Then he'd call Sara. Maybe she wouldn't talk to him. Maybe she would. He thought he would tell her this: "You can talk to plants, but they won't listen," and then he wouldn't explain what he meant. Maybe she could show him how to save the violets. He slept in his own bed, and when he woke in the morning, he couldn't remember any dreams, good or bad.

At lunch he wanted to tell Jermaine what he had decided, but Jermaine didn't come in. Gregory pushed a lone corn kernel through the creme with his fork, waiting for him until the cafeteria began to clear. He stopped a man on the way out who was Jermaine's coworker, asked about him, but he said he hadn't come to work. "He didn't call in sick, either, and I got a contract two inches thick to finish with him by tomorrow. So if you see him, tell him Roger's pissed!" the man said.

Gregory dropped his tray on the nearest table and ran to his office and the phone. The company directory had both Jermaine's number and address. Jermaine's answering machine said, in a subdued voice, not the one Gregory associated with Jermaine at all, "Thank you for calling, but I'm not at home. Please leave a message at the beep."

At Jermaine's apartment, after knocking, Gregory pushed the front door open. The apartment looked much like his own, a small living room, a kitchen to the left and a hallway that led to a bedroom. Gregory felt that he should be scared, or feeling silly and out of place, but he didn't. He knew what he'd find. And when he entered the bedroom, he wasn't surprised to see a plant/woman case open on the floor; and he wasn't surprised to see blood on the sheets that covered two bodies, a lot of blood; and he wasn't surprised, not one bit, that through the sheets that covered one of the humps, protruded thorns, thousands of needle sharp, translucent at the end, thorns.

O TANNENBAUM

CHRISTMAS IS ABOUT FRIENDS. YOU HAVE TO BELIEVE THIS AND NOT GET discouraged. Look around you. Everyone here is poor—some poorer than you—some are crazy, but look at them, eating turkey generous people donated, opening baskets full of clothes that are meant for them. All gifts of love. All symbols of human kindness. Today, of all days, you can't give up.

Here, pull up a chair. Grab a plate of turkey. Go ahead. Fill it up with dressing too. Everybody always shares. As long as I've lived, people have been kind. Maybe today I can give you a little in return for all that's been given me.

So there won't be any surprises, let me tell you something straight up front about me as an explanation. This Christmas Day, I turned twenty-one—it's my birthday, I think, but not for sure. It's different for me. Lots of people don't know for certain when they're born. They're abandoned at birth, so a birthday is assigned to them, probably one pretty close too. A baby, you can tell within a month or two how old they are, but that doesn't work for me. See, I have to count days, because for me, it's always Christmas.

Well, that's not exactly true. Lately it's been Christmas—the last five years ago or so, and for the five years before that, it was the last day of the Saturnalia. And before that, one kind of winter solstice celebration or another as far back as I can remember. My years, of course. Not your years. Really, for me, it's always Christmas.

Like this morning, I woke up in this shelter. The cot felt solid under my back, and the bed roll was worn but clean. Smelled old, you know, but not bad. Some folks were already stirring.

Guy next to me sat up coughing. Young looking fellow. Maybe my age, but a real dry cough that doesn't bring up anything, and he kept going for a couple of minutes.

"Got to quit these coffin nails," he finally said, lighting one up, tears still streaming down his cheeks. He took a deep drag. "Gonna be a good one today. I can tell," and he offered me a smoke. See, first thing that happened to me today was an act of generosity.

I shook my head. People moving all around. Elderly ones, or the touched ones, talking to themselves. Bundled up, mostly. Like that guy over there—three trashed coats and two grimy scarves. Hat pulled over the ears. It's warm in here, but homeless folk hold their clothes tight.

Gina entered my head then. I hadn't thought of her at first, and that made me sad, you know, 'cause every time we talk now it's probably the last. Without a miss for two-and-a-half months I've called her in the morning to say hi, to see how she is.

My months, that is, not yours. Like I said, every day is Christmas for me, and for me, two-and-one half months ago was 1915 when this soldier I met, Humphrey, asked me to call Gina. He sat next to me in the trench; I'd found out earlier in the day that we were twenty miles south of Verdun. German trenches were a hundred yards to the east, but you couldn't see them. Broken spirals of barbed wire, torn up dirt, a busted ambulance were all I could see. Night had fallen, and it had gotten very cold. A sentry walking by, head low, broke through a layer of fresh ice that had formed over the mud, so every step crackled, then squished. We had to pull our feet back to let him pass. The soldier's boots made a silly little squeaking sound when they pulled free.

Humphrey laughed. He was tired and scared, an eighteen-year-old Brit with a downy, blonde moustache and bloodshot eyes. He laughed at the ridiculous sound though, and then he started telling me about his family and his girlfriend, Gina. He talked for an hour, low and passioned and non-stop. He made me swear to contact her if he didn't make it home.

"It's Christmas," he said, and he didn't say anything about where we were or what we were doing. He leaned his head against his gun and shut his eyes and by the light of the winter moon told me about Christmas in Lancashire, where he was born. I wish you could have heard his voice, kind of low and broken. He was a lot more down than you. "They're roasting chestnuts," he said. "And eating quince pudding, and telling each other stories. My Uncle Charles will bring out a cask of stout—he makes it himself—and they'll tap it open. He'll pour pints all around. Charles and Aunt Edna will be pie-eyed and toasting to the King's good health. Gina will be with them." Humphrey paused for a long time at that. No other sounds up and down the trenches, just cold, milky light pouring down on us, and the air like ice razors pressing against our cheeks. Finally, he breathed, "Oh, Gina, my good girl, my black-eyed girl."

"Do they sing carols?" I asked. It had been a good day for me. Everyone clapped me on the shoulder. Ruddy faced fellows, mostly young, like myself, like you. "Merry Christmas, old sport," they'd say. "Separated from your company, are you?" and they'd offer me stiff shots of warm brandy from hip flasks that suddenly appeared.

"Yes," said Humphrey. "They sing 'O Christmas Tree.'" and he started to sing it, very softly, and I could tell he was crying. His voice, clean and clear, carried in that icy air, and it seemed like the only sound in the world, all tied up in the night sky and the moon and the barbed wire, and when he got to the part that goes, "They're green when summer days are bright; they're green when winter snow is white," his voice cracked, and he could go no further.

It was the saddest thing I have ever seen in my life: Humphrey slumped down in the bottom of the trench, lost and far from his home, from his Gina, the marvelous dark-eyed Gina who was hanging popcorn strings on a Christmas tree in a fire-lit room surrounded by Humphrey's parents and sisters and brothers and Uncle Charles and the homemade stout a million miles away.

And the echo of Humphrey's Christmas carol still rang in my ears, and I realized it wasn't an echo. It was the same tune, but the words had changed. Humphrey looked up too. He canted his head to one side and listened. Clear, so clear, as if the singer was in the trench with us, we heard a voice singing Humphrey's song. It sang, "O Tannenbaum, O Tannenbaum . . ."

Humphrey hopped up then, and so did I, and looked across the no man's land. A face looked back. A German face under a pointy helmet, and he waved a tiny, white handkerchief at us. Humphrey dug into his back pocket and waved his own handkerchief. I don't know who climbed out of the trench first, the German or Humphrey, but I followed Humphrey across the cratered ground to the broken lines of barb wire in the middle.

Humphrey didn't even pause at the wire. He stepped over it, his hand out, "Merry Christmas, old chap," he said.

"Fröhliche Weihnachten, mein Freund," the German said back, and they shook hands.

I stood behind them, arms wrapped around me against the cold. The moon, bright as any flare. All the way up and down the lines, as far as I could see, men were tentatively climbing out of trenches, walking toward the enemy, embracing, pulling out pictures to show each other.

Humphrey handed me a flask, his eyes shiny, his face alive with merriment. "It's Schnapps," he said. "It's Christmas Schnapps."

I fell asleep that night in the trenches, and I woke up the next day, a year later on Christmas in a hospital in London. Called Gina on the telephone. Told her I was a friend of Humphrey's. Found out he had died in January, but she was so glad to hear from me. Asked me if I was the "Yank" Humphrey had written to her about.

We talked a long time. It was another good day. In the hospital they brought in big baked hams. Cut them up in the wards. Even the sickest of the sick. Even the amputees and fellows who'd been gassed in the battle who couldn't hardly breathe, were happy. I made sure they sang "O Christmas Tree," because I knew I'd made a friend. For the first time in my life I could talk to one person from day to day. Gina told me to keep in touch. With the telephone, I could. No matter where I was on Christmas Day, I could call her.

So when I woke this morning, the man in the cot next to me offered me a smoke. A fellow from the kitchen told me that they'd be serving turkey and all the fixings in a couple of hours. Some kids from the high school were coming over later to carol with us. I asked him where the phone was. Yesterday—last year—Gina wasn't doing so good. Her heart, she said, was weak. "But you're sounding good," she had said.

"Yeah," I said. "The years have treated me well."

I made the call. She's in a nursing home in San Francisco. Moved to America in '57. I was afraid. The phone rang for a long time. Not many nurses on Christmas morning, and then someone answered.

I asked for Gina. Gina who? she asked, and I told her. "I'm new here," she said. "I don't know that patient." Papers shuffled around on her end. She put the phone down, and someone mumbled to her in the background.

You've got to understand. I've never known anyone for more than a day. A day is all I get. I don't understand why. When the morning comes, I wake up, and it's Christmas. Sometimes I won't sleep for a couple of days, but everyone sleeps. It can't be avoided. Maybe I vanish in the night. Maybe a year later I appear when no one is looking. Who can tell? I always wake up in a place where a stranger could go unremarked, an army, a hospital, a festival, a flop house and soup kitchen like this one. I don't know if it's a curse—there's lots I don't know—but all I get is a day a year, and I'm a stranger that no one knows.

Then Gina came on the line. It was her voice. I've heard her grow old. "Hello, old friend," she said. "Merry Christmas."

"Merry Christmas," I said.

Each year she's been there. Each year. She's ninety-six now. I'm twenty-one today. It's my birthday. In three hundred sixty-five years for you, I'll be twenty-two, but I want to tell you something. It's important I think.

I hear rumors of bad things in the world. I hear about wars; I've even seen some, but in my experience, human beings are good. They're generous. They share with strangers, and they reach out to someone they've only talked to on the phone once a year for eighty years. If you could just see things from my perspective, you'd understand, even without friends, people are good. There are reasons to hope.

You shouldn't give up. People will help.

And you know what else? I wonder if you could do me a favor. You could? Great. I wonder—would you mind if I phoned you next year, here? Do you think you could find your way back here on Christmas to take my phone call? It would mean a lot to me.

NOR A LENDER BE

ON A PARK BENCH NEAR THE SWINGS, THE OLD MAN IN AN OVERCOAT EYES the children. He's positioned himself carefully away from the parents who are talking amiably on a set of benches on the other side of the playground equipment. Near him, a pair of boys dressed in matching blue jumpers take turns going down the slide. The old man studies them for a while. They're maybe five and four, he decides, very sweet; they smile often; the same shade of blonde hair curls out from beneath their caps.

On the teeter-totters, a handful of older kids, around nine or ten years old, rise then fall in rhythm. They laugh in unison at some joke. Beyond them on the grass, a couple of teens throw a football back and forth. The old man sighs and looks at his hands. Liver spots mar the knuckles and make indecipherable patterns on their backs. He imagines things crawling under his skin, moving beneath the loose parchment of his flesh. He resists the urge to scratch his fingers. When he raises his left hand from his leg, it trembles slightly.

Underneath the slide, a little girl sits against a support pole, drawing patterns in the gravel. She's maybe eight, the old man guesses. Her blonde hair matches the boys going up the ladder. Her lips are thin and serious. She concentrates on what she's drawing, erasing a part of it and starting again. When she finally looks up, as if sensing she is being watched, her eyes are dark brown.

"Hi," she says, not lifting her finger from the spot on her drawing.

The old man glances at the parents on the other side. They're facing each other, chatting. Nobody seems to notice him or the child. He gestures to her—a come closer wave.

"Hey," he says. "Hey, little girl. Do you want to know a secret?"

She looks at her work for a moment, makes a final line in the gravel, then gets up, brushes the back of her dress and says, "Do you know one?"

"Sure," he says. "A good one. Come a little closer so I can tell you." He keeps his hands on his legs so she won't see the trembling. The trembling might frighten her. If she knew about the things under his skin, it might frighten her. If she knew what swam behind his eyes, it would drive her off.

*

The two observers, a black-haired woman in a gray pantsuit, and a man, sporting old-fashioned glasses, jeans and neatly pressed sport shirt had come into class at the beginning, taken seats in the rear, then not moved other than to whisper quietly to each other during William's lesson on *Hamlet*.

William paid them little attention. Visitors came to his class regularly: parents who'd just enrolled their kids, still suspicious of a live teacher instead of a computer DeskTop unit; media people with tiny cameras who'd film for their programs ("Retro-Teaching Survives in Colorado" was the title of a piece a week earlier); board of education members, each with their own agenda, etc. They'd make notes about the semi-circular desk arrangement, how much William talked, how often students responded. The minute details seemed to fascinate them. Sometimes old folk came in to wallow in nostalgia, to remember when all schools used to be like this.

William concentrated on the class of fifteen students; they were playing a quote game.

"So," said William, "If I were your boyfriend and you wanted to dump me, what might you say?"

Shelia, a sixteen-year-old with a splash of freckles across her cheeks and nose nervously raised her hand. "My Lord, I have remembrances of yours that I have longed to deliver?" She paused, pantomimed handing him something, then smiled when William took it. Her fingertips brushed his palms. She said, "I'd tell you that if I returned your ring or something."

William nodded again, leaning toward her. "Yes, Shelia. Exactly. But what if I denied it hurt me? What if I were a creep and said to you, 'No, not I. I never gave you ought'?" He said it gruffly, brusquely as if he really was irritated at her, as if he despised the idea of her.

"My honored Lord," she said, flushing. "You know right well you did. And with them words of so sweet breath composed as made the things more rich." She sighed. "I love that part."

William wandered around the room. The students watched him; he could feel their eyes—their attention—centered on him. It was always this way: the interaction, the game with the things he loved and the class, like opening a great oak door between them and the material, and he remembered again the first time he'd really understood Hamlet, facing the ghost on the stage, talking into the darkness, "King, Father, royal Dane. Oh, answer me! Let me not burst in ignorance."

William shivered. Literature struck him so immediately. He could feel it in the air, shimmering out of the texts on their desks. He said, "What if I were angry with someone and wanted to call him a name? Can any of you give me an insult?"

Jason, a skinny, pale boy said, "Bloody, bawdy villain! Remorseless, treacherous, lecherous, kindless villain!"

"Ouch," said William, grinning, as he stuck an imaginary dagger in his chest. Several students laughed.

Just as strong in room as the presence of Shakespeare were the kids, all of them awake for a moment in this play. William felt like a friendly conductor, punching their tickets on the Hamlet express. They'd boarded as they always did—a bit full of the world, distracted and fragmented, but the rocking of the iambic rails had lulled them into receptiveness. William had played Polonius for them at the beginning of class. He'd said, "I do know, when the blood burns, how prodigal the soul lends the tongue vows."

They'd been caught. By the time he'd gone back to "Neither a borrower nor a lender be," they'd dropped every concern they'd brought to class. It was just them and Shakespeare and William playing three-cornered catch. He closed his eyes to feel it washing over him, and he almost forgot for a moment what they had been doing until Rupert, a dark-eyed boy, cleared his throat before speaking. "What if I said that you were an old man whose face was wrinkled; your eyes purged thick amber and plumtree gum, and that you have a plentiful lack of wit?"

"I'd say, 'Though this be madness, yet there is method in it.'"

Red-haired Tracy said, "Do you think Hamlet was mad?"

Dirk, who sat behind her tapped her on the shoulder. "'I am but mad north-north-west. When the wind is southerly, I know a hawk from a handsaw.' Hamlet knew what he was doing."

Five hands shot up.

"In quotes only," said William.

A bell rang, ending class, and several students groaned in disappointment. They gathered books and headed to the door.

"Good night, sweet prince," said Rupert as he left. Jason prodded him and said, "Ah, ha. I knew it. Women delight you not."

Rupert's voice drifted into the classroom from the hall, "What a piece of work is a man. How noble in reason, how infinite in faculties . . ."

William chuckled and turned to his desk.

"How impressive," said the woman in the pantsuit. William jumped; he'd forgotten about his visitors. The woman rose and her companion followed her, standing slightly behind her to one side. "Victoria Baseman," she said, extending a hand. "Of the Reinhart Group. This is my intern, Isaac. We'd like to talk to you about what you're doing here." She looked around the room. Student art work covered most of the walls: painstakingly hand-drawn renditions of The Globe Theater, examples of

Elizabethan dress, and scenes from *Hamlet*. "The students appear to enjoy learning." Isaac, who might have been twenty and easily ten years Victoria's junior, took notes.

"That was . . . amazing. I was moved," said Isaac. Victoria shot him an annoyed frown.

William pushed the student's papers into a pile, trying to appear calm. The Reinhart group had swallowed Disney a decade ago, and had made massive strides into education in the last few years. Half the corporation schools in the country relied on Reinhart funding in one way or another, and they were one of the few companies who made money in the field since the privatization of schools thirty years earlier. "They're a good class. It's easier when they're motivated."

The woman consulted a data reader in her hand. "Looks like *all* your classes are motivated. Best test scores in the country."

"It's the school," said William. "The curriculum works."

Victoria snorted derisively. "False modesty. You've changed schools three times with a different curriculum each time. Your students excel when you're there. They're average when you're not. It's not the curriculum; it's you."

"I just teach them one day at the time. I've been blessed with good kids."

"The Reinhart Group thinks it's more than that. We've done extensive studies of student behavior—your students—and we've made interesting conclusions. Because of them, we'd like to make you a proposition." She sat on the edge of his desk.

"I'm happy here," said William. "I like the area." He pushed essays into his briefcase. "They pay me well."

Victoria put her data reader into her jacket. "Fifty years ago, you wouldn't have been so lucky." She turned to Isaac. "Fifty years ago teachers weren't paid by their successes. Good teachers, bad teachers, it didn't matter. They were paid the same."

"That seems silly," Isaac offered quietly, "Doesn't it? Why would anyone work hard?"

"Surprisingly, many of them did anyway. Teaching's more of an avocation than a vocation, wouldn't you say, William?"

William nodded. He wondered what she was leading to.

She continued, "But the schools weren't very good, just the same. When public schools collapsed and the corporations took over, good teachers were bid for. Bad teachers got better or quit. Generally education improved, and education became big business."

"Yes," offered William. "But there are still failings—whole groups of kids who are under served."

"Of course," Victoria said. "The corporate model has problems too. Applying management principles to classrooms hasn't made them all that much better, at least not as good as they need to be, despite the different approaches."

Isaac said, "You mean like individualized, home study."

"Yes, everything done at home through computers. No classrooms. No group contact. Interesting experiment," said Victoria. "An approach the Reinhart Group invests heavily in, but getting rid of the schools as structures hasn't done it. No, the problem is that every approach emphasizes curriculum."

Isaac looked puzzled, "Naturally. Curriculum and technique can be duplicated. It can be marketed. What else is there?"

"The teacher," said William.

Victoria nodded her approval. "Yes, the teacher. So we went big into teacher recruitment and training. That's why Reinhart is *the* major player in education. But it's time to make the next jump. It's time to get rid of the corporate model that relies on thinking of curriculum as product. The product model is dead."

Isaac said, "But what can replace it?"

"Yes, what?" said William.

"The pro-sports model is our new direction."

William sat on the edge of his desk. He'd read of something along these lines in the latest journals.

He said, "It's elitist, isn't it? Sell the superstar teacher to the high bidders? I'm not interested in teaching to a half dozen rich kids."

"Of course not," she said smoothly. "We know you've turned down similar offers. No, we're ready to take the next, logical step. The pro-sport model of education is like a pro-sports team. We need a franchise player, though, a Babe Ruth. Someone who is so much obviously better that success rests on that person's shoulder."

"How's that different? There's only one of me."

Victoria smiled, and William realized she'd led him to this question. He admired the technique; it seemed so Socratic.

"That's our new direction. We want you to be the franchise player, but not like those pro stars. You are a superstar teacher, the maestro of the blackboard. No one is any better. You're the best. But there's no profit in selling you *individually*. We can't make enough. We don't want to buy you; we want to buy your style. Then we can franchise it."

Isaac said, "And we're willing to pay you really, really well."

Do you know the story of Alice?" the old man asks. He leans close so his voice won't carry.

The little girl scrunches her hands in her lap. She doesn't appear uncomfortable, just interested in how her skirt wrinkles when she plays with it. "I don't know an Alice," she says.

The old man looks at the parents across the play area. They're still animated in discussion, not paying attention to anything beyond their talk. He doesn't see any police officers. A breeze rustles the willow behind them. He says, "Alice is a little girl, just about your age, and her story begins with a rabbit. Do you know what a rabbit is?"

"I've been to a zoo," she says. "I saw a cat and a porcupine there too."

"Of course you have," says the old man. "I knew you were a bright little girl."

"So, what about Alice?" she says.

"And inquisitive too. Oh, you're a bright one for sure." He settles back in the bench; he touches her shoulder gently. "Well, the rabbit is late to begin with, and he has a pocket watch. Why do you think he might have a pocket watch?"

"The rabbit has pockets?" The little girl covers her mouth and giggles at the idea.

"He's a special rabbit. Do you want to know all about him?"

"Oh, yes," she says. "My dad has a pocket watch too. It's on a big chain, but it's a lot more than a watch. He says it's his little assistant, and it's really expensive. He downloads it all the time, and I can't play with it. Tell me why the rabbit has one."

The old man checks the parents once again, slides toward her so their hips nearly touch and begins the story. Within a minute, he's forgotten about the crawling under his skin, the extra presence behind his eyes—he's into the story, and he's into her being into the story.

What sold William was Victoria's picture of the product: "Imagine your successes happening with students all across the globe. More and more kids in love with education, with learning, helped there by our simulacrums of you."

By this time they were sitting in the bar down the street from the school. Victoria had bought drinks for them all, and they'd talked about education for a couple of hours. The lights hung low and dim over the tables. Victoria's eyes glistened with interest, and her face glowed. After a while, William found her to be totally sympathetic to his views. "Teaching's about reaching," he'd said. "You have to touch the student with the material and your enthusiasm, or nothing happens."

She'd nodded encouragingly and ordered another round. Isaac took notes and moved empty glasses out of their way. "So how do you do it," Isaac asked. "Are you a stimulus-response man? Do you teach 'whole language'? Or are you into one of the more traditional, back to basics modes?"

William leaned back in his chair and crossed his hands on his stomach. Over the years he'd developed a slight paunch, but it didn't worry him; it made him feel comfortable, like Pooh Bear or Bilbo Baggins. It was the way he imagined a forty-year-old confirmed bachelor should look. He said, "When I first started teaching, I played around with lots of theory, but I don't think much about it anymore. I guess I'd have to say I'm pretty unconscious about technique. The kids are there; the material is there. I teach."

Victoria said, "Like Mickey Mantle."

"'Scuse me?" said William. He nearly missed the table with his elbow when he straightened up, and he realized he'd drank a bit too much.

"Mickey Mantle was a great player. Maybe one of the best hitters ever but not much of an intellect. One day he was giving a batting demonstration for a bunch of little leaguers, and he was trying to explain to them about foot placement and how to hold the hands and where the elbows should go, and the longer he talked the more tongue tied he became and the more frustrated. Finally he couldn't stand it any more and said to the bunch of little kids, 'Ah, hell. Just hit like this,' and he tossed a ball into the air and belted it over the fence. He couldn't explain it, but he could do it."

"Maybe I'll be no good for you then," said William. His face sagged with sadness and the bar darkened. He'd begun to think of Victoria and Isaac as friends. They liked education. They understood the passion of teaching. They liked him, and he wasn't going to be able to tell them how he did it. The money didn't matter. Victoria had painted a vision of thousands of students in love with literature. He imagined them lining up for play tickets, a new audience for Shakespeare and the rest, and now they were turning away all because he couldn't tell these nice people how he taught. "I don't have a method," he said, looking into the depths of his drink.

Victoria put a hand on his wrist. Her fingers felt cool and delightful, and William began to think of her like Shakespeare's dark-haired mystery woman who was a part of the sonnets. "You don't have to. That's the beauty. We can study your teaching while you're in the classroom. We can capture it and can it and reproduce it. All you need to do is what you've always done, which is to teach. We're not buying a technique. You could teach a technique, but no one could do what you do. What we want is for you to sell us your style."

A half an hour later, Isaac pulled a sheaf of contracts from his briefcase, and William signed them all.

Victoria said, "You're a rich man, William. You'll never have to work again, but you'll be reaching thousands. What a legacy. What a legacy."

Their knees touched under the table. William was sure that it was an accident, but he was thrilled just the same.

He didn't remember the ride home.

A week later, the technicians were waiting for William when he entered his classroom. They were white-suited and entirely business like. He could barely tell them apart as they placed dozens of silver dollar-sized disks on the walls and ceiling.

"They're transceivers, William." Victoria said. She wore white like the rest, and her black hair spilled over her shoulders. "We'll be recording everything you and the students do while our computers build a model of your responses to student cues. Our programmers tell me that this part of the process will last three months."

William scanned the room. The disks matched the wall's colors, and he could tell that they'd be easy to overlook.

"That doesn't seem like it'd give you enough, though. A bunch of vid of a teacher won't give you everything the teacher does. So much of it's internal." He was only half paying attention. Today he'd be starting with a new group of students, and his lesson plans filled his mind. Beginnings were so much fun, he thought. Starting them off right was part of the secret.

Victoria half sat on the edge of his desk. William liked the pose; it made her look long and sultry. It was distracting. He imagined writing her a sonnet.

"So how are we going to get more?" she said.

William recognized the strategy. She'd used it earlier on him. "You're being Socratic again."

She smiled.

He said, "All right, do the disks do more than vid?"

"Good question. Yes they do. What else do you think we need to capture your style?"

He turned the problem over for a bit before saying thoughtfully, "Teaching is mostly responding to the audience. What works great one time might crash and burn the next. So you've got to get inside my head, somehow. You need to see the students the way I see them, or it will be useless."

"You come to the point readily. So how are we going to get inside you?"

Something he'd signed on one of the contracts surfaced in his memory; most of the evening was lost to him now in a blur of pleasant drink and conversation. "A new technique, you said, I think. Some way to, umm, more closely monitor the environment."

"Your environment, to be exact," said Victoria. "We need to monitor you, so we've designed some very special nanotech to do the job. You'll need to be injected, of course, and it will be a few days before we have everything adjusted, but by this time next week, we will be getting a complete picture of the students and the classroom as you experience them. Not just visuals, but touch, smell, taste—all of it. All the subtle cues you use to teach from and how you respond to them."

Behind her, one of the technicians was preparing a hypodermic. She drew what looked to be a couple of cc's from a small bottle of cloudy, white liquid.

Victoria said, "It's really no different from what the doctor might give you to clear cholesterol from your system, or to hunt down cancer cells. Only these will attach along your nerve pathways. Totally painless, naturally. You won't even know they're there, but they'll broadcast to the transceivers while the computers build the model of your behavior. In three months, we'll have everything we need."

"That's sophisticated stuff." William bared his upper arm to receive the shot.

"It's proprietary. We'll have to keep you under surveillance outside of the school. Industrial espionage, you know. Afterwards, we'll neutralize it and you'll be free of our interference in your life. It's a small price to pay for the price we're paying you." Victoria patted him on the arm. "There. All done now. We'll clear out before your students arrive."

The technician said, "You might run a slight fever for twenty-four hours. The mechanisms will be duplicating and some people react to that."

William's arm felt warm at the injection site. It spread up his arm into his shoulder. Not unpleasant, but a little creepy, he decided. He felt as if he were being invaded, not like nanotech in the doctor's office, which didn't seem any different from medicine, but like his system was filling with spies. He decided he didn't like the idea of tiny transmitters seeing what he saw. It made his eyes itch to think of it, but he stayed calm. It's a silly reaction, he thought. Nothing will go wrong.

The police officer approaches the old man and his young companion on the bench while the old man recites the Lobster Quadrille for the third time. "Will you, won't you, will you, won't you, will you join the dance," he says to the girl. She looks up at him and smiles.

"I wish I could join the dance," she says.

The old man glances at the officer, who stands in front of them, his arms crossed at the chest.

The old man whispers to the girl, "Remember, the further off from England, the nearer is to France."

She recites back to him, "What matters it how far we go? There is another shore, you know, upon the other side." She claps her hands and laughs.

"Good girl," he says.

The officer clears his throat. "You're doing it again, William, aren't you?"

"What?" says the old man. "I'm just being myself."

"That's the crime," says the officer. "You're not going to make me cuff you this time, are you?"

William closes his eyes. He believes he can feel the nanotech moving around behind them, quietly capturing everything he does, still broadcasting the essence of himself to unseen transceivers. They're under his skin. They're coating his heart. "No," he says. "Not this time."

He stands and says to the little girl, "The book is called *Alice in Wonderland*. You can look it up if you want to know the rest of it. There are other books there too, like Shakespeare. Books for when you're a big girl. Make sure you read *Hamlet* when you're older. You'll like it."

"Thanks, mister," she says. "I will. Thanks a lot."

Within a week, William had nearly forgotten about the disks. He almost never looked for them. The students didn't mention them. He was into the ebb and flow of the class. As always, the kids started off as ciphers, completely unknown and blank. Some had gone through dozens of educational strategies before arriving in his room. All had been on a waiting list for at least a year. They won their spot by lottery. He was highly paid. His school marketed him and the other teachers on the staff through international advertising; like all other schools, they competed for the students, offering a program of study and a tradition of results.

William didn't care. He'd teach in a barn. He'd teach at a bus stop. Every concern dissolved in the face of students and the material. He was in his medium. He thought about sports superstars; did they play for the money? How could they? At the top of the sport, with no human peer, they had to play for love. That old basketball legend, Michael Jordan, going for the hoop, flew for the love of the game. William had heard stories that late at night Jordan used to strap on old tennies and head for the neighborhood civic center in Chicago to play pick-up ball. Some of the press knew it, but no one ever put it in the paper. At two in the morning he'd be setting picks and flicking passes to street players who came in to run hoops instead of hanging with the gangs. Jordan just loved to play.

So William ignored the disks. He moved from desk to desk. He set up small group discussions. A tap on the shoulder here, a well-timed smile there, and always the shades of literati that he brought back to life for the students: Shakespeare, Homer, Dickenson, Brontë, Carroll, and Twain.

The only disturbance in the beauty of the lessons happened in the quiet times in class. He'd be sitting at his desk, watching the students read, and he'd feel a shift under his skin, a subtle sliding like the slipping of a sheet of paper from the middle of a stack. Or a sudden irritation behind his eyes. He imagined nanotechs with legs, running from one nerve ending to the next, leaving tiny footprints on the back of his retina. Even at home, without the disks, he felt observed. They were with him, and they never went away.

William took hot showers. He scratched his skin sometimes until it was raw, then he'd scold himself for the silliness of it. At the microscopic level the nanotech operated in, he could never really feel them. They weren't doing anything. Still, he went through several bottles of calamine. In the quiet times of class, he'd sometimes feel like a fly in a web, and every disk held the end of one string. He squirmed slowly in the middle, connected by the radiant lines of the disks.

At the end of three months, Victoria and Isaac sat in the back of his room again. Except for technicians who came in occasionally to reset the disks, William had seen nothing of the Reinhart Group.

Victoria looked better than ever. She'd crossed her legs at the ankles, and William was keenly aware of her posture, the turn of her hand on the table, the tilt of her head, the half smile he imagined lifting the corners of her mouth when they met eyes.

"Bravo," she said, after he'd dismissed class and the last student had left. "A truly outstanding performance of the teacherly arts."

William blushed. "They were a good group."

Isaac said, "You have no idea."

Something in the way his comment sounded caught his attention. "What do you mean by that?"

Isaac cleared his throat nervously.

"Oh, it won't matter now," said Victoria. "Go ahead and tell him. It was partly your concept anyway."

Isaac held his clipboard to his chest. "We would have told you earlier, but we were afraid it would disturb your style. Maybe it wouldn't. You did fine with all the scrutiny any way, but this wasn't your normal batch of students."

"Not at all," said Victoria. William glanced between the two of them, confused.

Isaac continued, "We hand picked this class for a wide range of learning styles. Several of them were classic, reluctant learners. A couple were ultra-high achievers. We tried to mix them up as much as possible. We needed your reaction to all kinds of students, so this way we guaranteed it."

Victoria signaled to someone outside the door, and a group of technicians swarmed in and began removing the disks from the walls and ceiling. She said, "The students were nanotech primed also, the way you were. We recorded their perceptions of the class too. It truly was remarkable. Do you know that you respond to bored or drifting students *before* they know they're bored? I was stunned. It has been a phenomenal display."

"Oh, yes. About that. When will you . . . you know . . . remove them?" William resisted the urge to scratch his forearm. Even thinking about the germ-sized observers made him itchy.

"Right now, naturally." Victoria tilted her head to one of the techs, who immediately began preparing a syringe. "They would break down on their own in the next few weeks, but this will make sure that none of our competitors get hold of them."

"I wouldn't go to any of them." William drew himself up and straightened his tie. "It would be dishonorable."

Victoria stepped aside so the tech could get to William's arm.

"We're not worried about *you*, William. But our competition might not be so pure in spirit. You'd probably wake up in an alley with a tremendous bump on your head and a bruise on some vein from a sloppy shop-doc who just wanted your blood."

This shot hurt going in, but there was no warmth in his arm or shoulder like the first time.

The last tech cleared the room in a few minutes, and only Victoria, Isaac and William remained. Victoria shook his hand.

"Don't spend all your earnings in the same place, William. I doubt you could. It's been a pleasure working with you." She waved to Isaac, and he rose to leave.

William's throat suddenly felt dry, and he swallowed a couple of times. "You mean, that's it? We're all done?"

Victoria turned back to him. "That's it. But your contribution has been invaluable." She laughed. "Don't tell the accountants that I said that."

"I thought." William cleared his throat. "I thought we could talk over the project some more. Maybe during dinner." He coughed. "Or something," he finished lamely.

"Oh, William," she said. In the pause that followed, William felt like he was abruptly unanchored in his own room. The shot coursed through his veins, and it seemed he could feel the company's nanotechs being neutralized within his blood: a million deaths happening inside him at once. He realized he'd made a terrible mistake.

"You really are precious," she said.

The first time he wasn't arrested.

William had prepared for his next class as he always had, rereading, writing new notes, preparing new plans. He was excited about vid that he'd shot a month earlier in the recreated Globe theater in South Hampton. The New King's Men had played *Comedy of Errors, Henry the Fifth, As You Like It, The Winter's Tale, and Hamlet*. But as he bustled about his room, putting up posters (beautiful, brand new art prints that his Reinhart money paid for), rearranging desks and rehearsing his introductory lecture for the next day, he felt distracted. He'd stop to itch the top of his hand or to rub his eyes occasionally. Even though a check-up the day after the cleansing injection confirmed it, he imagined that not all the nanotechs were gone. It was a crawly sensation, alien-like and disturbing.

As he reached behind his ear to rub a bothersome spot, an official looking man in a gray suit knocked on his open door. After a brief introduction, mostly to assure the man that William was who was named in the papers he carried, the man served William with an injunction. Most of the multi-sheeted document was legal gobbley-gook, but the essential part was clear: "Because of considerable financial and competitive risk, and whereas The Reinhart Group did in good faith purchase the style, mannerisms, content and appearance of the aforementioned party, he shall be forever forbidden from using the same said style, mannerisms, content or appearance."

"Essentially," the gray-suited man said, "You are no longer allowed to teach."

"They can't do that," said William, sputtering.

The next day, however, he found that they could. The school's administration called his students and rescheduled them with other teachers. His classroom was given to someone else and his posters returned to him along with a note asking for his resignation. The principal, a woman of indeterminate age and colorless hair was very apologetic. "It's a copyright issue," she explained sympathetically. "They own the copyright to your style, and if we allowed you to teach, we'd be fined or face possible criminal charges." She offered him a handkerchief to wipe his eyes. "It's all very clear in your contract. You read the contract, didn't you?"

William shook his head.

"Oh, that's too bad. Well, you have plenty of money. You'll never need to teach again. You can enjoy your retirement. Travel. Read. Things could be much worse." She offered her hand, and numbly William shook it.

"They can't do this," he said again. His voice rose. "I'll take them to court. You can't confiscate a person's style!"

It took two years, and all the money that Reinhart had paid him, but he found out once again that they could.

Sitting in a book-lined office, William's lawyer, a scruffy-looking man who appeared perpetually unshaven but who was an old veteran of copyright law battles, and the absolute best man in the business, explained it to William their first conference. "The precedent is long established, but the most famous example is The Lone Ranger."

William said, "I'm not familiar with him." None of the books on the office shelves were literary. All were legal titles. Earlier when he'd tried to take one down, he'd found that they were merely decorative. The lawyer's computer stored the centuries of copyright law, rulings and precedents that the case would be argued from.

The lawyer said, "In the middle of the last century there was a television show called *The Lone Ranger*. When it went off the air, the actor who played the lead character couldn't find steady work, and he began doing promotional gigs as the

Lone Ranger. He'd wear the costume and show up at the opening of used car lots and shopping centers. The studio successfully prevented him from appearing in costume because they owned the character, they argued, not the actor." The lawyer stroked the stubble on his chin. "It's a sad case, really. I think about that guy sometimes, these old Lone Ranger costumes hanging in his closet, and instead of being a hero like he was in the show's heyday, he's just a broken down has been who couldn't even pick up a few bucks for appearing at the ribbon cutting ceremony for a fast food place."

"That's bleak," said William.

Surprisingly, at the trial, Isaac offered to testify on William's behalf. When it became clear that William could not beat the contract on its own merits, the lawyer tried to argue that William was drunk when he signed it. Isaac corroborated the drinking, but Victoria testified that William drank very little. On the stand she appeared imperious, unfriendly and very believable. The day after Isaac's day in court, he quit Reinhart and joined William's defense.

"I sat in your class that day and learned to love Shakespeare," said Isaac in way of explanation.

"But your job, Isaac," said William. "You didn't need to do that."

Isaac looked thoughtful, then furrowed his brow in concentration as he recalled, "Whither wilt thou lead me? Speak. I'll go no further."

Despite himself, William smiled. "Mark me."

"I will."

William said, "My next line is, 'My hour is almost come when I to sulphurous and tormenting flames must render up myself.' I hope it doesn't come to that."

"Alas," said Isaac. "Poor ghost."

But it did come to that.

They arrested William the first time for teaching *Through the Looking Glass* under an assumed name at a small, family school in Mississippi. He had no money for the fine and served ninety days instead. Reinhart lawyers successfully argued William should be isolated from other prisoners.

A year and a half later, they caught him guest lecturing on sonnet structure in a friend's classroom on the east coast. Ninety days again and a restraining order requiring him to stay one-hundred feet from school-aged children. William learned that Isaac had formed a small lobbying group and was trying to change the copyright laws.

A third violation earned him a monitoring ankle bracelet. A sympathetic former student removed it, which was supposed to be impossible, and the student wore it for two months while William taught night classes in Shakespeare through a city-run continuing education program. Three violations put William into the scoff-law category, and he served four years.

By the time he was sixty-four, William had spent more than half of the previous twenty years in jail, always in isolation. Teaching kids in the park had become his favorite technique. Cops knew who he was, and he'd developed a kind of infamy with them. Most of the time they chased him off. Occasionally someone new on the force or a grumpy veteran would haul him in, book him and hold him overnight. Victoria ascended to the Reinhart presidency and seemed to have long forgotten her project from years past, but the meticulous wheels of the company's legal division ground exceedingly fine and continued to prosecute him whenever he was arrested.

He'd sold his books long ago, and he couldn't afford net charges for computer access, so his reading was limited to the public library. Not that it mattered. Most of the works he loved, he'd memorized.

The only result of Isaac's years of work on William's behalf was finally a suspension of the isolation order in jail as cruel and unusual punishment, but the problems with the law never stopped.

So, there is no surprise in him when he stands and says to the little girl, "The book is called *Alice in Wonderland*. You can look it up if you want to know the rest of it. There are other books there too, like Shakespeare. Books for when you're a big girl. Make sure you read *Hamlet* when you're older. You'll like it."

"Thanks, mister," she says. "I will. Thanks a lot."

The script of what is said to him at the police station seems as familiar to William as any play. He knows his part within it.

He pulls his overcoat close to him as they lead him to his cell. Modern as the prison is, with its soft white walls and acoustic ceiling, it makes him cold, and when he's cold, the ghostly writhing of long-gone nanotech bothers him most.

The officer is curt, businesslike. "We have to double you up with someone tonight. A delusional kid. Shouldn't bother you." He opened the cell door. A boy no more than twenty sits on one of the fold-down beds, his back to the wall, legs drawn up, a shock of black hair hiding his eyes. He doesn't look when William takes his place on the other bed. The cell is narrow; William's knees nearly touch the gray blanket on the young man's mattress.

Even though the cells are soundproofed, a soft clatter of noises from up and down the hall reaches William. Somewhere, someone sings. Water gurgles in the wall. For a long time, William listens while thinking of lost classrooms, students shining from within, their own light coming through, reaching for him in his darkness. Memories are vivid and sad within him. He thinks of that last class before he'd signed the contract. If he'd only known, he would have done more with them, he thinks. He would have slept less, thought deeper about each lesson, concentrated harder on individual problems, made a bigger difference. They will always be the "last" class, he thinks. There will never be another. I will never close a door again and turn to face the faces that wait for me to launch their adventures.

"Why do you keep scratching?" says the young man.

William flinches. The voice sounded loud in the tiny room. He stops his hands. "I didn't realize I was. Sorry."

The man's eyes are still hidden behind his hair. "You're pretty old to be in here, aren't you?" He doesn't wait for an answer. "Pretty small room for two people if you ask me."

"I could be bounded in a nutshell and count myself a king of infinite space— were it not that I have bad dreams," says William.

"What's that?" says the young man.

William folds the blanket at the end of his bed into a pillow and rests his head. "Nothing. A bit from a play. You're pretty young. I suppose I could ask the same question. What are you doing here, if you don't mind my asking?"

The man laughs nervously. "I killed my uncle." He pauses as if waiting for William to comment. "Really, I did. Or at least I think he's dead. I hope so."

William closes his eyes. The bed isn't too uncomfortable: a lump under his hip that feels like it will bother him if he stays on it too long, but otherwise not bad. "You want to talk about it?" William asks, half hoping the man will not.

"He deserved it," says the young man. "Nobody would behave any differently in my situation. See, he married my mother."

William opened one eye and looked at the man. "Really?"

"Yeah. He married her, and I think he killed my dad to get him out of the way."

With some effort, William sat up. "Really?"

"My lawyer says that he can get me off, though. He says I'm crazy. See, I told him that my dad's ghost told me what to do."

"Did he?" William's voice cracks, and the walls of the cell begin to vanish. Everything focuses on the young man sitting with his knees up, hiding behind his hair.

"But you know what's really crazy?" The man leans forward and whispers, "I did talk to my dad's ghost." The man falls back against the wall. "Now that's a story you don't hear every day," he says. "That's one for the books."

William rubs his hand across his chest as if straightening a tie. He looks around him. The cell doesn't seem that small anymore. He pictures some posters on the wall, maybe the Globe Theater. Perhaps a playbill or two. "That is an interesting story," he says. "Maybe I can tell one too. It might mean something to you. What do you think?"

The young man shakes the hair out of his eyes. They are bright blue and young, very young. They look like a student's eyes.

"Sure," he says. "I have plenty of time."

"Have you ever heard," says William, "neither a borrower nor a lender be? This is the story that it came from, and it starts with three guys talking about the ghost of a dead king. The king's name is Hamlet, and it's about his son of the same name."

They talk all night, and when Isaac comes in the morning to bail him out, William refuses to go.

SHARK ATTACK: A LOVE STORY

WILLARD WAS DAYDREAMING ABOUT ELSA WHEN THE SHARK CAUGHT Benford, the new mail boy, directly in front of Willard's desk. Lost in his dream, Willard didn't look up from the stack of forms he was filling out mechanically. Bustle and commotion were standard fare at The First North American Trust Title Company, and the boy's silent waving of arms wasn't enough to distract Willard. Then the boy screeched.

Willard dropped his pen and instinctively pulled his feet off the aquamarine blue shag carpet. The shark, a small one if its head were an indication, probably five or six feet long, had Benford by the calf. He screeched again, then started slapping at the fish with a thick manila folder. Papers squirted from it into the air, spiraling about like sea gulls. The boy twisted in an effort to get loose and his pants tore along the seam. Willard saw a long stretch of white leg that ended at green boxer shorts.

"Help!" Benford said, his face an etching of pain and fear. He reached for Willard. Using his chair as a step, Willard climbed to the top of his desk, knelt on the desk pad and extended his hand to the boy.

"Grab on!" cried Willard, and their hands locked. For a second, he thought the shark had lost. Benford moved toward the desk, and his face beamed with hope. Then the shark regripped, shook back and forth angrily, sending ripples in the carpet that lapped against the other desks, and drug Benford under.

Benford's hand disappeared last, fingers still bent as if Willard had never let go. The carpet closed over him and the last papers drifted down to float on its now placid, blue nap. Then a dark swirl of red eddied at the spot, bloodying some of the pages. Within a few eye blinks, the color faded away and only the stained papers remained.

The attack lasted less than fifteen seconds.

Willard dropped his forehead to his hands.

When he had first seen a dorsal fin cutting through the carpet days earlier, he'd glanced around to see if anyone else noticed. Elsa, the prim title clerk he dreamed of in the desk beside his, didn't raise her head. A drooping of tight blond curls covered her eyes. Her cool looking, pale fingers moved efficiently to the next form and she began writing. The fin continued down the long rows of desks, avoiding a secretary carrying a stack of papers.

Later, he saw three fins circling the water cooler. They moved hypnotically around and around, and when Humphrey, the chief accountant, walked to the cooler for a drink, Willard bit down an urge to yell a warning. The fins widened their circle while the fat man filled and drank four tiny cupfuls of water. A bubble hiccupped in the large glass bottle each time.

No one else seemed to see them. He had attempted several times to tell Elsa. Once, he leaned toward her and almost spoke—the words were on his lips—but she glanced at him, her eyes bright, brown and shy, and he said nothing. He loved her eyes and the tiny wrinkles that radiated from their corners like she had spent time squinting at sunlight. Lifeguard eyes, he thought. Protective eyes.

In the year since she had joined the firm, he'd never had enough nerve to talk to her, and she had not spoken to him, even when he left funny little sticky notes on her computer screen like, "HELP! I'M DROWNING IN DOS!" She'd smile faintly in his direction, then pull the note free and tuck it into a desk drawer. He wanted desperately to talk to her now, to alert her.

A heavy slap next to his ear startled a scream out of him.

"What the hell are you doing, Willard?" bellowed Mr. Trusty, the office manager. He was wearing his favorite gray, pin-striped suit and an orange tie with the words, *Get your butt in gear*, printed over and over in black. "God damn it, Willard. You look like a seal crouched like that. Get off there right now." Mr. Trusty slapped the desk again.

"Yes, sir," said Willard, and he slid off the top into his chair. He braced his feet on a ledge in the desk so he wouldn't be touching the carpet.

"The deeds on the Hinson deal and the Arlington Estate have to be finished and at the bank tomorrow morning. I can't have you flipping out when there's work to be done. You'll stay late tonight."

The other workers began to clean their desks, putting folders into file cabinets and packing briefcases. It was quitting time. Mr. Trusty saw the papers strewn at his feet. His cold, gray eyes scanned the office. "Where is that little squid, Benford?" He kicked one of the pages. "Pick up this mess."

When Mr. Trusty turned and headed toward his office, Willard sucked in a sharp breath. The back of Mr. Trusty's jacket bulged slightly. Something between his shoulder blades pushed the jacket out, giving him a mild hunchback. Mr. Trusty grinned at another title agent a couple of desks away and said good night. His smile was full of teeth. Willard hadn't paid much attention to this before, but Mr. Trusty's face, when he smiled, was mostly shiny, white bone.

Other employees walked by Willard's desk. A couple nodded as they passed, but most didn't seem to see him. Their eyes were blank and, Willard realized with a rush, fish-like. Several of them had oddly bulging backs, and Willard wondered if this had always been the case and he'd never thought about it, or if the bulges were new. He watched one man, one he didn't know well—Quinton or Quigley—as he walked away. Before he reached the door, Quinton or Quigley placed his briefcase on a desk, bent down behind it, as if he were picking something off the carpet, and didn't reappear. A fin sliced between the desk legs and sank out of sight near the photocopy machine. Although the office was almost empty, briefcases rested on many desks.

Willard didn't know what to do, but he did know that nothing was going to get him onto the carpet now, not after what he'd seen.

He wished he was back in his bachelor's apartment with its comfortable chairs and neatly swept, beach brown, hardwood floors, where he'd sit at his kitchen table and work for hours constructing ships in bottles. Not ones from kits, but ones he made on his own from balsa stock that would go into antique wine bottles he'd buy at flea markets and garage sales. Using special glues and long tweezers, he'd place each pre-painted piece in its place, plank by plank, until finally he'd attach the tiny spools and pulleys and raise the toy sails. Willard imagined standing on their decks, the wind at his back, the solid thud of waves passing beneath the hull, the smell of birds and islands and exotic flowers in his nose, and beside him, Elsa, tanned and laughing and loving. Willard never sailed his ships alone in his dreams.

A fleet lined the living room on shelves he'd built specially for them, and track lighting illuminated his best ones like art work in museums. Only his landlord had seen the collection.

Now that it was after five, the office was mostly empty. The steady patter of computer keys, the ringing of phones and the shuffling of papers was replaced by the buzz from the florescent lights.

A soft sobbing attracted his attention. He turned. Elsa's hands hid her face and her shoulders trembled. She sobbed again.

"Elsa?" he said.

Her crying continued. "That poor boy," she said, finally. Her voice was low, and even though it was caught in a sob, melodious. "That poor, poor boy."

Willard almost leapt to his feet; then he remembered the carpet. "You saw!" he whispered in exultation.

She said, "It ate him right there." She dabbed a napkin under her eyes.

"How long have you seen?"

"Since the first, I guess." She pulled a book from a drawer in her desk. "I've been reading about them. They're just big eating machines, you know."

A tall, gray fin glided smoothly past Willard's desk. It slid through the carpet for twenty feet, then circled back. Another fin joined it, then a third and fourth. A glimpse of tail fin broached the carpet and a wide expanse of solid, dark back. By the size of the fin, Willard guessed the largest might be fifteen feet long.

"There are so many," said Elsa.

A weighty thud almost knocked Willard out of his chair. He braced his hand on the seat, and a fin scraped it. The knuckles shown white, then beads of blood welled through the skin. He scrambled to the desk top again. Elsa climbed to the top of her desk too.

"Why are they going after us?" asked Willard. "They never bothered us before."

Fins crossed back and forth in front of him. His chair rumbled away, snagged on the back of one of the larger fish. The shark turned in its path, shaking the chair off; then its broad head broke the surface, mouth agape, teeth glistening and it ate the chair, dragging it under in one bite.

"Feeding frenzy," said Elsa. "They're stirred up."

The carpet undulated from their passage. Strong, fishy smells filled the air, like seaweed baking in the sun.

"It must be the blood," said Willard. He pointed to the late Benford's papers on the floor, many darkly stained. A fin cruised through the middle of them, pushing some aside. "Maybe I can draw them off." He yanked some tissues out of a box and blotted blood off his knuckles. Squeezing, he coaxed a few more drops from each one, then wadded the tissues and threw them as far as he could. They fluttered down ten feet away.

He waited hopefully, but after two or three minutes, it was obvious that the sharks weren't interested.

"It's not enough," said Elsa. "We'll have to outwait them."

They watched the sharks' activity. It seemed they'd settled into a waiting mode of their own. Generally their circles were counterclockwise, although one would break the pattern and dash through the blood-stained papers once in a while, and several times the flurry of fins and splashing showed they were still agitated.

After a long time, Willard said, "Why didn't you tell me you saw the sharks days ago?"

She scrunched her knees around to make herself more comfortable. "Until you tried to help . . ." She gestured at the papers on the floor. "I thought I was the only one. Why doesn't anyone else see them?"

Through the western facing windows, the sun neared the horizon. Desks and computers cast long shadows across the blue carpet. Willard shrugged. "Denial, I guess, or they're with them."

She said, "Why didn't you tell me?"

He blushed, then turned his head away to hide it. He was about to say, "Because

I was shy," but a movement in the back of the office stopped him. He stood on his desk to see better. Coming toward them, a fin five feet tall wended its way between the desks. "I don't think we'll be able to outwait them after all," he said. "We're really in trouble."

The wave from its passage tumbled telephones to the floor. Desks rose and fell in its wake.

"Uh oh," said Elsa as she dug through the top drawer of her desk. She sat up holding a nail file.

"That won't stop it," said Willard. He imagined the shark that could have a fin that size. It'd swallow him and the desk and still want more.

Elsa stabbed her hand. She winced and stabbed it again.

"What are you doing!" shouted Willard.

"We'll have to divert them." She looked around the top of her desk, her hand dripping freely. The fin moved ponderously by. "Dang," she said. "Don't look." She unbuttoned her blouse, took it off and smeared the blood into it. "It needs to be fresh and there has to be a lot."

"Better hurry," said Willard.

The fin started back. Elsa wadded the blood-soaked garment into a ball, thought for a second, dropped a paper weight into it, and tossed it fifty feet away.

"It'll take a minute for them to notice," she said, "if they do."

Their reaction, though, was almost immediate. Three fins broke from the pack and headed for the blouse. With majestic grandeur, the massive shark ignored their desks in favor of the fresh scent. At least for the moment, no sharks were near them.

Willard's desk was twelve feet from Elsa's. He studied the carpet between them for sign of a ripple or any hint of a shark waiting below.

"Better do it," said Elsa.

He took a deep breath, jumped on the floor and onto her desk. She grabbed his arm to steady him. The fins closed in on the blouse.

"That won't hold them long," Willard said. "Should we go desk to desk, or sprint for the door?"

She looked panicked, and he could see the memory of Benford surfacing in her eyes. She steadied herself and said evenly, "Desk to desk."

Fifteen desks later, they stood in the tiled hallway that led to the elevator. Willard propped his hands on his knees and breathed in loud gasps. Elsa said, "I've never seen one out here. Have you?"

He willed his breathing to slow down. "No, but I'll feel better when I get home."

He straightened himself. She clasped her bleeding hand next to her chest in a fist. A streak of blood marred one side of her pink camisole, and she was shivering.

"Maybe you could come with me," he said, "and I could bandage that." He could hear his heart in his ears. It was only the adrenaline from the rush to the door that gave him the nerve to be so bold.

She looked at him sternly. "Turn around," she said.

"Excuse me?"

"Turn around."

Confused, he did. She pressed her hand against his neck, then felt his backbone to his belt. He remembered the bulges under some of the employee's clothes, and he understood.

"You're a nice man," she said. "What kind of floors do you have?"

He laughed. "Hardwood."

"I'd be happy to go home with you."

As they walked away, they heard the crashing of office furniture. Frustrated, the sharks had begun to feed on each other.

THE DIORAMA

BLACK! BLACK! HE'S PAINTING THE HOUSE BLACK!" OWEN GLARED through his picture window at Gary's house across the street. Emma, reading a *Roads West* magazine grunted as she pushed herself out of the recliner.

"You're smudging," she said. Owen pulled his hands off the glass, then she buffed his marks away with a handkerchief she produced from her jean's pocket. He thought about saying a woman her age shouldn't wear jeans, but decided he didn't want to start that argument again.

She said, "And that looks more like navy to me. No one would paint a house black." She tucked the hankie back in her pants as she looked out the window. "Of course, navy would be just as bad."

"Navy? You're out of your mind, Emma. He's painting it black, and he's doing it to spite me because of the houseboat."

"With all those trees in the way, I can't tell."

"I'm not talking about the trees. Who cares about the trees? I can live with trees. Can't you see what color he's using?"

"I'm old, not blind. Might be navy, might be black. Why don't you talk to him?" Emma walked back to her magazine, removed her brass page marker, sat down in the chair and then adjusted her reading glasses. "Not that he'll listen to you anyway."

"I will. I'm on my way right now." Owen slammed the heavy, burglar resistant door behind him.

He winced at the brightness of the unseasonably warm early October afternoon, and almost instantly a prickle of sweat formed on his forehead and the back of his neck. He tugged at the bottom of his tie while holding the knot firmly against his throat, buttoned his gray suitcoat's middle button, then checked the shine on his patent leather shoes for scuffs. When he reached the sidewalk he looked back at his own house, a sand tan with sienna trim, plain Colonial two-story, much like every other house on the block. He could see Emma reading inside. She didn't look up.

Owen marched across the street and onto the twigs and leaves beneath Gary's trees where the temperature seemed ten degrees cooler, and the paint-filled air smelled like silver polish. Gary perched awkwardly, high on an aluminum extension ladder. He sprayed paint onto the gutter and then pulled a foot wide swath of black down the side of the house almost to his feet. Then he sprayed the next section of gutter and added another broad ribbon of black to the side of the house. The asphalt shingles on the roof were already painted. From the spray gun in Gary's hand hung a rubber hose that led to a chrome and blue power sprayer hunched like a metal mosquito over a 5-gallon bucket, its proboscis buried deep in the paint.

Gary painted the five feet of siding from the corner of the house toward the first bedroom window while Owen, with his arms crossed on his chest, watched, waiting to be noticed. The window wasn't covered, and Owen wondered how Gary was going to avoid spraying the glass when he reached it, but Gary didn't break his rhythm: he continued the same pattern, painting the window and brown frame a solid, flat black.

"You can't do this," Owen announced. Gary looked down, his face covered with a dust mask and oversized goggles.

"Ah, Owen." He clambered down the ladder, dropped the gun in a bucket that smelled of lacquer thinner, pushed the goggles onto his forehead then pulled the face mask onto his neck. Where they hadn't protected his skin, his wrinkled face was gray with overspray and so were the few normally white hairs that fell out of his baseball cap. He was a tall, skinny man whose most notable features were his hands, long fingered and huge knuckled, arthritic looking; they constantly moved, picking things up, setting them down, rubbing his chin, scratching his chest. The two times Owen had talked to Gary, once at a homeowners' meeting and the other during a short but heated discussion on the street, he had found it hard not to watch them.

"Would you give me some help with the ladder?" Gary asked. Owen pushed his hands deep into his armpits and scowled. Gary shrugged, pulled the ladder upright and clanged it a few feet further down the house. He said, "Still steamed over the houseboat aren't you?"

"What are you doing?"

"Here? I'm painting, of course."

"No, I mean what do you think you're doing."

"You don't like the color?"

"Yes, I don't like the color. I hate the color. What are you doing?"

Gary bent over a box with four 1-gallon cans in it, pulled one out and pried the lid off with a screwdriver. He poured it into the 5-gallon bucket. "Color's a matter of taste, don't you think? But if it's any of your business, which it isn't, this is just an undercoat."

"You painted the window."

"No law against that. Now, at least, I won't have to clean it." Gary opened and emptied a second 1-gallon can.

"Don't think you're so smart. The Neighborhood Association will have something to say about this."

Gary "hmphed." He pushed the screwdriver into his back pant's pocket and slid the goggles over his eyes. "Coming from their impeached past president? Why don't you wait and see what it looks like when I'm done?"

"I won't like it, and they won't either, this breach of the covenants. We have a nice neighborhood."

"Depends on what you like, I guess." Gary covered his mouth with the dust mask. "You need a hobby, Owen. Retirement is making you an old man."

"Old man!"

"Well, I know it's an insult to the elderly, but it's the worst I can think of right now." He picked the spray gun out of the bucket, shook the lacquer thinner off and put a foot on the first rung of the ladder. "By the way, Owen, when I retired I gave all my suits and ties to the Goodwill, but even when I was working I wouldn't wear them on a Saturday." He climbed back to the gutter.

Owen's ear hurt from pressing the phone against it for ten minutes. Emma said, "Why don't you hang up and try later?" He turned his back to her. The city building's tape of music for people on hold started over, a medley of old Rolling Stone's tunes done with violins and French horns. He grimaced again at the coincidence of the first song, a syrupy, upbeat rendition of "Paint it Black."

The line clicked. "City Manager Lisa Younger here, what can I do for you this time Mr. Burrows."

"I pay taxes. I vote. I don't expect to be on hold until you get around to answering your calls. That's what you can do for me."

Momentarily, the line between them whispered with tiny sounds, ghost voices. "I'm sorry. They had a hard time tracking me down."

"Gary Guy's painting his house black. Stop him."

"The fellow with the houseboat and the hot air balloon? Really? Black?"

"Yes. Flat black." Owen stretched the cord from the wall phone so he could look out the picture window. "Trim, windows and front door. He started three hours ago and the front's all black now. Our covenants specifically forbid 'decorations that are not consistent with the general tenor of the neighborhood.'" Owen heard a shuffling of papers on her end.

Lisa said, "Decorations, according to city code, are 'Lawn ornaments and seasonal displays associated with holidays,' like Christmas lights or Halloween jack-o-lanterns. Paint is not considered a decoration. What do your covenants say about general upkeep?"

Owen thumbed through the fifty page pamphlet he had almost single-handedly drafted four years ago when he bought the first house in the subdivision. "Um. 'Home-owners will maintain paint, siding, brickwork or other accruements to the main structure in new or near-new condition.' There isn't anything specifically referring to color, but the *intent* of the covenants is to maintain the appearance of the neighborhood. He can't just willy nilly paint his house a different color. Earth tones! Natural earth tones are our choices. I give everyone who moves in a list of suggested color combinations if they decide to repaint. Good quality Sherwin-William colors."

"He's not done yet, you said?"

"No."

"Even if we could do something, which I'm not sure we can, as long as he's still in the act of painting we can't very well judge the final job. Maybe he's just putting on a first coat."

"He *said* it was an undercoat, but the windows and door . . . and the roof! He painted the roof, and it was already black. They don't get painted no matter what he's planning for the rest of the house. He's loony, and he's ruining the neighborhood. You've got to do something now."

"I'm sorry, Mr. Burrows. Maybe your homeowner association should meet with him. The city can't look at the house as long as he's still working on it. If there are no violations of the code, and your homeowners group doesn't appeal to us, there's nothing we can do. He's not doing any construction, is he? If he's building, then we could inspect the work."

"No, just paint."

"We're stuck, then. Sorry. If it's as bad as you say it is, someone else will complain too. With your history with Gary Guy, you might be better to stay away from him."

"I don't need advice, I need the city to do its job."

Owen pushed the cut-off button, ending the City Manager's chance to apologize again and made a mental note to send a letter to the city council about Lisa Younger's job performance. Emma stood at the window beside him. The setting sun seemed to rest on the peak of Gary's house and shined directly through the grove of oak, casting shadows into their living room. The house itself looked like a hole where a house had been, like the house had retreated backward and left a space that hadn't missed it yet.

Emma said, "A completely black house. You don't see that often. What a wonder."

A week later, the neighborhood association's meeting was a disaster, Owen thought. First, President Phuong Kim Nguyen hosted, and his wife served punch in plastic champagne glasses with detachable bottoms that were left over from their daughter's wedding two weeks earlier. Owen felt some obvious resentment from her, which he recognized stemmed from his opposition at the last meeting to the reception in their backyard on the grounds that the street would be cluttered with too many cars.

He was sure that she spilled the punch on him, and gave him a glass whose bottom kept dropping off, intentionally.

Secondly, Roger Bing, who he could always depend upon to second his motions, stayed home with a stomach virus, and thirdly, no one else seemed as alarmed about the painting of the house. Elston Newkirk, the elementary school principal, pointed out that Gary was still painting, and the house was obviously not going to be black when he finished. Elston said, "Why, just today, when I drove by, he was using brown paint."

The real mess, though, came from the next item on the agenda, the treasurer's report. Vonda Heaton read the total from the monthly income of association dues and the expenses, which, besides the normal landscaping service fees, included a large payment to Fenton and Associates, a law firm. Carol Craft asked to be recognized, stood, locked her eyes to a position four or five feet above everyone's head, her normal speaking stance, inhaled deeply and delivered a well-rehearsed speech. Owen saw her husband mouthing the words with her as she spoke.

"I believe that since the debt to Fenton and Associates was entered into by our past president illegally, such illegality being demonstrated by our homeowners group's decision to oust said president, that the aforementioned president should not only be personally responsible for the debt but also repay the treasury the money he used to obtain the initial consultation, such action being neither presented to or approved by said homeowners. Our bylaws giving the president such broad powers as to act without us should be amended retroactively."

Everyone applauded. All eyes were on Vonda. They scrupulously avoided looking at him.

Owen stood, picked up his coat, began moving toward the door and said, "Gary Guy's houseboat didn't belong on the street!"

"You didn't have to try and sue him with our money to prove it!" said somebody, maybe Elston. "Yeah!" yelled someone else, and then the room erupted in angry shouting. President Nguyen grabbed a brass chip-and-dip serving plate and clanged it repeatedly on the top of the coffee table, sending a spray of chip dust and guacamole onto the carpet. "Neighbors, neighbors," he said. The room silenced. His wife looked horrified at the coffee table finish.

"I hope your property values fall," said Owen, as he opened the door.

*

I'm not wrong about this, am I, Emma?" Owen looked out the window. "They hate me, and I did it for their good." He was sitting on the love seat that he had pulled in front of the picture window a week ago. A huge pair of binoculars rested on the windowsill within easy reach. The sun had set two hours earlier, but Owen could see Gary was still painting. A Coleman lantern on a stool to his side cast a harsh light filled with sharp-edged shadows.

Emma had been reading when Owen came in, her feet curled up beneath her on the recliner, and she hadn't glanced up when he sat down heavily. He heard her close her magazine. She moved onto the love seat with him, put her hand on his shoulder and said softly, "Of course not. You're not wrong. You're clumsy, though. You didn't use to be so clumsy. You used to take time to consider."

He shrugged her hand off. "They hate me." He picked up the binoculars and peered through them. Gary bent over a palette, dabbed a wadded rag into a color and applied it to the wall. "What the hell is he doing? Is that a tree he's doing? Here!" He thrust the instrument into Emma's hands. "You tell me what he's doing."

"Don't bark at me, Owen, and I won't peep at Gary Guy because you're mad at the homeowners." She handed him back the binoculars. "As a matter of fact, it *is* a tree. A California White Oak. Some people call it Valley Oak. I asked him about it."

"You *talked* to him? What are you doing talking to him? What was he doing in my house? The maniac might have strangled you, or . . . or . . . painted you or anything."

She laughed. "You are ridiculous sometimes. He'd been working all afternoon and I took over a beer. We talked for twenty minutes. He's doing a whole forest."

"A mural. The maniac is painting a mural on the *front* of a house in Cherry Hills. Across the street from me he is painting a mural like the side of a cheap restaurant? And you didn't say anything?"

"What would be the point? You haven't listened to me in years. And if you won't be civil, I won't tell you the rest."

Owen leaned toward her, opened his mouth to speak, sort of coughed instead, and fell back into the loveseat.

She said, "It's not a mural: it's a diorama, and he plans on finishing it by early November. He said he got the idea from the Museum of Natural History." Emma took the binoculars back and focused them. "See, he's doing a limb now. I imagine he'll be on a ladder later to get the high parts. The idea, he said, is to make the trees in his yard blend into the forest on the house. That way you won't be able to tell where one stops and the other starts, just like at the museum with the stuffed animals."

"Why would he do such a crazy thing? He can't sell a house like that. The city will have to act now. That used to be a beautiful house in a beautiful neighborhood."

"Oh, I'm sure he is going to change it back after November. He said that he won't need it after then."

"What does that mean?"

"Just that the project will be done, I guess, and he'll be able to go on to something else. You know he only flew the hot air balloon once. When he finishes one thing, he dismantles it and starts another."

"A balloon in his backyard was bad. The houseboat was bad. But they were only there for a little bit. He's ruining his house." Owen looked from Emma to the window suddenly. "Ha! The trees! The trees!"

"What? What?"

"He planted the trees a year ago. Are you going to tell me that he's been planning this project for a year? And that he will just clean it up when he is done? He must have some other idea in mind. No one works for a year on a whim. Everybody is the same. They all want to get something. Look at me. Years and years in the bank, and all that time I dressed nice, talked nice, and kept up appearances while you and I lived in rentals, one horrible rental after another, but I worked with a plan. We got this house because of that plan, and now we live in a neighborhood as good as anybody's. So I'll bet he's got some plan in mind. Nobody buys a beautiful house just to paint it black. Either he's after me, or he's crazy, or he's got some plan. Why he can't retire gracefully and enjoy the fruits of his labor is beyond me."

"He said he didn't want to die in that house."

"He's sick?"

"He said that the neighborhood looked like a mausoleum." She laughed again. Owen hated it when she laughed at him. "He said you looked like an undertaker."

"Well I say he looks like an idiot."

Emma walked away toward their bedroom. "Maybe so, but he's a nice man. Very polite. I liked his tree."

Four days later, Roger Bing and Owen draped their arms over the top of the fence separating their backyards from their frontyards. They watched Gary across the street on his hands and knees painting in some detail they couldn't discern. Roger wore a shapeless, floppy, wide-brimmed lady's hat that completely shaded his upper body. He had said, when the doctor scraped a small carcinoma off the side of his nose the year before, that he figured the sun was out to get him.

Roger said, "Have you been over there lately? He's got it so the ground just keeps going into the painting. Damndest thing. We're standing about five feet from the house looking at what he's done, and he says to me, 'See those five leaves?' and

I says, 'Sure, they're yellow.' And he says, "How many of them are real and how many of them are painted?' Well, this is quite a shock to me because I thought they were all real. So I studied them extra careful, like it's a driver test. Do you know we got to take that damn vision test every time we renew now? You'd think they're saying because we're over sixty-five we're incompetent or something . . ."

"What about the leaves?"

"Right. Anyways, I'm looking at the leaves, which are in a row, almost lined up, and I can't tell where the base of the house is! He's matched the colors. I mean, there are leaves lying on the ground from those damned trees of his, and he's painted leaves lying on the ground so they look the same. So I check them out from where I'm standing, and I say three of them are real. It's a guess. But he laughs at me and says, 'Only one is real.' I get down to look, and he's right. When I get close, it's obvious, but from more than five feet, you can't tell."

"That doesn't sound so great to me. Sounds like you shouldn't be driving anymore. What does it matter anyways? In another couple of weeks he's going to have to clean it all off. The city will get him, or the neighborhood association. The man's obviously mad." Owen pulled his own hat lower on his forehead. The grass seemed visibly wilted in the heat.

"What's going on between Emma and him?" said Roger.

"There's nothing going on. She gave him a beer and he gave her a earful about trees." Owen spoke languidly. The autumn heat made him feel lazy and slow.

"Oh."

A yellow jacket took off from its nest in Roger's gutter and flew almost in Owen's face before veering away. He waved a hand at it.

"When are you going to clean those things out? They start breeding and then you never get rid of them."

"Maybe next week." Roger didn't move. "I've seen her over there several times."

Owen suddenly became alert. "Really?"

"Sure. Ever since he started painting. Most the time in the morning. Don't you go to the Veteran's Hall in the morning? They sit on the ground and yak it up like a couple of gossips. 'Course I can't hear a word they're saying."

"Why should she do that?"

"Who knows. Maybe what's good for the goose is good for the gander." Roger turned his head on its ear and looked at Owen slyly. He was half smiling.

"That was a hundred years ago. And she's an old woman anyways." Owen paused. "And where do you get off with that kind of talk? I have half a mind to paste you one."

Roger sighed and put his chin back on his forearm. "It's just words, Owen. Just a joke." He straightened up. "I guess I ought to finish this lawn. If winter'll ever get here I can quit mowing."

Owen pushed away from the fence too. "Enjoy the Indian summer. Can't last." He headed for the back door.

Roger's voice drifted over the fence. "Even an old dog'll wander off sometimes, Owen."

The next morning, Owen settled into the loveseat next to the binoculars. From the kitchen came glassy clinks and dishwater swishing.

"Isn't it about time for you to go?" called Emma. He imagined her blouse sleeves were rolled up above her elbows and her hands were hidden deep in the murky water.

"Those old fogies. A few rounds of canasta and they're ready for naps. I'll stay home today." The noises stopped for a moment, then resumed.

"Are you feeling all right?" she asked.

He picked up the binoculars and focused them through the window. Gary appeared to be standing at what used to be the front step of his house, except now the gray sidewalk didn't stop at the door but continued on, curving slightly through a flowered meadow until it vanished a hundred yards farther in a dense thicket. All the trees, and there were hundreds of them now, glowed as if in direct sunlight. Their yellow and red leaves seemed almost a flame across the house. The shadows of the closest trees cast purple streaks across the meadow.

Gary pulled a note pad from his overall's pocket, flicked it open and consulted one of the pages. Then he bent down, tugged on what looked like a tent peg with a string running from it to the base of one of the trees and moved it over a couple of inches. He walked down the front of the house, first looking at his notebook, and then shifting each of the pegs with strings on them that stretched from the real trees to the wall.

The binoculars limited Owen's vision so that he could see nothing other than Gary's painting. The illusion of gazing into a mountain oak forest was almost perfect. The real trees blended into the painted ones. Owen rested the eyepieces on his cheekbones and peered over the lenses. The effect vanished. The neighboring houses, prim, plain and proper gave Gary's property a weird, surreal frame. But Owen had been looking through the binoculars for so long that it took him a moment to shake the impression that the forest was correct and that the neighborhood around it was out of place.

Owen's front door opened, and he sat up. His back popped and he lowered the binoculars gingerly to his lap. His elbows had stiffened. Emma stood, one foot in and one out. A picnic basket hung from her hand.

"What are you doing?" Owen asked.

She held up the basket and nodded her head across the street.

"How do you think it looks, you being seen over there while he's making a fool of me?"

"He's not even thinking of you, Owen. If you thought about yourself half as much as you think about him, maybe you'd see more."

"What do you mean by that?"

"Just that you should pay attention to your own house. That's all."

"So, you're siding with him. Is that it?"

Emma put the basket outside and sat on the doorsill. Owen could see the curve of her back and a fall of wispy white hair that covered her collar. She didn't say anything for some time. She said, "Do you remember right after we married when you wanted to take that job in Ontario, and I said it was a bad idea?"

Owen answered cautiously, "Yes."

"I made lots of excuses: I wanted my kids to be American; I didn't want to be away from my folks; I didn't like cold weather; I didn't know French. But the real reason I didn't want to go was because I was afraid of changing my picture of the future." She hunched over. Owen guessed that she had her arms wrapped around her knees, but he couldn't see for sure. "I had this vision of the way my life was going to go, and Ontario wasn't part of it."

"You were right. Ontario was a bad idea."

"Maybe, except we never had kids, my folks died, and I'm cold all the time now."

"You still don't know French."

"No, I don't."

"What's your point?"

"When we argued about going, you said that you didn't want to live, work and die in the same place. You said that if we didn't keep our options open to 'the magic of possibility,' we'd just fade away. 'The magic of possibility.' I remembered that. You always could turn a phrase." She started rocking. Her ear appeared, then vanished. He glimpsed the side of her face. "It seems to me that somewhere in the last fifty years, we've switched positions."

"I kept you in new clothes. You always looked good."

"I don't want that on my tombstone: 'She wore new clothes.'"

"Jesus! Everybody is talking about dying lately. What's this got to do with Gary?"

She turned, faced him and braced herself with one hand on the floor inside the house. Owen thought it a very girlish maneuver. It reminded him of when they had met. She had been sitting on the end of a dock at Smallee Lake, tossing stale donuts to the ducks. She had turned and looked at him like that when she felt his footsteps behind her.

"He's leaving, I think. Pretty soon. Maybe in the next couple of days. I don't want him to believe that no one cared. You know, he's been our neighbor for four years, and all he's gotten is anger. His wife dies and nobody brings him a casserole. Two months later you're threatening to sue him because he parked a houseboat where you could see it. It doesn't feel just."

"The damn thing blocked the whole street. You practically had to drive on my sidewalk to get around it."

"Well, you didn't have to bring in the lawyers. His children stopped him. He had this idea about selling the house and getting away, and it turns out that his children convinced a judge that he wasn't competent. Can you imagine that? He's on an allowance now. He sold everything to buy the trees."

"Where's he going?"

"I don't know. He says he's getting away from it all though, somewhere the children won't find him." She took a deep breath, held it, then let it out in a rush. "He's not crazy, but I think he believes he can walk into that painting. He hasn't actually said that's what he's going to do, but he talks like that's what he wants to happen. He tells it like a story. He said, 'What if the sun was just right?' I don't know what he means by that. But he said, 'What if the sun was just right? and my attitude was right, and I only had a few seconds where I could slip in?'"

Emma looked at him, as if waiting for him to contradict her, then continued, "When that doesn't work, he'll go someplace else. He's talked about a ranch in Washington where he used to go, an artist's colony. He said you don't have to be an artist to go there, that you don't have to be any more an artist than me, but that the people listen to each other, and they don't push each other around. Either way, his kids will be stuck with a house that needs a new paint job. That seems fair."

"You don't think that's crazy?"

"When he talks, he makes sense. He says you got to believe in what you're doing, and not care what other people say. He says he's on the edge of knowing enough to do what he wants to do and being too old to do it. He says that most people don't even know when they cross the border, but that's what it is. I like listening to him."

"I don't want you going over there."

"I know."

She got up, picked the basket off the front stoop, closed the door behind her and walked down their sidewalk, and across the street. Gary came out from beneath the trees and met her. She said something to him and he shaded his eyes, looking in Owen's direction. Gary waved, clearly a "come on over" wave. Emma stood motionless beside him, then she waved too. Owen clenched his jaw, straightened his back very stiff and didn't move.

*

In bed that night, Owen opened his eyes and read the time on the digital alarm on the dresser. 1:40 a.m. A distant hum from the refrigerator, and the measured ticking of the "antique" grandfather clock they had bought new at Penny's were all he heard at first. The less prominent background noises soon sorted themselves out: a train passing through a half mile away, a siren, a breeze wiping the house, his own pulse in his ears, and, finally, Emma's even breathing.

He had watched them eat their little picnic. Gary had spread a dropcloth under the trees; she had taken from the basket a thermos, a small cheese board, a quarter wheel of Longhorn cheddar (all that was left from a present from the Bings), a knife, two coffee cups and a box of crackers. They smiled often as they ate. Occasionally Emma looked over her shoulder toward him. He knew that she knew he was watching, so, eventually, he put the binoculars down and went to the basement. There, among lumpy, misshapen cardboard boxes filled with clothes they no longer wore and newspapers they intended to give to the Boy Scouts on the next paper drive, he found what he was looking for, a photo album.

Most of the pictures were from a trip they had taken during the summer of '63, twenty-six years ago, to southwest Colorado. Here was a picture of Emma at Four Corners with one foot in Colorado, one in Utah, a hand in New Mexico and another in Arizona. Here was a picture of Owen standing in front of a kiva entrance at Mesa Verde. He had one hand jauntily on his hip and the other pointed down the ladder. Here was a picture of the two of them at the base of Bridal Veil Falls near Telluride. The mist from the falling water nearly obscured them, and they were hunched over, their hands pulling their collars tight against their necks. They were laughing. He couldn't remember now who had snapped the picture.

He hadn't heard Emma come in, and he, in fact, did not come upstairs until the middle of the afternoon. She had been reading and did not acknowledge him when he passed through the room. Dinner was polite.

The album was beneath the bed. He thought about showing it to her in the morning. He thought about what it would be like to lay in the bed without the quiet, continuous presence of her breathing. Yes, he thought, he needed to pay closer attention to his own house.

Things would be better when Gary left.

A sound woke Owen up. Gray morning light faintly illuminated the dresser, the posts on the bed, a bentwood rocker with lace arm sleeves by the window, and on the wall a seascape Emma had painted years ago. He strained to hear the sound again.

There was silence. He knew she was gone without looking; he swung his feet out from under the covers and grabbed his robe from behind the bedroom door.

"Emma!"

He walked briskly from room to room. He wanted to run, but what if Emma stepped out of a door and saw him, running? What would she think? What would she say to him?

She would say, "Owen, why are you running? What will the neighbors think when they hear you were tearing around your own house at the break of dawn?"

He threw open a bathroom door and the spring doorstop buzzed on the rebound.

He paused at the top the stairs. The living room was empty. Her magazines were neatly stacked beside the recliner. His binoculars were in the case by the loveseat.

"Emma?"

He tiptoed down, suddenly afraid to make a noise. The carpet scratched at the bottom of his feet. The balustrade slid smoothly beneath his hand.

He looked into the kitchen. The rising sun flushed the curtain over the back door window. The light streaked the polished linoleum.

Then he ran.

The front door was ajar.

Slanting sunlight turned Gary's trees a mellow, softer color than Owen had seen before. He sprinted down the sidewalk, his robe untied, flapping behind him. The street stung his feet.

"Emma!"

He thought he saw a movement at the end of Gary's painted trail, the trail into the mountain forest, a flash of color like a ray of sun on the backs of two people a hundred yards away *in the painting*.

The leaves skittered beneath him. A breeze creaked branches in the trees above, and for an instant it seemed like the trees in the painting swayed too. The sun cast long shadows from the real trees that exactly matched the shadows painted on the meadow.

He skidded to a halt. "Oh God. Oh God. Oh God." He stood on the sidewalk, peering into the painting. In the distance the rising sun caught the face of a snowcapped range of mountains, reflecting orange and blue. A deep purple and black gash marked a pass, a place for the path he was on to go through. "Oh God!" He closed his eyes and ran forward.

The front door slammed him down on his rear, and his left cheekbone and eyebrow swelled his eye shut instantly.

He sat with his legs spread and straight before him, his hands braced on the sidewalk behind. His left hand hurt. He brought it up to where his right eye could see it. A chunk of gravel was imbedded in the middle of a broad, red scrape on the heel.

He shook the stone out and then felt his cheekbone and eyebrow.

He rolled onto his knees then forced himself upright. The doorknob was a bright, meadow green, but was easily visible this close. He turned it. Light spilled through into the empty living room. There was no furniture. In the kitchen he found a card table with one folding chair pulled up to it. A single plate and cup rested in the drying rack next to the sink. His lungs felt like they were filling up with water. Each breath bubbled.

His footsteps, soft as they were, echoed. He turned on lights as he went, and for a moment couldn't figure out why the house was so dark, until he remembered that the windows were covered with paint. Upstairs, in the master bedroom, was a bedsprings and mattress lying directly on the floor. The bed was made. All of Gary's belongings could have fit in the back of a small truck.

Owen sat on the edge of Gary's bed. He realized that the house was exactly like his. The design was the same. Without furniture, there was no difference. He lay down on his side, and then on his stomach. His knees were on the floor. His face pressed into the bedspread that smelled of lacquer thinner.

After a while, he got up, shuffled through the house turning off lights and shutting doors, locked the front door, crossed the street, went inside and sat in the loveseat. He stared out the window, unfocused for an hour. Eventually, he picked up the binoculars and pointed them at the forest. The left eyepiece he canted away from the swollen side of his face.

The next morning, just before dawn, Owen waited under the trees. He wore new hiking boots, new jeans, a bright blue backpack over a new flannel shirt, and his old yardwork cap. He shivered. Frost edged the leaves and a wind swirled some of them into the air. He could smell the inevitability of snow although there were no clouds. Indian Summer had broken.

A sliver of sun popped over the peak of his house. He adjusted the shoulder straps. Shafts of light fell through the limbs and remaining leaves of the oaks. He faced the painting, half embarrassed to be standing there but fully resolute to do something insane.

The light grew and he watched. The trees in the painting stood still, exquisite, convincing, but still. They never rustled like they had for an instant yesterday. The wind didn't touch them. He watched the shadows from the real trees. They didn't quite line up to the shadows of them painted on the meadow now. Where they first touched the house the difference was minute, a fraction of an inch, but perceptible. Yesterday, the shadows matched perfectly, but the earth had moved on. They shadowed the painting; they never lay down as if there were no wall there. When the sun cleared his house completely, he took off the backback and dropped it on the ground. He laced his hands on top of his head like a prisoner of war and walked home.

Later that morning, the phone rang. He listened to it for a long time, ten rings, before lifting himself out of the loveseat.

"Mr. Burrows? This is City Manager, Lisa Younger. I have some good news for you."

"Yes," he said dully.

"About the matter of Gary Guy's house, I had a man go by and take some photographs, and I think we can make a case that he's violated the city's sign code. We ought to be able to get the sheriff to serve him papers forcing him to change it, or we can condemn the property and do the job ourselves. Also, your homeowner's association president, Mr. Nguyen, came by with a formal request for the city to enforce your covenants. Either way we go, the place should be back to normal in a couple of weeks."

He said nothing for a moment, then he rubbed his forehead. "You can repaint it without his permission?"

"Yes."

"What if you can't find him?"

"It won't matter. We can condemn the house anyway."

"No."

"Excuse me?"

"You can't change the house." He gripped the receiver tightly. "The house has to stay the same. It has to stay like that for a year."

"But, Mr. Burrows, we wouldn't be involved if you hadn't given me a call. We've gone to a lot of trouble at your request."

He thought. "Do you know the law firm of Fenton and Associates?"

"Yes."

He extended the phone cord from the wall to the window so he could see Gary's house. "Well, if you try and change that house . . . that . . . work of art, I'll have a court order from them blocking you every which way to Sunday."

"Mr. Burrows, it doesn't fit into your neighborhood. It doesn't match the appearance of the other houses."

He started to speak, paused, and then said, "Who cares what the neighborhood looks like?"

Her voice was amazed. "You did. Have you lost . . . I mean . . . changed your mind?"

Owen saw his new backpack still sitting beside Gary's house. A pile of leaves partially covered it now. He made a mental note to go pick it up.

"We'll have to consider that possibility," he said.

THE COMEBACK

"The art of fiction is dead. Reality has strangled invention. Only the utterly impossible, the inexpressibly fantastic, can ever be plausible again."

> —Red Smith in the *New York Herald Tribune* commenting on the 1951 Giants snatching the pennant race from the Dodgers after being 13 1/2 games back on August 12.

THIS GAME WILL TEACH YOU THINGS. I CAN TELL YOU THAT.

In 1951, the underdog New York Giants beat the Brooklyn Dodgers in a best of three playoff set to go on to the World Series. A hundred years later, in 2051, our manager, Old Deacon O'Doul, who had a keen sense of baseball history, pasted that Red Smith quote on the locker room wall and growled at the boys, "We're only nine games behind and it ain't August 12th yet. If any one of you have an ounce of quit in you, tell me now so I can give up hope and start dusting off my fishing gear."

Baseball's changed some since 1951. Vids everywhere, floating over the field, watching the dugout. Heck, there's vids in the bat and the ball. The home audience can switch views whenever they want. Players are stronger. New ways of cheating. In 1951 you didn't worry about genetically enhanced players, that's for sure. You didn't worry about being traded to Buenos Aires or Cape Town. Nobody knew about guys like Spooky either or humanity evolving. But more about the game is the same than is different, and a coach yelling at his club in the locker room humbles ballplayers the same way in 2051 as any other time.

In the silence that followed, Spooky Earl Waters leaned over to me and whispered, "What 1930s ballplayer said, 'There'll never be another one like me?'"

I said, "Dizzy Dean."

But other than a leaky shower head dripping in the background there was no sound, and the team looked glumly at the floor. The speech worked; we took both ends of a double-header against Cincinnati that afternoon.

Spooky had a career day against Cincinnati. He stood next to Deacon in the dugout and called the defense before the pitch, "Second base, two steps left, one hop," or "Deep right center." Deacon would run through his signals, shifting an infielder to one side or the other, or he'd move an outfielder. Poor Cincinnati failed to get a single base runner in the opener; everything went straight to a forewarned fielder. Spooky didn't miss once. They were quite a pair, Deacon, the gray old man leaning over to get the call from Spooky, who looked like a towheaded kid, his brows all wrinkled up in concentration.

It was a great game: the reason I loved baseball in the first place. At the end, the sun cut across the field; the smell of infield dust and chalk and grass filled my nose, and the home crowd raised a ruckus.

In the nightcap, they only scored one run, and it was unearned. Blue Blackburn walked a pair in the seventh inning, and then scored the first on consecutive wild pitches.

At the end of the inning, Blue stormed into the dugout, knocked over the water cooler, and kicked the bats. He grabbed the front of Spooky's shirt, picking him up before anyone could stop him. "You lost my shutout for me you miserable excuse of a . . . prostate-rater!"

"Prognosticator," said Eddie "Crouch" Potato, our catcher, who put his hand on Blue's fist. "Put him down, Blue. You tossed those wild ones all by yourself."

Crouch was a quiet man, very gentle, but he weighed over two-hundred pounds with no fat. He looked like the kind of guy who'd crush your spleen if you crossed him. The year before we had a rookie pitcher who refused to come into the locker room after a game because he thought Crouch was mad at him for shaking off a signal. Blue was nearly two-hundred himself, but he knew it was a bad idea to rile his catcher, so he dropped Spooky and stalked down to the other end of the bench. "What good is he if he doesn't warn me about this kind of stuff?" As he went out to start the eighth, Blue slapped Spooky on the back of head. "Should have seen it coming, freak."

The vids picked up his behavior and replayed it on the big screen several times, which didn't help his mood. The crowd booed him.

Blue had won a lot of games, and he was a darned good pitcher, but he'd never earned a shutout. Not in Little League, not in high school or the minors. Never. It was just one of those weird things. Weird things are a part of baseball. Take Richie Ashburn of the '57 Phillies. He was playing in a game where a ball he fouled hit a fan. Ashburn, naturally was concerned, and he waited until they started to take the fellow out of the stadium. Then, on the next pitch, he fouled off again and nailed the same guy.

Afraid that he'd jinx himself, Blue never told anybody about the shut out, but we all knew he wanted it more than anything in the world.

Blue plunked the lead off batter in the shoulder. No good reason for it, he was just mad.

The part of the crowd hooked into the batter's point of view winced on the pitch. They passed their V.R. goggles around so others could see it themselves.

Blue wasn't the brightest pitcher I'd seen in my twenty years as equipment manager. Somebody once said, "Open up a ballplayer's head and you know what you'll find? A lot of broads and a jazz band." That was Blue.

He never really did figure out what prognosticators did for the club. In '51 they were still pretty new. I mean, the whole idea of psychic *Homo Telepathis*, which is what the papers called them, as a branch of humanity confused the heck out of a lot of people. Spooky and others like him who got little peeks into the future had only been in the league for a half dozen years or so at that point, and a few teams didn't even use them. Heck, some people argued they would ruin the game, but baseball's survived all kinds of change. I mean, look at the designated hitter and artificial turf! You still have to throw and hit and catch, for crying out loud.

I'd asked Spooky once why he only knew where hit balls were going but no other part of the game, and he kind of hummed and hawed without saying anything. He was a shy guy anyway, and darned small at a bit over five-foot, but he knew baseball like nobody's business—we'd swap trivia and stats all the time—and could tell a great joke. That's how he got hooked up with young Annabelle Martin in the front office. He made her laugh, and even though she was eight or nine inches taller than he was and looked like a model (which she had been her last two years of high school), it was understood they were an item. They'd meet for lunch in the hotel restaurant to split a sandwich when we were on the road. It was cute. I almost expected them to order one malt with two straws afterwards. At any rate, and not to get too far off the subject, Spooky said a hit ball released a distinctive and sharp flash in time he could track. Almost nothing else worked the same way, and he could only predict maybe twenty or thirty seconds into the future on a really good day, so he was no better at the race track than I was.

But he knew his trivia. Once I said to him, "Where'd the term 'Charlie Horse' come from?"

He grinned at me, that real open-faced smile where his face looks lit up from behind. "Charlie Esper. Pitched for the Orioles in the 1890's. He ran so badly his teammates thought he looked like a lame horse, and ever since then a player with a leg cramp uses his name."

I thought for sure he wouldn't know that one.

After the second win, Spooky danced a jig on a bench in the locker room. Deacon gave him a game ball; only Blue refused to sign it.

Of course, Spooky had his slumps. Like all ball players, percentages ruled him. Sometimes he'd have streaks too. Baseball's a streaky game; who can forget Joe DiMaggio, for the love of Mike? The day of the double-header against Cincinnati Spooky killed them, but other days he was useless. He carried a little towel, and if he wasn't seeing so good, he kept twisting it, like he was trying to wring out a vision of what was coming next. When his inner eye was working, he'd stick the towel in his belt or leave it on the bench.

After Cincinnati, Spooky went into a dry spell. About that same time, the tabloids ran a picture of Blue at a local dance place planting a big kiss on Anabelle Martin. She didn't look like she was struggling either, her eyes all bright and adoring. Don't know whether the slump had anything to do with the confrontation in the dugout or Anabelle, but I know Spooky started looking real distracted, and his eyes were red-rimmed.

He quit playing trivia with me, even when I tossed him some pretty easy chestnuts.

Over the course of the next few weeks, Spooky worked his way through towel after towel until they were no more than a tatter of threads. He got another from me and started on it. Didn't matter much to the club, though, even if he wasn't helping. We swept the Braves in four, split two games with the Mets, took all three against Tokyo in Tokyo and went twenty-four for twenty-nine to finish the season a half game back of the division-leading Chicago who hadn't played badly in the final stretch themselves.

And wouldn't you know it, our last game of the season was in Chicago to make up for a rain-out in July.

Blue won five of his six starts after Cincinnati, and Deacon scheduled him in for the Chicago game. All that winning didn't make him any sweeter, though. The gossip columnists were making a fuss about Blue and Anabelle, him being a big name ball player and all, and she being so young and glamorous. Blue would bring in the clips, mostly to get Spooky's goat, I think, and then he'd talk dirty about her to the rest of the guys loud enough for Spooky to hear.

Spooky moped around like a whipped dog. Like I said, his average dropped way off, and he started getting a lot of "false positives," where he'd tell Deacon to shift a player wrong; Deacon would flash the signals, and the ball would shoot through right where the fielder had been before. Deacon started to not trust in him so much. Still, Spooky produced in a couple of key situations. He never put down the towel though. Worried it pretty good, he did.

Most of the team caught on pretty quick to what was going on, but there's three or four like Blue on any squad, mostly second stringers, and they'd yuck it up at Spooky's expense. Crouch didn't like it, naturally, and he started tossing the ball back to Blue in the dirt or to the left or right so he'd have to step off the rubber until Deacon told him to cut it out.

"I don't know what's happening here, Crouch, but you're just hurting the ball club. I don't care what you think of the guy off the field, but he's a part of this pennant drive. You toss it up there nice and don't break his rhythm."

So it came down to the final game. Winner makes the playoffs. Loser gets to think about it all winter. After the national anthem, the team settled into the dugout except for Lemon Smith, our shortstop who batted lead off, and Crouch who was on deck. On the bench, Blue started spouting off about Anabelle. "I finally pegged her," he said to his cronies real loud.

Spooky sat up like he'd been shot.

The players around Blue chuckled and slapped him on the back while Blue worked a ball in his hand.

"Wasn't worth the wait, though," Blue said. "All those looks, and I don't think she'd been round the block before."

Somebody said, "How'd you know, Blue?"

He turned away to answer, so I didn't hear, but his buddies burst out laughing like they'd never heard something so funny.

"And get this," said Blue. "She thinks I *love* her. She's probably registering silverware patterns right now. Hell, I haven't spent two nights alone this month."

Made me sick just to hear it.

By this time, Lemon stepped up to the plate, so they turned to watch. A couple of them yelled encouragement. In the other dugout, their coach was signaling like crazy. The pitcher wound up, and as he delivered, their second baseman took off toward first. Lemon slapped a perfect line drive to the gap, but the second baseman snagged it on the run. Spooky's Chicago counterpart had anticipated the hit, and Lemon was out. Our next two guys went down swinging, so we took the field.

Spooky didn't move from his spot on the bench. Deacon looked around after a bit and spotted him. "Get up here, Spooky! We got a game to play, if you don't mind," he barked.

I'm no soothsayer like Spooky, or mind reader or anything else, but he was furious mad. I'd never seen him like that. His face got red and screwed up, and I could see it in the way he held his shoulders, how his hands moved in close to his side and clenched. I thought, it's a good thing Blue's a foot taller than Spooky, or Blue wouldn't have a chance.

Baseball players aren't supposed to let their feelings about each other get into their game, but it happens all the time. It's inevitable. Left fielder gets mad at the shortstop, so he quits hitting him for the cut-off, or third base is pissed at first base, so he short-hops his throws. When personal feelings *don't* enter the game, it's remarkable. Take the Tinker to Evers to Chance double play combo: Johnny Evers and Joe Tinker disliked each other so much, they didn't talk for two years, but there they are, a legendary pair of teammates. Most of the time, it's the other way around. Some days the game is *all* personality.

Blue coaxed a pop up out of their first batter. He walked the second, and the third grounded into a double play Lemon didn't have to budge an inch to pick up. Spooky didn't say a word. I don't think his head was in it. He was holding his towel, but when he wasn't glaring at Blue he was looking up at the club's sky box where management and their bigwig buddies watched. Of course, Anabelle would be up there too. I didn't figure they hired her for her computer skills. But I couldn't see anything behind the mirrored glass.

From the second to the fifth, Blue mowed them down. I don't think I'd ever seen him keener, catching the corners, running the ball inside if they crowded the strike zone. Change ups floated like marshmallows, sliders broke a foot away from the plate, and man, his fast ball was nearly invisible.

He was tight, though. I could see it in his jaw, the way he kept wiping his forehead with the back of his hand. It can't be argued, Blue was a competitor, and when the game was on, nothing existed for him but the ball and the batter. After five innings, I knew he was thinking about not just a shutout, but a no-hitter.

With two gone in the top of the sixth, their pitcher walked our first baseman, and he got all the way to third on a bad hop single through second base. Nothing a fielder can do about a bad hop. Spooky could call it, Deacon could signal it, and the fielder could be there, but a bad hop can go anywhere and get there fast. Bad hops are a part of the game. Ask Bill Buckner of the '86 Red Sox about bad hops. In the sixth game of the series, with two out in the 9th, Mookie Wilson tops an easy play grounder up the first base line, but the pill slips under Buckner's glove to give the Mets the game.

The ball does funny things.

Runners waited on the corners now; Crouch worked the count full, then fouled off five in a row. Finally, he planted the eleventh pitch into the twentieth row, straight-away center. We poured out of the dugout like the game was over, congratulations all around, and with a three run cushion, Blue looked like a man who'd stepped off death row.

I could feel the change in the dugout too. We started the game *pretending* to be loose. The loud jokes. The relaxed postures. They were a pose. But the way Blue was tossing them in there, three runs looked good. No one would say it, but I knew they were thinking cork popping and champagne baths. The playoffs seemed a blink away, and our remarkable comeback would be complete.

Spooky woke up on the home run too. He started twisting that towel around, watching the field a little sideways. Three pitches into their first batter, he said something to Deacon, and the old guy flashed signals quick as could be. As Blue delivered, left field turned and sprinted for the corner to catch what would have been a sure double at the wall a foot from the foul line. The crowd roared on the hit, then quieted to nothing.

Blue didn't look in, but he had to know he owed that one to Spooky. The second guy fanned at three high ones, and the third popped to shallow right. Our second baseman was camped under there before the hit, so we were out of the sixth.

Chicago called on their bullpen to shut us down through the top of the ninth, but Blue answered back with flawless control, the whole time with Spooky leaning against the rail, watching him.

In the stands, the crowd grew frantic. I could hear it in their cheers as batter after batter sat down. Blue walked one in both the seventh and eighth, but we got them in double plays Spooky set up. No one else reached. Deacon watched Blue too, but he was looking for a change in his delivery. Anything to indicate he was weakening.

"How are you doing, Blue?" asked Deacon at the end of the eighth.

"I can finish it." Blue draped a warmup jacket over his arm. He was so into his pitching, I don't think he knew any of the rest of us were there.

"What do you think, Crouch?" said Deacon.

"He's got more snap on the ball now than he did to start the game. He's on auto-pilot."

Deacon nodded, and I could see the wheels turning behind Blue's eyes. He had a sense of history too. A no hit shutout to win the final game of the regular season would make his name the answer to a lot of bar bets. So Blue led the team out of the dugout at the bottom of the ninth, three outs away from a berth in the playoffs.

Spooky took his place on the rail next to Deacon. Everybody else was up too. I could almost feel them willing the crowd to silence, sending all the bad luck they could to Chicago's batters, praying to the baseball gods.

Blue took his stance, and with three evil breaking balls sat the first batter down. I checked Spooky. He wasn't twisting the towel and he wasn't saying anything either. No hits? I thought. He looked up at the sky boxes again. I'd almost forgotten about Anabelle, but Spooky hadn't.

Somehow the ump saw four perfect strikes on the outside corner differently than we did, and he awarded the next man first base. He promptly stole second.

Deacon signaled for an intentional walk to put the double play possibility back on. Crouch set up wide to take the pitchout, but instead of tossing the ball out of the strike zone, Blue reared back and beaned the batter with a fast ball.

"What was that?" screamed Deacon. He hates purpose pitches, but I knew what was going on. Chicago's next batter loved to crowd the plate, and since we were going to put this runner on anyway, Blue must have thought, why not send the next guy a message? Maybe he won't dig in quite so deep.

Besides, I think Blue liked to hit batters.

The crowd stood. In the second tier, they stamped their feet so it sounded out like a quick, huge pulse.

I wanted one of Spooky's towels to twist myself, so I looked around for something, and there was his towel. He'd neatly folded it and it was laying on the bench. Deacon asked Spooky something, and Spooky shook his head. Deacon nodded, then signaled Lemon who slid to his left six feet.

I thought, double play ball, and I was right. The ball shot straight to Lemon, and he gobbled it up, but somehow he couldn't get it out of his glove, and when he finally did it slipped out of his hand to drop to his feet. By the time the play was over, the crowd was screaming and stomping too loud for me to hear anything else, and the bases were loaded.

Deacon started to walk over to the bullpen phone. It was only natural to pull Blue now. We needed two more outs, and Chicago had eight innings to learn Blue's timing, but Spooky grabbed his arm. I couldn't hear anything above the crowd. Spooky gestured and yelled, then Deacon yelled back. Finally he shrugged his shoulders. They went back to the rail.

Baseball is filled with incredible performances, like the '77 series when Reggie Jackson hit four home runs in four straight official times at bat. A player's not supposed to be that good. Later, I thought maybe Spooky had a kind of Reggie Jackson game to beat Chicago. Maybe more than twenty or thirty seconds of the future opened up for him just then, but I don't think he cared how the game played out.

No, considering what happened, I don't think he cared at all.

The bottom of the ninth. Bases loaded. One out, and Chicago had the potential winning run at the plate.

Blue's first pitch was a ball. Deacon flinched. The crowd roared. Now the pounding feet almost hurt. Our bench players crowded the rail. It all seemed so intense. My skin ached from the tension.

That's what you play baseball for, or course, for moments like that one.

Spooky, though, he didn't look tense at all. His fingers tapped lightly on the rail. One foot rested on the first step out of the dugout. He smiled, and I realized that was the first time I'd seen him smile since Cincinnati. He smiled, then he yelled something in Deacon's ear.

Deacon went through a complicated series of signals, all to Blue. I couldn't see most of them, but the last one was a hand to his right ear, the signal for "high." The player would have to jump to catch a ball over his head.

Blue nodded, then faced the batter.

Spooky turned to me and yelled, "Herb Score."

The name rang a bell, but I couldn't make the connection. Blue brought the ball up, held the pose for a blink, then unleashed a hellacious fast ball.

Every image that followed is blazed for me like those old time sepia photographs. Blue fell off to the right as he always does. The batter brought back his hands to swing, and as he started the bat forward, Blue recovered, his face a picture of desperation and hope, gathered himself and jumped up, glove above his head. Connection. The crack of a perfectly struck ball. A line drive up the middle just as Spooky had called it. But not high. Dead center.

Blue reached the top of his leap, anticipating the catch above him. His mouth was open. I don't believe he ever saw the ball. It caromed off his forehead with a horrible, wooden thud. The ball went up. Blue went down.

Behind him, Lemon charged forward. Caught the ball at his shoe laces. Fired to first to double off the runner.

We won.

They carried Blue off the field on a stretcher.

And all the while, Spooky never moved from the rail. He kept the same smile on his face, and I suppose everyone thought he was happy because we'd beat Chicago.

The myth is that in 1932, in the series between the Yankees and the Cubs, Babe Ruth called his home run hit, pointing where he was going to blast the ball in center field. It doesn't matter eye-witnesses don't back up the legendary story. It's the myth of the called shot that survives, and it's the story everyone knows.

After our game ended, and all the interviews were done, I looked up Herb Score. He was familiar to me because he led the majors in strike outs for the Indians in both '55 and '56. But he only had three games in '57. In the third game of the season a Yankee batter, Gil McDougald, blasted a line drive back through the box, shattering Score's cheekbone and ending his career as a ball player.

The story of Babe Ruth and his predicted home run is just a legend, but I know for a fact Spooky Earl Waters called his shot in the last game of the regular season in 2051. We won the game, but that was incidental. There was another contest on the field.

And that should end the story, but I really should mention the next day a grieving Anabelle Martin went to the hospital to pay Blue a visit. She couldn't get in because six other women were there arguing about who he loved most.

Spooky gave her a lift home.

Leo Duroucher said, "Nice guys finish last," but I say, a lot can happen in a season, and if baseball's taught me anything, it's that you should never count someone out until the last pitch.

Doesn't matter if it's 1951 or 2051. Those underdogs have a way of coming back.

FRIDAY, AFTER THE GAME

ARIEN NEVER CONSIDERED PLAYING FOOTBALL FOR WELLS HIGH TO BE *real* football even though the senses were accounted for: the concession stand oozed popcorn and hotdog odors; the home crowd roared at good plays and moaned for poor ones. The opposing players' stentorian breathing when they took their stance filled his ears. The helmet squeezed his head. Of course, he tasted the mouth piece's hard plastic; it was the only part of the game that *was* real. Despite the vividness of those senses, the grass beneath his fingers didn't feel grassy. All his hands sensed was hard or soft, warm or cold. No detail. No texture.

Also, he missed cheerleaders, mostly Margo. It wasn't that they weren't there; they were, stunningly beautiful, energetic, spirited, rousing the fans with intricate stacks and clever cheers, but as soon as the game ended, the field flicked out, and he was alone in his room, wearing his port gear. The cheerleaders were gone, including Margo.

The experience didn't satisfy him.

But after tonight's game, this could change.

Wells archrival, West Kimono High, owned the same six-and-two record, and the game would settle the league championship, but, more importantly two of West Kimono's players, Broncho Martinez, an offensive lineman, and Bernardino Li-Chen, an option back, lived within sixty miles, while Wells' quarterback, Harmon Byers, lived in Sante Fe, only forty miles from Albuquerque where Arien lived.

What were the odds, Arien thought, that *four* players from two opposing high schools lived within commuting distance? West Kimono's quarterback ported in from Fairbanks. He threw passes to a pair of wide receivers, one who connected in Buenos Aires, and the other played from Sydney.

Arien's senior class was spread over the globe, and were sim-students at Wells because their learning styles matched the teacher's techniques. They ported to classes in the morning, studied all day; then the athletes practiced, squaring off against virtual opponents for a couple of sweaty, afternoon hours.

Their proximity was rare, almost amazing, and out of that unique circumstance, the plot was born.

Harmon, who *looked* like a quarterback, classically chiseled cheek bones, long, smooth muscles bulging in his upper arms, always in his letter jacket, sat behind Arien in their Information Exploration class, a boring study of how and where to find problem-related data. The assignments mostly consisted of scavenger hunts for obscure facts: How was the *Maine* sunk? What were religious reactions to the discovery of Martian lichens? Miss Davenport said for the umpteenth time, "Finding information defines the modern thinker."

Harmon whispered in Arien's ear, "Are we ready?"

Of course, he wasn't really whispering in Arien's ear. Harmon sat in his port room at his home forty miles away whispering into Arien's virtual simulacrum.

Arien checked Miss Davenport. She lectured unperturbed. Harmon's "whisper" would register on her monitors—teachers received way more information about their students in a virtual classroom than they did in an old-fashioned one—but she still needed to pay attention, and Harmon's question was too vague to trip alarms.

Arien nodded.

Miss Davenport said, "What would be a productive sub-search routine to run if you wanted to know a foreign visitor's cultural differences while you made your initial introductions?"

After a pause, Martin, who sat to Arien's left, put up his hand. Arien moaned. Martin always answered questions, or asked them, or initiated discussion, or prompted debate, or looked interested, or otherwise kept the class moving. He was a Turing, an AI student. Most of the first week of school Arien spent discovering the Turings. Every class had at least a couple of them, digital shills who made the classes lively when the real students were sluggish.

After Martin answered, Miss Davenport moved on to another topic. Arien leaned across the aisle and said, "How'd you do on the test yesterday, Turing?"

Martin smiled—Arien thought he detected a nanosecond delay in the programming; the smile showed up a shade late—and said, "My name's Martin. Ninety-two percent. How'd you do?"

Arien considered lying, just for the reaction. If he said 60 percent, for example, the Turing would know that was twenty-five points low, and instead of whatever canned reaction the higher score would produce ("That's a great grade, Arien!" Fake smile.), the AI would have to decide how to respond to the lie, all the time behaving as if it didn't know it had been lied to. However, Arien knew the prank would get him a session in counseling inside of a couple of days where they'd poke and prod him about his self esteem.

"I did O.K."

"That's great, Arien." Fake smile.

The Turings were unfailingly chipper in class. Also, they never went out for football.

Margo sat in the front, a row to his left. She wore her cheerleading uniform today, taking careful notes in her perfectly formed script. She'd shown him her notebook once after he'd missed a day sick, each "i" dotted with a heart. Her head rested on her hand, and long, wavy red curls spilled down her arm. Rather than take his own notes, he studied her shoulders, the way she held herself tilted a bit to the side, her cheek's roundness.

He wished he could meet her for real, but he wasn't even sure where she lived. Her snail-mail address was an international post office box, which just meant the mail was forwarded elsewhere. Most people chose to keep their home addresses unlisted.

They'd gone to the virtual Homecoming together, which hardly counted. Parents and the school monitored the dances closely, and other than dancing, and a chaste hug at the end of the evening, they'd barely touched. It wasn't worth it. Although the port-suit was good for football's heavy impacts, a caress left something to be desired.

After class, they met in the promenade. Theoretically, conversations out of the room weren't monitored, but Arien, like most of the kids, didn't believe that. Comments were elliptic.

"Are you still going to do it?" Margo asked. She had a musical voice. Arien thought it sounded like a pipe organ, a small one, each note ascending through golden tubes. Sometimes they'd meet in study hall, and he'd ask her to read his notes back to him, just so he could hear her speak.

"It's a once-in-a-lifetime chance," said Arien. The passage between classes was airy and wide. Students strolled or gathered in small groups. Wells High adopted a classic Greek look this year—last year had been ivy league Victorian—so the walks were marble, and tall colonnades flanked doors into classrooms. The administrators at Wells reveled in digital remodeling. The teachers were the same way. Last week Davenport's class met in sawgrass-covered sand dunes with the ocean pounding away in the background. This week she'd gone to a kind of a post-Disney, pseudo-dental office burnished chrome and porcelain motif room under twenty-foot tall ceilings.

Margo held her books close to her chest, arms crossed over them, her expression serious. "Will the place work?" She'd suggested the site weeks earlier, when he'd told her about the plan.

Arien nodded. "There's enough light. The grass is flat. I lined out yard markers a couple days ago. The ground up chalk worked just like you said it would."

She said, "What if you . . . you know?"

He knew she meant to say, "What if you get caught?" a phrase that would surely alert a monitor.

They were at the door to his next class, Advanced Placement World History. "There would be a price to be paid. We won't get. . .you know." He thought about consequences. How many rules had he broken already? There was the stolen equipment, of course, and the lying to his parents about where he was going. The worst, though, the ones that might really get them, were the quarantine violations.

"It's just too paranoid," Arien said angrily. "I don't think I'm going to get the flu or a cold or something from everyone I meet. You know they used to play football in front of big crowds. A hundred thousand real people in the same stadium, and they didn't all get sick from each other."

Margo looked panicked for a second, then recovered. "Thanks. I hadn't thought about it that way. Maybe I can use that idea in my paper on archaic practices."

"Yeah," said Arien lamely. "Anything I can do to help." He kicked himself mentally for almost blurting out the plan.

She turned and started to walk away, then stopped. "I wish I could go," she said. "It'd be nice to spend some time with you."

Pressure constricted Arien's chest. She really liked him! He said, for the invisible monitor's benefit, "Well, study hard and you can get into this class too."

Coach practiced the new plays that afternoon, but they walked through the formations without hitting. On defense, Arien lined up to the left of the nose guard. For West Kimono, Coach had put in several twist plays where Arien switched places with the nose guard or the defensive end after the snap. Mostly Wells ran slants on defense, and the extra steps threw Arien's timing off.

Arien took his stance, almost helmet to helmet with the offensive tackle. On this twist he was supposed to go around the nose guard and into the hole between the other team's center and guard. They repeated the play a half-dozen times.

Football's a thinking man's sport, thought Arien. While he trotted around the nose guard, his heads-up display scrolled fundamental instructions. "Remember, a stalemate means the offensive lineman won. **NO ARM TACKLES!** Listen to the linebacker for the defense." The scrolling was endless, as were Coach's canned speeches playing in his ear, and Coach's real-time comments. A diagram appeared in front of him, showing where he was supposed to go and where he was now. His position glowed red.

"Arien! Get to your mark! If you're not there on time, they have an alley my grandmother could run through!" bellowed Coach.

After practice, Arien carefully disconnected himself from the portage. He put the helmet on its peg, pulled off the gloves, unzipped the sleeves, stepped from the pants and hung the suit on a hanger. The porting equipment filled one corner of the room. Arien's parents believed in waiting until technology was proven, so he didn't have one of the new units that was no bigger than a wastebasket. Regardless of the size, the ports worked the same way, transmitting data to the gloves, suit and helmet, creating any sensory environment. Within the outfit, he could run, swim, free fall, climb mountains, and hunt tigers, but mostly he went to school and played football.

It isn't *real* football, he thought, as he dragged the box from under his bed. His parents were locked in their offices, but still, they might come out for some reason, so sweat beaded on his forehead as he carried it down the hallway to the garage. It wasn't until he'd locked it in the trunk and returned to his room that he could breathe easily.

At their pre-game dinner, Mom said, "I don't see why he has to *go* to the musical revue."

Arien fought the urge to roll his eyes. "It's not a 'musical revue.' It's a retro-concert. The musicians play their own instruments, and you promised."

Dad said between bites, "We did wild things when we were kids, dear. He has a bio-mask. He'll be perfectly safe. You do have your mask, don't you?"

Arien nodded. "It's a state-of-the-art concert hall. They said all the air will be filtered and irradiated four times an hour. It's safe."

Mom looked doubtful. "Won't you be too tired after your game?"

Dad said, "He'll be fine. After we win, he'll have earned a little relaxation."

With any luck, Arien thought, he might be able to make the concert too. It was the concert that gave him the co-conspirators' addresses. He had ported to a chat room about it, a pleasant oak-shelved music library with deep-pillowed couches. Harmon was there, and Harmon had seen Bernardino and Broncho earlier. They all wanted to see the concert, and the plan was born.

After dinner, Arien showered. The suit seemed more responsive when he was clean, and the pounding water cleared his head. If Wells beat West Kimono, they'd qualify for regionals, but he had a hard time concentrating on the game. He thought about the box in the car. It wasn't too late to chicken out.

The first defensive playoff scrimmage convinced him he wouldn't.

As always, the stadium smelled appropriately grassy; the concession stand oozed popcorn odor; the home crowd roared appreciatively at good plays and moaned for poor ones, and opposing players' breathing when they took their stance filled his ears. It was *exactly* the same as the last game he'd played. The virtual playing field never changed, was absolutely regular. Shadows never varied. (They played under the lights.) Weather conditions always within parameters.

The West Kimono kickoff man returned the kick to their own twenty-five. Arien trotted in with the defensive unit. The linebacker called one of the twist plays they'd practiced. Arien put weight on his hand, ready to dash right on the snap (careful not to *lean* right or look right so as to give away the stunt). Their quarterback started his cadence. The ball moved. Arien jerked right. Drove around the nose guard. Turned toward the quarterback who'd backed to pass. Open ground. No protection for him. The twist worked! Arien plunged forward, already counting the QB sack on his stats. A hit from the side, and he was flattened.

They'd anticipated the twist and set up trap blocks. Arien stared through his face guard. The West Kimono man pointed at him. "Got ya," he said.

The hit was a surprise, and his side ached where the shoulder pads drove into him, but it didn't hurt anymore than any other hit. Arien pushed himself up, pulled grass out of his face guard. Another shortcoming in virtual football was the game had become risk free. No chance for *real* injury. The port suits gauged the strength of the blow and the ability of the athlete to absorb it. A couple of years ago there'd been a scandal in high school ball because a player actually broke a leg. For weeks officials suspended the schedule as they investigated. Eventually it came out that the boy had an undiagnosed calcium deficiency. The game was deemed safe once again, and play resumed.

Well-done trap blocks made a defensive lineman's life miserable. West Kimono mixed their blocking routine, sometimes taking him straight on, sometimes double-teaming, and every third or forth play, letting him through for a blindside. He didn't lay a hand on a runner in the backfield or even hurry the quarterback until almost halftime when he side-stepped a blocker, lowered his head, and buried it in the quarterback's ribs. They whistled him for spearing.

As the team filed into the locker room for half time, Arien looked for Margo. The cheering squad knelt on the sidelines, waiting for the band to play. No Margo. He wondered if she was sick.

Coach prepped them on defensive adjustments, adding two new alignments to their heads-up displays. Arien studied them. Pretty routine stuff. He supposed the game was exciting, the teams were tied at seventeen points each, but he was counting off the minutes until the end. The four players were supposed to meet an hour after the last snap. They'd have maybe an hour before heading to the concert. Would they show up?

Arien fidgeted on the bench. He didn't dare display the driving route. Coach would see he wasn't paying attention. Dutifully, he scrolled through the new plays. The band started their next song. Coach huddled them in the middle of the room. "Wells, Wells, Wells," they chanted.

The second half went their way. Arien flushed the West Kimono quarterback out of the pocket on their first possession, and the Wells safety ran the interception back for a touchdown. But time passed slowly. Arien kept checking the game clock.

Wells won. The crowd went crazy, and Arien ported home before anyone congratulated him. He peeled the suit off and headed for the garage.

"Good game, son. Enjoy the concert," called Dad as Arien passed his room. Dad held his port helmet in his hands. Mom still wore hers. "Go, Wells! Go, Wells!" she yelled, still at the stadium.

Arien punched the destination into the autopilot, and the car pulled away from their house. A projected map showed his progress as he moved through the neighborhoods. Arien liked to keep the windows transparent. The few cars he passed were opaqued. A light rain fell. Maybe they won't come, he thought. His stomach tightened. Arien had the greatest distance to cover, seventy miles. If everything went well on his end, he'd hit the super-way and make the trip in under thirty minutes. The others lived closer to the field.

The car turned into a retirement community. Lots of individual cottages with real windows, some with lights behind their curtains, then back into a newer area where the buildings crowded the streets, their unbroken faces as dark as the night sky behind them. Arien rubbed his arms briskly. He was only minutes away from the field, a long and wide grassy stretch at the back of a cemetery. He chewed his lip. If everyone showed up, they'd have maybe an hour. It had taken him about an hour to line the field, and he hadn't seen anyone. The tombstones at that end were all more than a hundred years old, so there were no visitors, but light poles circled the area and lined the path. They'd be able to see.

Under the cemetery entrance. Up the winding path through trees and crypts. Over a rise and into the older grounds. Some stones leaned, their names nearly worn away. They were the influenza stones. Thousands of them the same size and shape. The city left the field as a reminder–most victims were cremated, but these were buried, and the stones served as a monument.

Three cars were already parked when Arien pulled up. A skinny boy wearing a jacket looked up from his car's trunk and waved. Arien's motor turned off, and he climbed from the car. For a moment he considered putting on his bio-mask, but decided against it. If they were going to play, they might as well breathe on each other too. The boy looked familiar, but barely. He was baby-faced, and his wrists were thin. Arien guessed he might weigh a hundred-and-thirty pounds.

Arien said, "Harmon?" Rain drizzled down. He wished he'd brought a hat.

"Is that you, Arien?" the boy said. "Wow. I thought you were bigger." He pulled a set of shoulder pads and a helmet out of the trunk. "Did you bring the ball?"

Arien blushed. He'd tweaked his simulacra over the past few years to reflect what he wanted to be. After all, he played on the defensive line. It wouldn't do for him to appear unintimidating. But Harmon was a god in the classroom, a *quarterback* god, and this boy didn't look like he could toss a ball twenty yards.

Harmon said, "Broncho and Bernardino are here already. I don't know if we want to go through with this."

Arien opened his trunk. From the box he extracted his own shoulder pads, helmet and a ball, all ordered from an e-collectibles site. "Come on. We've gone this far. Don't you want to know what real hitting is like?"

Harmon swallowed nervously. "It's not that. Have you seen Bernardino?"

"Sure," Arien said. Then he thought about how he'd "seen" Harmon. The Bernardino he knew from the games was a lithe option back. Solid, quick footed. Soft hands that never fumbled. Arien had tackled him twice during the game, once for a fifteen-yard loss.

A chubby kid wearing shoulder pads that were too big for him, carrying his helmet in one hand and an umbrella in the other came around the cars. "Hi, guys," he said. "Is this Arien? I thought you were bigger."

"You're Broncho?" Arien almost said, "I thought you'd be more fit," but he bit his tongue. "Nice to meet you. Did you have trouble getting out?"

"Naw. Coach chewed on us for a while about losing, but he got disgusted early and dismissed the team. You really took us to town in the second half."

"You guys played a good game," said Arien. "Where's Bernardino?"

The other boys didn't say anything. Then Harmon pointed across the field. "Warming up."

In the darkness beyond where Arien had marked the sideline, a shadow moved. Then Bernardino stepped into the light.

He was huge! Six and a half feet tall. Two hundred and fifty pounds. Shoulders too wide for pads. "Hello, guys," he said, his voice a well-tuned avalanche.

"Wow," said Arien.

"Yeah, I thought so too," said Harmon. "I want him on my team."

"Sorry, boys. He plays with me," said Broncho.

"Wow." Arien had studied the old football films. Seen pictures of the greats. Bernardino looked bigger and stronger. He moved like he was barely containing an explosion.

"I apologize my simulacrum looks differently. The league handicapped me so I could play the game."

"They can do that?" said Arien. He felt like he'd discovered a new sin.

Harmon said, "Yeah, it's a parity thing. My dad knows all about it. He used to be on the high school activities board. Player's skills are augmented or limited so no one feels bad about being understrengthed or slow."

Arien shook his head. "Sheesh. Well, who would have guessed that? Let's play anyway. If we don't get started, the opportunity will be gone."

Bernardino grinned and picked up the ball. It disappeared in his hand. "We will kick off."

Arien helped Harmon into his pads. Then they trotted to the field's far end. Harmon said he'd take the kick. Arien would block. He looked up. The rain continued, the drops suddenly appearing in the light to splatter on his face.

This is the way it should be, he thought. No crowd. No virtual concession stand. Beyond the sidelines, rows and rows of tombstones glistened under the lights. The pads felt good on his shoulders, even if they didn't quite fit. They were weighty and sturdy and *real*.

In the mist, fifty yards away, Broncho looked like a midget standing next to Bernardino.

"Go ahead," said Arien.

Harmon raised his hand above his head, then dropped it. Bernardino kicked. The ball sailed out of sight as Arien charged forward. Special teams. His job was to give Harmon a clear path. His legs drummed. Rain tapped against his helmet, and a glorious rush of feelings consumed him. I'm playing ball, he thought. Real ball!

A dark mass moved down the field toward him. A tackler. Get him! thought Arien, his consciousness now reduced to instinct. Stop the tackler. Protect the ball carrier. He changed his angle, all his practice coming into the forefront. Even without a heads-up display, he envisioned the lines forming on the field. Bernardino converging on the ball. Harmon cutting behind Arien for protection. Broncho following the lead tackler, swinging to one side to drive Harmon away from the open area. Hit him low, thought Arien.

In the back of his mind, Arien analyzed the situation. Bernardino led the charge, his long legs chewing up distance. Broncho lagged behind. If he could engage Bernardino for an instant, he might be able to break the block and also take on the second defender. They would score a touchdown on the kick! There were only two men between them and the goal. Arien took on two players all the time during games.

For an instant, the scene was poised and beautiful. No virtual set pieces. No synthesized crowd urging them on. No simulacra. Real air. Real grass. Real inertia. Arien saw it as a painting, a grim look set in his features, shoulders hunched for the block; Bernardino getting ready to juke left or right around him. This was better than his imagination. Then the scene continued, Arien swooping forward, waiting for Bernardino to commit to one side or the other. Another stride. Bernardino grew, came closer, details focused: a button on his shirt, a string flapping on his pads.

He loomed.

He didn't juke.

The world went black.

Sometime later the world was still black. Arien's back felt wet.

"Do you think he's okay?" someone said.

Arien considered his position. For a while he thought the port-suit had fizzled out. Soon the screen would flicker and he'd be back in the classroom or at practice. He waited. A light patter of sound caught his attention. "What is that?" he thought.

"Maybe he's dead."

"I didn't mean to hurt him," said a deep voice.

Arien thought, "It's rain. I'm hearing rain. Why can't I see?" Slowly he raised his arms. The right one ached from the shoulder to the elbow. His hands met a smooth surface in front of his face. He turned it, and above the face guard Bernardino, Harmon and Broncho's concerned expressions floated.

Arien pulled the helmet off. Rain fell straight down, tapping against his skin. "That was a heck of a hit." He shut his eyes. "Did we score?"

"No," said Harmon.

"He dropped the ball and ran the other way," said Broncho.

"I'm sorry, Arien." Bernardino crouched beside him. "Can you move your legs?"

Rain stroked his face, sending drops down his neck. He thought about it for a while before sliding his feet toward him. "Yeah."

Bernardino looked so relieved that Arien nearly laughed, but breathing hurt, and he wasn't sure that he hadn't broken a rib.

"Maybe if I sat up," said Arien. They bent to help him. He wrapped his arms around his knees. Nothing grated in his chest, so he decided the rib was whole, but it wouldn't surprise him if he was bruised tomorrow.

In the rain, by the cemetery lights, the grass glistened. The ball rested in the middle, someone's helmet upside down beside it. If Arien could preserve an image, that was the one he wanted. The rain, a helmet, a ball—an unevenly lined field and four warriors (three a little smaller than he'd pictured them). He smiled.

"Someone's coming," said Harmon. A car crested the hill and pulled next to theirs.

"Oh, jeeze," said Broncho, "What if it's one of our parents?"

The headlights winked out and the door opened. In the rain, Arien couldn't tell who it was, but there was only one of them. He forced himself up, grimacing as he did.

The figure approached, wearing a bio-mask. It was a girl, a slender one in a rain coat. Arien didn't recognize her. She was shorter than he was by a couple inches, and the rain dampened her thin red hair—strands stuck to her forehead. Her nose was narrow, and her eyes, above the mask, were dark.

"Arien?" she said, in a voice like a delicate pipe organ. "Did I miss your game?"

"Margo?" Arien said. He dropped his helmet.

"I did, didn't I?" She put her hand to her mask, hesitated, then, looking at the other boys, removed it decisively. Her cheekbones were high, perhaps even a little sharp, and her chin wasn't as round as it appeared in class, but now that he'd heard her voice, he could see the Margo he knew.

"Yeah, it wasn't much of a contest."

Harmon said, "We did a kick off, but I don't think we're going to run any more plays. Maybe we could catch?" Broncho and Bernardino nodded.

Arien rotated his shoulder to a chorus of sharp pains. "I'll watch."

The other boys trotted onto the field. Holding the ball, Harmon set them on a line, called a cadence, then yelled, "Hike!" He faded back and threw a tight spiral to Bernardino. Arien whistled appreciatively. Harmon might be small, but he had good technique.

From the corner of his eye Arien glanced at Margo standing at his shoulder. Caught her looking at him.

"Missed you at the game," he said.

She scuffed the ground with her foot, and put her chin into her coat's collar. "I've been on the super-way since breakfast. I really wanted to see . . . you know . . . you guys play. I live in Toronto."

Broncho threw the ball this time. His wobbly pass didn't reach Harmon, who dove to make the catch. He came up laughing. "Look, grass stains!" He held his forearms up for them to see.

"That's a long way," said Arien. He didn't know what else to talk about. The Margo at school he could talk to for hours, but she wasn't *there* actually. He was safe behind his digital image.

"Was it worth it . . . to play like this?"

Bernardino threw the next pass. It knocked Harmon off his feet.

Her voice was the same. He thought about her sitting in class, about walking with her in the courtyards between their rooms.

"Yeah, I'm glad we did it. I don't need to do it again, though."

The silence stretched uncomfortably. Finally, Arien said, "There's a concert we're all going to. Would you like to go?"

He could hear the smile in her voice without turning to see it. "Oh, I'd love to. That would be lovely."

They didn't move toward the cars. They watched the three other boys playing catch, yelling with joy in the rain.

After a while, Arien took a shaky breath, then reached out slowly, blindly from his side, until he touched her hand. They touched. She nestled her fingers between his. He could feel her palm's silky texture, the fine strength in her hand and wrist. The rain had turned into a mist, and just before the boys quit throwing to each other to return to the cars, Arien, his heart careening in his chest, squeezed her hand.

She squeezed back.

THE SAFETY OF THE HERD

CRINGING FROM THE PRESS OF BODIES, SHOTGUN CITY DETECTIVE TOYAS Midtmann missed the beginning of the confrontation. He pushed his elbows against the commuters penning him in to give himself a little room, shutting his eyes against the mass of heads swaying to the tram's movement. A cop who loathes people shouldn't be a public servant, he thought. If he were a lion strolling alone across an African steppe where hills rose in the distance, shimmering in the heat, he would be happy. An uneasy murmur brought him back.

He eyed the tram securitycams, three black-lensed bubbles hanging from the roof. A red light blinked in two of them, but the one directly overhead looked dead, which either meant the vid *was* dead or the light didn't work. Regardless, the two toughs facing each other a few feet away weren't paying attention. Toyas squeezed between a couple of business types, trying to get close before things got worse. Everyone leaned away, though, and there wasn't room to move. Toyas shifted to get his stun prod out of its holster; but a heavyset guy in a gray overcoat trapped his arm against him.

A young tough said to an older man, "Are you pulling blade on me?" A skinart forest fire blazed on the young man's face and shaved head. Flame images circled his cool, blue eyes. He tapped his dueling knife's hilt that hung on his chest just below his shoulder, handle down for a quick draw.

The older one, dark-bearded, wearing pale leather, held his knife delicately between thumb and finger, sliding it slowly in and out of its chest sheath. "I'm pulling it."

"But are you pulling on me?"

Faces surrounded them, mostly Shotgun City domestics heading down canyon for day jobs. They pushed back, creating a four-foot arena. Behind them, the curious stood on their toes, peering over heads for a better look. The tram rocked, and through the windows, building after building whipped by.

The tableau froze, pale-leather holding his blade so an inch gleamed; fire-face resting a finger on the hilt. Toyas yelled, "Break it up! Police!"

Fire-face turned toward him, and the tram lurched. Pale-leather lunged forward, blade beside his ear.

Someone screamed. People pushed together so hard Toyas lost his breath. The tram slid onto the platform and stopped. Doors on one side opened, releasing the commuters. Behind him, other doors opened and new commuters pushed in. Toyas rode the crush out, panning the crowd for the two toughs. Nothing. People riding slideways and escalators. Others milled around soy and drink kiosks, steam rising from heating pans.

He almost tripped over the body ten feet later. Lying on his back, fire-face stared into the sky. Toyas felt for a pulse but knew the boy was dead. A stab wound just left of center bled little. The blade had gone straight to the heart, a rare thrust for a dueling knife, which by law could be no longer than three inches.

The neck was warm and placid. Sweat slick. Toyas guessed the boy died before he left the tram, but the crowd carried him upright to this point before he dropped. Fire images still crawled up his cheeks, licked his ears, flickered across his forehead, the skinart dyes following their programmed display, living on the dead skin. False fire. No heat. A woman brushed against him, her eyes locked forward; he was sure she didn't see him. "Step wide!" he called. "Crime scene. Step wide!" Still, they came. Crouched over the body, he saw knees and feet. A flattened cup leaked coffee until someone kicked it, and only the stain remained.

Toyas tongued a transmit switch on the back of a tooth and called for clean up. He ordered a tracer on the tram and a download of the securitycam files, but he held little hope they'd show much: backs of heads, fuzzy faces, motion—not enough for court-worthy IDs. Another corpse—fifteen to twenty a day on this tram line alone.

Tiny voices filled his ear: a rolling riot had spread to Idaho Springs, fifteen miles down canyon; there was a hostage situation in Dillon and another in Shotgun City. A dozen All Points Bulletins. Another cop called for a clean up while he waited. The violent recital: situations droned on. He half listened, tuning in to his calls and not the others, but he had nothing to do, leaning over the dead boy.

People stepped over the body. Toyas fended them off the best he could until clean up arrived. The human tide inexorably flowed, a herd on the move.

By the time he got to Bellamy Labs where he was to arrest Reanna Loveday for unauthorized genetic manipulation, it had turned into a suicide standoff.

Not much to the building itself. Undistinguished signs marked the slideway platform as private, and the afternoon's light reflected off the door's muted silver sheen. People in a steady procession on the slideway moved up and down canyon behind him. Toyas arched back; the sky, a luminous blue ribbon cut by walks and bridges, stretched between the buildings' tops. Trams scooted overhead on magnetic rails. The population's weight pressed around him, above him, below him; going its varied ways. It smelled of fish and deodorizers, of dusty, clammy skin that never saw the sun and slept too close together. This is no place for a Masai warrior, he thought.

I should be trotting across a grassy plain, spear in hand, my fate's master. Not that there are any Masai left, or grassy plains for that matter.

He imagined how easy it would be to pull his dueling blade in a crowded tram too and stab and stab and stab, for the room, for the dull hatred. He rubbed his hands together. He still felt the dead boy's sweat on his fingertips.

The door scanner okayed his warrant, opening to a wide hallway crowded with frightened lab staff. A young man in a medical smock turned to him when he came in the door. Something in his eyes struck Toyas. They darted wildly, and the man trembled. A skinart rose rotated slowly on his cheek, and Toyas thought about the dead tough, fire crawling on his head. "It'll be fine," said Toyas. "We do this all the time."

Sub-detective Clancey waved from the far end, looking small in his new uniform, his police academy chevrons still shiny. "She's blocked herself into a back office on the other side of her lab with a vial of something poisonous. Nobody knows what it is." He'd unholstered his stun-prod and slapped it nervously into his hand. "I figured I'd wait until you got here."

"Her lab's through there?" A skinny window beside the door revealed another hallway punctuated with doors.

Clancey nodded, then wiped his sleeve across his forehead. "She's got DNA stuff back there, they say. Maybe some wacky diseases. I don't know. Something exotic and incurable. Make your skin fall off."

Toyas shook his head. "Not a contract gene shop like this. Worst she could do is change your rhododendrons."

A shaky voice behind him said, "Her specialties are genetically-based animal behavior modification and natural vectoring. She finds traits we like from one kind of animal to replace traits we don't like in another animal."

Toyas turned.

Another man in a medical smock. Close-set eyes. Fiftyish. Name tag read "Hirhito Blevins." He extended a hand. "Loveday is working on the pigeon problem for the city. Wonderful mind. Wonderful, but touchy. She has a lab to herself. Over a hundred square feet of space, and she bullied the others out. Hates crowds, she says. Terribly inefficient. Three employees generally work a lab that size. We leave her alone, though. Genius can be eccentric."

Toyas tried to back away from the man, but the room was too crowded. "Can't you let these people go home? They'll just be in the way."

Blevins shook his head. "They're hourlies. Automatically docked if they leave the building."

Toyas rubbed his eyes and held back an urge to yell. Clancey downloaded the situation file and Loveday's psychiatric and work profiles into Toyas' palmtop. Intelligence rating off the scale, but mediocre school records. She'd worked continuously for the last four years, moving from one contract to the next—a rarity for most employees—flawless performance numbers. She must be good, Toyas thought. She'd tried killing herself when she was a teenager. Clancey peeked over his shoulder at the display. "See, she's serious about this."

Loveday's portrait came up. An unsmiling, thin-faced blonde in her mid-twenties. "Any clue what set her off?"

Blevins said, "I was talking, very calmly, and she started raving. Threw a clipboard at me. Totally unprovoked. She's unbalanced. Always has been, but we need her."

Toyas guessed the conversation wasn't that innocent but didn't say so. The case profile noted that Blevins had turned in the original complaint for unauthorized computer use. Loveday's user history showed hours of research on human gene patterns, mostly centering on socialization behavior. "This is all outside her specialty, isn't it?"

Blevins said, "Oh, yes. Completely misplaced effort. Her real gift is natural vectoring for animals. Most genetic manipulation happens under controlled conditions: a livestock breeding facility, for example, or a doctor's office. But sometimes we want to spread a genetic change where the subjects are difficult to reach, so we have to find a way to introduce and disseminate the mutagen naturally. A parasite or a disease. Something infectious, easily transferred, but not fatal. She was piggybacking a mutagen to a weakened form of avian influenza for the pigeon problem. This investigation into human genetic patterns is not a part of her contract. There are federal laws, and, besides, she stole computer time and lab space. It reflects on my evaluation."

Toyas gave his stun prod to Clancey, then opened the door into the empty hallway. His palmtop went back into its fanny pack. "Why'd she try to kill herself the first time?"

Clancey scanned his display. "Doesn't say, but her parents died two months before in a rolling riot." He read further. "Looks like they got caught at a restaurant. Six others died there too. The report doesn't implicate them. Might be a connection."

"Give me an hour."

The door closed. Toyas walked past open offices toward Loveday's lab. He turned off his earplug, and the crime litany stopped. His steps clicked loudly in the silence, and he realized for the first time in days, he couldn't hear a human voice. The police station rang with sounds; human commerce filled the shops and streets; his tiny Shotgun City apartment never completely shut out the slideway's rumble and the rise and fall of human murmur twenty-four hours a day. Everywhere he went, thousands of people within a mile of him. The entire Denver to Salt Lake City intermountain urban corridor crowded with them. They'd even filled the twin

Eisenhower tunnels that used to be a part of the highway system with apartments and shops to create Shotgun City.

He slowed to enjoy the moment. Took a deep breath. Here the air smelled anti-septic, scrubbed clean, slightly chemical, not close and clammy. Not like the tram. He walked in the middle of the hall and thought about extending his arms as wings; they wouldn't touch either side. In his apartment, he kept a recording of a Greater Flamingo taking off from the shore of lake Samburu—a tremendous bird fighting its way into the air. He could spin around here, his arms out, and not touch anything.

Toyas glanced back; in the window behind him, Clancey and several others peered through. He kept his arms down, but for the first time today he felt relaxed. If the tram hadn't been so crowded, if it had been like this hallway, the fight might never have happened. The flame-faced boy would still be alive, the fires washing over his lips and sweeping around his eyes. Before the fight started, the people close by had pushed away, but the people farther back had leaned in, not wanting to miss the action. Their heads bobbed between shoulders, craning for a view. A violence hunger. They wanted to see, and the ones close didn't want to be hurt, but none of them had reached forward to stop the fight. Toyas thought everyone on the tram should have been arrested. Co-conspirators. Accessories to a homicide.

Most of them wore blades. Old folks, children, clergy—it didn't matter. A knife was a fashion statement. Illegal to use outside the dueling halls, but people had them just the same. Toyas thought about his luck that the tram had pulled into the platform when it did. That close, blood's smell in the air, a chain reaction could have started. Everyone stabbing everyone else out of . . . what? Fear? Hatred? Hysteria? It didn't matter. Mass stabbings had happened before. Like a rolling riot. No explanation. Violence breaking out in one spot, spreading to another, leaving destruction and injury before moving on. Sometimes lasting for weeks and traveling for miles, like fire.

Loveday's lab door wasn't closed tight. Toyas pushed it open with his foot, let-ting the room unfold before him as the door swept wide. She wasn't there. A long table in the middle was clean, a clipboard on the floor the only sign of disarray. On the wall, between open cabinets filled with equipment, several posters hung. All historical scenes. In one, a herd of cows grazed at sunset, their backs golden in the slanted light. Another showed a hundred buffalo, their heads up and alert, as if a wolf had appeared just off the poster's edge. He touched it, and it crackled under his fingers. Real paper. Very expensive.

"Reanna Loveday?" Toyas called. He thought the partly closed door at the back of the lab must be her office. The light was off. "My name's Toyas. Shotgun City po-lice, Reanna. I need to talk to you. We don't want you to hurt yourself. Your friends are concerned about you."

"Blevins isn't a friend," said a voice from the dark. A bitter laugh. "He's an accounting geek. Right now he's adding up lost productivity." A shuffling noise. A click of metal on metal. "Toyas? Good, African name. Are you a rat or a snake, Officer Toyas?"

Toyas sat on the table's edge. He liked the empty room. He liked the posters. There was no reason to rush. Unless someone buzzed his palmtop, he was unreachable for the moment.

"I don't know. What's the difference?" he said. She didn't reply. "Must be nice to have a big place like this to work in." Blevins was right about the room: it was about ten by ten feet, which made it two feet longer and four feet wider than Toyas' Shotgun City apartment. "They said you were going to kill yourself."

Loveday didn't speak for a while. There was only one way out of the lab, and it was past him, so she wasn't going anywhere. Toyas stretched his legs.

"I might," she said. Her voice didn't sound stressed. Tired, but not stressed. Not like she was poised on the precipice. "Rats kill themselves. Snakes don't."

"Any particular reason?"

"Genetics. It's all in the genes."

"I didn't know animals could commit suicide," said Toyas. She actually sounded pleasant. A little stuffed up perhaps. She sniffed in the darkened office and blew her nose. "Do you want to come out here to tell me about it?"

"I don't like people. Did they tell you that?"

"Who does?" Toyas got up. Walked around the room. It was amazing. Step after step without running into someone. His knuckles brushed against the wall as he went by.

"Snakes do."

"Like people?"

"No, each other. You could fill a box with snakes and they wouldn't know the difference. Some of them spend the winter crammed into a little hole, hundreds of them. There was a story once of a Texas rancher who broke into a snake den while digging a cellar. Ten-foot-thick ball of rattlers snoozing away."

Toyas wrinkled his brow. The conversation had taken an odd turn. Still, standard procedure in a suicide situation was to keep the victim talking. "Snakes aren't people, though."

"My point exactly! At least most of them," she said, as if she'd won an argument. "But we can't avoid them! I had a reservation to go camping next month. I've held it for four years. Three days and two nights in a real forest. It's with a group, of course, but you can hike by yourself. There's a stream and a lake, they say. I've seen the brochure. There's a picture of one person, just one, sitting on a rock at a meadow's edge."

Toyas nodded sympathetically. For the last three years he had submitted requests to visit Mt. Kenya Park. He wanted to see *Kere Nyaga*, the Kikuyu name for Mount Kenya, the Mountain of Brightness.

She sneezed. "Sorry, allergies." She wiped at her nose. "They canceled my reservation."

"Why?" Toyas paused in front of a complicated computer display: twisted strands braiding among each other, numbered and lettered notation labeling the strand's bumps. He scrolled to the display's top. Human Gene Segment, L14d.

"People won't come out. Not enough snakes. Too many rats. They closed the park. They've closed all of them. There's no place to go to get away. There are too many people who are rats. We've got to get rid of the rats."

Toyas glanced sharply at the office door. Her voice sounded odd on the last statement, ominous or desperate. He remembered Clancey's fear that she'd made a disease. It was unlikely—anticipation of just such an event had prompted hundreds of checks in the system—but maybe she'd figured a way around the security. He reached behind him for his palmtop, and pressed the emergency call to bring a squad to isolate the building. This might not be just one detective talking a person out of suicide anymore. Soon, experts by the score would dissect her notes and computer, revealing everything she'd worked on in all the time she'd been here.

"That's why you wanted to kill yourself? Because you lost a camping reservation?" Keeping his tone calm, he clicked backwards through screen after screen of genetic code, but his fingers quivered on the keys. All beyond him, the cryptic notations giving no clue of her intent. Was this a suicide situation or a threat to public safety? "And what does this have to do with rats?"

"No. Not the camping." The ominous tone dropped away, and now she sounded exhausted, like she was giving up. "An experiment went wrong. I thought I'd solved a problem, but it didn't work. I couldn't change a rat. Physician Rat, heal thyself."

"Blevins said you worked with pigeons."

She laughed. "Those stupid pigeons. Do you know what the city wanted me to do? Stop pigeon droppings. Millions of dollars over the years cleaning buildings. They contracted me to change pigeon pooping behavior. I think I solved it. Pigeons poop everywhere. Cats are clean about it. A cut here, a splice there, and I'll have all the pigeons in the world scratching their droppings into the dirt. No, the experiment was with me. My self experiment failed. I'm genetically resistant."

Toyas transferred everything in her computer onto his palmtop. It only took a few seconds. The experts could look at it later if there was a need. He didn't see her own palmtop. Probably had it on her. Incriminating evidence might be there.

"Genetically resistant?" he said, mostly to keep her talking while he waited for reinforcements.

She sneezed again. "Yes. Not everyone's genes are malleable. Some resist mutagens better than others."

A chair scraped. Her pale hand appeared on the door jamb, and the door swung open. "Are you by yourself?" She stood in the shadows.

He nodded.

After several minutes without moving—he could feel her eyes on him, sizing him up—she said, "I'm agoraphobic. Really bad. You know, panic attacks." She slid around the door's edge, keeping her back to the wall. The palmtop picture didn't flatter her. Even in the lab's harsh light, her features were softer, younger, color high in her cheeks. "It's hard to breathe with you here." There was nothing in her hands—no poison or way to kill herself—nothing frightening about her. She might have a syringe in the lab coat, though, thought Toyas, something that would take just a pressure on the pocket to inject.

The file transfer finished. Toyas moved to the other end of the room. "Have you always been that way?"

She touched a button near the computer, and the double-helix on the screen cleared. "Since I was a kid. The doctors call it trauma induced social anxiety disorder. It got worse after my parents died. Rats in the box."

"Rats?" He checked his palmtop. The files were all there. Crisis intervention reported they were in the lobby.

She looked directly at him for the first time since she'd come out, her eyes bright, fevered. "Rats attack each other in a box. They're social, but you can't overcrowd them. They'll even bite themselves. Snakes don't. Herd animals don't. Pressed together in pens, they're content. Nothing bothers them. It's genetic. Mom and Dad died in a restaurant, killed with butter knives and forks. The box was too crowded. The rats got them. So, are you a rat or a snake?"

A bustle in the hallway behind him, and the door shattered inward. Loveday shrieked, leaping for her office door, but a tangle-burst got her. She went down in a tightening confusion of fine mesh that pulled her arms into her sides and bound her legs. Masked intervention operatives poured into the room, fifteen or twenty of them. There was little room to move. Toyas backed against the wall.

"Did she say anything?" someone shouted to him. "Did she make a threat?" Someone else pushed a re-breather into his hands, but he didn't put it on. Operatives opened drawers, poking gene-scanner proboscises into the depths, the hand-held units sucking air to their tiny, automated analysis chambers. "Nothing here," said one operative, the re-breathing unit muffling his voice. "Pigeon DNA," said another. "More pigeon. And cat. I have cat."

Blevins voice came from the door; Toyas couldn't see him past the officers.

"Those are authorized. We have papers for them!" Blevins followed the officers, showing them clearances for everything they found: dog, cow, octopus, mosquito, several others, but no snake. Toyas shook his head. Why no snake? That's what she said she'd been doing. There wasn't rat either.

Loveday kept shrieking wordlessly.

"What are you looking for?" said Toyas, flinching against her voice. "Can I help?" He sidled along the wall toward Loveday. Two officers held her down while a third ran a see-all over her tangle-webbed lab coat.

"Nothing in the pockets. She's clean." The officer searching her looked up at Toyas. "If she's made a pathogen, she needs a way to distribute it. Powder, pills, liquid spray—it could be anywhere. We've got a squad doing her apartment too."

Another officer ground his knee into Loveday's back, squeezing her screams thin. Toyas grabbed his collar and pulled him off. "She's not going anywhere," said Toyas. "No need to hurt her." Only the man's eyes were visible above his re-breather, dark and enigmatic. Toyas suspected the man liked what he had been doing. Loveday stopped screaming.

They ripped posters off the walls, scanned behind them; emptied cabinets, broke jars, poured out chemicals, cut open notebook covers, all efficiently. In fifteen minutes they'd taken the lab apart and found no deadly viruses or evidence that she'd worked on one.

An officer came out of her office, a melted palmtop in his hand. "She torched it," he said. "We may never know what was on this." He dropped it into a plastic bag for later analysis.

Toyas stayed close to Loveday, keeping his hand on her arm. "She just wanted to go to a park," he said under his breath. Knees and feet passed around him. He fended them off so no one stepped on her. It reminded him of the dead boy from the tram. No reason for all these people to be here, thought Toyas. They're scaring her, and it made his skin creep. Too much jostling.

Finally the officers stood around Loveday, discussing whether they should take her to the patrol house for questioning or to a hospital for observation. She breathed through her mouth. "Officer Toyas," she whispered. "I need to blow my nose." Stuffed up, her arms tight to her side, she sounded pathetic. Toyas found a tissue in his fannypack and held it for her. She blew noisily against his hand. When they picked her up, still horizontal, facing the floor, she rose until her red-rimmed eyes were level with his. "Thanks," she said, and sneezed in his face.

When the squad left, Toyas looked around the room. The litter had been swept up, but broken glass in a fine dust sparkled at the lab table's end. They'd taken the computer and her notes. A poster dangled from one corner on the wall. He pressed it back up. Sheep on a hillside, covering it so tightly he could see no grass, just backs and heads. In the middle, a single tree rose above them, its greenery a sharp contrast to the sheep's white and black.

Toyas couldn't sleep that night. The slideway's constant rumble bothered him. He could feel crowds passing past his doorway. He tried staring at his prints on the wall: a brightly lit view of Mt. Kilimanjaro, a sunrise on the Indian Ocean at the Kenyan coast, a lone giraffe. But it didn't help. After he turned down the light, he imagined his neighbor's breathing to his left and right. The weight from neighbors above seemed to bow the roof. Sometimes he heard them in bed, their apartment no larger than his own, moving rhythmically.

When he finally dozed, he dreamt of crawling in a tunnel, deep underground, moist dirt falling on his neck, slipping under his hands. After a dozen turns, the tunnel grew tighter until he squirmed on his belly. Then, the ceiling rose away. His fingers hooked over an earthen edge. A dim light glowed in the huge room below him, and it was filled. Thousands of naked people, intertwined, moving slowly in sleep—a giant people ball. The closest parted, as if they knew he was there, to give him a space in the mass. He slithered from the hole, put his hands on legs and arms, pulled himself in. No one woke, but they moved aside, let him burrow deeply in their phosphorescence. He pushed his knee against a shoulder, levered himself between two backs, their ribs and backbones sliding over him, swimming in people, and then he reached the middle. He rested. Everything tight and cozy, warm and friendly, until he heard a vibration, a quiet rattle rising in the mass. The leg above his head grew cool. Pressing against his side, a thigh thinned, became slick and scaled. Air buzzed, and pressure rose. He struggled to breathe. A fanged face pressed against his head, black marble eye unblinking. It slid by. All snakes, everywhere. No people. He gasped. Lungs ached. Arms trapped. No breath.

He flailed in the darkness, throwing his blanket aside. One hand slapped against the wall, and his neighbor rapped back a muffled curse. Toyas lay gasping, his throat coated and his nose stuffed up. By bed light he found tissue, but blowing didn't clear his nasal passages. A couple pillows propped beneath his head stopped the worst of the draining, and when the antihistamine and decongestant began to work, he fell asleep again, this time without dreams.

The next morning after he stepped outside his apartment door, he keyed for an update on Loveday. The palmtop showed they'd checked her in for observation. A couple screens later he found the hospital had put her in a private room. She'll like that, he thought. Other than disrupting the peace, no indictments had been issued. A blinking icon at the screen's bottom indicated "Under Investigation." Another one said, "Possible Biohazard." He clicked the unit closed, waited for an opening, then stepped on the slideway. Before he reached the Shotgun City limit sign and the end of the city's long tunnel, he'd sneezed half a dozen times.

"Sorry," he said each time to annoyed commuters. "Allergies." The decongestants kept his breathing clear, but his nose itched and he had a sore throat. Not bad, but it hurt to swallow.

He checked in so that headquarters would transmit his cases, a short list this morning, only three homicides. On the tram ride, he mulled over the dream, and as an afterthought checked on the stabbing from yesterday. As he'd feared, the securitycams didn't show enough to advance an investigation. No blood on flame-face's knife. No witnesses who could help. No specific similarities to other stabbings to indicate a pattern. Probably random, Toyas thought, one act of violence by a man who had never done such a thing before and probably never would again, not that finding the killer would help the dead boy anyway.

The tram missed the first Dillon platform. The rolling riot was too close. Police shut off the platforms, rerouted slideway traffic and shut down bridges and elevators through the district in an attempt to choke the fighting off. As the tram slid past the platform, Toyas saw yelling people standing on the edge, trying to get out. Rats and snakes, Loveday had called them. With no room to move, rats turned on each other. The box was too small. She'd asked him which one was he. That must mean I could be either, he thought. Not everyone hates the crowding. He sneezed again. Couldn't even get his hand up over his mouth in the tram's tight quarters. A lady in front of him flinched and wiped at the back of her neck.

The second Dillon platform passed, and the third. An angry mumble rose in the tram. People missing their stops would either have to walk up canyon to get to work, or they wouldn't be able to get there at all. Most employees were hourlies. They were paid only for time on the job, regardless of the excuse. Somebody pushed someone else, and for a few seconds shouting filled the tram. Toyas held his palmtop tight. With the right combination of commands, he could have the car flooded with sleepy-gas. He wondered how long ago it had been since he'd been gas-proofed, and if it would still keep him conscious. The yelling subsided, though, and he relaxed, swallowing in relief. It hurt.

His all-call squeaked in his ear, and headquarters queried him on his position. "Emergency override," the earphone said. "Debark at Silverthorne #4." He shrugged and worked his hand up to his face so he could wipe his nose. The tram followed a long curve in its track, making everyone lean. A man next to Toyas stumbled a little and caught Toyas' sleeve to keep his balance. "Pardon," he said.

"It's O.K." Except for his sneezing, Toyas didn't feel bad this morning. Not like yesterday when he might have thrown an elbow to keep the stranger off him. It's not their fault, thought Toyas. They're missing work.

He couldn't see a window. Somehow he'd ended up in the middle, but he knew the upper canyon complexes were passing by. In a minute, they'd be at Silverthorne and he could find out what the emergency was. In the meantime, he let the tram's gentle motion lull him. People pressed against him, moving with the sway. Very soothing.

Then, Toyas saw him, the pale-leather tough from yesterday. His hand rested on his dueling blade, a line of gleaming metal showing it was part way out of its sheath, and Pale-leather scowled around him, his dark beard disarrayed, his expression filled with hate. Toyas tongued a transmission and subvocalized a report. It took a few seconds to clear his stun-prod from its holster. He didn't want to be caught unprepared this time.

The tram slid toward Silverthorne station. Pale-leather glared at the crowd, his hand tight on the dueling blade, obviously within an instant of pulling it out. Toyas brought the stun-prod up, next to his chest. If the man drew the blade, Toyas figured he could just reach him over the intervening heads. They held the pose until the tram slowed down for the platform. Pale-leather closed his eyes for a moment, as if in relief, and Toyas felt suddenly inside the man's head. It was the closing of the eyes that did it. It wasn't people the man hated, but the pressure against him, the constant touching. He didn't want to hurt anyone, but he would. A rat in the box, ready to bite, his rodent-like instincts playing themselves through, nearly beyond his control, and Toyas knew that was him too, yesterday, an inch from stabbing out himself.

Doors opened, and a line of policeman waited on the platform, standing steady against the stream flowing from the car. Toyas maneuvered himself behind Pale-leather, letting the traffic carry him out. He reached to snag the man's shoulder when something grabbed him on both sides.

They spun him around, a policeman on each arm. Toyas barely saw the helmet coming before it was over his head.

"He's escaping!" yelled Toyas, and struggled to get an arm free. They held too tightly though, and through the helmet's glass, Toyas glimpsed Pale-leather stepping onto a slideway. The other officers formed a barricade around them that diverted foot traffic. Blevins' face floated into view as he sealed the helmet at Toyas' neck. A circulation fan kicked on, sending a sweet tasting wash of bottled air across his forehead. The policemen didn't say anything as they half-carried Toyas to a cruiser and pushed him into the holding tank. Blevins and an officer followed.

Blevins said, "Did Loveday cough on you? Did you touch her hands or face? How close did you get?" The officer ran a gene-scanner over Toyas' clothes. On the officer's shoulders were biotech chevrons and captain's bars. Toyas had never met a captain before. He searched for something to say.

"Oh, man," the captain said. "He's loaded."

Blevins paled. "It's not our fault. We admit no liability. Her actions were not sanctioned by the lab. Pure pirate stuff."

"What's going on?" said Toyas. His head wobbled, and he wondered blearily if the air in the helmet was doped.

Blevins ignored him. "If your people could have salvaged her palmtop sooner, none of this would have happened. Remember, we reported her. We deserve a medal."

The captain leaned back. A lurch indicated the cruiser had taken off. Where? Toyas wondered, sure now he was drugged.

"Shut up, Blevins," said the captain tiredly. "The courts will decide what to do with your company. In the meantime, how can we stop this?"

Blevins licked his lips. Toyas watched the man's lips part in slow motion, his tongue moving at quarter speed. Funny, Toyas thought, that their speech sounds fine, but they've slowed down so much.

"She tied the mutagen to a cold virus. That's her specialty, natural vectoring. Maybe we can quarantine the area, contain it all."

The captain kept his eyes closed, defeated. "We've ordered it already."

Toyas formed his words carefully. "Was it snake genes? She said something about snakes. Am I going to die?" The question felt academic, and he almost giggled.

Blevins looked at him. "No, not snakes. Why would you say that? It was a part of cow genetics. We don't know what part yet. We don't know what she wanted to do, but it's a human mutagen. She was immune."

Toyas' head dipped and circled. He was sure they could see it, although they didn't seem to notice. The world felt buttery and soft. He didn't even mind being transported to an unknown destination. In the background, the cruiser's hum sounded like bees, African bees, and he thought about Kenya, the great, wind-swept plains, and the long extinct animals. But not a lion. He pictured zebras instead, a congregation of them, heads down at the water hole. Toyas wished he were there, shoulder to shoulder in the population, at peace, taking water. He could almost feel them around him. The dust they kicked up a comforting layer on his back. The safety of the herd.

A tendril of fear eddied in him for a second. His lips parted heavily; he could barely shape the words. "They won't lock me up, will they?" He saw himself thrown in an empty hospital room. A viral contagion ward. No one to lean against. No one to reach out and touch.

Toyas held onto consciousness long enough to say, "Don't let them put me in . . . isolation."

SAVANNAH IS SIX

FOR AS LONG AS POUL COULD REMEMBER, HE'D SPENT THE SUMMER AT THE lake where his brother drowned.

This year, as they climbed in the van, Leesa said cryptically, "Savannah is six." Poul held his hand on the ignition key but didn't turn it. "I know."

Each year since Savannah was born, it got harder to come out. The nightmares started earlier, grew more vivid, woke him with a scream choked down, a huge hurting lump he swallowed without voicing. Poul took longer to pack the van; he delayed the day he left, and when he finally started, he drove below the speed limit.

They pulled into the long, sloping driveway down to the cottage just after noon. Leesa had slept the last hour, and Savannah colored in the back seat, surrounded by baggage and groceries. Her head was down, very serious, turning a white sky into a blue one. She always struck Poul as a somber child, for six, as if there was something sad in her life that returned to her occasionally. Not that she didn't smile or didn't act silly at times, but he'd catch her staring out the window in her bedroom before she'd go to bed, or her hand would rest on a favorite toy without picking it up, and she seemed lost. She was quick to tears if either parent scolded her, which happened seldom, but even a spilled drink at dinner filled her eyes, the tears brimming at the edge, ready to slip away.

Their cottage sat isolated by a spur of nature conservancy land on one side and on the other by a long, houseless, rocky stretch. He bought the place fourteen years earlier, the year after he married, from dad, who didn't use it anymore.

Only a couple of hours from Terre Haute, Tribay Lake attracted a slower paced population; county covenants kept the skiers off, so the surface remained calm when the wind was low. From the air it looked like a three-leafed clover, with several miles of shoreline. An angler in a boat with a trolling motor could find plenty of isolated inlets covered with lily pads where the lunkers hung out.

By mid-June the water warmed to swimming temperature—inner tubes were stacked next to the boat house for a convenient float—and the nights cooled off for sleeping. Poul and Leesa took the front room overlooking the lake. In the first years they'd opened the big windows wide at night to listen to crickets. Lately, though, he went to bed alone while she worked crossword puzzles, or she retired early and was asleep by the time he got there.

Poul knew the lake by its smell and sounds—wet wood and fish and old barbeques, and waves lapping against the tires his dad had mounted on the pier to protect the boat, the late night birds trilling in the hills above the lake, and an echo of his mother's voice, still ringing, when Neal didn't come back. "Where's your brother?" She'd asked, her eyes already wild. "Weren't you watching Neal?" She called his name as she walked down the rocky shore looking for the younger son.

Savannah closed her book and said, "I'm going to catch a big fish this year. I'm going to see him in my raft first, then I'll hook him. But I want to visit Johnny Jacobs and his kittens first." Over Poul's objection, Leesa had bought Savannah a clear bottomed raft, just big enough to hold a child, and it was all she'd talked about for weeks.

Poul said, "They won't be kittens anymore, Speedy. That was last fall. They'll be cats by now." Gravel crunched under the wheels. Leesa didn't move, her sweater still bunched between her head and the window.

Poul wondered if she only pretended to be asleep. It was a good way to not converse, and the lean against the window kept her as far away from him as possible. "We're here, Leesa," he said, touching her hand. She didn't flinch, so maybe she actually had been sleeping.

Leesa rubbed her eyes, then pushed her short, black hair behind her ears. She'd started dying it last year even though Poul hadn't noticed any gray. His hair had a couple of streaks now, but his barber told him it made him distinguished. At thirty-five, he thought "distinguished" was a good look.

"I'm going to walk down to Kettle Jack's to see if he has fresh corn for the grill. I like grilled corn my first night at the lake," Leesa said. Poul wondered if she was talking to him. She'd turned her face to the side, where the oak slipped past.

Poul pulled the car under the beat-up carport next to the cottage. Scrubby brush scraped against the bumper. Leesa opened the door and was gone before he could stop the engine. Savannah said, "I don't like corn on the cob. Can we have hot dogs?"

"Sure, Speedy." On an elm next to the cottage, a frayed rope dangled, its end fifteen feet from the ground. Summers and summers ago, there'd been a knot in the end and Neal hung on while Poul pushed him. "Harder, Poul!" he'd yell, and Poul gave another shove, sending the younger boy spinning. Poul looked at the rope. He didn't remember when it had broken; it seemed like this was the first time he'd seen it in years. With the door open now, forest smells filled the car: the peculiar lakeside forest essence that was all moss and ferns and rotted logs half buried in loam, damp with Indiana summer dew. He and Neal had explored the woods from the cottage to the highway, a half mile of deadfall and mysterious paths only the deer used. They hunted for walking sticks and giant beetles, or, with peanut butter jars in hand, trapped bulbous spiders for later examination.

Someone yelled in the distance, a child, and Poul jumped. He stood, his hands resting on the car's roof. Between the cottage and the elms beside it, a slice of lake glimmered, and a hundred feet from shore, a group of children played on a permanently anchored oil drum and wood decked diving platform, whooping in delight.

"I'd like mustard on mine, and then I'll go see the kittens," said Savannah. She had her duffel bag over her shoulder—it dragged on the ground—and was already moving toward the back door.

"Sure, Speedy," Poul said, although Savannah was already out of earshot. Poul arched, pushing his hands into his back. Sunlight cut through the leaves above in a million diamonds. He left the baggage in the car to walk to the shore. To his left, a mile away, partly around the lake's curve, Kettle Jack's long pier poked into the water. A dozen sailboats lay at anchor, their empty masts standing rock still in the windless day. Part way there, Leesa walked determinedly on the dirt path toward the lodge. Slender as the day they married. Long-legged. Satiny skin that bronzed after two days of sun. He remembered warm nights marvelling at the boundaries where the dark skin became white, how she murmured encouragement, laughing deep in her throat at shared joys.

Poul unpacked the van. Most of the beach toys went around front. He stuck the yellow raft on a high, open shelf in back of the cottage where rakes and old oars were stored. Maybe she'd forget they had it.

A screen slapped shut behind him. Savannah came down the steps. "I couldn't find the hot dogs, and something smells bad in the kitchen. I'm going to count fish."

Poul said, "Let's go together. Life vest first." He found one in a pile in the storage chest against the tiny boathouse. It had a solid heft that reassured him.

She pouted as he put it on. It smelled of a winter's storage, a musty, gray odor that rose when he squeezed the belt around her. "Guess you aren't the same size as last summer? Can't have you grow up this fast. We'll have to quit feeding you."

Savannah didn't smile. "Da-ad," she said.

Minnows darted away when they stepped on the pier. To the left, weeds grew up from the mucky bottom, starting as a ten-foot wide algae belt next to the shore, and waving languidly below after that until the lake became too deep to see them. To the right, white sand began at a railroad tie border six feet from the cottage and reached into the water, a smooth, pale stretch for thirty feet. It cost two hundred dollars every other season to have several dump truck loads of sand poured and spread to create the beach. A blunt torpedo silhouette a foot long moved toward deeper water. Probably a bass. Most perch were stockers in the lake, and a foot long blue gill would be a trophy. Only catfish and bass reached respectable size. Poul watched the fish gliding at the sand's edge, perfectly poised between the artificial beach and the lake's invisible depths. Once he'd stood at the same spot with Neal, fascinated by a three-foot long catfish, nosing its way beneath their feet. Through their reflections, through Neal's glasses and wide brown eyes and sun-blonde hair, and through Poul's dark hair and blue eyes, they'd watched its broad, black back. Later they'd baited huge treble hooks with liver or soap, but the fish never returned. Dad had told them some catfish lived longer than men. That same catfish might still be prowling the lake's bottom. Would it remember a summer of two small boys? Or was it now a ghost? Did old ones die to haunt the undersides of piers? Were there places even fish were afraid to go?

Poul shivered and glanced up. Savannah was on her stomach at the pier's end. Her knees not touching wood, her weight precariously balanced. His throat seized up, and he walked quickly, almost a jog (although he didn't want to scare her) to where she looked into the water. Poul put his hand on her back, holding her there.

Savannah's hands were flat out, fingers splayed, nearly touching the surface. Without a breeze the lake was smooth as glass. "Look, Daddy. I'm underwater. Do you think she sees me?" Her reflection stared at her, its hands almost touching her own, the vision of a little girl six inches deep, looking up.

Poul's tongue felt fat in his mouth, and it was all he could do to speak without a quiver in the voice. "Yes, dear. You're lovely. Now let's go in, and I'll find the hot dogs."

Savannah held his hand as they walked toward the cottage. The boards creaked underfoot. Through the wide gaps, water undulated in a slow, fractional swell. He shook his head. She'd never been in danger. Even if she'd fallen in, the life vest would have popped her to the surface, and he was right there. He wished he'd signed her up for swimming lessons during the winter. Poul kept his head down, watching his feet next to Savannah's, her white sneakers matching his small steps. She gripped his little finger, and he smiled. After lunch, he'd break out the worms and bamboo poles (anything to avoid the clear-bottomed raft). He'd have to dig up the tall, skinny bobbers and show her again how to mount the bait on the hook.

He remembered fishing with Neal. Dad used an open bail casting reel, sending his lures to splash far away, but they had as much action tossing their bait a few feet from the boat. Poul would stare at the narrow, red and white bobber's point, held upright by the worm's weight and a couple of lead shot. The marker twitched, sending ripples away. It twitched again. "Something nibbling you, Poul," said Neal, his own pole forgotten. "Yeah," said Poul, concentrating on the bobber, which wasn't moving now. He imagined a fish eyeing it below. Could be a bass, or maybe even a pike, like the stuffed one mounted on a board above the bar at Kettle Jacks, its long mouth open and full of teeth.

Savannah cried, "Help him, Daddy."

"What?"

She pulled away, dropped to her knees and poked her head over the pier's side, trying to look under. "Help him!"

"What, Savannah? What?" Poul knelt beside her; a splinter poked his shin. "Don't fall in now!"

She sat up, her hair wet at the tips where it had dipped. "Where'd he go? Didn't you see him? He was reaching up between the boards, Daddy. You almost stepped on him."

The sun dimmed, and everything around them faded. Only Savannah was clear. Dimly children shrieked on the distant diving platform. When he spoke, it sounded to him as if they were in a bubble: his faint voice travelled no more than a yard away. "What did you see, Speedy? Who was reaching up?"

Her lip quivered. "The boy, Daddy. He was under the pier. I saw his fingers right there." She pointed. "He was stuck under the pier, but when I looked, he'd gone away. Where do you think he went to, Daddy?"

Between the boards, the lake breathed gently, the surface smooth and untroubled. A crawdad crept along the muck. Poul watched it through the gap. "I don't think there was anyone there, Speedy. Maybe your eyes played a trick on you."

Legs crossed, her hands in her lap, Savannah studied the space between the boards for a moment. Slowly, she said, "My eyes don't play tricks." She paused. "But my brain might have imagined it."

Poul released a long, slow lung full of air. He hadn't known he'd been holding it. "If you're hungry, sometimes your brain does funny things." The sun brightened. Poul shivered, and he realized sweat soaked his shirt's sides. "Let's go in and have a hot dog."

She nodded. He had to open the porch door for her; it was a high step up, and her fingers barely wrapped around the nob. Neal had been so proud his first summer when he could grip it.

Later, while Savannah put mustard on her meal, Poul said, "Why did you think it was a *boy* under the pier if all you saw was his fingers?" Savannah swallowed a bite.

"He had boy hands. Boy hands are different. I can tell." She pushed the top back on the mustard.

In the evening, Poul walked to the end of the pier. A breeze had picked up, and on the lake, two sailboats glided side by side, their sails catching the sun's last yellow rays. Now all the lake was black. If he jumped in here, the water would barely come to his chest—it would be just over a six-year-old's head—but within a couple strides was a steep drop-off. The wind pushed waves toward him, a series of lines that slapped against the piles as they went by. He could feel the lake in his feet. Deep in his pockets, his hands clenched. Cottages on the far shore glowed in the last light, their windows like mica specks in carved miniatures. Behind them, forest-covered hills rose to the silence of the sky.

They'd found Neal ten feet from the pier's end, his hands floating above his head, nearly on the surface, his feet firmly anchored on the bottom. Poul stood on shore, his fists jammed into his armpits, and watched them load him in the boat, wearing the face mask and snorkel, limp and small, his arms like delicate pipes, his six-year-old skin as smooth and pale as milk, black boots on his feet. They were Poul's snow boots, buckled at the top and filled with sand.

Long after the sun set, and the boats disappeared and lights flickered on in cottages, music and voices drifted across the water, Poul came in to go to bed. On the porch, Savannah slept on the daybed. He checked the screens to make sure they were tight—mosquitoes were murder after dark—then locked the deadbolt, taking the key. Sometimes Savannah woke before he or Leesa did, and he didn't want her wandering outside. In the kitchen, he shook as he poured a cup of tepid coffee. A humid breeze had sucked the heat out of him. The cup warmed his hands. Moths threw themselves against the windows, pattering to get in. Leaves hushed against themselves. Years ago he'd sat at this same table, sipping hot chocolate, laughing at Neal's liquid moustache. That day they'd swam. The next they'd fish, and the summer at the lake stretched before them, a thousand holidays in a row.

Poul slipped up the stairs, keeping his weight on the side next to the wall so there would be no creaks. He left his clothes on a chair. Dock lights through the windows illuminated the room enough for him to get around without running into anything. A long lump on the bed, swaddled in shadows, was all he could see of Leesa. Except for his own breathing, there was no other noise, which meant she was awake. When she slept, she whistled lightly on each exhalation. From the beginning he'd found it charming, but never mentioned it, guessing it might be embarrassing. If he spoke now, he knew, she wouldn't reply.

Three years ago when they were at the cottage, she began suffering headaches at bedtime, or sore throats, or stomach cramps, or pulled muscles, or dozens of other ailments. That same summer she went from sleeping in just a pair of boxer shorts to a full, flannel nightgown. She'd start complaining about her night time illness before lunch, and after a while, he figured they were all a charade. The last time they'd made love had been a year ago, in this bedroom. He remembered her back to him, and he pressed against her; he could feel her muscles through the flannel, her hip's still delicate flare. She didn't move away, so he pushed against her again. It had been months since the last time, and the day had been good. She hadn't avoided him. She laughed at a joke. Maybe she's thawing, he'd thought, so he watched her, and when she went to bed, he followed. No chance for her to be sleeping before he got there. But she undressed in the bathroom, came out with the collar buttoned tightly at her neck, didn't look at him, and laid down with her back toward him. He didn't move for a while. They'd been married too long for him not to recognize all the ways she was saying, "No." Still, it *had* been months. He moved next to her. Outside, waves slapped upon the shore. The boat rattled in its chain.

It was the most loveless act he'd ever committed. Within moments, her whistling snore began.

That was the last time.

Why was she angry with him? Why had it gone so terribly bad? The closest they'd come to talking about it came that Christmas, after Savannah went outside to play in the snow, and he and Leesa sat wordlessly in the living room. He'd finally said, "What's wrong?" The sweater he'd given her draped across her hands; she didn't meet his eyes. "I don't like this color any more." Later he found the gift tossed in the back of the closet.

Whatever the source of the anger, it grew worse at the lake. The distance widened, and the nightmares came more often. He lifted the covers as little as possible and lay down. Leesa didn't react. Poul looked at the ceiling. A light from a passing boat swept shadows from one side of the room to the other. Its small motor chugged faintly.

Leesa wasn't whistling. He knew she heard the same motor. If her eyes were open, she'd see the same shadows. "Savannah scared herself on the dock today," he said into the darkness, the sudden sound of his own voice startling him. Only the cooling cottage's creaks and groans answered.

Hours later, still awake, he heard a noise downstairs. A muted rasp. He propped up on his elbows. Footsteps, then another scraping sound. A bump. Nothing for a long time. His eyes ached with attention, and saliva pooled in his mouth he didn't dare swallow. After minutes, he slipped from the blankets and moved from the bed, crept down to the living room, every shadow hiding an intruder, the pulse in his ear like a throbbing announcement. He turned on a light, flicking the room into reality, then into the kitchen where moths clustered against the screens. On the porch, Savannah lay atop her covers, sleeping. Scratch marks showed where she'd pulled a chair to the door. She'd unhooked the chain, but the deadbolt defeated her. Poul tucked her in, then he grasped the door knob to check the lock again. Slick brass felt cool under his palm. Savannah had sleepwalked. When she was three, she'd done it for a few months, but she hadn't done it since. The pediatrician said it wasn't uncommon, that she'd outgrow it.

Through the porch door's window, the eastern horizon glowed, turning the lake surface purple, but the dock was a black finger with a black boat's silhouette beside it. A muskrat swam, cutting a long V in the flat water.

The knob turned under his hand. It turned again. Whoever held it on the other side was shorter than the window. Poul slapped his head against the glass. A bare stair. He ran to the kitchen, banging his shin against a stool, breath ragged in his throat, grabbed the deadbolt key from its drawer, and stumbled back to the porch. Outside, he looked up and down the shore. A quarter mile away, his closest neighbor loaded fishing gear into his boat. Poul ran around the cottage. There was no one. Mindless, he sprinted up the long dirt driveway until he stopped at the highway, bent, with his hands on his thighs, gasping. Empty road vanished into the woods on either side.

He sat on the shoulder. A deep gouge in his left foot bled freely, and he realized both feet hurt. It took ten minutes to hobble back to the cottage, and wearing only shorts, he was profoundly cold. The sun bathed the cottage's front as he walked to the door. Grass cast long shadows. His own barefooted prints showed in the dew. Poul stopped before going in. Another set of prints led to his door, rounded impressions, small, like a child wearing galoshes, coming from the lake. Then, as if the sun was an eraser passing over the yard, the dew vanished.

Leesa took Savannah into town for lunch and shopping. They needed to stock the refrigerator and freezer, and Savannah decided she couldn't live without fruit juice in the squeezable packages.

Poul sat in a lawn chair at the foot of the pier for most of the morning. The sun pressed against his forehead and eventually filled him with lazy heat. Ripples caught the light, sending it in bright, little spears at him. Waves lapped the shore. The boat, tied to the dock, thudded hollowly every once in a while like a huge aluminum drum.

If he shut his eyes, it could be thirty years earlier. The sun beat the same way, and the same ripply chorus floated in the air. On the beach he and Neal had talked about deep sea diving and fish. Poul was frustrated. He had a wonderful face mask, fins to push himself along and a snorkel, but the mask was too buoyant. He could dive underwater, but he couldn't stay near the fascinating bottom where the catfish lived. So he had a brain storm. In the boathouse he found a pair of rubber snow boots he'd left from January when he and Dad had come to the lake to fix a frozen pipe. They were supposed to fit over shoes, so his bare foot slopped around. He held the top open. "Fill them up, Neal," he said.

His brother looked at them doubtfully. "Why do you want to do that?"

"Cause this will keep me from floating."

"Oh," Neal said with admiration. He used a yellow, plastic shovel to dump sand in. When it was full, Poul forced the bottom buckle closed. The sand squeezed his leg; he fastened the next one, and it was even tighter. Sand spilled over the top. After the last buckle, there was a strap that cinched the boot closed. It felt like his feet were in grainy cement; he couldn't even wiggle his toes.

Neal laughed when Poul tried to walk. Each foot must have weighed an extra ten pounds, and it was all he could do to shuffle forward. Poul adjusted his face mask and snorkel. "Wish me luck."

"Luck," said Neal. "Find the big catfish, okay?"

Poul nodded as he waded out. The water slapped higher on his body with each step from shore. When it reached his armpits, he put the snorkel in, then slowly squatted, his feet holding firm beneath him. He turned; underwater, the sand held ripples, a sculpture of the surface motion, while the underside of the surface undulated, meeting the beach at the shore. Then he stood, blew water from the snorkel and gave Neal a thumbs up. Neal waved back.

A few steps deeper, and the water line rose on the face mask. Another step and he was completely underwater, breathing through the snorkel. No fish, but a lot of suspended material, bits of algae. Exotic noises. A buzz that must have been a boat cruising along. A metallic clink that might be a chain under the diving platform a hundred feet away. His breath wheezing in and out of the snorkel. Other, unidentifiable sounds. Poul the adventurer, an explorer of undiscovered countries.

Then, a fish just at his vision's edge, much deeper, swam along the bottom. Poul froze, hoping it would come close, but it stayed maddeningly far. He moved toward it, sliding his foot only a few inches. It flicked away, then appeared again, still now, head on, as if it were watching him. An encounter with an alien would not have felt any more exotic. Poul leaned toward the fish, his hand out. A gesture of hello.

Water filled his mouth, straight into his throat and he was choking. It hurt! Eyes tearing, he looked up. He'd gone too deep. The top of the snorkel was below the surface. Blind panic! He flailed his arms, trying to swim up, but his feet didn't budge. He jerked, screaming through the snorkel. No air! No air! He turned toward shore, and took a step. He took another, then blew hard, clearing the water and breathed in gasps. Without pause, he continued toward shore. When he was shallow enough, he ripped the face mask off and sucked one huge breath after another. By the time he got to shore, his throat quit hurting, but he wanted to get away, to lay down and cry. He could feel it in his chest, the horrible pressure of no air, the moment when he didn't dare inhale.

"Did you see a fish?" Neal asked. He was sitting with his toes in the water, arms wrapped around his knees. "Was it totally cool?"

Poul shook his head, hiding his tears by unbuckling the boots. He scraped his feet pulling them out. Later that day Dad would smear first aid cream on them, his eyes unfocussed, his hands shaking.

Poul left the boots on the beach and went into the woods to cry. He'd never been so scared. He'd never been so scared! And when he returned an hour later, Mom was walking up the shore, calling Neal's name. "Where's your brother?" She'd asked, her eyes already wild. "Weren't you watching Neal?"

Poul rose from the lawn chair; he could feel the nylon webbing creases in his backside. Neal was six, he thought. Savannah is six. The two facts came together with inevitable weight. For years he hadn't thought much about Neal's death. Every once in a while, a memory would flare: the two of them talking late at night, after they were supposed to be asleep, the model airplane Neal had given him for his birthday, the words carefully inscribed on the back, *For mi big brother. Luve, Neal.* Neal trusted him, looked up to him, but most of the time Neal didn't exist anymore. Then Savannah was born, and Neal came back, a little stronger each summer. Maybe that's what Leesa sensed: the younger brother, dead within him.

Savannah is six, Poul thought, and Neal has been waiting.

He went through the cottage and made sure the screens were tight. It wouldn't do for the house to be filled with mosquitoes when Leesa and Savannah returned. For a moment he held a pen over a notepad in the kitchen, but put it down without writing. A beach towel went over his shoulder, and he walked to the end of the pier. Standing with his toes wrapped over the edge, a breeze in his face, felt like leaning over an abyss. Beyond the drop-off, he saw no bottom. The big fish were there, the fishy mysteries he'd left to Neal.

He dove in, a long shallow dive that took him yards away without a stroke. Water rushed by his ears. Bubbles streamed from his nose. He came to the surface, treaded. From his shoulders to his knees, the lake was warm, a comfortable temperature perfect for swimming, but from the knees down it was cold. Neal hadn't known how to swim, he thought. To even go on the pier, Dad had made him put on a life jacket, and Poul was the older brother. How many times had he been told to *protect* him, to watch out for him? And it didn't matter what he'd been told, Poul *wanted* to keep his brother safe. At the playground, he listened for Neal's voice. When someone cried, Poul stopped, afraid it was Neal. Loving his brother was like inhaling.

Neal went into the lake; he never came out. Neal must have hated him, Poul thought. At the end, he must have cried out for him, but Poul didn't come. He didn't warn him.

Poul swam deeper, put his face down, eyes open. Without a mask, his hands were blurry. Beyond them, blackness. How deep? Were there pike? He imagined a ghost catfish, its eye as broad as a swimming pool rising toward him.

But try as he might, Poul couldn't drown himself. He floated on his back, letting his feet sink until his weight drew his face under, and just when the time came to breathe, he kicked to the surface. He couldn't let the water in. Swimming parallel to the shore, he passed Kettle Jack's, swam by dozens of cottages like his own until his arms tired. Each stroke hurt, his shoulders burning with exhaustion, but they never quit working. The lake let him live, and Neal never came up to join him. Poul waited for a hand (a small hand) to wrap around his ankle, to pull him down where six-year-olds never grow older. Instead, the sun moved across the sky until Poul was empty. Completely dull, drained and damaged, he turned toward shore, staggered up a stranger's beach, and walked on the lake road toward his cottage, staying in the shoulder, where the grass didn't hurt his feet.

If Neal didn't want him, who did he want?

This far above Kettle Jack's was unfamiliar to him, but the look was the same: long, dirt driveways that vanished in the trees below, or led to cottages camped along the shore. Old boats sprawled upside down on saw horses. Bamboo fishing poles leaned against weathered wood. Station wagons or vans parked behind each house. Towels drying on lines. Beyond, in the lake, sailboats cut frothy wakes; the wind had picked up, although he didn't feel it much here.

He started walking faster. Leesa and Savannah would be home by now. He wondered what they were doing. Leesa never watched Savannah like he did. Her philosophy was that kids take care of themselves, generally, and it's healthier for a child to have room to explore.

He hadn't realized how far he'd swam. Way ahead, the tip of Kettle Jack's pier poked into the lake. Maybe Savannah and Leesa would walk there to see Johnny Jacob's kittens. But it was hot, and Savannah hadn't swam yet. Yesterday she'd fished. Today she'd want to swim. He could see the scene. Leesa would pull into the driveway. Savannah would put on her swimsuit to go out on the beach. She had sand toys, buckets, shovels, rakes; little molds for making sand castles. Leesa would set up a chair, lather in sun lotion and read a book. Savannah could be in the water now.

Poul broke into a jog. How idiotic it was to leave the cottage, he thought. No, not idiotic. Criminal. If vengeance waited in the lake, if some sort of delayed retribution haunted the cold waters, why would it care for him? Where would his suffering be if he drowned, like Neal, relieved of responsibility at last? He was running. Kettle Jack's passed by on his left. It was a mile to his cottage. He'd swam over a mile! And maybe that was the plan: to get him out into the lake and away. Suddenly he felt as if he'd lost his mind. What was he thinking? What sane father would dive into the water away from his daughter? Savannah is six, he thought, and she needs her daddy.

The van was parked behind the cottage. Poul ran to the front, his breath coming in great whoops. Empty lounge chair. Sand toys on the beach. A child's life vest lying next to the boathouse. No sign of her. He yelled, "Savannah!" as he went through the door onto the porch.

Leesa sat at the kitchen table, eating a sandwich. "What's wrong with you?" she said.

"Where's Savannah?"

"Puttering around in that raft I bought her. We had a heck of a time finding it."

"I didn't see her!" he said as he ran out of the kitchen.

Out front, he scanned the lake again. Boats in the distance. No yellow raft. He had a vision: Savannah paddling, looking at the bottom through the clear plastic. Sand, of course; she'd see sand and minnows. Then she'd move farther out, her head down, hoping for fish, not aware of how far from shore she was going. The water would get deeper. She'd be beyond the sand, where the depths were foggy and dark green. "What is that?" she'd think. A moving shadow, a form resolving itself, a face coming from below. The little boy from beneath the pier.

Poul pounded down the dock, scanning the water to the left and right. Leesa followed.

"She was right here a minute ago! I've only been inside a minute!"

At the dock's end, Poul stopped, within a eye blink of diving in, but the water was clear as far as he could see. Even the sailboats had retreated from sight.

"Maybe she went to see the kittens," Leesa said.

"With the raft? She wouldn't go with the raft!" Poul's voice cracked.

A bird flew by, wings barely moving. It seemed to Poul to almost have stopped. His heart beat in slow explosions. Leesa said something, but her meaning didn't reach him, the words were so far apart. Then, a round shape pushed from beneath the pier. At first he thought it was the top of a blonde head, right under his feet, and it moved a little bit further, becoming too broad to be a head, and too yellow to be blonde. It was the raft. He could feel himself saying, "No," as he bent, already knowing Savannah wouldn't be in it. He tugged on its handle. It resisted. Who is holding on? It slid out. No one held it. Six inches of water in the bottom made it heavy.

"Savannah!" Leesa screamed. Then the bird's wings beat twice and it was gone. Poul's pulse sped up. The lake had never seemed so empty. He remembered Dad, who had stood at the end of the pier, mute, when they pulled Neal out. Now he stood on the same board.

A high voice called from the lake, a child. Poul looked up, his skin suddenly cold. It called again, and Poul saw her, lying on the diving platform a hundred feet away. Savannah.

He didn't know how he got there—he didn't remember swimming, but he was up the diving platform's ladder, holding his weeping daughter instantly. She nestled her head under his chin and shook with tears. Before she stopped, Leesa arrived in the boat, and they both held her.

Finally, when Savannah's crying had settled into a sob every minute or two, Leesa said, "How did you get out here, darling? You scared us so."

Between shuddery breaths, Savannah said, "I didn't mean to go so far, and I couldn't get back. I paddled really hard, but I fell out. The wind pushed the raft away."

She looked from Poul to Leesa, her eyes red-rimmed and teary.

"I swallowed water, Daddy. I couldn't breathe."

Poul swallowed. He could feel the snorkel in his mouth, the solid, leaden ache of water in his lungs.

Leesa gasped, "Thank God you made it to the diving platform. We could have lost you," and she burst into tears herself.

Through Leesa's crying, Savannah looked at Poul solemnly. "I didn't swim, Daddy. The little boy helped me. He took my hand and put me here." Savannah rubbed her eyes with the back of her arm. "He kissed my cheek, Daddy."

Poul nodded, incapable of speech.

"He looked like the boy in your baby pictures." She sniffed, but seemed more relaxed, her fear already becoming vague. "My eyes didn't play tricks on me."

Poul spent the sunset sitting on the end of the pier, his toes dipping in the lake, surrounded by the watery symphony. Aqueous rhythms beating against the wood, lapping against the shore. And fish. He sat quietly, and the fish came: a school of blue gill, scales catching the last light in a thousand glitters swirling in front of him and then were gone. Later, when the sun had nearly disappeared, a long, black shape glided by, its eye as big as a quarter, a long row of teeth visible when it opened its mouth. Poul had finally seen a pike.

He sighed, pushed himself up and found Leesa in the kitchen. She'd already put Savannah to bed in their room upstairs.

She looked at her coffee cup dully. It was almost hard to remember what he'd loved about her when they'd first met, then she turned her head a little and brushed back her hair, and for a second, it was there, a picture of Leesa when they were young. Before Savannah. Before coming to the lake had become so reluctant. The second disappeared.

He pulled a chair out for himself and turned it around so he could lean his arms on the back. She didn't speak. Poul shut his eyes to listen to the woods behind the cottage. The air there was always so moist and living, but it didn't penetrate into the kitchen. With his eyes closed, he could swear he was alone in the room.

"I want a divorce," Poul said.

Leesa looked at him directly for maybe the first time in a year. "Why now?"

The low, slanting sun cut through the trees behind the cottage, casting a yellow light in the room. He knew that on the lake it highlighted the waves, but didn't penetrate the depths. Fisherman would be out, because the big fish, the serious fish moved in the evening. The evening was the best time to be on the lake, after a hard day of swimming, of hiking in the woods where he'd played with Neal, and just before they went to bed to tell each other stories until sleep took them, two brothers under one blanket lying head to head, and they dreamed.

Poul said, "When you realize a thing is bad, you've got to let it go or you'll drown."

SATURN RING BLUES

OLD JELLY ROLL MORTON'S SOULFUL VOICE FILLS THE BUGLIGHTER'S cabin.

Nothing more mournful and perfect than a good, solid dose of the blues while you're waiting at the edge of the ring for the start of the race. That and the cloud-striped surface of Saturn turning below, the dusky-edged ridge of the rings above, catching a little of the reflected light, and between them both the sharp-eyed light of the stars. Lots of sad stringed guitar and bent-note blues harp, and his whiskey voice down deep. It's a pool hall voice.

I met Elinor in a pool hall. She had an attractive way of blowing chalk dust off her knuckles that caught my eye. We racked up games till the bar closed. Only thing I can beat her at. I see the angles clear. "You got those angle eyes," she said.

It's true. I even like my hull transparent. Most of the equipment's behind, all that stuff that shapes the forces around the buglighter, keeping me safe from danger, and, when the need arises, pushing me where I want to go. So with the hull clear, I'm sitting alone and pretty in the stars. That's the way I feel, just like those blues songs tell me: "Lordy, I'm all by myself since my baby done left me."

Lots of buglighters can't do it—perch in the clear like I do—too much space around them. It's hard on the heart. Elinor said to me, "Virgil, you're too much of a sit down and look around kind of guy." She would know, I guess. Of course I wasn't paying attention at the time; we were playing pool and I said, "Shh. I'm concentrating."

The starter's voice interrupts the music: "Flyers, welcome to the 17th annual Greater Circumference of Saturn Ring Runners Challenge, 2,500 Kgram class. Five minutes to race time."

A hundred meters around, dust motes spark off the bubble that contains me. Zap, zap . . . there go a couple more. That's where we get the name, buglighter, little bits of ice and rock, zappin' like firecrackers in the forces surrounding us. In five minutes the race will start, and I'll adjust the bubble. Instead of flicking that ring sand away, it'll suck it in, transform it in an instant, and shape the pulse into comforting thrust, rolling me around the inside of the ring on fission fire in my perfect sphere of protecting energy, sort of like a transparent cue ball bounding off the bumpers of the ring. From the start, all the way around again, about 578,000 Kmeters, or roughly 15 times the circumference of the Earth.

Over my shoulder, Elinor's buglighter is all aglow. She's a hot one, her. She likes to start these races fast, so she's storing energy in the field. She's always got a plan. Plan ahead, that's her. She didn't see me in her future, I guess. Cut me loose clean. She likes to fly light.

"Gotcha on my backside, Elinor G.," I say on a private channel, figuring that it won't hurt to assay some warmth in her direction.

"Cut the chatter, Delta Mud," she says. That's my ship, not me. Feel that way most the time though, just as low down as can be. So I turn up the music. Little bit of Brownie McGhee and Sonny Terry, "Blues from the Lowlands." I got 'em too. Got 'em bad. Don't know why you're sayin' no to me, Elinor G.

Nothing to do then except study the course ahead, sending out some high-imaging radar. It shows me what to miss—klunking into a chunk of ring matter bigger than a football or so at 50,000 kph would put a dent in my day, and, of course, it'll send that rock flying like a cannonball in the opposite direction—but, it doesn't show me where to go: the rich sand and pebbles I can eat up and convert to thrust. That's the art and joy of ring running: dodging the big ones; following the fuel, shooting fast around the ring without spinning out.

My first two chords are clear, but after that, I'll be checking as I go: thousands of kph, glimpsing ahead for widow-makers on the high wire edge of the ring. It's only a kilometer wide, generally, at least only a kilometer of usable rock.

Ring racing is in the chords' progression and rhythm—like the blues—cutting across the arc of the orbit's circle. The way I fly, the shorter the chords, the faster the ship. Look and blast, look and blast. Can't look while you're blasting (too much interference); can't blast without looking (otherwise you'd be sure to fetch up against some pocky chunk of rock, big as a barn and your race would be over forever). It's a funny looking race, if you diagram it. Put two circles on a piece of paper, one inside the other, and the outside one not too much bigger than the inner. That inside circle is Saturn. The outside one is the inner edge of the ring. Now, take a ruler and draw a straight line that connects two points of the outer circle without crossing the inner circle. That's one chord. If you keep drawing chords, you end up with a polygon that goes around the planet. That's the race.

My angle of entry into the rings is shallow, and most of the bigger rocks are deeper in, so I minimize risk while maximizing speed. Elinor, though, she takes these long chords, building up speed on each one; each one dives her deeper into the ring. It's scary genius at work to watch her fly.

So I keep the chords short to play those high speed blues. I take out my c-harp and blow a few chords of my own—still nothing better than a Marine Band harmonica. Well engineered instrument, the harmonica: light, compact, fits in the hand, feels cool on the lips. Good acoustics in a buglighter too. Echoes back in nice and tight, like singing in a shower. I try out a new line for my Elinor Blues. "Elinor, Elinor, you don't be coming round anymore." A common blue's pattern is statement, repeat and a variation. Got the statement and repeat down pat, but don't know a variation yet. I try one out. Five minutes is a long time for a race to start.

> Elinor, Elinor, you don't be coming round anymore.
> Elinor, Elinor, you don't be coming round anymore.
> Been five long years, baby. Waitin's been such a chore.

Can't think of her as "baby." She's all hard muscle and physics-brain bright. Give her enough numbers and just enough fuel, and she could with one solid blow, dead-stick the rest of the way a course from the moon, Rhe, to Titan and not miss her orbit slot by a couple of meters. But every guy singing the blues calls his baby, baby.

The signal starts the race. Elinor and a couple others blast on the dot, brightness enveloping their buglighters, glowing like acetylene teardrops. My ship gathers in sand, sucks in a larger pebble or two, most of the mass converted into energy. Screen shows I've got a clear shot deeper into the ring. Greater chance of crashing into something, but the usable detritus is thicker. Let it go all at once. The good, solid thump of the nuclear explosion behind me pushes me into my seat. Thank God for inertia dampers, otherwise I'd be a thin jelly on the back wall of the cabin.

Right off, rocks start clattering against the bubble, lost in bright sparks. I've gained speed, moved up in the orbit, further into the dust.

We run the race on the inner edge of the "B" ring, the bright one you can even see from Earth with a reasonable telescope. The "C" ring below is much thinner. Hard to guarantee you'll find rock to blast with when you need it. The "A" ring is farther out; it's got that cool gap in it where the moon, Pan, orbits.

In my monitor, I see Elinor's ship. She's taken a long chord as her first jump, crossing all that mostly empty space. It's a shorter distance to go around, as I mentioned, but a riskier tactic.

"You like a brief life, Elinor?" I say.

"Brief and bright," she says.

I do some quick calculations and whistle in appreciation. She'll dive into the ring for a couple of hundred Kmeters before she'll have the energy for her next blast. Her radar can't penetrate that deep. Too much intervening sand.

"Going for the record?"

"Already got it," she says.

And she does; won last year, and I pulled up a lame second.

Time for the next blast. Race like this is an art. Sort of a mix between orbital mechanics, demolition derby and pool; the whole thing done with your heart gripped firmly between your teeth so you don't lose it.

"Going slow there, Delta Mud," she says, but I can't answer before I slam through the burn. Bubbles go white and glorious as they store up the energy, then release it all at once. Can't hear it, naturally, though my music gets fuzzy during; way too much radiant activity to avoid that, and the inertia dampers don't completely mask the thrust of it. My seat presses hard into my back. I feel every wrinkle in my shirt.

Monitors are clear. Nothing in my way, so I set up for the next chord.

"Eaten any cold dinners lately?" I say.

"No," she says. "Have you?"

I let that question hang out there a while. It's a friendly response, if I hear it right, and probably because she's got an early lead. Use to be I'd go visit her for dinner pretty regular, and we never did get right to eating it. One thing lead to another, you know, and the dinner would cool off.

So an answer takes a bit of thinking. Is she opening the door here? Are all those cold, cold nights looking out at lonely stars about to come to an end?

I wish I could see her. You know, to watch her face. She's got this way of letting the corners of her mouth twitch up when she's making a joke. It's real subtle. Lots of folk don't notice. And she shakes her head sometimes, like she's getting hair out of her eyes, though her hair is spacer-short.

How's she looking now? What I need is a deep-imaging radar of the heart. Something to peer in there to check on those pocky rocks drifting unseen.

She's about to end a chord, so I check her progress.

Ring racing is the hardest kind there is. *Straight* races . . . well, they're simple. Thrust behind mass, and don't miss. Best technology wins. Pilot might as well stay home (singing the blues). But here—whew! Faster you go, the more dangerous it is. More chances for mistakes. Less time for decisions. All the time risking spinout, missing the ring, flying off with better than escape velocity and no mass anywhere to grab.

She's in the ring now. Gathering energy. Blasting. Her trajectory changes, and she's shooting back out the ring to the relatively clear space beneath.

I've got some time. She'll be checking the path ahead, figuring her next burn.

I make sure the transmitter is off, blow the harmonica some more—make the harp sing:

> Elinor, Elinor, saw you walking in the stars.
> Elinor, Elinor, saw you walking in the stars.
> Venus at your toe tips; your fingers touching Mars.

She said, "I think I can cut four chords off last year."

I shake my head. "You'll be sucking Saturn's atmosphere. Not worth the speed you lose."

She chuckles. "For you, maybe. Have you checked the competition?"

I hadn't bothered. She's the only other ship I care about, but I tapped the display and the others popped onto the grid, way behind.

"Looks like it's just you and me."

"And the record," she adds. "How's it feel to be the second best flyer in the rings?" She's laughing. Pure speed does that to her.

"When you're beat by the best," I say, "Who cares about the rest?"

"That's sweet, Virgil."

I'm into my next burn. Speed's up, so the bubble fairly crackles, sending dust and tiny rocks in all directions and storing energy. I let it go, and the chair kicks into my back, snapping my head into the support. Inertia dampers are good, but most ships let their thrust out more gradual because they carry mass to convert to energy with them. Buglighters don't carry anything but some maneuvering fuel.

All the rest is gathered in, then, wham, released in a hurry.

A few chords later, speed's way up, and my work's harder. Soon as the interference clears, I check the radar for rocks, plug in the new numbers, and let the computer go to work with trajectories and mid-course corrections. While it crunches numbers, I've got nothing to do but think.

Blues are perfect for space, and I'll bet if B.B. King or Howlin' Wolf or Muddy Waters were alive today, they'd be buglighters. All that other music, well, it has beginnings and ends, but not the blues. You can take any song and run it for hours with variations, letting it build or slide down low. It's back porch music, smokey pool hall music, buglighter music. You can tell when you're in a spacer bar by the music. It's all guitars and bass and c-harp bent over those blues notes. Every tune's despairing, but kind of funny too, sort of like cruising in the rings. Part of it's deadly serious, and then you have to laugh. Blues and buglighting and my love for Elinor are just too ironic to keep a straight face.

See, when you're singing the blues, you start off all sad and lonely, but after a while, you're into the music. You forget why you started the song, and you're just doing the song. And buglighting, you forget why you started or where you're going, and you're just flying the chords. There's music in them. Music in the light and the rhythm. Music in the rainbow of colors when the distant sun catches the rings just right. Music in the shadows and darkness behind Saturn. It's the blues, man; everyone knows it's the blues.

We go like this for awhile. I blast three times for every two of Elinor's. It's kind of sobering watching her eat up the distance. She's got so much speed, and it's building. I'm going about as fast as I feel I can go. My burns now just get me into the new chord; they don't add much velocity.

But that's the way it's always been. Old Elinor is always a jump or two ahead of me.

"Doesn't look like you're going to give me a race this year, Virgil."

"It's a long way around," I say.

"I'll have a drink set up for you when you get in," she says.

I'm a ways from my next turn, so I switch to her monitors so I can see what she sees. It's scary. Her angle of attack is high. She can only see a third of the distance into the ring that she penetrates.

"Assuming you make it," I say.

Her screen is graying out as she enters the ring. A couple of big rocks glow off her path; they're no danger, but I've never seen stuff that big moving by so fast. She's busy, so I don't say anything and switch back to my own monitor. She fades out as she gets deeper. I won't see her till she exits, and I check my own course again. Looks like clear sailing to me.

"Uh, oh," she says.

I shouldn't be able to hear her yet. I check the screen. She's there, going the wrong direction, outside of the ring. A spinout.

"You all right?" I ask. Silly question, really. If she wasn't, I wouldn't have heard anything at all. She wouldn't be on the monitor.

"Shoot," she says.

I'm running her numbers through the computer. She's got way too much speed, and she's moving away from the ring. My calculations show she can't push herself back to it either.

"What happened?"

"Hit something," she says.

"How's your system?" I check the emergency bands. She's already sent a "come-hither" to the outer stations. I send one too.

"Smells bad in here," she says, and she chuckles. "I think I burnt some stuff out. Nothing vital. Heck of a shot. Must have been a good sized chunk."

"Great race while it lasted," I say.

"Yeah," she sounds preoccupied. I roll through my next burn. Our courses are fairly close now, but I'm inside the ring trailing her, and she's outside the ring, rising fast, way faster than me.

"Have you run the intercepts?" she says.

I hadn't, so I plug in the numbers. They don't look good, and I do them again. I whistle.

"Yeah," she says. "I don't think anyone can come get me in time."

"Your bubble still sound?" I say. My fingers are dancing over the computer keys, inputting data, asking for alternative scenarios. What happens if she uses her maneuvering fuel to slow down? What happens if she tries to push herself back into the ring? None of them look good.

"Yeah." She sounds sad. I'm not sure if it's because her chances are dim or because she's out of the race.

I switch out of our private channel. Titan station is chattering away to miners on Pan to see if they can raise a ship in time, but they aren't geared for quick takeoffs, and the moon is in the worst place right now for them to mount a rescue. They can get to her, but it would be hours too late. If she'd been going a reasonable speed, no problem, but she's got way too much velocity. Without a steady supply of fissionable mass, her buglighter will shut down and she'll freeze solid. Buglighters aren't built for empty space. They're ring-runners.

The other racers are talking too. Somebody says he'll chase her, which is plain stupid because he'd never catch her, and even if he did, what good would it do? He couldn't bring her on board. He couldn't bring mass out to her.

"I'm going to try braking," she says. "It'll slow me up, and maybe someone on the outer rings can catch me."

"No, don't," I say. "Not yet. Save the fuel."

My imaging radar shows me the ring ahead, mostly fuzz since it's pebbles and sand with a few bright spots that represent bigger rocks. I'm looking for the right sized rock on the edge of the ring. Idea's forming. Nothing looks good, though, so I kick through the next burn and start scanning as soon as I'm clear.

"What do you have in mind?" she says.

"Shh. I'm concentrating." I'm thinking about angles, mass, velocity and risk, so I'm not paying much attention to conversation.

Rock can't be too big. It'd kill my ship, and I couldn't give it the speed it'd need to catch her. Can't be too small either. The impact would turn it to dust, and it wouldn't give her enough energy if any of it did reach her buglighter. And the whole idea is a little wacky anyway. The odds of making the shot are incredible. Quite a bit worse than running two bumpers to sink the eight ball in the corner pocket.

On the monitor, a likely candidate pops up. It's on Elinor's edge of the ring. Not too deep. Chances are I can line up on it, not be deflected on the way in, and it won't be deflected on the way out. Hitting right, though, that's the problem. If I miss by even a fraction of an inch, the rock could spew away at a useless angle; Elinor will be in the same fix, and my buglighter will be too busted up for a second shot.

Once the problem's in the computer, it controls my maneuvering jets. I'm running the radar on tight scan now, checking the rock, trying to get more info on it, and the numbers are coming back good.

"What are you doing?" Elinor asks. I know she can see my buglighter on her monitors. She can do the same trick I did earlier and have her monitors display what I'm seeing.

I don't say anything. Not much I can do at this point anyway, but I'm running a second set of calculations, just as an exercise really, since I'm committed to the collision at this point. Thought it would be interesting to do the math though, to see how much energy my bubble will have to take. The figures come back. They're somewhat above what the specs say the ship will handle. Specs are conservative, I hope.

"Veer off," she says. "Virgil, this won't work."

I check my straps and buckles. Inertia damper is going to get a workout here. "Set your bubble up and get your maneuvering jets ready," I say. "Don't know how close I can get this to you. You might have to chase it." I rotate the buglighter so I'll take the force from behind.

Ship's counting down for me: 10 seconds to impact . . . 9 . . . 8 . . . I turn up the music, a little George Thorogood tune, "Bad to the Bone."

5 . . . 4 . . . 3

Sunlight's glistening off the inner edge of the ring flashing past. Gets a man thinking.

When I wake up, it's silent and dark. My neck hurts. Left elbow is locked up. I touch it gingerly. Shirt's torn there, and it's damp. Don't know what might have hit it. But I've got breathing air, and it's not cold. Pebbles are zapping at the bubble boundary, so more's good than bad here. I'll have to thank the designers of the buglighter for the slop built into their tolerance specs.

Computer doesn't answer to voice controls, but when I flip the auxiliaries on, the monitors glow again and start spewing out a list of damages. Radar won't come up, though, and neither will the radio. Some whiffs of fried circuitry float in the air, so I shut down the main routines and go to the backups.

After a few minutes, the radio crackles and I hear Elinor. "Virgil," she says. "Can you hear me, Virgil." She sounds like she's crying. Radar's still blank. Can't tell if I helped her or not.

"I'm here," I say.

Nothing over the radio for a bit. I'm scrambling to get the radar online. Can't tell how fast I'm going or if anything nasty is in front of me.

"You're a hell of a pool player," she says, finally, and I don't hear any crying in her voice now. "I didn't have to use but about half my fuel to intercept the rock."

"Luck," I say.

She snorts. "It was coming pretty darn fast too. But I got enough of it to make a good burn. I'll be back in the ring in plenty of time."

"You're the master in the ring," I say. Radar starts working, and I do a quick scan. Lost lots of velocity. No ship-killers on the screen though. A mini-burn keeps me in the mass field. Don't need a spinout of my own to cause problems.

"Looks like we're both out of the race."

"Could be worse, Elinor." I laugh. My elbow aches, and I unbuckle myself so I can get to the first aid station.

"I owe you big time," she says.

"You'd have done it for me." The first aid diagnostic gives me a once over, suggests a pain medication and alerts the Inner A Station that I'm injured.

"Might have tried," she says. "Couldn't have done it."

"Well, I was motivated."

I ease myself back into the chair, swallow the pain meds and set a nice, slow, easy course back to the station, letting the computer do all the work.

"I've been thinking about that," she says. There's a long pause here. "Maybe we should get together and talk about it some. You know, you could drop over for dinner or something."

I smile. It's been a long time coming. Nights have stretched, and I've played a lot of harmonica in the meantime. Around my ship, little blue glitters of rock and ice catch the reflected light off Saturn. I should be home in a few hours. It'll take her considerably longer.

"I'll think about it," I say, and switch my radio off.

Nothing's more quiet than the silence in a buglighter when your heart is in a turmoil and you're not sure if the one you want wants you. I've charted that course before.

The harmonica fits easily into my hand. A tap or two against my leg clears it out, and I try a few notes. They sound good. They always do.

I know how I'll answer. She probably knows it too. But in the meantime, let *her* sing a little of those Saturn Ring Blues.

ONCE THEY WERE MONARCHS

From the guard tower, Müller watched Bates circulating among the children in the shallow end. Bates was a fat thirteen-year-old whose bulging fingers turned to pale prunes after a half hour in the water, and whose rounded shoulders glowed dull red with perpetual sunburn. He often cruised the shallows in crocodile mode, his nose barely out, his bleached blue eyes evaluating each child before moving on.

Müller scrunched his hands into fists, thinking how good it would feel to squeeze the little pervert's neck, but he also welcomed the distraction from the lonely heights of the guard's chair. Mostly, life guarding left him too much time to contemplate isolation, his alienation from the screaming children, from the boring regularity of human rhythms. He thought of his unique position, high above the water's surface, looking down on all he surveyed as he had in the old days from mountaintops or from the circling giddiness of summer thermals beneath his wings. But mostly he felt the loneliness of the unending masquerade.

A handful of butterflies fluttered above the oleanders by the pump room. Müller thought about Monarchs and Viceroys.

"Good job yesterday," said Mr. Regin as he walked by the tower. "Quick thinking!" The old man's sandals flapped against his feet as he headed for the exit gate.

A long-haired boy wearing cut off jeans climbed from the deep end to Müller's left and dashed for the diving board.

"Don't run," growled Müller automatically, scrutinizing Bates as he drifted down to the rope that kept non-swimmers from the deeper water. The August, Sacramento sun's heat sank into Müller's skin like a heavy, sweltering blanket while the light glared off waves around Bates in a million, stabbing points. Müller turned his hands over, releasing his fists so they took the sun in his palms. It penetrated all the way to his bones, and he could feel his strength building, his animal inside churning for release, and still he watched Bates.

Müller had warned the pool manager the day before, after he'd pulled the Seigurd boy out of the water. Everyone thought Seigurd was drowning, but after a few seconds, Müller realized the child was having an asthma attack. A quick search of his towel revealed an inhaler, and twenty minutes later the kid was doing cannon balls off the high dive. "The Bates kid is a sicko, Raquelle. He's stalking the little girls all the time." His gravelly voice sounded too loud to him in the manager's office.

Raquelle hadn't looked up from the guard schedule on her desk. "Both Ray and George want the Fourth off, and Janille can't teach her Mom-Tot lessons next week. She's taking driver's ed. Can you cover?"

Müller thought about a double or triple shift on the Fourth of July, the crowded pool, non-swimmers whom he didn't know showing up the one summer holiday; the sun, like a blowtorch in the sky. "Sure. Now what about Bates?"

Raquelle glanced at him, zinc oxide coating her nose white. "Has anyone complained? Has he touched anyone?"

Müller looked around the room. Raquelle had a shelf full of sun screen by the sink; he smelled a fruity layer of it on her skin. Several floppy brimmed hats hung from a chair by the door along with a thin, light-colored blouse she wore to protect her arms outdoors, although she hardly ever guarded anymore. "I've got a feeling about him."

Raquelle shook her head. "He seems like a good kid to me. Probably should lay off the sweets. Has anyone had him in a lesson or talked to his parents? Maybe they could tell you something."

"I asked. He's never signed up for one, and I don't think he has parents. He walks to the pool."

Raquelle dismissed his concern with a wave of her hand. "You're a good guard, Müller. That was a nice piece of work yesterday with the Seigurd boy. I checked your records. You've been here, what, eleven years?"

Müller nodded, sighing. Raquelle was the fourth manager at the pool since he'd signed on. When someone noticed his longevity, it was time to pack his bags and go to a place they didn't know him, where they'd think he was just another late twenties guy slumming as a life guard and swim instructor. Maybe he'd move to San Diego and do some beach guarding.

"Keep an eye on him if you're worried. And for crying out loud, put up your umbrella. Your skin will turn to boot leather in this heat."

"I'm working on my tan," he said.

Müller squinted against the sparkle off the water. His eyes teared a little, but he stayed focused on Bates. Now the boy had sidled along the gutter until he was behind the Lindsey twins, a couple of blonde-headed, blue-eyed nine-year-olds in matching, pink bikinis who were tossing a ball back and forth between them. They shrieked as the ball went up, jumping to catch it before it hit the waves. Bates submerged, staring for a long minute before coming up for air. In the glare, Müller lost him. The surface caught the sun like an oily mirror, and Müller rubbed the back of his hand across his eyes to clear them. For a second, as Bates surfaced, he didn't look like a young teenager at all. For a second, as the water tumbled off his head, and the fractured sunlight pierced Müller's vision, the boy's skin turned color, a streaked yellow like an old bruise, and where the flesh had been smooth before, it became lumpy as if it were covered with warts. Not little warts, but fist-sized things on the edge of rupturing. For a second, Bates didn't look human. He turned, as if sensing Müller's attention, and the eyes behind the goggles were bulbous. Malice filled them.

Then Müller blinked, and his pulse pounded in his throat. He nearly roared, because now he knew what the creature was. The flickering reflection stopped, and Bates peeked up at him dully, a fat boy on a hot day wandering in the pool.

Something tapped Müller's foot. Beneath her hat, Raquelle shaded her face with her hand. "You looked pretty serious there for a second, buddy," she said. "Something bothering you?"

Müller scanned the few bobbing heads in the water. It was so hot that even being in the pool didn't beat the heat, and play had become listless. The pink-bikinied girls abandoned their game of catch and floated on their backs, eyes closed, blonde hair like nimbuses around their heads, their fingers interlocked so they wouldn't lose contact with each other. They floated in perfect X's, their feet spread, their arms splayed out. Müller had watched them hold this pose for minutes at a time on other days. Best little back floaters he'd ever seen. Some kids were rolling up their towels, readying for the 1:00 break, where the pool was cleared for ten minutes. On really hot days the least crowded time was between the 1:00 break and 5:00, when parents returning from work brought their families in.

Müller said, "Do you know about the Viceroy butterfly and the Monarch?" He nodded toward the colorful display above the oleanders. "Birds find the Viceroy tasty while the Monarch is bitter, so the Viceroy has adopted the Monarch's coloring. Birds leave the Viceroy alone now."

Raquelle looked confused. "And your point is?"

"There are all kinds of examples in nature of protective coloring and mimicry, like the walking stick or the scorpion fly. Sometimes the illusion is to protect the individual; sometimes it's to make it easier to prey. There's a preying mantid in Malaysia that looks like a flower. It eats the insects that come to pollinate it. We even have myths about imitators: the wolf pretending to be Little Red Riding Hood's grandmother, for example."

Raquelle nodded. "You're thinking about the Bates kid still, aren't you?"

Müller shrugged.

"You think he's a forty-year-old in a thirteen-year-old's body?"

"Something like that," said Müller. "He's a troll."

Bates had slid around to where the Lindsey twins still floated. He kept five or six feet away from them, but as the girls slowly revolved in the water, Müller could see he maneuvered himself so when he submerged he could look between one of the girl's legs.

Raquelle studied the tableau before her. "You sure you're not imagining it? I'd hate to confront a kid. Parents, you know, and libel suits. The city sent a memo on just this thing a week ago. He's not doing anything."

Bates sank so only the top of his head was visible, like a tiny hair island in a sun-beat ocean. He turned slowly too, but when he faced the girls, he paused slightly. He looked longer, and a waggle of his fingers moved him slightly closer.

"We just haven't caught him yet," said Müller. "You've got to be patient."

Raquelle clicked her fingernails against the base of the guard stand. "Tell you what. You take a break before you turn into beef jerky, and I'll take the last fifteen minutes. I'd like to watch him for a while."

Müller swung easily out of the seat and dropped to the deck five feet below it. Raquelle mounted the ladder. "How come you know so much about bugs? Are you a student?"

Müller grimaced. "Sort of. For mimicry to work, there can't be too many mimics. The base population has to outnumber the imposter by a huge percent or the adaptation breaks down."

"I don't get you. What does that have to do with anything?"

Müller checked the pool one more time. It was almost empty now: Bates, the Lindsey twins, a handful of older kids in the diving well . . . that was it. "I was just wondering how one Viceroy butterfly would find another among all those Monarchs."

Raquelle shook her head. "You're a strange bird, Müller. Get out of the sun for a while."

In the guard room, Müller checked the job board. This late in June, most positions were filled; even the inner-city rec programs in L.A. weren't advertising. He only looked at jobs south of San Francisco. Years ago he'd been in northern Europe, and the seasons didn't bother him much. Now that he was older, though, he sought the southern sun. Even here, in Sacramento, the rainy winter that never dipped below freezing bothered him. It took a couple of weeks of 90° weather in May for him to shake off the winter chill.

He wrote down a few phone numbers, then slouched into a vinyl-webbed deck chair. Summer was coming on, and the heat was beginning to fill him. By late August, it would be all consuming, and the drive to find another like him would make him restless. He brushed a finger against his lip and smiled, thinking about how soft it was. Even now, after hundreds and hundreds of years of hiding in a human body, he marveled at how fragile they were. That they ever threatened him and his kind on their mountain heights amazed him. But they did, and after a century of warfare, humanity had won. Saint George and all the rest like him won.

Only protective coloration and mimicry saved the remaining few. A little magic, a lot of swallowing of pride, and a desire to survive. They spread out. They fit in. They lost touch with each other. How does a Viceroy tell another of his rare kind from the overwhelming population of Monarchs indeed? And how long would it be before a wolf in sheep's clothing would forget what it was like to be a wolf, before he might fall in love with the flock? He wanted to fly above them again, like a tremendous hawk on the hunt, waiting to drop into a long stoop, but he didn't want *them* anymore; he'd been among them too long, he'd *been* one too long. Now, he only wanted to soak up sun and store it, he wanted to find one of his own, and he wanted to guard them, because they were weak, because they protected their young, and because he could. The little boy yesterday with asthma, for a second, Müller had thought he might die, and the thought scared him deeply. It scared him more than any horse-mounted knight ever had.

He folded a towel to put behind his head and rested. Beyond the guard's room, the sounds of the summer pool went on: the steady hum of the pump and filters, the occasional slurp of water through the skimmers, a vibrating thrum of the diving board, followed by the two-beat splash of someone entering the water. He smelled water steaming on the sun-washed cement, the acrid bite of chlorine, and fresh-cut richness of grass in the park around the pool.

Being a life guard suited him. For hours he did nothing except store sunshine. He could sit without moving a finger; only his eyes shifted as he scanned his area of responsibility. And beneath him, the human stories unfolded: there, a teen couple discovered each other while dangling their feet in the water; there, a mother struggled to watch her three boys, all under eight years old, at the same time; there an elderly woman jogged in the shallow end, practicing what she'd learned in the water-aerobics class. People were magnificent at a pool. They were physical and playful and emotional. And some of the time, they too lay still and let the sun fill them.

Then, every once in a while, he stirred to action. A child slipped on the deck and needed tending. Someone in a swim lesson got over his head and needed saving. Boys were too boisterous or young lovers were too amorous or someone lost a parent. And today, of course, there was a Bates, a special problem.

He drifted into a light sleep, dreaming about the undersides of clouds and a forest beneath him like a green, swaying sea.

After a while, outside, he heard crying. He sat up and pushed the door open with his foot. On the verge of grass by the baby pool, one of the Lindsey twins was holding the other. "I don't know why he would do that," said the one between sobs.

The other said, "I don't know either."

Beyond them, the guard chair sat empty; Raquelle stood on the edge of the diving well, chatting with a couple of the kids in the water. Müller wondered how long she'd been standing there.

Without thinking, Müller found himself kneeling by the girls. "What happened?" he rumbled. The girls stared at him, eyes red rimmed and teary.

"Nothing happened," said the crying one.

"It was nothing," said her sister, sobbing a little herself.

"I'm just sad."

"She's sad."

One turned her head toward Bates as he climbed out of the shallow end and headed for the locker room. She shivered a little and held her sister closer.

Müller couldn't move. Inside, things roiled around, raging, raging, but he had to contain them or everything would be lost, so he couldn't move. He knelt by the girls, not speaking for several minutes until they quit crying. Bates had vanished into the locker room but hadn't come out. Raquelle called the break to clear the pool while she tested the water's chemistry, and the handful of kids that were left headed to the concession stand at the other end, away from the locker rooms.

Finally, Müller stood. He was very close to the edge; in all his years, he'd never been this near to letting go of the mask. In his hands he could feel the claws wanting to come out. In his jaws, the long suppressed teeth ached beneath his gums. The ancient way of rending swirled about him. He could see it, could taste it, like a warm, thick soup squeezed from animals' heads.

The locker room door closed behind him. Listening quietly, he heard Bates around the corner toweling off, humming something discordant in a flat key, the notes bouncing off the slick tile and cinder block. Müller closed his eyes and sniffed the air. Chlorine. Hand soap. Mildew. Bates, the odor of sweat and bubble gum, and beneath that, something nasty: the smell of rotted mushrooms under a bridge, what they used to call blood mushrooms, deep red and damp. It was a troll's smell. But nothing else. They were alone in the locker room. The only light came through grimy skylights that dropped foggy shafts of white into the moist air.

Müller locked the door. The click echoed. Bates quit humming.

"Is anyone there?" said Bates, his voice a little quivery after several long moments of silence. A leaky shower head plinked water onto the cement.

Müller couldn't help it; a low growl bubbled out of him. It vibrated through the room.

Bates squeaked, then edged his way along the lockers until he stood directly in a shaft of light and could see Müller standing at the door.

"What do you want?" said Bates. He held his towel to his chest, as if it were a shield, and his goggles dangled around his thick neck.

A part of Müller wanted to say something to him. After all, they were both long lasting remnants of a time gone past, but the fury stilled the small part of him that contained his voice. The larger part of him moved away from the door and toward the fat boy. Bates stepped backwards, and suddenly his eyes narrowed.

"I know you," Bates said, and his voice dropped an octave. He stepped away again, and out of the skylight illumination. For a second, the illusion dropped, as it had when Müller saw him in the pool, and the creature underneath showed through. Now that Müller knew what to look for, it was easier not to be fooled. The clammy, sunburned skin covering the troll shifted, and Müller saw the heavy arms infested with ragged hair and rock-like warts. And the face beneath the face was filled with teeth—two short, heavy tusks dropped out of the corners of his mouth, pulling the lips apart so the cracked, uneven teeth in the middle poked in every direction and were revealed.

"You all are dead," said the troll. He dropped the towel and moved behind a bench, keeping it between him and Müller who continued to advance. "You're extinct, and there aren't many of us left either. It must be hard on you."

He didn't sound like a young boy now. Pretense was gone. The voice gurgled out of Bates' ancient throat, and his stony fingers clenched and unclenched as he kept his distance, moving toward his gym bag on the floor.

"We could share them," said Bates. "How long has it been since you've eaten well? Let me take one, one of those little girls for example. There are two of them—they're the same—one won't be missed. I'll take her to the forest and play my game, then you could have her. We'd both be served."

Müller pushed the bench aside. He eyed the troll's arms; they were inhumanly long and heavily muscled. The troll had changed himself less to fit in. The protective coloration only affected his proportions and surface appearance; he was still mostly troll with all his subterranean powers: his stone backbone and cold earth strength. He still could be incredibly powerful. If they grappled, Müller knew the troll would win. Müller's wings were buried too deep; his hands had been hands for too long while the talons had wasted away. So little was left that wasn't memories, but still, he came forward, the heat from a thousand hours of summer sun coalescing inside him.

Bates stopped at his bag, straddling it, his hands nearly brushing its handles. "The little girls are soooo tasty," he said, and in one motion, plunged his rock hand into the bag, coming out with an obsidian knife a foot long.

"But you'll never know, lizard!" and he jumped forward.

Müller stood still, something quivering inside him, building. His skin could barely hold it, it felt so big, begging for release.

The troll kicked aside the last bench.

The sun stored within Müller focused, became hard, ascended.

Bates raised his knife.

Shaking with the joy of it, Müller opened his mouth as if it were the old days, and unleashed the flame. It roared and roared and roared. And for a minute, the locker room could have just as well been a meadow in front of a castle, and the troll a lance wielding knight charging toward him. For a moment it was like it had always been.

And then it was done.

The sun shone like a white pupil in a blue eye and beat down. Müller stretched on the guard chair so all of his stomach caught the light. He rested his head back so his neck was warmed while he watched the pool. His hands lay palms up, gathering in heat, and within him an empty pocket began to fill again slowly, not like the old days where he'd find a warm boulder on the shoulder of the great mountain to spread his wings, to collect the sun in leathery gulps. No, he was smaller now, and these things took longer, but it still felt good. It felt very, very good to connect this way to earth and light, to the rhythms of the old sol's might.

"The boys' locker room smells bad," said Raquelle. Müller didn't move to look down at her, but he knew her face would be hidden under her floppy brimmed hat. "Can you check it out on your next break?" she said.

Müller breathed deeply, filling his lungs with hot summer air. Beyond the pool, wavy lines rose off the streets. He could see them swaying from black, shingled roofs. "When I'm on my break. Yes."

"Probably a kid lit some trash. I don't know why anyone would play with fire on a day like today. Wouldn't surprise me a bit if it were 115 degrees. Not even 2:00 yet. We ought to close, it's so hot. I'm pumping in city water now to cool the pool."

"It's a beautiful day. Perfect time to be on the tower," he said. In the diving well, the two swimmers who remained were splashing water on the board before they got out to do their dives. Even from here, Müller could see the dark splotches on the cement shrinking. A butterfly fluttered past. It looked like a Monarch, but he couldn't tell. It might have been a Viceroy. He smiled.

"Jeeze, you're a strange one, Müller." Raquelle moved herself so she stood in his shadow, the smell of sunscreen strong on her skin. "You remind me of a woman I guarded with in San Bernardino last year. She's worked that pool forever, they told me, and the hotter it is, the longer she stays out. Regular sun worshiper, she is."

Müller straightened in his seat and looked down at Raquelle intently.

She continued, "There are whole weeks of weather in San Bernardino that make today seem cool. I couldn't stand it."

The first diver went off the board. The second scurried out of the pool, stepping quickly to keep his feet cool as he headed for his turn.

"You've got to like the sun if you're going to guard," said Müller. "Maybe I should look that woman up. She sounds like a kindred spirit."

The diver bounced the end of the board twice to get extra height. At the top of his arc, he grabbed his knees and bent his head back in a tremendous cannon ball. Water flew everywhere, and the sun turned the spray into a flash of rainbow. For an instant, sparkle, color and the reflected diamonds of a million suns hung in the air.

"Yes," said Müller, settling back in his chair. "I might have to go to San Bernardino."

ORIGIN OF THE SPECIES

ROMULUS STOOD UNDER AN ELM IN THE MOON-WASHED SHADOW OF THE long, green sward between Gray Mountain Golf Course's ninth fairway and the Gray Mountain Country Club, listening to the tinny dance music of Pinehurst High's prom. He pried chunks of bark off the tree absently with his fingernail, but his focus was on the building, pink light leaking from the windows, a hundred shiny windshields catching the moon in the parking lot beyond, and the sad-leafed whisper of the wind. Shadows passed between the light and the windows, couples dancing, heads close together, gliding by during the slow song, and Romulus wondered which one was Fay with her date, what's-his-name, the troll.

He looked through the leaves at the moon, three days short of being full, and he scuffed the ground in disgust. Since September, when Student Senate scheduled the dance, he'd known. All the full moons were marked on his day-planner, mixed in with deadlines for college applications, baccalaureate, Senior Academic Awards night and graduation. There it was, a perfectly circular moon on the Tuesday after prom, and he'd known he would be standing outside, skin a little itchy, jaw aching, watching the dance.

When Romulus was a freshman, Dad told him it was regressive genetics catching up. They'd sat in his bedroom, Romulus' wildlife posters covering the walls, Dad, a little embarrassed, telling him the facts of life.

"You're getting to that age, son." Dad pressed his hands on the tops of his knees and locked his elbows straight, clearly uncomfortable.

"I know, Dad." Romulus scooted farther away on the bed. Dad's weight pressed the mattress down, and no matter where Romulus sat, he felt like he was an inch away from tumbling into him. And Romulus *did* know. He'd known for years, listening to his parents talking late at night, marking their calendars, Dad slipping out at dusk the nights of a full moon. What kid wouldn't know?

"You're going to start noticing girls more. You're a sensitive boy," Dad said.

Romulus blushed. It was true, he did. They'd walk by him in the halls, their backpacks hanging off one shoulder, intent on conversations with each other, and he'd catch himself staring at the almost invisible hair on a naked wrist, the curve of muscle in a neck. But most of all, it was their smell. For the longest time he hadn't known what it was. Once a month, or so, depending on the girl, he'd catch a stray whiff beneath the shampoo and perfume and hair spray, and his muscles would tense. He hoped to god Dad wasn't going to say anything about that. That would be too much. He'd rather jump out the window than listen to Dad fumble his way through an explanation of the smell.

Instead, Dad launched into an oblique reference to evolution and the origin of the species. "The genes mixed, son. I know what they told you in your science classes about where man came from, but they don't know the half of it, the magical half."

Romulus let out a relieved sigh. Dad wasn't going to talk about girls after all. Instead he talked about elves and harpies, goblins, giants and humans. "The dominant breed won out and all were assimilated. Everyone's human, more or less, but sometimes a regressive gene rises to the surface. Do you know what I'm trying to say?" He put his hand on Romulus's knee. "You're a special kid. There are others like you, some just like you, some from the other races, a little bit of old ancestry, the old mythologies, in everyone, more or less."

"Sure, Dad. Thanks for clearing this all up for me. I've got to do my homework now. Okay?"

"Oh, good." Dad let out a noisy sigh, like he'd just set down a great weight. "So you know why things are the way they are?"

"Yeah, I got it."

Then Dad left. Romulus didn't do his homework, but lay in bed instead, his hands clasped behind his head, staring at the ceiling, thinking about smells.

So he started paying attention to the lunar calendar his freshman year, and as time wore on he grew a few inches, filled out in the chest, found he needed to shave, and the week of the full moon he didn't schedule anything at night. Was Dad right? he wondered. Was *everyone* descended from mythological creatures? Sometimes he wandered the halls during passing period, or he sat in class and tried to figure where the other students came from. Was the cheerleader part elf? Was the junior class president's great, great, great, great (and so on) grandmother a gorgon? She was frightening enough, and there was a snakiness to her hair when she stood in the wind. He sniffed her, but she smelled purely human. He'd never identified anyone's deep ancestry until he smelled the troll in the boy who liked Fay, and that was a pure scary fluke. They'd bumped in the hall. The troll shoved him off, and in the shove Romulus had smelled him. A line of associations clicked—an instinctive recognition—but so strong that for a second the boy's hands were twisted claws, and his incisors hung from his mouth like stout tusks.

Romulus hadn't known whether to run or snarl. And what bad luck! Of all the boys in the school, the troll had to ask Fay to prom.

It wasn't his fault the stupid Student Senate decided this date for the dance. He leaned against the tree. Fay hadn't understood, really, when he told her he couldn't go to the prom. She'd smiled. Was sweet about it. Maybe she even believed him when he stammered his excuses. So she made the date with the troll. Romulus squeezed his eyes shut in frustration. The music changed to a faster beat. Shadows bounced against the window. A couple boys slipped out the doors and walked to their truck, avoiding the security cop in the parking lot. Even from a hundred yards away, Romulus smelled the beer. They only stayed in the truck for a few minutes, then headed back to the dance.

Romulus left the lawn and walked the neighborhoods, choosing streets randomly. He hid from cars—it was long past curfew, and he didn't want to explain to a policeman what he was doing. Sometimes a dog chained in a back yard caught wind of him and howled. He didn't howl back, didn't even growl, but he wished one would break free. They could run the blocks together, or they could stand face to face, teeth showing in the moon. "This is mine," their postures would say. Maybe the dog would leap, go for his throat. Romulus closed his eyes and felt the night air on his cheek, the stoney road beneath his shoes. Or maybe *he* would leap and the dog's throat would be in *his* teeth. He could almost feel the pulse in his mouth.

It seemed for hours that he walked, often with his eyes closed, not paying attention to where he was, trusting his nose to lead him. When a car turned the corner ahead of him, and he dove into a bush, he was surprised to find he was directly across the street from Fay's house. The car parked. It was the troll's convertible, top down, looking low, black and ominous in the moonlight. Fay and the troll walked to the porch.

"I had a nice time," she said, her hands in his between them.

"Me too." The troll wore a letter jacket over his tux. Even from the bushes across the street, Romulus could see the multiple brass bars glistening in the porch light showing how many times he'd lettered: football, wrestling and track. A thick-necked, thick-wristed, thick-headed wunderkind with perfect balance and the fast twitch muscles of a cheetah. A vague suggestion of Harrison Ford in his chin and smile. A careless black lock of hair that fell across his forehead in an unkempt way that some girls found charming.

Romulus was loath to think Fay could fall for this, but as the two talked, their faces came closer and closer together like an inevitable collision, two lambent planets closing on each other in the night sky, until they were kissing, and Romulus turned away, a bitter tear in each eye.

Later, after Fay went into her house and the troll drove away, Romulus walked back to Gray Mountain Country Club. Other than empty beer cans and broken glass in the parking lot, nothing remained of the prom. He wandered onto the golf course, fell asleep on the third green, and when he woke in the morning, stiff from tiredness and the cold, he saw his own dew-drawn silhouette in the grass.

In the hallways that Monday, Romulus moved listlessly from subject to subject, avoiding Fay until finally he ran into her between Calculus and Mythology, a class they shared.

They talked outside the door. "Did you do your homework?" she asked.

He nodded. They were supposed write a report on a character from Camelot. He'd chosen Uther Pendragon. As always, he found himself staring. Her complexion fascinated him, absolutely exquisite, like polished silk, pale and smooth, dark-blue eyes, a hint of copper in her blonde hair. He thought about a willow wand swaying on a river bank. Looking at her was like listening to water dance over rounded rocks, all foam and bubbles and deep, still pools.

Fay glanced into his eyes, then looked away. "I don't think teachers should be allowed to make assignments on prom weekend."

"You didn't get yours done?" His palms sweated just talking to her.

Fay shook her head.

"You can have mine. I've got an A in there already without it."

Fay smiled. "Really? You'd do that?"

Embarrassed, Romulus put his head down. "It's no big deal."

She put her hand on his arm. "That's the nicest thing I think anyone's ever offered to do for me, but I better face the music on my own." She stood on her tiptoes, kissed him on the cheek, then slipped around the doorway into the room.

Students streamed past him, intent on beating the tardy bell, but Romulus didn't move. Slowly, he brought his hand up to his face and brushed his fingertips where she'd kissed him.

During class, Romulus barely listened. He focused instead on Fay, who sat a row over and two seats in front of him. The troll sat beside her. Halfway through class he passed her a note. She read it quietly, wrote something on it, and passed it back. The troll nodded and put the note in his folder. Mr. Campbell talked at length about the search for the historical King Arthur. In despair, Romulus turned his attention to Campbell. "The real King Arthur, if there was one, may have lived in 5th Century England, a hero because he drove out barbarian invaders. Much of our knowledge of King Arthur came from a historian, Geoffrey of Monmouth, who in the 12th Century set down the reign of British kings. He made most of it up, evidently. But it's through Geoffrey that we first learn of Merlin."

Romulus wrote names and dates disconsolately until Campbell said, "The death of Arthur and disappearance of Merlin are the end of wizardry in the world. Belief in mythological creatures fades with every passing century." He said it within another context, but the words reminded him of something his dad had said about evolution and the magic. Romulus wondered if the biology classes ever touched on this alternate explanation for changes in the species.

Quickly Romulus wrote his thoughts below Campbell's facts: "What if Merlin's disappearance *caused* the downfall of mythological beings?" He thought he'd ask Dad about it later.

Fay concentrated on her own notes. The troll wrote something on a slip of paper, and with a husky whisper, handed it to the boy behind him, a freshman who somehow had been assigned this senior level class—Romulus had stepped between the boy and a pissed off football player earlier in the year, but other than a grateful "thank you," they didn't talk—and he gave the paper to Romulus, muttering, "Pass it on." Behind Romulus sat one of the troll's wrestling buddies. Romulus often found himself a courier for their stream of letters, mostly directions for the weekend's parties. The torn paper sat, message up, on the desk—the troll hadn't bothered to fold it. It read, "I'll nail her tomorrow night." He'd scrawled a lopsided happy face below, its eyes two squashed circles. Romulus' fingers curled up, revolted by the thought of touching it.

Something whacked the back of his head.

"Hand it back, dog breath," hissed the wrestler.

Romulus grabbed the note, twirled in his seat and banged it on the desk. The wrestler leaned away, a startled look in his eyes. He said, "Hey, I was just joking."

After a few seconds, Romulus broke his glare and faced forward, and he heard a sigh of relief behind him.

"Boys?" said Campbell.

"Sorry, sir," said Romulus.

For the rest of the period, the note ran through his brain: "I'll nail her tomorrow." The happy face looked more and more evil in his memory. He opened his text to the illustrations, and wasn't surprised to see a resemblance between the drawing and the book's woodcut of a troll.

After class, in the hallway once again, Romulus pushed his way through the crowd until he caught up with Fay, but once he reached her side, he wasn't sure what to say. The certainty he'd had in class faded. Maybe the troll was talking about someone else. How could he ask her what she was doing tomorrow night? She carried her books against her chest, her chin down, as if she were mulling over something.

"Fay?" he said.

She looked up, smiled at him. "Hi, Romulus. Isn't your next class the other way?"

He blushed; he could feel his face heating, and the heat embarrassed him even more. It was all he could do not to turn away, but he had committed himself now. He had to know.

"I wondered if you wanted to go to the Senior Choral Recital. It's tomorrow at seven." As the words slipped out, he knew he'd never be able to keep the date. At seven the sun was still up, but it was a two hour concert.

Her expression fell. "Oh, I'm sorry. I can't. Not tomorrow. I . . . have other plans."

In the pause he heard the truth. The troll's note *was* about her. And he knew where they'd go too: Chaney Park, a spot on the bluffs overlooking town. It's where the troll always took his dates. He was legendary about it.

Fay smiled again, her face perfect in the bustling hallway. Her eyes glistened. Even as his heart ached, he marveled at her eyes that were brighter than they should be, as if they reflected a crystal light no one else saw. Then he caught a hint of her smell. Like everyone else, she smelled of shampoo and deodorant, but underneath was her own essence, a spring-drenched forest, nothing fleshy at all.

"I'd like a rain check, though," she said. "Ask me again another night."

Romulus blinked in surprise, and she was gone. Just kids bumping against each other, making their way from room to room.

That night the moon rose in Romulus's window, white and fat and unblinking. His lights out, he sat on the edge of his bed, breath short, skin on fire. Inside he was all pressures and cramps, legs trembling. Dad would know what to tell him, but Dad had stolen out the back door when the sun went down. The moon had never seemed so large; it was larger than the window, and the light had never seemed so potent, so penetrating. Romulus scratched at his chest, popping buttons. Where the light touched felt better, not cooled, but caressed in warmth.

Romulus whined, biting in the sound he really wanted to make. He pulled his clothes off. A part of him worried his mother would come to check on him, and what would she think, him standing naked in the pale, moonlit square in his room? She'd caught him in the bathroom the other day, staring in the mirror. She'd said without pausing, "Your father plucks his, you know."

"What?" he'd said.

"Most people have two eyebrows." She leaned past him, buffed a spot on the counter, then left.

Confused, he'd looked at himself again. Although he hadn't been thinking about it at the time, he'd always considered his eyebrows his best mark, in a lupine sort of way, and the shadow between them a distinguishing feature. Dad plucked his?

Of course, he was his father's son—she wouldn't be surprised to see him naked in the moonlight either. Still, he worried she might come in. The other part, though, saw himself leaping through the window. He thought, I must go to the forest. Already the trees quivered, waiting for him. And in the trees they would expect him, the entire panoply: elves, fairies, goblins and giants. The other creatures lost in mythical, evolutionary time.

But there would be trolls there too, and dragons. All the old maps said so: in the unexplored areas, here there be dragons.

From the moon-tinted hills beyond town, a thin howl rose in the light. Very lonely. Very far away.

Romulus tried a howl back, a tentative utterance that couldn't have made it past their front gate.

He did it again, louder. It hurt tearing through his throat that wasn't quite shaped for it, but it felt good too. Once more. A door popped open across the street, and a neighbor stuck his head out. Romulus buried his head in a pillow. No way Dad heard that, he thought, but he didn't try it again; and when the moon rose high enough so the light was not so obvious, he curled on the floor to fall asleep.

The day passed miserably until Mythology, where he hoped he could figure a way to warn Fay, but no matter how he thought to phrase it, his message sounded unbelievable. In the classroom's afternoon mugginess he doodled at the bottom of his notes. Fay split her attention between Campbell, who moved meticulously through the history of the Knights of the Round Table, and the troll, who smiled slyly at her when she turned toward him.

"Many retellings of Arthur's legend say that after the boy king took the throne at fifteen, and under Merlin's tutelage, he rid his country of monsters and giants," said Campbell.

Romulus sketched a sword rising from a lake. If he had Excalibur, he thought, he would rid this classroom of a monster himself.

When the bell rang, Fay continued writing her notes. The troll stood beside her, put his hand on her shoulder, then spoke softly in her ear. Romulus scrunched his toes in his shoes to keep himself from springing from the desk.

That evening Romulus finished dinner, told Mom and Dad he needed to take a walk, and went out the back door, but not before he caught a knowing glance between them.

Chaney Park was a six mile hike up a gravel road that rose too steeply the last three miles to bicycle, and Romulus figured he could be where kids parked by 8:30 or so. There was no question about using the car. He shuddered to think of himself behind the wheel, driving a two thousand pound vehicle, and the moon pouring through the windshield like a million biting ants.

The houses on his street were new brick and crisply-painted bi-levels, but a block over was an older neighborhood, where the roofs rose to steep peaks, and every house sported a single attic window, a lone eye watching him trudge toward the edge of town. Behind him the sunset flared orange and yellow, but before him only the bluffs' tops caught the last pale sliver of daylight, and they didn't hold that long. The woods below already swam in shadows. He crossed the railroad tracks; the blacktop changed to dirt, and soon, thin-trunked trees rustling with spring growth lined the path on both sides. He trudged up a long hill. At the crest he looked back, the town spread out behind him, stretched along the river, a tiny fiefdom at this distance. Streetlights could just as well be campfires, the baseball stadium glowing on the other side of town, a castle. He turned and walked into the dale beyond, losing the town and the day's final glow at the same time. A few stars twinkled in the sable blanket.

Romulus took deep breaths. He hadn't walked at night out here before. He felt keen, sharp. Another breath. Oak. Old oak that had started growing before the town existed. There were other smells he recognized too: fox, a shy one who must have crossed this path only seconds before he came into sight; and squirrel, and damp ferns dripping into moldy leaves, some so deep in shadow that winter's frost was only inches below.

In the distance, wheels crunched through gravel, and engine noise rose above the murmuring forest. Romulus loped off the road and into the brush, around a great ball of roots from a fallen tree. He gripped two gnarled, woody wrists and peered out. A moment later a car roared by, radio blaring a steady rap thump. A snatch of laughter and a beer can clattered against a rock. Then dust.

He waited until the air cleared before stepping from behind the tangled dead fall. In the hills above, the car's rowdy passage rose and fell. Hands jammed deep into his pocket, he continued his walk, thoughtful, now that the car had gone. What if Fay wanted to be with the troll? There would be nothing to warn her about. This trek to Chaney Park could be seen as little more than stalking her. There wasn't much he could do anyway. Still, he pushed onward, leaning into the road's steepness, taking each hairpin turn with measured deliberateness. His legs buzzed pleasantly, and he felt as if he could go forever if he had to. With his eyes closed, he imagined trotting along through the forest, tireless, behind deer maybe, waiting for one to drop from exhaustion. He smiled at the image. Several more times he leapt into the covering woods as more cars drove by. He didn't see the troll's car.

Finally the road leveled, but the trees surrounded him thicker than ever, leaning over the road and blocking the stars. It wasn't until he reached a clearing and the forest opened before him that he realized he'd made the top. The moon sat on the horizon, a bloat egg, rich and ivory and huge again, as it had been on Sunday in his room, but now there was no window between him and it.

A full moon in the height of its glory. Romulus had never felt its light so intensely. A breeze swept through the tree tops and the oaks creaked. He looked around for a high place, then saw one, a jumbled pile of boulders that made a miniature mountain to his left. He ran to its base, his wavy, gray shadow flowing over grass and brush and branch. Up he clambered, hands down, like feet, fingernails clicking, leaping from rock to rock until he gained the summit. No forest blocking the moon now. He howled. Not self consciously, but a full-throated paean to the night sky. "Oh," he said afterwards, and he crouched so his hands took part of his weight. Was this the way it was for Dad? thought Romulus, or am I even closer to the past than he is? Could I actually *change*?

He felt the animal shape beneath his human one moving about. Then the sky darkened as a cloud crossed the moon's face. Romulus shook his head to clear it, and he looked about him for the first time. To the east there was no sign of the town, but he knew if he walked a little bit farther along the road, he'd be at Chaney Park, where the bluff offered a view of the entire valley.

A car's headlights cut through the trees below, and in a few seconds, the car itself passed, turned toward the park, and vanished into the forest, its taillights glimmering long after he'd stopped hearing it. The moon was a hand's-width above the horizon. How long had he been on the promontory? Moaning, he ran down the boulders, careless of injury, hit the road at top speed, and raced toward Chaney Park.

Three cars and a van rested on the picnic area's lined asphalt, noses pointed toward town, but none of them were the troll's convertible. Romulus crossed the back of the narrow lot in the tree's shadows. From one car a muffled conversation mixed with the wind. A sticker on the van's bumper proclaimed, IF WE'RE ROCKIN', DON'T COME KNOCKIN'.

Past the parking lot the road turned to dirt again to wind up the hill. Every fifty feet or so a private picnic area opened on the left or right, complete with a split-log table and iron charcoal pit. The first one was empty; a rusted pickup occupied the second. Romulus stayed low, just off the path, walking in the soggy remains of last year's leaves, his nose telling him as much as his eyes. The breeze caressed his face. Other cars waited ahead; he could smell them, the still warm engines, their tires, cigarette smoke. Then he caught it, a distinct whiff of the troll. He growled. A girl's quivery voice in a car ten feet away said, "What was that?" Romulus crouched even lower in a run, his hands nearly touching the ground.

Then, ahead, clearly in the forest's silence, he heard Fay. "Don't!" she said. "I don't want . . ."

The road rose. At the crest he saw the final picnic spot in the clearing fifty yards below, the troll's car in the middle, top down, bathed in moonlight. He paused. Where was Fay? He could smell her perfume, and he smelled troll. Romulus spotted them in the back seat, the troll's dark letter jacket blending into the shadow; he was struggling, holding Fay down beneath him. Her hand rose above him, like a drowning person. Cloth ripped.

Romulus charged toward them, his lips pulled away from his teeth in a noiseless snarl, but everything suddenly felt underwater and syrupy. It took an hour for his foot to hit the ground and an hour for the next. Fay's hand froze in the air like a marble statue. Slowly, it seemed, so slowly, he came closer.

The troll laughed, the throbbing sound coming to Romulus almost too low to hear. More cloth ripped. A button, a fine pearl colored disk, flipped lazily into the air. Only ten yards away now, but every step seemed to cover less distance.

Then the air about the convertible changed. Even in his urgency, breath tearing through his throat, his teeth aching to bite something hard, Romulus slowed. The air changed, centering on Fay's hand. A circle of moonlight ten feet around slid toward her. It was as if the light wasn't light at all, but a thin coat of paint, funneling to her hand. For a moment it seemed as if the stars themselves swarmed, each touching her hand until it shone with potency, and her palm turned down. Her elbow crooked as if she were about to embrace the troll. Romulus stopped, nearly touching the car. Now he could see it all. The troll had pushed her back, trapped her legs with his own, pinned her with his weight, one arm stuck behind her, his lips pressed against the side of her face. Her eyes were closed, but not in fear—Romulus had time to study her—she was concentrating. The light flowed down her arm, filled her face. She glowed from within, like a porcelain nightlight. Then all the brightness emptied from her hand in a cascade of sparks, slamming into the back of the troll's head.

He stiffened.

Romulus stepped back, covering his eyes.

When he opened them, he had to blink away a black spot in the spark's shape to see Fay, now sitting up. She'd rolled the troll onto the car's floor, and her feet rested on his back.

"Dang," she said. "Just look at my blouse." She pulled the torn front together, then zipped her jacket.

She turned to Romulus and said in a voice no different than if she'd run into him in the mall, "What brings you to Chaney Park this time of night, Romulus?"

Her face still glowed, and something glimmered in the back of her eyes, very sharp and ancient. She combed her fingers through her hair. Romulus noticed her ears. They were distinctly pointed. He'd not seen that in her before.

"It seemed a good night for a walk," he said lamely. The troll snorted beneath her feet, then settled into a comfortable sounding snore. "What *are* you?" Romulus said.

She stood on the back seat, brushed her hands down her pants in short, brisk strokes.

"Fairy, I think. At least that's what my mother says. And you?" She jumped out of the car to land beside him.

Romulus tried to answer, but all his words had been sucked out of him. He attempted to speak a couple of times, but nothing came out.

Understanding came into her eyes. "It's the moon thing, isn't it?" She looked into the sky. "That's why you couldn't go to prom. Oh, I should have figured it out earlier. But I still don't know why you're here tonight."

Finally Romulus said, "I couldn't sleep." His voice rose at the end, as if it were a question.

Fay glanced at the troll, then back at him. She shook her head. "You're sweet, Romulus." She looked thoughtfully into the car for a moment, then pulled the keys out of the ignition and threw them into the forest. "Would you like to walk me home? I think I've lost my ride."

Romulus nodded dumbly, so happy that if he had a tail to wag, he would wag it a thousand miles an hour.

They started toward town, leaving the sleeping troll and his car behind.

Romulus took a deep, deep breath of night air. He could smell everything, all of it, leaf, branch and tree.

Fay cleared her throat. "You're not going to try to bite me, are you?" She sounded only half-joking.

Romulus let the air out in a relieved rush. "Oh, no! Not you."

"Good," she said. "That would make it tough for us to date." She moved next to him.

They walked down the winding dirt road, hands not touching, but very close, both so full of moonish power they thought they'd burst.

NIGHT SWEATS

July 31, Friday Afternoon: Moving In

IN SPACE'S FAR REACHES, RED-SHIFTED RADIATION MARKS THE UNIVERSE'S BE-ginning, a microwave ghost forever lingering after the Big Bang. When ama-teur astronomer Meadoe Omura puts her eye to the telescope to see her favorite nebulas, she travels backward in time, and light travels both ways. On August 6, 1945, a great flash illuminated Hiroshima. Photons, radiation, a radio pulse blasted into space. Years and years later, an attentive observer on one of Earth's nearer star systems might catch the twinkle. The past made present, living in the eye.

What has passed does not disappear; it recedes, ever fainter, but never gone, remaining, a ghost. Like what lived in the old house in Harriston that Meadoe bought, like what lived in Meadoe.

In 1945, her grandfather worked a job on Hiroshima's outskirts, excavating defense bunkers, when the sky turned bright, so terribly bright, and seconds later the dirt buried him and the others. The story stuck with Meadoe and when she was a little girl she had nuclear nightmares: a bomber's high altitude roar, the peace of an early morning city, a mushroom cloud rising and rising. She thought about Hiro-shima a lot, as she studied the stars, when she read quantum physics.

But today Meadoe wondered, should I have bought the house? She stood on the porch, the new key unfamiliar to her touch. It cost so much. The apartment was fine. I could have taken another path than this one, like an electron. She thought about uncertainty. In quantum physics it meant that one could never tell both where an electron was *and* how fast it was going. It seemed an electron was in all the possible places at the same time. She'd tried to explain that to Joan, her therapist, once, but by the time she got to tachyons, a particle that appeared to travel backwards in time, Joan's eyes glazed over.

Of course, in my case, she thought, the uncertainty principle just means should I have signed a thirty-year mortgage?

What had looked like pleasant landscaping swallowed the house, and the house itself leaned over her, large and quiet.

Her radio was already unpacked—the movers must have set it up—so she turned it on and an oldies station playing a big band number crackled into life. She opened boxes until late.

After eating part of a casserole, after screwing in the new deadbolts, after finding a nightshirt and blankets and a bedroom lamp, Meadoe went to bed.

She fell asleep before she had a chance to hear any sounds her new house made.

At 4:30 a.m. Meadoe woke. For a while she lay still, trying to figure out where she was and why she was so warm. Her blanket felt pounds too heavy, and her arm under the pillow buzzed with the numbness of sleeping on it wrong. A streetlight cast a pale white shaft alive with dust motes through her window. She decided she was awake for good and might as well unpack some more.

Meadoe sat. "What the heck?" she said into the strange room. Her nightshirt clung to her, and when she pushed the blanket aside, it was soaked. She wrapped her arms around herself and shivered. When she stood by the bed and looked down, there, in sweat, was her outline.

August 1, Saturday Morning: Therapy

Joan said, "The key to your present is in your past." She consulted her notes, her briefcase open on the couch. Curtains still weren't hung, but the house had begun to look like home. Books were dusted and in the bookcase; her antique hook rug covered most of the living room floor.

Joan flipped to a new page and clicked her pen. "You're still virgin."

"Thirty-two years and not a tumble." Meadoe kept her hands still in her lap. Old ground it might be, but she didn't feel comfortable discussing it.

"You told me something happened in high school." Joan flicked back a few pages. "Christopher Towne. Basketball player. You knew him from church. He liked the same books you did. On the third date at the Deer Trail Park picnic area he tried . . ."

"Yes, but he stopped."

"Before he started, did you want him to?"

"What?"

"Start."

Joan hadn't asked that question before. Deer Trail Park sat at the end of a long dirt road south of town. When they'd pulled into the parking lot, Christopher dimmed his lights to keep them from shining into other cars. She picked out Ursa Major and Minor through the front windshield. Beyond the city, the stars glittered so clearly. Meadoe shut her eyes.

"I knew kids made out there. I suppose I wanted to."

"You suppose?"

"I wasn't really sure what making out involved. I was fifteen. Nobody had talked to me about it. I thought it would be like *Wuthering Heights*. I never thought about sex. I still don't."

Joan coughed. Meadoe knew she did that to cover a snicker. "So, you thought one of you would die and the other would pine forever? That's ambitious for a third date."

It had been in early November, a few days before her birthday, which is why she remembered—the first cold night of the fall. Windows were fogged in the other cars. Chris had taken her to a movie, then headed to the park without asking.

"No, what I like about *Wuthering Heights* is the second part anyway, after Catherine dies and Heathcliff keeps searching for her. *Wuthering Heights* is a bad example. Maybe I thought we'd hold hands. You know, and then kiss on the porch when he dropped me off."

Joan wrote in the notebook. "Sheesh, were we ever that young? Hadn't you ever had a sexual fantasy with Christopher in it before? You knew you were going on the date; you'd been out with him twice already; didn't you think about anything more extensive than holding hands?"

They *had* held hands. He turned the engine off and moved next to her. Her hands clasped in her lap, like they were now, and he gently pried one free. She remembered she'd almost giggled at that, partly from nervousness, and partly because it all seemed so awkward. His fingers slid between hers; she couldn't tell if it was her sweat or his.

"I played with dolls still when I was fifteen. I read *The Girl Scout's Guide to the Stars*," said Meadoe. "I know it sounds silly, but I thought of myself as a little girl. Holding hands was the extent of it. Maybe carving our names in a tree."

She'd thought she should sigh when he squeezed her hand, but she didn't. Her neck muscles bunched; blood pounded behind her eyes. Now that they were *there*, she longed to leave. Her lips snapped as they parted. "I want to go now," she tried to say. Nothing came out. Chris slid closer. Her left hand was trapped in his; her shoulder pressed against the door, and he leaned to kiss her. There was no place to go, so she let his cheek push her head back to kiss her. It seemed bizarre. No passion within her. If he'd stop, she could ask him if it felt weird to him too. Kissing her hand would be as romantic as this. Rubbing a washcloth over her lips would feel no different. His breath heated her neck, and her shoulder ached where the door pushed into it.

Chris leaned against her harder, turned toward her and wrapped his left leg over hers, forcing her knees apart, pinning her to the seat. He kept kissing her mouth, then the side of her face, breathing hard. "Meadoe," he gasped. His hand worked its way into her blouse. Meadoe tried to twist away from the door, but she had no strength;

it was as if her spinal cord had been cut—total paralysis. In her head she chanted "I want to go home now," in a Dorthyesque way, as if tapping her ruby slippers together would take her from the car.

Joan said, "So when do you think your emotional self caught up with your physical self?"

Meadoe shook her head, her eyes still closed. Chris pulled his hand from her blouse, popping a button. He tugged her belt with one hand and pushed her hand against him. "Meadoe," he said again, his breath full of after-dinner mint. Finally, she found her voice. "I want to go home now," she said. "I want to go home!"

"This is home," said Joan.

Meadoe opened her eyes, fingers digging into the chair. "Did I say that out loud?"

Joan looked at her thoughtfully. "I think we've covered enough ground for today. But I'll tell you what, when we meet again I'll want to know what you are *really* afraid of." Joan closed the notebook and put it in her briefcase. She put on her jacket. As Meadoe opened the front door for her, Joan said, "Meadoe, there's two kinds of people who say they don't think about sex—the ones who do and lie about it, and the ones who do but repress it."

August 1, Saturday Afternoon: The Wallpaper

Standing on the porch, her arms filled with contact paper to line the kitchen drawers, Medoe fumbled with the lock. The new deadbolt resisted turning at first, then suddenly released. Meadoe imagined for a second someone on the other side had twisted it for her. The radio played the oldies station where the announcer said, "And now Glenn Miller and his band playing 'Boulder Buff,' featuring Billy May on trumpet." Uneasy, she looked around the room. It wasn't like her to leave the radio on. Nothing in the living room was out of place, the back door was securely locked, and the windows were latched.

She sat on the edge of her bed to kick off her shoes. For fourteen years she'd lived in the apartment two blocks from the library. In this new setting, her own furniture looked changed, as if someone had stolen her belongings and replaced them with clever counterfeits. Even the air felt alien and smelled strange.

The bed felt good though, so she flopped back. A dozen chores waited. More unpacking, setting up the telescope, but her motivation was shot. Is it true, she thought, that I'm thinking about sex all the time and don't know it?

Through the uncurtained window, the afternoon sun cast a square of warm light on her legs. She was trying to make patterns from the swirls and texture in the ceiling plaster when she noticed the wallpaper in one corner had peeled away from the wall. Changing the wallpaper topped her project's list, so she levered herself out of bed, slid a stool under the corner and pulled off the first layer. Several sheets stuck to it. The room's history unpeeled in wallpaper. Under a pale yellow, a horrible brown and white geometric; under that, a green marble pattern; under that, a solid pink. The base wasn't wallpaper however. After clearing several feet—the paper fell away easily—she stood back. A movie poster: *The Outlaw*, starring Jane Russell and Jack Beutel. No date, but old, and the paper was laminated to the wall. Licking her finger, she rubbed at a spot, cleaning it. A varnish, she guessed.

A half hour later, all the wallpaper lay crumpled on the floor, and an entire collage was visible: from ceiling to floor and wall to wall, posters, magazine covers, newspapers and pin-ups, carefully arranged, varnish protected, in beautiful condition. Hand drawn scenes: girls in bathing suits and war planes: whoever assembled the display was an artist. *Life* magazine pictures of models on beaches: July 9, 1945, a dark-haired woman wearing a striped two-piece suit, her hand to her brow as if looking into the ocean; April 17, 1944, Esther Williams standing in front of a giant sea shell; Rita Hayworth sitting on a towel, August 11, 1941. The magazines cost a dime. Other Rita Hayworth images, mostly from movie magazines including a *Time Magazine* painting of her, one hand over her head, her other behind her as if the artist had caught her in a twirl, her dress billowing, showing a lot of leg. Ingrid Bergman looked doey-eyed on a *Casablanca* poster, but most of the women she didn't recognize: Martha Raye, Betty Grable, and Maureen O'Hara. Unfamiliar movies: *Four Jills in a Jeep, Destination Tokyo* and *Haunted Honeymoon*. In the background, the radio announcer talked about "our boys in the Pacific." Meadoe cocked her head to listen, but a song started, "The Boogie Woogie Bugle Boy of Company B." She rubbed her arms, suddenly chilled.

To one side, surrounded by war news, a striking drawing of a Japanese woman pursing her lips at a microphone, a rising sun flag behind her. Bare shoulders, half turned, the flag snapping in a wind. Underneath, the card read, "Tokyo Rose." Meadoe touched her own face whose high cheekbones and slanted eyes were mirrored in the drawing. Of all the drawings, this was the best. More life—a sensuousness in the mouth, in the twist in the neck.

"He did a lot of work here," she said to herself. Clearly this was the effort of a young boy. Pin-up girls and war photos. She looked for dates. Nothing past July, 1945. Everything was vivid, though. No fading. The display must not have been up long before being covered. Why?

The setting sun touched her neighbor's roof; she glanced at her watch. There was time to set up the telescope for a little early evening viewing. Tomorrow she could tackle the collage's mystery.

Once the sun set in the back yard, the air cooled quickly and mosquitoes buzzed. Meadoe slapped at her bare leg as she tightened the viewfinder bracket that held the equatorial mount. The counterweight nearly slipped from her hands when she maneuvered it onto the shaft, but soon she was making the fine adjustments to the viewfinder and the clock drive.

A breeze rustled the lilac. Meadoe rubbed her arms. In the moon's sterile light, the neighborhood metamorphed into a black and white photograph. Shadows too black to peer into. Trees without color. She thought again about the pictures on her bedroom wall, and turned to look at the house. Gray, moonlit shrubbery rustled. Moon reflected off the back door. The pale green siding now looked white. Meadoe rested her hand on the telescope, at ease for the first time in several weeks. Moving's stress had taken more from her than she thought. It would be a relief to return to work.

She brushed her fingers over the telescope's thin metal, an old friend. They'd spent hours untangling the universe's many twined lights. As long as she had the telescope and the night sky, she'd never be truly unhappy, regardless of whatever Joan said about unacknowledged desires. She chuckled in relief.

Then, a movement caught her eye. She stayed her hand on the telescope. Had something behind her bedroom window shifted?

Whatever it was, it wasn't moving now. Standing stone still, she studied the window. Was that a reflection off wavy glass? Or was it a face looking out? Her eyes froze open; she couldn't take them off the image. Had she locked the front door? She knew she had, or at least she was pretty sure she had. She *always* locked the door when she came in. Of course, she always turned off the radio when she left, but hadn't it been on when she came home?

Keeping her head steady, her eyes focused on the window, she took a step to the left, away from the telescope. The face disappeared.

She stepped back. Moonlight did reflect from the window; the glass was wavy, but it didn't look like a face now, only like shimmery glass. There's no way I could mistake that for a face, she thought. There's no way. She moved again, tried to see a forehead in the reflection, a cheek's curve, the dark shadow under a nose. Maybe it was there, but the moon had advanced in the sky a tiny bit. Maybe the image required an exact alignment of light and viewer. Maybe there was no image at all, only nervousness about a new house.

Never looking away, she unscrewed the counterweight and slid it off the shaft; its bulk filled her hand reassuringly. The porch door creaked. Meadoe reached around the corner to turn on the light. Shadows fled, and within seconds moths fluttered against the screens. She repeated the move on the back door; the back of her hand and wrist screaming their vulnerability when she stuck them in the dark to find the switch.

Light flooded the empty room, and the rest of the house was just as empty. In her bedroom, feeling foolish, she put the counterweight on her dresser.

The posters on the wall almost glowed. Meadoe sat on her bed again, as she had in the afternoon, and studied them. Ingrid Bergman looked wistfully into the distance. Fred Astaire danced across a ballroom floor. The wolf man glared straight into the camera. Planes diving. Battleships sailing. **VICTORY IN EUROPE** trumpeted a headline. It's practically a museum, she thought. A moment in time captured on the wall. She thought of her own photographs taken through the telescope, also snapshots in time. The scale was different; some of her subjects were millions of years away, but the principle was the same. Captured time.

She squinted at the wall. There was a pattern in the design, an order. Not straight lines, but lines nonetheless. The *Life* covers formed three curves; the hand drawings two more; the movie poster swept in their own arc. News articles and war photos filled the gaps but created a sight line too. It took her a while to decipher the underlying purpose, but as she lay on the bed, letting her eyes roam from image to image, it became clear. All lines led to Tokyo Rose. No matter where one started, the natural flow was to the Japanese beauty.

Later, she read with all the lights on, then decided that was silly. She checked the doors and windows again, flicked the living room and kitchen lights off. With only her reading light on, she closed the book and rested it on her chest. She listened with half an ear to a radio drama about someone named the Great Gildersleeve. Some of it was pretty funny, and it took her mind off sounds she couldn't identify: a metallic rattle that might be a pipe expanding, a thump and buzz that might be the refrigerator cycling, a dog barking. There wasn't enough light to see the posters now, and the window was a gray square leaking moonlight. She worried that someone might look in, and she laughed. No matter what side of the window I'm on, I'm scared of the other! Tomorrow she would hang curtains.

She turned off the radio and the light and slipped into a dream. It seemed she'd slept for a long time, and she knew she was dreaming. In the dream she rested on a white beach, like one of the models on the cover of *Life*, like Rita Hayworth, and the sun beat down hot, oppressively hot. Overhead a plane rumbled across the sky, too far to identify, but clearly military, a B-29 maybe. She rolled. In the dream she shifted away from the sun, but she felt blankets on her shoulders and knew she rolled in bed too. It was so hot. I should find some shade, she thought. I need sunscreen. Waves hissed in the dream. Heat shimmered off the sand blurring the horizon.

Someone stood beside her. It was too hot on the beach, and it robbed her strength, but she could feel him standing there. For a long time he said nothing, and she thought, if only he would set up an umbrella.

Then, he touched her back. His hand was smooth, and the overheated skin felt instant relief. She closed her eyes against the brightness, could feel sand beneath her cheek. The hand moved. It stroked to her shoulder blades and down to the base of her spine spreading coolness the whole way. Meadoe moved into the stroke. Then softly, a voice in her ear.

"Do you trust me?"

She woke, screaming, and the bed was sweat-soaked again. She had to flip the mattress before putting on dry sheets.

In the morning, her linen drawers were open and once folded clothes piled messily within.

August 2, Research: Sunday Morning

The library didn't open until noon on Sunday, so Meadoe disarmed the alarm system before entering. The lights were off. Flyers from different publishing houses touting their newest releases covered her desk, and she moved them aside to give herself room to work. The Real Estate/Assessor's Office didn't have a web page but the City and County Records Office and Building Permits did. She punched in her address. After a few seconds search, a list of names and dates scrolled onto her screen with her name at the bottom. From 1928 until 1945 the house had two owners: the Belascoes who owned it until 1940, and the Shirleys who owned it until September of 1945. Since then the house had changed hands seventeen times. The realtor said young couples bought the house, and then moved out when they had children. Meadoe tapped her fingernail against the keyboard. She typed in her neighbor's address to the north, a house that looked very much like hers from the street. Three owners since '45. The house to the south of her, four owners in the same time period. Across the street, two owners. She checked another dozen addresses in the neighborhood. None had more than four owners since the end of World War II.

Scrolling back up the screen, she returned to the Shirleys. Howard J.T. Shirley bought the house in May of 1940. Margaret L. Shirley cosigned the loan. Wife? Mother? Sister?

A name search for Howard J.T. Shirley brought her to a Shirley genealogical site where she found he died in 1982. Margaret L. Shirley, his wife, died two years later. The site listed one child, Nathaniel Shirley, born January 15, 1929, died August 6, 1945. He was sixteen when he died, the same day the atomic age opened its awful eye over Hiroshima. Meadoe could hear her father's voice, thickly accented, "Your grandfather dug all day for the rest of his friends. Dirt covered their faces. There were scars on his arms from broken glass in the rubble."

Nothing turned up on a search of Nathaniel's name.

The historical archives were in the basement. Turning on lights, Meadoe worked her way to the local history shelves. On the top row, Harriston High School annuals. Nathaniel smiled from the juniors section in the 1945 book, and the little hairs on her arms stood straight up as they had when she'd pulled down the wallpaper. She wished she'd brought a sweater.

Nathaniel had light hair with a shiny, sculpted look that most of the boys sported. Glasses. He wore a dark tie, white shirt and dark jacket. Varsity track. Art club. She thumbed through the annual. Grainy black and white photos of football games and victory gardens. At the homecoming dance, several boys were in uniform. Some downtown Harriston buildings in the background of the homecoming parade were familiar.

Prom pictures were in a copy of the school paper, *The Lions Roar*, stuck in the back of the book. On the second page, she found Nathaniel, his arm around a pretty girl with dark hair like her own, but curled instead of straight, hanging to her shoulders instead of trimmed to just under the ears. The caption read, "The Prom's best couple: Junior Nathaniel Shirley and Senior Erica Weiss."

Meadoe went back to her computer. If Nathaniel did the wall art, he didn't enjoy it long before he died. Why did people move in and out of her house so often? Thoughtfully she typed in a search for "ghosts and poltergeists." Her research offered numerous explanations for ghosts and hauntings. One source suggested that ghosts wanted attention. That's why so many of them threw things. Another argued that poltergeist phenomena was caused by the emotional upheaval of someone in the house, generally a pre-adolescent girl. Was she effectively pre-adolescent? Could her house be responding to her? One ghost hunter said ghosts recreated the circumstances that held them to the earth. Another maintained ghosts existed because they had unfinished business.

In the August '45 *Harriston Independent*, on the second to last page, she found Nathaniel under the headline, "Truck Strikes Local Youth." He'd been crossing the intersection of Harriston Boulevard and Broadway when a milk truck hit him. The paper reported Nathaniel died at St. Joseph hospital that afternoon of head injuries. Beside the article was the same class picture she'd seen in the yearbook looking so formal, so young in his coat and tie.

Before going home, she stopped at the video store.

"Do you carry *The Outlaw*, with Jane Russel?" Meadoe asked.

The teen cashier keyed the title into his computer and shook his head.

"*Four Jills in a Jeep*?" On the wall beside her, Meadoe counted at least 60 copies of the latest release. "How about *The Haunted Honeymoon or Destination Tokyo*?"

"Nope." He hit a key that brought up more information about the films. "Jeeze, those are old. You'd probably have to order them special."

"*Casablanca*?"

"That we have. Two copies. The film's in black and white though. I'm supposed to tell you that because some guy rented it last year and raised a stink because he thought it was defective."

At home she phoned Joan. "I've got curtains to put up you can help with, and a video to watch if you aren't doing anything."

"I'll bring wine," Joan said.

In the middle of the afternoon, the whole ghost theory seemed suspect. Certainly the apparition in the window could have been her imagination, and maybe she'd messed up her own clothes in the dresser in the middle of the night. She'd never done that before, but she'd never moved into a house of her own either, nor had she had night sweats.

Which was Joan's point an hour later as they hung the bedroom curtains. "There's numerous medical reasons for profuse sweating. You're young for it, but it could be early signs of menopause."

Joan pushed a hook into the drape's back while Meadoe held the fabric up. None of the windows were standard width, and the curtains really should have been special ordered, but Meadoe couldn't afford that. Custom curtains were on the lengthening list of home improvements. She tried to keep her tone light. "Oh, no. It couldn't be that. My grandmother had a child when she was forty-three." A medical condition? she thought. Her father spent four months in a hospital dying of colon cancer when she was twelve. She remembered how frail his arms became—how thin his face. Cancer killed her grandfather too. Slow mushroom clouds erupted in his lungs, a part of Hiroshima's omnipresent past.

Joan took three hooks from her chest pocket and moved down the drape, pushing each one in. "That's the benign explanation. Anxiety provoked by severe repression could cause it too—a purely psychological symptom—but night sweats can accompany diabetes, M.S., AIDS, polio and a half dozen other things I can't think of off the top of my head. First things first, we ought to get your estrogen checked."

In Meadoe's bedroom, Joan examined the wall for a long time, touching some of the pictures, then moving back with her head cocked, as if she were in an art gallery. "Whew! And you think this was all done by a sixteen-year-old?"

"No more than a month before he died." Now that Meadoe had seen the pattern that drew her eye to Tokyo Rose, it seemed it should be obvious to Joan too, but Joan didn't seem to notice it.

"I always liked '40s hair styles. They struck me as more . . . deliberate. This low maintenance look we all go for now just isn't as romantic. There must be a half a can of hair spray on that woman's head. Oh, look at that." She had found Tokyo Rose. "She looks a little like you, Meadoe. Did you notice that? She's beautiful."

"We all look alike to you." Meadoe laughed.

"There's more of the west in you than the east, girl." Joan put a stool under the curtain rod and hung the drapes. "There, now you won't be wondering about peeping Toms in the shrubbery."

Over a glass of wine, Meadoe told Joan about her scare the night before and the dream. Meadoe looked into her glass as she spoke. Remembering the touch on her back raised new goosebumps. She could still feel the fingers over her skin.

"Doesn't the timing of these things strike you as fortuitous?" said Joan. "I mean, it's pretty obvious that the evening I bring up a delicate topic in our session—ask you what you fear most—your subconscious supplies fears. Of course, the face in the window is symbolic in some way. It could be your repressed self looking out at you, or it could be Christopher Towne coming back in your imagination." Joan laughed. "Or it could have been a funny trick of light. Not everything has a psychological explanation. The dream now, that is interesting. What were you wearing in it?"

Meadoe shook *Casablanca* from its plastic box and put it in the VCR. "I don't know. I suppose a bathing suit. He touched bare skin."

Joan settled onto the couch after slipping a coaster under her wine glass. "How do you know that he was a he? You said you only saw feet."

"I . . . I don't know that either. In the dream I assumed it was a man."

Meadoe sat on the couch. Joan moved over to accommodate. It was more of a love seat than a proper couch, not large enough for Meadoe to stretch out to take a nap on.

"And you said when he touched you in the dream you liked it? I'd say that was a good sign. It's obvious the dream has sexual overtones, and you welcomed them."

"The sun was hot. I was burning up, and his hand was cool. Do we have to talk about it? The movie has started."

Black and white maps appeared on the screen with a voice over. Lines traced a path through Europe to Casablanca. The narrator said of refugees without visas in Casablanca that their fate was to "wait and wait and wait." She thought about Nathaniel Shirley. What if he was a ghost in this house, caught in his sixteenth year, and like the refugees, looking for a way to escape?

An Englishman wearing a monocle said, "We hear very little, and we understand even less." Meadoe nodded. That made sense. She hadn't seen *Casablanca* before, and it struck her as funny. The music seemed overstated, and the acting stilted. A plane flying in one scene was clearly a model, and the Germans were stereotypical. She wondered how Japanese were portrayed in other films from that era.

Then a woman walked into the cafe. Ingrid Bergman. The prefect of police said to her, "I was informed you were the most beautiful woman ever to visit Casablanca. That was a gross understatement." Meadoe leaned forward. It was true. She *was* beautiful. A fragility in the face. Flawless skin. A half smile that changed her appearance from somber to knowing. The pictures on Nathaniel's wall didn't do her justice.

Joan picked up her wine glass and sipped from it. Somewhere in the film Meadoe stopped thinking of it as stilted. Her own wine warmed on the table. At the end she cried so hard that Joan put her arm around her until Meadoe giggled at the ridiculousness of it.

"It's all right," said Joan. "There must be something in the story that speaks strongly to you. That's why movies are such a powerful medium. They help us live the tales we can't tell ourselves."

An hour after Joan left, Meadoe didn't feel tired at all. Normally she was in bed by 9:00 before work, but her mind raced with a million thoughts. With the curtains up, the house seemed homier, more enclosed and safer. She picked up a book, reread the same page twice without understanding a word; put it down. She looked into all the rooms for the tenth time, and then decided a shower might relax her. Afterwards, wearing a robe, she poured herself another glass of wine and started the video again.

She noticed details she missed the first time. The young woman who sought Bogart's help was in the opening crowd scene hopefully looking at the plane overhead. Every time an Italian military officer appeared in the film, everyone ignored him. Senor Ugotti said to Bogart, "I have lots of friends in Casablanca, but just because you despise me, you're the only one I trust," which made Meadoe smile. There were jokes in the first half of the film she hadn't got earlier. She poured more wine, feeling a pleasant torpor steal over her and closed her eyes. One of the books about ghosts said spirits were doomed to replay the circumstances of their deaths over and over. Is it like video, Meadoe wondered, or can it be changed? Bogie never gets the girl.

In the film, Sam sang "As Time Goes By." Meadoe drifted. The tune went on and on. "And you must remember this, a kiss is but a kiss, a sigh is but a sigh." She felt she wasn't on her living room couch anymore, but in a theater watching *Casablanca* on a movie screen, back row. Silhouettes of heads filled the seats in front of her, the woman's hair curled and styled. A curl of her own hair blocked her vision. But my hair is straight! she thought. She shook her head to move it. Buttered popcorn smells. After shave. Plush underneath her hands.

Bogart stared down a glass of whiskey. "Of all the gin joints in all the world," he said.

Slowly, Meadoe realized someone's hand was on top her left one, the fingers clasped around her hand, very proper and gentle. She didn't move, but let it rest there. It didn't make her feel anxious. Her stomach didn't tighten. This is a good dream, she thought; no contact phobia. Joan would be proud.

At the roulette wheel, the young woman's husband won a lot of money. Bogart had rigged the game so they would win and she wouldn't have to make an unnamed sacrifice to save them both. Everyone congratulated Bogart, and he squirmed. Meadoe sighed. The scenes no longer seemed to be in order, but she liked it just as much. She leaned a little to rest her head on her companion's shoulder. The theater air washed her in warmth, very warm, and sweat trickled down the side of her face. She didn't mind though. She was comfortable. "Yes, Ugotti, I do respect you more," said Bogart.

Her companion turned in his seat. She knew it was a he, and his hand came across her to stroke her other arm. His breath touched her cheek, but she kept watching the movie. Bergman told her husband she'd been lonely in Paris, but she didn't tell him about Bogart. She didn't tell him she'd fallen in love.

The hand on her arm moved. It stroked the side of her breast. Now Meadoe wasn't really watching the movie. She heard it behind closed eyes. Everything was gentle. Not like the time with Christopher Towne. Very slow. And the air almost burned, as if she faced an oven, but the hand was cool and slow and pleasant. She knew she sat on her own couch in her own livingroom—she knew she was dreaming—but she also was in a theater. Both places at once. Not alone in either place.

Sam sang again, "It's still the same old story, a fight for love and glory, a case of do or die."

Meadoe sighed. Made a small sound in the back of her throat. Heard herself make it and thought, I'll have to be quiet, or I'll wake myself from this dream.

The hand moved again, to the front of her blouse, parting the cloth (doesn't it have buttons? she thought), and the coolness was on her bare breast, holding it lightly, barely stroking. She turned to offer herself more easily, her breath caught high in her lungs, her skin a thousand times more sensitive than she'd ever felt it before.

Then a loud click. She sat straight up on her couch. The video had finished and ejected. She shook suddenly and realized she was covered with sweat, literally dripping, and the front of her robe was open.

She showered again before going to bed.

Monday morning, on the way to the library, Meadoe bought the video.

August 3 and 4, Monday and Tuesday Night: In the Interim

It took willpower to undress for bed both nights. Even with curtains, Meadoe felt watched. Pictures of her parents on her dresser seemed to have been rearranged.

The medicine cabinet door opened on its own accord. No matter where she tuned the radio, it eventually played oldies. She listened to Chet Huntley read the news from a station she couldn't get in the car and there was no listing for in the newspaper. It played polka favorites for an hour at 7:00.

When she finally turned out her light, she lay rigid on her back, hands at her side, looking at the ceiling. Did a floor board creak? Did the spoons drawer rattle in the kitchen? She thought, if I shut my eyes and then open them, will a face be staring into my face? Dare I sleep? Can I?

Then so softly at first, so imperceptibly she wasn't sure it hadn't started much earlier and she'd dismissed it, a voice talked steadily. It rose and fell. No words she could distinguish, but it lasted a long time. When it broke off, she stopped breathing, listening as hard as she could. Then sobbing. A young man's muffled weeping as if it were miles away. It was hardly there—no more than wind against the house; no more than a whisper of a sheet dropping across a long, long room, but it was beside her too.

When she slept, she didn't dream. She woke refreshed.

August 5, Wednesday Afternoon: An Interview

Meadoe stood in front of the impressive house for a long time before ringing the bell. What if she decides I'm a loon? She stepped off the porch, thinking she might be able to slip away, when the front door opened. An elderly woman with thin, white hair, heavily powdered, held the doorknob.

"You're the young lady who called from the library? I'm Erica Weiss. Come in. Come in. I've made coffee." Her voice was surprisingly full considering her age, and Meadoe entered the living room.

"Thank you for having me." Dozens of framed pictures hung on the walls from long wires attached to the ceiling molding. The room smelled of vanilla and hand lotion. It wasn't an unpleasant smell but a strong one. While Erica went to the kitchen for the coffee, Meadoe examined the pictures. There were photographs of family groups wearing late 1800s clothing sitting on the grass. Servicemen looked out from some of the pictures. Wedding portraits, graduation photos, parties, snowfalls. Meadoe recognized a younger Erica in one picture standing with what might have been parents. One was of her wedding. The groom wore a formal military uniform.

"I lost Robert in 1983," said Erica, carrying a tray with cups and a coffee pot. "We'd just inherited the property from my mom and dad. He had a stroke while adding the garage."

"I'm sorry." Meadoe sat on the edge of the couch, unsure how to ask her questions, unsure, now that she was there that she wanted to ask them.

The elderly woman said, "It's a long life, but you've got to live every minute of it. We had a few good years." She balanced a cup on her knee and filled it with coffee, then filled the other and handed it to Meadoe. "I contributed to the oral history project a few years ago. Young man with a tape recorder came out and asked questions for a couple hours. Nice fellow, from the university. Don't know what he did with all that blather."

The coffee nearly blistered Meadoe's lip. She blew across it and took a sip. A rich blend with a hint of licorice. "This is more for me than the library, I'm afraid. I wanted to talk about high school, about Nathaniel Shirley. I moved into his house."

Erica put her cup on the table, then hid her hands in her lap. "What made you come to me?"

"Your picture together in a yearbook. I found drawings in the house that were his. Good art."

Erica swayed a little, and when she reached for her coffee, her hand shook with a palsy Meadoe hadn't noticed earlier. "He never drew me. I asked him to once, but he said he didn't have the skill yet. He wanted to get me right." Her voice quivered, not nearly as full as it had been at the door. She wiped at her eye. "Sorry, the infirmity of age. So many old friends have passed. I guess Nathaniel was the first."

"Can you tell me about him?"

"It was a long time ago." In the parlor a clock chimed the hour, six mellow gongs. Afternoon sun fell in a narrow strip along the carpet in front of the living room window. Meadoe drank again, almost holding her breath, barely noticing the scalding liquid.

"We started dating at the beginning of my senior year; he was a junior. Many of the older boys had left to Germany or the Pacific so the girls dated younger. He was a beautiful boy. Did you see his picture? He had long fingers, like a sculptor. I thought it was just a fling, of course, so I had a beau at Homecoming." Erica sighed. "Girls now don't understand what it was like then, I think. If a girl today likes a boy, she just asks him out. The feminists have it right; it's a better system, but then—oh, then—a girl sat by the phone. He took me to Homecoming, and we had fun, but I didn't fall in love until the next week. We were in choir. One morning I walked into the room, and there was a drawing of Tokyo Rose on the blackboard, a huge one done in colored chalks—he could really draw Tokyo Rose—and underneath he had written, "Erica Weiss is lovelier than Tokyo Rose." He didn't sign it, but we all knew, even the teacher. She didn't erase it. It stayed there all period."

Meadoe considered the room, the woman. It was hard to imagine her as a high school senior. In the pictures, she was pretty, curly black hair, bright eyes peeking at the camera. Meadoe couldn't see the young woman in the old one. "I don't know how to ask this; it sounds rude, and I don't mean it to be, but I need to know. Were you two . . . serious? I mean . . . were you close?"

"Very close." Erica looked at Meadoe and blushed. "Oh no, nothing like that. It was 1945, after all. Not today. We never . . . not ever. Good girls didn't."

"That's not what I meant to imply." Meadoe tried to smile, but that was exactly the question she wanted answered. The pinup girls. The touch on her back, the sitting on the couch in front of *Casablanca* were so sexual.

"Well, we were people, of course. Young people. I think most old folk forget how high their juices used to run, and the young ones, of course, believe they've invented sex. We thought about it. We wanted to, but I was firm. I was proper." She looked past Meadoe at the pictures on the wall. "Most of the people I grew up with are dead now. I have their photographs." She paused. The clock ticked. Meadoe cupped her coffee, warming her hands. "During the war young kids had less opportunity than they have now. They chaperoned the dances. My mother called slow dances, 'vertical fulfillment of horizontal desires,' and the chaperones separated you if they thought you were too close. We thought about it though, what with the boys going away to war. Some girls absolutely thought it was their patriotic duty."

"But you didn't?"

"No, we never did." She looked miserable. "I graduated in '45, and I was going to go to college. He still had a year left, but he told me he was signing up that summer, the summer he died."

Talking about his death seemed to have exhausted her, so Meadoe helped put away the coffee cups.

"Did you see *Casablanca* with him?"

Erica closed a kitchen cabinet softly, hiding cups and saucers by the row. Meadoe believed most were never used, that the old woman took out the same cup or two everyday but never any more. The house seemed bigger now, and more empty.

"We did. At the Denham for an encore showing. It was a couple of years old by then."

Meadoe remembered the popcorn, the quickening of breath. "Did you sit in the back row?"

They walked toward the front door. Erica paused. "Funny question." She rubbed her brow in thought. "Yes . . . you're right. We did. How did you know?"

Meadoe shrugged.

They said goodbye, but before Meadoe moved to the porch, Erica put her hand on Meadoe's arm, stopping her. The old woman's eyes were watery and pale, her gaze steady. "In August that year, my aunt in Fort Collins became ill. My mother left me alone in the house for three days. I was eighteen. She said she trusted me. For the first time since Nathaniel and I started dating we had an empty house. I was going to go to college. He was joining the army. I called him. He was coming to see me when he had his accident."

Meadoe nodded dumbly. The woman's grip was intense. Her mouth grim. "He never would have been in the intersection if I hadn't called. All these years, all these years I've known, Nathaniel Shirley died because of me."

August 5, Wednesday Evening: A Visitation

Meadoe left her car in front of Erica's house and walked home, deep in thought.

Erica's look stayed with her. The old woman's grip on her arm. The way she said "Nathaniel." Never "Nathan." His whole name over and over again. When she'd spoke her final words it was if all the time between had been erased. As if only moments before she'd hung up the phone and sat in her empty house waiting for a boy who never arrived.

A half hour later as the dusk deepened, she rounded the corner onto her street. No cars were parked in front of the houses for once, and none of the neighbors were in the yards. Dinner time, she thought. But as she walked, she slowed. No cars. No people. Just the elms' lazy sway, the stillness of summer lawns, the day's last heat baking through the sidewalk. She turned to look behind her. For a moment nothing moved, and she marveled. This could be 1945, she thought. I have no evidence otherwise. Nathaniel might have seen his street just like this. A plane hummed away in the sky. Sunlight caught it there, way above her, like a golden cross: a four-engined golden cross. She thought, is that a B-29? But when she blinked, it became a jet. A car turned up the street, a mini-van that turned on its lights as it passed, and the moment vanished.

At first in the darkness inside her house, Meadoe didn't notice the disarray. Silverware on the kitchen floor stopped her. Drawers were open. Canned goods scattered across the counters. Couch cushions were on the floor. Art hung crooked on the walls. Meadoe, clutching her hands to her chest, moved into her bedroom. Sheets on the floor. Dresser drawers open—one was across the room—her clothes emptied from them. Windows and doors were locked. Nothing missing. Nothing broken. Meadoe picked up methodically. Why would Nathaniel act out this way? Was it because she visited Erica?

August 5, Wednesday Night: Anniversary

Later, she prepared for bed carefully: a long bath, a single candle lit on the tub's edge, the remains of the wine Joan left. The radio played a nonsense song, "Mairzy doats and doazy doats and liddle lambzy divey." She washed her hair in the tub, sinking back until the water covered her ears, muffling the radio. Everything in her bunched together in tight fists, her stomach, her lungs, her back muscles, as if a race were about to start, but she forced herself to go slow. The wine tasted good. Warm water held her in its hand. Time felt mushy and possible.

She thought about the night of August 5, 1945, where the Enola Gay waited for its atomic payload; its crew slumbered in the barracks, while Erica Weiss's mother packed for a trip to Fort Collins. Erica lay down to sleep, thinking about a phone call, thinking about long kisses held on a porch, thinking about a sculptor's fingers sliding across her shoulder, touching her cheek. Nathaniel Shirley stared at his collage until midnight, hearing planes in his ears, watching Ginger Rogers spinning across a dance floor. "Here's looking at you," Bogey said at an airport in the fog. Nathaniel's eyes always ended at Tokyo Rose, her dark hair, the twist in her neck. He thought about touching that hair, except it was never Tokyo Rose he touched in his imagination. It was Erica; her hair curled and smelling of shampoo. Meadoe's grandfather in Hiroshima slept. Old, old light from stars so distant a million lives might have come and gone glittered in the sky.

Meadoe rubbed herself dry. Left the door open. She felt his eyes on her. Pulled on panties and a night shirt and headed for bed. She remembered the *Casablanca* dream where she sat in the theater. In the dream she'd directed herself. She'd turned so her companion could touch her. In the dream she'd had free will. In the dream she'd had curly hair.

11:55 p.m. The clock flicked to a new minute. Meadoe lay on her back, eyes part open but drifting, just on sleep's edge, pleasantly buzzed. A wine glass sat on the night table where she could reach it. The radio played in the background, soft dance tunes, horns and clarinets. Big bands. Meadoe licked her lips. Felt herself doing it, knowing that she was almost asleep. A bead of sweat trickled down her forehead. Under the covers, heat pressed her on all sides. Moving slowly, concentrating on the buzz like a pressure point behind her eyes, she pushed away the blanket so only the sheet covered her.

In a dream now, she sat in her front parlor. Sun poured through the front windows. The house was almost intolerably hot, and even leaving the doors open didn't help, but Erica, wearing a thin cotton blouse and shorts, didn't consider it. Mother had been gone for two hours now. She wouldn't be back for three days. Erica's hair stuck to the side of her face, but it was nervousness, not the heat. On the table, the phone waited.

Nathaniel could be here in thirty minutes. Erica thought about his laugh. The way he touched her face. How when he was in the room she felt watery inside and hoped that he would hold her. The phone clicked when she lifted it.

In Meadoe's home, the bed creaked; She incorporated it into the dream, turned it into a creaky chair. Erica held the phone, listening to the dial tone, in the dream, and Meadoe moved aside without opening her eyes both in her bed and in Erica's front parlor. A weight lay beside her, scarcely breathing, and the air baked in the room. For a moment, nothing moved. The dial tone hummed. Meadoe's heart pounded in her ears. A tug on the sheet. It slid off. Erica dialed the operator, waiting between each digit, trying to stay calm. A jostle in the bed. Lips on Meadoe's neck. She scrunched her eyes tight, forcing herself to stay both in the dream and in her bed. A pressure moved off her arm; a hand, moved down her side, over her hip and then rested on bare leg. Meadoe breathed a sound at the touch, tried not to move. What if the hand went away? She desperately did not want to wake.

Meadoe held the phone. Pushed her curly hair away from her eyes. One ring. Two rings. In her bed, the nightshirt pushed up, uncovering her belly. Caressed, she pushed into the weight beside her. Felt his length, the heat of him. The hand moved off the middle of her chest. Slid down. Sweat coated her. She floated in it. The fingers paused at her pantie line. She wanted those fingers to keep moving. Wanted his touch.

She talked on the phone too. Nathaniel said he'll come.

Erica . . . Meadoe . . . Erica . . . she didn't know who she was, breathed hard. He'll be here soon, Meadoe thought. Mother is gone. Mother is gone. He'll be here soon.

The fingers stayed still, but the heel of the hand moved closer so Meadoe knew the fingers must be bent, his beautiful, sensitive sculptor's fingers. She gasped, not afraid now that he would hear, and then the fingers slipped farther down.

Meadoe moaned, reached and grabbed the wrist, preventing him from going any lower. "Wait," she said into her room's hot, dark air. "Wait."

Erica put on her shoes. She thought, I should wait. But she opened the front parlor door, rushed. In the dream, Meadoe/Erica ran up the street. Her house was closer to the intersection than Nathaniel's. She should get there first. Her feet blurred beneath her. Up the long hill, made the intersection. He was not there yet. Traffic held her for a minute. Cars, trucks, military vehicles. She crossed.

Meadoe held the wrist. She ached, but she didn't let it move.

A minute later, she saw Nathaniel. He was running, but when he noticed her standing there, he slowed to a walk. A grin stayed on his face. The smile was infectious, and Erica smiled back. They hugged at the same moment across the globe a bomber dropped its single bomb. Roared frantically away. Meadoe Omura's grandfather lifted dirt by the shovelful from the bunker. Around him, other workers moved wheelbarrows, carried brick, mixed cement.

The traffic light changed, Nathaniel started across, but Erica held him back.

A milk truck slammed through the red light and continued down the road. Erica smiled even broader. The bomb burst and the atomic age arrived. Quantum theory made real.

Nathaniel said, "Wow, good thing nobody was in the street."

Erica nodded. She didn't let go of his arm.

"Pretty warm out, don't you think?" Nathaniel said.

Erica shaded her eyes. "A bit. Maybe we can go some place out of the sun?"

"Do you have something in mind?"

"Oh, yes," she said, and they walked toward her house.

In her bedroom, Meadoe held the hand still under her belly, and she walked hand in hand with Nathaniel down Harriston Boulevard. They went in her front door. A brief kiss. A fumbling with buttons and snaps. They laughed in the afternoon's warmth, nearly stifling in the house, oblivious of heat and atomic bombs and milk trucks.

Meadoe forced her eyes open to the bedroom's darkness. Their laughter rang in her house, echoey and distant. Moonlight slanted through the window, gathered in a form lying beside her.

His eyes were open, staring into her own across the years. Young eyes, long dead. They blinked.

"I'm not who you think I am," said Meadoe.

The voice barely made it to her ears. It could have been no more than a breeze outside. Her own heart thudding in her veins. As light as a lover's touch. "I know, Tokyo Rose," he said, then the room was empty and twenty degrees cooler.

August 8, Saturday: Final Reel

"So you haven't seen evidence of the 'ghost' since Wednesday night?" Joan pulled her notepad from a briefcase. She was in her therapist's mode now, harder, more brusque than Joan the friend.

"No. He's gone." Meadoe leaned back in her chair.

"How can that be? You didn't change history. He still died on August 6, 1945. You told me Erica Weiss believed it was her fault, that she still believes it, so why would he disappear?"

Meadoe smiled. "I don't know, really, but I don't think I changed history. I changed the ghost. It's quantum physics, like I told you before—the uncertainty principle. Individual electrons are in all possible positions. History plays itself out in all ways."

"Parallel worlds?" Joan wrote on the pad, and Meadoe couldn't tell if she was taking her seriously or not, but she didn't care. Couldn't Joan feel it in the house? How much sweeter the air was? How much easier it was to breathe?

"Maybe, but I don't think it's that simple. Parallel spirits maybe. The worlds aren't discreet. Nathaniel intersected here. I just showed him another way it could have turned out."

Joan tapped her pen against the page. "You sound different. What's going on?"

"Remember last week when you asked me what I feared most?"

Joan nodded.

"I found out what it was, and I conquered it."

"In the dream?

"In the dream." She remembered holding Nathaniel's hand back. She'd said, "wait," and he'd stopped. The power was in her then; it was in her now. She had control. "Come on, I want to show you something in the bedroom."

"What?"

"You'll see."

In the bedroom, Joan looked around. "Did you clean the windows? It seems brighter in here."

Meadoe shook her head. She hadn't noticed it before, but Joan was right. The room was brighter. She sat on the edge of the bed, waiting. Joan paced the room.

"Look at the collage," said Meadoe.

Joan contemplated the wall and found it almost immediately. "Where's Tokyo Rose? And who is that? How did you get that picture under the varnish?"

Meadoe smiled. She'd seen it Thursday morning when she awoke, happy, nearly ready to sing, and she'd lain in the bed in languid glory. Her eyes followed the Life covers to the drawing, only it wasn't Tokyo Rose anymore. Smiling from the penciled portrait, as stunning as any of the movie stars, a black-haired girl, curls waving around her ears. Erica Weiss. In Nathaniel's hand, a date, August 7, 1945.

Joan said, "He was already dead."

Meadoe bounced against the bed's edge. "Just in this world, Joan. Just one of him."

WHAT WEENA KNEW

WEENA WADED AWAY FROM THE OTHERS INTO DEEPER PARTS. CURRENT pulled at her tunic, threatened to take her feet from the bottom, but she wasn't ready yet. Maybe one of the others would see her and ask why she was alone, what she was doing so close to the dangerous waters. No one did, even though she stood still for some time, letting her fingers rest in the stream, the cool flow pushing them aside like little fish fins. She squinted against the sun's glitter; each ripple caught a diamond point and tossed it against her vision, so the stream's middle didn't look like water at all but more like a glittery ribbon, gently squirming before her.

She licked her lips—they were dry—and even though the day was not yet hot, her forehead felt flushed.

No one will come. They don't care, she thought. They're more concerned with gathering flowers, eating fruit and making love until the sun sets. She closed her eyes. Would it be frightening to fall into the glittery ribbon or glorious? Would she rise up at the end, a thousand diamond points herself, a sparkling display that none could bear to look at lest they go blind? A step deeper. Water reached mid-way up her chest; it tugged her hands. Come with me, it said. Come deep and stay.

So she did, and the current took her. For an instant, it was peaceful, the floating as her feet rose from the gravel, and she knew she'd chosen well. No more nights hiding away. No more mornings convinced the Fear was a dream, that missing friends weren't missing at all, just hiding. She marveled at how light she felt. The river held her like a cloud; a child could not ask for a cradle so soft.

Then, she inhaled. It burned! Her eyes popped open. Her arms waved and feet kicked. Another rush of gagging water down the throat. It wasn't supposed to hurt! Her face broke the surface. She screeched, glimpsed her friends, then tumbled back under again. Roaring in the ears: current pushing through rocks, waves slapping on waves in the turbid middle. Her hand flailed in the air, tantalizingly above the water, but no movements of her arms or legs seemed to move her up. Her tunic's weight dragged. Then an upswelling pushed her face free for another peek and a half-swallow of air mixed with foam. No one on shore had moved! They weren't going to help her!

But she knew they wouldn't; it wasn't their nature.

A calmness crept through her. She hurt still, but an inner part relaxed. This was the last. The river gripped her and drew her to him, and she understood she would not be coming back up. Light faded.

Then a vise clamped her upper arm. A surge. A tremendous force, and she was clear of the stream. Air! There was air to breathe, but all she could do was cough. She was being carried. Her cheek rested on skin. Huge arms wrapped her close until they were on the bank. Gently, her rescuer put her down. Rock warmed her back; her hands lay flat in the heat; her head dropped onto the warmth. Against the sky stood a figure strangely shaped. Weena's vision swirled—she could barely focus— but before she passed out she saw in wonder, he was a giant.

Weena's life appeared no different from the other Eloi. She was raised by the mothers, played with the other children, learned in time not to eat poisonous berries, grew to adult height, lay with the boys when she wanted, loved the sun and feared the night. If there was a variation, it was in her absentmindedness, her willingness to explore beyond the gray home's grounds, to mourn the loss of friends. She cried, which puzzled the others greatly. In the mornings when some Eloi were missing, and the others went off to bathe or play in the grass, she sat by herself. There weren't even words for what she was feeling, but the friends were gone. In the dark the Morlocks came and took them. They would never return. There were no words to explain the space in her chest. It ached in emptiness. Then, later, there was another emotion she had no name for. She envisioned herself rising above the Morlocks, fear banished, the sun in her hands, striding toward them, and they fled.

After he made sure Weena was not going to die, the giant donned strange clothes fastened together with round pieces of bones. Weena watched him dress, all fear of the night for the moment banished. He was *huge*, almost her own height again taller than she was, and broad and strong. The face was rounded and lined with wrinkles near the eyes and corners of his mouth. Oddly enough, his hair was straight. His speech baffled her. When she couldn't answer him, he shook his head, gave up and wandered away. Weena followed, staying out of sight. Soon she saw that he appeared to be exploring with purpose. He walked in widening circles, stopping only when he came to the river, then reversing himself. Buildings interested him, even the empty ones no one had lived in for as long as Weena could remember. Even the dark buildings no one entered.

He moved with such purpose! She'd never seen anyone go from place to place as if one were more important than the other.

Who was this alien creature? What did he want here? How was it he could go into the dark without fear?

Weena resolved to find out more. She searched the bushes for flowers to string together until she'd made a necklace big enough. Her nimble fingers wove them together. If the giant saved her from the river, he would not hurt her now, and if he didn't fear the darkness, maybe she would be safe with him. When she finished, she approached, and he let her put the flowers around his neck. They spent the afternoon sitting in a stone arbor, where Weena soon learned some of his speech, but not enough to ask questions. He taught her his words for rock and grass and tree and everything he could point at around him, and then taught her hand and foot and face.

When, in the afternoon, the giant went wandering again, Weena tried to stay with him, but his pace was too fast, and he was going too far from the gray home. The sun moved toward the horizon, and even though Weena cried out after him, he did not return. She fled to the gray home just as the sun touched the horizon. A chill shook her as dusk poured over the land. The giant was alone outside, and night was coming.

No one asked her who he was or what he wanted. The Eloi chatted idly among themselves, and even though Weena had spent the most extraordinary afternoon, not one questioned her. She tried to tell some of them, "The giant went into the dark buildings! The giant has stayed outdoors after the sun set!" but none seemed interested. *She* would have been fascinated. If someone told her such a story, *she* would hang on every word.

Late in the evening, long after the Eloi had gone to sleep, Weena sat up watching the shadow on the wall that was the door into the gray home. Would he return, or would something else come through the door tonight? The moon was over three quarters gone. In a few nights, there would be no moon. It would do no good to run. All she could do would be to lie still and hope they passed over her. It was all any of them could do.

Then, a figure came through the door. Weena gasped; he was so sudden. She'd almost forgotten already how large he was. He found a place and lay down. She rose, walked carefully among the sleeping Eloi, and joined him. At first, he seemed surprised, but he let her rest her head on his arm, and soon he was asleep. Weena stayed still, her eyes open. Even his breathing was big; he rumbled behind her. She could feel the heat broadcasting from his chest. His hand, only a foot from her face, lay palm up, each finger a massive curve of strength. She put her hand on his; hers was tiny.

When Weena was young, before she learned about the night, she built a dam on a stream. The rivulet wound its way down a shallow gully behind the gray home until it joined the larger waters. She didn't want to walk all the way to the river to bathe. It seemed so silly. By the time she returned, she'd be just as hot as she'd been before, so she gathered round stones and put them in the water. Methodically she built a wall, and as the wall grew across the stream, the water rose. After the sun was nearly done for the day, a good sized pool had grown behind her wall.

In the morning she took some friends to see it. "Look," one said, "Weena has found a pool for us to play in."

"I did not find it," she said. "I built it."

"Why would you do that?"

Weena didn't have an answer. How could she explain the feeling she had while watching the water rise? Bit by bit it swallowed the bank upstream. Gradually it deepened. Her heart filled too. There was a joy in seeing the rushing water stilled. If the wall was bigger, everyone from the gray home could bathe here. They could bathe wherever they found a stream!

But she couldn't say that. Her friends splashed in her pool for the day, and the next day they walked to the river the way they always had. Weena knocked a hole in the wall.

In the morning, the giant ate with the Eloi, trying to talk, but they became bored shortly and no one remained but Weena. She told him the word for each fruit, for the drink, for the table and cushions, for door and window. He told her his words. Soon they left together, and she followed him as he continued exploring buildings, fearlessly plunging into darkened structures, some that Weena knew contained Morlock passages, but despite her pleas he didn't seem concerned.

Where did he come from? What secret did he possess that made him so fearless? The longer she followed, the more amazed she became. In the afternoon, he took them to the winged statue. He walked around it. Weena sat on a smooth stone bench and watched. He pushed on the bronze base, and from his expression, she knew he was frustrated. Clearly he wanted in. Why would he want that? This too was a Morlock place. If he could open it, he would only face a passage into the dark where no Eloi returned.

Weena hopped off her bench. The giant had placed his ear against the base, then rapped his knuckles against the metal. He moved a foot farther and did this again. Weena touched his back. "What are you looking for? You will wake the Morlocks."

They didn't have enough language to understand each other yet, but he showed her tracks in the lawn. Something heavy had rested in the grass twenty feet from the pedestal. The giant pantomimed dragging an object and pointed to the marks on the ground. She understood. Something of his had been pulled into the Morlock passage, and they'd shut the door to it. After a long series of gestures and using the few words they both knew, she began to understand that the Morlocks had stolen a "vehicle," something the giant traveled in. Weena tried to imagine what the vehicle would look like. Where would he go in it, and why weren't there marks in the grass that showed how the vehicle got there? The lawn was soft from rains and hail storms over the last few days, even their feet left prints, but there was no sign that showed how the vehicle arrived. Did it fly? Weena asked him if he came out of the sky. It took a few tries before he understood what she was asking. He laughed, a booming sound that startled her at first, and he shook his head.

Weena patted his hand, having no words to say to him. If she could just learn what he knew, maybe she could face the night. For the first time since she'd given herself to the river, she shook off its chill. Her throat didn't feel constricted by the water's rush. She could breathe.

That evening, despite her protests, he slept away from the gray home, in the open. Didn't he know about the new moon? But he was determined to sleep on the grass near the winged statue. Weena struggled within herself. He lay down without fear. Shut his eyes. He didn't care if she came or went. He was a giant, safe within himself. She looked at the complex shadows in the bushes, the darkening horizon, and lay down beside him.

Weena learned about boys while gathering flowers one morning in the spring. She'd followed a group of children, and as they spread out down the hill, they separated until she was alone with a boy she didn't know very well. He slept in a different home and had other friends, but he was nice. He smiled at her as they walked together around a pile of vine-choked rubble. Weena smiled back, then moved into low bushes to pick handfuls of yellow blossomed Cheek-daisy.

Something soft hit her ear. She looked up. The boy tossed a flower at her and smiled again. She threw one back, and soon they were wrestling in the soft grass.

Weena knew what was happening. The more experienced girls talked about it, and the adults made love in the open, but she had never done it herself. Some girls said that it hurt the first time. She was frightened, just a little, as she pulled her tunic up around her waist, but it didn't hurt hardly at all, and it was over before she had time to think much about it. Still, it seemed special, and they stayed together for the rest of the day, holding hands and kissing.

The boy's name was Tomey, and when the evening fell, Weena asked him to sleep in the gray home. As the darkness deepened, they snuggled into sleep among the other Eloi, his knees fitting neatly into the backs of her legs and his arms wrapped warmly around her chest.

Then, later, when all was nearly black, something woke her. She didn't move. None of the Eloi did. They never did. The Fear was upon her, cutting her from her muscles, paralyzing her. In the pitchy dark, ghostly figures moved among them. Slyly they slid through the room, hunched over, pale shadows among the deeps. One approached her. It's dry foot scraped the floor. This close, its breath rasped. Its hand touched her shoulder, and she came loose inside. Couldn't move. Couldn't inhale. It reached behind her, pushed its hand along her back and pried Tomey off. His arm pulled out from beneath her; his other dragged across her chest.

Then the Morlock was off, carrying Tomey like a dead thing across his shoulder. Tomey never made a sound.

In the morning, no one talked about their missing friends. Weena looked around her. They rose, ate their fruit, spoke among themselves, made ready to bathe or to play outside. She couldn't speak to them. Instead a pressure built inside her, it filled her lungs, eddied into her throat and pushed at the back of her eyes. Then she wept. Some looked at her as they left, but no one asked her to explain. When they were all gone, the huge room echoed with her sobs.

Over the next couple of days, Weena learned the giant's language as he learned hers. As he continued his explorations, she watched him carefully. He *knew* things; he had an attitude about things. At a brown structure, nearly covered with trees and prickly bushes, a stuck door stymied him. Weena waited to see what he would do. His approach fascinated her. He didn't come to an obstruction and give up as the Eloi did— he worried the problem until he solved it. How would he act here? The door to the brown structure had always been closed. The building was impenetrable; everyone knew that, but the giant dug at the door's base, pulling rock and dirt out by the handful. He jammed his fingers into a crack and tugged again. The door moved! Not enough to let him in, but it had never occurred to her to change the door's condition. The giant found a stout branch, worked it into the wider gap and pulled back on it. Slowly the door gave way. He dropped the branch, then squeezed into the building. Weena looked at the branch for a long time. It was like looking at the stream behind the gray home when she was young. There was a problem: she didn't want to walk to the river to bathe. There was a solution: dam up the current until a pool formed.

Weena crouched by the branch, ran her fingers along the rough bark, fingered the place where the door had stripped it to the green wood. She rubbed the sap between her fingers. It smelled fresh. The Morlocks—now there was a problem, she thought. Was there a solution?

The giant emerged, his face smudged.

"It's empty," he said. "What happened to your people? They built these wonderful structures." He waved his hand. From where they stood, she saw a half dozen other buildings. Some were homes where Eloi slept at night. Some were like the brown building beside them now, abandoned, useless, *dark* places where Eloi never went.

"We do not build," she said. "They have always been here since the day the world was born."

He shook his head. "No, dear Weena. They were built by people. Your people I suspect, thousands of years ago. By the descendants of my people." He looked sad and said more to himself than to her, "What happened to us?"

By the afternoon, Weena was too tired to follow the giant any further. She returned to the gray home to eat. Thoughtful, she munched a fruit in the warm light that poured through the windows high on the gray home's walls. A boy she recognized but had never talked to sat beside her. "You speak with the giant. What does he say?"

She looked him over. He was younger than her by a year or two. Bright eyes. Curious eyes, something she didn't see in the Eloi ever. In the days she'd spent with the giant, no one had asked her about him. "He asks a lot questions," she said.

"About what?"

"Why do you want to know?"

Around them, other Eloi ate or played or talked their idle chatter.

He squirmed in his seat, didn't meet her eyes. "I'm sorry if I'm bothering you. It's just . . . well . . . sometimes I . . . wonder about things."

The silence stretched between them. She could tell he was on the verge of bolting. "So do I," she said.

He looked up gratefully. "Really? I thought I was the only one."

"What is your name?" she said.

"Blythe."

"I am happy to meet you, Blythe."

She spent the afternoon answering his questions until evening came, then she went outside to find the giant, who continued to sleep away from the gray home, fearless to the approach of the new moon and the Morlocks.

On his fifth morning with Weena, the giant marched to one of the Morlock portals, a low, circular wall around a bottomless shaft, protected by a sturdy, stone cupola. There were dozens of them in the area.

"I'll come back, Weena," he said, and kissed her on the forehead.

At first Weena didn't understand what he intended, but when he threw one leg over the wall, she grabbed his shirt sleeve and pulled him back. "You can not go down. The Morlocks live there."

He shrugged her off and vanished into the shaft. Weena peered down after him, her limbs shaking. He was already many feet deep. He smiled at her, then continued the descent. Weena watched after him until she could see him no more. A dull thudding vibration came from below, and she could feel air being drawn into the shaft.

Until this time she thought her interest in the giant was to find out what he knew, to learn from him, but as she peered into the blackness, she realized she worried about him. She didn't want him to be hurt.

She sat on the grass near the cupola, determined to wait. Soon, Blythe came and sat beside her. It seemed obvious that he'd been watching them from some hidden place.

"Will he come back?" he said.

"How can he?" Weena plucked a blade of grass, wrapped it tight around her finger until the grass broke.

"He is a giant," Blythe said with confidence.

Weena thought about this with wonder. "Yes, he is," but she didn't believe that he would return.

"He will teach us how to protect ourselves from the Morlocks."

Astonished, Weena looked at him. Although she'd thought such things, she'd never heard anyone say them.

But Weena didn't believe the giant would return until some time later when his hand appeared at the wall's edge, and he crawled out to collapse on the grass.

Crying with joy, Weena kissed his hands and face until the giant laughed at her and hugged her close. Then he fell back and slept. Weena sat with him, holding his hand until he woke much later.

That afternoon the giant went exploring again with renewed purpose. He wouldn't tell Weena, but something he'd seen underground clearly bothered him. In each building, he examined the doors, the broken windows. In many he found Morlock passages, and he left in disgust. Unlike his trips before, when Weena tired, he picked her up and let her sit upon his shoulder.

Weena wrapped her arm around his head. He set out away from the gray home in a straight line, and his long strides swallowed ground at a dizzying speed. After a while, she could see they were heading toward a distant building, a huge, green structure in the hills that no Eloi she knew had ever visited. Soon, though, the sun slipped behind the hills, and the air grew cool.

"We need to go back," she said. Overhead the first stars glimmered through the dusk. She clung tightly, but he didn't answer. He appeared tireless. Weena wondered if they would walk all night. Could the Morlocks even catch them at this pace? Would they dare attack him? He'd gone straight into their lair and emerged unscathed. Maybe he couldn't be hurt. Maybe they feared him as much as she feared them.

She thought about this as the night swept over the land. Maybe he had no secrets to discover. If all that protected him was his size, then she might as well return to the river and let herself drown. She remembered the moment of peace, the comforting water's roar as she floated downstream. Then she remembered the first gagging swallow. She shuddered. Was drowning better than the Fear when nothing could move her, when her arms and legs betrayed her, when the Morlocks walked among them?

Still, the giant pushed forward. Weena rested her cheek against his head, closed her eyes against the thousand stars and fell asleep.

In the morning they set off again.

After they had covered some distance, he said, "I come from far away."

Weena walked beside him. He had thrown away his shoes and seemed to have picked up a limp. She chose her words carefully. He didn't talk about himself much. Most of their conversations were about her or the Eloi. "I know. You came in your vehicle the Morlocks stole."

He stopped, sat down and rubbed the heel of one foot. A purple bruise marked it. He massaged it gingerly. "My vehicle doesn't travel *distance*," he said. "It travels in time."

Weena didn't know what to say, so she smiled and nodded.

"My house used to be by the winged statue, where we saw the marks from my vehicle. I didn't move an inch, but I traveled many . . ." He searched for a word. "Lifetimes. Many, many lives passed while I rode. So many that the world was different. None of these buildings were here. There used to be a city, London, and I lived there with others like me. We ruled great machines in my city that would do our work for us. Make tools for us. Take us from place to place without walking. We could send messages across tremendous distances to learn what was going on in other parts of the world."

He kept talking about where he came from while Weena puzzled over the idea of travel through time. How could one live many lifetimes? And there was only one question that mattered, though. "Were there Morlocks?"

He shook his head. "We had our own demons." The green building stood on a hill beyond a tree-filled valley. They would be there after a short walk. The giant looked across the valley, past the building, as if he didn't see it standing there. "We fought them. We didn't wait for them to consume us." He wiped his mouth. "Mankind was never meant to be cattle."

"I don't understand . . . cattle?"

"Of course not," he said, shifting his gaze to her. He looked tired. She wondered if he'd slept the night before. "You live on milk and honey. *You're* the fatted calf. What does the herd think about when they're in the holding pens, when they're led up the long ramp to the slaughter house?"

His face flushed. Weena touched his hand. She didn't know all the words he used, but she got the sense of them. "You fought your Morlocks?"

"In a manner of speaking, yes." He squeezed her hand. "I don't know why I should tell you these things, sweet Weena. You are not equipped to understand them. Evolution has robbed you of reason. You live a beautiful life here. A beautiful, thoughtless life with something ugly underneath. Maybe it's best if I don't paint a different picture." He stood, grimaced when he put weight on his foot. "It's better when you are happy."

She thought, but I'm not happy! I'm frightened all the time. What can you teach me? What do you know? But she didn't know how to ask the question. He took her hand, and they started down the hill toward the green building.

Weena walked beside him struggling with a new thought. They *fought* their demons, he said. If he would only show her how.

The green building was tremendous! Weena had never seen a structure so large. The first room's ceiling was vague in shadow, and long spears of hazy light cut through broken windows high above the floor. The giant paused beside a pile of bones so old that many crumbled when he touched them. "This was a dinosaur. We're in a museum," he said. At one side of the room, he cleared dust from sloping shelves. Weena peered around him. The shelves were glass, and within the boxes were stones and animal teeth and other items she did not recognize. The giant moved excitely from display to display, knocking a perfect storm of dust into the air.

He said, "Here is sulphur. If I could find saltpetre, we could build a little surprise for the Morlocks." But he didn't explain what he meant. He moved from room to room, casting about from one side to the other. Weena trailed him, hushed and expectant. He would find a tool they could use against the Morlocks. They wouldn't need to fear the night of the new moon any longer!

But as the giant continued to search farther into the green building's depths, he found nothing useful, and the rooms grew progressively dark. Weena stayed closer, trying to see into the rooms' unlit corners, wary of the cavernous shadows beneath the tables and machinery they passed. Several times she saw narrow footprints in the dust. The giant didn't notice until a stealthy pattering of footsteps echoed in a room. He grabbed Weena's hand, looked around until he found a metal bar protruding from a rusted, useless machine. He broke it off, hefted its weight. "Now I have something," he said.

Weena bit back her disappointment. All this way for a club? No tools like he'd spoke of? No machines that would jump to his bidding? Just a club? Having clubs would not save the Eloi, even if she could convince the others to use them. Once the sun set, the Fear would petrify them, just as it had immobilized her when Tomey was carried away. The Eloi could not defend themselves in the dark.

The giant said, "We will be out of here soon enough, little Weena." Now he moved from room to room with refreshed urgency. Weena stayed close. Dirt blocked the light through most windows, and the afternoon was wearing away. In a nearly undamaged gallery, the giant found something that pleased him: in an unbroken case, a box of matches. He danced with delight, kicking clouds of choking dust off the floor. In another case, he found a sealed jar that when opened exuded a pungent odor. He was nearly as pleased with this new discovery. "Camphor," he said. "It burns."

Weena didn't know the word, "burns," but she recognized the matches. He'd amazed some Eloi with them in his first days, scratching them against a rock and then showing the yellow, dancing light at its end. Why he was happy to find them, she could not decide. More importantly, the sun through the windows was failing. Tonight was the new moon, and she'd seen too much Morlock sign within this cavernous building. Soon they'd be rising from their subterranean hiding places, and the giant had found nothing helpful other than a club and his glowing toy. Could he protect her? Would he protect her?

At the river, the Eloi had watched her swept down stream. She'd screamed, and none of them moved. Why would the giant help her now? Why had he saved her at the river? She held his hand as they retraced their path through the building until they emerged through the broken doors. The sun rested partly below the horizon. By the time they reached the forest's edge, it was fully night. Oddly the giant had gathered sticks and branches until his arms were full. Weena's eyes ached with trying to see into the woods. There! Was that a white shape moving? There! Another one. Even the giant noticed them slipping from shrub to shrub. The forest air rustled with their passing. Leaves crackled under unseen feet on all sides.

The giant set the branches in a pile on the ground. He scratched one of his matches into its tiny, yellow light. Weena hadn't seen a match at night before. It was surprisingly bright. Then he pushed it into the branches. Twigs grew yellow with a luminous vapor. Branches glowed, and a moving, sinuous presence rose from the wood. Weena leaned forward, fascinated. What is this? she thought. It's beautiful, like the sun captured on the ground, like the diamond ribbon in the stream's center. It threw light into her eyes. She reached for it. The giant stopped her, but she'd already felt its heat. It *is* the sun, she thought. He can make day! For a moment, she forgot the pressing dark around them, the rustling steps just out of sight.

"It's a fire," he said. "Didn't you know?" She heard the surprise in his voice, as if what was happening was a common occurrence.

Soon all the branches crackled in flame. Every once in a while a sharp pop sent sparks flying from the damp wood. An ember landed near her foot, pulsing with heat like a tiny heart.

"Come on." He grabbed her hand and pulled her into the wood. She turned to look back. The burning had crept from the pile of branches into the brush beside it. Fire writhed in the leaves, but it grew smaller the farther they walked. "If we get beyond the forest, we'll be safe enough," he said.

Weena looked up. Through the trees there was no trace of moonlight. Only the occasional star peeked through. She could feel the urge building inside, the Fear, that yelled at her to lie down. Avoid notice! it said. Become still and small and you will live. Something soft touched her neck. She twisted away, slapped against the giant's leg, but she couldn't see. Was it a leaf?

Twigs snapped around them. Indistinct voices, animal voices, murmured in the dark. Weena jerked her attention to each new sound. She was touched again. Her throat froze.

Then the giant let go of her hand.

There was nothing else to do. There was no way to resist the Fear anymore than she could stop from blinking if dirt flew in her eyes or she could stop from inhaling when the river her swept her away. She dropped to the ground. Lay quiet, the Fear said. Be dead. They will pass you by.

But another voice in her mourned. She had lost. The Morlocks would have her. There was nothing to learn from the giant with his long strides and strange clothes and talk of vehicles that traveled through time. He was just a big man with a club, and what good was a club to the Eloi who reacted to threats in the dark by falling down?

A Morlock hand touched her. A horrible soft hand that crept down her arm, around her waist. She couldn't see; it was black as a cave. Weena felt regret through the Fear. If she could cry now, she would cry for herself. None of the Eloi would.

Then, a flash of light. The Morlock hissed, let go and ran away. Cracking her eyes open a tiny bit, she saw the giant light some of the camphor, and the little flame was enough to drive the Morlock back. He pulled branches out of the trees, piled them on the flickering patch. Soon a smoky fire illuminated the trees around them. Still, Weena could not move. She felt the Morlock's hand on her.

The giant picked her up, spoke to her, but she kept her eyes shut. Fear filled her. Closed her throat. Don't let them know you are alive, the Fear said. Soon the giant put her down. He sat beside the fire, and within moments his chin dropped to his chest. He slept.

For a long time Weena stayed on her side, her arm trapped beneath her, her face pressed into the forest floor's dry leaves, watching the fire. Gradually, the Fear left. The cheerful flame leapt through the branches. Green leaves curled, caught fire and vanished in smoky puffs. She crawled next to the giant. On the ground next to him was his box of matches. He must have dropped them. Weena held them close, put her head against the giant's leg. The fire bathed her in warmth. Pungent smoke blanketed them. Watching the flames was mesmerizing. They danced like river waves, always moving in place.

She woke to an uproar. The giant was shouting and all was black. The fire was out! Weena heard him running, yelling incoherently. A creature rushed by her, and then another. The woods reeked with Morlocks, their strange cries rent the air. Her body locked into place. Something stepped on her foot as it ran toward the giant. A metallic crunch silenced one voice. Even gripped by the Fear, Weena smiled. So the giant's club worked for him after all. The Morlocks can be stopped. Her smile slipped away. None of the Eloi would ever know. And what good was the knowledge? They came out at night, when the Fear ruled.

More blows in the dark. Not so loud now. The giant moved away from her, by the sounds of it, fighting Morlocks the whole way. She believed he would survive them. He had gone into their home armed with nothing and emerged. With a club, the giant would be unassailable.

Only now she was alone. Maybe they wouldn't find her, if she stayed absolutely rigid, but Morlocks filled the woods. Their footsteps, their cooing voices were everywhere. When the giant escaped, they would take her.

Weena fought against the Fear. If she could only move. The matches were in her hand. A little movement, hardly any effort at all would light one. She could save herself. The box rested against her fingers. I can grip it, she thought, and she forced her fingers to close around its square shape. A triumph! Had any Eloi ever struggled like this before? Giving in was so much easier. Do nothing. The danger will pass. Her breath came in short gasps now. She pictured the sun beating down the grassy meadows, the diamonds in the stream. Painfully, she rolled onto her back. Real pain, like forcing her limbs into unnatural position. A moan escaped her. Weena scrinched her face in effort so hard that she saw red in the darkness.

A roaring sound began to overwhelm the Morlocks' shouting. She couldn't hear the giant any more. Like a wind through the trees, it came, and Weena suddenly opened her eyes. The red was real. The forest was on fire. Their first fire must have spread, and a bright wall of light flowed toward her through the trees. It released her, the light, and her muscles relaxed. She sat. A Morlock broke into the tiny clearing, its broad eyes streaming tears; it slammed into a tree, twirled in pain, and ran on straight toward the flame.

Weena stood, brushed twigs and leaves off her tunic. The fire didn't leap from tree to tree quickly. She had no trouble staying in front of its progress. Every once in a while, other blinded Morlocks would stagger past, some toward the fire, some wandering in circles. She stayed away from them.

When morning came, parts of the forest still burned. Weena could not find the giant. Exhausted, finally, she walked toward the home, but it was miles and miles away, and she didn't have him to carry her. By the time the sun was overhead, she was too tired to go on, so she stretched out on the grass. Wood smoke filled her nose, and she slept.

Blythe met her at the winged statue as evening fell. Footsore and hungry, Weena sat on the bench she'd rested on days ago when the giant had knocked on its metal walls.

"The doors were open earlier, and there was a machine behind them," Blythe said. He sat next to her on the bench. "The giant went in. Then the doors closed. The Morlocks must have got him."

Weena put her hands behind her and stretched her back. She had never walked for a whole day before. Her body was a medley of aches and surprising stiffness.

"I don't think so, not if he got to the machine first," she said. The giant had told her he could travel through time. She imagined him vanishing from the Morlocks' grasp, just as they descended upon him.

"Either way, he's gone," said Blythe. His shoulder slumped. "We've learned nothing. We're just as helpless as before." He looked at the sun as it slid below the horizon. "The night's coming. We should go to the home."

In the distance, the hills glowed pink. A line of skinny clouds in the west flamed brightly in the sunset.

Weena said, "No. We should gather wood and pile it by the home's door." She fingered the box of matches. There were enough to get them through this new moon, or they could keep the fire burning constantly. They had time to solve the problem of making fire for themselves.

"What good will that do? We need the giant to save us," said Blythe.

Weena looked at him. The giant had said that her people had built the structures. They had commanded great tools. Once the night had been theirs. If she could see it; if Blythe could see it, there would be others.

"No, Blythe, we don't."

THE INFODICT

SANJI KEPT A SPIDER ON MARLYSS CONSTANTLY, AND HIS CONCIERGE prompted him with updates. As Sanji sold forty cases to the crosstown outlet, it scrolled her location when her car passed under a traffic vid at Divisadero and Pine.

At the moment, he was in his office, deep in his leather chair, feet up, but it wouldn't matter if was at home or at the park or on a flight; when the info flowed, he swam in it.

Earlier in the day he'd played back some of her phone calls. Last week she'd said, "I'd love to have dinner with you." He replayed it several times, her liquidy contralto. "I'd love to . . . I'd love to . . . I'd love to . . ."

Where's she going? Sanji called up her travel patterns for the last week, Mondays for the last month, and every 5th of the month for the year. Numbers rolled through the air between him and his desk, everything he'd gathered on her since they'd started dating a year ago. No match. He okayed the delivery, quick scanned for reservations she might have made or credit blips. Nothing. He red flagged the time for later analysis just as it reported her at the Divisadero and Lombard.

"You watching Marlyss again, bud?" said Raymond. "You're obsessive." Raymond sat on the edge of Sanji's desk. As usual his tie didn't match his shirt, and the suit coat should have been retired years ago. Rather than getting a hair implant, he had combed thin strands over the bald spot.

"Where's your specs? Don't you work here anymore?" Sanji minimized the Marlyss profiler, but kept the program running in the background. New numbers showing this afternoon's inventories, shipments and condition of the delivery fleet popped up. All in the green. He stood, smoothed the front of his jacket, checked his look in the mirror. Businessman perfect. Just the right part in the hair. A meticulous, trim appearance.

"I get buzzed if there's a problem." Raymond pointed to the flesh-colored button in his ear. "I'm just a P.R. flak. Non-essential paperwork only. Short of a complete emergency, my job could be done by a high school intern." He shrugged. "Let me take you to lunch."

Sanji's own earphone squeaked a high pitched, short-speak message about highway traffic and truck travel time. With a pressure on his desk handplate, Sanji alerted the drivers.

"I've got the expense account. I'll pay." Sanji put his desk on auto mode, which handled routine calls, rerouted e-mail and forwarded everything to the Concierge, a black, wallet-sized case attached to his belt.

Sanji checked the daily specials at Reefers, a favorite spot for the business crowd, and ordered while they walked. "What do you want?" Above them thin clouds filtered the San Francisco afternoon, softly lighting apartment buildings and trees.

Raymond said, "Don't you ever turn that thing off? I thought I'd decide when we got there."

Sanji laughed. They wove through the lines in front of the fast food kiosks. "You're a positive Luddite. We can have the food waiting, cooked to our specification, eat and be out in fifteen minutes. Don't you know they hate customers like you?"

They turned down a long hill, each step jolting Sanji's specs as they flashed that Marlyss had used credit to park her car at a lot just off Divisadero and Marina Boulevard. Weather numbers scrolled up: sixty-five degrees, 86 percent humidity and gusty breezes off the bay. Probably cold as hell. A list of small restaurants and shops within walking distance appeared, all in historic San Francisco, most without vid security he could tap into. He checked her med monitors. Pulse over 100 and steady. Respiration elevated. She was walking. Blood sugar a little low. Probably going to lunch herself. But why downtown? Why the change of habit? Did it mean anything about their relationship? He wouldn't know where she was until she paid for something.

Sanji ran a quick check on her infosystems. As far as he could tell, she hadn't accessed any data about him since dinner last night. Did that mean she didn't care?

"Maybe I don't know what I want yet," said Raymond

"That's the point. You could be deciding now. You're not a very good multi-tasker." Other pedestrians walked around them. Most wore specs. Many of them working, sub-vocalizing communiques, their eyes flitting back and forth as they read data.

Raymond looked from building to building. Sanji knew Raymond was interested in restored architecture. Why he didn't access the info off the net was beyond him. Raymond actually liked to *see* the structures.

Raymond said, "So, did you ask her?"

Sanji wrinkled his brow. It was such a direct question. "Yes, last night."

"And?"

They crossed the street and entered Reefers. "Good afternoon, sirs," said the door as it opened for them. "Your table is ready."

A line shimmered on the floor leading them into the restaurant. On the walls, outdoor footage of a rock concert surrounded them. The soundtrack was just loud enough to make other patrons' conversations unintelligible.

Sanji said, "She wants to think it over. She'll tell me tonight. I'm thirty-two. You'd think I wouldn't be so nervous."

"Thirty-two and never been married. As far as dating goes, you're practically a teenager. Thinking it over's better than a no." They sat. "Can I get a menu?" Raymond said to the table.

A minute later a waiter, looking miffed, delivered a paper version of the day's offerings. "Are you new to Reefers, sir? We have a much more attractive electronic display tailor made for our Concierge customers."

"You'll just have to come back, son. I left mine at work," said Raymond. The waiter's jaw dropped, and Raymond added, "You must be the new one. I've eaten here twice a week for four years."

The waiter did the peculiar mid-focus, twitchy stare someone got when checking a readout in his specs. "Who *are* you, sir?"

Raymond smirked. "I pay cash."

"Ah, one of those," said the waiter with a sniff, as if everything was clear now. He stalked away.

"Where do you *get* cash?" said Sanji.

"If you go to your bank in person, and present identification, it's still available. Mostly they keep it around for international travelers."

Sanji shook his head. This was another of Raymond's oddities. He was so consistently dependable, however, that management had decided he was eccentric rather than weird.

"But why go to the trouble?"

The waiter appeared again, an order tablet in hand.

"I haven't decided yet," said Raymond, and the waiter turned on his heel. "That boy isn't going to get a tip."

Sanji toyed with his napkin. Around them, others were eating their meals, their conversations lost in the projected concert's ambient noise. On the wall, a new band mounted the stage. A sea of heads stretched from the foreground to the stage's base.

Raymond said, "That's Woodstock. The 2014 one. I love the classic footage. The other night they showed the old Who concert that ended in a riot. Pretty strange to be eating shrimp in the shell while watching cops beating kids over the head with batons."

"It's the atmosphere," said Sanji. He called up the Marlyss profiler again. Her pulse was down, but he had no fresh information on her other than she only had fifteen minutes left on her parking. The day after being asked to marry, she goes off on a strange errand. The question was, what was on her mind?

"Is it work or Marlyss now?"

Sanji snapped the display off guiltily. "How'd you know?"

"Your eyes get all spastic."

Sanji sighed. "How can you stand it, not being connected? Do you know where your wife is this instant? Have you checked on your children this morning?"

Raymond put the menu down. "Now that I'm ready, where's that waiter? No, I haven't checked them. I don't know how you do it. You can't eternally keep your fingers on everyone's pulse. It'll drive you crazy."

Marlyss's heart rate blinked onto the display again. The Concierge reported it had remained unchanged for the last ten minutes. Analysis indicated she was sitting or standing, probably eating lunch. Was she alone? Something fluttered in Sanji's chest. "I have a right to all the information that's available. That's the law. What would be crazy would be not taking advantage of it."

Sanji's ear plug beeped a pay-attention as new displays scrolled across the bottom of his specs. The Far Eastern division reported a markdown in raw material pricing. If he ordered now, he could cut 7 percent on manufacturing, invest the savings in interest-bearing bonds for an extra percent and a half. He thought for a couple seconds about whether the numbers could drop more, decided that they might, but not much, placed the order and shifted funds into the right accounts. In the meantime, a tiny vid window opened up in the upper left corner of his vision. The spider had found Marlyss. In the grainy picture from a bank's security camera she walked up the street, gripping her coat closed at her neck. The breeze whipped her long, red hair in front of her face.

A quick query placed the bank a half block from her car. The Concierge listed three restaurants that were her most likely lunch spot. All touristy sea food places. But she hadn't *paid* for anything. If she wasn't eating lunch, what was she doing there? She walked out of the first camera's view, and the Concierge switched to another camera that caught her back as she walked up the block, then out of sight around the corner.

"You're not going to make it until this afternoon, are you? Man, you are practically comatose when you pay attention to that thing. You're an infozombie. They have twelve-step programs for your problem."

Sanji squirmed. "You can never get enough good data. That's why all information is public. Nothing is private."

"Maybe that's okay for business activities or government policy. You're trying to read her mind. Ah, there he is."

The waiter reappeared, looking bored.

"What's the catch of the day? The menu didn't list it."

Rolling his eyes, the waiter said, "Orange Roughy."

"I'll have that then."

Sanji leaned forward. "You don't get it. If you love someone, you want to know everything you can. How else will she know I care?"

"They used to call that 'stalking.'"

"That's ridiculous. Stalking is following her around. Threatening her. All I'm doing is accessing available data, which is my right. She knows I can do it—everybody does it—in fact, she probably expects me to. This is the information society."

"All I know is in matters of the heart, the more you know the more you don't know."

Sanji sat back. The waiter arrived, pushing a cart, their meals steaming. He put the plates in front of them. When he left, Sanji said, "What the hell does that mean?"

Raymond smiled, cut into the Orange Roughy. "It means that sometimes you don't want to know what's on the menu until you get there."

For the rest of the meal, they ate quietly while rock crowds cheered on the walls. Numbers rippled across Sanji's vision: delivery times, work schedules, stock prices. His ear plug whispered status reports. When he finished, he couldn't remember what he'd eaten.

At work Sanji set a countdown clock in his specs' upper right corner. Four hours until he met Marlyss. She went home. No vids in her house, but her security alarm reported when she disarmed it, electricity consumption went up as she turned on lights, water usage indicated she'd showered. Then, nothing. Her pulse perked along steadily. Her Concierge was in sleep mode.

He drummed his fingers on the desk, baffled. Why wasn't she checking on him? In the year they'd dated she had *never* checked on him as far as he could tell. From her point of view, their entire relationship was based on conversations and the time they'd spent together. No wonder she can't answer the question: she doesn't know me, he thought. A stomach twinge hit, and he flinched. His own med readouts indicated indigestion and suggested an antacid. He wondered what he had eaten that would cause that; he couldn't recall anything spicy. Last night had been the same though, and it wasn't food related. He told her goodnight, the echo of his proposal fairly hanging in the apartment's air. Her hand rested briefly on his, her fingers warm and long and fine. "I need to think about it," she said.

After she left, he laid in his bed staring at the ceiling, thinking about her beside him. He rubbed his palm over the sheets on what would be her side. They were cold and smooth and empty. He tried to recapture the moment before he asked her, when the words were formed but he hadn't spoken them yet. Even now, only minutes later, he could hardly believe he'd had the nerve to do it. Then the twinge. Stomach acid reflux. She wasn't there, and maybe she never would be. His guts tied up inside him, but he didn't get medicine. He put on his specs, activated the Concierge, started the data streaming. Green text flowing across his eyes. Quick-speak chirps in his ear. After a while, he connected the spider for Marlyss. It picked through the megamillion information strands, and soon he swam in her numbers. All of them. Medical records, shopping purchases, paychecks, tax returns, utility bills, loans, bank statements, school, everything. And the vids he'd saved. Marlyss at the mall. Marlyss in the park. Marlyss coming and going from a thousand places, all captured digitally, stored somewhere, and retrieved, by him.

But nowhere—not a clue—on how she would answer his question. Sanji clenched the sheets. How could the answer not be there? What was left to know?

His eyes grew dry watching the clock count down. He blinked and shook his head. Scrolled through jewelry catalogues, screen after screen of wedding rings. Checked travel brochures. South American beach resorts. European tour packages. What would she like? Briefly he connected with a flower shop, then broke it off. She said she wanted time. Flowers would seem pushy. Or would they be romantic? What was in her head?

He imagined a sensor planted in everyone's brain. Readouts cunningly tailored to track emotion and thought. *That* would be information worth having. There would be no need for guesswork.

Irresistibly, with glacier-like gravity, the clock unwound the minutes.

Marlyss waited for him in front of the Maritime museum. In the dusk behind her a restored schooner attached to the dock with three permanent gangplanks, thrust its bare masts into the cloudy sky. Sanji walked quickly. The wind cut through his jacket, and he realized he hadn't been near the sea in months. She'd suggested Fisherman's Wharf for their rendevous. "I like the seagulls," she'd said.

He'd correlated seagulls to her database and found she'd papered the first apartment she'd rented, years before they met, in Seascape Serenity, a pattern of lighthouses, chambered nautiluses and seagulls.

"I missed you," he said as they hugged, and he regretted the words immediately. It'd only been a day. He sounded needy.

"Me too." She held his hand and they strolled toward the shops and tourist attractions. In the bay to their left a cargo hovercraft surrounded by its self generated mist, thundered past Alcatraz. He sensed the unanswered question between them like a malignant djinn.

Glumly he noted the temperature and weather report to give himself something to watch. Even though she walked beside him, he couldn't resist replaying "I'd love to have dinner with you." To give himself courage, he triggered the loop: "I'd love to . . . I'd love to . . . I'd love to . . ."

Beside him, she was a silent cipher, red hair spilled over her jacket, most of her face obscured. Just the edge of her cheek and a bit of her nose visible from the side. Something didn't look right about her. As they walked, he glanced from the corner of his eye several times. Finally it occurred to him. She wasn't wearing her specs! He ran a quick check. Her Concierge was still in her apartment.

Casually he reached up and pulled his own off. He blinked against the breeze hitting him square in the face for the first time. They went into his pocket. He shut down his Concierge, and his earplug went dead.

Sidewalk stands they passed sold cheap T-shirts and San Francisco trinkets. Crab and beer smells escaped the restaurants. Tourists waited in lines for tables. She led them into a maze of souvenir displays and then onto a boardwalk overlooking a small marina. Private fishing boats bobbed under the dock lights. It was nearly night. The buildings cut the wind, and Sanji didn't feel as cold.

Marlyss said, "I come here sometimes when I want to think." She sat on a wooden bench and when he sat beside her, she looked straight at him for the first time since they'd started walking. Her hand went to his cheek. "Sanji." She traced a line from his temple to the corner of his mouth. "I've never seen you without your specs."

And they were kissing, her lips soft against his, her breath quick against his skin. After a minute, he realized she was crying. His face was damp with it. He touched a tear from below her eye with wonder.

She said, "They told me you were an infodict. My friends told me you were . . . emotionally isolated." She giggled, a surprising sound in her throaty voice. "Oh, Sanji, I would love to marry you."

And they kissed again, long and silent. Sanji felt the waves beneath them lapping against the pilings, rocking their bench the tiniest bit. Seagulls cried in the bay. He held her close. She trembled, and he trembled too. It was all so huge, the emotion within. In the night, in the artificial light, the boats moved in elegant witness to the moment. Sanji knew he would remember this instant forever.

He didn't know how long they'd sat before Marlyss straightened and pulled away from him. She wiped her face. "I need to tidy up a bit. Do you mind? There's a restroom just around the corner. I won't be a minute."

"Of course not," he said, and even these little words felt different, because now he was speaking them to the woman who'd said yes. Everything was different now: the quality of air, the quality of sound, all of it. "I'll be right here," he said.

She kissed him on the cheek, smiled, and walked to the corner of the building, her footsteps loud against the boards.

Sanji leaned back, the bench a firm support behind him, and he stretched his legs. He sighed. It was good.

Then he noticed a small box halfway up the light pole on the dock across the water, a police unit, an infrared camera turned on only at night for security. Of course, the police would watch closely at night, when most crimes occurred. He looked around. The area was thick with surveillance. Accessible surveillance. His hand snuck into his pocket, caressed his specs. He twitched the Concierge back to life.

Yes, there he was, in reds and blacks as the camera saw him. He expanded the search, jumping from camera to camera. There was the front of the building he sat behind now. There was the side. There was the door to the public restroom. Sanji backed up the infrared vid a couple of minutes. There was Marlyss, entering the restroom. Sanji turned the spider up a notch. Water ran in the restroom. A hand dryer pulled energy.

He thought, what's she thinking now? Is she sorry she said yes? Will she always love me? It would take a lot of data to know. The information would have to flow fast and furious. Yes it would.

When she came out, he put the specs back in his pocket, but the Concierge was ready. The spider was running, and it would never rest.

THE LAST AGE SHOULD
SHOW YOUR HEART

:::::blink:::::

MARVELL CHECKED HIS CLOCK AND POWER SUPPLY. FOURTEEN THOUSAND years had passed, and the beach-ball sized maintenance machine had six minutes stored before he would have to enter sleep mode again. Other figures flicked through his engineered consciousness: two percent less of the twenty-seven hundred square miles of his photoelectric grid was active than had been there the last wake time, but most of the bad sectors were much farther than six minutes away. They showed as tiny black dots on the power grid's smooth green representation in his display, almost all of them to his west. The sun's energy output had reduced too, by .04 percent. His sensors displayed it as a dull red plain on the other side of the grid, filling half the sky, only a dozen miles above, its wrinkled, gassy surface sliding by at orbital velocity. If nothing else changed, he'd be out for seventeen thousand years, clinging to the sun-encircling grid, gradually storing energy, before waking again. Could he get to the nearest bad sector and at least repair it before shut down?

And where was ThreeAndrea?

At the cost of ten seconds of wakefulness, he powered up the locator. She was on the west edge of her grid, fifteen minutes away, inactive. Somewhat closer than she had been fourteen thousand years ago. What were the odds they would ever be awake at the same time? Sacrificing a few more seconds, he ran a diagnostic on her grid. Nearly the same rate of degradation.

He set course for the nearest bad sector to his east, uncoupled from the system, the copper crimps snapping open in unison, then released the pulse that would send him toward the repair. To conserve time, everything on him powered down, except his awareness, but that drew the most energy. He recited poetry during the drift from billions of years earlier, his favorite works in a long dead language from a long dead species, whose connection to the Makers was lost in history. Had they once traded? Had there been interstellar commerce? Were the Makers their descendants who'd moved from sun to sun, carrying the poetry with them until it ended up here? There was no way to know. The authors were gone, their star not even a distant memory.

Only the literature lasted, not the lengthy path it had taken to end up within him.

Marvell's memory banks were extensive, and in the super cold on the grid's shadow side, he only needed to expend a nanowatt to plumb his memory's depths. "Had we but world enough, and time," he thought, and he let the words cycle over and over. Then he threaded another line through it, "the grave's a fine and private place, but none I think do there embrace." Marvell had taken to mixing and matching his poetry, choosing favorite lines only, since there was hardly the luxury of the entire poem. Funny, to long for embracing, he thought.

He tried to remember if he'd dreamed. It seemed unreasonable that in fourteen thousand years of sleep he hadn't dreamed, but he couldn't come up with a single image in the silent time while he'd been shut down. He wouldn't know the time had passed at all except his clock reminded him, and that in the blink the power grid had gained a few more black spots, but he felt it, hanging on him, like a heavy ebony blanket, the psychic time of the years passing while he clung beneath the grid, millions of years old, much closer to the end of his life than the beginning.

The timer told him he had arrived. Visuals brightened. Above him, the power grid glided past, a great, opaque sheet between him and the sun, capturing every stray radiation, converting it to electricity and storing it in his batteries, but now there was almost nothing to capture. The sun was only mildly warmer than the space around it. He slowed himself, unlimbered his arms. As always, links were broken in the fabric above. Time was cruel. The Makers had built the grid to last forever, and it had certainly outlasted them, but forever is an unreachable goal. His sensor-laden fingers found the ruptures, wove them together in automatic competence, measured their capacity.

If he could have shrugged, he would have. All the grid's connections were thinning, breaking down, the essence of their mass sublimating slowly. He paused while his subtle intelligence did the calculations. Idly, as he waited, he scanned the system. On each corner of his orbiting fiefdom rose the old power transmitters that used to beam the gathered energy to the Makers' planet beyond, but he'd long since lost contact with them. No heat from it. No light. There was no way to sense it, and there hadn't been for millions of years. The towers remained, their mechanisms useless. He recited a bit of verse: "Look on my works, ye mighty, and despair."

The calculations finished. "Gather ye rosebuds while ye may," he thought. "Old time is still a-flying." If he was lucky, he might wake up another three or four times. The race was between the sun reducing to so little output that the grid couldn't convert it into electricity, or the grid itself failing utterly.

His arms folded back into his shell. The crimps reanchored. He wondered if ThreeAndrea would see that he'd moved closer to their shared border. Would she do the same calculations and come to the same conclusion. When was the last time he'd talked to her? There wasn't time to access his records. Screens faded to black. Sensors powered down.

Just before his six minutes ended, he said to himself, "That age is best which is the first, when youth and blood are warmer; but being spent, the worse, and worst times still succeed the former."

::::: blink :::::

Seventeen thousand years, almost exactly, and he only had five minutes. More of the grid was down. As it had been for several of the last cycles, it was falling apart faster than he could repair it. His duty was clear. The bulk of bad sectors was to the west. The most efficient plan would be to head for the heaviest concentration and begin repairing there. Already he'd mapped out the best course. He could extend the grid's life by thousands on thousands of years. The sun would go out eventually, but it was dying at a slower rate than the grid, and it was possible that it could flicker into renewed life, that deep inside, where the gravity-tortured physics became unlikely, the chain reactions could push themselves into momentary brightness. Not long-lived, for sure, but the sun could pulse. It had before, and if it did, the power would flow. He'd be able to stay alert indefinitely to completely repair the system.

His job was to outlast the dormant periods.

He scanned for ThreeAndrea. She was on the west edge of her grid, only four minutes away. She must have headed straight toward him during her last active period.

Oh, for the heady days when the sun glowed brightly and energy flowed in abundance! He never slept then, cruising along the grid's protected side, making sure the towers beamed their power to the Maker's planet safely below them. Then, a chain of grids encircled the star like a huge ribbon, and there were thousands of mechanisms like him, sentient, self-aware, independent machines devoted to repairing the inevitable breakdowns. He'd seen pictures of the sun as viewed from the Maker's planet, a beautiful, bright light in the sky with a narrow stripe cut through its middle, the grid's shadow. Now, as far as he could tell, ThreeAndrea and he were the only ones left, two small robots, mending their sections. Then they had power to spare, in constant communication, swapping poems, conversing about their jobs, about their lives. No one lives a limited life, he thought. Our lives are as important as any. He felt a longing to hold onto his, lonely as it was.

But as the sun waned, they went increasingly into sleep mode. He hadn't spoken to her for millions of years (although he'd only been aware of a handful of them), and he realized he might never speak to her again.

Seconds ticked relentlessly, and he didn't move. There were dead patches between ThreeAndrea and him. He could go closer to her, but it wouldn't be efficient. A thought crossed his mind: there are no more Makers. I have no responsibility to them, but the grid called. His programming and habit pulled at him to go west, away from ThreeAndrea and into the heart of the damaged system.

And what would be the use of going her way? She could well move farther from their shared border. He couldn't lock onto her grid any more then she could lock onto his. The connections would be incompatible. To leave his area would be suicide.

A snippet of John Donne surfaced in his memory, "For the first twenty years since yesterday I scarce believed thou couldst be gone away." It was the poem that ended with, "Yet call not this long life; but think that I am, by being dead, immortal. Can ghosts die?" ThreeAndrea liked John Milton, although she dwelt more on the last works of the Makers. The sad dirges to themselves, made as they dug deeper and deeper into their planet, pursuing the heat at the core, breathing air transmuted from minerals and rock, their own atmosphere having long ago frozen and fallen to the surface. He decided, set a course, unclamped and released a pulse.

Duty ruled out. He must repair as much damage as possible.

Then he remembered a bit of Shakespeare, "Let me not to the marriage of true minds admit impediments . . . Love alters not with his brief hours and weeks, but bears it out even to the edge of doom."

Seconds ticked away, much more important to him than distance. The clock ruled what was left of his life. Above him, the blank-slate grid scooted by. Every passing instant was a crisis, a turning point, a crux, a moment lost and a trial of resolution.

Fully formed, the thought leapt before him, I don't need to be duty's fool.

Before he calculated fuel, before he could even determine if what he wanted to do was possible, he unshipped an arm, reached up and grabbed the grid. His metal shell snapped into the black surface. Ripples stretched along the metallic fabric. Connections broke. In a second, more damage was done to the grid than had occurred in the past hundred thousand years. But his momentum slowed until he stopped, and the grid rebounded, pulling him back. Marvell let go at the end to the bounce, sending himself in the other direction, toward ThreeAndrea asleep on the border.

Only three minutes left. The math was unforgiving. He'd have to stop considerably short of her. By the time he'd recharged himself, she would be long gone. His errand was futile. Still, he plotted the best angle, made a small correction, set his timer and waited. Another poet drifted through his mind, "Now let us sport us while we may, and now, like amorous birds of prey, rather at once our time devour than languish in his slow-chapped power," and if Marvell could have smiled, he would have.

He slowed, clamped. Dug up some Shakespeare to meditate on while he was shut down, if there was a chance for dreams: "In me thou see'st the twilight of such day as after sunset fadeth in the west, which by and by black night doth take away, death's second self that seals up all in rest."

::::: blink :::::

ThreeAndrea hadn't moved. Marvell noted that first. Then, the time, sixty-four thousand years. He'd reduced the grid's capability that much? No. His damage wasn't that big, and the decline in functioning sectors was as predicted. It was the sun, even dimmer now, throwing out less usable radiation, cooling in the universal heat sink. There would be no chance for a saving pulse. The last burst of radiation truly had been its ending gasp, and the decline was comparatively swift and inevitable. Too small to nova, not even enough mass to become a neutron star, it would just continue to fade, like a filament in a light bulb caught in slow motion. Neutrons would break into protons and electrons, and, eventually, those too would go their separate ways, joining the background heat that was all that remained of the universe, but this was unimaginably far into the future, even for an intelligence as old as Marvell's.

Was she dead? Marvell activated his sensors, spending precious seconds of consciousness. She'd done no repairs to her grid as far as he could tell since she'd activated last. More chilling, though—she hadn't budged from where she'd anchored on the closest edge of her grid. He had three minutes to act. Quickly, he unanchored, recalled the course, released a pulse, then turned his sensors off. The numbers said he would reach her with seconds to spare.

Nothing to do in the seconds left but to recite poetry, a little Yeats. At first he considered "Sailing to Byzantium," and then "The Second Coming," but he couldn't imagine a birth in his future, not even the grim one with a rough beast slouching toward Bethlehem to be born. He chose instead some Gerald Manley Hopkins. It called to him pictures of a life he'd only imagined on planetary surfaces he'd never walked on. There were so many terms in it he hadn't experienced, but there was something in the tone:

> Nothing is so beautiful as spring,
> When weeds, in wheels, shoot long and lovely and lush;
> Thrush's eggs look little low heavens, and thrush
> Through the echoing timber does so rinse and wring
> The ear, it strikes like lightnings to hear him sing.

He kicked the sensors back on, slowed himself to a stop, reanchored. Her shell looked whole. The nearly invisible seams where her arms folded into her body appeared clean. No outward damage, but that didn't reflect what might have gone on inside. A critical relay could have broken, or, he thought, she could have ended it herself. They both had the capability. He could shut himself down forever easily enough. Is that what she had done? Why hadn't she moved? How could he communicate with her?

Only seconds remained before he shut down. What could he do? If he could have, he would have wept in frustration. Instead, he extended his arm, his mechanical manipulators, loaded with sensors and so like fingers stretching out to touch her. She was a shade too far. No time to bring it back. One arm out, inches too short, Marvell retreated into sleep mode.

::::: blink :::::

Marvell woke to poetry, and for a moment it puzzled him. It didn't come from within him. He hadn't called it up, but there it was, running through his brain, "When I consider how my light is spent ere half my days in this dark world and wide, and that one talent which is death to hide lodged in me useless, though my soul more bent to serve therewith my maker . . ." He recognized the poet, John Milton.

"ThreeAndrea?" he said. Slowly, far more slowly then he ever remembered, his systems came to life.

"Yes, I'm here."

"How . . . ?" His instruments showed power flowing through his outstretched arm. Finally a visual glowed. ThreeAndrea's hand joined to his, sending electricity into him. His power storage units were empty. "How long has it been? My clock isn't functioning." Several submechanisms weren't responding either. The thruster seemed to be cut off, and although he could sense the arm still stored into his side, it wouldn't respond to a diagnostic.

ThreeAndrea said, "Almost thirty thousand years for me. Somewhat less for you." Her voice was as he remembered it, different from his own, lighter. She spaced her words irregularly. He'd always wondered if it was an error in her programming, or if she did it on purpose to be unique. She continued, "You anchored into an inactive sector, or it broke soon after you arrived. There was no way for you to recharge."

"I thought you were dead. You didn't move."

For seconds she didn't reply. He continued scanning himself. No power. No propulsion. No way to move his arms. He couldn't access his grid to see what new damage there might be.

Then she said, "I was afraid you wouldn't come."

He had no answer for that. "How much time do we have?"

"I haven't been repairing, just storing. Four minutes between the two of us. I can't move you, though. The only way for you to stay active is hooked to me."

"Well, then don't let go." He could feel the power coming from her, and it tingled oddly. His system had to reroute it, and it wasn't exactly the same as he was used to, as if the electricity was flavored by passing through her. It wasn't unpleasant.

"I won't. Have you looked down?"

If he could have shook his head, he would have. He realized that since the Maker's planet had stopped responding, he'd spent every waking period looking up, examining the grid, peering at the diminished sun beyond.

"I don't have the power to," he said.

"Look through mine," she said, and she clicked open relays that allowed him access to her scanner.

The field that was the universe was absolutely blank. An empty distance, devoid of radiation and light; nothing was out there. "Where are the stars?" Marvell said.

"They're gone."

"All of them?"

"All of them."

"Then this is the last?"

"As far as I can tell."

"Walt Whitman would be sad," Marvell said. "He wrote, 'I wandered off by myself, in the mystical moist night-air, and from time to time, looked up in perfect silence at the stars.'"

"He got the silence right," said ThreeAndrea.

Marvell tried to access his clock. It still wasn't working. "How much more time?"

"Not long."

"What's the condition of your grid? Will we wake again?"

Marvell sensed her withdrawing as she consulted her system.

"We might, but it's all grown so old."

He knew she meant the grid, the sun and them. Everything.

"Are you afraid?" Marvell asked. He studied the blankness below them. It was totally featureless, without depth or meaning. All the stars that once shone gone at once, finally. The long play ended.

"Not now. It's just sleep mode," ThreeAndrea said.

"I can feel your hand, you know," Marvell said. His sensors recorded the pressure of her manipulators against his own. Sensitive to the last, his fingers caressed the metal texture, brittle in the deep, deep cold.

"Yes, I hoped you could."

::::: blink :::::

PERCEPTUAL SET

MARGO SAID, "IF YOU REALLY WANT TO KNOW HOW A MAN WILL TREAT YOU, watch how he eats his cheesecake."

Janet poked at her dessert. "That's ridiculous." The second shift filled the cafeteria. From their table near the wall, the narrow room curved up to the other end as it followed the mining and processing ship's long arc, but Janet's attention was on Crew Chief Alec Maier. She noted he'd chosen the cheesecake too, but he ignored it as he listened to a pair of his miners arguing about relief time and compensation for lost work. He never glanced her way.

Janet put her fork down in disgust. "You can't make a decent cheesecake with rehydrated dairy products. I should have had lunch in my quarters."

"Did you get new scans on the Gargoyle?"

"Where did you get that name?" Janet whispered. "A Strieberist will hear you, and I'll be fending off missionaries again."

"Nut cases. If they had their way, we'd give up on the whole ark project and wait for rescue instead."

Janet remembered how the recruiters sold her on graphic presentations of the ark ships heading for the stars, fleeing the mutagen-wracked Earth, packed from end to end with everything necessary to colonize distant planets. Without the asteroid mining projects, the arks would never be built. They had needed her cartography skills, and now she was the go-to person in the department.

"Maybe, but they see alien fingerprints on everything. I don't care what the company says about hiring diversity. They make my life miserable. You're not supposed to know anything about it anyway. It's secret," Janet said.

Margo dipped a piece of bread into her coffee cup, then popped it into her mouth. "People talk to me. I'm the therapist." Like most of the crew, she'd long ago given up on the regulation work clothes, wearing instead a loose T-shirt and shorts. Her hair was a close-cropped brunette that matched her dark-brown eyes. She grinned while chewing. The only time Janet saw her with a serious expression was when she studied psychiatric profiles. Then, her brow would wrinkle and she'd push her fingers into her cheeks as if trying to squeeze understanding out of herself. "So, is it an alien space station?"

Janet thought about not answering, but Margo's security clearance was higher than hers, and if she really wanted to know, there'd be little Janet could do to stop her. "No, but it's darned weird. The clearer the scan, the more it looks like a head to me, just like the Ceres' flyby recorded." The first clear photos showed a face on the asteroid. At first it seemed as if it was *all* face, but later shots showed it was more like a cameo carved into a larger surface. She'd enhanced the images, then turned in her report.

Margo snorted. "Face, my foot. It's your perceptual set. Giovanni Schiaparelli thought he saw water channels on Mars in the 1800s. He was *prepared* to see evidence of life, and he found it. It's like that head on Mars obsession at the end of the twentieth century. Put three dots and a line on anything, and people turn it into a portrait. That's called 'feature extraction,' taking info you're familiar with and ignoring the rest. A water stain sits on a wall long enough, someone sees the Virgin Mary. Do you ever notice the Virgin Mary doesn't show up on walls in Muslim countries? This asteroid is no different from the rest, an odd-shaped rock we can run through the mill for metals, fuel and chemicals. The Ceres' flyby takes a long-range shot by accident, and third-rate administrators with more imagination than good sense turn shadows and a jagged protrusion into an alien artifact. We're taking a tedious trip for nothing, and I'll be dealing with disappointed alien hunters for months."

"The main office doesn't think it's nothing. You don't divert an entire mining operation on a whim."

Margo said, "Maybe not, but you're on a deadline. If you don't figure out exactly what it is before we get there, the radicals will get the upper hand. There's more than one Strieberist in administration."

Janet watched as Alec pushed his dessert to the side and started sketching on his napkin. The workers leaned over his shoulder so they could see what he was doing. She admired the way he concentrated while writing on the small surface.

"He's monofocused," said Margo.

Janet turned away. "You're the monofocused one—I'm not watching him. The probe should be within ten kilometers in an hour. We'll get even better pictures then."

"Sheesh, it's half a kilometer long. How close do you need to get before you see it's an ordinary object?"

"That's another thing. The Gargoyle has almost no albedo. I mean, most asteroids are darned dark anyway, .03 or so, but this one's a lump of coal. If it hadn't occluded Ceres, we would have never seen it. That's not natural."

Margo shrugged her shoulders. "A black asteroid, big deal. There, now look at that one." She lifted her chin toward a miner at a near table. He wore his coveralls with a strap down. Sweat marked his shirt in a pattern mirroring his work suit's pressure points.

"What about him?"

"Watch the cheesecake."

Janet thought the man had a rugged competence. Like most miners, he carried the ship's spin-induced gravity carefully, as if he wasn't sure that anything he set down wouldn't drift off. He pulled the plate with the cheesecake toward him. Then keeping one hand on the plate, he trimmed a third of the slice off with his fork, lifted, swallowed, took the second third, lifted, swallowed and finished the last third, all in fifteen seconds.

"Whew!" Margo said. "That was business-like."

"What does it tell you about him?"

Margo raised an eyebrow. "Isn't it obvious? He doesn't take time for the finer things in life. A woman would be wise to steer clear of him."

"Maybe it means he was hungry. You're a loon."

"And you think a football stadium-sized rock has been shaped into a head. So how did Alec eat his?"

Janet turned to look back at the crew chief, but he and the two miners who'd been arguing with him were gone. His cheesecake sat untouched.

Margo said, "You work with him all the time. Why you have to turn it into such a big deal now that you've decided you're interested is beyond me. What do you guys talk about on those long jaunts in the jalopy?"

"That's business. He's thinking about where the operation will anchor. I'm thinking about navigating and mapping. There's nothing romantic about riding the jalopy from the ship to the next mining site."

"You can't read clues into his every behavior . . ."

"You just told me to look at how he eats his cheesecake, for crying out loud!"

Margo went on, ignoring the interruption. "Yesterday he asked you to pass the salt, and you spent the next two hours deciding what it meant. Tell him you think he's cute."

"I'm thirty, not sixteen. Maybe you could tell him."

Margo laughed. "Oh, that's very thirty. If you give me a note, I'll pass it to him."

Janet looked at her suspiciously. "Does he ever talk about me?"

Margo shrugged. "Maybe."

"I should have never kissed him," said Janet. "He doesn't like surprises."

"He saved your life!"

"Yeah, and there's that, too."

*

In the cartography lab, Janet shuffled through the new prints. Chief Cartographer Lindsey London held one in her lap, biting her lip.

"It's difficult to ascribe these formations to natural forces."

Janet put a half dozen scans on the table end to end, each one revealing a different look at the asteroid as the probe passed. "Those aren't formations, they're features. It's a face. Two faces, actually, one on each side."

Lindsey stood so she could see the entire set. She was a severe woman in her fifties, rigorous in habit and demanding. She cleared her throat, then rubbed her forehead. Like many on the ship, she suffered from sinus infections. "I suppose it would be hard not to draw that conclusion. They do look like faces." She moved a print closer to her. "Darned ugly ones too."

With enhancements, the asteroid's edges were clear, the shadows and highlights easy to distinguish. Janet turned the photo so the orientation made sense to her. On the asteroid's edges, jagged spikes jammed so tightly there appeared to be no space between them. They crossed each other in random arrangement. With the probe close, details stood out. Janet estimated each spike might be ten or fifteen meters in diameter at the base, although she couldn't see where they anchored, and none were shorter than fifty meters as they tapered to blunt points. Were they crystal structures? What could cause this? If the entire surface were covered with the spikes, it would be difficult to land. There was no place a ship could put its legs down for a secure anchor. In the spike field's middle, however, the face filled a third of the space. It rose from the pointy surface, a nearly perfect ovoid.

Janet turned the photo again, squinting at the new angle. "I don't know about ugly. It looks scared."

Lindsey glanced again. "If it is an alien face, how would we recognize its emotion?"

"How *else* would you describe that?"

The mouth was reptilian and gaping, stretching across the ovoid's bottom, a dark, crooked gap. A slit where the nose would be, and the eyes thrust wide open, like two almonds far apart, pupils dug into the spherical surfaces. Janet squinted at the photo, trying to see it without the starry background. "I don't know what makes me think it, but this is a frightened expression. Whoever carved it knew what fear looked like."

"It's not the same on the other side." Lindsey handed her another scan.

Here the mouth bared huge, stone teeth. The eyes were narrower. Janet shivered. It reminded her of a dog she'd tried to pet once, until its lips curled back and the snout became all fangs and a shuddery growl.

Janet said, "So, are you still going to argue this isn't a manufactured object?"

"I'm not telling the company we've found an Easter Island head in the asteroid belt, but I'm willing to say it's anomalous and deserves further study. Until then, no one Earthside knows about this."

Janet raised an eyebrow.

"Not my decision," said Lindsey. "Word from upstairs. Even on board there aren't a dozen people who know why we've changed our schedule."

Janet started an accelerated animation of the odd object on her computer. It revolved so the two faces alternated. The fearful expression rotated past, the shadows stretched across the stone skin, darkening the mouth, shifting shadows across the eyes so for a moment, they seemed to move. Then the spiny border filled the screen. The fearful face's profile cut across the stars as the second face rotated into view.

"It's a solid hunk," said Lindsey. "Not a rubble pile."

"That's my guess. I read the light bouncing off it—there's darned little—and it comes up nickle-iron. No magnesium. Some iron-silicates."

"Nickle-iron should be brighter. Why's it so dark?"

The second face came into view. As frightened as the first one looked, this one threatened. The same alien features. A different emotion.

"Maybe it's painted."

Lindsey didn't laugh. "Send the probe down to get a sample from the surface of a face. Keep it away from the spiky areas. There *might* be a coating, or it could be just a dark ore, a type of asteroid we haven't observed. If there are others with this little reflectivity, we might never see them. While we're waiting, get a complete map worked up. We're going to want to anchor the drills and mill."

"Has anyone considered the asteroid might be a message?" Janet swallowed dryly. Lindsey didn't like her orders questioned. "If it is artificial, whoever put it there didn't want it to be seen, and if it was seen, they didn't want it to look attractive. Maybe we should leave it alone."

Janet sent the photo probe's data into the mapping programs. She watched the asteroid continue its rotation on the screen. Fearful, angry, fearful, angry.

"Not with Strieberists in upper management." Lindsey stood behind her, her hands on the back of Janet's chair. "Are you going to be able to concentrate on this?"

Janet tore her attention from the Gargoyle. Lindsey's question didn't make sense. "Excuse me?"

"Are you going to be sharp? Everything here has to be perfect. Our reports, perfect, when we send this to the company. There will be political ramifications if this turns out to be artificial. I can't have you mooning over the Crew Chief instead of doing your work."

"I am *not* thinking about that man!"

Lindsey shrugged. "So you say."

"I do say!" Janet's face flushed. She bent over the keyboard, tapping the instructions that would separate the sampler probe from the mapper and send it to the surface.

Janet jogged up the ship's long curve, enjoying the track's yielding surface as it cushioned her bare feet. Behind her, footsteps approached, so she moved to the side, her shoulder nearly brushing the wall to her left until the runner passed. Here the ceiling was low, cutting off the view of the passage sixty meters ahead. She could never shake the feeling she was running uphill. At least, it appeared that way, a steady climb in front, and if she looked behind, a steady climb the other way. Running in the circular station was like perpetually hitting the bottom of a rounded valley. Across the broad sidewalk to her right, she passed doors, hallways and windows. The Infirmary, a long section marked with red crosses at either end rolled by for the third time. Once more would make a five kilometer workout, her required aerobic ration.

Without the kiss, Alec wouldn't be a problem. It happened a week ago. He'd been reading an asteroid's assay numbers and a mathematical map that showed stress lines, faults, and probabilities of mass shifts once they began operations. The top sheet of papers on a pile near the edge of his desk slid off, fluttering to the floor. They'd both reached for it, her hand on his shoulder as they bent down, and when she looked up, he was there, an inch away. It must have been something in his eyes, or maybe she could feel his muscles tense under his shirt, or maybe it was just a short circuit in all her thinking processes, but she leaned the slightest bit, pressed her lips to his, and then the moment was gone. He bolted straight up, knocking the remaining papers into the air. She fell back, banging her elbow on the chair's edge, and as she grabbed the sore spot, she saw his expression, eyes wide in fear (or disgust?). He spluttered something incoherent, face red, then fled the room.

She blushed to think about it.

More footfalls behind her. She moved to the side again, slowing in thought. The maps showed the Gargoyle was an almost perfect sphere, varying no more than a few centimeters in diameter measured through the poles or the equator, another good argument it was artificial. Bodies this small didn't have enough gravity to pull them into round shapes. Most asteroids were rugged, irregular, nearly solid nickel-iron chunks, or jumbled carbonaceous chondrite rubble piles. The only way she could think to form a small, spherical body in space would be to heat the entire mass to a liquid state, and like a water drop floating in a no-gravity chamber, it would pull itself into a perfect globe. But the Gargoyle wasn't a smooth, spinning bowling ball; it was a designed object. Still, there was a blessing in the shape: figuring orbits around it would be easier. The last asteroid she'd sent a probe to was shaped like a four kilometer long dog bone with an eccentric wobble, and the gravity going around the long end was three times that of circling the narrow middle. She'd used a lot of the probe's fuel keeping a consistent distance away from it while she mapped.

Alec spoke almost in her ear, "When I run toward the spin I feel faster."

Janet stumbled, then recovered her stride. She tried to speak, but what came out instead was a cross between a cough and an exclamation that sounded like "Gack!"

"It's a funny thing," he said, as if she'd made no sound at all. "I know it doesn't make a difference which direction I go, but when I jog into the spin, it's like the ship rotates beneath me. Going the other way is like trying to catch up, and my strides seem shorter." He had a pleasant speaking voice.

"Have you tried timing it?" she asked finally.

"Same time both ways. Doesn't change how it feels, though."

They ran side by side for a minute without speaking. Janet thought of a dozen things to say, but nothing sounded natural. She almost said, "How do you like cheesecake?" The thought made her smile. Margo would be pleased if she had. When another jogger approached, going the other direction, Alec dropped behind to let him pass. On his chest, the jogger wore the familiar green and white Strieberist button that read, "They are waiting."

The infirmary slid by again on her right. Janet stayed in her rhythm. Why was he talking to her? Had he come behind her on the track by coincidence, or did he want to be with her? Was he just a nice guy who talked to anyone? What was she supposed to read into this encounter?

And he had saved her life. Of course anyone might have noticed the flaw in her space suit before they'd gone on that mission, but he was the one that caught it. How could she date a man who'd saved her life? It was too corny. Knight in shining armor stuff. It put them on unequal footing.

She cleared her throat and said, "This makes me think of a hamster in an exercise wheel."

He didn't answer.

She said, "Where the wheel goes round and round, and the hamster works like crazy to go nowhere."

Without slowing, she glanced over her shoulder. He was gone. She sighed. Just as well. The probe would be near the Gargoyle now, and she wanted to be there when it touched down. It would take several hours to start sending back its analysis, but she felt more in control if she was in the lab while the probe worked.

For a while, the mapper tracked the sampler on its way, showing the tiny craft approaching the Gargoyle, puffing out compressed air to control the descent and to match the slowly revolving asteroid's spin, but the orbiting mapper would be on the other side when the sampler made contact. Sweat tickled Janet's forehead. Landing a probe on an asteroid was tricky business, even with automated routines and computer assistance. There was almost no gravity, so the asteroid didn't help orient the probe, and the probe's kinetic energy remained the same, so a percentage point miscalculation would slam it into the solid surface, and third, she'd chosen the angry face to land on. Now that the probe was within a few hundred meters, all the details were clear. There were lines in the expression, taut skin pulling away from its mouth, a tension in the cheek area, all in black and gray relief. The lifeless pupils seemed to track the probe in as it approached. Dark pocks scarred the surface, as if the face had been disease ravaged. Watching the expression grow larger was unnerving.

"You're closing a little fast," said Lindsey.

"I've got to anchor the probe or it'll just bounce off. If you were standing on the surface there and twitched your toes, you might achieve escape velocity."

The face swelled until there were no discernable features, just the pocked skin. Then the probe's shadow, its spider-like feet reaching closer and closer. Touchdown. Janet sent the signal to fire the anchor bolts in case they didn't deploy on their own. She took half a breath in relief. The probe continued. The feet broke through. Shards flew toward the camera, then nothing. No image.

Lindsey coughed. "That's expensive equipment. What happened?"

Telemetry came in fine. The machine's little nuclear heart still beat. Janet ran through a handful of tests. The internals looked green, but there was no video, and she couldn't tell what the probes' attitude was. "The face must have been a shell. If it's spikes underneath, the probe could be wedged between a couple. The arms are stuck. I can get the sampler to deploy, but it's not reaching anything. For all I can tell, it might be pointing straight up and be nowhere near the surface."

"Can you shake it loose? Take it up and bring it down again?"

Janet shrugged. "I can't tell which way we're facing. Without the video I can't see, and with all the metal around it, radar orientation won't work. It could wedge in deeper. We'll have to wait for the mapper to come around so we can see it. I can bring it in close for a good look, but it won't be in position for several hours."

Later, after she'd made the adjustments in the mapper's orbit, she leaned back in her chair and watched numbers march down the screen. Lindsey had gone to a management meeting, leaving Janet alone in the cartography lab. She tapped her fingers on the table edge. Above the monitor hung the Gargoyle's two clearest images. Fearful and angry.

Was this first contact? The long-sought evidence that mankind wasn't alone in the universe? She knew they were on the edge of something tremendous, but a voice kept creeping into her thoughts, coming from just behind her, not out of breath at all, saying, "When I run toward the spin, I feel faster." She wondered if Madame Curie thought about laundry while she was discovering radiation, or if Buzz Aldrin found himself contemplating a crabgrass problem in his lawn while the Eagle was going down. This would be so much easier if she just knew what he thought of her, but the messages were enigmatic. One day he ignored her, the next he went out of his way to say hello.

She shook her head and studied the mapper's data. Some measurements didn't make much sense. The Gargoyle's magnetic field was what she expected for a body of its size, but there was a ghost image underneath the main one, as if there were a second magnetic source within the asteroid. Deep radar imaging didn't help either, although there were four tiny bright spots on the surface: one on each face and at the poles. She programmed the mapper to take closeups of one of the spots when it made its nearest pass.

The intercom crackled. "Hey, roomie. Cracked the mystery yet?"

Janet said, "Hi, Margo. Nope, and we've just a few hours before the Gargoyle will be at eyeball distance. Some Strieberist working outside's going to catch a glimpse, and we'll have a riot. And you know what's funny? They were right all along. The Gargoyle is alien. Lindsey is confabbing with the upper mucky-mucks about what it might be and what to do about it."

"What's your guess?"

"Maybe it has religious significance." Janet thought about the Sphinx and the pyramids, ancient structures from a long gone civilization. It was hard to imagine why an advanced, technological society would build such an inaccessible shrine. "I lost the sampler probe. It's as if whoever designed it didn't *want* anyone to land on it. I don't know what the ship's going to do when we get there. We won't be able to anchor easily, and it's too big for a controlled melt. We could set up every mirror on board, and it would still take a hundred years to heat it enough."

"When administration says 'jump,' we're not supposed to ask why. Maybe their interest is scientific."

Janet laughed. "Not a chance. If it isn't profitable, they won't do it. They must figure the Gargoyle is a treasure chest."

"Why the faces?"

"To scare off the superstitious?"

On the monitor, video from the mapper streamed by as the asteroid grew in size. Closest approach would be in a few minutes. Janet shivered. No matter how she looked at it, the effect was creepy, like a hedgehog wearing a lizard mask. "Whoever made this was more advanced than us, and it was a tremendous effort. There's some practical purpose here."

"Could it be a tomb like for the pharaohs?"

Janet started at Margo's echoing her thought. "Were going to have to find out. Lindsey will insist on a complete investigation. I'll take the jalopy over for a personal touch. Standard procedure is to pull the ship within ten kilometers, but I'll bet we won't get closer than a hundred on this one. It'll be a long flight."

The mapper's monitor began spitting out images as it gradually swept past the asteroid. "Gotta go," Janet said and broke the connection. First, she looked for the probe. Underneath the face's left eye was a new, dark blemish. What sunlight there was dropped straight into the hole, and she could see the probe canted to one side. A tough angle, but now that she knew, she could get it out on its own power, assuming the jets weren't bent. She rubbed her chin, then directed the camera at what she'd thought were pock marks. They were all holes. They must be from smaller asteroids colliding with the Gargoyle. How long had it been tucked into this orbit? Why weren't there any large meteor strikes? Every asteroid they'd surveyed showed a long, violent past, filled with collisions, but other than these small holes, the Gargoyle was unmarked. She wondered if Texas-sized Ceres, which led the Gargoyle in its long route around the sun, absorbed most of the rocks that should have pummeled the smaller body.

The mapper continued across the surface until it was over a shiny spot the radar had picked up. An image assembled itself on her screen. She enhanced it, then sat back, shaking her head. It was a couple meters wide by a meter high and appeared to be made from polished rock or metal. Even with the monitor's fuzzy resolution she could see illustrations and writing. She contacted Lindsey to tell her the Gargoyle had a plaque.

The jalopy was an awkward looking rhomboid assembly of tubes, compressed air jets for propulsion and maneuvering, and several tool chests loaded with prospecting and mapping equipment. Inserted in the middle were two lightly shielded pods for the pilot and passenger. Alec and an equipment handler were already in the launch bay checking the supplies when Janet walked in.

Alec said, "This doesn't look like a mining operation to me. They ought to be sending an archaeologist." He scowled as he inventoried a locker and then slapped it shut.

"Probably," said Janet, raising her eyebrows. Rather than risk upsetting him more, she moved to where her suit was stored. What's wrong with him? she wondered. Soon, though, she was into the rhythm of getting ready for the mission. Every new asteroid required an initial human survey. There were too many variables in hooking the mining operation up to rely on robot reports. Asteroid composition could vary from one spot to another. A seemingly solid rock could be deeply cracked, or might be a dozen loosely melded pieces. Many turned out not to be suitable for easy mining. Too many silicates, not enough clean ore, not a clear site to base operations. For every five or six asteroids they visited, the ship would pause at one, but tons of usable metal could then be extracted, milled, smelted and shaped, then sent on the long, elliptical path that ended in lunar orbit for assembly into the ark ships. At the same time, chemical processes produced fuels and other usable products. Mining the asteroids reminded her of the Eskimos who used every part of a slaughtered sea lion.

Janet and Alec had worked as a team for three years. It was possible to do the whole job without talking, but they never had. She worked her way into her suit. Next to her, Alec pushed his arms into the thick, clumsy sleeves, his face just as dark and angry as it had been when she walked in.

"Ready," he said a few minutes later. Janet nodded. An assistant hooked her onto the hoist that lifted her over the jalopy and into her pod. Soon they were alone in the launch bay as the engineers left, closing the airlock doors behind them. Her suit stiffened as the chamber was evacuated, then the launch doors opened beneath them. The ship's spin provided the initial velocity. All that was necessary was to orient the ship and time their release, work that didn't need their input. Although launching was routine, it was a team effort, with dozens of others making the trip as smooth and safe as possible.

Janet triggered a private communication line as soon as the vacuum was established.

"What's wrong with Alec?" she asked.

Margo answered. "I thought you'd never get back to me. I've got his med readouts. Elevated pulse and respiration. He's scared. Xenophobia."

Alec's shadow moved in his pod's translucent shell as he checked the instrumentation. Beneath them, the stars scrolled past. "What's our transit time?" he asked.

Janet flipped to his frequency. "Twenty minutes. They pulled us closer than I thought they would." She clicked back to Margo. "Scared? I thought he was mad. You should have seen his expression." Her finger rested on the manual releases as she watched the launch countdown. She'd press her button at the correct time as a backup to the computer. "If he's that bothered, should he be going? I can't have him making judgement errors."

"He's not *that* scared. Check your own readouts."

Above her head, among a plethora of information, were her numbers, all elevated.

The countdown reached zero, and Janet pressed the button, dropping the jalopy from the mining vessel. Her stomach did the familiar lurch from the 1G environment to weightlessness. She rotated her pod so she faced their target, almost invisible in the fathomless black. During the trip, she stayed busy directing the craft to the Gargoyle's surface. In the few jobless moments she had to contemplate their mission, she listened to space's sound, which wasn't silent at all. Her suit hummed and whirred. Air hissed in the helmet's close confines. Behind it, her pulse throbbed. From the unmarked distance, the Gargoyle appeared, grew large, and soon filled the sky.

To anchor, she chose a spot in the spike field on the angry face's side. Unlike the probe, it wasn't her intention to fire explosive bolts into the surface. Instead, she would allow the craft to settle onto the spikes. Up close, they didn't appear as regular as they had in the vids. Micrometeor strikes had scarred them. Some were broken or cracked. Others bore smaller blemishes, like bullet holes. The distant sun's light through the spike forest cast awkward, impenetrable shadows, hiding the base structures.

The jalopy glided a few meters over the spikes until the edge of the angry face appeared on the horizon. Janet slowed the exploration craft until the spikes beneath them matched their speed. They descended onto two blunt tips, and the ship canted to rest on the shattered end of a third.

"We're here," she said. Not a quote for the history books, she thought.

Alec let loose a long, relieved breath. "You wouldn't believe what I've been thinking."

Janet powered the jalopy down, unbuckled herself, hooked a safety line to her belt, and pushed herself from the pod. "Try me."

"It's so obviously artificial. I thought it would open fire. I'm a little jumpy."

"It's dead, Alec." Janet laughed to herself. Odd thoughts had crossed her mind too.

Alec hooked himself in and floated to a tool locker in the Gargoyle's minuscule gravity where he equipped himself with a specimen hammer and sample sacks. "I'll get pieces from these spike tops, then move down to the base."

Janet nodded, then remembered to say, "Yes," as she jetted toward the face's edge, twenty meters away. From this angle she could see it was a thin plate resting on the spikes. She braced herself between two stone spears to examine the material. A hand-width's in thickness, it didn't appear to be either stone or metal. More like black porcelain than anything else. She smacked the top with her hand, but the leverage was bad, and all she succeeded in doing was losing her grip. For a second she floated, unanchored, then she grabbed the edge again, this time to hoist herself to the surface. At this angle, she couldn't tell it was a face. Every few meters, a hole marked the smooth surface, and her light revealed the spikes below. She glanced back to see Alec stuffing something into a sample sack. He waved, then attached his safety rope to a different spot. His voice crackled in her radio. "Looks like typical nickle-iron to me, a dark deposit on top, lighter underneath."

"So they made it from an asteroid."

"Would appear so."

"Okay. I'm going to the forehead to check out the plaque."

Alec grunted, a preoccupied sound. He chipped a bit from one spot, played out the slender safety cable, then glided to the next.

The Gargoyle's gravity was negligible. If she dropped a hammer, it would take minutes to complete its fall, so she drove an anchor bolt into a spike, attached her original line to it so there was now a path from the jalopy to the face's edge. When she reached the plaque, she'd place another bolt. Some asteroids had so many safety lines running across them, they looked like they'd been netted.

A gentle push from her back unit slid her across the Gargoyle's face, past its twisted mouth filled with spiky teeth, past the deep gashes that were its nose, across an eye's smooth bulge, to a knee-high platform on the forehead's edge.

"I'm moving toward the surface," said Alec. His breathing sounded regular, his voice clipped. Janet guessed if she could take his pulse now, it would be normal, while her own heart pounded in her ears. This was an alien artifact, concrete proof there were other sentient beings in the universe. She twisted her hand control to emit gas in a tiny puff that slowed her.

It was a plaque, just as the probe's flyby had shown, packed with symbols, illustrations and hieroglyphics. The largest illustration dominated the plaque's middle: at the top, a diagram of the Gargoyle. Next, a cutaway view showing the asteroid's interior with an odd symbol at the center. She thought about the funny magnetic readings. Was it a storage chamber? Then, a larger circle around the Gargoyle without the cutaway view. A planet? An orbit? The last illustration showed the circle fragmented into broken lines and a series of intersecting lines where the Gargoyle had been. An explosion? She clicked pictures from several angles, then crouched to see how it was fastened onto the platform.

Her gaze was on the horizon.

A screech in her helmet.

Alec shot up from the asteroid's surface, maneuvering jets on full, pushing him away from the asteroid. The safety cable, which was anchored sixty meters from him, snapped taut, pulling him into a parabola. First up, then parallel to the surface, then just as quickly, straight down. He disappeared into the spike field. Too fast.

"Alec?" she transmitted. She'd already detached her safety line, pushed hard away from the plaque toward where he'd gone in, and without thinking, made the corrections that killed a spin she'd picked up. She slapped the emergency "come hither" button, sending an automatic call for help, while flipping through displays until she found his suit telemetry. Pulse, fine. Breathing, fine. Air pressure, fine. She took a few deep breaths of her own. Suit temperature, fine, but falling. Partial system failure.

Questions from the ship. Nothing they could do now. She shut communications down. Concentrated on maneuvering. If she overshot, she'd waste too much time slowing, reversing direction, accelerating, then slowing again. A man in an unheated suit in shadow would freeze. She tried to remember how much time he might have. Couldn't come up with it. Too long since the refresher course. Most suit accidents were instantly fatal.

It wasn't until she paused over the spikes where he'd vanished, that she wondered what had thrown him off the surface in the first place. She directed a light down. His lower torso was visible, feet up, the rest was caught between two spikes as thick as tree trunks. No movement.

He'd yelled, a frightened yip. And his jets had been on, so he hadn't been tossed up, he'd jumped and then blasted. What scared him?

His safety cable pulled at the suit's side, as tight as a piano wire. She unsnapped it carefully, keeping her hand and head clear as it whipped from sight. Working by her helmet light, she inspected the damage. Alec's momentum had jammed him into the space between two spikes. The cover to the power unit on his back was cracked and bent. Whatever was broken inside, she wouldn't be able to repair it from here. The quicker she could extricate him and get him back to the ship, the better. She pulled herself around so she could look into his faceplate. In the middle was a blood spot matching a welt on his forehead. His eyes were partially open, with white slivers showing. He didn't react to the light in his face or to shaking.

The asteroid's surface, where the spikes were anchored was a couple meters below them, but too far for her to push him. She tried bracing her feet on the spikes' steep sides, but there wasn't enough grip and her feet slipped on every effort. Her breathing sounded harsh in her ears. "Damn it, Alec." She rested for a second, her head down.

This deep in the spike forest, the sun didn't penetrate. For the first time, she looked around her. Black, heavy columns leaning every way, marked by shadows that barely showed on their charcoal-like surfaces.

She scanned part way around before she saw it.

A scream stuck in her throat. By reflex, her legs pushed. If she'd been touching, she too would have flown straight up, but she'd drifted just enough that she kicked against nothing.

It was an alien figure, face like the one on the surface, peering around a spike, angry as hell, arms raised, claws extended.

By the time she'd scrambled to the other side of the columns that held Alec, she realized it couldn't be alive, but it took a long minute for her to approach, heart thudding, mouth dry.

The alien was a statue made from the same material as the asteroid. Its skin was polished, details sharp, like finely worked obsidian, her height, heavy in the chest, a short, hairless tail. Beyond it, others crouched behind spikes; some charged, carved in attack. Their frightening forms filled the forest. Janet guessed there was more statuary on the reverse side, mirroring the fright of that face. Angry or frightened. Nothing in between. She took pictures by habit.

Putting the camera away, she pushed herself above the spikes, then jetted to the jalopy. If she could free Alec, she could plug his suit into the exploration craft's power system and get around the break in his own.

It took a few frantic minutes to unanchor and lift off. She tried to eyeball where he was, then realized she hadn't marked the spot. The spikes' tops all looked the same, uniform in their randomness. She started the jalopy forward in the general direction while she tracked down his suit's signal. Soon she was above him. With the jalopy anchored again, she fastened a cable to the sturdy frame, then dove down where he was still stuck and unmoving. Not looking at the statue reaching toward her took will power. Getting Alec off the asteroid was a solvable problem, immediate, without the ambiguity of the message the statues sent. Were they alien gods, represented in stone? Were they art? Were they important at all? It didn't matter now. She fastened the cable to Alec's suit, then measured several meters of slack. Using the jalopy to pull him out by a straight pull wouldn't work. The compressed air jets didn't generate enough thrust. She'd need to use the jalopy's weight and momentum to jerk him out. She played out more cable, cinched it, then headed up.

The jalopy moved away from the spikes. Janet watched her speed and orientation so she didn't drift. It had to be a vertical lift off or she risked pulling the unconscious man across the spikes instead of up. Acceleration was slow. Return trips always took longer than going out.

One meter, two, three, four. How much cable had she left? Five, six. A gentle jolt shook the jalopy. Slowly, Alec rose from the spikes. Janet hit the auto-routines to get them back to the mining ship, then reeled him in. Soon he sat in his pod, plugged into the jalopy's power. His suit temperature rose. She stayed beside him, directing her light at this faceplate, waiting for the frost inside his helmet to melt.

He coughed, a sudden sound in her radio. His eyes opened, then squeezed back shut.

"How do you feel?" she asked. Her hands shook a little. Post emergency shock, she thought. Margo would explain it to her later.

"I saw a monster," he said thickly. He closed his eyes, and lolled his head against the helmet's side.

*

Medics hustled Alec away from the dock, and Janet had just removed her suit when she was summoned to Lindsey London's office. Lindsey waited inside, a tissue in hand and wearing a pained expression. Behind her were two upper-management types she barely recognized. One, an older man whose hair had gone pure silver around his ears, mirrored Lindsey's discomfort, though Janet doubted a sinus infection caused his; the other, wearing a Strieberist button, smiled widely.

"Oh, you are so lucky," he said, "to be the first person to land on an alien artifact. Let me shake your hand." He squeezed hard, and for a second Janet thought he was going to hug her too. "Your life is in for a change. When the media gets a hold of this, you'll be the most famous person in the solar system."

"We can't jump to conclusions," said the older one. "It may not be alien."

Janet looked at him in disbelief.

Lindsey said, "I did a calculation based on meteor strike frequency on its surface. The Gargoyle's been in space at least three million years." She blew her nose. "Give or take a million."

"Even if it is . . . extraterrestrial, whoever left it certainly isn't around now," said silver hair. "This find shouldn't impact our basic mission. We'll leave it to scientists who are better equipped."

The Strieberist shook his head. "No, no, no. Don't you understand that this removes the need for our mission? The aliens left this for us to discover. It's their invitation to us. What else could it be? We should find out where the Gargoyle came from, and then bend our efforts to contacting them. It's mankind's most heroic quest yet."

"That's a *scientific* question. We are a *business* operation," said silver hair. "We have neither the expertise to investigate the artifact or the authority to abandon our mining efforts."

"What are you talking about? Investigating? I've never seen a more uninviting spot in my life." Janet looked from one to the other. "Did you see the pictures of the statues on the surface? Have you looked at the plaque?"

Silver hair cleared his throat. "There's some argument about what the plaque means. There appear to be several kinds of writing and diagrams. Our analysts compared it to the messages we attached to our deep space probes early in the space program."

"Which we included to introduce ourselves to other intelligences." The Strieberist sat on the edge of Lindsey's desk. "I agree with that analogy."

Lindsey called up the plaque on the wall monitor. "You saw it close, Janet. What were your impressions?"

"I didn't get to look at it long." She moved to where she could study it closer. The marks made no sense. She thought there would be little chance she could decipher the plaque's intent if it was written in Chinese, and that was a heck of a lot closer culturally to her than this communique. "The only thing I recognize is the diagram in the middle, with the Gargoyle, but I don't think we need the plaque to understand the big message, which is to stay away. I've never seen a clearer no-trespassing sign in my life."

The Strieberist bristled. "There is a message here, and it's a welcoming one to an *intelligent* race. The expressions might represent their smiles. Our evolution is obviously different. What makes you think we could recognize facial expressions in whatever they descended from? When we decipher the plaques, you'll see. There will be formulas for super-science. Maybe faster than light technology, or bio-break-throughs that will revolutionize human life. See there?" He pointed to the cutaway diagram of the Gargoyle. "They've buried something for us. Why else would they show the asteroid's interior unless they wanted us to get it?"

Janet thought about perceptual set. The Strieberist saw what he expected to see. "In New Mexico there's a radioactive waste dump in the salt deposits. When the government chose the site, they had two worries: one, how to keep the waste from leaking out, and two, how to keep people, generations down the road, maybe long after any record of what was buried there had been lost, from digging it up. The problem was any monument they left could be misinterpreted. It's like the pharaohs' tombs. They were all looted. You can't trust that anything left over great stretches of time won't eventually be disturbed."

She pointed to the diagram. "You know what I think that is? Something deadly. The circle around it in the next diagram is the sun. The last diagram shows the sun exploding. Maybe they had a war and made a sun killer that couldn't be destroyed. Maybe it's their toxic waste. The faces are angry and fearful. Maybe those emotions and expressions are universal. Run away and be afraid."

Lindsey nodded. "If there is something in the Gargoyle, we'd want to study it much longer before opening it up. I'm including a recommendation in my report to quarantine the site."

"That will be my suggestion too," said silver hair.

The Strieberist slapped the desk. "My people won't put up with this. We have a right to know what is inside this artifact."

Janet looked from Lindsey to the older man to the Strieberist. It was a political struggle, and they weren't going to listen to her now. Whatever happened, it might take years to resolve. She remembered the statues at the surface, how they scowled and grimaced, how their hands were poised to rend, and she shivered. If they believed her theory, there was no way they could ever know what was inside the asteroid. She thought about Pandora and Bluebeard's wives.

"I would like to go check on Alec," she said.

Lindsey nodded, then turned back to the argument. As Janet left they were shouting at each other.

Thick bandages wrapped Alec's hands, and a slimy ointment had been smeared on his ears and nose.

"It's frostbite," Alec said. "Another ten minutes, the doctor tells me, and I'd have been frozen to the core."

Janet pulled a chair next to him, not sure what to say.

"They showed me your pictures from the Gargoyle. It was a statue I saw, wasn't it?" His face reddened slightly.

"Anyone might have reacted the same way, Alec. I'm just glad I was there to get you back." She put her hand on his arm.

"You saved my life. That's a pretty big deal."

She shrugged. "It just makes us even."

He leaned back and closed his eyes. "What are they saying about it?"

"I think they're going to haggle for a while, and then somebody will open it up."

Alec shook his head. "If I put one of those statues in the conference room, it would change a few minds. We need to do something to stop them."

"Someday we can, but not today. Today you need to get better. There'll be a lot of arguing among folk with a bunch more pull than we have before anyone makes a decision." Janet was already imagining the report she would turn in. If the Streiberist was right, she and Alec were famous now, the first humans to land on an alien arti- fact. Their voices might be louder than they would be otherwise. She smiled. There was reason to hope.

A technician wheeled in a cart with a food tray. "Time to eat," he said. "We got you stuff from the cafeteria. No dietary restrictions for you, so dig in." He put the tray across Alec's lap before he left.

For a minute Alec looked at the meal, then at his wrapped hands. He laughed. "I can't hold anything. I don't suppose you could feed me?"

Janet reached across Alec to pick up the fork. On the tray was meatloaf, corn, a roll, and a piece of cheesecake.

He kept his eyes on hers through each bite, and he never tried to move the arm she held. His face fascinated her, how his mouth worked, how he swallowed. Once she wiped his chin and he nodded his thanks.

When she got to the dessert, she cut off a fork full and held it out for him.

He shook his head. "No. Too big," he said. "Cheesecake has to be eaten in small bites."

Janet smiled. Maybe she was seeing what she wanted to see. Maybe this was her perceptual set, but she didn't think so.

It was all she could do not to say, "You know what this means, don't you? We're not alone."

She trimmed the piece and fed it to him delicately.

THE STARS UNDERFOOT

I N THE MIDDLE OF THE NIGHT, DUSTIN EDGED AWAY FROM THE FROZEN SHORE, careful to keep his weight evenly on both feet. The quarter mile wide lake had only started freezing a week ago, and no one had made it more than a yard before the ice cracked. Yesterday Kenyon Parker had fallen in up to his knees, and while the gang laughed, he'd run for home, his lips blue with cold. But the temperature had been bitter all day, and once the sun set, the thermometer plunged below zero. I'll be the first across this year, Dustin thought. There's an advantage to being small. He shuffled forward, the ice so thin, he could almost feel it sag under his weight.

A deep breath froze the inside of his nostrils, and it tickled when he wrinkled his nose. So he did it again. I've already established the season's record. I've got to be twenty feet out, he thought. It was hard to tell by starlight what the distance was, so he flicked his flashlight on to check. Yep, twenty feet if it's an inch. Underneath him, trapped bubbles slid away like little jellyfish. The ice was remarkably clear. Dustin crouched, pressed the light against the ice, and played it across the bottom, across silt covered sticks and muddy boulders, much deeper than he was tall. He turned the light off. If anyone in the houses surrounding the park saw him, they would call the police for sure. Last year, *days* after Mike Liddle had made the first crossing, Dustin had been walking alone across the lake, and a lady stuck her head out her back door to yell, "Get off the lake, young man. It's not frozen." Dustin looked down at his feet, at the milky smooth expanse as solid as a marble floor. "Call the Pope, then," he'd called back. "It's a miracle," which he'd thought was a pretty clever thing for a twelve-year-old to come up with.

Of course, Mike Liddle had been a hero all winter last year, and Kenyon Parker was one for falling in this year, but no one had ever attempted a night crossing to open the season. No one had ever done it alone. Dustin checked under his coat where the camera was protected from the cold. When he reached the middle, he'd take a picture. Ten bucks at the one-hour developing place, and his name would be carved into neighborhood history.

A splash at the lake's far end. Then, quacking, as if the ducks were right beside him. House lights reflected off the unfrozen part of the lake where they swam, looking like little puppet figures, most with their heads down. Overhead, stars glittered with icy twinkles so sharp that Dustin thought he could surely touch them. He shuffled forward, wary of the slickness, farther from shore, closer to the lake's middle. Another quick check through the ice. His flashlight penetrated deeply, but couldn't reach the bottom now. Green particles drifted through the beam. He wiped the light with his sleeve, standing still, listening to the night sounds. A half hour earlier he'd removed the screen in his bedroom window, lowered himself out, and hiked the mile to the park, crunching through ice-encrusted leaves strewn on pale sidewalks. He'd never walked through the town at night, and now, in the midst of the lake's smooth emptiness, the sounds were amplified: cars shifting gears on streets blocks away, a dog barking, distant laughter from a party. And lights seemed more intense too. Not just the stars, but windows in the homes whose backyards faced the lake. Some glowed in a flickery blue that said a television was on. Rich yellow light poured from others. The air smelled of woodsmoke. Dustin exhaled carefully because he didn't want to disturb the symphony with his own sounds. His glasses fogged from his breathing, so he turned a little into the breeze, and they cleared. The night had never seemed so pure and clean. If he'd known it would be like this, he would have snuck out every night, and he told himself that in the future he would. I'm a superhero, he thought. I'm outside of space and time. I move where no one sees or hears me, while I see and hear all. He chuckled, and it sounded loud in the brittle cold.

A series of snaps, like tiny firecrackers, radiated away from his feet on the next step. He stopped, hands held from his sides as if he were balancing, and his heart raced. I'm in danger! No one knows I'm out here! He shuffled a few feet further, away from the weak area, then stood as motionless as a statue, his hands still out. The ice glittered. It was the stars, perfectly reflected. He stood on a starry table spread beneath him, and he thought about astronauts and space walks. Even the quality of air tasted different, more animated, more primordial. He felt like an explorer, in the center of his own town; he'd discovered a new wilderness. "Trailblazer," he said. "Dustin Boone," the crackling ice already forgotten.

Being small bothered him. He'd never been a hero in anything. Even his friends picked him last when they chose sides, like he was the little brother they had to play with. And the teachers only tolerated him at school, where he earned "C's," because his mom and dad would ground him if he had a "D." He read too much and paid attention too little. He'd stare out the window, cheek resting on his hand, where the mountains rose cool and blue on the horizon, and he imagined undiscovered countries. He watched late-night science fiction and horror movies on Friday and

Saturday, when his parents let him. Never the hero. Always the dreamer, the reader, the observer.

A breeze scurried across the surface, kicking the dusting of snow into glowing spirals. Dustin's eyes watered, so he blinked them clear. For a second, he thought a beam of light had flashed up through the ice just in front of him. He blinked again. Nothing other than the little crystal whirlwinds dancing across the lake. He swayed. The stars beneath and above, the wind that switched from front to back, the sense that he wasn't standing on anything substantial dizzied him. For a second, he was afraid he might fall. Surely that would send him through the ice. He remembered rocks they'd thrown into the lake yesterday, orange-sized stones lobbed high that vanished with ragged claps, leaving uneven holes where the water boiled for a second, then was still. The light appeared again, twenty feet away, a distinct glow below the surface.

He moved toward it, careful to keep his feet always against the ice, his body awash with goosebumps. How could there be a light *under* the water? He looked up. Maybe it was a reflection, a plane, a planet, but only the hard-edged stars filled his vision. Maybe it was a ghost, and that nearly stopped him, but maybe it wasn't. He continued on, eyes so wide that he thought they might freeze that way.

The light changed in intensity, dimming, almost disappearing, then growing strong again. It was a beam now, cutting through the water beneath Dustin, so that for a second he saw the floating algae he'd seen early, suspended green specs, then the light pointed away from him. Dustin could see the source, a bright spot three or four feet deep. He held his breath. Could it be a new kind of fish, something that only came out in early winter, never observed before?

Dustin was an imaginative boy. He played by himself in the yard for hours, building kingdoms, then tearing them down. He wrote stories in the back of notebooks, not showing them to anyone. His full life was mostly a secret from his acquaintances. He'd read at family parties, not so much to escape the meaningless chit chat, although that was an advantage, but because he yearned to visit secret worlds. In the books, he saved the day. He solved the problem. He turned the tide. He was not an ordinary boy, because an ordinary boy would not be out on a barely frozen lake in the stars; an ordinary boy would not hope that a picture taken in the middle of the night would make him a hero to his friends.

So he was not ordinary, because an ordinary boy would have run away from the light instead of sliding ever closer, and an ordinary boy would have surely screamed when he saw the light was a flashlight, and holding the flashlight was a hand, and that the hand was attached to an arm wearing a coat somewhat like Dustin's own, and the boy that was wearing the coat stood on the ice just as Dustin did, but upside down, like a bat, walking under the water, pointing his light ahead of him, moving his feet carefully, as if he too might slip and fall.

"Hey!" yelled Dustin. His voice echoed from the nearby houses, and the ducks fluttered in response, swimming to their pool's far side. "How can you do that?"

The boy under the ice paused, then swung his light to and fro, as if he'd heard, but didn't know where the question had come from.

Dustin crouched to see better. The soles of the boy's shoes were under Dustin's mittens. Dustin realized the boy didn't look wet. His coat wasn't water sodden, and his hair, from what he could see by the boy's light, was neatly combed. He had a pleasant face, maybe only a year or so older than Dustin, and he wore glasses, but he looked puzzled as he turned slowly, shining his flashlight all around him.

"I'm here," yelled Dustin.

The boy turned his flashlight down. Suddenly Dustin couldn't see. The light blinded him. He threw himself away, slipping on the ice, and there was a sudden cracking. Dustin kept moving, trying to see what was happening. His hands were wet! The ice was broken. He lay flat, spreading his weight, trying to see past the great, black circle that was the flashlight's afterimage.

Something splashed, more ice cracking and a vague scream. No, not vague, muted, like a scream with the volume turned down, a distant sounding "Help! Help!" only ten feet away.

Dustin turned on his flashlight. The boy's legs stuck through the ice and kicked wildly into the air. A movement above him caught Dustin's eye, and he flicked his light toward it. At first, he couldn't tell what it was, then he recognized the boy's flashlight rising from the lake, sinking into the stars. When it turned, its beam glowed dully, then winked out.

Then the ice broke more, and the boy lurched farther into view, his elbows visible now, thrashing at the ice. Dustin glimpsed his face, pulled from the water, and it was frightened, cheeks bulging in a held breath. The boy kicked himself down and tried to pull himself under the surface, but the ice kept breaking. The face appeared. He choked, then lunged down again.

Dustin thought about moving farther away, to keep the cracked ice as far from him as possible. He could retreat to the shore. Whatever was happening here was beyond his ability to understand or explain. Who would believe it? But he didn't move. He watched, his hands bunched into fists so tight he could feel his fingernails digging in, even through the mittens. "Get back!" he yelled. "Get back!" and he didn't mean "get away," but "get back to where you are safe."

The boy floated up, until only his hands remained in the water, flailing. Dustin imagined in a moment, the boy's struggles would weaken. He'd go limp and slowly follow his flashlight into the sky.

Knowing that it was stupid, thinking that the boy drowning in air was probably a hallucination, Dustin left his light on the ice pointed toward the boy and pushed his way forward.

Wet ice. Broken ice. He broke through the ice five feet away. Water. Water like liquid fire, soaking through his pants, weighing down his coat, pulling him deep. Dustin kicked himself forward, so shocked by the water's temperature he couldn't inhale. He kicked himself forward, then grabbed the other boy's wrist that was now a foot above the lake. Dustin pulled hard. The boy moved toward the water, while Dustin's sinking stopped. He pulled again. The boy's face was against his own. They'd both lost their glasses, but by the flashlight's pure light, he saw the boy's eyes, an inch from his own, and they were pleading. Now the boy's head was underwater, while Dustin was clear of the lake to his armpits. He climbed the boy like he would climb a float toy, pulling himself up while pushing the boy down, and the boy helped, thrusting himself deeper. He grabbed Dustin's leg, pinching the skin through his winter pants.

But they weren't stable. Dustin felt the roll begin, and his head was underwater, a thousand cold needles piercing his scalp and peeling back the skin. A scramble to get back on top, desperate to be *above* the water. Knees collided. Hands grabbed coats, tugged, struggled, until there was an equilibrium again, Dustin's head high.

For a moment, he didn't think about saving the boy. Anything to get out of the strangling cold. He'd taken two choking gulps in a row. Coughing ripped his throat, and already his arms felt leaden, his hands like wood. His face burned. He climbed the upside down boy. A promised land of unbroken ice beckoned in front of the flashlight. Dustin reached toward it, careful of their balance, gathered in water and pushed it behind them. They moved a couple of inches. The boy's legs shook under Dustin's hand, but he reached into the lake too, his hand appearing out of the water, mimicking Dustin's movement, and they moved again. Working together, they paddled toward the unbroken ice.

Even Dustin's brain felt cold and sluggish, his thoughts disconnected. Why can't I keep climbing, he thought, until I'm standing on the bottom of his feet and he's standing on the bottoms of mine? We could *walk* out of danger if we always stepped where the other stepped, and the vision seemed so dreamy, for a minute he thought they were already doing it, which frightened him more than anything that had occurred so far because his hand had stopped paddling. He was just holding on, shivering so hard that it was if his muscles had locked up. He forced himself to paddle again. Every inch in the core of him hurt, but he couldn't feel his arms or feet now at all. He had to watch to be sure they were still moving.

The unbroken edge moved closer. The flashlight was only ten feet away. He touched the solid surface, slid his hand across it. Nothing to hold onto, and they almost tipped again. He reached, a little farther this time. For an instant, his wet mitten stuck to the ice, pulling the edge against their hips, but the mitten broke loose. The boy's boot shifted under Dustin's armpit. How could they get back onto the ice without shattering it? Dustin shut his eyes tight, his head so cold that his thoughts flowed like thick jelly. He could push away from the boy and fall flat. If the ice held, he'd be safe, but the boy would be in the middle again. Dustin looked down. The boy held his legs in nearly the same manner. It could work if they leaned at the same time. They'd fall to their sides of the ice, their legs still in the water, but maybe they could scoot to safety. Dustin put his hand flat on the surface. The flashlight beam shone directly on it. If the boy looked, he would see it, a mittened silhouette through the ice. Would he understand?

Breathing hurt. Razor-like crystals seemed to cut into his lungs, his throat. The boy moved—the balance shifted—and through the ice, Dustin saw him reach. Their hands faced palm to palm, only an inch apart. Dustin let go of the boy's leg and twisted as he fell, so that he landed on his stomach. A loud snap. Somewhere, the ice cracked, but it held beneath him. He pulled a knee out of the water, slid forward a few inches. Got the other knee out. Slid. He was clear of the hole, five feet from the flashlight. The boy on the other side pushed forward too.

The light revealed him. Blue eyes to Dustin's brown. Frightened. Hurting, but alive, inhaling. Dustin pushed himself to his hands and knees. If I don't move, I'll freeze to death he thought. He staggered to his feet. Shuffled to the shore, two hundred yards farther, his coat and pants weighing him down, then lumbered toward home as if Jupiter's gravity was holding him down, water turning to ice in his hair.

What seemed like hours later, he stood in his shower, still in his clothes, his skin tingling in the heat, his un-numbing fingers and toes screaming. Every muscle complaining, he peeled away the coat, dropped the ruined camera to the tile.

I was a hero tonight, he thought as he sat among his lake-soaked clothes, the shower water pounding down, the steam filling the bathroom.

He thought, being a hero isn't about what happened; it's about what didn't. I was a hero tonight, and he was too tired even to cry.

That happened much later that night, and many nights after, when he woke from a dream, where the boy on the other side was dead, his eyes creamy pale and wide, only an inch away beyond the ice, and the boy was him.

THE YARD GOD

A WEEK AFTER HER TWENTY-SECOND BIRTHDAY, DEMI SAT EXACTLY IN THE middle of the yard between the oak tree carpenter ants and the elm tree blacks, trying to make peace. The war had raged since May's first warm days thawed the soil, and just like last summer centered on the area beneath the sycamore, where the tent caterpillars dropped to the ground and made easy prey. The afternoon sun cast long shadows so her silhouette reached nearly to the chain link fence between her and the street. She pulled at her skirt again to cover her knees. If Mom looked out the kitchen window and saw her sitting cross-legged on the lawn, she'd be sure to yell at her. Not that it was likely Mom would look out. Since January she'd spent more and more time on the couch, surrounded with hot water bottles and warming blankets and medicines.

Even with the ants warring, Demi was happy. One time, when Mom was in a good mood, she'd held Demi on her lap and said, "Life is full of happy-sads. You're my happy-sad." But Demi didn't understand what she meant. You're either one or the other, Demi had thought.

Demi closed her eyes to feel the ants' minuscule lives better. It took a lot of relaxed concentration. She sensed them like tiny red spots in the hundred yard radius of her awareness, the nest to her left, a loosely tangled ball of thread burrowing into the oak's dead roots, filled with scurrying ants, and the other nests under the elm, reaching nearly a yard deep, with passages more complicated than any human building, even more confusing than the community college's hallways where Demi attended remedial night classes for adults. She was taking Introduction to Reading for the third time.

In the lawn between the two colonies, ant trails wended their ways between the blades. She watched the ants moving to and fro, some foraging, some carrying food, and some battling over a tent caterpillar that wasn't quite dead yet. Demi bit her lip. There was plenty of food for both populations. No need for them to kill each other. But another one died, and then another, their tiny lights winking out in her mind. The only place they didn't fight was at the gift rock on the garden's edge where trails from both tribes intersected. Here they piled seeds, wisps of grass, and once, by Herculean effort, a shiny dime. Demi collected the tiny offerings every day and broadcast her thanks.

She sent soothing signals to them, directed them toward dead beetles, spilled garbage in the alley. "There's feasts awaiting!" she broadcasted, and some turned aside from the combat, but others ignored her. Demi sighed. She put her hands behind her and arched back to let the setting sun bake her face. When she sat very still and quieted her mind, she sensed the entire yard, all the vibrant lives scurrying, burrowing, flying, lying in wait around her, from the sluggish pink haze of earthworms like fat yarn in the dirt, to her favorite, the bright yellow nimbus that was the barn owl in the oak.

Behind closed eyes, she saw Ethan's bilious green aura long before he spoke. As he entered her field of vision, she ordered the wasps off who'd been resting on her shoulders. He moved slowly along the fence and stopped. Maybe he was looking the other way, she hoped, but she straightened anyway, wrapped her arms around her chest and tried to stay small. If I don't make a noise, maybe he won't know I'm here, she thought, but she could feel him staring at her. Had her skirt moved above her knee again?

The miniature life lights winked out, leaving the red-tinted blackness of light through her closed eyelids.

"Hey, little darling. What 'cha doing, sitting in the sunshine like a flower?" His voice reminded her of the squishy sound in the kitchen drain.

She opened her eyes. His arms draped over the fence. He was all smiles and oily hair. Wide-set swampy-brown eyes. Untrimmed, ragged fingernails with burger grease under them. They'd been in school together until the third grade when they started holding her back. Now he lived by himself in what had been his parents' house, two doors down. Twice in the last month she'd caught him peeping in her window. Stiffly, she stood, turned away and marched toward the house.

"Don't go, Demi," he whined. She centered her gaze on the back door's peeled paint, tried not to hear him, but it was like he'd put his mouth to her ear. "Just 'cuz you're retarded don't mean we can't have a special time. I'd be better company than your dead-end mom."

The door slammed behind her. Faintly she heard his last shot, "You won't be twenty-two forever!"

She checked the stove while trying to figure out what Ethan meant. Nothing there. She took a package of dried noodles from the cabinet, poured water into a pot and set it on the stove.

Her mom coughed in the next room. "Demi! Where've you been? I've needed to pee for a half hour."

"Coming," Demi said. The dark living room smelled of old blankets and too much breathing. Mom sucked on a lozenge, her thin lips pursed, the skin on her face stretched so thin that she almost seemed like a skull already. Demi pulled the covering from Mom's thin legs, then put an arm behind her to lift her up.

"Be gentle," Mom gasped.

"Sorry." Demi lifted her, a feathery weight with no substance. Demi remembered a moment from years ago when Mom towered over her, her hand open and coming down. The hard slap. "You're stupid!" Mom had shouted. Demi couldn't recall what Mom had been so mad about. Maybe Demi had spilled the sugar or not picked up her toys. In those days, Mom had been a bulky, ominous presence in Demi's world. "I'll try to be better," Demi had said. Mom hit her again. Later that time, or maybe some other—they got mixed up in Demi's mind—she had sat in the middle of her bed trying to figure out how to make Mom happy. "I'm a bad baby," Demi had thought, and she wept, thinking about how much she loved her mom.

Even then she sensed the other lives: the carpet mites, a family of mice behind the walls, spiders, termites, centipedes, rolly-pollies, cockroaches, bees, all in or around the house, and they were a great comfort. To entertain herself, she made two flies weave an intricate flight before her, cavorting in loops and dives and pretty patterns until they were too tired to stay aloft and they settled on the floor.

Demi helped Mom untie her pajama bottoms and supported her until she sat on the toilet. "Oh, baby, it hurts," moaned Mom.

After Demi carried her back to the couch, Mom said, her voice querulous again, "When's dinner? I think I might be able to eat something today."

"Good, Mommy. Doctor Davis said you needed food to get better."

Mom smiled wanly. "Some beef noodles, maybe."

When Demi got back to the kitchen, she stopped in front of the stove and stood numbly for a few minutes, not thinking, just staring into a middle distance somewhere beyond the kitchen but short of eternity.

A synapse snapped to life in her brain, and she looked around her as if she'd never seen the room before. "What are you doing, you dumb cluck?" she asked herself.

"Dinner, Demi," came Mom's voice from the living room.

"Ah." Demi looked at the water in the pot for a while, then dipped her finger in. Cold. Shaking her head, she turned the stove on, then carefully set the timer for ten minutes.

Outside, Ethan had gone. Demi settled back into her favorite spot. The sun dipped behind the tenement across the street, but light bathed rooftops. The ant war had ended. In the corner under the eaves, a garden spider glowed in her mind like a tiny sun. It must have just fed. With her eyes closed, Demi in her backyard was no different than an astronaut floating in space, the piercing light of a thousand lives beating from every direction. Lines of ants walked the long paths in the grass, heading toward the gift rock. Wasps orbited her. She could even feel the somnolent owl gazing down on her sleepily. In the yard, she felt loved.

Her awareness deepened, penetrated the grass, felt the dandelions' vegetable glow. Even soil fungus wafted a faint light. Something wasn't right. She probed around her. Some part out of place or misfocused. After a while, she found it. The owl was hurt, its wing nearly broken. How did it get back to its high perch? Demi could feel the damaged muscles and the owl's hunger. Had it been like this for a long time without her noticing? She concentrated mightily, gathered a little light from all the lights, sending it toward the owl. Gradually, the hurt mended, while every insect and animal and plant within her globe of awareness was slightly reduced.

She smiled. The owl thanked her in its mute manner. The other lives thanked her for their sacrifice. Demi gave and she took away. She showered them with her affection, and they received it with insect joy.

The stove timer buzzed too soon, and Demi went in to finish making dinner.

"I can't eat this." Mom dipped a spoon into the bowl, stirred it around until a coughing fit took her. When it ended, she said, "My stomach hurts."

Demi sat with her hands in her lap. "Maybe if I blow on it for you? That always makes it better."

Mom closed her eyes and grimaced. "It's not hot, dammit. The smell's making me pukey again. I need my medicine. Come here, girl." Mom waved her hand toward her.

Demi thought, Mom's clothes are getting so big! The blouse's cuff gaped like a cave, while Mom's wrist looked like a pale branch sticking out.

Mom said, "I'm going to pin the prescription to your shirt. Here's the money. You'll have to wait for the pharmacist. It's just two blocks. You can do that, can't you?" Mom exhaled minty lozenge breath, but underneath some other smell lurked, slate-hard and relentless, like the vegetable drawer long after old cabbage had gone blue and liquid.

"A cup of ice first," said Mom. "My throat gets so dry."

After filling a glass with ice cubes, and leaving it on the table by Mom's couch, Demi put her jacket on. A streetlight flickered as she went out the front door, illuminating a pickup truck on cinder blocks and a trash pile that hadn't been collected. A mongrel dog worried something from the pile and hurried down the street with it between its teeth. Demi pulled the jacket close around her neck. She didn't like the neighborhood at night. Boys hung out on the corners or porch steps and called her names, but Mom needed her medicine. How else would she get better? Demi steeled herself. Her mother depended on her. I'm a good daughter, thought Demi.

At the pharmacy, the clerk gave her change for a ten, although Demi was sure she'd paid with a twenty. Outside the store, Demi counted the money twice. A car rolled by, blank faces ignoring her on the other side of the windshield. If she came back with the wrong money, Mom would be mad, and that would only make her worse.

She went back in.

"I made the right change, dunderhead," said the clerk. He leaned against the register, his thumb hooked into an apron string. Overhead, the bare flourescents buzzed.

Tears swam behind Demi's eyes. "Mommy gave me twenty dollars, mister. We need that money. Mommy's sick."

"Shit. Everyone has a story." The clerk shooed her away with one hand. "That was a ten spot. Take a hike."

A large black woman came from behind an aisle, a clipboard in her hand. The clerk didn't see her. He sneered, an ugly expression that pressed his eyebrows together and made her think of Ethan. "You got a problem, take it up with management."

The black woman stepped forward, reached past the clerk, startling him, and opened the register. She looked into it for a second. "You don't have a ten in there, Gerald. Give the lady the rest of her money."

The clerk stuttered momentarily. "You going to take this rum-dumb's word over mine?"

The woman snorted impatiently, then counted out two five dollar bills. "I don't have to, Gerald. You don't have a ten in the drawer. But if I did, I probably would. Why don't you clean out your locker? I'll cut you a check tomorrow."

Demi felt a flood of relief as she stuffed the bills into her pocket.

The woman smiled at her, pulling her face into a friendly map of creases and dimples. She said, "I just bought this store, darlin'. Got one of those investment zone loans. Too bad they couldn't loan us some good help. I'm Marjorie." She put out her hand.

Demi shook it gratefully. "Demi's my name. I've always lived here. My mommy's sick. I've got to take her the medicine."

She rushed from the store without waiting for an answer. What a nice lady, she thought, and for the first time in weeks the neighborhood looked good to her, the moths circling streetlights, the parked cars like indolent hippos taking naps beside the sidewalk. She whistled part of "Pop Goes the Weasel" as she walked, not paying attention.

Ethan caught her as she passed an alley. No warning. One second she was whistling, and the next, he had his arm over her shoulder, squeezing her to him.

"What's a firefly like you doing out on a dark night like this, Demi?" he said. She could smell beer on his breath, and he reeked of cigarette smoke.

Her skin went scaly cold, and she tried to shrug him off. "Stop, Ethan. I don't like it."

He dug his fingers into her upper arm and kept her close. They were a long way between street lights. No cars. No pedestrians. Every porch was empty. He steered them into the alley. "Don't you get lonely, Demi, day after day hanging out with your mother? I've seen you, you know, sitting at your dresser just starin' into space. Don't you get lonely?"

"Let me go, Ethan. Mommy's waiting." But he held tight and moved her into the deep shadows between the houses. Her legs moved mechanically; her arms seemed incapable of motion. Then, he was pushing her down onto an old mattress that smelled of mildew and dog fur.

"Give a kiss, won't you, sunshine." He pressed his lips to her neck.

Demi turned herself inward. It was like she was at the doctor's office for her yearly visit. "Feet in the stirrups," Doctor Davis would say, and she went away in her mind, far away from the cold instruments, the uncomfortable pinches. She'd listen to the office music, look at the ceiling tiles, imagining she was a cloud floating over plowed fields in winter, everything covered in white, lined into squares. Where are the farmers in winter? Isn't it peaceful, drifting along, disconnected?

Vaguely she felt buttons being undone. Ethan said something incoherent. He pinned her hands above her head, digging her knuckles into a brick wall. She heard crickets. Watched a high haze rush across the band of stars visible between the roofs. It was like the doctor's office, but she was frightened, so frightened that the balloon that was herself shrank up, became a peanut deep, deep inside her, and it was crying.

Ethan's voice from far away said, "We'll have to do this again, buttercup."

It took a long time for the tiny, tiny Demi, who'd fled inside herself, to come back outside to look. At first she was only aware of the smelly mattress. A button dug into her back. She rolled, reached to feel the spot, and was puzzled to find her skin was bare. Her shirt was hiked up around her armpits. Slowly, she pushed it down, then tried to sit. She moaned. Her muscles ached; her crotch burned, and when she felt down there, her fingers came away wet. "And me without a plug, you dumb cluck. What would Mommy think?" she said.

Mommy's alone! she thought, but even with that thought to rush her, it took several minutes to adjust her clothes. A muscle strain in her neck sent searing sparks whenever she tried to look to her left. She limped from the alley and headed home.

When the door clicked shut, Mom sat under the reading light on the couch, blanket-covered and shapeless, her eyes hollow and dark. She opened her mouth to speak, but nothing came out. After a painful swallow, she croaked. "I could have died twice in the time you've been gone. Where's my medicine?"

Demi's hand flew to her mouth. "I had it."

Mom turned her face to the wall, sighed in disappointment, then breathed shallowly without speaking.

She should yell at me, thought Demi. I've been bad. I lost the medicine, but it's not my fault! Not my fault!

Demi shuffled down the street, head down, her eyes scanning the sidewalk and gutter. The prescription came in a white sack with the pharmacy slip stapled to it. She hoped the streetlights would be bright enough to find it. How could I drop it? It must be in the alley. But the closer she got, the slower she went. What if Ethan was there again? Behind the houses and dumpsters and busted-down garages of the alley, impenetrable shadows could hide a dozen Ethans. She stood on the sidewalk, facing the tunnel of graveled darkness and broken glass, closed her eyes, and forced herself to relax. Gradually a sphere of lights brightened around her. It was as if she was coming from an arc-lit room to a dim cave. Her eyes adjusted, and the world that emerged was beautiful, all soft, fuzzy, living lamps that as soon as she saw them, they saw her. A slinky, purple cat wove around a trashcan. Two aqua-colored rats peered at her from beneath a stack of broken pallets. Sleeping flies, creeping millipedes, huge water roaches waving silver antennae in her direction, but no Ethan.

She found the package by the mattress, the paper torn, the plastic bottle smashed, and all the pills crushed to powder.

There was nothing she could do. The pharmacy would be closed by now. She was a bad daughter, and it wasn't her fault. That's all she could think. Not my fault . . . not my fault. She thought about Ethan holding her, stopping her from going home with her delivery. The cat fled. Insects froze as she strode by.

Demi walked toward home, fists clenched, eyes closed, navigating by mental vision until she passed Ethan's house. She stopped by his mailbox. Her globe of awareness encompassed the house. Cockroaches swarmed in his unclean kitchen; termites gnawed at the floor joists, and in his bedroom, she sensed the long, sickeningly green light of Ethan himself, lying in bed. She hated him. "We'll have to do this again," he'd said. He'd destroyed Mommy's medicine. She rubbed her hand against her neck where he'd kissed her. Won't someone protect me from him? she thought. He's a bad man. He needs punishment, and those thoughts ran over and over until a kind of calm came to her. She relaxed. Her vision had never seemed this clear. All the house's lives stood out as brilliant beacons. She sorted through them until she found what she wanted: in the attic, five black widows; in Ethan's box springs, a brown recluse. He's bad. He made me unhappy. Ethan has hurt me, she broadcast.

Demi had no plan. She didn't think that far ahead, but she knew what she felt at the moment she felt it. When the sun was high in her yard, and the lives surrounded her with love, and seeds covered the gift rock, she felt love. When Mommy scolded her or turned away or sighed her deep sigh, Demi felt despair. When she looked at Ethan, she felt simple hate. That's all. No plan. But she knew what was going on as the spiders began to move, climbing from their attic webs, crawling out from the bed springs. The deadliest bite, the brown recluse, he didn't react to, most people don't. It continued to bite Ethan while Demi watched until he rolled in his sleep, crushing it. Forty minutes later, though, when the black widows reached him, he did scream, and his screaming followed her down the street as she walked to her own house. It wasn't until she shut the front door that she heard him no more, but by that time she wasn't thinking about Ethan. He'd slipped from the plate of her awareness. It wasn't until she was inside that she remembered she still didn't have Mommy's medicine.

"Mommy?" she said to the dark room. In the kitchen, the clock ticked. The refrigerator kicked on with a noisy rumble. "Mommy?"

Demi rubbed her hand along the wall until she found the light switch. Mom lay on the couch, propped by her pillows, head to one side, mouth open.

"Mommy?"

Demi's mother didn't move. Her hand dangled below the blanket's edge. Two small pieces of melted ice floated in the cup behind her head.

Her fingers to her cheek, Demi crossed the room slowly to kneel by Mom. She took Mommy's wrist and held it like she'd seen doctors on television, but she didn't know what to feel for.

Demi sat on the floor, her back to the couch, holding Mommy's hand. She'd never looked at the room from Mom's point of view before. This low, Demi couldn't see what was on the kitchen table top. She couldn't see the clock on the table by the door, but she could see her baby pictures. Mom had put them on the wall below the front window's curtain. Demi cocked her head to the side. Three pictures hanging from the wall at knee level: Mommy cradling Demi in a yellow-checked comforter. Demi sitting in a sandbox, holding a blue bucket. Demi on a swing, clinging to a chain with one hand while trying to get a sucker into her mouth with the other.

She closed her eyes. Mommy loved her after all. Gradually, Demi opened her mind to her other world, the household zoo, the backyard jungle, teeming with life, flowing in multicolor dots, and she realized her mother still glowed, dimly, a pulsing watery blue not much brighter than a fungus or a cloud of gnats, but she still lived.

The owl had been hurt, and Demi made her better. It had never occurred to her to try to help Mom this way. The yard world and Mommy's world were separate. The animals and insects loved her; they brought offerings to gift rock. Mommy . . . well, Mommy was strong. Mommy loomed in Demi's memory like a moving mountain, all loud voice and raised hand.

Demi concentrated on Mommy's color, willing it to grow. She gathered all the light she could, reaching beneath the soil to worms, taking from crickets, stealing from the ants. Frantic, the mice in the wall fled to the far corners of the house, but kneeling by her mother, Demi found them and emptied them. Their lights winked out. The ant colonies died, destroyed more thoroughly than the greatest ant war could have ever destroyed them. Wasps settled in their nests, never to fly again. Spiders dropped from their own webs. A bat, flitting through Demi's inescapable grasp fluttered once, then dropped to the yard, its light extinguished.

Inside Demi's head, the wire of her talent heated white hot, twisted under the strain. She'd never done anything like this before. Directing flies to dance, healing the owl, hating Ethan were like baby steps.

Still, Demi reached for more. Mommy's light wasn't turned up enough. Demi opened every living faucet she could reach, grass, flowers, trees, moss, algae, and the life flowed toward her mother until in Demi's mind, all was black except for Mom, who blazed like a blue ocean.

At the end, the wire snapped in Demi's head. She gasped, for Mom's light disappeared. Demi opened her eyes to be sure Mom was still there.

Mom twitched. She closed her mouth. Demi squeezed her hand, and Mom squeezed back.

"Mommy?" said Demi, feeling the pressure of Mom's thin fingers against her palm, watching her eyelids flutter.

"Is it breakfast?" said Mom. "I'm ready to eat something. Maybe an egg."

Demi bit her lower lip. She rested her forehead against Mom's arm. "Oh, yes, Mommy. I can make some eggs."

Mom pulled a lungful of air in and let it out, as if she'd never breathed before. "Good." Mom let go of Demi's hand, opened her eyes and looked at her daughter. "For Christ's sake, Demi, your clothes are a mess. If you've been outside like that, I'll die from embarrassment. Can't you at least take care of yourself?"

Demi's cheeks flushed. "Yes, Mommy. I'm sorry."

"And don't burn down the kitchen either."

Demi fled to the stove, made the eggs and fed her mother, who ate with enthusiasm.

When Mom leaned back to rest, Demi slipped into the backyard. The morning sun had just crested over the neighbors' rooftops. She went to her favorite spot, where grass crackled under her hands as she sat.

Demi sighed with exhaustion. Her back hurt, and raising her hand to rub her sore neck sent a medley of sharp pains along her side. Gradually the sun revealed more and more of the yard, and Demi realized the grass was brown-tinged and there wasn't a nearby sound. No crickets or grasshoppers or buzzing wasps. The air throughout the yard was cool and quiet. A handful of leaves dropped out of the elm, skittering onto a layer of fallen leaves that were already there. Leaves coated the ground beneath the sycamore and oak too. On the gift rock, a few ants lay curled between the seeds.

Mom's voice came from the kitchen. "Dammit, Demi. You left the stove on!"

Demi looked beyond the ants. Dead grass, dead flowers, dead bushes and dead trees. She closed her eyes and relaxed into her private seeing place. Nothing appeared. It was like probing the gap left by a pulled tooth. She knew something had been there once, but it was gone now, as dead as her yard.

A shadow flicked across her face. She looked up. The owl circled the dead oak, crossing the sun again, its huge wingspan blocking the light for an eyeblink. When it settled on a branch, a dozen leaves rained down. The owl folded its wings to its side and looked at her, locking gazes. Demi felt she could walk up to the owl and touch it. It would let her. There was no hate in the scrutiny, no condemnation. It bobbed its head, dropped off the branch in a long swoop directly toward her. A wingtip brushed her forehead as it passed, and then it was gone. The caress was a gentle one, not a hello or goodbye, but an acknowledgment. Even if she could never see them the way she had before, the ants would return. The grass would renew, and in her backyard, saplings would grow.

Mommy's alive, Demi thought, and she couldn't understand why she was crying.

THE LAST OF THE O-FORMS

BEYOND THE BIG RIG'S OPEN WINDOW, THE MISSISSIPPI RIVER LANDS rolled darkly by. Boggy areas caught the moon low on the horizon like a silver coin, flickering through black-treed hummocks, or strained by split rail fence, mile after mile. The air smelled damp and dead-fish mossy, heavy as a wet towel, but it was better than the animal enclosures on a hot afternoon when the sun pounded the awnings and the exhibits huddled in weak shade. Traveling at night was the way to go. Trevin counted the distance in minutes. They'd blow through Roxie soon, then hit Hamburg, McNair and Harriston in quick secession. In Fayette there was a nice diner where they could get breakfast, but it meant turning off the highway and they'd hit the worst of Vicksburg's morning traffic if they stopped. No, the thing to do was to keep driving, driving to the next town where he could save the show.

He reached across the seat to the grocery sack between him and Caprice. She was asleep, her baby-blonde head resting against the door, her small hands holding a Greek edition of the *Odyssey* open on her lap. If she was awake she could glance at the map and tell him exactly how many miles they had left to Mayersville, how long to the minute at this speed it would take, and how much diesel, to the ounce they'd have left in their tanks. Her little-girl eyes would pin him to the wall. "Why can't you figure this out on your own?" they'd ask. He thought about hiding her phone book so she'd have nothing to sit on and couldn't look out the window. That would show her. She might look two years old, but she was really twelve, and had the soul of a middle-aged tax attorney.

At the sack's bottom, beneath an empty donut box, he found the beef jerky. It tasted mostly of pepper, but underneath it had a tingly, metallic flavor he tried not to think about. Who knew what it might have been made from? He doubted there were any original-form cows, the o-cows, left to slaughter.

After a long curve, a city limit sign loomed out of the dark. Trevin stepped on the brakes, then geared down. Roxie cops were infamous for speed traps, and there wasn't enough bribe money in the kitty to make a ticket go away. In his rearview mirror, the other truck and a car with Hardy the handyman, and his crew of roustabouts closed ranks.

Roxie's traffic signal blinked yellow over an empty intersection, while the closed shops stood mute under a handful of streetlights. After the four block long downtown, another mile of beat up houses and trailers lined the road, where broken washing machines and pickups on cinder blocks dotted moonlit front yards. Something barked at him from behind a chain link fence. Trevin slowed for a closer look. Professional curiosity. It looked like an o-dog under a porch light, an original form animal, an old one if his stiff-gaited walk was an indicator. Weren't many of those left anymore. Not since the mutagen hit. Trevin wondered if the owners keeping an o-dog in the backyard had troubles with their neighbors, if there was jealousy.

A toddler voice said, "If we don't clear $2,600 in Mayersville, we'll have to sell a truck, Daddy."

"Don't call me Daddy, *ever*." He took a long curve silently. Two lane highways often had no shoulder, and concentration was required to keep safe. "I didn't know you were awake. Besides, a thousand will do it."

Caprice closed her book. In the darkness of the cab, Trevin couldn't see her eyes, but he knew they were polar-ice blue. She said, "A thousand for diesel, sure, but we're weeks behind on payroll. The roustabouts won't stand for another delay, not after what you promised in Gulfport. The extension on the quarterly taxes are past, and I can't keep the feds off like the other creditors by pledging extra payments for a couple months. We've got food for most of the animals for ten days or so, but we have to buy fresh meat for the tigerzelle and the crocomouse or they'll die. We stay afloat with $2,600, but just barely."

Trevin scowled. It had been years since he'd found her little-girl voice and little-girl pronunciation to be cute, and almost everything she said was sarcastic or critical. It was like living with a pint-sized advocate for his own self doubt. "So we need a house of . . ." He wrinkled his forehead. "$2,600 divided by four and a half bucks . . ."

"Five hundred and seventy-eight. That'll leave you an extra dollar for a cup of coffee," Caprice said. "We haven't had a take that big since Ferriday last fall, and that was because Oktoberfest in Natchez closed early. Thank God for Louisiana liquor laws. We ought to admit the show's washed up, cut the inventory loose, sell the gear and pay off the help."

She turned on the goosenecked reading light that arced from the dashboard and opened her book.

"If we can hold on until Rosedale . . ." He remembered Rosedale when they last came through, seven years ago. The city had recruited him. Sent letters and e-mails. They met him in New Orleans with a committee, including a brunette beauty who squeezed his leg under the table when they went out to dinner.

"We can't," Caprice said.

Trevin recalled the hand on his leg feeling good and warm. He'd almost jumped from the table, his face flushed. "The soybean festival draws them in. Everything's made out of soybeans. Soybean pie. Soybean beer. Soybean ice cream." He chuckled. "We cleaned up there. I got to ride down Main Street with the Rosedale Soybean Queen."

"We're dead. Take your pulse." She didn't look up.

The Rosedale Soybean Queen had been friendly too, and oh so grateful that he'd brought the zoo to town. He wondered if she still lived there. He could look her up. "Yeah, if we make the soybean festival, we'll do fine. One good show and we're sailing again. I'll repaint the trucks. Folks love us when we come into town, music playing. World's greatest, traveling novelty zoo. You remember when *Newsweek* did that story? God, that was a day." He glanced out the window again. The moon rested on the horizon now, pacing them, big as a beachball, like a burnished hubcap rolling with them in the night, rolling up the Mississippi twenty miles to the west. He could smell it flowing to the sea. How could she doubt that they would make it big? I'll show her, he thought. Wipe that smirk off her little-girl face. I'll show her in Mayersville and then Rosedale. Money'll be falling off the tables. We'll have to store it in sacks. She'll see. Grinning, he dug deep for another piece of beef jerky, and he didn't think at all what it tasted like this time.

Trevin pulled the truck into Mayersville at half past ten, keeping his eyes peeled for their posters and flyers. He'd sent a box of them up two weeks earlier, and if the boy he'd hired had done his job, they should have been plastered everywhere, but he only saw one, and it was torn nearly in half. There were several banners welcoming softball teams to the South-Central Spring Time Regional Softball Tourney, and the hotels sported NO VACANCY signs, so the crowds were there. He turned the music on, and it blared from the loudspeakers on top of the truck. Zoo's in town, he thought. Come see the zoo! But other than a couple geezers sitting in front of the barbershop, who watched them cooly as they passed, no one seemed to note their arrival.

"They can't play ball all day, eh, Caprice? They've got to do something between games."

She grunted. Her laptop was open on the seat beside her, and she was double entering receipts and bills into the ledger.

The fairgrounds were on the north edge of town, next to the ballfields. A park attendant met them at the gates, then climbed onto the running board so his head was just below the window.

"There's a hundred-dollar occupancy fee," he said, his face hidden beneath a wide-brimmed straw hat that looked like it had been around the world a few times.

Trevin drummed his fingers on the steering wheel and stayed calm. "We paid for the site up front."

The attendant shrugged. "It's a hundred dollars or you find some other place to plant yourself."

Caprice, on her knees, leaned across Trevin. She deepened her voice in her best Trevin impersonation. "Do we make that check out to Mayersville City Parks or to Issaquena County?"

Startled, the attendant looked up before Caprice could duck out of sight, his sixty-year-old face as dusty as his hat. "Cash. No checks."

"That's what I thought," she said to Trevin as she moved back from the window. "Give him twenty. There better be the portable potties and the electrical hookups we ordered."

Trevin flicked the bill to him, and the attendant caught it neatly in flight as he stepped off the running board. "Hey, mister," he said. "How old's your little girl?"

"A million and ten, asshole," said Trevin, dropping the clutch to move the big rig forward. "I've told you to stay out of sight. We'll get into all kinds of trouble if the locals find out I've got a mutant keeping the books. They have labor laws, you know. Why'd you tell me to give him any money anyway? We could have bought a day or two of meat with that."

Caprice stayed on her knees to look out her window. "He's really a janitor. Never piss off the janitor. Hey, they cleaned this place up a bit. There was a patch of woods between us and the river last time."

Trevin leaned on the wheel. Turning the truck was tough at anything less than highway speed. "Would you want trees and brush next to where you were playing softball? You chase a foul shot into the undergrowth and never come back."

Beyond the fairgrounds, the land sloped down to the levee, and past that flowed the Mississippi, less than a hundred yards away, a great, muddy plain marked with lines of sullen gray foam drifting under the mid-morning sun. A black barge so distant that he couldn't hear it chugged upstream. Trevin noted with approval the endless stretch of ten-foot-tall chain link between them and the river. Who knew what god-awful thing might come crawling out of there?

As always, it took most of the day to set up. The big animals stinking of hot fur and unwashed cage bottoms, in their eight-foot-high enclosures came out of the semi-trailers first. Looking lethargic and sick, the tigerzelle, a long-legged, hoofed animal sporting almost no neck below an impressive face filled with saber-like teeth, barely looked up as its cage was lowered to the soggy ground. It hooted softly. Trevin checked its water. "Get a tarp over it right away," he said to handyman Harper, a big, grouchy man who wore old rock concert T-shirts inside out. Trevin added, "That trailer had to be a hundred and twenty degrees inside."

Looking at the animal fondly, Trevin remembered when he'd acquired it from a farm in Illinois, one of the first American mutababies, before the mutagen was recognized and named, before it became a plague. The tigerzelle's sister was almost as bizarre: heavy legs, scaly skin and a long, thin head, like a whippet, but the farmer had already killed it by the time Trevin arrived. Their mother, as ordinary a cow as you'd ever see, looked at its children with dull confusion. "What the hell's wrong with my cow?" asked the farmer several times until they started dickering for the price. Once Trevin had paid him, the man said, "If'n I get any other weird lookin' animal, you want I should give you a call?"

Trevin smelled profit. Charging $20 per customer, he cleared $10,000 a week in June and July, showing the tigerzelle from the back of his pickup. He thought, I may not be too smart, but I do know how to make a buck. By the end of the summer, Dr. Trevin's Traveling Zoological Extravaganza was born. That was the year Caprice rode beside him in a child's car seat, her momma dead in child birth. In August, they were going north from Senetobia to Memphis, and at eleven months old, Caprice said her first words: "Isn't eighty over the speed limit?" Even then there was a biting, sardonic tone in her voice. Trevin nearly wrecked the truck.

The crocomouse snarled and bit at the bars as it came out, its furry snout banging against the metal. It threw its two hundred pounds against the door and almost tipped the cage out of the handlers' grip. "Keep your hands away," snapped Harper to his crew, "or you'll be taping a pencil to a stub to write your mommas."

Then the rest of the animals were unloaded, a porcumander, the warped child of a bullfrog that waved its wet, thorny hide at every shadow; the unigoose, about the size of a wild turkey atop four tiny legs, shedding ragged feathers by the handful below the pearl-like glinting horn, and each of the other mutababies, the unrecognizable progeny of cats and squirrels and horses and monkeys and seals and every other animal Trevin could gather to the zoo. Big cages, little ones, aquariums, terrariums, little corrals, bird cages, tethering poles, all came out for display.

By sunset the last animal had been arranged and fed. Circus flags fluttered from the semi-trailer truck tops. The loudspeakers perched atop their posts.

The park attendant wandered through the cages, his hands pushed deep into his pockets as if he hadn't tried to rip them off earlier in the day. "Y'all best stay in your trucks once the sun sets if you're camping here."

Suspicious, Trevin asked, "Why's that?"

The man raised his chin toward the river glowing red like a bloody stain in the setting sun. "Water level was up a couple days ago, over the fences. The levee held, but any sorta teethy mutoid might be floppin' around on our side now. It's got so you can't step in a puddle without somethin' takin' a bite outta ya. Civil Defense volunteers walk the banks everyday lookin' for the more cantankerous critters, but it's a big old river. You got a gun?"

Trevin shrugged. "Baseball bat. Maybe we'll get lucky and add something to the zoo. You expecting crowds for the softball tournament?"

"Thirty-two teams. We shipped in extra bleachers."

Trevin nodded. If he started the music early in the morning, maybe he'd attract folks waiting for games. Nothing like a little amusement before the heat set in. After a couple minutes, the park attendant left. Trevin was glad to see him walk away. He had the distinct impression that the man was looking for something, probably to steal.

After dinner, Caprice clambered into the upper bunk, her short legs barely giving her enough of a reach to make it. Trevin kicked his blanket aside. Even though it was after 10:00, it was still over ninety degrees, and their wasn't a hint of a breeze. Most of the animals had settled in their cages. Only the tigerzelle made noise, one long warbling hoot after another, a soft, melodic call that hardly fit its ferocious appearance.

"You lay low tomorrow. I'm not kidding," said Trevin after he'd turned off the light. "I don't want you driving people off."

Caprice sniffed loudly. "It's pretty ironic that I can't show myself at a mutoid zoo. I'm tired of hiding away like a freak. Another fifty years there won't be any of your kind left anyway. Might as well accept the inevitable. I'm the future. They should be able to see that."

Trevin put his hands behind his head and stared up at her bunk. Through the screen he'd fitted over the windows, he could hear the Mississippi lapping against the bank. An animal screeched in the distance, its call a cross between a whistle and a bad cough. He tried to imagine what would make a sound like that. Finally he said, "People don't like human mutoids, at least ones that look human."

"Why's that?" she asked, all the sarcasm and bitterness suddenly gone. "I'm not a bad person if they'd get to know me. We could discuss books, or philosophy. I'm a mind, not a body."

The animal cried out again in the dark, over and over, until in mid-screech, it stopped. A heavy thrashing sound followed by splashes marked the creature's end. "I guess it makes them sad, Caprice."

"Do I make you sad?" In the truck cab's dim interior, she sounded exactly like a two year old. He remembered when she *was* a little girl, before he knew that she wasn't normal, that she'd never "grow up," that her DNA showed she wasn't human. Before she started talking uppity and making him feel stupid with her baby-doll eyes. Before he'd forbid her to call him Daddy. He'd thought she looked a little like her mother then. He still caught echoes of her when Caprice combed her hair, or when she fell asleep and her lips parted to take a breath, just like her mother. The air caught in his throat thinking of those times.

"No, Caprice. You don't make me sad."

Hours later, long after Caprice had gone to sleep, Trevin drifted off into a series of dreams where he was being smothered by steaming Turkish towels, and when he threw the towels off, his creditors surrounded him. They carried payment overdue notices, and none of them were human.

Trevin was up before dawn to feed the animals. Half of keeping the zoo running was in figuring out what the creatures ate. Just because the parent had been, say, an o-form horse didn't mean hay was going to do the trick. Caprice kept extensive charts for him: the animal's weight, how much food it consumed, what vitamin supplements seemed most helpful. There were practicalities to running a zoo. He dumped a bucket of corn on the cob into the pigahump's cage. It snorted, then lumbered out of the doghouse it stayed in, not looking much like a pig or any other animal Trevin knew. Eyes like saucers, it gazed at him gratefully before burying its face in the trough.

He moved down the rows. Mealworms in one cage. Grain in the next. Bones from the butcher. Dog food. Spoiled fish. Bread. Cereal. Old vegetables. Oats. The tigerzelle tasted the rump roast he tossed in, its delicate tongue, so like a cat's, lapped at the meat before it tore a small chunk off to chew delicately. It cooed in contentment.

At the end of the row, closest to the river, two cages were knocked off their display stands and smashed. Black blood and bits of meat clung to the twisted bars and both animals, blind, leathery bird-like creatures, were gone. Trevin sighed and walked around the cages, inspecting the ground. In a muddy patch, a single webbed print a foot across marked with four deep claw indents showed the culprit. A couple partial prints led from the river. Trevin put his finger in the track, which was a half-inch deep. The ground was wet but firm. It took a hard press to push just his fingertip a half inch. He wondered at the weight of the creature, and made a note to himself that tonight they'd have to store the smaller cages in the truck, which would mean more work. He sighed again.

By 8:00, the softball fields across the park had filled. Players warmed up outside the fences while games took place. Tents to house teams or for food booths sprang up. Trevin smiled and turned on the music. Banners hung from the trucks. DR. TREVIN'S TRAVELING ZOOLOGICAL EXTRAVAGANZA. SEE NATURE'S ODDITIES! EDUCATIONAL! ENTERTAINING! By noon there had been fifteen paying customers.

Leaving Hardy in charge of tickets, Trevin loaded a box with handbills, hung a staple gun to his belt, then marched to the ballfields, handing out flyers. The sun beat down like a humid furnace, and only the players in the field weren't under tents or umbrellas. Several folks offered him a beer—he took one—but his flyers, wrinkly with humidity, vanished under chairs or behind coolers. "We're doing a first day of the tournament special," he said. "Two bucks each or three for you and a friend." His shirt clung to his back. "We'll be open after sunset, when it's cooler. These are displays not to be missed, folks."

A woman in her twenties, her cheeks sun-reddened, her blonde hair tied back, said, "I don't need to pay to see a reminder, damn it." She crumpled the paper and dropped it. One of her teammates, sitting on the ground, a beer between his knees, said, "Give him a break, Doris. He's just trying to make a living."

Trevin said, "We were in *Newsweek*. You might have read about us."

"Maybe we'll come over later, fella," said the player on the ground.

Doris popped a can open, "It might snow this afternoon too."

"Maybe it will," said Trevin congenially. He headed toward town on the other side of the fairgrounds. The sun pressured his scalp with prickly fire. By the time he'd gone a hundred yards he wished he'd worn a hat, but it was too hot to go back.

He stapled a flyer to the first telephone pole he came to. "Yep," he said to himself. "A little publicity and we'll rake it in." The sidewalk shimmered in white heat waves as he marched from pole to pole, past the hardware, past the liquor store, past the Baptist Church—SUFFER THE CHILDREN read the marquee—past the pool hall and auto supply shop. He went inside every store and asked the owner to post his sign. Most did. Behind Main Street stood several blocks of homes. Trevin turned up one street and down the next, stapling flyers, noting with approval the wire mesh over the windows. "Can't be to careful, nowadays," he said, his head swimming in the heat. The beer seemed to be evaporating through his skin all at once, and he felt sticky with it. The sun pulsed against his back. The magic number is five-seventy-eight, he thought. It beat within him like a song. Call it six hundred. Six hundred folks come to the zoo, come to the zoo, come to the *zoo*.

When he finally made his way back to the fairgrounds, the sun was on its way down. Trevin dragged his feet, but the flyers were gone.

Evening fell. Trevin waited at the ticket counter in his zoo-master's uniform, a broad-shouldered red suit with gold epaulets. The change box popped open with jingly joy; the roll of tickets was ready. Circus music played softly from the loud-speakers as fireflies flickered in the darkness above the river. Funny, he thought, how the mutagen affected only the bigger vertebrate animals, not mice-sized mammals or little lizards, not small fish nor bugs or plants. What would a bug mutate into anyway? They look alien to begin with. He chuckled to himself, his walking up the sidewalk song still echoing: six hundred folks come to the zoo, come to the zoo, come to the zoo.

Every car that passed on the highway, Trevin watched, waiting for it to slow for the turn into the fairgrounds.

From sunset until midnight, only twenty customers bought admissions, most of them ball players who'd discovered there wasn't much night life in Mayersville. Clouds had moved in, and distant lightning flickered within their steel-wool depths.

Trevin spun the roll of tickets back and forth on its spool. An old farmer couple wearing overalls, their clothes stained with rich, Mississippi soil, shuffled past on their way out. "You got some strange animals here, mister," said the old man. His wife nodded. "But nothing stranger than what I've found wandering in my fields for the last few years. Gettin' so I don't remember what o-form normal looks like."

"Too close to the river," said his wife. "That's our place right over there." She pointed at a small farm house under a lone light just beyond the last ball field. Trevin wondered if they ever retrieved home run balls off their porch.

The thin pile of bills in the cash box rustled under Trevin's fingers. The money should be falling off the tables, he thought. We should be drowning in it. The old couple stood beside him, looking back into the zoo. They reminded him of his parents, not in their appearance, but in their solid patience. They weren't going anywhere fast.

He had no reason to talk to them, but there was nothing left to do. "I was here a few years ago. Did really well. What's happened?"

The wife held her husband's hand. She said, "This town's dyin', mister. Dyin' from the bottom up. They closed the elementary school last fall. No elementary-age kids. If you want to see a real zoo display, go down to Issaquena County Hospital pediatrics. The penalty of parenthood. Not that many folks are having babies, though."

"Or whatever you want to call them," added the old man. "Your zoo's depressin'."

"I'd heard you had somethin' special, though," said the woman shyly.

"Did you see the crocomouse?" asked Trevin. "There's quite a story about that one. And a tigerzelle. Have you seen that one?"

"Saw 'em," she said, looking disappointed.

The old couple climbed into their pickup that rattled into life after a half dozen starter-grinding tries.

"I found a buyer in Vicksburg for the truck," said Caprice.

Trevin whirled. She stood in the shadows beside the ticket counter, a notebook jammed under her arm. "I told you to stay out of view."

"Who's going to see me? You can't get customers even on a discount." She gazed on the vacant lot. "We don't have to deliver it. He's coming to town next week on other business. I can do the whole transaction, transfer the deed, take the money, all of it, over the Internet."

One taillight out, the farmer's pickup turned from the fairgrounds and onto the dirt road that led to their house that wasn't more than two hundred yards away. "What would we do with the animals?" He felt like weeping.

"Let the safe ones go. Kill the dangerous ones."

Trevin rubbed his eyes. She stamped her foot. "Look, this is no time for sentimentality. The zoo's a bust. You're going to lose the whole thing soon anyway. If you're too stubborn to give it all up, sell this truck now and you get a few extra weeks, maybe a whole season if we economize."

Trevin looked away from her. The fireflies still flickered above the river. "I'll have to make some decisions," he said heavily.

She held out the notebook. "I've already made them. This is what will fit in one semi-trailer. I already let Hardy and the roustabouts go with a severance check, postdated."

"What about the cages, the gear?"

"The county dump is north of here."

Was that a note of triumph he detected in her voice? Trevin took the notebook. She dropped her hands to her side, chin up, staring at him. The zoo's lights cast long shadows across her face. I could kick her, he thought, and for a second his leg trembled with the idea of it.

He tucked the notebook under his arm. "Go to bed."

Caprice opened her mouth, then clamped it shut on whatever she might have said before moving away.

Long after she vanished into the cab, Trevin sat on the stool, elbow on his knee, chin in his hand, watching insects circle the lights. The tigerzelle squatted on its haunches, alert, looking toward the river. Trevin remembered a ghastly cartoon he'd seen once. A couple of crones sat on the seat of a wagon full of bodies. The one holding the reins turned to the other and said, "You know, once the plague is over we're out of a job."

The tigerzelle rose to its feet, focusing on the river. It paced intently in its cage, never turning its head from the darkness. Trevin straightened. What did it see out there? For a long moment the tableau remained the same: insects clouded around the lights that buzzed softly, highlighting the cages; shining metal against the enveloping spring night, the pacing tigerzelle, the ticket counter's polished wood against Trevin's hand, and the Mississippi's pungent murmuring in the background.

Beyond the cages, from the river, a piece of blackness detached itself from the night. Trevin blinked in fascinated paralysis, all the hairs dancing on the back of his neck. The short-armed creature stood taller than a man, surveyed the zoo, then dropped to all fours like a bear, except that its skin gleamed with salamander wetness. Its triangular head sniffed at the ground, moving over the moist dirt as if following a scent. When it reached the first cage, a small one that held the weaslesnake, the river creature lifted its forelegs off the ground, grasping the cage in web-fingered claws. In an instant the cage was unrecognizable and the weaslesnake was gone.

"Hey!" Trevin yelled, shaking off his stupor. The creature looked at him. Reaching under the ticket counter, Trevin grabbed the baseball bat and advanced. The monster turned away to pick up the next cage. Trevin's face flushed "No, no, no, damn it!" He stepped forward again, stepped again, and suddenly he was running, bat held overhead. "Get away! Get away!" He brought the bat down on the animal's shoulder with a meaty whump.

It shrieked.

Trevin fell back, dropping the bat to cover his ears. It shrieked again, loud as a train whistle. For a dozen heart beats, it stood above him, claws extended, then it seemed to lose interest and moved to the next cage, dismantling it with one jerk of the bars.

His ears ringing, Trevin snatched the bat off the ground and waded in, swinging. On its rear legs, the monster bared its teeth, dozens of glinting needles in the triangular jaw. Trevin nailed the creature in the side. It folded with surprising flexibility, backing away, claws distended, snarling in a deafening roar. Trevin swung. Missed. The monster swiped at his leg, ripping his pants and almost jerking his feet out from under him.

The thing moved clumsily, backing down the hill toward the levee fence as Trevin swung again. Missed. It howled, tried to circle around him. Trevin scuttled sideways, careful of his balance on the slick dirt. If he should fall! The thing charged, mouth open, but pulled back like a threatened dog when Trevin raised the bat. He breathed in short gasps, poked the bat's end at it, always shepherding it away from the zoo. Behind him, a police siren sounded, and car engines roared, but he didn't dare look around. He could only stalk and keep his bat at the ready.

After a long series of feints, its back to the fence, the nightmare stopped, hunched its back and began to rise just as Trevin brought the bat down in a two-handed, over the head chop. Through the bat, he felt the skull crunch, and the creature dropped into a shuddery mass in the mud. Trevin, his pulse pounding, swayed for a moment, then sat beside the beast.

Up the hill, under the zoo's lights, people shouted into the darkness. Were they ball players? Town people? A police cruiser's lights blinked blue then red, and three or four cars, headlights on, were parked near the trucks. Obviously they couldn't see him, but he was too tired to call. Ignoring the wet ground, he lay back.

The dead creature smelled of blood and river mud. Trevin rested a foot on it, almost sorry that it was dead. If he could have captured it, what an addition it would have made to the zoo. Gradually the heavy beat in his chest calmed. The mud felt soft and warm. Overhead, the clouds thinned a bit, scudding across the full moon.

At the zoo, there was talking. Trevin craned his head around to see. People jostled about, and flashlights cut through the air. They started down the hill. Trevin sighed. He hadn't saved the zoo, not really. Tomorrow would come and they'd leave one of the trucks behind. In a couple of months, it would all be gone, the other truck, the animals—he was most sorry about the tigerzelle—the pulling into town with music blaring and flags flapping and people lined up to see the menagerie. No more reason to wear the zoo-master's uniform with its beautiful gold epaulets. *Newsweek* would never interview him again. It was all gone. If he could only sink into the mud and disappear, then he wouldn't have to watch the dissolving of his own life.

He sat up so they wouldn't think he was dead; waved a hand when the first flashlight found him. Mud dripped from his jacket. The policemen arrived first.

"God almighty, that's a big one." The cop trained his light on the river creature.

"Told you the fences warn't no good," said the other.

Everyone stayed back except the police. The first cop pushed the corpse off its stomach. Its little arms flopped to the side, and it didn't look nearly as big or intimidating. More folk arrived: some townies he didn't recognize, the old couple from the farmhouse across the ballfields, and finally, Caprice, the flashlight looking almost too big for her to carry.

The first cop knelt next to the creature, shoved his hat up off his forehead, then said low enough that Trevin guessed only the other cop heard him, "Hey, doesn't this look like the Anderson's kid? They said they'd smothered him."

"He wasn't half that big, but I think you're right." The other cop threw a coat over the creature's face, then stood for a long time looking down at it. "Don't say anything to them, all right? Maggie Anderson is my wife's cousin."

"Nothing here to see, people," announced the first cop. "This is a dead 'un. Y'all can head back home."

But the crowd's attention wasn't on them anymore. The flashlights turned on Caprice.

"It's a baby girl," someone said, and they moved closer.

Caprice shined her flash light from one face to the other. Then, desperation on her face, she ran clumsily to Trevin, burying her face in his chest.

"What are we going to do?" she whispered.

"Quiet. Play along." Trevin stroked the back of her head, then stood. A sharp twinge in his leg told him he'd pulled something. The world was all bright lights, and he couldn't cover his eyes. He squinted against them.

"Is that your girl, mister?" someone said.

Trevin gripped her closer. Her little hands fisted in his coat.

"I haven't seen a child in ten years," said another voice. The flashlights moved in closer.

The old farmer woman stepped into the circle, her face suddenly illuminated. "Can I hold your little girl, son? Can I just hold her?" She extended her arms, her hands quivering.

"I'll give you fifty bucks if you let me hold her," said a voice behind the lights.

Trevin turned slowly, lights all around until he faced the old woman again. A picture formed in his mind, dim at first but growing clearer by the second. One semi-trailer truck, the trailer set up like a child's room—no! Like a nursery. Winnie-the-Pooh wallpaper. A crib. One of those musical rotating things, what cha' call ums—a mobile! Little rocking chair. Kid's music. And they'd go from town to town. The banner would say THE LAST O-FORM GIRL CHILD, and he would charge them, yes he would, and they would line up. The money would fall off the table.

Trevin pushed Caprice away from him, her hands clinging to his coat. "It's OK, darling. The nice woman just wants to hold you for a bit. I'll be right here."

Caprice looked at him, despair clear in her face. Could she already see the truck with the nursery? Could she picture the banner and the unending procession of little towns?

The old woman took Caprice in her arms like a precious vase. "That's all right, little girl. That's all right." She faced Trevin, tears on her cheeks. "She's just like the granddaughter I always wanted. Does she talk yet? I haven't heard a baby's voice in forever. Does she talk?"

"Go ahead, Caprice dear. Say something to the nice lady."

Caprice locked eyes with him. Even by flashlight he could see the polar blue. He could hear her sardonic voice night after night as they drove across country. "It's not financially feasible to continue," she'd say in her two-year-old voice. "We should admit the inevitable."

She looked at him, lip trembling. She brought her fist up to her face. No one moved. Trevin couldn't even hear them breathing.

Caprice put her thumb in her mouth. "Daddy," she said around it. "Scared, Daddy."

Trevin flinched, then forced a smile. "That's a good girl."

"Daddy, scared."

Up the hill, the tigerzelle hooted, and just beyond the fence, barely visible by flashlight, the Mississippi gurgled and wept.

ITS HOUR COME ROUND

BAD NEWS SHOULD BE HELD TO THE END, DON'T YOU THINK? ESPECIALLY the kind that unbalances everything else you've said, erases it even? So I'll wait until I've told you about how I love working in the orchards in the spring. We hoe around the tree trunks, loosening the soil for rain and fertilizers; we rake away twigs and dead leaves, and a few dried apple husks that are all that's left after the winter, until the ground beneath the trees is smooth and clean and almost holy.

I love climbing the long ladders to inspect the buds. Are they green yet? Have they begun to bloom? I love the pace of prison work. An old-school lifer named Blue Buck Johnny told me once, "Drink plenty of water and walk slow. You're going nowhere fast." He started his term in Soledad fifty years before I met him, before the Mars colonies, before the 21st Century was properly rolling. Soledad was the last of the big houses where they warehoused criminals. No real treatment there, hormonal, psychiatric, genetic or otherwise. No ET. Just a bunch of maladjusts teaching each other how to be bad. That's when they held cons for "time served" rather than reforming them. They grandfathered Blue Buck into the Mola Correctional Facility. He was never going back to the world, but he didn't mind. He liked the inside and the shunt that stifled his urges.

So do I, sometimes. Did I mention I read poetry too? Yeats, I read him a lot, but I like Houseman and Neruda and Walt Whitman too. I speak the poems out loud to the bare branches when I'm hanging on a ladder, looking for beetle bore holes or frost damage.

I love breathing spring air. It's rainy here in the valley, not your California rain that settles in for months, where you don't see the sun from January to May, but the sudden Colorado rain that sweeps up the valley in a heady gust that smells of Utah canyons and wet grass. The wind comes across the treetops, bending the far ones first, so they shake their heads, and then the next and the next and the next, until it's on you, loaded with dust and litter and fat, stinging drops that make dark bullet holes in that perfect dirt beneath the trees.

I love all that, and I love people too. Can you believe it? There's slang for people inside: white guys are peckerwoods, and most affiliate after a while. AB's a popular choice, the Aryan Brothers. Blacks go for the BGF, the Black Guerilla Family. Border Brothers for the Hispanics, or the NF, Nuestra Familia—they're northern Hispanic. The BGF is the power broker at Mola. Even the guards step lightly around them. You want something done, you go to the family. Prisons may be different from Blue Buck Johnny's day, but the power games, intimidation and supply and demand are the same.

I, of course, don't affiliate. They've got names for me too. This is the bad news I've been holding back. It doesn't matter that I like the sun on my face, or on any ordinary day I'm the most generous guy in the world, or I have parents and a sister I love, or in the fifth grade I won a citizenship award for collecting the most tin cans for the senior center fund raiser. I'm a cho mo. A diddler. A chester. A BGF lord named Grover Lincoln Douglas outed me at lunch my first week here. Grover said, "This peckerwood's name is shit. He's on a drug charge." I didn't know what he meant then; I'd never done pharmaceuticals in my life. Later I found out a "drug charge" was shorthand for, "He drug them out of the sandbox." I'm a child molester, and a child died.

See, I told you. It doesn't matter what else I say. You might have even started to like me. I might have invited your sympathy. The man loves books. He appreciates nature. He has a pleasant, measured voice. I could have been your friend until you heard that. No matter how long my story is, the one deed will color the rest of my words. My life is measured, evaluated and overbalanced by that one fact. Some mistakes never go away.

But there, now you know.

This spring, my fourth at Mola, I first saw Chika Achutebe as she arrived on the morning bus. I watched from a treetop when the stringer of fish, all newbies, filed by to housing orientation, their shunts so fresh that infection still streaked their biceps. Chika's blonde afro stood out, her dark face shining beneath it, all Arabic and sleepy eyed. I thought she was on depress already, but that's just the way she looks. There were seven fry, a big shipment. Blue Buck told me at Soledad they'd get fifty cons on a bus, and they'd get a couple busses a week, all men. No coed populations then! No wonder time was so violent. Hard to imagine that much fresh meat, and Soledad was just one of hundreds of lock-ups. Of course, most of the cons were returners. Revolving door justice. Lots of recidivism back then, before they started grading the prisons. Before the shunts and ET and that whole therapeutic cocktail they've cooked up to keep us from coming back.

So these really were cub scouts, so scared they didn't know if they should shit or go blind. But I picked out Chika; she was huddled up on herself, shoulders pulled in, hands squeezed so tight together, and taking little steps like she was afraid that if her feet got too far in front of her they might not come back. Gang bangers checked them out as they went by. Grover Lincoln Douglas leaned on his hoe (the long-handled kind for breaking up dirt), marking who to recruit. Couple of the Aryan Brothers worked as trustees, handling paperwork for the transport bulls, and they wracked up the possibilities too.

You'd think in a controlled environment like this there wouldn't be much violence, and there isn't. The shunts, ET and therapy out the wazoo work, but it's still dangerous. You don't go from crime to cure in a day, you know. Some urges don't ever go away, and most the cons are Coving it, Crimes of Violence. When you get off on hurting people, you're an ET candidate for sure. Mola pulls a Clockwork Orange on you and that old blood music never sounds the same.

It would be a week before I saw her again—it takes the medboss that long to put them on a program—but then she was out. Best chance I have to make friends is to break in the new ones, so they know me before they know my time. I'm gregarious by nature. Talkative. It's a craving the shunt doesn't manage.

We met at breakfast. "Can I sit here?" I asked. The cafeteria is big enough for two hundred, but there are only eighty prisoners and a dozen staff members at Mola. Blue Buck told me Soledad housed over 7,000. Hard to believe there was that much crime. Here, big windows open onto the orchards. Some of the apples had blossomed all white and pink in the sunlight, and I could see apricots and peaches farther off. Pancakes that morning. The room smelled of maple and sizzling butter.

"Yes, thank you," she said without looking from her food.

Up close she was even more striking. Hair so blonde it was nearly translucent. Classic cheekbones. Skin as dark and smooth as chocolate pudding. Heavy, long lashes over those sleepy eyes. Narrow shoulders. Trim figure under the khaki work shirt. My shunt kicked in. Sometime you can feel it: a tiny click under the skin as a microdosage releases. Sexual depressant. I hadn't had a hard-on in four years.

She said, "Sometimes I wake up in the middle of the night, and I'm sad." She looked toward the windows, but I don't think she was seeing anything. Her eyes were red-rimmed. "I used to have a dog named Fardel, but she's gone now. When I wake up I think I hear her barking, but it's never her."

Her voice was tiny and soft. She frowned when she turned back. "If I got a puppy, I'd name her Fardel Two, because she would be the second." There were no lines in her face, no worry marks above her eyebrows, no creases anywhere. Absolutely pure, unwritten-upon skin.

"How old are you?" I said. My shunt clicked again, and then twice more. Different doses. My brain fuzzed a little bit; the room got sort of whispy and underwater.

"Twenty-seven," she said in the voice of a ten-year-old. "Twenty-eight this June. How old are you?"

"Thirty-six," I whispered. "Thirty-seven in November." She's retarded, I thought. What could this little girl have done to earn a stay at Mola Correctional?

*

The medboss ordered an unscheduled ET for me that afternoon. I was stacking bug powder for spraying next week. "Empathy Training, 3:00, Knavely," she said. She wore scrupulously clean pants suits, razor-like creases pressed into the legs and arms. Short, black hair, streaked with gray, like a maiden aunt. A pleasant smile that showed her gums, although she didn't smile often. Old-fashioned glasses.

"Yes, boss," I said, without breaking rhythm.

The Adjustment Center dominates the housing yard. Single-story prisoner bungalows line the four streets that lead to the circle drive around the AC. From the air, I imagine Mola looks like a sniper scope. An eight-foot-high fence to keep deer away from the fruit circles the compound. Inside that, a two-hundred-yard clear zone to the trees, the orchards; then the roads, which form the crosshair, the Adjustment Center in the middle. Administration, medical services, counseling, parole and the warden's office fill the upper floors while ET takes the entire basement. A placard next to the entrance reads, "NEITHER NATURE NOR NURTURE IS DESTINY." They're serious about it too.

My hand barely shook as I signed in. This would be my seventy-eighth ET in four years. One a day for the first month, and then one a month after that. I knew the drill.

Take a chair. Strap my feet in. Plug the IV into the shunt. It's pretty easy once you've practiced. The access port is under a skin fold on the bicep. The shunt itself, an inch wide and three inches long, is buried in the muscle. You don't feel it after the first few weeks. Hard to believe it analyzes the patient, makes dosage decisions, transmits and receives all in that little unit.

The medboss bustled in, checked my straps, then locked down my hands and chest. She looked me in the eyes before lowering the diving bell over my head. "Pretty routine now, eh?"

I nodded, feeling anything but.

Empathy Training. I don't know what you've read, but it's not like that. Not virtual reality. Not "Electro-psychotropic Simulation." It's total immersion in fear and pain.

The helmet came down, covered my eyes, fastened under my chin. My shunt rattled a complicated series of clicks in my arm. I waited for the scenario. Different one each time. I have no idea how they make them. Then, I'm squatting on a beach, packing sand with a little shovel. My feet are tiny. I slip them into a puddle and squish the water between my toes. The sky's bright, the sand is crisp and smooth, lazy waves slide toward my castle to slip back into the sea. Tomorrow's my birthday, I think, and I'll be seven. Seven, seven, seven, I sing to myself. A shadow covers my work. I look up at a dark silhouette. My mouth goes dry, and he picks me up. Already I'm scared. My legs don't straighten. I stay curled, shovel in hand, and he carries me that way, hustling me toward the bathrooms.

I know it's chemically and electrically induced anxiety. The diving bell reaching into my cortex, stimulating the right reflexes, but it feels real, not simulated. I'm genuinely terrified. Sometimes I scream. After ET I can't talk from the hoarseness, but this time I'm silent. The door opens and closes. He turns the light off. My head bangs on something, a bathroom stall maybe.

He's so big. I'm small and weak and scared, scared, scared. Wet myself scared, and I do. My pants come down. He turns me and my chest is pressed against the ceramic edge of the toilet bowl in the dark. A noseful of unflushed urine smell, my face nearly in the water. Then I scream. His hand's on my mouth. I can't breathe. It goes on.

It goes on.

It goes on.

When the diving bell came off I was weeping. "Oh God oh God oh God," I heard myself saying.

"I know," said the medboss. "I know, Knavely." She was not unkind. It was the job.

"Why don't you just kill me?" I gasped.

The chest belt fell away, and I leaned forward, still strapped at the hands and ankles, to throw up. They'd hose the room down later. The medboss patted me on the back until I finished.

"There's no such thing as a throw-away person," she said.

I staggered out of the AC. His hands still on me. My ribs hurt. My ass hurt. I was afraid to feel back there. Surely I'm bleeding, I thought. Sometimes cons develop bruises. There was a guy in here a couple years earlier on an assault and battery beef whose face would be puffy, his eyes black, after ET. Psychosomatic symptoms. Stigmata. No one touched him, but he'd take days to heal.

Nobody talked to me as I walked through the apple trees, through the peaches and apricots, past the last tree and into the clear zone. The fence was two hundred yards away, but I wasn't trying to escape, nor going for a "bush pass." No one escapes Mola. I kept walking. There was a proximity guard in the AC. I was on a grid, and when I got far enough away from the center, long before I reached the fence, it knew.

Tears rolled down my face. My legs shook. I did that to someone. Who was I? There's this poem by Yeats where he says, "What rough beast, its hour come round at last, slouches toward Bethlehem to be born?" There was a beast in me, or I was the beast, I don't know, but how can one live with knowledge of what he has done when the victim's pain is so fresh? And so, for the seventy-eighth time, I walked toward the fence until the proximity alarm sent a signal to my shunt. It clicked. Suddenly, I was drowsy, and unconsciousness washed over me. Vaguely, I felt myself falling, but I don't remember hitting.

Sometimes a con pisses a bull off, and the guard orders a cho mo double feature. Not all the staff at Mola is as compassionate as the medboss. There's sadism; there's violence, even with the shunts. Sometimes it's the inmates; sometimes it's the staff. On goes the diving bell and the poor bastard gets a long load of my normal treatment. Nothing worse than being a diddler in prison. Nothing worse than being one, period.

By the next afternoon, I was in the trees again, pinching buds. I culled out every other one so the crop would be more robust. It was non-thinking, physically trying work involving moving the ladder often and climbing up and down it scores of times.

Maybe I was the only one not to hit on Chika the first day—most cons aren't at Mola for COP stuff, crimes of passion, so they don't get chemically castrated every time a sexual thought crosses their minds—or maybe it was just another of nature's cruel tricks, but when I came down the ladder the umpteenth time she waited for me.

Even the way she wore her clothes was childlike. An adult makes adjustments, draws the shoulders square, smooths away the wrinkles. Not so with Chika. She'd missed a button three down from her collar. "Can I watch?" she said in her little girl voice.

I shrugged. "It's a free prison." The day after ET, I'm not nearly as chatty. It's sort of like that old joke about not wanting to belong to a club that would have you as a member. A person who wanted to talk to me probably wasn't worth talking to.

She sat cross-legged at the foot of the ladder and played with her shoelaces. "I have a tree at my house, but there's a table for tea and two chairs."

Not many branches left to do on this tree. It'd take me another twenty minutes to finish, but I was tired. When I reached the ground, she moved aside by scooching on her bottom.

"My new bed's nice," she said, her expression totally innocent.

I leaned back against the tree a yard from her and slid until I was sitting too. She looked around, her slender fingers cupping her knees, hair like a halo, wide-eyed, as if she was on a field trip.

"Do you have any idea why you're here?" I asked.

She ducked her head. "I did a bad thing I shouldn't have. They'll keep me until they're sure I won't do it again. That's what my attorney told me." She said "attorney" carefully, getting each syllable right. "What are you here for? Did you do something bad too?"

Nothing I could say to that. There is this phrase, "Do your own time." It means, mind your own business.

"Yeah, I did something bad too." I wanted to hold her. She trembled even though the day was warm, pulling her arms in close. It was weird: her size and build said she was adult, but her expression and posture said she was a child, a frightened kid who didn't know who to turn to. I kept my hands firmly still. Everything in me wanted to reach out to comfort her. I could picture it, her leaning into me, her blonde hair against my face. I shook my head and moved a few inches farther away, waiting for the shunt to click, to save me, but it didn't, so I tried to think about the night that put me here.

The funny thing about it is that I could hardly remember the actual event. For so long, my life had been bound up in Mola's orchards that everything before, my schooling, my work, my marriage, my own children, my crime, seemed to belong to someone else. All I kept from that former life is the burden.

She shifted on the ground so she faced me more, her knees apart, ankles crossed. "Do you get scared at night, Knavely?"

Before I go to sleep sometimes, there's an image from the trial that gets me. It's the mother. I'd been sentenced like everyone else to an RTL, "reformation to life." They were taking me from the court when the mother leaned out of the crowd at the door, her face white and dead. "I hope you never sleep peacefully again."

After sentencing I'd gone straight to surgery for my shunt. I didn't know if I slept peacefully or not. When I stayed awake too long, the shunt took care of me, then I slept. Who knew if it was peaceful?

"I get scared," Chika said. "People moan, and I ask them if they're all right, but they don't hear me. I think they're having nightmares."

In my unit people moan. Six cons per apartment. Blue Buck told me that prisons used to be noisy all the time. People screaming, doors clanging. Never a quiet moment. Mola's not like that. No slamming, barred gates. Much calmer. Half the pop's on depress, though, so it's hard to tell what it would be like otherwise. From where Chika and I sat I could see a dozen other cons just standing among the trees, too tanked to make a move. Sometimes in the summer I'd go and turn them if it was a sunny day. They could get a bad burn if they weren't wearing a hat.

Chika leaned toward me and whispered, "A man comes to me every night. He wants to get in, but I won't let him. I can't see his face."

I found myself standing over her—I have no idea how I leapt to my feet so fast. I yelled, "What?" She fell back in the dirt. Her hands covered her mouth, and she cried.

"No, no. It's okay. I'm sorry . . . I didn't mean to startle you." Sweat dripped into my eyes. I wiped my face with the back of my wrist. A steadying breath, then I counted to ten slowly.

Chika rolled to her side away from me, drew her legs in, and sobbed. I squatted beside her until she suddenly relaxed. Her shunt had dropped a load. When she sat up, her eyes glazed over. It was as if I'd never said anything.

"My new bed's nice," she said again. "I like pink sheets."

Her thumb went into her mouth.

"She's mentally incapacitated," I said. "She shouldn't be here."

The medboss sat behind her desk in her corner office. She could see half the facility through the floor-to-ceiling windows. "I'm not in a position to judge," she said. "The courts found her competent. Chika's very high functioning, considering her IQ, capable of making choices. She's made some poor ones."

I forced myself to stay calm. Sun bathed almost the entire office, warming my legs. It would be only a couple hours until nightfall.

"I think she needs protection. She's not safe."

The medboss consulted her records. Screen after screen flickered by. When she stopped, it wasn't at Chika's profile; it was mine.

"Knavely, I appreciate your concern, but, really, she's much safer in here than she'd be outside." She studied my charts. "You have a parole hearing next week. I'm recommending your release. What do you feel about that?"

I didn't even have to think. "No. I'm not ready."

She appraised me from her chair, her dark eyes steady behind her glasses. "The state pays us to cure you. If you recid, we lose money. If we keep you too long, we lose money. When the therapy team says you're turned, and the board agrees, out you go. Assuming we did our job, you're a new man, society is safe, and you can get on with your life. You'll be relocated, renamed and be given a whole new background. The state wants you to have the best chance possible of making it."

My tongue stuck to the top of my mouth, and I had a sudden flashback to yesterday's ET session. The room smelled like unflushed toilet. "I haven't been punished enough."

"We can't punish you, Knavely. Punishment is old-school. This is a reformation facility. All we're worried about is a relapse. Do you think you'll commit another crime?"

I thought about Chika. I wanted to hold her, but there's lots of ways to hold someone. "I'm not confident."

The medboss shrugged. "Nothing's certain. All we can do is look at your profile.

I'm recommending dismissal. I'll bet you clear 369, and we'll collect triple bonus." She smiled, lots of gums. If I didn't recid in thirty months, the prison received performance pay. Sixty months later, they collected again, and ninety months earned them a third. A full 369. Mola Correctional guaranteed their freebirds.

"But what about Chika?" I said. My legs shook. I doubted I could stand.

The medboss turned back to her display, called up Chika's charts. "Oh, I wouldn't worry about her. She's tougher than she looks."

"She's just a little kid. She can't make decisions for herself."

Outside an inmate crew unloaded smudge pots from a flatbed. The prediction was for a frost tonight, and if it was too cold for too long, the buds would die. There wouldn't be a crop. Rather than look at the medboss, I watched them wrestling the unwieldy furnaces into position. A pressure itched at the backs of my eyes.

She said, "Five months ago your 'little kid' killed her father with an ice pick. She decided to do that."

"Surely it wasn't premeditated," I said.

"Daddy was tied up. The coroner testified she took two hours to finish him. Don't know what started her, but she had plenty of time to change her mind along the way. I wouldn't paint too pretty of a picture of her in your mind. Your girl has some anger management issues."

After dinner I walked Chika to her dorm, trying to decide what to do.

"I like you, Knavely," she said, and held my hand.

The hairs flew up on the back of my neck. My arm went rigid as an impulse to jerk it away was answered by a fear of frightening her again.

We stopped at the door. In the orchards, the bug lights were on. So was the one hanging from the dorm's gutter, five feet away. A cool, polar light washed over the wall, turning the windows into icy squares. Bugs zapped themselves into ash all around us. A front was coming in, and I felt frost in the air. They'd be lighting the smudge pots soon. Chika didn't let go.

"I don't want to talk to that man again," she said. She kept her head down, so I could just see the top of her head. Her feet shuffled on the cement. "He scares me. He said, 'I can be your honey, Chika.'" She looked at me, her eyes shiny, reflecting bug light blue.

"Tell the dorm bull you don't want visitors."

She giggled. "What's a dorm bull?"

"The guard in your unit."

She squeezed my hand, serious again. "No . . . not the guard."

And then I knew, it wasn't an inmate.

A faint squeaking filled the night air behind me. Bats dipped and circled through the trees. She watched them, the corners of her mouth turned up in delight. "Did I tell you I had a dog?" she said. "His name was Fardel."

"Yes, you did."

"I like animals. I'm going to ask them for a puppy."

I was ready to go. How could I help tonight? And what about tomorrow night, and the one after? The medboss said she'd recommend parole. I might not even be here in a week.

"Could you stay with me, Knavely?" she said. "If you're with me, the man won't come." Her grip was intense. "I could . . . do things for you."

My gut twisted. "No," I said. "Oh, no. I can't." I paused, waiting for the shunt. This was when it should click, sending a soothing dose through my veins, but it didn't. Was she a child or an adult. And what was I? I felt a stirring. Holding my hand, Chika looked at me, pleading. I gasped, "You'll be fine. Really. You'll see," and I disengaged my fingers.

There's no curfew at Mola, but most go to bed early. A hard day in the orchards'll take it out of you. I walked from Chika's apartment, afraid to look back. She'd still be on the porch, her bed awaiting her, and the long night. The late shift moved between the trees, carrying torches. A few smudge pots were lit, and an oily smoke eddied in the cold air. Without a coat, I shivered.

Grover Lincoln Douglas and three of his BGF cronies bunked in the last unit on North Street. I went in without knocking. Cigarette smoke twisted around a desk lamp in the middle of their card game. He put his cards down when I moved into the light.

"I need to buy something," I said.

"What do you have to offer?" He spat on the floor.

"Name your price."

Grover leaned back in his chair. Shadows surrounded him. Only the beds' edges were visible, then I realized that two of them were occupied. Eyes glinted, watching like coyotes.

He glanced at his cards on the table as if he'd rather be playing, then folded his hands across his chest. "It might be too expensive for you. What do you think I have to sell?"

"Protection."

He laughed. "Nothing can buy you that, Cho Mo. No soul here would slap your back if you were choking on a chicken bone."

"It's not for me."

His chair flopped forward so he could rest his elbows on the table. "That's different. Maybe we can deal. It just so happens a pair of fish I know have a desperate urge you can help them with, and they're willing to owe me big for the privilege."

I swallowed, knowing what he was talking about. Grover specialized in fulfilling urges.

Grover said, "No charges. Not a word." He drew a finger slowly under his chin.

We worked out the arrangement. Last thing I said was, "She stays safe. No predators. No coercion."

"I'll put the word out." He tilted his head and looked up at me, eyes narrow. "Funny request for someone on a short ticket. I heard you're riding the 369 out soon. Why should you care?"

It was a tough question. "Sometimes I don't know why I do stuff, but I've got to do it anyway."

A coyote grunted on one of the bunks, "Ain't that the truth."

Grover picked up his cards, "Be at the peach tree blind in twenty minutes."

I nodded and left. By now all the smudge pots were fired up and the orchards stank of kerosene and diesel smoke. No wind, so there was a chance the buds wouldn't freeze, even if it dropped into the mid 20s.

There are several blinds at Mola, places where surveillance cameras don't reach. Activity happens there in private. While I walked between the night-blackened trees, I thought about Grover and the shunts. He'd been out of the world for fifteen years. Whatever he'd done, the medboss and the rest of the staff weren't convinced he wouldn't do it again. They were planning on kicking me after only four years on a manslaughter and molestation conviction. Some folks must be harder-wired for their lives than others. I walked a slow circuit around the orchards, checking the smudges, thinking about reformation, redemption and punishment. Mola only offered one. The others I'd have to find on my own. Dull yellow flames undulated within the smudges, belching warm smoke. A con nodded in acknowledgment as I went by. He must not have recognized me.

Grover and two others waited at the peach tree blind, a distant fence light illuminating their heads and shoulders but leaving the rest dark. He was talking to them. "Here's the package. You take your shot, best you can. I'm not responsible for administrative follow-up. You can't perform, it's your fault, not mine. Payment in full on your side regardless."

They nodded. Both held something a foot-and-a-half long. Hard to tell in the shadows. Probably rubber hose. The light showed their faces clearly enough, though. Fresh fish. One I recognized from Chika's bus. Young, hard, wary. Asian eyes on him; a twisty scar across his cheek and the corner of his mouth. The other was bland, peckerwood suburbia. Straight teeth in his smile. He smiled now. "I want to go first," he said.

As I said, there's violence in Mola. Not much, since meds and therapy work hard to stomp it out, and, of course, recidding in prison is a short route to another month or two of daily ET, but the urge is there, even when there's little opportunity.

Suburbia said, "Are you scared, asshole? I like it better when they're scared." He popped the rubber hose across the palm of his other hand. "Grover here says I can't kill you, but he didn't say I had to leave anything for anyone else either." He whacked his palm again.

He looked at Grover. Grover nodded. Suburbia stepped forward, his smile wider, eyes bright. I didn't flinch. Maybe somebody had molested him when he was young. Maybe he was abused. All those nurture arguments. Or maybe nature programmed him for violence. Too much of one hormone, not enough of another. Maybe a genetic flaw. Lots of reasons people behave the way they do. There's no discussion of evil in technological corrections, no room for it, and no treatment.

He got close, exhaled in my face. "Damn, this will be good!" He breathed hard. Licked his lips, working himself up. Raised his hand, and I could see the hose clearly—he'd jammed glass shards in it.

The hose would hurt, when it hit, the glass would rip, and I would deserve it. I clasped my hands behind me so I wouldn't protect myself by reflex.

Then, his eyes crossed. It would have been funny in any other context. When his eyes crossed, and all the tension went out of his face, he sagged as if he'd been erased inside. Shunt magic. He struggled for a second, raising his hand again, but the hose rocked loosely. He gasped, then dropped his arm to his side. "Damn," he said, no force behind it. "This isn't fair."

"I told you that might happen," said Grover.

"Huh?" said Suburbia. He sat at my feet. "Can't shtand anymo'." With his legs crossed, he fell over backwards, his eyes shut. A soft snore bubbled in his throat.

Grover looked at the other one. "Your turn slant-eyes."

The boy murmured under his breath, chanting a mantra. "Stay calm," he said. "Stay calm," but his brow oozed sweat. His shunt was already working on him. He approached anyway, hand pressed against his stomach, hunched a little like a washerwoman. In the mellow light, he grimaced, paused, then shuffled forward another couple steps. "Oh," he moaned. "I'm gonna be sick." The rubber hose plopped onto the dirt, and he shambled off, bent almost double now, into the swirling smoke.

Grover laughed. "You did those boys a favor, Knavely. They're seeing the errors of their ways through you. Bet they're out of here a year earlier each because of this." He picked up the hose. "You get what you want, and I collect my fee anyway."

I took a shuddery breath. They'd been so close. Another step, and either would have been on me. The strong arm. The quick lash, and I'd get my inadequate payback, but they'd faltered. Reformation without punishment. The medboss would send me into the world unmarked. My hands unclenched. I hadn't realized it, but my fingers had been squeezed so tightly my fingernails had dug into my palms. Blood seeped from both.

"Pity to waste the opportunity, though," Grover said.

The hose whistled in the air, and the first blow took me across the chest, knocking me against a tree. The second snapped a rib. My hand went up, and he broke my wrist. Grover reeled back drunkenly. His shunt must have been dumping everything at once, but he came forward again, arm high, and I looked up in time to see retribution coming down.

The medboss sat at my bedside, peering over the glasses that had slid to the end of her nose. "So you fell off a ladder?"

I nodded, the thick dressing clinging to my face. The drainage tube running out of my cheek brushed my neck.

"And this happened in the middle of the night, not only shattering your cheekbone, but also breaking a pair of ribs and your arm?"

From the high infirmary window, only clouds were visible. I turned away from her to look at them. My head made the maneuver in a pulsing, oceanic slosh that didn't settle down for several seconds after I'd stopped moving.

"How's the crop?" I said carefully. Talking sent razored slivers through my jaw.

In the corner of my eye I could see her studying me. Her hands came up and templed against her lips. "No frost damage." She sighed. "You know, we can't help anyone if you stick to this story. We don't know what happened out there. I have some medical clues. I know what the shunts did, but I don't know why they did it. I don't know which of my records correlate to what you're covering up. There's sick folk in here. The only way to treat them is through knowledge."

I shrugged, and that hurt too.

Two weeks later I met Grover under the apple trees, thick with blossoms now, and the air so pollen-filled my eyes watered. He worked a weed pick, uprooting anything small and green with a twist of the wrist.

"I hear you're on the next bus," he said without looking up.

"They're waiting for me at the gate." My arm ached hollowly from where they'd removed my shunt. "I never said anything."

Another weed popped out. He ground it under his heel. "That's why your baby's still sleeping alone."

"Good." A breeze knocked down some petals. They drifted down like pink parachutes, pattering around us.

Grover scratched his chest. "You taking a beating won't bring back that dead kid."

My throat went dry.

He said, "The kid's still dead, and in a week or a month or sometime, Chika will find some horny bastard who won't scare her too bad when he asks her to sit in his lap. You get a honking scar out of the deal. A useless gesture won't redeem you Cho Mo."

"In time, the scar will fade," I choked out.

"Yeah, but why the bother? What's the point?"

Another breeze blew through the boughs. No petals fell this time, but they all fluttered, a vast pink comforter whispering overhead. I said, "You've got to do what good you can do, regardless of who you are."

I didn't see Chika on the way out. I never said goodbye, but as I passed Administration, the Asian kid with the twisty scar staggered from his first ET, tears streaming down his face, his eyes unfocused and desperate. He saw me, changed direction, caught me by the shoulders.

"They didn't tell me it'd be like that! I'm not . . . human," he said. "That night in the orchard. I'm so sorry." He rocked his head from side to side, mouth open, until he fell to his knees, then tipped to his side. "They should destroy me," he blubbered. He pulled his knees into his chest, fell to his side, then wrapped his arms around his legs, burying his face. "I'm a mad dog."

The long road from Mola stretched in front of me. At the end I could see the checkout booth and the bus. I knelt beside him, patted him on the back while he shivered. Grover was right: nobody could bring the dead child back, and nobody could forgive me either. All I could do was wait for the scar to become a part of my face and then accept it as my face.

"There are no throw-away people," I said.

THE SOUND OF ONE FOOT DANCING

SHOOK THE CHAINS HOLDING THE SOUND STAGE'S SIDE DOORS LOCKED, THEN started the long walk through the darkened studio to check the front. The day had been a full one. Mr. Sandrich, the director, had the crew knock down the Lincoln Day set and assemble the Fourth of July one. He didn't like three of the flats, and they had to be redone. The dancers and extras got antsy, and all the while reporters were trying to get in to interview Fred Astaire about how he felt about yesterday's declaration of war. In the meantime, one of our cameramen had a son on the Arizona, and he didn't come to work because the Navy hadn't told him whether his boy was alive or not, so I doubled as studio security and camera grip. I'd been thinking about quitting, you know, joining the war effort and all.

It was 3:00 in the morning, and I should have been going home myself, but a percussive tapping from the Holiday Inn set kept me here. Tired as I was, I had to smile. Astaire was practicing by himself again. It didn't matter when Sandrich called the day, Astaire stayed to work. I'd heard he weighed 140 pounds when the picture started. The Paramount doctor said he was down to 126 and prescribed thick steaks, which were delivered from the commissary every night at 7:00. He hardly touched them.

The front doors were locked too, so I found a chair in the dark beside the set and watched Fred Astaire dance. Only one overhead spot was turned on that isolated him in its lighted circle. His hands were in his pockets, and he danced with only one foot. The taps flew briskly, different rhythms, slow at first, a quick rattle, then a steady syncopation. He switched, so now his other foot beat out a rhythm. His head was down. I'd seen him do this before, a dancer's warmup. Soon, though, he started moving on the stage, more ice skating than dancing, in and out of the light.

I relaxed into the seat. The steady tapping of his flashing feet lulled me and excited me too. No one could be so tired that watching Fred Astaire wouldn't wake him. Without music, he made tunes. Without a partner, he made a duet. His hands were out, practicing one side of a routine I recognized. It was the part from *Flying Down to Rio* where he and Ginger Rogers danced across seven white grand pianos. He hummed the tune, turning, turning, dipping and sliding, in the light and out. I could almost see Ginger, dress flying, anticipating his moves. He'd told me once, "Of course Ginger was able to accomplish sex through dance. We told more through our movements instead of the big clinch. We did it all through dance."

Astaire accelerated. His feet hardly touched the stage, while his tapping seemed not to come from him, but to be an accompaniment. I'd seen him dance many nights, but not like this, one hand curled around an invisible waist, the other in the air, holding an invisible hand. Round and round. Through the light, brilliantly lit, and than back to the dark, a gray shape swirling, tapping, humming his musical part.

Then, he stopped. "Where'd you go?" he said, his voice echoing in the empty studio. "Where'd you go?"

I cleared my throat. He jumped. He didn't know I'd been watching. "Where'd who go, Mr. Astaire?"

"Is that you, Pop?" He shaded his eyes from the spot and peered toward me.

"Yes, sir. Nice dancing, sir."

"Where'd the girl go?" He looked at his empty hand, puzzled.

"Girl, sir? We're alone. Studio's locked up."

"There was a girl . . . about yay tall. Dark hair. Round face." His voice trailed off. "We were dancing."

I stood, my skin as cold as marble. "You must be tired, sir. It's time to go home."

He looked at me, his forehead and cheeks white in the spot, his eyes deeply shadowed. Then he glanced behind him as if he'd heard a noise. "I was holding a girl, I could have swore . . ."

I rattled my keys. "It's been a long day, Mr. Astaire. I'll open the door for you."

When he was gone, I crossed the cavernous space, past the Valentine Day's set, through the little tree-lined road for the carriage ride, where Bing Crosby sang "Easter Parade" to Marjorie Reynolds, through the Holiday Inn set itself—the Christmas tree was next to the piano; they'd do the "White Christmas" bit this week—and then to the north doors.

They were secure, I knew they were, but I checked them anyway. When I came to the door, my hand trembled. The big deadlock turned stiffly—the door wasn't used much—and I pushed it open with my shoulder. Outside in the California night I saw a narrow alley, a low wall, and on the other side, shining in the star light, the glistening mausoleums and tombstones of the Hollywood Memorial Cemetery. Rudi Valentino is buried there, and so is Douglas Fairbanks. I also saw Lillian's grave, not so new now, tucked away inconspicuously next to the gaudier displays.

Lillian, who answered a call for dancers last year, another anonymous girl hoping for a movie part, who lined up with the rest, who made the first cut because she wasn't too tall, or too short, or too fat, who waited for her chance to dance, and when they called her name she stood, took her spot on the stage, put her hands on her hips, poised for the music to begin, like a thousand other girls over the years. I watched her because I always watch the dancers' auditions. Except this time, for this girl, before the music started, she swayed and fell.

I sighed. Lots of girls faint. They stand around all day, their hopes in their throats, and then their turn comes. So I walked forward, fingering the smelling salts in my pocket. She'd come to, another embarrassed performer. But she didn't. The studio doctor got there within minutes. The other dancers, all hopefuls, surrounded us. "She's gone," the doctor said.

A dancer shrieked. "It was just sleeping pills! It couldn't have killed her."

I learned that day how strong, how *obsessive*, the Hollywood dream is. Lillian had looked like a shoe-in for the part. If she flubbed her audition, then the other dancer thought she'd have a better chance, so she'd slipped her the drugs.

The doctor told me later, "Lillian must have had a weak heart, Pop, for her to collapse that way."

I don't know what killed her, but I don't believe it was a weak heart. Not *her* heart.

Lillian's tombstone glowed grayly among the others. There's something in the real dancers, like Fred Astaire, that won't quit, some steel-barred determination that keeps them on their feet long after the rest have gone to bed. I looked up and down the alley, the door's handle cool under my hand. "Go to sleep," I said into the empty night. "Go to sleep, Lillian. Quit coming back."

Most of the sound stages at Paramount have a haunt or two. It's an old studio. The first film was shot here in 1917, DeMille's *The Squaw Man*. Valentino shot *The Sheik* here in 1921, and *Wings*, which won the first ever Academy Award for best picture, was filmed here in 1927. Casts by the hundreds have come through Paramount's gates. All those dreamers filming dreams. But doors swing open on empty stages. Equipment moves. An actress can walk from one spot to another ten feet away and suddenly shiver. "It's so cold here," she'll say, her hands wrapped round her arms.

I saw Lillian the first time a week after she died, her back to me, standing in an open door. "You can't be here, Miss. We're closed," I said. Then she turned, and I recognized her as she faded away. She returned two or three times a week, looking sad. I followed her once, walking slowly from set to set. At the end she met my eyes. I blinked, and she was gone.

I asked around. None of the other security guards knew about her. Only me. I thought, why me? Why do I always see her? Was it because I held her head as she died on the stage, so young, so unfulfilled, still waiting for her musical cue? Was that it?

When I returned to the sound stage at noon, filming had already been going for four hours. Jimmy, the morning guard, told me that Astaire was waiting at the gates at 6:00 and danced for two hours before the rest of the cast arrived. Firecrackers popped within the studio.

"He's doing the Fourth of July routine again?" I asked.

Jimmy shook his head, then nodded. "The man's unstoppable."

There was applause as I approached the set. The camera crew and extras clapped. Astaire stood in the middle of the stage surrounded by wisps of firecracker smoke. "Not right yet. Let's shoot it again," he said. Then he took his starting position behind the curtains.

Mr. Sandrich looked like he wanted to say something, but he swallowed the thought, shrugged and said, "Cue the music. Take twenty-one. Cameras, action."

Astaire came through the curtains, all movement and rhythm and timing. This was supposed to be a spontaneous routine. In the story, Marjorie Reynolds, his partner, doesn't show up and two important Hollywood executives are in the audience. He grabs a handful of pocket torpedoes, and as he dances, he throws them against the ground, an explosive counterpoint to his own pyrotechnics. It's the most amazing dance routine I'd ever seen.

He turns. Bam! He skips twice, does a half pirouette. Bam! Bam! He lights an entire string of firecrackers, then dances among the explosions. All to the music. All looking like he was making it up on the spot. It was stunning.

When he finished, he didn't even appear to be breathing hard. Everyone applauded again. My hands sting with enthusiasm.

"No. It's still not right. Let's do it again." He disappeared behind the curtains.

A familiar voice said over my shoulder, "Pop, he's getting so thin, I could spit through him."

"Yes, sir, Mr. Crosby."

He shook his head in wonder as he walked away toward the sound proof practice rooms. Martha Mears, Miss Reynolds' voice double, was with him. They'd been working on the harmonies for "White Christmas" since last week.

All in all, Astaire did the firecracker routine for the cameras thirty-eight times and it was late at night before he said it was good enough. Only the essential crew members were left in the studio.

"Go home, boys," he said. "I want to get in another step or two."

The lights shut down, except for the spot he'd danced to the night before. I checked the doors. In the year since she'd died, I'd never seen Lillian dance. She walked or stood. She found me, then locked her eyes on mine, straining to communicate a mute message from beyond her grave I never understood.

Tapping came from the stage again. One foot.

"Hey, Pop," he said as I took a seat in the dark. "Let's see if we can get a curtain call from our mystery dancer."

He beat out his complicated, one-footed rhythm, hands deep in his pockets again. "You know, my character in the film is searching for a dance partner." He changed to the other foot without breaking the beat. It scraped, skipped, heel-toed, variation on variation. "I know what it's like to look for a partner. One dance. One supreme dance to glory." He sounded whimsical. "Sometimes when the music starts, it's like . . . well . . . it's like . . ." He trailed into silence, his eyes tracking off stage. "Ahh," he sighed.

I couldn't see her! Why couldn't I see her? Astaire glided to center stage. Offered his hand. Curled the other around the small of her invisible back.

I've seen Astaire dance with Ginger Rogers, with Eleanor Powell, Rita Hayworth and Grace Kelly. He's redefined what a human can do with his body to music. But I'd never seen a dance like this. Not before. Not since.

And they danced. The room grew cold. Not just a spot, but the whole studio, thousands of square feet. My exhalations were frosty plumes. I found that I was crying, the tears freezing on my cheeks, and I suddenly felt like an intruder, a peeping tom. I left. Walked through the Holiday Inn interior. The Christmas tree glittered in the little light. Bing Crosby's pipe lay on the piano top. I could almost hear him singing, "I'm dreaming of a white Christmas . . . where children listen for sleigh bells in the snow."

Then I exited. Now I stood in the Holiday Inn exterior. Impossibly, the snow machine above turned on. Oatmeal flakes tumbled down around me. I was freezing in a fake snowstorm while Fred Astaire danced with the ghost of dead girl who never made it into the pictures.

I unlocked a north door. Crossed the alley. Leapt the low wall, then walked home through the Hollywood Memorial Cemetery. I never went back to the studio. I mailed my resignation.

They released *Holiday Inn* in August of 1942. A Japanese U-boat shelled a Santa Barbara oil refinery in January. Corrigedor fell in May. We beat the Japs at Coral Sea and again at Midway, but the losses were terrible. I tried to enlist. The Army wasn't interested in a prematurely gray, heavy, flat-footed thirty-two-year-old ex-security guard.

In September, finally, I went to see the movie. Someone told me that they'd seen me in the film, and I remembered that on a lark they'd used me in one scene. Didn't even change my name. I'm standing at a security door when the filming of the final Holiday Inn sequence starts, and I tell Fred Astaire and his agent they can't come in. I have one line. Behind the door, Bing Crosby and Marjorie Reynolds finally get together. If you watch the movie, you'll see me.

But that's not what's important.

I settled into the theater seat. The movie was pretty popular. That song, "White Christmas," just seemed perfect for our boys overseas, but this was a weekday matinee, and I almost had the house to myself.

It's a sweet story. I'd almost forgotten. Bing Crosby loses his girl to Fred Astaire, and then he has a bad go of it as a farmer, then he tries show business again at Holiday Inn, a nightclub only open on holidays. Crosby meets Reynolds, and they fall in love, only to have Astaire come along and try to steal her too. I waited for the Fourth of July number. How would it play on the screen? Would anyone see that Astaire used thirty-eight takes to look like he'd made it up on the spot?

The scene approached. There's an ensemble song and dance number before Astaire's firecracker routine. I was watching, my eyes half closed. A line of girls comes onto the stage from one side, a line of guys from the other. They're singing a patriotic tune about the Fourth. The guys group at the back of the stage singing the bass line. Half the girls split off into the audience, the other half, six girls, have formed three pairs, backs to the camera. The first pair faces the audience to sing, "Let's salute our native land." The next pair turns, "Roman candles in each hand." Then the last pair sings, "While the Yankee doodle band."

I don't hear any more. I'm standing in the theater, pointing at the screen.

The girl on the right is Lillian. She sings and dances through the rest of the scene. It's Lillian.

Astaire danced her right into the movie. He got her a part. Rent the video if you don't believe me.

I never saw Fred Astaire again.

After Astaire died at eighty-eight, Mikhaile Baryshinikov said, "It's no secret we hate him. He gives us complexes because he's too perfect. His perfection is an absurdity."

They buried him at Oakwood Memorial Park not far from Ginger Rogers' grave.

I wish they'd put him at Hollywood Memorial, where his real partner rests, the one who danced her way into *Holiday Inn*. The only one light enough on her feet to match him, step for step.

THE BOY BEHIND THE GATE

As you are now,
So once was I.
As I am now,
So you shall be.
Prepare for death and follow me.
—from a tombstone in the
Central City Cemetery

CENTRAL CITY: TODAY

PINE TREE TOPS CREAKED OVERHEAD, BUT THE AIR DIDN'T MOVE IN THE granite-strewn gully as Ron hiked up the steep gulch. He consulted his compass, then rechecked the map. Another hundred yards above him should be The Golden Ingot #9, and if the rusted mining equipment he'd been climbing over and around for the last ten minutes were any indication, the map was right. He scanned the ground, his eyes aching from sun and dust. The backpack, heavy with a powerful flashlight, rope and bolt cutters thumped against his kidneys. Was anything out of the ordinary? Was there any sign? A patch of cloth? A child's shoe? Could Levi have walked this far? Ron imagined the eight-year-old being towed up the mountain, hand-in-hand with the stranger who'd taken him. Would Levi have been crying, aware in his little boy way of the danger he was in?

Ron closed his eyes. He wanted to imagine Levi scared. He hoped he was scared to death because the alternative . . . Maybe he'd been wrapped in a blanket or a plastic sheet slung over the man's shoulder. They knew who the man was, Jared Sims, but Levi wouldn't have known. Ron shivered and continued climbing.

A jumble of cable, thick as his wrist and so rusted that wherever the metal crossed itself it had corroded into one piece, blocked his path. Ron scrambled partly up the gully's slope around it. Piles of yellow and white mine tailings humped up above him, and soon he topped out to the relative flatness of the claim. The old map he'd photocopied in Central City had shown him where the mine was; it wasn't marked on the USGS maps. Most of the abandoned mines and shafts had been filled in. Too much chance of some tourist wandering around old mining property, snapping pictures of busted down mills and what was left of miners' cabins, and then stepping on some rotten boards covering a shaft a hundred feet deep. So over the last twenty years, the state and park service had been closing the properties. Still, the Gilpin County mining district had been huge, and thousands of claims had been made. There were hundreds of openings even now for someone to find if he knew where to look. Perfect, mysterious holes blasted into the mountain, timeless monuments to long-dead miners' hopes. Perfect places to hide a little boy you didn't want found. Here, at the Golden Ingot #9, except for the rust, it could be 1880 again. He half expected to surprise a dozen miners waiting for their turn in the bucket and the long ride down the shaft.

Ron kept his eyes down. Little chance that there'd be a footprint in the yellow gravel, but it didn't hurt. Maybe Levi would have dropped something for him to find. It seemed years ago, but it was only last winter that Ron had read him *The Lord of the Rings*. The hobbit, Pippin, had broken from the orcs and dropped a sign that he was still alive, a beautiful beech-tree leaf brooch. Levi had said, in his little man's voice, "That was very clever of him, Daddy, wasn't it?" Ron remembered Levi's head resting on his arm while he read. He could almost feel the weight of his little boy leaning against him until they got to the end of the chapter. "Read some more, Daddy. Read some more," he'd said sleepily.

A pile of boards laying almost flat looked hopeful. Ron lifted the end of one. It creaked as it rose slowly, pulling a dozen nails from the rotted plank beside it. Dust slapped into the air after Ron moved it aside and dropped it. The next one showed a shaft's edge. A minute later, he'd cleared most of the boards. The pile looked like it hadn't stirred since Grover Cleveland held office, but since he was here, he was going to check.

The afternoon sun showed only six feet of shaft wall, while the rest was black. Was the bottom only a dozen feet away, or was this one of those deep, deep holes reaching hundreds of yards down?

As always, as he had scores of times since the police gave up looking ten days before, he crouched at the shaft's edge, cupped his hands around his mouth and called into the darkness, "Levi! Levi! Are you there, son?"

Wind stirred sand behind him, blowing a little over the edge where it glittered in the sunlight, then disappeared. Only the breeze's sibilant hiss answered him.

*

CENTRAL CITY: 1879

Images flitted in Charles' mind as he stayed motionless in his bed, listening to the boy's even breathing on the floor beside him. It was the small hours of the morning, when time came unanchored, and memories piled willy nilly atop one another. Charles could see them all: his wife dying, the Laughlins, the McGarity's, the bloody hands in the mine. The fireplace coals had long since died, and the moon's thin line outside the window cast almost no light through the muslin drape. He'd light a candle if he dared, but if he did, the boy's eyes might be open; he might look at him through the flickering light and know that he knew.

He couldn't sleep. No, not that. Charles would dream, and in his dreams he'd see the Laughlin children burning up, their red skin baking from within. "Scarlet fever," the nurse from Idaho Springs had said. "Poor things."

Charles had stood at the Laughlin's door that morning, a basket of bread and clean sheets hanging from one hand, blinking at the darkness in the room. Only the sun behind him provided light. They'd covered the one window, and the cabin smelled close and moist and sweaty sick. The nurse sat by three-year-old Lisa to his left. Against the back wall lay Evelyn with her mother sitting beside her. The baby's crib rested in the opposite corner. William Laughlin sat at the rough-hewn table in the room's middle, resting his forehead in his hand.

The boy crept around Charles, even though he'd told him to stay with the mule. His arm wrapped around the back of Charles' leg, and he leaned into the room. Charles put his hand down to push him back, but he didn't. He didn't like touching his son, the stranger who lived with him every day. Lisa panted under the blankets, blonde hair plastered to the side of her face. Four-year-old Evelyn turned to the wall, her chest still for a moment before she drew her next wheezing breath. Her mom, a hint of the scarlet flush across her own cheeks visible in the sunlight, pressed a wet cloth to Evelyn's forehead.

"The little one?" Charles said.

William Laughlin shook his head without moving his hand. "She went during the night." He coughed. It sounded wet and pathetic.

"I brung some things," Charles said. He stepped deeper into the room, and the atmosphere pushed back. Outside, the sun shone bright and men filled the valley, moving surely from mine to mill, loading ore wagons or carrying supplies. Blasting echoed off cliff walls above, and Clear Creek murmured like watery wind. But here, the air felt dead with fever.

William draped a hand over the basket's edge. "You're a right Christian, Charles."

"You going to your shift?" Charles moved back. The heat in the room oppressed, and he didn't want to breathe so close to the sick girls.

"I'll be along."

Charles retreated to the porch. The boy leaned over Lisa, his legs bright in the sun pouring through the door, while his upper torso faded in the room's shadows. He drew a finger across the little girl's forehead, through her fevered sweat. He stood, facing his father, his finger up as if he'd erased chalk off a blackboard. For a moment he looked at Charles as if surprised to see him still waiting for him, then he put his finger in his mouth.

When they crossed the footbridge over the creek, Charles said, "Why'd you do that, boy? I told you to stay out."

The boy held onto the mule's bridle, his head not even coming up to the mule's chin. "They'll burn, Papa."

Charles nearly stumbled, then glanced at the boy. He wore an old, flannel shirt too big for him with the sleeves rolled up. Pale, skinny arms. Dark hair cut above his eyebrows. Dark eyes. He was given to long, unblinking looks. A serious mouth, like his mother who died bringing him into the world eight years before.

"I'm glad he's out of me," she'd said in the moment before she died screaming.

"What do you mean, boy?"

"I put the death in them." He held up his finger that had touched the girl as if in proof. "Just like the other lambs."

"Don't talk like that." Charles pulled the bridle from the boy's hand, his own hand shaking. "You go on home, and I don't want to see a mess in the cabin when I get back. Sweep the floor."

"I can smell the fire," the boy said before turning toward their cabin.

Charles thought about his son all day, deep in the mine, as he worked the single jack, bent low in the tunnel only three quarters of his height, placing the steel bit against the stone, pounding it a bit deeper with each blow, rotating it each time to clear the bit. Pausing just before he drove the hammer home. The angle had to be perfect. The placement, perfect. He had to judge before he struck. Striking without looking could shatter the drill. There was always the pause before the hammer came down to be sure he was doing the right thing. So there could be no mistake. It was a feeling of good or bad in the way the drill stood. Charles considered his judgement with the hammer to be his only genius. He never struck wrongly. *Clang!* The hammer would fall against the rod. Rock dust crumbled from the hole. *Clang!* He'd hit it again, his strong right arm driving the blow home. Numbing work to create a hole for the charge. He could raise the hammer all day with that arm; the work had made it larger than the other one, a giant's arm, but he couldn't shape the boy with it. He couldn't even hold him.

The boy had been bad from the beginning. His wet nurse took sick and died. After that, no one would help Charles, so he fed the child himself with goat's milk, certain that the first winter would kill him, having no mother to care for him, but as winter filled the mountains with snow and cutting wind, even as influenza swept through the camp taking many babies, the boy thrived. He was walking by the next summer, and Charles would leave him locked in the cabin when he worked his shift, half expecting to find the toddler dead on his return. But every day the boy met him, a little taller, a little stronger, and never smiling.

Setting the powder took a half hour. Each hole had to be filled with the proper amount. Then the fuse cord had to be measured. Charles worked methodically. This deep in the mine, the stale air hurt his lungs and gritty rock coated his eyes and tongue. He checked the candle burning brightly in its shadowgee stuck in the wall. When he set the last charge, he retreated to the bucket lift, covering his nose and mouth with a soaked bandana to protect against the dust. After the blast, he stood with head bowed, breathing through the wet cloth.

Charles wanted to love him. He tried. The weather in the boy's heart was cold, though, and hugs meant nothing to him. He never played. He never cried. And always, around him, children died. Diphtheria. The grippe. Typhoid. The croup. Pneumonia. Whooping cough. Small pox. Lingering diseases. Wasting illnesses. The cemetery filled with tiny corpses.

The ore cart rattled on the rails as Charles pushed it toward the broken ore. For the rest of his shift he'd fill the cart, take it back to the lift, empty it and return for another load. No candles lit the path, but that didn't matter. Charles didn't mind the dark most days, but today he couldn't stop thinking about the boy. What does the boy do while I'm at work? What does he daydream about? Charles imagined him wandering through the camp, looking for children.

In the spring he'd taken the boy to a funeral. Seamus McGarity had lost both his boys and his wife to dysentery three days apart. McGarity, his kin and friends circled the coffins, two tiny wood boxes and a long one. During the prayer, Charles looked down at his boy dressed in mourning black. The corners of the boy's mouth turned up and his eyes were shining. At the ceremony's end, the boy dropped dirt in each grave. Surreptitiously, he also put a handful of grave soil in his pocket.

"Lucky your kid's doing good," McGarity said to him the next day as they waited for the bucket to take them down the shaft. His lunch pail dangled from his hand, and the miner looked exhausted, as if he hadn't slept for a month. "He came by a week ago. Found him sitting by the door."

"What did he want?" Charles wished he could pat McGarity on the shoulder. How would it be to lose your whole family? There'd been other men whose children died who drank themselves to death. The other miners stood away from them. People died in the camps all the time, but it wasn't easy to be next to the bereft, not at first.

McGarity didn't answer for a while. He stared out over the valley, but he didn't appear to be looking at anything. Finally he said, "Caleb used to sing his little brother to sleep. I don't think he knew I was listening. 'Amazing Grace' it was. Learned it from his mom. He had a nice voice for a ten-year-old."

They found McGarity at the bottom of a shaft a week later. Was he drunk and fell in, or did he jump?

At the blasting site the dust still hung in the air, surrounding the candle in a pale globe. Charles hefted ore into the cart. My boy's not human, he thought as each rock crashed against the metal. Methodically he bent and lifted, bent and lifted. Not human. Not human. Charles pictured the boy with his finger in his mouth, salty-bitter from the Laughlin girl's scarlet fever sweat.

After a while Charles stopped loading. His hands stung. He stepped next to the candle's feeble light and held them up. Blood ran down his wrists from his ragged fingertips. Dully he realized he'd not worn his gloves. And a certainty came to him, a gravestone solid conviction: my boy's a monster!

Charles lay in his bed, motionless. The boy breathed evenly on the floor below him. Only the sliver-moon lit window floated in the dark. Charles kept his eyes wide open. If he shut them, even for a second, the boy might stand. He might lean his unsmiling face close. The boy might run his finger across Charles' forehead.

"I see you burning, Papa," the boy would say. He always called him Papa, like it was a curse.

And dawn was hours away.

Ron sat in his van on the abandoned mining road near the boulders the park service had used to block the path, his map spread out on the seat beside him marked with X's for mining claims. From Central City there were so many. The historical marker at the town limits proclaimed THE RICHEST SQUARE MILE ON EARTH. He shook his head. If only it were that small.

Starting at Black Hawk at one end of the valley to the other end of Central City was a couple of miles. Mine tailings spotted the slopes on both sides. Then there were the gulches: Chase, Eureka, Russell, Lake, Pecks, Fourmile and others the map didn't name with mines of their own, and the road went on to the ghost towns of Yankee Hill, Ninety Four, Alice and Kingston. Nevadaville was only a stone's throw to the west. He could almost see the honeycomb of tunnels.

Ron smoothed the map, but his attention shifted. On the floor, barely visible in the blue dusk of sunset, a red plastic building brick lay canted on its side. He stretched around the steering wheel, crinkling the map with his elbow, and picked it up. The brick had almost no weight sitting on his palm. He straightened, put the brick on the dashboard.

They didn't have building bricks when he was a boy. His dad had given him Lincoln logs, and over the years, Ron's dad had added to the set until they filled a box almost too big to fit under his bed. Ron made forts and villages and fences and barns. Two short logs crossed over each other served as cannon. His dad came into his room one night and they built a tower together, half as tall as Ron.

Years later, when Levi was six, Ron had said to his dad, "You never told me how much fun being a father would be."

"I didn't think of it at the time," his dad said.

Ron fingered the building brick. He'd never made a tower with Levi.

The sky grew dark, and Ron didn't move. He thought about putting Levi to bed. "Have good dreams," he'd say. For forty nights now, Levi had not had Ron to wish him a bedtime without nightmares. He thought about throwing a baseball back and forth. He remembered reading to him, book after book, Levi's head resting against Ron's arm as they sat on the couch.

Ten days ago the Denver detective in charge of the investigation said, "We're giving up the search, Ron. You're going to have to face the possibility your son is dead. Sims killed his victims. We know that." They sat in the detective's temporary office in the Gilpin County Courthouse. Ron struggled to remain calm. The detective didn't look over twenty, and it was clear Ron made him uncomfortable.

"He didn't kill them right away," Ron insisted. "The Perez girl he kept in his basement for a week. In Colorado Springs he kept that baby in a storage garage for four days. His house was in Central City. My boy is in a mine somewhere. It's logical." Ron held a crumpled flyer. HAVE YOU SEEN THIS CHILD? Levi smiled from the page, a strand of his black hair across his forehead, his dark eyes turned toward his cake before he blew out the candles.

With the detective, Ron had walked through Sims' house, a restored turn-of-the-century Victorian gingerbread with no closets. Posters covered the living room walls, all children. Except for the kitchen, blocked with yellow crime scene tape and the outline of Sims' body on the floor, the rooms were meticulously tidy. Magazines on the coffee table were fanned out perfectly, the same half-inch overlap on each. On Sims' dresser in the bedroom, a line of brass padlocks stood like sentinels in a military row. They were the only decoration. Ron wondered what could make a man like Sims. Couldn't love have saved him? Love, pure love, might have kept Sims from hating, just as pure love would find his son. The police didn't love Levi enough to find him.

The detective shook his head. "If he hadn't shot himself, we could ask him. But he did. We've had crews up and down the area. If your son were there, we would have found him. He might have lasted a week without food. Only a couple days without water. It's been a month. Sims buried his victims. I'm sorry to have to say it this way, but I'd guess your boy is in a shallow grave."

Ron gripped the arms of the chair to keep from leaping at the man. "There's bonds between a father and his son. I'd know if he had died."

"The department can arrange counseling, if you request it," the detective said.

"You're not a father, are you?" Ron looked past the detective. Black and white photographs hung on the wall behind him: men standing before a wagon, holding shovels and lunch boxes; a long shot of Central City down main street when it was still dirt; the front of a school, forty or fifty children sitting on the steps, their severe looking teacher standing behind them with her arms crossed.

Ron touched the hard edge of the plastic building brick sitting on the dashboard and thought about the kids in the school a hundred years ago no different than his own boy, all dead by now for sure, and Levi who might not be. Razor-edged stars filled the sky through his windshield. The air had cooled, caressing his face through the open windows. This far up the rutted road he couldn't hear traffic from the high-way or crowd noise from the casinos that filled Central City. He canted his head to hear better. Something clicked repetitively in the distance, maybe a night bird or a locust. He wondered if locusts lived this high. For a long time he rested his finger on the brick and listened. The night vibrated with its own muttering. Unidentifi-able sounds that he guessed might be the breeze sliding over rocks and through the scrubby grasses. A high squeak that might be a bat. He couldn't tell. The mountain was perfectly black and the cloudless sky danced with stars that provided no illu-mination.

He turned on the ceiling light to read the map. If someone saw him from a dis-tance, he thought, he'd look like a time traveler in his craft, light glowing through the windows, unattached to the Earth.

Eventually he turned the light out and fell asleep sitting up, his head pillowed on a jacket against the door, windows still open so he could hear if Levi should call.

Charles slipped out of the cabin before dawn, the eastern sky just barely lighter than the west. The wind came up the valley, and in it he could hear the stamp mills thrumming as they crushed ore.

He trudged up the switchback trail toward the mine, his hands heavy, his head heavy. Had any child the boy met lived? There weren't that many children in the camps. The school in Nevadaville had 150 students last year, he'd heard, but there were 10,000 miners in the district. Central City had a small school and so did Black-hawk. Charles had never sent the boy, but he was supposed to go in the fall. The town was growing. More families came in every day. They were building churches.

At the top of the hill, he paused. From here in the pre-sunrise grimness, most of the town was visible in purples and blues. He couldn't find his own cabin though. Then, he gasped. A black aura like a cloud hid it from him, and for a moment it seemed as if it grew tentacles that flowed down the dirt roads, over the wooden sidewalks, sniffing at each door. The wind rippled the cloud's top, then blew in his face, carrying the smell of a crypt and the fevered dampness from the Laughlin cabin.

Charles shook his head. There was his cabin! There was no black cloud. He held his hands over his pounding heart. Am I going mad? A hallucination! But the question echoed hollowly. This was not madness. He'd seen the cloud as a vision, a sign. He backed up the trail, afraid to take his gaze away from the cabin.

When a man's dog goes wild, he shoots him. It's his responsibility. What was his responsibility as a father of a monster?

When Charles worked the mine that day, he stuffed his pockets with candles, and he kept one lit no matter where he was. The shadows beyond the weak candlelight were like the shadow creeping from his own house.

If Sims had locked Levi in a mine, it would have to have several qualities, Ron thought as he shouldered his pack. Pine lining the mountain top glowed in the morning light, but the sun wouldn't touch the valley's bottom for another hour. Ron checked his map and began the long hike up the old road. It had to be both close enough for him to get to, but far enough off the beaten track that it was unlikely anyone would find it. It had to be far enough back that even if Levi screamed for help, no one would hear him. There would be food and water. The question was, how much food and water? Sims wouldn't have planned on leaving Levi with over a month's supply.

Each step up the road felt like the ticking of an immense clock counting down. How much time was left? Was Levi even now crouched against a locked gate, light leaking around the edges, on the brink of death by thirst or starvation? If he ran out of water, might there be water in the mine itself that he had been drinking to keep himself alive? Ron thought about *Tom Sawyer*, not the hijinks of the little boy, but the awful image of Injun Joe trapped in McDougal's cave. After Ron's dad had read him that part, Ron had nightmares for months about eating bats while trying to carve through a thick wooden door with a broken knife.

Ron quickened his pace, his calves burning, keeping his eyes open for evidence of tunnels not on his map. He'd followed dozens of faint trails to dead end mines in the last ten days, peered down scores of open shafts, rattled the locks on handfuls of metal gates, always looking for a sign, always listening for Levi's voice. He crossed from the valley's shadow into the sunlight, and even this early in the morning the rays heated his shirt. It would be a hot one today.

The road ended at the tumbled remains of a small mill. Busted beams pointed skyward, a skirt of rotten wood at their feet. Ron rested for a moment, his hand against a gray post. Splinters flaked onto his skin. Behind the ruin a narrow path vanished over a ridge. Weeds grew into the twin grooves that were too narrow for an automobile. He imagined steel-rimmed wagon wheels and a cart of ore making its way down the road behind a team of horses. Time seemed irrelevant here. It could be 1880 again, or 2080; the mountains wouldn't know the difference. But he wasn't timeless, and the clock counted; every minute passed was another minute that Levi suffered alone. Could an eight-year-old die of fright? What if he believed his daddy had forgotten him? Ron whimpered at the thought.

His photocopied map called this the Sunderson Mill. Above it were several mines: West Yellow Dog, New Baltimore, and Crossroad. Ron spread the map over his knee. Small X's indicating digs crowded the gulch. There could be ventilation shafts, drainage tunnels, powder storage crypts, false starts, dead ends and full-bore excavations that needed checking.

It would take all day.

"Come with me, boy," said Charles, his hands shaking. It had taken him several minutes to push open the cabin door. He couldn't shake the impression of the cloud he'd seen around his house in the morning. It seemed to hover still, insubstantial, but present just the same. The sun shone mutedly through it, and the air felt cooler than it did ten feet away.

"It won't work," said the boy. He sat on the edge of his bed, his dark hair disheveled, his gaze steady and challenging.

Charles swallowed hard. "What won't work?"

"What you are planning." The boy came toward him, across the cabin's single room.

Charles backed away into the sunlight, gripping the hammer hanging from his belt. The weight of his satchel tugged at his shoulder. For a second he envisioned beating the boy down where he stood, before he could get away. He forced his fingers from the hammer.

"We are taking a walk."

"I know." The boy strode past him and up the road out of town.

Charles watched him, his breath caught in his throat. Suddenly the air seemed to clear, and the sun pressed against him. Had it always been this way around the boy? Had he been in a daze from the moment the child was born?

It was as if the boy followed a trail traced for him in the dirt. He walked in the road's middle, barely giving way when a wagon came toward him. The horse's nostrils flared at his smell.

Charles caught up to him when they turned onto the Sunderson Mill Road. The mines above it had gone bad the year before, and the mill was closed.

"The mountains hold things, Papa." The boy's hands hung straight at his side, as if he were standing at attention, not hiking a steep road.

He had no words to say to him. Am I the monster? thought Charles. The boy's mother wouldn't want this. Have I done something to deserve a curse? Every step hurt. Part of him wanted to run away. He could do it: leave the boy on the road, catch the new train out of town, and be in Denver before anyone knew. His family lived back east.

Another part denied that anything was wrong. Charles thought, what if I'm insane? My boy is strange, for sure, but he's not evil. What child growing in the mountains with a dead mother and a father who worked the mines wouldn't mature differently?

And a third part wanted to fall on the boy like a bear and rend him, bloody bone from bloody bone.

"Keep going," Charles said when the boy slowed at the mill. The windows were already broken and its door hung askew.

"Don't you love me, Papa?" he said. The boy looked at him sardonically. "A Papa should love his son."

The trail climbed as quickly as stairs for a hundred yards, while the afternoon sun touched the mountaintop before them. Charles choked on the words, "Of course, I love you." And he knew that he did. He loved him even as he wanted to kill him, even as he was afraid. Was this right? He thought of sick children sweating in their fevers, dead children. "They'll burn, Papa," the boy had said.

At the ridge's top, the trail flattened and split. Winding to the right, it led to West Yellow Dog, a fifty-foot drift that started with a yard-wide vein of quartz and wire gold but petered into low-grade ore that wasn't worth the cost of the powder to extract it. The middle trail ended at the New Baltimore, a failed attempt to find West Yellow Dog's wire gold by coming at it laterally. Charles had worked the New Baltimore for six months before the owners shut it down.

He'd never been in the Crossroad on the left trail, but, as the hard rock Cornishman who told him about it said, "The claim was snakebit from the beginning." The rumor was that the first prospector had been drilling into the rock to set a charge, and when he hit the drill for the last time, it disappeared into the rock. There was a tunnel already there. A silly story, but the claim didn't pay out, and there had been accidents.

They took the turn to the left, around a granite wall, out of the sun and into the stone bowl that held the mine. Rock surrounded them on three sides, like a small arena. The sound of Charles' hard-soled boots echoed. At the far side, a metal gate held closed by a clasp lock marked the mine's entrance.

"You're going to be staying here, boy." Charles removed a chisel from his satchel, set its edge against the lock, raised the hammer, then paused. Always he judged before he struck. Was the chisel set correctly? Would the hammer do its job? There could never be a strike without the pause for judgement, where a mistake could be saved. The metal's sharp report reverberated off the rocks. Another blow broke it, then Charles pulled the door open; it screeched against the stiffness in its hinges. He'd never seen a mine entrance like the Crossroad's. The floor looked worn smooth, as if thousands of feet had marched on it through the years. How had the miners done that?

"Don't you love me, Papa?" the boy said again.

Charles didn't look at him. From his satchel he removed a blanket, candles, a small bundle of food and a water bottle. "I'll be back tomorrow."

"You must not be my Papa." He didn't sound insincere this time. "My Papa loves me. He'll find me, my Papa."

"Just get in!"

Charles could barely see the new lock he put on the door through the tears.

Behind the iron gate, he heard the boy move, a large sound, as if what stirred in the tunnel had suddenly grown huge. He fell back. Impossibly, the door stirred in its iron frame, and for a second Charles thought the inch-thick bolts might pull from the rock. He scuttled away. Even at the edge of the granite arena, when Charles looked at the mine entrance, he could hear the boy behind the gate, breathing loud, his heart throbbing. The sky grew dark and the air thick. A noxious cloud seeped around the door's edges, filled the stone chamber, its tendrils crawling on the floor toward Charles. The boy said, his voice full of old mining timbers and cold, wet stone a thousand feet deep, "Papa?"

Charles fled.

West Yellow Dog had been dynamited. All that remained of its entrance was twisted ore cart track. Ron searched the cliff base to both sides. A niche three hundred yards to the right might have been where they stored powder, but it was only ten feet deep and didn't have a door. Below the mine, partially hidden behind scrubby pine growing between the rocks, he found a small tunnel barely tall enough for him to enter on his hands and knees, but twigs and dirt blocked the way a few feet in and it smelled of marmot. Ron sat on his haunches outside the hole and closed his eyes against the sun.

He'd know if Levi had died, wouldn't he? A father and son had a bond, he'd told the detective.

Within his view, visible only because the sun cast long shadows, several foundations rose from the grass in the clearing below the slope. There must have been a small community here, or they might have been part of the mining operation. At the Gilpin County Courthouse, Ron had looked at pictures of the town from the 1880s, and beside them were modern shots taken from the same spot. The buildings changed. Trees changed. But the rocks and mountains stayed the same. He trembled. To the mountain, time didn't exist; all times were interchangable. He glanced at his watch. To a little boy dying in a mine, every second stretched like skin on fire.

He pushed himself upright.

The New Baltimore had a park service gate on it. Ron slowed as he approached. Covered in dust, the remains of a broken lock lay on the ground. He rubbed the scratches in the metal. No rust. Someone had been here this summer.

"Levi!" His voice sounded hollow and out of place.

The gate gave reluctantly, its base dragging over the rock as he pulled it open. Moisture seeped from the walls a few feet in. Resting one hand on the black-slime ceiling just above his head, he shone his flashlight on indistinct footprints on the muddy floor. Back in the depths, a watery *plink-plink-plink* broke the silence. The tunnel split. To the right, a pile of rock and broken timbers blocked the way. To the left, the passage sloped downward for another twenty feet before ending at a pool of water. The footprints led here. Ron played the quivering light across the surface, penetrating to the bottom. Rocks. More timber. Metal so heavily rusted he couldn't tell what its original shape had been. No wrapped bundle. No horror-story patch of white that resolved itself into a face.

He released a pent-up breath. Why had someone broken into the mine? Turning, he studied the walls and ceiling. A slippery, unhealthy looking fungus covered the surfaces, and the stagnant air smelled rotted and mildewed. Near the ceiling to the left of the pool, a patch of rock peered through the growth, as if it had been brushed clean, and above it, a crack wider than his fist swallowed the light. Ron reached in, touched plastic. He found four bags in the crack, about a pound each. A whiff of the first one showed he'd uncovered someone's stash.

Ron left the bags on the floor. Ten minutes wasted.

According to his map, all that remained was the Crossroad. It took a half hour of backtracking across the gulch's east side before he found a faint trail that led to a gap around a rock wall.

He spotted the lock on the door on the other side of the stone arena as soon as he rounded the corner, a brand new, brass padlock, like the row of them on top of Sims' dresser. He ran without thinking about it. Old metal door, not park service.

Ron ripped off his backpack, fumbled for the bolt cutter, gripped the handles and squeezed. The lock snapped.

Was now the moment when he would know? Ron had dreamed of finding Levi in a thousand ways. Bad dreams, in some, where Levi was dead. Either dead over a month, or even worse, dead a few days. He'd be starved or dead from thirst or exposure. In some dreams he was alive but sick, damaged from exposure or the time alone. In one dream Levi didn't know him, his mind gone. What could be worse than an eight-year-old driven insane by abuse and fear? In that dream, Ron loved his son back to sanity. No evil could be so bad that love could not change it to something good.

Ron tore the lock from the hasp, jammed his fingertips into the gap between the door and the frame. Pulled.

In the good dreams, Levi waited. "Daddy!" he would cry. He always called Ron "Daddy," like it was a blessing.

The door swung open.

Charles didn't even try to get to sleep. Sitting at the table in his cabin, the tiny slice of moon providing the only light again, he thought about the locked gate and the boy behind it. His intention was to never return.

He thought, what's the greater evil? Every time he closed his eyes, he saw dead children, a fingerprint on their foreheads; he also saw the boy at the Crossroad, staring at a candle, maybe, or sleeping. What kind of dreams would a bringer of death like him have? But Charles was evil too. The boy, no matter what else he was, was his son. A father should take care of his own. One time when Charles was young he locked a storage shed on his father's farm. A week later his father sent him to fetch some tools. The storage shed stank, a solid wall of putridness rolling out when Charles opened the door. A cat had been locked in, its mouth gaping open, dry as dust, the stomach burst. If he had known, wouldn't it have been merciful to have killed the cat a week earlier?

Charles looked through the darkness to his own bed. He couldn't imagine sleeping again. The boy behind the gate moved in his mind. The room was so black, Charles could almost see the boy without closing his eyes. Like the cat, the boy was locked in. But the cat wasn't the devil. No, not by a long shot. Maybe a creature like the boy thrived on the black air behind the gate. Could such a thing be killed by an act as simple as being shut into a mine? What if it could do some magic to save itself?

In a sudden vision, Charles saw himself as an older man walking down a street. A beautiful carriage clattered by, the horses' hooves loud on the bricks. In the vision,

Charles glanced up. Sitting in the carriage was his son, grown now, and the look he gave from the carriage was full of hate.

Charles made a fist on the table, alone in his cabin in the midst of the night and moaned. The boy was behind the gate. "I'm cursed," Charles said to the four walls. Already he felt the guilt like a blood-soaked blanket settling over his head, suffocating him.

He's a boy dying slowly, my son, Charles thought. He's a monster who can save himself in some evil way.

Like the New Baltimore, the Crossroad was wet. Footprints showed clearly in the mud. Little prints. A child's shoes.

"Levi!" Ron's eyes strained to see into the mine, pulse throbbing huge in his chest. "Are you there, son?"

He took a few steps down the tunnel. Where was Levi? Ron turned on his flashlight. The powerful beam cut into the air showing the path curving away before him. His feet slipped on the muddy floor as slick as polished marble, and suddenly he felt scared, as scared as he'd ever been in his life. His breath puffed out in a plume before him. Every instinct told him to run. The mine didn't feel right. The air clung to his arms like icy cockleburs, and he had to brace himself with a hand against the wall. Then the floor shook, but it wasn't just the floor; everything jolted or quivered. Every cell in his body flinched. He wasn't sure if he had turned around and was heading out. He thought, the world has shifted.

He stepped forward again. Where am I? Where am I going?

A voice came from the tunnel before him, a little boy's voice.

"Papa?" it called.

Ron rushed forward, his fear forgotten. He would greet him with love like he'd never known.

"Papa?"

His son was coming home.

Charles stood at the Crossroad gate. He'd pulled it open, but he wouldn't step inside. No, he was too frightened for that. He couldn't *see* the boy, or all would be lost. He had one chance to make it right, and only one.

"Boy?" he yelled into the mine.

For a long time there was no sound, then Charles felt a peculiar twitch, like the mountain had shrugged. The air itself contracted, and his ears popped.

He shook his head. Whatever else was going on, he could not be swayed.

"Boy?" he shouted again.

A voice came from far back in the mine. "Daddy?" it cried. "Is that you, Daddy?"

Small feet splashed through the mud, growing louder.

"I knew you'd come, Daddy," the voice exclaimed, very close now.

Charles stood by the door out of sight, his hammer raised high, paused above him. When the boy stepped out, he would bring it down. Oh, yes he would. He would end it here.

And all would be right.

DO GOOD

Dedicated to Richard Vernon, Marshall Strickland, and Edward Rooney

VICE PRINCIPAL WELCH STUDIED THE EMPTY HALLWAY FOR AN HOUR, WAIT-ing for ghosts. He stood loosely, leaning against a wall, arms crossed on his chest, as if watching the Homecoming dance from an out-of-the-way corner. An empty school is a quiet thing, but it is not silent. He felt as if he'd put his ear to a seashell, except the seashell had swallowed him, and the waves rolled, almost forty years of them.

He'd unlocked the front door at 4:30 in the morning, turned off the alarms and slipped in. The lockers echoed his footsteps, while a security light at the end of the hall provided illumination, reflecting a thick, moon-white stripe from the middle of the waxed floor and a bright star on every locker handle. The hallway smelled of books and old paint. Out of habit, he looked at his pocket planner. Nothing sched-uled until 7:30. He sighed, then put it away.

Years ago, when Welch took the vice principal job, Principal Robinson, who retired and died the year after, had taken him to a bar on the far side of town where Lincoln High parents seldom gathered. He told him after their third beer, "That school's been there since 1902, Welch, and it started with greatness. We'd have been the state football champs in our first year, but the wingback broke his leg in the last game. Think of its tradition. What are you going to add, Welch? How are you going to make a difference? What are they going to say about you when you're gone?"

"I don't know," said Welch, his voice sudden and unexpected in the hall-way's quiet.

At 5:30, the heating system kicked on overhead, and a series of sharp pops ran down the ducts. Lilly, the head custodian, would be coming in soon, turning on lights, unlocking doors, opening the school to the Monday parade. He reached into his wallet for a ten dollar bill, smoothed it against the wall and wrote, DO GOOD. He thought for a second, then added, LAUGHING JACK. From his coat pocket he took a roll of tape, put an inch-long piece on one end of the bill, then walked down the hall. He closed his eyes, spun around a few times, and then stopped, his hand holding the bill in front of him, finger pointed. Locker 457. His master key opened the door. Books covered the bottom: A.P. ENGLISH, CALCULUS, MODERN U.S. HISTORY, a senior's locker, a senior who evidently didn't have homework over the weekend. Magazine photographs of body builders were stuck to the door's inside along with a valentine neatly inked, TO KIKI FROM HER BUDS. He taped the ten dollar bill next to the valentine before closing the door.

Down the hall, a row of lights flickered on. Lilly had started her rounds.

Welch sighed and headed toward the second floor to his office. No ghosts this morning. Not a one, but that didn't mean the school wasn't haunted. As he walked up the stairs he could feel the crush of students coming down, all those faces across the years streaming around him and through him.

"Good morning, Mr. Welch," said Pamela Howel, the Principal's secretary as she paused outside his door at 6:00, early as always. He glanced up from the bi-monthly incidents summary. She carried a briefcase in one hand and a cellphone in the other. Perfectly coifed black hair. Wire-rimmed glasses. Narrow, thirtyish face. Metabolism and personality of a hummingbird. She'd taken the job in September and had already remade the office in her image.

"Hello, Pamela. Good weekend?"

"Nope. Visiting in-laws. Don't forget I need your intention sheet for next year on my desk by Friday."

Welch checked his planner. Written next to Friday's date was the reminder about the retirement intention form.

"Are you going to hang it up?"

Welch shrugged.

"Not that we want you to go," she said before dashing to her office.

Fifteen weapon violations since March 1. Eleven knives, a ninja throwing star, a broken bottle, a BB gun and a sawed off pool stick. Twenty-three fights. Vandalism in the football weight room. Six car burglaries. A fire in the girl's bathroom next to the cafeteria. An attempted suicide. Four incidents of senior hazing, each involving duct tape. And then the folder filled with complaints about Beau Reece, a mouthy second-year freshman who weighed maybe eighty pounds. Welch sighed and pushed it to the side. All in all, a pretty calm two months. He raised his pen to sign the report.

A movement caught his eye. A student in the chair next to the desk crossed his legs.

Welch looked up. No one sat in the chair. He blinked. The skin on his arm prickled as if all the tiny hairs had been tugged. Was it someone he knew? That was the problem: after so many years, it seemed he knew everyone he met. They could be former students or retired teachers or parents he'd met years before. Every face sparked a vague familiarity.

Welch put his head down to look at his papers again, trying to achieve the same state of mind he'd had the moment before, but the chair remained stubbornly empty.

He'd started seeing students who weren't there the week before Christmas break. At first they were a motion in the corner of his eye, but now he saw them straight on. He thought of them as ghosts, but they were more like remnants of the absent. He saw last year's graduates and kids from his first years of teaching, and, occasionally—he shivered to think of it—the dead too.

Twenty minutes later, a pair of noisy baseball players on their way to the gym for before-school throwing practice passed his door. Phones rang. Voices murmured. Doors opened and closed. An unbroken succession of students streamed by. He locked his door behind him, did hall duty until the final bell emptied the passage, hurried a handful of the tardy to class, then slipped into the only empty desk in Miss Knapp's room for a quick evaluation. Thirty-three students filled the rest of the room. A few glanced at him when he sat down. A slender, shiny-cheeked girl who didn't look a day over twelve years old, moved her backpack so Welch had room for his feet.

At the blackboard, red-haired Miss Knapp smiled nervously in his direction. She was fifty or so years old, come late to teaching after decades in the private sector. This was her third year in the building, her tenure year. If her evaluations were good, her job would be much more secure in September. He nodded and opened his notebook.

When Welch was a young teacher, he noticed students stopped talking when he passed. Not all the time, but often enough that when he heard a hushed, "Shh! It's a teacher," he longed to step up to them and ask them to share the secret. He wanted to tell him that five years ago he'd been like them. He was still seventeen in his heart.

It grew worse when he became vice principal. It spread to the teachers. Now he'd been vice principal for so long, he no longer recalled what teachers stopped talking about when an administrator came near. He'd asked his sole friend, Coach Qualls, who taught mythology and the humanities, about it once. "You're the troll, Welch. No one loves the troll."

Miss Knapp trembled slightly as she copied an assignment on the board.

Her fear annoyed him. I'm just a regular guy, he thought. I'm the fellow across the street. He waited until she looked at him, then he frowned and wrote in his notebook, PICK UP GROCERIES TONIGHT. She paled and asked the class for their attention. Welch wrote, BROCCOLI, RYE BREAD and MUSTARD as if he'd just noticed a critical deficiency in her technique.

He stayed ten minutes until she handed out a worksheet. He had four other teachers to evaluate before first hour ended, so he noted in his planner that he'd observed her class, then rose to leave. Miss Knapp put her book on her desk. "Mr. Welch?"

They talked in the hallway outside the room.

"Can I do anything for you, Mr. Welch? Is this about Beau Reece?" Miss Knapp hid her mouth with her fingertips while holding her wrist. "I didn't see him today, but Friday he provoked the seniors again."

"No. Just a drop-in visit." Welch thought she might be an attractive woman if she didn't suck her cheeks in. He wondered if she was scheduled to supervise the dance this weekend. They might have a chance to talk more casually there.

"My methods, do you think they're sound?"

Suddenly, he felt guilty and mean. He shouldn't have written in his notebook like that. "Yes, of course. You're doing fine." He searched for a more specific observation. "I'm impressed with how you hold the attention of such a full class."

Her eyes darted to his notebook. He could tell she didn't believe him, not for a second. "Oh," she said hopelessly, "my next class is much larger."

"Really? Where would they fit?" He leaned around the corner and looked into her room. Half the desks were empty. The students slouched over their worksheets, their pens a litany of scratching in the silence. The desk where the shiny-cheeked girl had sat was unoccupied, no backpack on the floor. His face felt cold.

"Are you okay, Mr. Welch?"

Welch squinted his eyes shut and rubbed his forehead. "Yes. Have a good day." But as he moved away from her room, he knew she wouldn't. She'd worry all morning about what he'd seen in her room. She'd complain to her friends at lunch, and when she taught in the afternoon, she wouldn't be quite as effective as she would have been if he had never visited. Maybe it would be better if she wasn't coming to the dance. He envisioned two hours of polite conversation filled with bitter subtext.

In Mr. Mendez's Algebra I class, Welch watched the students' backs bent over their work. He'd come in quietly, and only a pimply-faced boy whose purple-penned notes were unreadable noticed when Welch took a seat. Mendez continued sketching a long equation on the board. "The formulas never lie," said Mendez. "Even imaginary numbers tell the truth."

Welch sat for several minutes, his record book unopened. Mendez taught in Lincoln High's original wing. The ceilings rose ten feet, and rather than the anonymous white tiles and flourescent lighting that marked the new wings, a dozen light fixtures hung down, each bright bulb surrounded by a green reflective collar, like a bed of metal and glass daisies growing from the ceiling. A hundred-year-old math room, thought Welch. Over and over, the same lessons: Balance the equation. Seek the lowest common denominator. Chart the axis. Solve for X.

Were any of the students here the least bit . . . nebulous? Welch leaned forward, stretching his trembling fingers toward the pimply student's arm. Mendez kept lecturing. Welch realized the man hadn't faced the students the entire time. The class could sneak out, and Mendez would never know. Welch's hand approached the boy's arm, close enough to touch his sleeve.

Will my fingers slip through?

Welch could see the pores in the boy's hand, the tendons in his wrist.

The boy looked up, his eyes wide, watery and brown. "Yes, sir?"

"Nothing, son. Keep up the good work."

Welch grabbed his notebook, and his pen clattered to the floor.

"Ah, Mr. Welch has joined us," Mendez faced him, chalk in one hand. "Perhaps we could show him the magic of the quadratic."

All heads turned to look at him. Welch backed out of the room. "No, no. I'm just leaving." He fled to the safety of the empty hall, breathing hard. He realized he hadn't touched the student. Now he'd never know.

Coach Qualls, grading papers in the teachers' lounge, looked up when Welch walked in. His bulk swallowed the kid-sized plastic chair. "You all right?" he asked. His jowls were huge and covered with a perpetual five o'clock dusting of white stubble. At sixty-four years, he was the last staff member who'd been in the building longer than Welch.

Welch sank into a seat of his own. "Yes, of course."

They sat for some time. Qualls moved from paper to paper, check-marking mistakes. Welch looked out the lounge's window, but it faced the side of the school across the open quad below. Sun washed the bricks. No trees or birds or open sky. Just a white wall from top to bottom. Dim sounds from the band room drifted up, throbbing bass notes and the drums. They started and stopped a dozen times, the same thirty seconds of music.

"I turned in my intention form for next year. Time for me to check out," said Qualls. "Are you going to be the old man?"

Welch opened his planner. He hadn't written down anything from Mendez's class, and he wondered if he could count it as an official observation. "Did you accomplish what you wanted by going into this profession?"

Qualls paused, his pen in the air. "Ah, it's one of those days."

"It's just I wonder sometimes if I've done anyone any good. What's my role in the grand scheme? You told me once in the fairy tale that is the school, I'm the troll. I've thought a lot about that." Welch pushed the heels of his hands into his eyes, lighting a thousand sparkles behind his closed lids.

"Was I drunk?" Qualls scratched his chin thoughtfully.

"No. We were between third and fourth hour on a Tuesday."

"Oh, yes. I remember. In the school's mythic landscape, you are in the troll's niche. The teachers are knights, the students are all potential heroes, and you are the dark underpinning. Loved by no one. Intimidating to all. If we just had a bridge to put you under, you'd be perfect."

"That will look damned unimpressive on my tombstone. 'Here lies Vice Principal Welch, friend to none. Troll to the end.'"

Qualls checked the clock. "Five minutes to the bell. I'm going before the halls crowd up." He stuffed the papers into a briefcase that snapped crisply.

"So, are you a knight? Do knights get to retire?"

Qualls flourished his red pen. "Not me. I'm a wizard, and I'm off to wield my spells one more time. There are kids out there ready to be charmed and bewitched."

For a second, poised at the door to the rest of the school, Welch thought Qualls did look like a wizard under his bushy, white brows.

"I'm seeing ghosts, Coach," said Welch, but Qualls was already gone.

The coffee pot hissed. Above it, on the bulletin board, a sign hung from one thumbtack. DARE TO BELIEVE IN CHILDREN. Stapled beside it, his contribution to the effort, a list of students he'd suspended and a reminder to teachers to provide them with makeup work.

At the end of the day, long after the volleyball team had departed from their spring practice in the gym, and the booster club had left the cafeteria, and the students constructing the set for the musical had put away their power tools and paint brushes, Welch roamed through the school, turning on lights as he went. He checked his pocket planner. Nothing left on the day's schedule. I'm off the planner, he thought. I'm beyond my time. He'd been in the building for the last twenty hours, but he felt restless and antsy instead of tired.

He shook the thought away. Which one would it be tonight? He jangled his keys in his pocket. To his left the lockers gave way to tall windows that looked into the business computer lab. Screen savers swirled in the lab's darkness. He turned right into the freshman hall. Lockers on both sides. Doors into classrooms topped by teacher's names and their subjects. Miss Knapp had added a big smiley face by her name. Welch grimaced when he saw it. Maybe if he dropped a note in her box tomorrow it might make up for his visit to her class.

He stopped by the locker closest to her room. His keys dangled, clinking against the metal. Inside, a cigarette-smelling jacket hung from the hook above a paperback copy of *The Odyssey*. He wrote, DO GOOD on the ten dollar bill he took from his wallet, then signed it, CYCLOPS. When he reached to stick the bill to the inside of the door, he paused. A piece of tape, brittle with age, clung to the spot he always placed the bill. How many years ago had he opened this locker, hoping his gift would make a difference?

It didn't matter. That student had long ago graduated.

Before he could move, though, an arm reached through him, seemed to extend from his own elbow, and stuck a five dollar bill to the spot. The new tape melted into the old and became one.

Blood rushed from his face, and his skin erupted into goose bumps so violently that he thought he might faint. The spectral hand closed the locker, but it was open too, both doors visible to him. Then footsteps echoed in the hallway. Welch turned to see a man walking away. It was himself, darker haired, wearing the horrible gray and red plaid jacket he'd given to the Salvation Army in 1978. Wrestling against his paralysis, Welch forced himself to stir so he could follow, but the man's figure faded into the shadows at the hall's end and the sound of footsteps became the pounding of his heart in his ears.

Welch blinked once, hard, then licked his lips. Of course, it made sense. Still, he was unnerved. He shuddered when he turned back to the locker. The ghost bill had disappeared, and now the locker had just one door, the open one. He put the new tape over the old, then shut the locker as softly as he could, flinching at the mechanism's loud click.The next morning he started with the Beau Reece folder. Three teacher complaints against him in the previous week. Tardiness, insubordination and inciting a shoving match in the locker room. The two seniors swore Reece started it, but by the time the P.E. teacher arrived, Reece had vanished and the seniors were pushing each other. "I don't doubt the Reece kid had something to do with it," the P.E. teacher said.

As the halls emptied into the first period classes, Welch waited outside the band room, where Reece played the clarinet. The bell rang, and the stragglers hurried to their destinations, casting fearful glances Welch's way. He ignored them. Where was Reece? A few minutes later a student opened the band room door and put the attendance sheet in the folder. The teacher had marked Reece absent.

Ditching or tardy, thought Welch. He checked his watch. Fifteen parent call slips waited on his desk. Last week's athletic eligibility reports needed to be sent to the state for validation. A dozen obligations crowded his planner. He was days behind in teacher evaluations. And, of course, the intention form for next year brooded in his "to do" box. Retire or hang on? What should he do? He filled a cup with coffee in the teacher's lounge, then let himself into the sound booth overlooking the stage. He sat so he could see over the balcony to where the choir practiced. The sopranos stood and held a high note, a long, trembling, wordless vowel. Welch sighed, closed his eyes, letting the cup warm his hands. The altos joined in, then the baritones and bass. Sometimes, when he felt particularly discouraged, after he'd disciplined the umpteenth student for the day, he'd go to the choir room or to the band, or he'd wander through the art classes' galleries, or he'd open the shop's storage room so he could see the shelves and chests and tables students had made. He'd run his hand over the polished joints and glassy smooth wood. The kids can do great things, he'd think. They can be marvelous. But he never worked with those kids. The ones who waited outside his office were the tardy ones, the insubordinate and combative, the criminals.

The bell rang. Welch jumped, spilling the now cool coffee down his leg. He'd fallen asleep. Could he do anything good today? Could he make a difference? He wiped his pants dry as best he could, straightened his tie and headed for the attendance office.

"Can you get me Beau Reece's phone number and his attendance folder?" he said to the secretary, a girl who'd graduated from Lincoln three or four years earlier. She handed him the papers without smiling. When she was a seventeen-year-old junior, he'd suspended her for three days for smoking in the girls' locker room.

Naturally, the number was no longer in service. Welch drummed his fingers on his desk, the phone in his other hand. He looked through Reece's attendance records. Although he often skipped classes, he hadn't missed a whole day of school until yesterday. Today didn't look good for him either.

Miss Knapp knocked on his door, looking distraught.

"Have you got a minute?"

Welch nodded. He hadn't put a note in her box yet. Maybe he could just tell her he thought she did a good job.

She sat in the chair next to his desk. "I know you're working very hard to help me be a better teacher, Mr. Welch, but I don't think you get to see the best of me." She kneaded her hands in her lap without looking at him. "I'm a nervous person, Mr. Welch. I'm fine with the kids. When you're in the room, though, I get all tied up."

Welch couldn't speak. He stared at her hands, squeezing so tight the muscles in her arms quivered. He wanted to put his own hands over them and hold them gently. He'd say. "You're going to be an excellent addition to this staff. You already are."

What he said instead was, "Maybe I can arrange for someone else to observe you."

Knapp stood, keeping her hands clasped. "I don't mind you observing me. I just can't teach when you're doing it." Her expression was unreadable, somewhere between misery and confusion. She left the office like a penitent, head down. The whole encounter hadn't lasted thirty seconds. The phone in his hand began beeping, so he hung it up.

Down the hall, he used his key to enter the faculty bathroom. The intercom clicked on for the morning announcements, a litany of club meetings and graduation reminders for seniors. Above the urinal someone had written SQUELCH WELCH. It wouldn't be so bad if this was a student bathroom. He smeared the ink with his thumb.

"Hate graffiti, don't you, son?" said Principal Robinson as he passed behind

Welch and let himself into a stall, closing the door behind him. Robinson's belt buckle clinked loudly in the tiled room.

"I'm having a bad day."

"It's the Reece kid, isn't it?" Robinson's voice rose over the partition. "He's the burr under the saddle. You straighten him out, and the other irritations will go away."

Welch closed his eyes and leaned forward, resting his forehead against the cool tile. "Maybe. But if I suspend him, what good will that do?"

"You've got to find him first."

The toilet flushed.

Welch looked at the partition. There were no feet visible below it.

He gasped, then leapt to the door, breaking the latch when he banged it open. No one sat there. In the bowl, the water swirled.

Welch stepped back and bumped into the wall. His legs shook and he almost fell. Then, suddenly, he laughed. The water slowed its circular path and grew still while Welch's laughs subsided to chuckles. He wiped tears off his cheeks. Now he knew a secret, not that he'd ever heard anyone ask it, but he knew. Ghosts used bathrooms.

He started to laugh again. It welled within him, but he clenched his jaw tight against it. He could see himself in three of the mirrors above the sinks, his wild eyes; his disheveled hair. "I'm hallucinating," he said. "I'm going to wake up in my bed, and I'll be twenty-two again, wondering if I should go on the motorcycle trip into Mexico with Harold." Welch remembered his brother's postcards that came every week his first year of teaching and how he put them aside while planning lessons.

"Now I'm talking to myself in the bathroom." Welch stepped to a sink, washed his face. He straightened his tie, then dabbed a paper towel at his chin where a single drop of water glistened. Maybe when I open the door, he thought, there won't be a school there at all. It could be a desert or an ocean or a blank wall. He remembered the white wall across the school's courtyard through the teacher lounge window. How many years had he spent staring at that featureless expanse?

He pushed the door open tentatively. Pamela Howel strode toward him, a clipboard under one arm. She had her "I have to deliver a hand grenade" expression.

"We have a situation, Mr. Welch."

Welch nodded, but he started making his strategy. If I visit every one of Reece's classes, I'm bound to run into him. I have a quest, a mission to turn this boy around. I don't have to be the troll. I can be Odysseus. Ten years of war. Ten years of exile, and then a just reward. He smiled as he headed toward his office, picturing Reece's schedule sitting on his desk.

Howell grabbed his arm earnestly. "Did you hear what I said?"

Surprised to see her still there, he shook his head.

"The boy who tried to commit suicide last week named you in his note. The school board put you on their schedule for tonight. You need to be there at 7:00 sharp." She pivoted on one heel and went back the way she had come.

Welch reeled; he couldn't even remember the kid. He rubbed his fingers hard into his forehead while scrinching his eyes closed. Nope. No memory at all of his connection with the boy. One thing at a time, he thought, as he wrote in his planner, SCHOOL BOARD MEETING, 7:00, SUICIDE.

First, find Beau Reece. Outside Reece's second class, Welch stood by the doorway, hands in his pockets, watching students enter. Most ignored him. Some looked at him curiously. A few kept their eyes averted. The stream slowed. The bell rang. No Reece.

Welch walked off school grounds to "skid row," where the smokers, skateboarders, goths and dropouts went when they were ditching class. He flushed a couple out of the high jump pit by the football field, encouraged three boys sitting on their skateboards in the alley beside the track to move on, then strode behind the convenience store across the street from the high school, surprising a pack of kids smoking, mostly tobacco, but he caught a whiff of pot too. Eyes went wide as cigarettes disappeared behind backs. Most of them had been in his office at one time or another.

"Have any of you seen Beau Reece?" he asked without real hope.

No answer for a long minute.

A boy wearing black leather pants and a spiked dog collar said, "He played with the jazz band yesterday before school."

Reece didn't go to any of his classes yesterday. Welch assumed he must have been sick. "Really?"

The boy nodded. The rest of the group stood silently, little whiffs of smoke curling behind them. "He missed this morning," the boy added.

"Thanks," said Welch, then he turned toward the school.

"Umm . . ." a girl with a violet top knot but shaved close above her ears said. "Aren't you going to yell at us to get back to class?"

Welch looked up at the perfect cotton-ball clouded sky. He shrugged. "Do what you want."

Ten paces away though, he stopped and went back. The kids hadn't moved. "All of you are underage to be smoking. Throw those things away, and I'll forget I saw you." He tried to bluster, but it came flat and without conviction.

"Are you all right, Mr. Welch?" asked the violet top knot.

Welch sighed as if he'd been punctured. "Just get away from the store. They're business folks and you kids leave a mess back here."

When Welch reached the school, he looked at the convenience store. None of the kids had left.

For the rest of the morning, he patrolled the building in a daze. He pulled the records of the student who'd tried to commit suicide, but Welch's encounter with him had been in December when the boy had been suspended with three others for throwing snowballs at the busses. Even when Welch looked at the boy's picture, he couldn't remember him. Why would he name me in a suicide note? wondered Welch, and what did the school board want? He walked a long circuit from the agriculture building, past the swimming pool, then out to the driver's ed. course. In all his years in education, he'd never been teacher of the year, or even teacher of the month. He'd never been recognized by the board for an "Excellence in Education" award. He'd never been asked to speak at graduation. No one ever gave him a yearbook to sign. Maybe the board would ask for his resignation, or worse, the ignominy of a forced retirement.

What did Odysseus feel like after twenty years? Cursed by the gods. All his men dead. Not even sure his wife remembered him. Hope must have dwindled within him, thought Welch. What did the troll under the bridge feel? How did he feel about his place in the world?

He added up all the sick days he'd never taken. If he handed in his retirement intention sheet now, he could call in sick for the rest of the year and not even go to the school board meeting. Who needed the grief?

The bell rang, sending the students to lunch. Welch walked on the left side of the hall against the flow of traffic, glad for the contact when students bumped into him, even if they did shoot him annoyed glances. At least they were real, and he was real too. A short boy passed on Welch's right. Welch grabbed the boy's shoulder.

"Beau?" he said, but it wasn't him.

School ended. The busses left. Teams practiced. Clubs met, and, gradually, the building emptied. Once again, Welch wandered the hallways. The sun, low in the sky, sent long beams of light through the windows next to the doors and down the main hall. Only one day in the spring the windows lined up with the sun on the horizon so the light reached all the way to the other end.

He felt like he walked in a tunnel of light as he fingered the ten dollar bill in his pocket. In fifteen minutes he would have to leave. His planner was very exact about it: SCHOOL BOARD MEETING, 7:00, SUICIDE.

Years and years earlier he'd started taping money to the inside of lockers, one or two bills a week. Sometimes more if there were a lot of kids through his office. DO GOOD, he wrote, but in all that time he'd never heard anyone talk about the mystery presents. He never heard what the kids did with the cash. It reminded him of standing on the edge of the Grand Canyon, flicking pebbles over the edge. They vanished into the depths without a sound. How come our *good* deeds never come back to haunt us? He checked the slip in his hand. Beau Reece used locker 1209.

The doors behind him crashed open, flooding the hall with sun. The silhouetted form of a half-dozen boys filled the space, and hard-soled shoes clicked against the floor.

"What are we gonna do?" cried one. As they came closer, Welch could see they were football players carrying a boy on a stretcher. For a moment Welch was disoriented. Football in the spring? Football ended months ago.

"I think his leg is broke," said another. They rushed by Welch. Dirt and grass stains marred their thick sweaters with an "L" sewn to the front.

The boy on the stretcher moaned, his face streaked with tears. "I'm sorry, guys," he said.

"We can't be best in the state without our wingback," said a third.

"Welch could save the day," sobbed the boy on the stretcher. "He could carry the ball for us."

"What?" stammered Welch. "What did you say?"

But the team hurried down the hall, the sun glaring on their backs, and they dissolved into dust motes before reaching the end.

The hallway dimmed as the doors closed. Welch looked back at the windows. The sun touched the horizon, a perfect, crimson globe beyond the glass. In minutes the hall would be dark and it would be next fall before the sun lined up once more. He glanced at his watch. Time to go.

Taking a deep breath, he found Beau Reece's locker. He flattened the bill against the metal and wrote DO GOOD. He thought for a second about signing it ODYSSEUS. He shook his head. Odysseus didn't fit. If he was anyone from that story, it would be Paris, whose bad judgements destroyed heroes, so he signed it, THE TROLL.

The key slid into the lock, but the door resisted. Welch leaned into it to take the pressure off the internal mechanisms so he could pop the latch. The door swung open. Then, slowly, a body fell out. A ghost in the locker! Welch thought, his heart fisted tight. He took it in at once. The band of duct tape around the body's torso, pinning his arms to his side. The tape around the ankles. The broad band of dull silver across the ghost's mouth. And still, it fell, until at the last second, Welch stepped forward and caught it before it hit the floor.

A solid weight in his hands, Welch sat back in surprise. No ghost. It was a real boy, a small one, unconscious or dead. Welch pressed his fingers to the boy's throat where a pulse beat firmly. He worked his fingers under one edge of the tape, and carefully pulled it away from the child's mouth.

It wasn't until the kid opened his eyes blearily and croaked, "Mr. Welch?" that he realized he held Beau Reece.

Near midnight, while sitting in the hospital's waiting room, it occurred to him he'd missed the school board meeting. It didn't matter. He couldn't help smiling.

The doctor told him Beau was dehydrated but would be fine. "Don't you have rules against hazing?" asked the doctor.

The glass pneumatic doors from the parking lot wheezed open. Coach Qualls and two other teachers came in.

"What are you doing here?" said Welch. Qualls looked so misplaced, and Welch realized in three decades he'd only seen him at school.

"The night nurse is the superintendent's wife, and she called him. His cell phone went off right in the middle of his closing comments. We came straight over. Good work, man." Qualls slapped him on the shoulder.

Welch shrugged. "Just luck, really."

Qualls sat next to him. "That's not what I heard. The secretaries told me you'd been looking for Reece since yesterday. Good instincts, I'd say."

Welch sighed and let himself sink deeper into the chair. The day had been a long one. Another teacher walked in, and before the doors closed, Miss Knapp entered, rubbing her coat sleeves against the cold of the spring evening.

"You were all at the meeting?" asked Welch. Through the doors he could see other teachers in the parking lot heading toward them.

"Sure," said Qualls. "Weren't you supposed to be there too? That kid who tried to commit suicide named twenty-four of us in his note. Typical school board over-reaction. They wanted to talk to us about sensitivity. Did you hear how he tried to do himself?"

Welch shook his head. The room filled with teachers.

"Four bottles of antacid pills." Qualls laughed. "He thought an overdose of anything would kill him."

The superintendent of schools joined the crowd, spotted Welch. "It's caring educators like yourself who make us proud to be teachers." He squeezed Welch's hand. "Forty years in education, and you're still making a difference. You saved that boy's life."

A news truck pulled up to the doors.

Welch stood next to Qualls. Teachers filled the room. Qualls raised his hand and waved, then slowly dropped it, turning toward Welch.

"What?" said Welch.

"It's the darndest thing."

"What?"

"I thought I saw Principal Robinson. For a second I thought it was Robinson over there."

Welch sighed. "It happens to me all the time."

"Where's this Welch fellow?" said a man with a television camera tucked under his arm.

"Must be a slow news night," said Welch, suddenly so embarrassed that he looked for a door to duck into, but the teachers surrounded him.

Afterwards, when the television crew departed, and most of the teachers had trickled away, Miss Knapp approached him, still in her coat.

"This was marvelous." She looked around the room. "So many of us came."

Welch didn't know what to say. Outside of the school, he had no words for her. But he wanted them, words that wouldn't make her nervous. Surely he could talk to her about subjects other than attendance and discipline and teaching strategies.

Something in her expression seemed strained, then a realization dawned on him. "Qualls did this, didn't he?"

Miss Knapp blushed. "No . . . oh, no. We really were glad to come, really. Well . . . he said you'd been a little down. You're not angry, are you?"

Welch shook his head. They stood without speaking for a few seconds, then she put out her hand. "I have to get going. Congratulations, though. You did a good thing. Will you be at the dance Friday?" Her delicate and cool fingers rested against his palm.

Dances featured ear-crushing music by groups he didn't recognize, gate-crashers from other schools who had to be tossed out, kids who came to the school drunk or who snuck into their cars for a beer or a joint before trying to get past him, and afterwards there would be torn confetti and crushed paper cups and decorations to be taken down. That's the way it always was. But he also knew the dance floor would be full of students and ghosts. He could live with the ghosts. And for the real kids? Warm hands on bare backs during the slow songs. Shy smiles. Genuine laughter. He would stand to the side, arms crossed on his chest, watching, like a knight on a castle wall.

"Save a dance for me," he said.

It was his place.

A FLOCK OF BIRDS

THE STARLINGS WHEELED LIKE A GIANT BLANKET FLUNG INTO THE SKY, like sentient smoke, banking and turning in unison. They passed overhead so close that Carson heard their wings ripping the air, and when the flock flew in front of the sun, the world grew gray. Carson shivered even though it was only early September and warm enough for a short-sleeved shirt. This close he could smell them, all dark-feathered and frantic and dry and biting.

He estimated maybe 50,000 birds. Not the largest flock he'd seen this year, but one of the bigger ones, and certainly bigger than anything he'd seen last year. Of course, the summer before that he didn't watch the birds. No one did. No chance to add to his life list that year. No winter count either. The Colorado Field Ornithology office closed.

He leaned back in his lawn chair. The bird vortex moved east, over the wheatgrass plain until the sun brightened again, pressing pleasant heat against the back of his hands and arms. He was glad for the hat that protected his head and its middle-aged bald spot. This wasn't the time to mess with skin cancer, he thought, not a good time at all. He was glad his teeth were generally healthy and his eyesight was keen.

The binoculars were excellent, Bausch & Lomb Elite. Wide field of vision. Top notch optics. Treated lenses. He'd picked them up from a sporting goods store in Littleton's South Glenn Mall. Through them the birds became singular. He followed discrete groups. They swirled, coming straight toward him for a moment, then sliding away. Slowly he scanned the flight until he reached the leading edge. Birds on one half and sky on the other. They switched direction and the leaders became the followers. He took the binoculars away and blinked at their loss of individuality. In the middle, where the birds were thickest, the shape was black, a sinuous, twisting dark chord. One dot separated itself from the others, flying against the current. Carson only saw it for a second, but it was distinctly larger than the starlings, and its wing beat was different. He focused the binoculars again, his breath coming fast, and scanned the flock. It would be unusual for a single bird of a different species to fly with the starlings.

Nothing for several minutes other than the hordes streaming by, then the strange bird emerged. Long, slender wings, a reddish breast, and it was *fast*. Much faster than the starlings and twice their size. The cloud shifted, swallowing it, as the entire flock drifted slowly east, farther into the plains.

The bird looked familiar. Not one from his journals, but one he'd seen a picture of before. Something tropical perhaps that had drifted north? Every once in a while a single representative of a species would be spotted, hundreds, sometimes thousands of miles from where it was normally found. The birder who saw it could only hope that someone else confirmed the sighting or that he got a picture, otherwise it would be discounted and couldn't be legitimately added to a life list. If he could add a new bird to his list, maybe that would make things better. A new bird! He could concentrate on that. Something good to cling to.

The flock grew small in the distance.

Carson sighed, put the binoculars back in their case, then packed the rest of his gear into the truck. He checked the straps that held his motorcycle in place. They were tight. The tie-down holding the extra batteries for the truck and motorcycle were secure too. From his spot on the hill he could see the dirt road he'd taken from the highway and the long stretch of I-25 that reached north toward Denver and south to Colorado Springs. No traffic. The air above the Denver skyline was crystalline. He strained his ears, tilting his head from one side then the other. He hadn't heard a car on the highway behind him all afternoon. Grass rustle. Moldy-leaf smells, nothing else, and when he finally opened the truck's door, the metallic click was foreign and loud.

Back at his house in Littleton, he checked the photoelectric panels' gauges inside the front door. It had been sunny for the last week, so the system was full. The water tower showed only four hundred gallons though. He'd have to go water scavenging again in the next few days.

"I'm home," he called. His voice echoed off the tiled foyer. "Tillie?"

The living room was empty, and so were the kitchen and bedrooms. Carson stepped into the bathroom, his hand on his chest where his heart beat fast, but the sleeping pills in the cabinet looked undisturbed. "Tillie?"

He found her sitting in the back yard beneath the globe willow, still in her robe. The nightgown beneath it was yellowed and tattered. In her dresser he'd put a dozen new ones, but she'd only wear the one she had in her suitcase when he'd picked her up, wandering through the Denver Botanical Gardens two years ago.

He sat on the grass next to her. She was fifty or so. Lots of gray in her blond hair. Slender wrists. Narrow face. Strikingly blue eyes that hardly ever focused on anything.

"How's that cough?" he asked.

"We never play bridge anymore, Bob Robert."

Carson stretched out. A day with binoculars pressed to his face and his elbows braced on his knees hurt his back. "Tough to get partners," he said. Then he added out of habit, "And I'm not Bob Robert."

She picked at a loose thread in the robe, pulling at it until it broke free. "Have you seen the garden? Not a flower in it. A single geranium or a daisy would give me hope. If just one dead thing would come back."

"I've brought you seeds," he said. "You just need to plant them."

She wrapped the thread around her fingertip tightly. "I waited for the pool man, but he never came. I hate skimming." She raised her fist to her mouth and coughed primly behind it twice, grimacing each time.

Carson raised his head. Other than the grass under the tree, most of the yard was dirt. The lot was longer than it was wide. At the end farthest from the house a chicken wire enclosure surrounded the poultry. A couple hens sat in the shade by the coop. No pool. When he'd gone house hunting, he'd toyed with the idea of a pool, but the thought of trying to keep it filled and the inevitable problems with water chemistry made him decide against it. The house on the other side of the privacy fence had a pool as did most of the houses in the neighborhood, now empty except for the scummy pond in the deep end. In the spring he'd found a deer, its neck bent unnaturally back, at the bottom of one a block over. Evidently it had jumped the fence and gone straight in.

"Are you hungry?" Carson asked.

Tillie tilted her head to the side. "When will the garden grow again?"

He pushed himself off the ground. "I'll fix eggs."

Later that evening, he tucked Tillie in bed. The room smelled of peppermint. From the bulge in her cheek, he guessed she was sucking on one. In a little-girl voice, she said, "Can you put in my video?" Her expression was alert, but her eyes were red-rimmed and watery. He smiled. This was as good as she got. Sometimes he could play gin rummy with her and she'd stay focused for an hour or so before she drifted away. If he asked her about her past, she'd be unresponsive for days. All he knew about her came from the suitcase she carried when he'd found her. There was a sheet of letterhead with a name at the top: "Tillie Waterhouse, Marketing Executive," and an athletic club identification card with her picture and name. But there was no Tillie Waterhouse in the Denver phone book. Could she have wandered away from the airport when air travel was canceled? The first words she had said to him, when she finally spoke, were, "How do you bear it?"

"Did you have a good day?" He turned on the television and pressed rewind on the VCR.

Her hands peeked out from under the covers and pulled them tight under her chin. "Something magical is going to happen. The leaves whispered to me."

The video clicked to a stop. "I'm glad to hear that," he said. The television flickered as the tape started, a documentary on the 2001 New York City Marathon a decade earlier. It opened with a helicopter flyover of the racers crossing the Verrazano-Narrows Bridge into Brooklyn. The human crowd surged forward, packed elbow to elbow, long as the eye could see. Then the camera cut to ankle level. Feet ran past for five minutes. Then it went to face level at a turn in the course. The starting crush had spread out, but the runners still jogged within an arm's length of each other, thousands of them. Carson had watched the video with her the first few times. The video was a celebration of numbers. Thirty thousand athletes straining over the twenty-six mile course through New York City's five boroughs.

"Here's the remote if you want to watch it again."

"So many American flags," she said.

"It was only a month after that first terrorist thing." Carson sat on the end of her bed. Some runners wore stars and stripes singlets or racing shorts. Others carried small flags and waved them at the camera as they passed.

"I won't be able to sleep," she said.

He nodded. "Me either."

Before he left, he pressed his hand to her forehead. She looked up briefly, the blanket still snug against her chin. A little fever and her breath sounded wheezy.

Later that night he made careful entries in his day book. A breeze through the open window freshened the room. He'd spotted a mountain plover, a long-billed curlew, a burrowing owl and a horned lark, plus the usual assortment of lark, sparrows, yellow warblers, western meadowlarks, red-winged blackbirds, crows, black terns and mourning doves. Nothing unusual beside the strange bird in the starling flock. Idly he thumbed through his bird identification handbook. No help there. Could it actually be a new bird? Something to add to his life list?

Tomorrow he'd take the camera. Several major flocks roosted in the elms along the Platte River. He hadn't done a riparian count in a couple months anyway. After visiting the distribution center, he'd go to the river. With an early enough start, he would still have ten hours of sun to work with.

He shut the book and turned off his desk light. Gradually his eyes adjusted as he looked out the window. A full moon illuminated the scene. From his chair he could see three houses bathed in the leaden glow, their windows black as basalt. His neighbor's minivan rested on its rims, all four tires long gone flat. Carson tried to come up with the guy's name, but it remained elusive. Generally he tried not to think about his neighbors or their empty houses.

He couldn't hear anything other than the wind moving over the silent city. Not sleepy at all, he watched the shadows slide slowly across the lawn. Just after 2:00 a.m., a pair of coyotes trotted up the middle of the street. Their toenails clicked loudly against the asphalt. Carson finally rose, took two sleeping pills and went to bed.

"The woman who stays with me is sick," said Carson. He rested his arm against his truck, supplies requisition list in hand.

The distribution center manager nodded dourly. "Oh, the sweet sorrow of parting." He hooked his grimy thumbs in his overalls. Through the warehouse doors behind him Carson saw white plastic wrapped bales, four feet to a side, stacked five bales high and reaching to the warehouse's far end. They contained bags of flour, corn, cloth, paper, a little bit of everything. Emergency stores.

Carson blanched. "It's not that. She just has a cough and a bit of fever. If it's bacterial, an antibiotic might knock it right out."

"T.B. or not T.B. That is congestion, Carson," he said, laughing through yellow teeth. Carson guessed he might be fifty-five or sixty.

Carson smiled. "You're pretty sharp today."

"Finest collection of video theater this side of hell. Watched Lawrence Olivier last night until 3:00 or 4:00." The manager consulted his clipboard. "No new pharmaceuticals in a couple months, and I haven't seen antibiotics in over a year. I could have my assistant keep an eye open for you, but he hasn't come in for a week. Lookin' sickly his last day, you know?" The manager rubbed his fingers on his chest. "Could be that I've lost him. Have you tried a tablespoon of honey in a shot glass of bourbon? Works for me every time."

A car pulled into the huge, empty parking lot behind Carson's truck, but whoever was inside didn't get out. Carson nodded in the car's direction. Evidently they wanted to wait for Carson to finish his business.

He handed the manager the list. "Can you also give me cornmeal and sugar? A mix of canned vegetables would be nice too."

"That I've got." The manager hopped on a forklift. "Tomorrow may creep in a petty pace, but I shouldn't be a minute."

When he returned with the goods he said, "The quality of mercy is not strained here. I'm not doing anything this afternoon. I'll dig some for you. Few months back I heard a pharmacy in an Albertson's burned down. Looters overlooked it. Might be something there. I've got your address." He waved the requisition list. "I could bring it by your house."

Carson loaded boxes of canned soup and vegetables into the truck. "What about the warehouse?"

The manager shrugged. "Guess we're on an honor system now. Only a dozen or so customers a day. Maybe a couple hundred total. I'll bet there aren't 50,000 people alive in the whole country. I'll leave the doors open." For a moment the manager stared into the distance, as if he'd lost his thought. Behind them, the waiting car rumbled. "You know how they say that if you put a jellybean in a jar every time you make love the first year that you're married, and you take one out every time you make love after that, that the jar will never be empty? This warehouse is a little like that."

When Carson started the truck, the manager leaned into the window, resting his arms on the car door. This close, Carson could see how greasy the man's hair was, and it smelled like old lard.

The manager's smile was gone. "How long have you known me?" he said, looking Carson straight in the eye. His voice was suddenly so serious.

Carson tried not to shrink away. He thought back. "I don't know. Sixteen months?"

The manager grimaced. "That makes you my oldest friend. There isn't anyone alive that I've known longer."

For a second, Carson was afraid the man would begin crying. Instead, he straightened, his hands still on the door.

Tentatively, Carson said, "I'm sorry. I don't think I've ever asked what your name was."

"Nope, nope, no need," the manager barked, smiling again. "A rose by any other moniker, as they say. I'll see what I can find you in the coughing line. Don't know about antibiotics. Come back tomorrow."

It wasn't until Carson had driven blocks away toward the river, as he watched the boarded up stores slide by, as he moved down the empty streets, past the mute houses that he realized, other than Tillie, the manager was his oldest friend too.

Sitting on his camp chair, Carson had a panoramic river view. On the horizon to the west, the mountains rose steeply, only a remnant of last winter's snow clinging to the tops of the tallest peaks. Fifty yards away at the bottom of a short bluff, the river itself, at its lowest level of the season, rolled sluggishly. Long gravel tongues protruded into the water where little long-legged birds searched for insects between the rocks. A bald eagle swept low over the water going south. Carson marked it in his notebook.

Across the river stood clumps of elm and willows. He didn't need his binoculars to see the branches were heavy with roosting starlings. Counting individuals was impossible. He'd have to estimate. He wondered what the distribution manager would make of the birds. After all, they had something in common. If it weren't for Shakespeare, the starlings wouldn't be here at all. In the early 1890s, a club of

New York Anglophiles thought it would be comforting if all the birds mentioned in Shakespeare's plays lived in America. They tried nightingales and chaffinches and various thrushes, but none succeeded like the 100 European starlings they released in Central Park. By the last count there were over two hundred million of them. He'd read an article in one of his bird books that called them "avian cockroaches."

He set up his camera on a tripod and scanned the trees with the telephoto. Not only were there starlings, but also red winged blackbirds, an aggressive, native species. They could hold their own against invaders.

Carson clicked a few shots. He could edit the photos out of the camera's memory later if he needed the space. A group of starlings lifted from some of the trees. Maybe something disturbed them? He looked for a deer or racoon on the ground below, but couldn't see anything. The birds swirled upwards before sweeping down river. He thought about invaders, like infection, spreading across the country. Carp were invaders. So were zebra mussels that hitchhiked in ships' ballast water and became a scourge, attaching themselves to the inside of pipes used to draw water into power plants.

It wasn't just animals either. Crabgrass, dandelions, kudzu, knotweed, tamarisk, leafy spurge and Norway maple, pushing native species to extinction.

Infection. Extinction. And extinct meant you'd never come back. No hope.

Empty houses. Empty shopping malls. Empty theaters. Contrail-free skies. Static on the radio. Traffic-free highways. The creak of wind-pushed swing sets in dusty playgrounds. He pictured Tillie's video, the endless runners pouring across the bridge.

Carson shook his head. He'd never get the count done if he daydreamed. Last year he spotted 131 species in the fall count. Maybe this year he'd find more. Maybe he'd see something rare, like a yellow-billed loon or a fulvous whistling duck.

Methodically, he moved his focus from tree to tree. Mostly starlings, their beaks resting on their breasts. Five hundred in one tree. A thousand in the next. He held the binoculars in his left hand while writing the numbers with his right. Later he'd fill out a complete report for the Colorado Field Ornithologists. A stack of reports sat on his desk at home, undeliverable.

He couldn't hear the birds from here, but their chirping calls would be overwhelming if he could walk beneath them.

A feathered blur whipped through his field of vision. Carson looked over the top of his binoculars. Two birds skimmed the tree tops, heading upriver. He stood, breath coming quick. Narrow wings. Right size. He found them in the binoculars. Were they the same kind of bird he'd seen yesterday? What luck! But they flew too fast and they were going away. He'd never be able to identify them from this distance. If only they'd circle back. Then, unbelievably, they turned, crossing the river, coming toward him. The binoculars thumped against his chest when he dropped them, as he picked up the camera, tripod and all. He found the birds, focused, and snapped a picture. They kept coming. He snapped again, both birds in view. Closer even still until just one bird filled the frame. Snap. Then they whipped past, only twenty feet overhead. And fast! Faster than any bird he'd seen except a peregrine falcon on a dive.

His hands trembled. Definitely a bird new to him. A new species to add to his life list. And the bird he'd seen yesterday couldn't be a single, misplaced wanderer, not if there were two of them here. Maybe a flock had been blown into the area. He knew Colorado birds, and these weren't native.

He stayed another hour, counting starlings and recording the other river birds that crossed his path, but his heart wasn't in it. In his camera waited the image of the new bird, but he'd have to transfer it to the computer where he could study it.

Tillie was in bed. Beside her, on the night stand, were packets of seeds. She hadn't moved them since he'd brought them to her in the spring. The television was on. There were, of course, no broadcasts, so gray snow filled the screen, and the set softly hissed. Carson turned it off, darkening the room. Sunlight leaked around the closed curtains, but after the brightness outside, he could barely see. In the silence, Tillie's breathing rasped. He tiptoed around her bed to put his hand to her forehead. Distinctly warm. She didn't move when he touched her.

"Tillie?" he said.

She mumbled but didn't open her eyes.

Carson turned on her reading light, painting her face in highlights and sharp shadows. He knelt beside her. Her lips were parted slightly, and she licked them before taking her next rattling breath. He wanted to jostle her awake. She slept so poorly most nights that he resisted. The fever startled him. As long as it was just a cough, he hadn't worried much. A cough, that could be a cold or an allergy. But a fever, that was a red flag. He remembered all the home defense brochures with their sobering titles: FAMILY TRIAGE and KNOW YOUR SYMPTOMS. "Tillie, I need to check your chest."

His fingers shook as he pulled the blanket away from her chin. Her neck was clammy, and underneath the covers she was sweating. She *smelled* warm and damp. Clumsily he unbuttoned her nightgown's top buttons, then he moved the light so he could see better. No rash. She wasn't wearing a bra, so he could see that the tops of her breasts looked smooth. "Tillie?" he whispered, really not wanting to wake her. Her eyes moved under her eyelids. Maybe she dreamed of other places, the places she would never talk to him about. Gently he rubbed his fingertips over the skin below her collarbones. No boils. No "bumpy swellings" the brochures described.

Tillie mumbled again. "Bob Robert," she said.

"I'll get some aspirin and water." He pulled the blanket back up. She didn't move.

"You're nice," she said, but her head was turned away, and he wasn't sure if she was talking to him or continuing a conversation in her dream.

As he poured water from a bottle in the refrigerator, he realized that it would be difficult to tell if Tillie became delirious. If she started talking sense, *then* he'd have to worry about her.

The distribution manager had said to come back the next day, so there was nothing to do other than to give her aspirin and keep her comfortable. She woke up enough to take the medicine, but closed her eyes immediately. Carson patted her on the top of her hands, made sure the water pitcher was full, then went to his office where he printed the pictures from his camera. The last one was quite good. Full view of the bird's beak, head, neck, breast, wing shape and tail feathers. Identification should have been easy, but nothing matched in his books. He needed better resources.

Driving to Littleton library meant passing the landfill. Most days Carson tried to ignore it—it reminded him of Arlington Cemetery without the tombstones—but today he stopped at the side of the road. He needed a place to think, and the broad, featureless land lent itself to meditations. Last year swarms of gulls circled, waiting for places to set down. The ones on the ground picked at the remnants of flags that covered the low hills. The year before, wreaths and flags and sticks festooned with ribbons dotted the mounds while earth movers ripped long ditches and chugged diesel exhaust. Today, though, no birds. He supposed there was nothing left for them to eat. No smells to attract them. The earth movers were parked off to the side in a neat row. Dust swirled across the dirt in tiny eddies that danced for a moment, then dissipated into nothing. The ground looked as plain as his back yard. Not a tree anywhere or grass. He thought about Tillie searching for a geranium.

He looked up. The sky was completely empty. No hawks. Could it be that not even a mouse lived in the landfill?

What would he do if she left? He leaned against the car, his hands deep in his pockets, chin on his chest. What if she were gone? So many had departed: the girl at the magazine stand, the counter people at the bagel shop, his coworkers. What was it he used to do? He could barely remember, just like he couldn't picture his wife's face clearly anymore. All of them, slipping away.

He slid his fingers inside his shirt. No bumps there either. Why not, and were they inevitable?

A wind kicked across the plain, scurrying scraps of paper and more dust toward him in a wave. He could taste rain in the air. Weather's changing, he thought, and climbed back into the car before the wind reached him.

Skylights illuminated the library's main room. Except for the stale smell and the thin coating of neglect on the countertops and the leather chairs arranged in cozy reading circles, it could be open for business. Carson saw no evidence that anyone had been here since his last visit a month ago. He checked his flashlight. Sunlight didn't penetrate to the back stacks where the bird books were, and he wanted to make sure he didn't miss any.

On the bulletin board inside the front doors hung civil defense and the Center for Disease Control posters filled with the familiar advice: avoid crowds, get good sleep, report symptoms immediately. The civil defense poster reminded him that PATRIOTS PROTECT THEIR IMMUNE SYSTEMS and the depressing, REMEMBER, IT GOT THEM FIRST.

The cart he found had a wheel that shook and didn't track with the others. It pulled to the left and squeaked loudly as he pushed it between the rows. In the big building, the noise felt out of place. Absurdly, Carson almost said, "Shhh!" A library was *supposed* to be quiet, even if he was the only one in it.

Back at the bird books, he ran his flashlight across the titles, all his favorite tomes: the Audubon books and the National Geographic ones. The two huge volumes of Bailey and Niedriach's *Birds of Colorado* with their beautiful photographs and drawings. He placed them in the cart lovingly. By the time he finished, he'd arranged thirty-five books on the cart, every bird reference they had. He shivered as he straightened the collection. The back of the library had never felt cold before.

At the checkout desk, he agonized over what to do. When he was a child, the librarian filled out a card that was tucked in the book's front cover. Everything was computerized now. How was he going to check the books out? Not that it was likely anyone would want them, but it didn't feel right, just taking them. Finally he wrote a note with all the titles listed. He stuck it to the librarian's computer, thought about it for a second, then wrote a second one to put into the gap he'd left in the shelves. He added his address and a p.s., "If you really need these books, please contact me."

Before going, he wandered into the medical section. Infectious diseases were in the 600 area. There wasn't a title left. He took a deep breath that tickled his throat. It felt odd, so he did it again, provoking a string of deep coughs. It's just the dust in here, he thought, but his lungs felt heavy, and he realized he'd been holding off the cough all day.

Carson stopped at the distribution center on the way home. The parking lot was empty. He wandered through the warehouse, between the high stacks, down the long rows. No manager. No assistant. Last year Carson had hauled a diesel generator into a theater near his house. He'd rigged it to power a projector so he could watch a movie on the big screen, but the empty room with all the empty seats gave him the creeps. He'd fled the theater without even turning off the generator. The warehouse felt like that. As he walked toward the exit, his strides became faster and faster until he was running.

As the sun set into the heavy clouds on the horizon, he accepted the obvious. Whatever Tillie had, he had too. She breathed shallowly between coughing fits, and, although the fever responded to aspirin, it rebounded quickly. The aspirin helped with his own fever, but he felt headachy and tired.

Sitting beside her bed, he put his hand on her arm. "I'm going to go back to the Distribution Center tomorrow, Tillie. He said he might find some medicine."

Tillie turned toward him, her eyes gummy and bloodshot. "Don't go," she said. Her voice quivered, but she looked directly at him. No drifting. Speaking deliberately, she said, "Everybody I know has gone away."

Carson looked out the window. It would be dark soon.

Tillie's arm burned beneath his fingertips. He could almost feel the heated blood rushing through her. "I've got to do something. You might have pneumonia."

She inhaled several times. Carson imagined the pain; an echo of it pulsed in his own chest.

"Could you stay in the neighborhood?" she asked.

He nodded.

Tillie closed her eyes. "When it started, I watched TV all the time. That's all I did, was watch TV. My friends watched TV. They played it at work. 'A Nation Under Quarantine' the newscasters called it. And then I couldn't watch any more."

Carson blinked his eyes shut against the burning. That's where he didn't want to go, into *those* memories. It's what he didn't think about when he sat in his camp chair counting birds. It's what he didn't picture when he bolted solar cells onto the roof, when he gathered wood for the new wood stove he'd installed in the living room, when he pumped gasoline out of underground tanks at silent gas stations. Sometimes he had a hard time imagining anything was wrong at all. When he drove, the car still responded to his touch. The wind whistled tunelessly past his window. How could the world still be so familiar and normal and yet so badly skewed?

"Well, we keep doing what has to be done, despite it all," he said.

"I was innocent." Her gaze slid away from his, and she smiled. Carson saw her connection to him sever. The shift was nearly audible. "I don't want to see the news tonight. Maybe there will be a nice rerun later. *Friends* or *Cheers* would be good. I'll go to the mall in the morning. The fall fashions should be in." She settled into her pillow as if to go to sleep.

Carson set up a vaporizer, hoping that would make her breathing easier, then quietly shut her door before leaving.

Crowbar in hand, he crossed the dirt expanse that was his front yard, stepped over the dry-leafed hedge between his yard and the neighbors. The deadbolt splintered out of the frame when he leaned on the crowbar, and one kick opened the door. The curtains were closed, darkening the living room. Carson wrinkled his nose at the house's mustiness. Under that smell lingered something rotten, like mildew and bad vegetables gone slimy and black.

He flicked on his flashlight. The living room was neat, magazines fanned across a coffee table for easy selection, glass coasters piled on a small stand by a lounge chair and family photos arranged on the wall. Three bedroom doors opened into the main hallway. In one, a crib stood empty beneath a Mickey Mouse mobile. In the second, his light played across an office desk, a fax machine and a laptop computer, its top popped open and keyboard waiting.

The third door led to the master bedroom. In the bathroom medicine cabinet he found antacids, vitamins and birth control pills, but no antibiotics. When he left the house, he closed the front door as best he could.

An hour later he'd circled the block, breaking into every house along the way. Two of the houses had already been looted. The door on the first hung from only one hinge. In the second, the furniture was overturned, and a complicated series of cracks emanated from a single bullet hole in the living room window. In some of the houses the bed sheets covered long lumps. He stayed out of the bedrooms. No antibiotics.

His chest heavy, barely able to lift his feet, he trudged across the last lawn to his house where one window was lit. Whatever the illness was, it felt serious. Not a cold or flu, but down deep malignant, sincere, like nothing he'd ever had before. This was how he felt, and he'd started in good shape, but Tillie hardly ever ate well. She never exercised. Her system would be especially vulnerable. He pictured his house empty. No Tillie gazing over her cards before drawing. No Tillie wandering in the yard, looking for a single geranium to give her hope. "How do you bear it?" she'd asked.

Tillie was sleeping, her fever down again, but her breathing was just as hoarse. In his own lungs, each inhalation fluttered and buzzed. He imagined a thousand tiny pinwheels whirling away inside him.

Carson started the New York City Marathon video, then returned to the chair next to Tillie's bed. He wet a washcloth then pressed it against her forehead. She didn't move. "What a celebration of life," said the announcer. "In the shadow of disaster, athletes have gathered to say we can't be beat in the long run." A map of the course winding through the five boroughs appeared on the screen. Then a camera angle from a helicopter skimming over the streets showing the human river. At one point a dozen birds flew between the camera and the ground. "Doves," thought Carson, feeling flush. Even his eyes felt warm, and when he finally rested his head on Tillie's arm, he couldn't feel a difference in their temperatures.

He dreamed about bird books spread across a desk in front of him, but he wasn't in his office. Other desks filled the room, and at each one a person sat, studying books. In the desk beside his, a man with tremendous sideburns that drooped to the sides of his neck picked up a dead bird, spread its wing feathers apart, scrutinizing each connection. He placed the bird back on his desk, then added a few lines to a drawing of it on an easel.

"Purple finch," said the man, and Carson knew with dreamlike certainty that it was John Audubon. "A painting is forever, even if the bird is not." Audubon poked at the feathered pile. "It's a pity I have to kill them to preserve them."

"I'm searching for a bird's name," said Carson. Some of the people at the other desks looked up in interest. He described the bird. "I've only seen three of them flying with European starlings."

"Only three?" Audubon looked puzzled. "They flew in flocks that filled the sky for days. Outside of Louisville, the people were all in arms. The banks of the Ohio were crowded with men and boys, incessantly shooting at the birds. Multitudes were destroyed, and for a week or more the population fed on no other flesh, and you saw only three?"

Carson nodded.

"With European starlings?"

Carson was at a loss. How could he explain to Audubon about birds introduced to America after his death? He said instead, "But what is the bird's name?"

"Purple finch, I told you."

"No, I mean the bird I described."

Audubon picked up his pencil and added another line to the drawing. He mumbled an answer.

"Excuse me?" said Carson.

More mumbling. Audubon continued drawing. The bird didn't look like a finch, purple or otherwise. His lines grew wilder as the bird became more and more fantastic. He sketched flames below it with quick, sure strokes, all the while mumbling, louder and louder.

Carson strained to understand him. What was the bird? What was it? And he became aware that the mumbling was hot and moist in his ear. With a jerk, he sat up. Tillie's lips were moving, but her eyes were shut. What time was it? Where was he? For a moment he felt completely dissociated from the world.

Two aspirins in hand, he tried waking her up, but she refused to open her eyes. Her cheeks were red, and in between incoherent bursts of speech, her breathing was labored, as if she were a deep-sea diver, bubbling from the depths. Her forehead felt hot again. A sudden shivering attack took him, and for a minute it was all he could do to grit his teeth against the shaking. When it passed, he swallowed the aspirins he'd brought for her. Maybe there might be antibiotics in one of the houses a block over.

He put on a coat against his chills, grabbed the crowbar and flashlight, then crossed the street. In the night air, his head seemed light and large, but walking was a strain. The crowbar weighed a thousand pounds.

In the second house he found a plastic bottle marked PENICILLIN in a medicine cabinet. He laughed in relief, then coughed until he sat on the bathroom floor, the flashlight beside him casting long, weird shadows. Only two tablets, 250 mg. each. They hardly weighed anything in his hand. What was an adult dosage? Was penicillin the right treatment for pneumonia? What if she didn't have pneumonia, or she did but it was viral instead of bacterial?

Carson staggered back home. After fifteen minutes, he was able to rouse Tillie enough to take the pills and the aspirin. Exhausted, he collapsed on the chair by her bed. He put his head back and stared at the ceiling. Swirls and broad lines marked the plaster. For a moment he thought they were clouds, and in the clouds he saw a bird, the narrow winged one that he'd seen by the river, the one Audubon said he knew, and suddenly, Carson knew too. He'd always known, and he laughed. No wonder it looked familiar. Of course he couldn't find it in his bird books.

Smiling, holding Tillie's hand, he fell asleep.

A pounding roused him.

Thump, thump, thump. Like a heartbeat. His eyelids came apart reluctantly and gradually he focused on the length of bedspread that started at his cheek and reached to the bed's end. Without moving, without even really knowing where he was, he knew he was sick. Sickness can't be forgotten. Even in his sleep, he must have been aware of the micro war within. It surged through him, alienating his organs, his skin. The machine is breaking down, he thought.

"Someone's at the door," said Tillie. She stirred beside him. "It might be the pool man."

Carson pushed himself from the bed, his back cracking in protest. His legs felt wooden. How long had he been next to her?

She was sitting up, blankets over her legs, an open book face down under her hands. "You've been sleeping, Bob Robert," she said brightly.

He put a hand against her forehead, then against his own. "I'm not Bob Robert." She was cooler, and the wheezing in her chest didn't sound quite as bad. The empty penicillin bottle sat on the night stand beneath her reading light. Could antibiotics work that fast? Even if they did, one dose wouldn't cure whatever they had. She'd relapse. He'd get sicker. He needed to find more.

A pounding from the front of the house again.

He stood shakily, his chest aching on each breath.

"I'll be back," he said.

"Oh, I'm all right. A bit of reading will do me good." She opened the book. It was one from his office. Sometime during the night she must have gotten out of bed.

Carson braced himself against the hallway wall as he walked to the front door, hunched over from the illness. His head throbbed and the sunlight through the front window was too bright.

"Carson, are you in there?" a voice yelled. "Birnam wood has come to Elsinore," it shouted.

Through the pain and fever, Carson squinted. He opened the door. "Isn't it Dunsinane that Birnam comes to?"

The warehouse manager balanced a box on his hip. "I saw the damndest thing on the way here." He started. " Jeeze, man! You look terrible."

Carson nodded, trying to put the scene together. The manager's truck was parked next to his own in the driveway. The sun lingered high in the sky.

How long had he been sleeping? Carson forced the words out in little gasps. "What are you doing?"

Grabbing Carson's arm, the manager helped him into the living room onto the couch. "I found the antibiotics I told you about," he said. "It wasn't in the pharmacy. The place burned to the ground." The manager ripped open the box lid. Inside were rows of small, white boxes. Inside the first box were hundreds of pills. He plucked two out. "But in the delivery area behind the store, there was a UPS truck chock full of medicine."

Carson blinked, and the manager offered him a glass of water for the pills. When did he get up to fetch the water?

"Your chest is heavy, right, and you're feverish and tired?"

"Yes," croaked Carson.

"I can hear your lungs from here. Pneumonia, for sure, I'll bet. If we're lucky, this'll knock it right out."

Carson swallowed the pills. Sitting, he felt better. It took the pressure off his breathing. Tillie had looked healthier. Maybe the penicillin helped her, and if it helped her, it could help him.

The manager walked around the room, stopping at the photoelectric panel's gauges. "You have a sweet set up here. Did you do the wiring yourself?"

Carson nodded. He croaked, "Why aren't you at the warehouse?" The light in the room flickered. Ponderously, Carson turned his head. Through the picture window, it seemed for a moment as if shadows raced over the houses, but when he checked again, the sun shone steadily.

Without looking at him, the manager said, "Time to move on. That warehouse paralyzed me. I've been waiting, I think. Olivier's Hamlet said last night, 'If it be now, tis not to come; if it be not to come it will be now.'"

"What was he talking about?" asked Carson.

"Fear of death. Grief," said the manager. "The readiness is all, he said. Ah, who is this?"

Tillie stood at the entrance to the hallway. She'd changed into jeans and a work shirt. Her face was still feverish and she swayed a little. "Oh, good, the pool man," she said. Without pausing for a reply, she waved a handful of packets at them. "I'm tired of waiting for flowers, Carson. I'm going to plant something."

Confused, he said, "It's nearly winter," but she'd already disappeared. He rubbed his brow, and his hand came away wet with sweat. "Did she call me Carson?"

Shadows hurried across the street again, and this time the manager looked too.

"What is that?" asked Carson.

"I was going to ask you." The manager stepped out the door and glanced up. "I saw them on the way over. They're funny birds."

Carson heaved himself out of the couch. His head swam so violently that he nearly fell, but he caught himself and made it to the door. He held the manager's arm to stay steady.

Overhead, the flock streamed across the sky, barely above the rooftops. Making no sound. Hundreds of them. Narrow wings. Red breasts.

"What are they?" asked the manager.

Carson straightened. Even sickness couldn't knock him down for this. The birds zoomed like feathered jets. Where had they been all these years? Had there just been a few hidden in the remotest forests, avoiding human eyes? Had they teetered on the edge of extinction for a century without actually disappearing despite all evidence to the contrary? Was it conceivable to return to their glory?

Carson said, "They're passenger pigeons."

The manager said, "What's a passenger pigeon?"

It's an addition to my life list, thought Carson. Audubon said they'd darkened the skies for days. Carson remembered the New York City Marathon. The people kept running and running and running. They filled the Verrazano-Narrows Bridge.

"I guess sometimes things can come back," said Carson.

The impossible birds wheeled to the east.

NOTES FROM THE FIELD

S O MUCH HUMAN LANGUAGE IS UNTRANSLATABLE. AFTER I'D SCANNED AND tagged my latest subject, she talked non-stop.

She started by saying, "I don't do this often. It's my rule to get to know someone before we . . . you know . . . sleep together." And she continued as she pulled up nylons, wiggled into a short-skirted black dress and adjusted her hair. My equipment recorded it, of course, for later analysis and synthesis with the rest of the field data. She told me about her sisters and how they were married, "Except Susan, who has been living with this realtor in Seattle for two years, so she's practically engaged," and then went on about her job while she reapplied makeup. When she went into the bathroom, I checked the tag's status; the monitor showed it had already attached itself to the fallopian tube, where it would stay, transmitting data for about six months until it broke down into undetectable biological components.

Upbeat, bright, until she was ready to go, she asked me what about half of them do. "Will I see you again?" Her face seemed poised, carefully blank.

I shrugged. A useful gesture, communicating messages in a wide range.

She took a deep breath, a shuddery one, and looked away, which often means the subject is on an emotional edge. I hadn't seen it coming. I hardly ever do. Reading human facial expressions is my hobby, not part of my mission, but I don't feel I'm very good at it. She looked around my apartment, at the art prints in frames, at the expensive stereo equipment, at the new furniture, which reinforced my masquerade as a young business executive, and said, "Don't mind me. It's all blather."

I've discovered humans in the bars are often lonely, a little desperate. The sex is an amelioration.

Blather: In this context, probably meaning language that covers or replaces the message the sender would prefer to communicate. Although all human languages possess words used in this way, there is no Lasarént equivalent.

The last *Lasarént* abduction of a human for examination and tagging occurred in 1967 near San Antonio, Texas. The three other extrasolar races quit the practice before 1964. They attracted too much attention. Memory adjustments weren't perfect. That's the nature of technology, imperfection. So the plan to study humanity entered its second phase, infiltration. Still, abduction stories appeared in the tabloids. For a while there was considerable bickering among the four races about who was cheating, but it became evident that human behavior is often delusional.

My first field experience coincided with our last abduction. The human lived in Tremaine, an hour's drive from San Antonio along a twisting, graveled road. We stalled his truck, anaesthetized him and moved him to an exploratory vehicle. Some tests require a lively nervous system, however, so he was brought near consciousness. He looked at us from the table, eyes half closed. "Jesus, Mary, son of a bitch. It's the goddamned Rapture."

I've been in the field ever since, over thirty years.

Rapture: In this context, probably meaning a religious experience of being transported to heaven. Some confusion here over his use of the article "the" instead of the more commonly expected, "a." Other terms for this include "the final reward," and "coming home." See "euphemism." Beyond that, the utterance resists translation.

For three weeks I'd been collecting information and tagging specimens in singles bars in the Old Town area of Sacramento when I ran into a *Trosfrilla* operative. My bioenhancements and cosmetic surgeries, some of them quite radical and painful, allowed me to pass as a male human. I had the more difficult task of studying females. *Lasarént* field operators disguised as females, using similar techniques in tagging males, reported as many as three or four specimens a night. One evening I attracted two females to my apartment at the same time, which nearly overloaded my scanning equipment, but other nights I only collected notes. In other countries, of course, we use practices appropriate for their cultures.

A converted riverboat, the Sleepy Jean Grill and Suds, permanently docked near the Port of Sacramento, was the next bar on my schedule. A place couldn't be visited too often, or I might have to deal with a previous contact a second time. There is no scientific need to scan the subject twice once it has been tagged, but females I'd met previously often ruined my chances for a new encounter by talking until the bar closed. I parked in the lot, and crossed a gangplank over the water to enter.

Inside, the bar stretched the length of the narrow room and was made of weathered barn planks, heavily varnished. Neon beer signs flashed behind Venetian blinds. No cover. A local hangout. Hard to get to if you didn't know it was there. Grill behind the bar to the side, where a cook flipped burgers and fried potatoes. Lots of cooking odors, beer and a mossy undertone from the river. Red lights. A small dance floor flanked by large speakers at one end, a pair of pool tables at the other. Tables in between. In a larger singles bar I'd have better luck attracting someone, but I had plenty of data from those venues. Now I was more interested in atypical cases.

The lights caught my attention—they were nearly the hue of the spring time

Lasarént sky—and the water smells reminded me of my birth den in the bank of the far *Hydrash*. Before the crowd arrived, I could feel the current flowing beneath the boat, rubbing the aged wood. As soon as I entered, I knew I would return. I took a table in the middle and asked the waiter for two place settings. It was one of several techniques to interest women, the empty chair. Some women can't resist a single man, nicely dressed, aesthetically pleasing (we'd spent years perfecting attractive proportions in the lures—a fractionally small shift in eye placement, nose size or teeth arrangement can make a lure successful or a failure—my human face had been altered numerous times). She can't resist if it's obvious his date has not arrived.

The empty chair is a passive technique. It depends on the women coming to me, as do several other ruses such as reading a book, or taking notes. A tape recorder on the table will sometimes work, or a camera. What doesn't work is looking unoccupied. A man who clearly just waits is shunned. Scanning the bar doesn't work either. A man looking for a woman never finds her. There are active techniques too. Many of them. Almost all involve some pretense for conversation, not just, "Nice weather we're having, don't you think?" but anything that asks the woman to contribute something of her own. Even something as simple as, "Great jacket. Where'd you get it?" can be a beginning. After that, the evening scripts itself around drinks, dancing, more conversation until it's obvious she is willing to come to my apartment. Often there needs to be an excuse to go, either to see the art prints, or to admire the view from the balcony, or to listen to music. Rarely will either of us be straightforward: "Let's go somewhere private for sex." Humans are interesting in this behavior. Important matters to them aren't discussed directly.

I've been among the humans for years, "sleeping together" numerous times. Never have I discussed my matters of importance. We have no middle ground.

"Sleeping together" does not involve sleeping. It is sex, often times on a bed (which is used for sleeping too!) but one female told me we'd "slept together" when we didn't make it past the clothes closet. Fortunately the scanning equipment covers the entire area equally well.

I was part way through a salmon steak, which I'd developed a taste for, when the woman sat at my table.

"I hate to eat alone, do you mind?" she said. Blonde hair cut short. Dark eyes, hard to see the color in this light. According to human conceptions of physical beauty, I guessed that she didn't have to eat alone often. She was almost six feet tall, my height. Slim. Plain, blue shirt worn loose. White pants. White boots tucked under the pant's legs. Not standard dress for a singles place, but the Sleepy Jean wasn't typical, as I said. Two motorcycle types at the bar watched her for a moment before turning back to their drinks.

"Not at all," I said. "Have you ordered?"

She brushed hair off her forehead. "Don't mind if I do."

Normally, meeting a woman is not this easy. Even though the bars exist for social interactions, humans are wary at first. They don't trust each other. It seemed clear to me, though, that this one was bound for my apartment, so I field-scanned her. A tiny unit on my wristwatch would tell me if she'd been tagged before and give me an overview of her suitability for our studies.

She was *Trosfrillan*, one of the other extrasolars, which explained her height. How they got a nine-foot tall, six-limbed creature into this package amazed me. My modifications, painful as they were, were not as drastic.

"Damn!" she said, looking at her own watch.

We didn't speak for a while. The *Trosfrilla* study humans in much the same manner as we do. They are interested in travel patterns. Mating rituals. Work/recreation ratios. Sleep/wake cycles. Biochemistry. The normal field data for any species. Past difficulties prevent us from sharing our findings, though there is now some effort to consolidate the work. Our races evolved on different planets in the same system. There had been wars in our past. We were competitors.

I looked around the bar again. The motorcycle guys hunched over their beers. A couple shot pool at a table at the bar's far end. Beneath me, the floor moved subtly, responding to the river's flow.

"My name's Arlyss," I said. My *Lasarént* name would damage a human throat.

"Trudy," she said. "Have you been down long?"

"Off and on for thirty-some years. I haven't been off-world for eleven years now."

The waiter came by and took her order. I ate more salmon. The mimicked human gestures came almost naturally to me, often times revealing my emotions in ways I would never display when in my *Lasarént* body. I found myself smiling. It had been a long time since I had talked to someone without pretending. "Yourself?" I said, when the waiter left.

"Only five. I'd been doing Seleneological surveys when this opportunity came up. It was a change." She shifted in her seat. "I'm uncomfortable in this form."

I nodded. Gravity was wrong. Not all that different, only 1.2 heavier, but it was *wrong*. A different molten core beneath me. A different wash of magnetic influences. The stars at night, wrong.

She didn't wait for her meal. "I have to go. Quotas."

I felt a unfamiliar urge within me as she rose. A few more people had entered the bar, taking other tables, all humans who could never know who I was. Their faces moved strangely, in their human way: too many horizontal lines, when they closed their mouths or eyes, the eyebrows, the hair line, all oddly horizontal. It frightened me to recognize their feelings in their faces—that I couldn't really remember what a *Lasarént* face looked like. I wanted her to stay. She wasn't *Lasarént*, but we shared a sun. "Why did you come here?" I said. The bar was small. Even when it was full, it would be as unlikely a place for her work as it was for mine.

She pushed her chair under the table. I noticed her fingers. Their sculpting was perfect, nails exactly human-like. The *Trosfrilla* have six fingers on their manipulating hands. She lost part of herself for this transition too. "The river reminded me of home." She floated her hand away and indicated the whole bar. "The light—did you notice?—it's like *Trosfrilla*."

"I saw," I said, but she was already striding away. The bikers watched her again.

Clearly I made her uneasy. If she wanted to scan and tag a human, she would be as successful here as she would be anywhere else. It wasn't the quota that drove her away. It was me. I wondered about *Trosfrillan* morality. Did she consider her work embarrassing? Was this a perversion in her eyes?

Bestiality: Sexual relations with an animal. Humans consider this to be of the lowest sort of behavior. The background for this revulsion is untranslatable. Is there a Trosfrillan equivalent?

As it turned out, I made a contact that night, a woman playing pool by herself. I put quarters on the rail, shot eight-ball with her until closing.

Pool is an elegant game, maybe one of the best of the human recreations. I get lost in the velocities and angles, the cue in my hand, the felt's smooth plain, the ball's muted click. We played evenly. She set up for a shot then stood back each time, as if she were shooting it twice. Called her bumpers. A rhythmic pattern she never varied. She clicked her tongue appreciatively when I made a good shot. After a while, I got the impression she didn't care about the score. She watched the rolling ball like I did, as a physics demonstration. Something beyond personality. Humans startle me sometimes with their depth, and I wished I could talk to her about myself. Last call for drinks surprised me.

We left together, and she said, "Where's your car?" I'd scanned her earlier. Twenty-seven years old. She showed evidence of having borne children. Impossible to tell more until she was at the apartment, where the equipment was better.

She didn't talk as we drove away, but she looked out the window. Her unsmiling reflection flickered in the streetlights. Her breathing was even, hands still in her lap. "You have protection?" she said when we pulled into the parking lot.

I nodded. Of course it was designed not to interfere with my measurements or the placing of the tag. Human diseases didn't threaten me, and I sterilized myself between encounters to not spread contagions. I'm the definition of "safe sex."

Later that night I drove her back to the Sleepy Jean. After she shut the car door, she leaned in the window. "My name's Margaret."

"Sorry," I said. "I'm Arlyss. I forgot to ask."

"I thought you should know."

I stayed in the parking lot, listening to the river. It started to rain. Big drops slapped against the windshield and splattered on the upholstery. A stream of muddy water crossed the parking lot to empty into the river between the anchored boat and the shore. The lights had been turned off, but the beer signs still glowed, glinting redly in the rain pools. I hadn't thought of *Lasarént* for years, not like this.

I once read a bumper sticker on a truck parked outside a Chicago dance club: "Save time: go ugly early." No translation available.

The next night, at Shatterday's, a huge singles lounge in north Sacramento, I saw Trudy again. She was on the crowded dance floor, as far as I could tell, by herself. Now that I knew she was *Trosfrillan*, I could see it in her movements. Their backs have twinned vertebrae. Even in her near perfect human form, she danced distinctly. People gave her room. More than a few watched her, men and women.

I held my beer tightly, waiting for it to warm to a drinkable temperature. Even though I had been in the bar for an hour, I'd made no attempt to hook up with anyone. I contemplated the music, which is not artistic to my ear, but I find it beautiful that they *have* music. It tells me perhaps we will get along when this race breaks free from its planet, when we reveal ourselves to them. There has to be something worthwhile in a species that devotes so much time to music, and invented pool. And they dance, of course, which speaks well for them, even when it's clear that much of the dance I see is variations on mating rituals. All posturing and invitations.

Trudy's dance had none of that in it. Pure movement for the love of movement. The *Trosfrilla* have hierarchies of dance, achievement levels that take years to master, as do the *Lasarént*. In the mythology of encounters between our two races, there is a story of a war settled by a long dance. They danced the peace in, goes the tale.

"Do you want to dance?" said the woman. Short, a bit plump by human standards. I checked my watch. Young. Twenty-one. Untagged. Her friends sat at a table a few yards from mine, hiding their giggles. I don't believe they thought she would have the courage to ask me. She danced well, for a human. At least she moved energetically. The song ended, and we waited for the next. She kept her hand on mine to keep from losing me in the crowd. We danced again. I made frequent eye contact. Responded to her changes in posture. Human dance: postures and invitation. I read her. She read me. Others jostled us. The music pounded in its numbingly unchanging beat. As always, I felt disconnected. I didn't know her. She would never know me. No point of synchronicity in our lives. I could imagine her in my apartment in an hour or two, trying to close the distance. For me, what happened in the apartment was clinical.

What a fruitless pursuit on her part, even if I was human. I'd seen the same kind of face before. Sad, under the laughter. What would be the best she could hope for? That I wouldn't leave her at the end of the evening? That I wouldn't be in another bar on another night dancing with someone else? And then what would she have? Humans don't meet in the mind as do the Lasarént. She would never press her back into the muddy wall of a den on the banks of the Hydrash, side by side with the family line. She'd never know ecstasy as the fleshy tendrils grew between us, from back to back, burrowed in, transferred genes and nutrients and emotion. She would never touch minds with her den mates in orgiastic communion all winter long.

I almost walked away from her. But a hand pressed against my thigh, and a voice whispered in my ear, "How do you handle the loneliness?" I turned. It was Trudy, already dancing away into the crowd.

What loneliness? I thought. I am a scientist on a mission. My work is my companion. We danced more. I bought the plump woman drinks.

At the apartment, she clung to me after I'd tagged her. "I was afraid I was too ugly for you," she said.

I told her truthfully, "You are as beautiful as any woman I've seen."

"You wouldn't kid a kidder?" she said, and tears wet my chest when she pressed her face there.

"You wouldn't kid a kidder": To lie to someone who lies. This is one of many funny/ sad utterances humans use, like "He has a face only a mother could love," and "She's built for comfort, not for speed." Emotionally untranslatable.

The next night I sat in Bullsnappers until closing. Twice women asked me to dance. I declined. Sitting back, I watched the bar's rhythm. Men and women in groups, leaning over tables, lined up at the bar, standing besides one another at the edge of the dance floor, mostly not talking, but together. Loud music. Too loud for conversation, but sometimes someone would touch another's arm, and they'd push their heads together. She'd shout something. He would nod.

People got up, danced, sat down. Patterns emerged of touch and laugh and movement. Strobes flashed in the ceiling, and I watched the dance floor. Legs rearranging. Pelvic rotations. The sinuous flow of a skirt's edge around a twirling woman. Bass beat, down deep, bouncing in my chest. No pause between songs, and the pattern started again. Hands on backs, shifting. Thighs pressed against thighs under tables. A kiss on a cheek. A bathroom door opened, and harsh light silhouetted the figure coming out.

It was all too loud, chaotic, and . . . alien. I couldn't integrate here. Hadn't integrated for so long I wasn't sure I could. Nothing felt right. I left cash on the table and pushed my way to the exit. Faces blurred. Strange faces loud with horizontal lines and teeth and darting eyes, watching each other, watching me, and knowing nothing.

Outside, I breathed raggedly. Barely made it to my car. At the apartment, hands shaking, I ran a diagnostic. Maybe one of the implants was breaking down. Maybe, after all this time, my *Lasarént* immune system was rejecting the grafts, or it could be an acquired allergy. I had too many symptoms, but the equipment reported nothing wrong. Everything normal. For the first time in my field experience, I sedated myself and remained unconscious for several days.

On a Wednesday night, I returned to the Sleepy Jean. Same red lights. Same soothing murmur under the boat. No one in the bar besides the bartender, a cook and myself. I took notes idly about peanut shells on the floor, and how they cracked underfoot, about lingering odors beneath the obvious ones: perfumes, sweat, detergents, petrochemicals. The chair's surface was cool and smooth, and I realized for the first time that it was an imitation of leather.

Around the room, numerous fakes and imitations. On the walls, old movie posters, but, on close inspection, not the originals. Baseball mitts hanging from the ceiling, just like ones I'd seen in several other bars to provide "atmosphere," along with old road signs, car license plates, a pair of snow shoes, a boat oar, a stuffed peccary, several fishing poles: all pretending to be random, as if the bar grew to be this way instead of being designed. The beer mugs done in an old-fashioned style. The bartender dressed as a riverboat captain. Fakes. I scribbled into my notebook. So much of the integral human experience involved fakery, which was no different from what happened between them. For years I'd watched them come into bars, pretending to be at ease or happy or interested or interesting, and it all covered something else. Like their language.

I put my notebook down and shut my eyes. If I ignored the glassy clink behind the bar, shut out the alien cooking smells and odd gravity; if I concentrated on the river's swishy passage under the boat and the dim red light through my eyelids, I could almost imagine faraway *Lasarént*. What season was it there? Would the rivers be running high now on their winding flow to the shallow seas? Would the hills be oozy and wet under the reddish sun? I licked my lips, tasted the river's moisture on my tongue. Rested my head on the chair's back to feel the moving water better.

I stayed that way for a long time.

Footsteps thudded on the floor. I felt them, and I scrinched my eyes tighter, trying not to break the feeling, but a chair scraped back, and someone joined me at my table. The problem with the vacant chair is it invites company. I thought about sending the person away. Another specimen for the database didn't seem that important right now. What would be the use of one more tagged woman, moving through her life, tracked by invisible *Lasarént* field scientists? What would be the good of me committing one more act of human fakery?

It was Trudy.

"I expected to find you here," she said.

I touched her hand. "That's good work."

She held it up to herself, fingers straight. "They hurt all the time, you know."

I didn't, but I said I did.

The bartender asked her if she wanted something, and she ordered a beer. When he turned away, she said, "Enzyme treatments make it palatable—even my digestive system was changed—but they drink it too cold."

"Mine too. When I started, all the food was shunted to a storage stomach. I emptied it after meals, but they decided that was too cumbersome—shipping food to me twice a month—so I have earth-analog bacteria implants and a processor that converts it for me."

"Ouch," she said. "All that biologically?"

"Most. I'd attract a lot of attention in an Earth hospital if they X-rayed my insides, though."

She laughed. I admired the perfection of her guise. No evidence of vestigial scales. The missing limbs. The loss of height. The loss of eye stalks. *Trosfrilla* biotechs must be true artists.

The door opened and a dozen men and women poured into the bar. A coed softball team, wearing black and yellow T-shirts, talking excitedly.

I didn't want her to go again. The players settled around two tables, calling for beer and pretzels. One of them plugged money into a juke box, and the Sleepy Jean suddenly became noisy and too crowded.

"Can we go someplace quiet?" I asked.

She nodded. What thoughts were going through her *Trosfrilla* brain? We were no longer enemies, technically, but she could learn nothing about Earth people from me. I could learn nothing from her. Our conversation made no scientific sense. We'd gain nothing from it. She was not a human woman. I could take no readings or plant a tag. Still, I wanted to stay with her.

She followed me in her car to my apartment. I turned the equipment off before she entered. No point in letting my superiors know I'd entertained a *Trofrillan* operative.

I said, "Can I get you something to drink?"

Trudy moved into my apartment unlike anyone who'd entered before. She dropped the human role; her feet slid across the carpet, more like her own gait, and her hands went to her jaw line that she rubbed hard. She said, "Water is fine, if it's warm." The heels of her hands ground into the side of her face. "It hurts all the time, here. I'll be glad to go home."

I poured the water and one for myself. Through the door I could see her examining my things. She pushed aside an art print to study the thin plate of scanning equipment behind.

"What's your range?" she called.

"About fifty feet."

She grunted and let the print swing back into place.

"Do you have any music?" she said. "Real music?"

I had several CD's of recordings I'd made from *Lasarént*. The stereo couldn't do the full tonal range justice, but it captured the mutating harmonics and asynchronous rhythms well. We sat beside each other on the couch. Through my picture window the sun set, a red sunset, and I smiled at that. Trudy stayed motionless, her fingers curled on her thighs, her wrists bent slightly, like a Praying Mantis. I smelled nothing *Trosfrillan* on her, only shampoo and perfume.

Around us the human city teemed with its activities. In the building, doors slammed—I felt their distant echoes—feet pattered down the hallways. Outside, traffic pushed past, all individually guided, most cars holding only one person. Busy. Horns and engine noise beat against the glass. A siren whining. But in my apartment, the red sun bathed everything warmly, and the music currents swept by, gentle and chaotic, like the river beneath the Sleepy Jean, like the far *Hydrash*. My scanning equipment was off. My position was no longer clinical. I wasn't collecting.

Trudy rubbed her face again. Underneath the mock skin (Beautifully engineered! Only a well equipped lab that knew what to look for would be able to detect its extraterrestrial origin), I guessed her reshaped skull ached along its alien lines. She grimaced, a very human gesture of pain.

"Here, let me," I said. In the kitchen, I filled a pan with warm water and found a washcloth. She watched me soak the cloth, then press out the excess moisture.

"I don't think we should," she said. Her hand rested on my forearm. "Thank you for the thought, though."

Still, she didn't resist when I placed the cloth against her cheek, let the warmth rest there for a moment, and then pushed my thumbs gently into the muscles. Her dark eyes locked on my own. When I went back to the bowl to reheat the cloth, she sighed and shut her eyes. I straddled her on the couch so I could massage both sides of her face equally. She moved her head against the pressure, so I could tell where she wanted it. Gradually, the apartment darkened, and the red sunset behind me went from vermillion to purple to sable. My thumbs kneaded her cheek bones, pushed into the ridge of her jawbone, circled under her ears—the skin caressed the covered bones, a whole tiny landscape of knobs and valleys and smooth plains, over and over.

She said, "Do you miss winter on *Lasarént*?"

My back ached with memory's loss. The den filled and dark and close. The hormonal changes engendered in the moist soil and shared air, and the timeless eruption of tendrils in my back, burrowing through the mud, finding other tendrils, growing and intertwining until we joined, all of us, in one organism; one birthing, breathing, thinking organism that waited out the winter in warmth and communion and unity. The integration.

I couldn't say anything, but swallowed the human sob in my throat while my thumbs orbited endlessly on her face.

Her hands went to my shirt, unbuttoning. In the darkness I saw her eyes glinting, staring again at me. I massaged the skull above the ears; her hair tickled my wrists. She held my ribs and pulled me closer, her breath hot on my chest, then she reached around and put her hands on my back.

"Here?" she said, her voice mellow against the music.

"Higher," I said, and moved down so she could reach.

The *Trosfrilla* know our anatomy; they know us. One can't go to war for generations without learning of the enemy, and she knew. She knew. Her fingers traveled up and down beside my back bone, digging until she found the buried tendril-pods, chemically suppressed, but still there, sensitive to stimulation, and she rubbed them gently.

When the music ended, I fell away, exhausted.

We breathed deeply in the now silent room, city lights glittering beyond the window, the traffic slowed to its night time murmur.

"Thank you," she said.

"Does it hurt as bad?" I touched the side of her face.

She didn't look at me. "Not as bad. And you?"

Of course there had been incomplete satisfaction in what she'd done, not like a full nesting, but she knew the tendril-pods were there. She'd touched them and reminded them they were alive.

"That felt good," I said. "Thanks."

Trudy rose from the couch, and I knew she was leaving.

She got to the door before I said, "Will I see you again?"

By the dim city light, she paused, her back to me—things remained that way for many heart beats—then she shrugged.

"Why?" she said.

I tried not to weep, my alien form overwhelming me with reflexive emotion, and I suddenly understood something human.

"Don't mind me," I said. "It's all blather."

THE LONG WAY HOME

MARISA KEPT HER BACK TO THE DOOR, HOLDING IT CLOSED. "ANOTHER few minutes and they will have made the jump. You can go home then."

"The war has started," said Jacqueline, the telemetry control engineer. Her face glowed red with panic. "I don't matter. The mission is over. They made the jump *four hours* ago."

Marisa swallowed. If Jacqueline grabbed her, there would be little she could do. The woman outweighed her by thirty pounds, and there were no security forces to help. "Jacqueline, we've come so far."

The bigger woman raised her fist. Marisa tensed but didn't move. Her hands trembled behind her. For a moment, Jacqueline's fist quivered in the air. Beyond her, the last of the mission control crew watched. Most of the stations were empty. The remaining engineers' faces registered no expression. They were too tired to react, but Marisa knew they wanted to leave just as badly.

Then Jacqueline dropped her hand to her side. Her eyes closed. "I don't make a difference," she whispered.

Marisa released a held breath. "We're part of mankind's greatest moment. There's nothing you can do out there." She nodded her head toward the door. "We can't stop what's happening, but we can be witnesses to this. There's hope still."

Several monitors displayed a United States map and a Florida one inset in the corner. Both showed bright yellow blotches. "Areas of lost communication" the key read underneath. Major cities across the country; most of the southwestern coast and northeastern seaboard, glowed bright yellow. In Florida, yellow sunbursts blotted out Miami and Jacksonville. As she watched, another one appeared on Tampa. She glanced at Mission Control's ceiling and the half dozen skylights. At any moment the ceiling could peel away, awash in nuclear light. She expected it, expected it much earlier, but she'd stayed at her station, recording the four-hour-old signals from the *Advent* as it sped toward the solar system's edge, already beyond Neptune's orbit. Would she have any warning? Would there be an instant before the end that she would be aware that it had happened?

Jacqueline sat heavily at her console, and Marisa returned to her station. The data looked good, but it had looked good from the beginning six years earlier when the massive ship ponderously moved out of orbit, all 14,400 passengers hale and hearty. There had been deaths on board, of course. They expected that. Undetected medical conditions. Two homicides. Two suicides, but no major incidents with the ship itself. The hardware performed perfectly, and now, only a few minutes from when the synchronized generators along the ship's perimeter powered up to send the *Advent* into juxtaspace, Mission Control really was redundant. Jacqueline was right.

The room smelled of old coffee and sweat. Many of the controllers had been at their stations for twenty hours or more. As time grew short, they split their attention between their stations and the ubiquitous news displays. A scrolling text readout under the graphics listed unbelievable numbers: estimated dead, radiation readings, cities lost.

Marisa toggled her display. She wanted readouts on the juxtaengines. Mankind *was* going to the stars at last, even if there might be no Earth to return to if they could duplicate the ship to bring them back. "It's easy, having no family," she said under her breath, which wasn't quite true. Her grown son lived in Oceanside, a long commute from southern L.A., but they only talked on the phone at Christmas now. She had to check his photograph to remind himself of what he looked like. A station over, an engineer had his head down on his keyboard, and he sobbed.

Dr. Smalley was the only controller who appeared occupied. He flicked through screen after screen of medical data. The heartbeats of the entire crew drew tiny lines across his display. He looked at Marisa. "We won't know what happens when the shift happens. What will their bodies go through? What a pity they can't signal through the jump."

"If they make the jump at all," moaned Jacqueline.

"We'll know in three minutes," said Marisa. "Regardless of what happens here, we will have saved ourselves."

Dimly, through mission control's thick walls, sirens wailed up and down. The building vibrated, sending a coffee cup off a table's edge and to the floor.

"Maybe if we'd spent the money here, where it could do some good, we'd never come to this," said Jacqueline. "We bankrupted the planet for this mission."

Dr. Smalley studied the heartbeats from the ship. "They're excited. Everyone's pulse is high. Look, I can see everything that's happening in their bodies." He waved a hand at his display. "Their individual transmitters give me more information than if I had them hooked up in a hospital. I wish I was with them."

"Everyone wishes they were with them," said Marisa.

Jacqueline said, "Don't you have a word for it, Doctor, when the patient's condition is fatal, so you decide to try something unproven to save her? That's what we're doing here, aren't we? Humanity is dying, so we try this theoretical treatment."

The countdown clock on the wall showed less than two minutes. The floor shook again, much sharper this time.

"Please, a few more seconds," Marisa said to no one.

So much history happening around her: the first colonial expedition to another star system, and the long feared global nuclear conflict. The victor had to be the explorers. The names passed through her head: Goddard, Von Braun, Armstrong and the rest of them. It was a way to shut out the death dealers knocking at the door.

"It's an experiment," said Jacqueline, edging on hysteria. "We've never sent a ship even a tenth this big. We've never tied multiple juxtaengines together. What if their fields interact? Instead of sending the ship in one piece, it could tear it apart."

"It's too expensive to try out," Marisa snapped. "It's all or nothing."

"You've been listening to the defeatists," said Dr. Smalley. "The theory is perfect. The math is perfect. In an instant, they will be hundreds of light years from our problems."

Marisa clutched the edge of her monitor. The countdown timer clicked to under a minute. I'm a representative of mankind, she thought. For everyone who has ever wanted to go to the stars, I stand for them. She wished she could see the night sky.

Dr. Smalley hunched toward his computer as if he were trying to climb right through. Jacqueline stared at the television screens with their yellow-specked maps. The images wavered, then turned to gray fuzz. She pressed her knuckles to her mouth.

"Ten seconds," said Marisa. "All systems in the green."

The countdown ticker marched down. Marisa remembered a childhood filled with stories of space, the movies and books set in the universe's grand theater, not the tiny stage lit by a single sun. If only she could have gone too, she could have missed the messy ending mankind had made for itself. The first bombs exploded yesterday morning. Over breakfast, she'd thought it was a hoax. No way people could be so stupid. But the reports continued in, and it wasn't a joke, not in the least.

Eyes toward their readouts, the control engineers monitored *Advent's* last signals. Already at near solar-escape velocity, the *Advent* would leap out of the solar system, riding the unlikely physics of juxtaspace.

"Three . . . two . . . one," someone said. Marisa's screen flipped to the NO SIGNAL message. Analysis indicated the ship had gone. A ragged and weak cheer came from the few engineers in the room.

"She's made the jump," Marisa said. She envisioned the *Advent* obscured in a burst of light as the strange energies from the juxtaengines parted space, allowing the giant ship its trans-light speed journey. For a moment, the space program existed all on its own, separate from the news broadcasts and progress reports, far from the "Areas of lost communication."

"No," said Dr. Smalley. "There should be no telemetry now. They're gone." He touched his fingers to his monitor. Marisa moved to where she could see what he saw. The heart beats on his screen still registered. Brain waves still recorded their spiky paths. He flicked from one screenful of medical transmissions to the next.

"How is that possible?" said Marisa. Jacqueline stood beside her. Other engineers left their stations to crowd behind Smalley's chair.

"They're getting weaker," said Jacqueline.

"No, no, no," said Smalley. His fingers tapped a quick command on his keyboard. A similar display with names and readouts appeared on the screen, but this one showed no activity in the medical area.

"What is that?" asked Marisa. How could there be transmissions? The *Advent* was beyond communication now. They'd never know if she reached her destination. Light speed and relativity created a barrier as imposing as death itself.

"It's their respiration," said Smalley, his voice computer-calm. "They're not breathing." He switched back to the heartbeats. Many of the readouts now showed nothing. A few blinked their pulses slowly, and then those stopped too. Smalley tapped through screen after screen. Every pulse was now zero. Every brain scan showed a flat line.

Marisa's hands rested on the back of Smalley's chair. She could feel him shaking through her fingers. "Check their body temperatures," she said.

He raised his head as if to look back at her. Then he shrugged in understanding. The new display showed core temperatures. As they watched, the numbers clicked down.

"Is it an anomaly?" asked someone. "Are we getting their signals from juxtaspace?"

"The ship blew up," said Jacquline.

Marisa said, "No. We would have received telemetry for that." She held Smalley's chair now so she wouldn't collapse. "It's their real signals from our space." Her face felt cold and her feet numb. A part of her knew she was within an instant of collapsing. "The *Advent* left, but it didn't take them."

Jacqueline said, "Worst case scenario. It was a possibility that the multiple engines wouldn't work the same way as single ones. We dumped everyone into space." Her voice cracked.

"They're dead," said Marisa as the room slowly swooped to her right. I'm falling, she thought. What would a telescope see if it could see that far? After the flash of light? Would it see 14,400 bodies tumbling? What other parts of the ship didn't go?

Her head hit the floor, but it didn't hurt. Nothing hurt, and she was curiously aware of meaningless details: how the tiled floor beneath her felt gritty, how ridiculous the engineers looked staring down at her. Then, oddly, how their faces began to darken. What a curious phenomena, she thought. The fraction of a second before she knew no more, she realized that their faces hadn't darkened. It was the skylights above them. They'd gone brilliantly bright. Surface of the sun bright.

We're not going to the stars, she thought, as the heat of a thousand stars blasted through the ceiling. She would have cried if she had had the time.

Who has died like this? So sudden, the walls shimmered. Then they were gone. The air burst away, much of the ships innards remained, but twisted and ruptured. Torn into parts. The stars swirl around us, and all the eyes see. We all see what we all see, but there isn't a "we" to talk about, just a group consciousness. The 14,400 brains frozen in moments, the neurons firing micro-charges across the supercool gaps. And we continue outward, held together loosely by our tiny gravities, sometimes touching, drifting apart, but never too far. Pluto passed in hardly a thought, and then we were beyond, into the Oort cloud, but who would know it? The sun glimmered brightly behind us, a brighter spot among the other spots, but mostly it was black and oh so cold. Time progressed even if we couldn't measure it. Was it days already, or years, or centuries? Out we traveled. Out and out.

Jonathan shifted the backpack's weight on his shoulders as he tramped down the slope toward Encinitas, then rubbed his hands together against the cold. He'd left his cart filled with trade goods in Leucadia, and it felt good not to be pulling its weight behind him. The sun had set in garish red an hour earlier, and all that guided his footsteps was the well worn path and the waves' steady pounding on the shore to his right. No moon yet, although its diffuse light wouldn't help much anyway. When he'd crested the last hill, though, he'd seen the tiny lights of Encinitas' windows and knew he was close.

He whistled a tune to himself, keeping rhythm with his steps. The harvest was in, and it looked like it would be a good one this year for Encinitas. They'd wired two more greenhouses with grow lights in the spring, and managed to scare up enough seed for a full planting. For the first time they might even have an excess. If he could broker a deal with the folks in Oceanside, who lost part of their crop with leaf blight, it could be a profitable winter.

A snatch of music came through the ocean sound. Jonathan smiled. Ray Hansen's daughter, Felitia, would be there. Last year she'd danced with him twice, and he imagined her hand lingered as they passed from partner to partner, but she was too young to court then. Not this year, though. It was going to be a good night. Even the icy cold ocean breeze smelled clean. Not so dead. Not like when he was a boy and everyone called it the "stinking sea."

He slowed down. The gate across the path should be coming soon. It stopped the flock of goats from wandering off during the summer. In the winter, of course, they were kept in the barns so they wouldn't freeze. Yes, Encinitas was a rich community to be able to grow enough to feed livestock. Felitia would be a good match for him. She was strong and lively, and her father would certainly welcome him warmly if he was a part of the family. Goat's milk with every meal! He licked his lips, thinking of the cheese that was a part of the harvest celebration.

But what if she didn't want him?

He slowed even more. What wasn't to want about him? He was twenty, and a businessman, but it wasn't like he was around all the time to charm her, and a year was a long time. Maybe she didn't want to travel from village to village, carrying trade goods. And she was a *bookish* girl. People talked about her, Jonathan knew. That was part of her charm. He buried his hands under his armpits. Did it seem unusually cold suddenly, or was it fear that made him shiver?

The gate rattled in the breeze, which saved him bumping into it. Fingers stiff, he unlatched it. Clearly now, the music lilted from over the hill. He hurried, full of hope and dread.

"Jonathan, you are welcome," said Ray Hansen at the door. Hansen looked older than the last time Jonathan had seen him, but he'd always seemed old. He might be forty, which was really getting up in years, Jonathan thought. Beyond, the long tables filled with seedling plants had been pushed to the wall. Everyone in the village seemed to be there. The Yamishitas and Coogans. The Taylors and Van Guys. The Washingtons and Laffertys. Over a hundred people filled the room. Jonathan smiled. "I've come to see your daughter, sir."

The older man smiled wanly. "You'll need to talk to her about that."

Jonathan wondered if Hansen was sick. He seemed much thinner than Jonathan remembered him. Probably the blood disease, he thought. Lots of folks got the blood disease.

The band struck up a reel, and couples formed into squares for the next dance. The caller took his place on the stage. Felitia, in a plain, cotton dress sat on the edge of a table at the far end of the long room, swinging her feet slowly beneath her. Jonathan edged along the dance floor. The music drove the dancers to faster and faster twirls, hands changing hands, heads tossing. He apologized when a woman bumped him, but she was gone so fast he doubted she heard.

Felitia watched him as he made the last few yards, her blues eyes steady, her blonde hair tied primly back. Was she glad to see him? Surely she knew why he was there. He had left her notes every time he passed through Encinitas, and her replies that he retrieved the next trip were chatty enough, but noncommital. She could have been writing her brother for all the passion he found in them.

He sat next to her without saying anything. Now that she was beside him, the speech he'd practiced sounded phony and ridiculous. The villagers rested when the music ended, talking quietly to themselves. On the makeshift stage, the band tuned their instruments. The two guitarists compared notes, while the trumpet player discreetly blew the spit out of his horn.

"This is nice," said Jonathan. He winced. Even that sounded stupid.

"Yes." Her hands were together in her lap. "How were the roads?"

The band started another tune, and soon the crowd wove through the familiar patterns.

"Fine, I guess." Jonathan decided that the best move would be to leave the room. It was one thing to think grand thoughts while pulling his cart down the seashore roads, but it was quite another to confront her in the flesh. "I did good business in Oceanside."

"It must be interesting, seeing all those places."

Jonathan swelled. "Oh, yes. I've been even further north than that, you know. I even went to San Clemente once. A few of the buildings still stand. I wanted to press on to Los Angeles, but you know how cautious the old folks are."

She looked sideways at him.

He cleared his throat. "Just along the beach. Nothing inland, of course. It's ice from the Santa Ana mountains almost to the sea, but they say the snow field is retreating. It's getting warmer, they say."

Felitia sighed. "The dust went up; the dust will go down. I don't know if I believe it. They can call it 'nuclear winter,' but it's more like nuclear eternity to me." She watched the dancers, her face lost and vulnerable. "Encinitas seems so small."

Jonathan gripped the table's edge. What he wanted to ask was on the tip of his tongue. Everything else sounded trivial, but the timing wasn't right. He couldn't just blurt it out. A thought came to him, and with relief he said, "I brought you a present." He slung his backpack off his shoulders and set it between them. Felitia peered inside when he opened it.

"Books!" She clapped her hands.

He dug through the volumes. "There's one I thought you might like especially." At the bottom he found it. "We need to go outside so I can give it to you." He tried to swallow but couldn't. Nothing he'd ever done before felt so bold.

She held his hand as they walked away from the dancers. Her fingers nestled softly in his.

Felitia put on a coat and picked up a storm lamp before they went out the back door. The flame flickered before settling into a steady glow.

"What is it?"

Wind pushed against his face, tasting of salt. It could snow tonight, he thought.

First snow of the season. He pulled the book out of his jacket and handed it to her. "Here's as far as you can get from Encinitas."

She opened the book, a paperback edition of Peterson's field guide to the stars and planets. By the storm lamp he could see a color print of the Cone Nebula, a red, clouded background with white blobs poking through.

"Oh, Jonathan. It's beautiful."

Their foreheads touched as they bent over the book.

She turned her face toward his. "My father told me about stars. He said he saw them when he was a boy, before the bad times."

Jonathan glanced up. "My dad said we were going to the stars. His mom helped launch the *Advent*." The uniform black of the night sky greeted him, as indistinguishable as a cave interior. "He said the sky used to be blue, and the sun was as sharp-edged as a gold coin."

He looked down. Felitia's face was only an inch from his own. Without thinking about it, he leaned just enough to kiss her. She didn't move away, and his question was answered before he asked it.

Later, holding her against him, he said, "They say when the dust clears, we'll see the stars again."

And on a calm night, four years later, after Ray Jr. had gone to sleep, Jonathan and Felitia stood outside their house in Oceanside.

"Can you see?" said Felitia. "Do you think that's what I think it is?" She pointed to a spot in the sky.

One hand on her shoulder, Jonathan pulled her tight. "I think it is."

A bright spot glimmered for a second. Another joined it.

They stayed outside until they both grew so cold they could hardly stand it.

We feel space. Neutrinos pass through like sparklers in the group body. Gravity heats our skin. We hear space, not through the frozen cells of our useless ears, but through the sensitive membrane of our group awareness. The stars chime like tiny bells. It has a taste, the vacuum does, dusty and metallic, and it doesn't grow old. We go farther and farther and slower and slower, until we stop, not in equilibrium; the sun won. Gradually, we start back. Apogee past. The Oort cloud. The birthplace of comets. How many years have we gone away?

"Relying on the old knowledge is a mistake." Professor Matsui faced the crowd of academics in the old New Berkeley lecture hall. The new New Berkeley hall wouldn't be done until next year. After a hundred and twenty years of use, this one would be torn down. He would miss the old place. "We overemphasize recreating the world we know from the records, but we aren't doing our own work. Where is our originality? Where is our cultural stamp on our scientific progress?" He was glad for the new public address system. His voice wasn't nearly as strong as it had been when he was young.

Matsui watched Dr. Chesnutt, the Reclaimed Technologies chair. He appeared bored, his notebook unopened on his study desk. Languidly he raised his hand. "Point," he said. "Would you have us throw away our ancestor's best work? When we allocate money, should we assign *more* on your 'original research' that may yield nothing, or should we spend wisely, investigating what we *know* will work because it worked before? When we equal the achievements of the past, then it will make sense to invest in your programs. Until then, you divert valuable time and valuable funds."

Pausing for a moment to scan the crowd, Matsui took a deep breath. Were the others with him or against him? The literature department was evenly split between the archivists and the creative writers. Biology, Sociology and Agriscience would lean toward him, as would Astronomy, but the engineers, mathematicians and physicists would cast their vote solidly with Chesnutt, and, as the former head of the School of Medicine, he had probably coerced everyone in the department to vote his way. "Obviously we must continue the good work of learning from the past, but if we throw all our effort, and funds, into that, we risk creating the same mistakes that destroyed their world. You pursue their wisdom without worrying about their folly. Will you follow them down the road that led to nuclear annihilation?"

Chesnutt chuckled. "You can raise the 'nuclear annihilation' demon all you like. As you know, there is no agreement among historians about what caused the great die-off. The nuclear exchange may have been the last symptom of a much deeper problem. We will only avoid their fate if we learn from their triumphs."

Heads nodded in the audience.

Matsui finished his speech, but he could tell Chesnutt had called in all his favors. It didn't matter what value his arguments had, the Research Chair would not gain funding this year. He'd be lucky to hold his committee assignments.

After the meeting, Matsui left the lecture hall in a hurry. He didn't want to deal with the false condolences. The bloodsuckers, he thought. They'll be looking for strategies to make my loss an advantage for their departments in some way or another.

A breeze off the bay cut through his thin coat, sending a translucent veil of clouds across the night sky, and tossing the lights dangling from their poles.

"Wait, Professor," called a voice.

He grimaced, then slowed his pace. Puffing, Leif Henderson, an assistant lecturer in Astronomy, joined him.

"Good speech, sir."

"I'm afraid it was wasted."

"I don't think so. We've got a couple Chesnutt supporters in the department, but I can tell you the grad students aren't interested in making their names in the field by rediscovering all of Jupiter's moons. The younger ones want to do something new."

Matsui pushed his hands deep into his pockets. Maybe he was getting too old for the back-stabbing politics of the University. "Chesnutt has a point. Old Time learning casts a huge shadow. We may never be able to get out from under it, and it doesn't help that whenever original research makes a discovery, the intellectual archeologists dig up some reference to show it's been done before. There's no impetus for innovation."

Henderson matched Matsui's steps. "But the Old Timers didn't know everything. They didn't conquer death. They didn't master themselves." The young man looked into the night sky. "They didn't reach the stars. We should have been receiving the *Advent's* signals for the last fifty years if they made it, or even more likely, they would have come back. They have had four hundred years to recreate their engines."

"I like to think they arrived, and we just haven't built sensitive enough receivers, or maybe three hundred and fifty light years is too far for the signal. What they have to wonder is why *we* haven't contacted them, why we didn't *follow* them. The world has gone silent."

The sidewalk split in two in front of them. Astronomy and the physical science buildings were to the right. Administration was to the left. They paused at the junction.

Matsui looked down the familiar path. He'd walked that sidewalk his entire adult life, first as a student, then a graduate assistant, and finally as a professor. From his first day in the classroom he had valued creative thought. That is what the academy is about, he had argued. The Old Timers accomplished noble feats, but they are gone. We should make our own mistakes.

"The world is changing, Henderson. The population will be over one billion in a decade. We survived an extinction event four hundred years ago, so we missed being the last epoch's dinosaurs. We fought our way out of the second dark ages. As a species, we must be fated for greatness, but we're so damned stupid about achieving it." He kicked at the ground bitterly.

Henderson stood quietly for a minute. In the distance, the surf pounded against the rocks. "It's a pendulum, Professor. This year, Chesnutt won. He won't always. If we're going to push knowledge forward, we will escape our past. We'll have to."

Matsui said, "Not in my lifetime, son. It's so frustrating, as a character, humanity has desires. It must. But what they are and how it will go about getting them will remain a mystery to me. There's a big picture that I can't see. Oh, if only there was a longer perspective, it would all make sense."

Henderson didn't reply.

"I'm sorry," said Matsui. "I'm an old man who babbles a bit when it gets late at night. I wax philosophic. It used to take a couple pints of beer, but now cool night air and a bad budget meeting will do it. You'll have to forgive me."

Henderson shuffled his feet. "There's a move in the department to name a comet after you."

Suddenly, Matsui's eyes filled with tears. He was glad the night hid them. "That would be nice, Henderson."

Matsui left Henderson behind, but when Matsui reached the faculty housing, he didn't stop. He kept going until he reached the bluff that overlooked the sea. Condensation dampened the rail protecting the edge of the low bluff, and it felt cold beneath his hands. Moonlight painted the surf's spray a glowing white. He thought about moonlight on water, about starlight on water. Each wave pounding against the cliff shook the rail, and for a moment, he felt connected to it all, to the larger story that was mankind on the planet and the planet in the galaxy. It seemed as if he was feeling the universal pulse.

Much later, he returned to his cottage and his books. He was right. Chesnutt replaced him on the committees, but Matsui wasn't unhappy. He remembered his hands on the rail, the moon like a distant searchlight, and the grander story that he was a part of.

Thoughts come slower, it seems, or events have sped ahead, and we want to sleep. Maybe we have spread out, our individual pieces, a long stream of bodies and ship parts, and odds and ends: books, blankets, tools, chairs, freeze dried foods, scraps of paper, the vast collection of miscellany that humanity thought to bring to a distant star. Or maybe the approaching sun has warmed us. The super-cool state that kept consciousness and connection possible is breaking down. But we know we are accelerating, diving deep into the system that gave us birth. It's been a long trip, out and back, the 14,400. Our individual dreams forgotten, but the group one survived: to travel, to find our way out of the cave, to check over the next hill top. We feel an emotion as the last thoughts fail: something akin to happiness. We're going home.

Captain Fremaria sat on a blanket with her husband on the hill overlooking the launch facility. The lights illuminating the ship had been turned off, but she knew crews were working within the enclosed scaffolding, fueling the engines, running through the last check lists, making sure it would be ready for the dawn liftoff.

"It's just like another test flight, darling," she said to her husband. "I've flown much less reliable crafts." Her heart took a sudden leap as she thought about the mission. She could hear the rockets igniting in her head. Could she do it? The idea of climbing atop the thousands of pounds of propellant had never sounded so foolhardy as it did now. When she was training, the flight remained a theory, an abstraction, but with the ship so close and the schedule coming to its close, she felt like a condemned woman.

"Don't remind me," he said. "I just want to know that you'll be safe. I need a sign."

She sighed. "I wouldn't mind one myself." She did not have to climb aboard the ship. No one could force her to. In fact, she wouldn't really be committed until ignition.

"It's too much history." He moved closer to her so his hand rested on hers. "Mankind returns to space after all these centuries. Everyone wants to know about the impact of this moment. Will we go to the moon next? Will we go to Mars? What will we find there of the old colonies?" He snorted derisively. "I just want to know that you will come back."

Fremaria nodded her head, but he wasn't looking at her. In three hours she would report to launch central, where they would begin preparing her for insertion into the craft that would carry her into orbit. The mission called for ten circuits around the Earth, then a powerless drop back into the atmosphere, where she would fly the stubby-winged ship to a touchdown at Matsui Airbase.

"I won't be that far away. If you could take the train straight up, you'd be there in a couple hours."

Her husband chuckled, but it sounded forced.

For the first time in weeks, the wind was calm. Fremaria had watched the weather reports anxiously, but it looked like the launch would take place in perfect conditions. Not a cloud marred the flawless night sky. The horizon line cut a ragged edge out of the inverted bowl of pristine stars.

"I've never seen it so clear," said her husband.

A green light streaked across the sky.

"Make a wish," said Fremaria.

"You know what it is." He squeezed her hand.

Another meteor flamed above them, brighter than the first.

"That's rare," said Fremaria. "So close together."

Before he could reply, a third and fourth appeared, traveling parallel courses.

"It's beautiful," he said.

She arched her back to see the sky better. "There isn't supposed to be a meteor shower now. The Leonids aren't for another month."

A spectacular meteor crossed half the sky before disappearing.

Fremaria leaned into her husband's shoulder for support. For almost two hours the display continued, often times with multiple meteors visible at once, some so bright that they cast shadows. Then, the intensity dropped until the sky was quiet again.

"Have you ever seen anything like that?" Her husband asked. "Have you even ever *heard* of anything like that?"

"No." She thought about the mysteries of space. "It's a sign."

He laughed. "I guess it might be."

Fremaria glanced at her watch. "It's time for me to go." She brushed her pants after she stood. Her husband held her hand again, but her thoughts now were in the ship. She ran through the takeoff procedure. No mission went without a hitch. They would be depending on her to make corrections, to shake down the craft. A good flight: that was all she wanted, and then a next one and a next one. They began the walk down to the launch facility.

She thought about the centuries. The *Advent* was supposed to go to the stars. Had it made it? No one knew, but they were going again. Her flight would open the door again.

"Are you scared?" her husband asked.

Fremaria paused on the trail. The ship waited for her. She could see that they had cranked part of the scaffolding away from it. Soon it would stand alone, unencumbered. She would sit in the pilot's chair listening to the countdown, prepared to take over from the automated controls if needed. What an experience the rocket's thrust would be! What a joy to feel the weightlessness that awaited her! To break free. To take the first step to the long voyage out.

"I'm ready to go."

A single meteor flickered into existence above them. It glowed brilliantly in its last moment. They watched its path until it vanished.

"They don't last too long, do they?" he said.

Fremaria glanced at the ship, then back at the sky. "No, but they travel a long way first. There's something to be said about making the long trip."

THE ICE CREAM MAN

KEEGAN CHOSE A SONG FROM THE TRUCK'S JUKEBOX AFTER HE CROSSED 6th Street going south on University Blvd.: "You are My Sunshine." It was his Thursday route. The music boomed through the loudspeakers, echoing from the late 19th Century houses. Within a minute, doors opened, people wandered down their sidewalks and waited for him on the street. He muted the song as the truck slowed to a stop. Even through his dark sunglasses, the sun was too bright. Every reflective surface bounced the light in painful intensity. He squinted against the intrusions.

An old lady in a broad-rimmed hat that shadowed her face and a lacy blouse that covered her neck to her chin looked up at him. "Do you have strawberry today?"

He handed her a cone with a single scoop.

The tip of her tongue touched the treat. She closed her eyes and sighed. "Best strawberry ice cream in the world."

He snapped his fingers. "Overripe strawberries are the secret. They're sweeter. You're lucky they're in season."

The lady put a pint of bourbon on the counter. "Will this do?"

Keegan held it to the sunlight, where it glowed like golden honey. "That's a couple weeks worth, darling."

She blushed. "I need a box of .22 longs if you have them. Something's been in my back yard the last few nights."

Keegan searched below the counter. "Short rounds, short rounds, short rounds." He moved the small boxes aside. "Ah, here we go, .22 longs. That would make us even."

Behind her frowned a middle-aged man with a tiny black mustache like a charcoaled thumbprint below his nose. "Where do you get the ammo, hairlip?"

Keegan resisted the urge to cover his mouth. He smiled instead. "It's all in trade. I have something someone wants. Somebody else has something I want. What do you want?"

"Nobody trades bullets. They horde them." He looked suspiciously at the truck. "And how do I know your ice cream is any good?"

Another man a couple folks back in the line said, "Are you going to order, Rich, or are you going to be a pain in the ass? Doesn't matter if it's good or not. You can't get ice cream anywhere else."

The man scowled. "Vanilla."

Keegan turned his back to get another cone from behind him. He rubbed his nostril with his thumb, and as he scooped the ice cream he pressed the thumb firmly into the frozen ball before plopping it into place. "There you go, mister," he said. "Since it's your first time, it's on the house."

The next customer wanted a double scoop of chocolate, which Keegan let him have for a nearly full bottle of powdered cinnamon.

"Can't get enough good spices," said Keegan to the man who'd defended him. "How are you doing, Laird?"

Laird leaned on the counter, his tanned arm a sharp contrast to the polished aluminum, liver spots sprinkled across the top of his hand like the map of an island chain. "Pretty good, Keegan. You put a booger in his ice cream, didn't you?"

Keegan grinned. "I didn't charge him."

"Maple walnut for me, if you have it."

The ice cream rolled smoothly into the scoop. Keegan liked the cold air caressing his wrists. It felt better than the waves of heat rising from the asphalt outside the truck, and it was only 11:00. Good for business. Hard to work in.

Laird licked a drip off the cone before it reached his hand. "Can't really blame the guy for his bad temper. He moved in a month ago. No territory. No prospects. Some muta-bastard broke into his house and tore up most of his stores, so he's feeling pinched."

"Is he thinking of scavenging north of Colfax Avenue?" Keegan closed the freezer lid. No need to let the product melt, and the truck used less fuel if the refrigerator unit wasn't working the whole time. "I wouldn't recommend going alone."

"You don't seem to have trouble."

Keegan swept a damp rag the length of the counter, keeping his eyes down. "I know the area."

"Speaking of that, did you find the item I asked for?"

"It's rare. Really rare." The rag swung loosely in Keegan's hand as he leaned against the cabinets, squinting through his sunglasses at the sunlight outside the truck's dark interior. The last two people in line, a middle-aged couple he'd served several times before, wiped their foreheads in unison. Like most folks, they didn't look at his face. He wanted to cover his mouth again.

Laird sighed. "All right. I can double the sugar for next month." He leaned forward to whisper, "I found a cache you wouldn't believe. Geezer who'd filled a double-car garage with goodies before kicking off."

"Great." Keegan pulled two boxes of 12-gauge shotgun shells from under the counter. He rattled them before putting them down. "Got a project?"

Laird pocketed the boxes. "Nope. The boys on the Colfax fence say they're having breakthroughs every night. I want more punch for my dollar. Whatever tore into Rich's house went through the bars on his window. Something new south of the fence, evidently. One of these days I'm afraid I'm going to stumble on a mutoid that's all teeth, scales, tentacles and bad attitude, and I don't want to face it with a popgun."

"You could move to the country like everyone else."

Laird turned to look down the street. Many of the houses were boarded up, their windows staring into the street like blind eyes. On other houses, bars covered the windows and doors. Barbed wire separated them from their neighbors. "What, and leave all this? There's still a lot of scavenging to do before I start scratching dirt for a living. Besides, farms have mutoid problems too." He licked the last of the ice cream out of the cone. "Could you sweeten this up?"

Keegan dropped another scoop on the cone.

Laird said, "The ammo question was dumb. You know the one I want answered?"

Keegan looked at him through his sunglasses.

"Where do you get the cream? The last true cow died twenty years ago."

"I have good freezers."

Laird laughed. "See you next Thursday." He walked away, waving as he went.

The last couple both wanted raspberry, but Keegan didn't have any. They settled for a scoop each of chocolate macadamia nut. He placed the set of four sundae glasses they'd brought on the floor. The woman looked suspiciously at her cone.

"Just ice cream in that one, ma'am," he said.

When he drove away, he flicked the music back on, "Little Brown Jug." A couple blocks later, a new crowd gathered. By 1:00 he was sold out.

Driving the ice cream truck had been Keegan's first job out of high school. In the dispatch office, Old Josh Granger had handed him the route and an inventory sheet along with the keys to the truck. "Drive slow in the neighborhoods," he said. "Nothing sadder than a little kid who can't catch the ice cream truck."

Keegan nodded.

"Not that there's kids anymore." Granger sat heavily on a stool, cupping his hands over his knees. "God, I remember when the five-year-olds would chase me down. Scads of them. Couldn't even get their change up to the counter. Little hands holding money. Do you remember kids?" Granger looked out the window onto the lot where the trucks were parked. Canvas covered six of them. "You're what, eighteen? No, you wouldn't. You're one of the last batch."

Keegan ground the toe of his sneaker into the cement. "They'll find out what's causing it. I heard the news the other night. They're making headway."

Granger sighed. "Do you have a girl?"

Keegan blushed. "They don't seem to take to me." He scratched his nose, covering his mouth.

"Humph! Sorry, son. Maybe it's for the better. Save you the heartache. No ultrasound horror show. No little bundled buried in the back yard for you . . ." He trailed off. A muscle in his arm twitched, but he didn't seem to notice. "Nobody gives you guff about it, do they?"

"No, sir. They're all real nice." Keegan thought about the whispers in the school hallway. Once he'd heard an entire conversation. "Do you think he's a mutation?" someone had said. "Nah," said someone else. "Cleft palate. It's just a birth defect."

Granger said, "Don't they have operations to fix that?"

"I had it. You should have seen it before."

For the rest of the summer, Keegan drove the truck. Kids his own age and older waited for him. In the shadows, they hardly noticed his face. "I want a bomb pop," one would say. "Ice cream sandwich," said another. For a summer he drove the town, music filling his ears: "Home on the Range" and "London Bridge" and "The Yellow Rose of Texas," calling, calling, and the folks came out, remembering in the music what it must have been like to be five. He imagined them as children, running after him, their eyes on fire, laughter in their throats. It was the best summer of his life. Then, in August, the company went under, and he had to turn in his keys.

When he left his last inventory in the dispatch office, Old Man Granger sat unmoving on his stool, staring off into an unfocused middle distance.

"Here's my paperwork, sir. I filled everything out."

Granger didn't speak.

"I rinsed out the freezer wells too. The truck's clean." Keegan resisted an urge to pass his hand in front of the old man's eyes. "Well, I got to go."

When Keegan turned back to close the door, Granger finally spoke. "Don't ever drive too fast." He could have been talking to himself. "You don't want to leave the kids behind."

It was thirty years before Keegan would drive an ice cream truck again.

The University Boulevard and Colfax Avenue enclave ended south of Cherry Creek, about fifteen blocks from Colfax. Keegan drove through the empty neighborhoods, his music turned off, the ice cream gone, and the boxes of traded goods packed securely behind him. He rested his wrists loosely over the top of the wheel, avoiding road debris with long, sweeping curves. Here the remains of homes sat back from the sidewalk on top of short, weeded slopes. The frame houses that weren't burned to the ground sagged forlornly, holes gaping in their roofs, an occasional glass shard still clinging to a window, catching the sun. The brick homes fared better, though their roofs swooped to black holes too. Nothing worth scavenging in them now, unless there were secrets buried in their basements. Too close to University. Inside, all the drawers would be pulled out, the sheet rock rotted, wallpaper hanging in ragged folds, their owners either dead or moved to the country to raise crops.

Keegan sighed, checked the fuel gauge, and turned north. A slinky, black form, ten feet long, flowed across the road on short, powerful legs, before vanishing behind some bushes. The sun was still high in the sky. Keegan whistled. Most of the mutoids were nocturnal. He hadn't got a good look at it, but it moved like a predator. Either it had broken through the Colfax fence, or it came out of the Platte River wastes a couple miles west. Keegan slowed the truck.

It appeared again, beside a house, placed a foot high on the worn wood, then pulled itself up. When its front paws reached the gutter, its hind feet were still on the ground. Then, without a break in rhythm, it poured onto the roof, defying gravity in its sinuous path. Before it disappeared over the peak, it looked at Keegan, small eyes buried in a broad, black skull, like a bear's. That high, poised in the sun, it no longer appeared black, but a deep, regal purple.

Back on University, two fence men pushed the barrier aside to let him through.

"Saw something big on the road back there," said Keegan.

"Like a low-riding black panther?" asked the fellow hoisting a scoped rifle.

Keegan nodded.

The man shaded his eyes to look up into the truck. "I got a shot at him yesterday, walking bold as brass in front of those shops on 6th Street. Nothing to eat in the enclave except us, so we've organized a hunting party for tomorrow. Find him and then go north for a bit. Clean out the worst of them."

"About time we went north," said the man's partner, wearing thick glasses and a cowboy hat. "The leave-them-alone and they'll-leave-us-alone policy sucks." He hefted his rifle, a military issue weapon with a curved magazine. "We need as much replacement ammo as you can get us when you come next week. If we're going to clean the area out, we'll be jacking quite a few rounds."

"Tomorrow, you're hunting?" Keegan wondered if they heard the quiver in his voice.

"Couple hours before sunrise. We've got forty rifles. Figure we can make a sweep as far north as 30th Avenue. Some hotheads on the committee wanted to burn everything in that direction, but we figure a lot of the best stuff is up there."

Keegan tapped his fingers on the steering wheel. University Blvd. stretched in front of him. The tops of trees in City Park a couple blocks ahead waved in a breeze that didn't touch them on the street. "No need to go *beyond* the fence, is there? The majority aren't dangerous."

Rifle-scope man looked at him curiously. "Us or them, buddy."

Keegan nodded. "I'll see what I can do."

The afternoon routine was the same as always. First he unloaded the truck in the converted bank building's garage, putting the consumables in the steel-doored storage room, then placing the rest on the shelves except for the glasses he took into his living quarters to add to his display, two rooms of ice cream art under the lights. His favorites were ruby glass banana split plates, casting red shadows beneath them. Then there were the tall sundae glasses, fluted sides and poutylipped tops. Fine ice cream bowls of delicate china. Scoops by the dozens, some mechanical (one with a heating element for ease in carving hard-frozen treats), another of ivory, another with knuckle protectors, another with mother-of-pearl inlay in the handle. In the next room he had the pictures: ice cream trucks from all over the world. Psychedelic ones, and plain ones, and ones that looked like motorized tricycles, and ones shaped like cones or ice cream men or hot dogs or popsicles. Today, though, he didn't pause to admire the collection. The men were coming!

But what could he do? He spent a couple hours in the ice cream room, beating eggs, adding sugar, stirring in cocoa powder and cream and vanilla. All the variations: chocolate almond, blueberry, mango sorbet, cinnamon, and a triple batch of plain vanilla. Pouring the mixture into the ice cream makers. Turning them on. His hands smelled of chocolate. The air smelled of sweet cream.

He checked the diesel generator and the diesel tanks. Finally, he made a round of the building. All doors bolted. All windows barred. The last shred of afternoon light cast lines across the bank's lobby, dust an inch thick on the counters where the tellers used to sit. His heels clicked loudly as he walked from window to window.

By the time night had fully fallen, Keegan had restocked the truck, opened the garage, and pulled onto the street. Lights off, he headed north.

He liked the city better at night. The shadows grew velvety, and reflections were soft moonlight or starlight. At 24th Street, ten blocks north of Colfax, he turned the music on. Not nearly as loud as he did during the day. In the dark the sound seemed to carry farther. "Popeye the Sailor" he played, then "Rock-a-bye Baby."

From out of the empty houses, they came, slowly at first, and then eagerly. Some shambled. Some wobbled on uneven legs. Some trotted, their stony hoofs clicking the cement. Keegan pulled over, went to the back, opened the door above the counter, his scoops tucked into his apron.

"What'll it be?" he said to the first one.

"Chocolate," the creature croaked, its horny bill clacking together.

"What have you got for me?"

The three-fingered creature put a box of .45 caliber shells on the counter.

"Where'd you find them?" said Keegan as he swept them out of sight.

"Chocolate," it said again.

Keegan shrugged, then filled a cone. "Whatever suits you."

When the creature reached for the cone, Keegan pulled it back. "Listen," he said. "Go north tonight. It won't be safe this close to Colfax."

"Chocolate!" it snapped.

"I'm not kidding. You've got to get out of the neighborhood." Keegan pictured the scene before sunrise. The men would carry torches above their heads, watching for eye-shine in the dark. Guns would explode. The mutoids wouldn't run. Most of them didn't know better. Most of them were harmless, the warped children of warped children. Some time a couple generations back, their parents might even have been human. Or maybe their ancestors were dogs or sheep or the zoo animals. Nothing bigger than a rat had bred true since Keegan had been born. There was no way to tell, and why could some of the mutoids speak? Was language passed from the ones who'd been born in human houses and then hidden? Not everyone could give up their twisted offspring so easily. Not every parent could smother a child in its sleep. "Will you go?"

Behind the creature a line had formed. An ape-like animal with an alligator's face, its loose muscles hanging from the back of hairless arms, held a small keg Keegan knew was full of cream. Behind it a three-foot tall crab with a shiny blue shell dangled from a stubby-fingered claw a basket full of eggs. Reluctantly, Keegan gave up the cone. The beast popped it into its mouth in one bite, hummed contentedly for a few seconds, then moaned as it put its hands over its forehead, eyes squeezed shut.

"I've told you that you get headaches that way," said Keegan.

The thing nodded as it staggered off.

"Don't stay home tonight," Keegan yelled.

"Cinnamon maple," said the ape, its voice a hissing lisp, when it put the keg on the counter. The heavy cream sloshed inside. Keegan didn't want to think what kind of mutoid produced it.

"The men are coming with guns," said Keegan. The ape's long fingers wrapped the bottom of the keg. He tilted his head to the side as if thinking about Keegan's news.

The ape said, "More cream tomorrow?"

"No, not more cream. You are in danger." A thin cloud slid across the surface of the moon, darkening the street. Keegan glanced up. Dozens of mutoids crept through the houses' shadows. They were stalking him, he figured. The tyranny of the sweets. They heard the music. Most of them were small, youngsters. Were they the sentient ones, waiting for a chance to go for the ice cream? And how sentient were they? North of Colfax the boundary between the self-aware and the purely animal blurred.

"I'll bring cream," said the ape.

Keegan bent down in frustration, resting his head on the counter.

The crab said, "They're simple people." It spoke with a slight English accent and a whir behind its voice as if a tiny windmill nested in its throat. By standing on the tips of its delicate claws, and with a stretch of the clawed arm, it rested the basket of eggs on the counter. Once Keegan had asked it where it got the eggs. "Really old chickens," it had said.

"You'll be hunted," said Keegan. "We've got to get everyone out of here, north of 30th."

"Some might go." The crab clicked its claws together. "The smarter ones. Not many. Are you sure the men are coming? They've never come before."

Keegan nodded.

The crab's eye stalks quivered. Was that nervousness, Keegan wondered. Or was the crab laughing?

Turning north, the crab waved a claw. "It's dangerous out of our neighborhood. There are territories to consider. Borders to be crossed. Not everyone is so friendly as they are here."

"The men won't be friendly either."

"Some of us have talked about burning them out, but we figured if we waited long enough they'd die on their own," said the crab. It sounded meditative.

Keegan nearly dropped his scoop. "What . . . what would you do to me?" He couldn't read an expression in the crab's eyes or immobile mouth. Overhead, the cloud cleared, and for a moment the moon shone strongly, driving the shyest of the young mutoids back to shadows' shelter.

"You're not one of them." It clicked its claws again. "Do you have any sherbert?"

Numbly Keegan scraped a bowl full for the crab. "Don't eat it too fast," he said out of habit.

The crab sidled away.

"You'll get them to go north?" Keegan called. "You'll warn them?"

"Those that listen."

The next mutoid plopped a box of .30-06 shells on the counter. "Vanilla," it grunted. "With sprinkles."

"You have to leave," said Keegan. He shouted to the rest of them in line, to the hidden mutoids across the street. "They're coming to kill you! You have to run."

But none of them seemed to understand. Only the crab, and he was gone. By the time Keegan scraped the last of the ice cream out of the last bin and trade goods covered the truck's floor, he was nearly weeping. It was after midnight. Within a few hours, the Colfax fence would open and the men would march through, their guns cradled, the safeties off.

Exhausted, Keegan leaned on the counter. The street was empty now, and the only movement was the subtle moon-cast edge of shadows crossing the asphalt. Somewhere in the distance a thing howled, a long yodeling uluation that ended like a baby crying.

After a long while, he pulled himself into the driver's seat, started the engine and headed home. Fifteen minutes later, the garage door lowered automatically behind him. For a moment he considered not turning off the truck. It would be easy to leave the motor running in the closed space, to sit with his eyes shut. He could turn on the music and mix the carbon-monoxide sleepiness with "When the Saints Go Marching," or "Greensleeves."

"Us or them," the man at the gate had said. "Us or them."

Keegan turned the ignition off. Mechanically he unloaded the truck, putting the cream and eggs in the refrigerator, sorting through the ammunition, putting the other odds and ends in boxes. When he finished, he looked at the clock. 2:30.

The safe thing to do would be to go to bed. He would need to move his business north. No matter how thorough the men were, they were few and the mutants were many. They wouldn't all be wiped out. He could build a new route in the downtown area, maybe, where the broken skyscrapers crawled with life.

Or maybe he could stop the men.

Keegan opened one of the storage rooms off the garage, turned on the light, scanned the walls filled with equipment: rifles, shotguns, pistols, M-16s, bandoliers, sniper scopes, night vision goggles, gas masks, trip mines, hand grenades, Kevlar jackets, bazookas and mortars. All trade goods that had come in the last year. Boxes of ammo reached to the ceiling. Some shells had spilled. Their brass casings caught the ceiling light. He couldn't walk without kicking them.

He picked up an M-16, turned the heavy and unwieldy thing over in his hands, and realized he'd never fired it. Wasn't even sure if he had clips to load it.

And what good would it do? He wasn't a soldier. He couldn't kill. "Us or them," the voice said. "Us or them." Keegan could hear it in the room quiet as a whisper.

"Who am I?" he said out loud. He smoothed his hands over his apron, sticky with the day's work. They still smelled of chocolate.

*

An hour's labor refilled the truck. All the ice cream he could fit. Boxes of sugar cones. Keegan checked the clock again. Almost 4:00. They'd be at the gate by now.

Steering by moonlight, he pulled onto the street, heading north. "Row, Row, Row Your Boat" pumped out of the loudspeakers, turned loud. The first mutoid stepped from the door of a house in front of him. Keegan nodded his head, but kept rolling. Soon, another joined him, then a third. The music switched to "Song of Joy." Keegan turned left onto 19th Street, cruising at walking speed. Doors opened. Mutoids crawled from under cars, out of manholes, from behind walls, big ones, little ones, ones that were so misshapen they were hard to look at, and still Keegan drove on, cutting back and forth through the blocks. He beat time on the steering wheel. How far could the music reach?

Old man Granger had said, "Don't ever drive too fast. You don't want to leave the kids behind." Keegan watched through the mirror. Would they keep following? By now the street was crowded. When he reached University again, he turned north. Behind the music, did he hear a gunshot? How far back were the men?

Twelve blocks to go. Fourteen or fifteen if he wanted a cushion. At this speed he could feel broken glass crunching under the wheels. Slowly he passed moonlit cars' rusted-out shells, drooping road signs. A three foot tall mutoid with a body and head like a frog supported on a pair of slender legs, trotted alongside the truck, waving a box of rifle shells.

"Keep coming," Keegan called. They rolled through the 24th Street intersection. "Song of Joy," finished. In the pause between tunes, the patter of feet sounded like rain. "It's a Small World" covered the noise. Another sharp crack from behind, then, two more over the music. Definitely gunshots.

Ahead of him, a bus that had been turned on its side years ago nearly blocked the road. He steered the truck to the left to go around, over the sidewalk. A shadow stirred on top. Keegan leaned forward to look through the window.

The black creature he'd seen the day before arched its head high, its stubby front claws clasped across its chest, like a giant otter. Slowly, the truck passed the bus, within a few feet of the creature. It cocked its head to one side, as if listening to the music, and Keegan was struck again by its graceful posture, an almost regal pose with the moon-filled clouds behind it. The mutoid parade moved to the side of the houses, as far away from the beast as they could, but they kept following.

A dim reminder of gunshots rang out again. The creature looked south, then dropped to all fours before flowing off the bus, onto the street, toward Colfax Avenue, toward the men. "Don't go," Keegan whispered, but the long, black mutoid vanished into shadows.

Keegan didn't pull over until he was past 33rd Street. By the time he'd opened the counter, the crowd had gathered around. Their bodies bumped against the truck. Over their heads, Keegan saw more coming.

He wiped the counter clean. A dog-like face peered up at him, the creature's tiny, pink hands holding a screwdriver for trade. Keegan slung the rag over his shoulder. He grabbed a scoop. "What'll it be?" he said.

When the ice cream ran out, the sun was two hours into the sky and Keegan's wrists burned. He blinked against the daylight. The last mutoids wandered off, cones in hand or paw or claw or tentacle. But he hadn't heard a gunshot for some time. He closed the counter. As he drove home, he turned on the music to the inside. "The More We Get Together."

Five days straight labor replaced most of the ice cream, but Keegan was low on ingredients. It was time to head south again. He'd hadn't unloaded the truck since his all-nighter, and it took an hour to sort the ammunition and knick-knacks. He opened an unused storage closet to stow the overflow, mostly .22 short and longs, but also an assortment of larger calibers, several boxes of shotgun shells, and four clips of what he guessed were M-16 rounds. The mutoids were *good* at scavenging, digging deep into basements and warehouses and abandoned homes.

A dozen men including Laird stood at the Colfax fence as he pulled up. They slid the barrier aside to let him in.

"What's going on?" Keegan asked.

Laird rested his hand on the door. "The boys were eager to see you." He frowned. "Seems they were pretty successful on their trip last week, and they're raring to try it again. Acquired a bit of a blood lust, I figure. Rich there is leading the posse."

Keegan stiffened as he recognized the man with the short mustache from the week before. "How successful?"

Rich joined Laird at the truck. "Not bad, hairlip. Didn't get as many of the bastards as we might have liked, but we got a trophy out of it." He gestured to a tarp on the sidewalk ten feet away. A man next to the shape pulled the tarp back, revealing a broad black head and sleek neck. A chaos of flies descended on the corpse.

"Getting ripe too," Rich added.

Keegan opened the door, stepped onto the street. The sun leaked around his sunglasses, and his eyes teared instantly. He wiped his cheeks with the side of his hand. Up close the fur really was more purple than black. Even a week dead, the creature's muscles stood out, as if with a flex of will, it could rise, throw off death's shroud and rip them apart.

Rich said, "We need to trade for more bullets, though. Our supply is low."

Keegan touched the creature's head. Its eye was gone. Just a raw socket remained. He remembered it standing on the bus. Why had it gone toward the men? What drove it south? He smiled. There had been young mutoids then, or at least small ones. Ones he'd never seen before, like children. The truck played "Love is Blue," and "Music Box Dancer," and "Fly Me to the Moon" while he handed them ice cream. All of them gave him something. He flicked the trade goods behind him, not even looking to see what he was getting. There were so many. He'd scooped and scooped and scooped.

Rich said, "I'll bet there's a lot more of them out there, maybe more big sons of bitches like this one. Took all of us to drag him back this far."

Laird touched Keegan's shoulder. "It's an impressive specimen, isn't it? The men said it didn't even try to run. Stood in the middle of the street as if daring them to go past."

"Impressive, hell," said Rich. "It's us or them."

Keegan said, "Yeah, he's something."

Rich kicked the body. "You got more ammo, ice cream man? We've hunting to do."

The ice cream man's back cracked when he stood. I'm getting old, he thought. The rest of the men faced him, none of them under fifty. The last of their kind. We're all getting old.

"So, what about it? How many bullets can you get for us?"

Keegan thought about the little ones running after the truck. Some of them could speak. Some just pointed at a picture of a flavor. They held their hands open, ready for their treats. He thought about the rooms full of trade goods at the bank, the shiny shells on the floor.

"Scavenging's been tough," said Keegan. "I don't think there's any ammo to be had."

As he left he played "Who's Afraid of the Big Bad Wolf," and within a block the people came out for their ice cream.

ECHOING

THE SEMI'S ENGINE ROARED STEADILY WHILE THE HEATER POURED WARMTH on Cliff's ankles. His headlights cut into the snowstorm, flakes coming hard. He rubbed his eyes and stifled a yawn. There hadn't been another truck or car for the last hour on the long stretch of I-25 between Trinidad and Albuquerque, but he wasn't surprised. Christmas Eve in a snowstorm, who would be moving then?

The road unfolded. No tracks. Every twenty seconds or so he passed a highway reflector on his right. He moved the truck closer to the middle, or at least what he hoped was the middle. Snow dove from the darkness, slashing straight toward him, blindingly white. His knuckles ached from gripping the steering wheel. It had started snowing when he pulled out of Denver after dinner, soft at first, and glowing in the late afternoon light. The radio had played an instrumental medley of carols. Cliff hummed along, thinking about his family waiting in Albuquerque. After he checked the shipment in at the warehouse, he would climb into his car and drive home in plenty of time to be awakened by the kids. Denver to Albuquerque: eight hours on a good night.

Cliff downshifted, but the snow swept in just as hard, erasing distance. Sometimes it didn't look like snow coming toward him; it looked more like streaks of darkness exploding from a black center, wiping out the white. He blinked and shook his head. If this were a normal storm on any other night, he could find a pullout, park the truck and sleep until dawn, but the last weather report he'd heard said highways were closing behind him. They'd stopped traffic between Denver and Colorado Springs twenty minutes after he'd traveled that route. "Looks like our first big winter storm, folks," the DJ said.

Cliff twiddled the radio dial. Nothing but static now. Most times he picked up stations the whole way.

Last year a trucker froze to death in a pullout thirty miles from Taos. No CB, just like him. No cell phone. The storm closed the road, and two days later when the plows broke through, they found him wrapped in a sleeping bag in his truck's cabin. Cliff hunched over the steering wheel. They weren't going to find him like that because he wasn't going to stop. Nothing would prevent him from getting home to his kids.

Still, the snow shot from the darkness. When he switched on his brights, it was worse. He thought about being alone, about the long distance. What if, he thought, the snow wasn't snow at all, but stars? What if I were flying through the galaxy, passing stars . . .

. . . passing stars? Watch Commander Tremaine shook his head. For a moment the flying stars in the viewvid made him think of snow, but he hadn't seen snow for the last third of his life. What he'd seen instead, between long sleeps, were representations of stars scooting through the wall-covering viewvid during the long journey from one edge of the galaxy to the other, 100,000 light years, past one hundred billion stars at 2,000 times the speed of light.

He checked the [M]-space figures again. This couldn't be right! He refigured them. The ship didn't know where it was. Through the mental interface the computer wailed, scared into incoherence. Sometime while he'd been sleeping, they'd been thrown off course. Stars zipped by. Some swelled, became perceptibly larger. How close were the stars coming? The ship was off course! Tremaine shuddered. Even in [M]-space, they could not go *through* a star. The collision would create a spectacular display, destroying not only the star, but swallowing up its neighbors. The ship was supposed to slip *between* the stars. Their course had been designed for that. The passengers slumbering in the long-sleep cots in the holds depended on that, and so did he. After the long trip was done, he would find a place in the cots himself for the return voyage home where his family waited.

He broke open the emergency console, concentrating on the scores of steps necessary to slow the ship, to bring it below light speed where it could recalibrate itself. Be calm, he thought to the computer, and its keening voice silenced for the moment. Tremaine didn't look up. He watched his hands instead. Anything so he wouldn't see the cascading stars. He could almost hear them: deep gravitational wells and surging gases compressed to unimaginable density at their cores. They hissed in his imagination as they went by. As he worked, he wondered if the star that would kill them all would be visible. Might he have a chance to see it, appearing as small as the others at first, then growing out and out in the vidview's display as the computer scrambled to keep up with the data it was representing? Would he have time to flinch?

He'd quit working. His gaze locked on the viewvid. Stars appeared from nowhere, still at first, picking up speed as they moved from the center. His eye caught on one, followed it until it vanished to his left. Picked up another, followed it too, until it missed. A beautiful representation, if it weren't so dangerous. Of course, if he really could look out a window, he wouldn't see anything. Light in [M]-space wasn't light anymore. Nothing his senses could respond to existed in [M]-space, and what he thought of as the ship's movement was only a metaphor for what was happening. His understanding of [M]-space itself was metaphoric. It changed reality and the perception of reality. Still, the computer showed him a starfield, the ship rushing forward, a thousand near misses a minute.

Tremaine breathed hard. What would it be like to see one appear and never move, only grow? He felt like a child for an instant, staring forward, mesmerized. The sense that he was someone else, someone younger, a girl, gripped him. He shook his head. What if just for once, the screen changed . . .

. . . the screen changed. Brianna flinched. For a second the pixels spreading to the edge of the screen didn't look like pixels to her anymore: not plain white specks on a flat black background (her dad's 17-inch flat screen monitor), but glowing, moving, three-dimensional diamonds, and the black wasn't screen-black; it was palpable black. She let go of the monitor, then fell back into Dad's leather office chair. For a second, she'd been someone else: a man, panicked at a console, afraid, so afraid. Afraid of what? Brianna breathed hard in the dark room. Through the closed door she could hear the Christmas party. Aunt Agnes sang something off tune. Her brother, Ray, played the piano in accompaniment. He was so much better than Agnes that he made her almost sound good.

Brianna rubbed her eyes. She played the screensaver game often. Once after smoking some of Ray's stash. Once when she'd snuck home from school to miss a sophomore English test on *Julius Caesar*. Mostly when she wanted to get away. Her therapist had asked her once what her personal motto was. "Everyone has a motto. It's what guides them in how they behave in the world. Mine is 'Make everything right.' I struggle with that," said the therapist, a perky woman who rubbed her cheek when she paused between words. Brianna wondered if the cheek ever became chapped. "So what's *your* motto, Brianna?"

Without thinking, Brianna said, "Ignore them, and they'll go away." And what she thought was, it's about isolation. It's about not connecting to anyone or anything, like Sylvia Plath who wrote a poem describing her stay in a hospital after a suicide attempt. Plath liked the sterility of the room. She despaired when friends brought her flowers because they broke up the porcelain and steel solace of white walls and shiny, tiled floors. Brianna loved that poem. "I'm an eyeball on a pillow," said Brianna to the silent screen, "just observing." Plath tried an overdose to kill herself. Brianna rested her hand on the drawer in her dad's desk where she'd put the baggie full of barbiturates. Light blue capsules with pink logos. Ten times more than the job required.

The door to the study opened behind her. Brianna pulled her arms close, hiding in the office chair. The door closed. She'd already taken a dozen pills. If they found her now, it would be too soon. The pill's acrid bite lingered in the back of her throat.

"I don't know where she is," said her father. "She's going to miss the eggnog."

Brianna sighed in relief. If it wasn't the eggnog, it would be the popcorn balls, and if it wasn't that, it would be the Christmas video. Probably *It's a Wonderful Life* again or *White Christmas*, which wasn't nearly as good as *A Muppet's Christmas Carol* that they never watched, even though she asked for it every year.

On the screen, the stars seemed different again, sweeping away from the vanishing point in the monitor's center. Brianna leaned forward. The room felt cold, her chair rigid, and the stars came too fast, too fast by half. She gasped for breath. It couldn't be the pills working already. She'd just taken them. The screen game was about going somewhere else, leaving her life, but it had never *worked* so well. These weren't pixels. They weren't even stars anymore. She cocked her head to the side. What were they? Snow? Her breath came out in a visible plume. Was a window open? That couldn't be it, or she would be freezing. For a second she could feel a winter's coat on her arms, her hands gripped a steering wheel, her foot reached forward to find a brake pedal. There was too much speed. It was dangerous. She had to slow down. Where was the brake . . .

. . . where was the brake? Cliff pressed so slowly. The wheel squirmed under his hands. It must be pure ice beneath the snow, and his headlights didn't show what waited on either side. Ditch or cliff, it didn't matter; the shoulder that would grip his tires and send him into a deadly jackknife threatened more. Gently he pumped the brake. A reflector appeared on his right, so he was on the highway—for a second he hadn't been sure—and he still could be home for Christmas morning, but he'd have to be oh so careful. The speedometer needle crept downwards: thirty miles per hour, twenty-five, twenty. He downshifted, letting the clutch creep out so as not to break the tires' traction with the road. Now the snow swirled, no longer diving toward his windshield, but twisting in the headlights. The snow wasn't that deep. No more than a few inches. If he could make his way from reflector to reflector, he could find his way home.

His watch said 3:30. Five hours until dawn. At this speed he'd make Albuquerque by . . . he checked his watch again. How long ago had he gone through Trinidad? He remembered the lights at the edge of town, blurred by the whirling storm, and Raton Pass, he was pretty sure . . . yes, Raton Pass for sure, but had he made Maxwell yet? It was only another twenty-five miles or so. Had he gone through? He shook his head. Surely he had. But what was the last exit he'd seen? So many little towns off the highway: Springer and Colmor, Levy and Wagon Mound. He knew he hadn't reached Wagon Mound yet.

Cliff leaned forward, pressing his chest against the wheel, close to the windshield. I-25 was a broad road, clearly marked. There was no way he could be lost, but he thought about the way exit lanes curved off so gradually, and they were lined with reflectors too. Could he be heading away from Albuquerque? He tried to picture the map. What if he'd taken the Springer exit without realizing it, and he was headed east now instead of south? No way to tell, and nobody would know where he'd gone. If only he'd pass a sign, a lighted building, a marker of any kind.

He thought, should I stop? At least now I'm still on the road. The engine will idle for twelve or thirteen hours. Plenty of heat. Surely someone will come along before then (but what if this isn't I-25? What if I've lost the interstate and this is state highway 56? Eighty miles of empty back road that never gets plowed).

He stretched away from the wheel. The backs of his arms hurt, and he realized his jaw was clenched. What can you do if you're lost except to press on and look for a landmark? Through the steering wheel, he could feel the road, still slicker than slick . . .

. . . Watch Commander Tremaine wiped the sweat off his forehead, slicker than slick. The ship was slowing. He imagined the eddy of [M]-space behind them, like a boat's wake, spreading evenly from their passage, washing up against the stars. The psychic disruption wouldn't matter. Life was so rare that a million systems wouldn't feel the ripple, but he'd never heard of a ship slowing as fast as he was slowing his. Tortured reality could be catching up to them now. He watched his hands. Were they blurring at the edges? He glanced up. The stars weren't coming toward him anymore; they gyrated in their paths, curving randomly. [M]-space was catching them. How could he trust anything he saw or did? Even his thoughts could become scattered, the neurons flowing unpredictably. The confusion was already there: for an instant he thought he was a young girl; for a blink he was driving down a long, snowy road. Or was it confusion? Could he be close to a world with sentient life, connecting to them through the no-space of faster-than-light travel? Causality stripped away. Trembling [M]-space turning distance into concepts no farther apart that two thoughts.

He pictured the passengers, helpless in their cots. What dreams could [M]-space's backwash cause them? Would they sense his fear? Would that be the last thing they knew, his fear quivering on disaster's edge? How could he find their way home?

Tremaine held a sob close in his throat. He didn't have to see the controls to slow the ship. He'd trained through the procedure a thousand times. He let his reflexes take over. Fear didn't matter if he kept moving. But the ship would know that he was scared. It would respond.

Now the starfield slowed, or maybe his perceptions speeded up? No, no, they had to be going slower now; he'd completed so many steps. He closed his eyes. Just feel my hands, he thought. Fingers on controls. Push this one. Slide this one over. Listen to the calibrations reset. I want to go home. Everything must be done right so I can go home. Where am I?

Through the mental interface, Tremaine felt the computer struggle. A trillion stars! It needed an orientation, a landmark, a point of view to start a search. How long would it cast about in its memory trying to find a match? Cliff could grow old and die while it sorted through the images, the old star charts.

Tremaine imagined his wife, a tall woman waiting at the edge of the woods where they'd met. At night they looked at the stars, and in the day everything was green. He could smell trees, so pungent, green on green, he could smell it, and there was music . . .

. . . playing behind the closed office door. Brianna opened her eyes. The feeling she was someone else possessed her so strongly, she nearly threw up. Ray had switched to "Angels We Have Heard on High." Strong bass line countering the melody. He held the high notes before dramatically entering the chorus. The room smelled of pine. Dad had bought a real tree this year, and no matter where she went she couldn't escape the resiny odor.

"I'm not lost," whispered Brianna. "If I open the door, I'll be home. That's all I have to do. I'm home now."

But that wasn't the lost that she felt. With her eyes closed she'd broken contact with Earth, for a second, as if she'd been cut loose and was spinning. "Where is the galactic center?" she'd thought. She clenched her fists. On her fingertips she could still feel the dials and levers and touch pads of what . . . a ship . . . a slippery road without a landmark . . . and there was something about [M]-space (she almost giggled at the sound of term), but where am I? This is *way* out of control. What would my therapist think of this?

There is an answer, she thought. Her hand crept toward the desk drawer. There's no confusion in the baggie. But her motion stopped when she touched the handle. In the room beyond, they sang, *Angels we have heard on high, sweetly singing o'er the plains, And the mountains in reply, echoing their joyous strains.* She leaned toward the monitor. The stars had stopped moving, or at least they were moving very slowly now. What did the screensaver represent? All the time she'd looked at it, she'd only thought about where she was going, never about where she'd come from. What star had she started from? Where was she? (A tiny voice said, "Yes, where are you?" and she felt again the panic of the man at the console. "I need to know where you are.")

Brianna shook off the sleepiness growing in her. The room seemed so dream-like. It was the drug spilling into her like ink in water, spreading away, darkening the center. Languidly, she touched the enter button, and the screensaver blinked off. She chose her encyclopedia program. Typed in "Milky Way." A schematic flickered into focus on her monitor, spiral arms spinning away from the thickened blob of a middle, a little arrow pointing to a place halfway out on one of arms, closer to the edge than the middle. "You are here," it said, and Brianna took a deep breath. "I am here," she said. She switched to a picture of the night sky, the Milky Way, like light leaking around the edge of a closed door . . .

. . . Where am I? thought Cliff. The truck barely moved now. His heater worked better at seventy miles an hour. At this speed he had to wipe frost off the windshield with his coat's sleeve. It would be so easy to stop, but he had another vision: his truck parked not at the side of the highway, but in the middle. What if another truck, later in the night when things had cleared a little, came barreling down the road? It wouldn't have time to swerve when the bulk of his truck loomed up through the snow. But I want to stop. He was so tired that he didn't trust what he saw in the head-lights. Fantastic shapes forming in the drifting flakes. Faces. He tried to think of his family, his wife, his son, his daughter, but they seemed so far away. They were the dream. Endless snow, a cold that bit through his coat, that numbed the backs of his legs, that was reality. He thought about hypothermia, dementia, the end of reason. There's rest, he thought, in a bag full of blue pills with pink logos.

Cliff punched his leg hard with a closed fist. The pain, for an instant, felt good. Cleared his head. What was that thought about pills? He could see them, resting in a desk drawer, Christmas piano playing in the background. I'm in trouble, he thought. She's in trouble too. She's *stopped*, parked in the middle, waiting to freeze.

He punched his leg hard, twice, twisting his fist when he did to sharpen the sting. It's just a road, and I'm a few miles from *somewhere*, if I can keep going, but within minutes the snow ceased to be snow again: it fashioned itself into hands reaching to get him, into the backs of monsters blocking the road. Vertigo gripped him, and an impression that he was falling straight down instead of driving forward surprised a scream out of him. The storm was a mouth; he saw it open, teeth at the edges, swallowing him and the truck whole, but he couldn't stop. He drove on. I saw it! He wept in fear. Hallucination or not, I saw it . . .

. . . Tremaine closed his eyes and opened them again. What had he seen? For an instant, it was there, a schematic of the galaxy, an arrow pointed on one spiral arm. The girl had thought, "You are here," and then he'd seen a photograph of the stars. If he could align what he'd seen, just an approximation, the computer might be able to do the rest. He concentrated on the memory, the gauzy middle of the galaxy, the arrow, the long strands circling away, and the computer watched what he watched. The diagram was such a rough location, but the computer hummed contentedly while it worked, because even a rough guess eliminated the near infinite number of wrong choices.

For the first time since Tremaine had realized the ship was off course, he relaxed. The stars in the viewvid weren't moving now, and he wondered which star held the girl with the diagram. In answer to his question, without breaking its rhythm, the computer brightened one dot on the display. Tremaine enhanced the image. A plain star, unremarkable to look at. On further magnification he noticed an unusual ringed planet in the system. That wasn't where she was. Third planet from the sun, almost a double planet, its moon was so large. Maybe if he concentrated, he could send her a thank you, although she'd never know for what. When he tried to see what she saw again, he only saw stars moving, and beneath the stars, a bag full of blue pills with pink logos. No galaxy. No arrow saying, "You are here." On the viewvid he studied the planet's blue face until the computer whistled happily. It had located them. Reluctantly, Tremaine clicked off the display while the computer recalibrated their course. I'm going home, he thought. They would be on their way soon, and he had duties . . .

. . . What duties? thought Cliff. Where did that thought come from? All that kept him going was habit, now. Nothing he saw could be trusted. The reflectors, when they came seemed too far or too near (or too high or the wrong color). Was this hypothermia? He imagined his brain settling into a solidifying jelly, growing colder by the minute. For a second he thought the snow was stars, and he thought he could set a course by them, but now it was just snow again, flying through his headlights.

I could pull off, let the snow pile up. It would be so easy. His hands barely held the wheel, and his eyelids slid closed on their own accord. It's dark in here. So comfortable to fade away into sleep, into dreams where a piano played "Angels We Have Heard on High" and a Christmas tree beyond a closed door smelled of pine resin and popcorn strings and people laughed at a joke he didn't hear.

The truck can recalibrate itself, he thought. But if I keep moving, it will find my way home. . .

*

. . . I'm already home, thought Brianna, aren't I? The sense of *home* formed within her, a longing for it. A vision of a forest with a woman someone loved; a Christmas morning so far away, and so wished for. *Home*, like she'd never thought of it before. She reached around her. There were the office chair arms; there was the desk, although they seemed vague, and she was so cold. She wrapped her hands around her arms, the skin stiff as marble.

How could this be? She gasped. The pills were working. She could barely move. After a long struggle, she put her feet on the floor. If she could get out of the office, maybe, and into the other room where it was warm, they could save her.

I'm alone, she thought, and I'm lost. The highway will never end. I'm in snowy hell. Her hands rested on the steering wheel. There was no place to go, only the truck cab stuck in front of clouds of dancing snow. (I'm *not* in a truck—I'm in my dad's office) The steering wheel's solidity seemed more real than the computer monitor. Frost on the window. The low rumble of the geared-down diesel engine. The accelerator and the clutch, more real than the office carpet beneath her feet. I'm going to sleep, she thought, but I have to get to my family . . .

. . . my family. Cliff forced his eyes open. If he slept, he'd never get home. He imagined opening the front door on Christmas morning. "I'm home," he'd say into the empty room, and there would be a giggle: his son behind the couch, his daughter behind the chair, waiting to surprise him. His wife smiling in the hall, just out of sight.

I've got to get home, he thought . . .

Yes, said Brianna in the darkness of her dad's office. I've got to wake up . . .

They both hunched forward. Stay focused, they thought. Keep moving . . .

Brianna staggered out of the chair. Braced herself on the desk's edge. She wept with fatigue . . .

Cliff waited for the next reflector. There it was. The speedometer hardly twitched, but he was still going forward. The road ended somewhere, as long as he didn't stop. . .

How far away was the office door? Brianna couldn't see it. She couldn't see anything now. Why not? The headlights were on. The reflectors marked the road, if she just kept them to her right. (Don't stop now, came the thought through the diesel noise—there's a light ahead).

There's a light ahead; it came from under the door, where the piano played . . .

There's a light ahead, beyond the headlights and the crashing snowflakes; it's a gas station next to the highway . . .

Brianna grabbed the doorknob. It twisted beneath her hand. The door was opening. The light poured in, and the piano played "Angels We Have Heard on High." Before she entered the room, she thought, how many times has he played that song? Maybe he's played it all night.

She stepped into the light . . .

. . . light in the darkness. The sign said WAGON MOUND GAS AND CONVENIENCE. Cliff edged the truck onto the exit ramp. People sat in the café. He could see them, drinking coffee. Beside the window, under the wreath they'd painted on the glass, waited a phone booth topped by six inches of snow.

He could call his wife.

When he stepped out of the truck, the wind picked up. For a second, the snow came straight at him, unswerving lines, glittering in the parking lot's light, like stars sweeping past a starship. He was a Watch Commander. He was a young girl hoping to escape. In the last tremor of [M]-space, he was the three of them, trying to get home.

Cliff beat his hands together against the cold.

THE MIRACLE AT RAMAH

Being a part of a recently translated manuscript
found near Ain Feshkha and the Dead Sea.

NOW THERE CAME OUT OF JERUSALEM AN ORDER FROM KING HEROD, who heard of the birth of a king for the Jews, that all the male children under the age of two be put to death in Bethlehem and the region around, thus fulfilling what was spoken by the prophet Jeremiah:

> *"A voice was heard in Ramah, wailing and loud lamentation, Rachel weeping for her children; she refused to be consoled, because they were no more."*

Herod gave this command to the chief of his legion, who gave it to his commander of the guards, who gave it to the captain of the watch, who gave it to Flavian Aurelius, the Roman sergeant of the guard.

Flavian gathered a force together, thirty much hated conscripts of mean disposition and rightfully earned cruel reputations, to march on Bethlehem and enact the command. Flavian led them on horseback while they walked, as was proper for his station, and when the soldiers reached the town, he gave them their orders:

"King Herod, our rightful ruler and representative to the great Roman Empire, of which I am a citizen and you are not, has decreed that all male children of two years and under be put to death on this day. To assure that this is done efficiently, which will reflect well on me and one day remove me from the onerous duty of leading Hebrew swine, Greek cutthroats and low lives such as yourselves, you men will block the roads out of the town and you twelve will come with me to each house to find and kill all male children. As is befitting a man of my stature and origin, I will not go into the houses, but let any man emerge from a home that has a child within without blood on his spear, and I will cut him down."

Thereupon, Flavian drew his Roman sword and shook it at his men.

Now within that command was a young murderer named Yehudi of Hebron who was taken from the prison in Jerusalem to serve in Herod's ranks. Yehudi was surprised at the order. "Why kill children?" he thought, but he quickly banished the idea and replaced it with his favorite motto, "Take care of yourself." And though he had never harmed a child, he looked at the heartless expressions on the other men's faces, and he knew that he would do what he must do.

So Flavian split his command and when the appointed moment came, they marched up the hill to the first house.

At this time, two Greeks served in Flavian's unit, Eustace and Ignatius. Eustace was a broad shouldered man with many scars who had slaughtered Hebrew trouble makers without a flinch of conscience. He entered the first house. At nearly the same time, Ignatius, a smaller man who had made a name for himself with a knife in the alleys of Nablus, entered a house across the dusty road. From both places came much shouting and wailing.

Another Hebrew in the troop, Seth of Ashquelon asked if they should help the two men in case they were overwhelmed. Flavian smiled viciously and said, "If the pigs can not hold their own, then they deserve to die, but if one is killed, then we will slay everyone in the house and their neighbors too."

This was truth, for Flavian had enacted such a policy many times before and was well known for his willingness to apply his vengeance broadly. Hence, resistance to the rule of Jeruselum was seldom encountered.

When the two men emerged, Flavian shouted, "Show me the blood on your blades."

And they did. It coated their spears. Their hands and arms dripped. Blood stained the edges of their robes.

Yehudi of Hebron looked upon the pale but resolute faces of the Greeks and read nothing there. He thought, "Killing a child must be easier than I thought, for these two have done such a thing and appear unmoved."

Eustace said, "The women will not put their children down."

And Flavian said unto him, "Then plunge your spear deeply. One Hebrew vermin less to breed is service to Rome and Herod."

Now, as they marched up the hill to the next houses, a great wailing arose from both behind and before them, for the purpose of their mission had spread quickly, and frightened faces appeared at many windows.

"Kill your Roman master!" shouted a voice. Another shouted, "Spare our children, oh sons of Israel!"

But the company was resolute. Once again, men entered the houses and the screaming was horrible to hear: screams of men, screams of women and the shrieking of children. "Show me your blades," demanded Flavian when they came out.

And as the command advanced up the street, Yehudi knew that he too would soon enter a house to kill a child. He steeled himself for the task. He remembered that he would, "Take care of yourself."

By now, many men's spears were bloodied. Yehudi wondered if the blood of children would look different from that of others, and he could see it did not.

And so it came to pass that it was Yehudi's turn to go in. He pushed open the unbolted door—for even to block the door against the King's will would earn a household death—and looked down upon a man and woman on the floor sheltering a tiny bundle, crying in fear. The woman called out in a loud voice, "Go away and spare our baby." The man said nothing, but held his wife tightly and put his body between Yehudi and the child.

"Stand," said Yehudi, "Or I will kill you as you lie." And his voice was stern, and his heart was as of stone. Outside of the house, Yehudi heard the screams of others. Such weeping he'd never experienced. In every house, a child; in every house he imagined a bundle of death.

And the woman rose, holding the shrieking child to her. Yehudi drew back his spear, for he could see that Eustace was right, the woman would not put the child down and would share his death.

And lo, the child was wrapped in swaddling clothes of purple hue, and Yehudi stayed his thrust. The household was poor. Little food graced their shelves. The table was old and battered. From the mattress of straw's appearance, Yehudi could tell it had been many times turned, but the child was swathed in purple, a year's wage even for him as a part of Herod's guard.

Then Yehudi said to the woman, "You must wail as if to raise the dead." And she looked upon him without understanding. "Scream, you fool," he said, and he placed his own hand over the end of his spear. Yehudi did not expect the cut to hurt as much as it did, but he needed enough blood fool to Flavian who waited outside. So, as the woman screamed and the man joined her, both loud enough to cover the sounds the baby made, Yehudi wiped the blood on his blade and arms. He stained his robe with it, then closed his wounded fist over the spear's shaft to staunch the flow.

"When we leave," he said, "take the child away and hide him."

Outside the house, Flavian said, "Show me your blade."

And Yehudi did.

And so the troop continued up and down the streets of Bethlehem, and within the afternoon they visited all the houses, leaving behind them much lamentation and sounds of sorrow. In the places Yehudi entered, he killed no children, but continued to put fresh blood on his spear. He much berated himself for his foolishness too, for this was no way to "Take care of yourself," but a part of him felt much misery for the dead babies in the other houses.

On the edge of Bethlehem, Flavian Aurelius dismissed the twelve who had done the killing, and he led the rest toward Jerusalem. Yehudi looked at his fellow soldiers who were sore tired and bloodied, and he felt no kinship with them. By now, the crying from the little town had ceased, but the echoes of it still rang in Yehudi's ears.

Then Eustace, who had been the first to enter a house, fell to the road. All gathered around him and Yehudi bent down to aid him. Eustace's lips were pale, and his skin was cool to the touch. The man opened his eyes when he felt Yehudi's presence, and said to him, "I had to show him blood on the blade." The Greek opened his hand, and lo, a deep cut, much bloodied was there. And Yehudi was amazed.

"Me too," said Yehudi. And one by one, all the other men in the company, every single man, opened his hand. Each thief or murderer, despised by all Hebrews as minions in the service of Herod, showed the mark of his own blade on the palm of his hand.

And so it came to pass that the words of the prophecy were fulfilled and Flavian Aurelius carried out the wishes of Herod. The twelve men became known as the butchers of Bethlehem. But late at night, when none of the Roman guard could see them, and no one could report their actions, each was welcome into the inns and homes of Bethlehem.

And it was good.

ONE DAY, IN THE MIDDLE
OF THE NIGHT

Two Dead Boys Got up to Fight

R EDMOND CAME OUT OF COLDSLEEP FAST, AN AMPHETAMINE AND NEURO-stimulator crashload whacking about his head and limbs like fire alarms. Even before his pod opened he ran security on Grant and found his sleep-pod was warm, bios off. A quick check confirmed what Redmond feared: they were thirty-seven years too soon; everyone else slumbered on, teetering so close to death's edge that their bodies forgot to age. Just the two of them were awake on the *Atonement*, a half million ton starship slowly accelerating toward Zeta Reticuli with enough colonial equipment and frozen, fertilized ova to seed a new world, and Grant meant to kill him.

Pulling sensors off his chest and arms, Redmond cursed under his breath. He'd programmed the system to alert him much sooner, when there was any change in Grant's readout. Grant must have figured a way to fool part of Redmond's security, or he'd weaseled a gimmick into the meds to wake him quicker. Either way, his plan wasn't good enough, or Redmond would be dead now.

The computer told him every door between the north and south sleepbays was locked. So, unless Grant was already in the south sleepbay with him, he had time to prepare a defense, and if he didn't get him that way, to hunt him down.

Maybe Grant *was* in the chamber with him. Maybe he was standing beside the pod, waiting, rage in his eyes and something deadly in his hands. Redmond watched the countdown before the pod opened. One minute to go. He drummed his fingers on the luminescent, slick inner surface, glowing a thin crimson around him. He imagined Grant poised outside. Redmond reached beneath his thigh and wrapped his fingers around the zoology supply tranquilizer gun he'd smuggled into the pod. Cool metal felt ominous against his palm.

He couldn't picture shooting his brother, but it was time to end this.

*

Back to Back, They Faced Each Other

The sleeproom was empty. Redmond sat, his gun in hand, and surveyed. Half the crew slept in this end of the ship; the other slept nearly a mile away. That way a catastrophe might not take them all. They'd be able to continue. A movement in the corner of his eye startled him. He tracked the gun toward it. It was a maintenance robot rolling toward a bot tunnel, an aperture barely large enough to accommodate the eighteen inch tall and two foot wide machine. Redmond shuddered. The round-shelled mechs reminded him of cockroaches, really big ones, scuttling behind the walls. The bot scooted through the hatch that opened with a distinct, pneumatic wheeze. Even that sounded insect-like and horribly organic.

He moved to a workstation, keeping his gun raised, and woke the rest of the system. Vid monitors flickered into life.

"Where's Grant?" he said.

"There is no one named Grant aboard the ship," said the computer.

He nodded. That made sense. With the doors locked and under Redmond's command, Grant would have to go outside. He could be in transit now, incredibly vulnerable. Redmond accessed the meteor defense system. It wouldn't take but a few commands to control the cannons manually and threaten him as he made his way along the hull. But the computer couldn't find him. "No external activity detected," it said. Redmond checked the vids and other sensors. Nothing.

Suspicious, he called up the exterior suit inventory. They were all there.

"Where's Grant?" he said again.

"There is no one named Grant aboard the ship."

"Grant Mayer, when did he wake up?"

"Redmond Mayer is the only member on board with that last name. Would you like to see a crew roster?"

Redmond thought the computer sounded mocking, and he squeezed his eyes shut in frustration. "Damn." Generally he liked the computer; it was Grant who hated it, although he was just as genius in programming as Redmond. Grant once said darkly, "What does it think about the hundred years we're asleep?"

Redmond glanced at the north sleeproom's vid. A pod gaped open, a mirror image of his own.

"Computer, where is the crew member who exited pod N49?"

"N49 has never been occupied."

"Double damn." It took him several minutes of going through the records, but he discovered it quickly enough. Every mention of his brother had vanished, neatly erased. As far as the computer was concerned, Grant didn't exist, and if he didn't exist, then the computer wouldn't track him. All Grant had to do was stay away from the vids. He had free reign and was effectively invisible, which is just the way he'd want it. Redmond keyed in a find and repair routine. Now that he knew the computer had been tinkered with, he could search out the changes and neutralize them. A progress counter winked into existence, but it couldn't tell him when the routine would finish. It was possible the changes were too deep or too well hidden.

Redmond rubbed sweat from his forehead and glanced up. Everything was perfectly still: the pods with their comatose cargo, the conduits running overhead, the shadows on the wall, but Redmond felt an expectancy, as if the ship were holding its breath, waiting for him to move. This was the stillness of the stalk, of the patient wait.

Drew Their Swords and Shot Each Other

Four long corridors, interrupted every fifty feet with doubled airlock doors, stretched between the north and south ends of the *Atonement*. As far as Redmond could tell, all the doors were secured, and only he could open them. Before preparing himself for the long sleep, he'd spent hours and hours programming subroutines into the computer for just such an eventuality as this. Theoretically Grant would be marooned in the north end or trapped between two doors in one of the corridors.

Of course, according to theory, Grant couldn't exit his sleep-pod before Redmond did, and according to theory, he couldn't erase himself from the computer. Redmond stared at the monitors thoughtfully. Were they accurate? Were they showing real time, or had Grant figured a way to have them display empty rooms as he walked in front of them? For that matter, were all the doors truly closed? He toggled a key; the doors showed locked and airtight. Could he trust the computer? After all, he had hidden his work from everyone else, yet Grant had subverted at least part of it. He wished he could ask it if it were trustworthy so he could listen to its tone of voice. Maybe he could hear a lie if it existed, but that was Grant kind of thinking. Grant talked to the computer like it lived. He called it the Blind Man. "All vids and no eyes," he said. It was his eccentricity. Every crew member developed one.

The back of his neck prickled, and he twirled, gun up, so close to squeezing off a shot that he couldn't believe the dart didn't slip away. The sleepbay was empty. One hundred pods in four rows filled the room's middle. Air whispered out of the vents, the sole sound other than his breathing. Normally when he was awake, so were the forty-nine other members of his shift. He hadn't been alone in the ship from the time the trip started a thousand years earlier. Since he was awake two weeks of every hundred years, he'd experienced about five months of travel time, but it still felt as if he'd been on board his entire life. He could barely recall another time where the gray walls didn't bind his existence. They cradled him and comforted him. They held him close, focused him, concentrated him. His imagination coalesced into a ship-shaped, palpable entity a mile long, no wider than the largest room, just as it molded his creativity and hopes, his knowledge and his fear, but mostly his fear.

No one can understand you more and hate you for it than a brother, Redmond thought. It's a mile long ship, and there's no place to go. Once the hatred exists, hiding it is hard. Ignoring it is impossible. After a while, there doesn't need to be a reason. But he remembered it in the top bunk twenty-two years ago—if he didn't count the thousand years they'd dozed—in the top bunk and who would sleep closest to the wall. Redmond slept on the edge when he was seven, forced there by his brother, facing the room's empty middle, Grant behind him, whispering, "The monsters will eat your face, Redmond. They'll eat it, and I'll have time to run." Redmond believed only the knowledge that their parents were in the next room kept Grant from throttling Redmond in his sleep.

By breakfast they were the wonder twins again, competitive, cooperative, and grades ahead of the pack.

The computer told him all of his routines were in place. The complex was geared to Redmond's voice. Grant wouldn't even be able to get basic information, and certainly not control. Or, at least from here it appeared Grant didn't have control. It was impossible to know. The *Atonement*'s computers were so huge, decentralized and redundant that no one really understood the system. Redmond had never felt so paranoid.

Where was Grant, and what was he doing?

Two doors led from the sleeproom. One opened into living quarters, workstations, the power plant and engines behind him; the other would take him to workshops, the ova repositories, the cafeteria, hydroponics and gym. Beyond them waited the corridors with their locked airlocks. If Grant had passed through, he could go around the sleeproom and get him from behind. Redmond dogged the back door so it couldn't be opened. Wearing a visor with a computer interface and heads-up display, he toggled the other door open. A vid showed the room beyond was empty, but he didn't completely trust the information. The door sighed on its hinges. He waited for a minute before moving; his ears ached from listening.

Staying next to the wall, Redmond peeked around the door. The vid was right.

After the workshops, he stalked between the cafeteria's empty tables. He paused to cycle through the vid views again. Two hundred and thirty-seven cameras in total. Three had failed since the last crew had done maintenance thirteen years earlier. The next crew wouldn't be up for twelve years. They'd have two weeks to fix or replace the broken equipment, check their course, and nurse the ship into another twenty-five years of automated competence before the third of the four crews woke.

The ship had already lasted a thousand years, and it had three thousand to go. By the time they arrived at Zeta Reticuli, every part of her would have been remade. Only the crews and cargo would be original equipment. Camera failures were common, but he'd have to check each one for Grant. Redmond glanced around. No dust on the tables—the bots took care of that—but the ship felt utterly abandoned, like a museum after hours, or a morgue. It made him feel like a child again, like he did when he was fourteen, separated from his tour, hiding from Grant with half a Roman brick pried from an ancient wall along the Appian Way for protection, ready to smash Grant's teeth to the back of his throat if he had to, but a teacher came by first. For as long as they had fought, there was always a third party in the way, as if an intelligent fate kept them from tearing each other apart and goaded them into excellence.

As he passed the tanks in hydroponics, he checked fluid levels, pumps and chemical balance from habit. The computer cared for it, of course, but the plants were vital to their existence. Besides handling the air, they manufactured pharmaceuticals, cleaned the water, provided fresh food, and anchored the *Atonement*'s tiny ecosystem.

He tapped his fingers against a vat of brine shrimp swirling about under their own lights. When Grant erased himself from the computer, he made himself a nonentity. It wouldn't track him. It ignored his med signals. There was no way for the computer to directly recognize him, but maybe there was an indirect way.

Redmond sat on the floor between the shelter of two tanks so that he could see the doors. He called up the ventilation readouts. If Grant breathed in one room long enough, Redmond might be able to find him.

It took him a while to get the computer to display the readouts the way he wanted. He looked for oxygen demand. Air circulated in all the rooms, but the computer adjusted for need. Finally, a tiny difference in one segment of the C corridor showed up. Something produced carbon dioxide there. Redmond checked the vid for that segment. Nothing visible, but Grant could be in the blind spot beneath it. Still, the computer showed secured airlocks, so Redmond's plan must have surprised Grant as he rushed from the north end to the south. The doors would have flashed a stay-clear, then closed. Grant wouldn't have been able to stop them.

Maybe the thing to do would be to go back to the sleeproom, climb into his pod, and resume the long sleep. When the next crew woke, they'd find Grant's remains. Redmond could manipulate the computers to show anything he wanted. He scratched his chin. That was Grant kind of thinking.

He shook his head. No, he had to end it now. Leave the computer records intact. They'd show that Grant had started it. Redmond had acted in self defense. When they reviewed the records, they would know.

How long had Grant been trapped? He was clever, and he knew the ship intimately. Was there a way out of the passage other than the airlocks? Was there anything in it that could be used as a weapon? The computer showed that segment's emergency locker's manifest: food, water, some tools. No obvious deadly weapons. But Redmond would have to be careful. He would take all precautions. Grant was malicious in his intellect. He was three minutes older, but it was three minutes of planning, three minutes to get a head start on his brother emerging a shade later.

Leaving hydoponics behind, Redmond moved into the corridor.

At each airlock, he rechecked the vids and oxygen uptakes; Grant wasn't moving. The next segment looked empty, and the tiny warning light above the airlock glowed yellow, meaning there was pressure beyond, then flashed to green when he activated the door. After the ten second cycling sequence, the twinned, massive, metal doors swung open to reveal another long section of empty corridor. A second maintenance bot scuttled out of sight in front of him, disappearing with a creepy squeak. Redmond squatted at the bot's tunnel entrance. It wasn't very big, but a determined man might squeeze into it, and once in he could feasibly bypass the blocked corridors. Of course, he'd have to get through the safety features in the tunnels too—they had their own airlocks—but he could do that without tripping the alarms Redmond had set up.

A few minutes search revealed no tampering within the maintenance tunnels. There weren't vids in them though. Still crouched by the entrance, Redmond chewed his lip. The closer he got to the segment with the elevated carbon dioxide, the more nervous he became. Catching Grant in between doors was too easy. In fact, this was Grant's style, to let Redmond think he was winning until the end.

Something rattled beneath his hand. He threw himself backwards, slamming a shoulder into the wall in the process. Flat on the floor. Gun ready. Breathing in gasps through his mouth. He laughed in relief when the bot reemerged from the tunnel. It rolled on its hidden wheels to the corridor's middle, twirled until it faced him, its tiny vid eyes unblinkingly aimed. Redmond's laugh died in his throat. When the crew was awake and they all busied themselves with their two week regimen, the bots almost never came out. He could ignore them, but now he realized he was awake during bot time.

The machine pirouetted, then rolled down the corridor back the way Redmond had come. He laid his head on the deck, weak with relief.

He pushed himself off the floor. Another few minutes, and he would have him. Redmond licked his lips. The long feud would be over. Dimly he considered again how he'd explain this to the rest of the crew. He didn't worry about punishment. Grant was the dangerous one, the diabolical one. *Grant* had broken protocol by emerging from the pod too soon. *Grant* had reprogrammed the computer to hide himself; that would show his intent. Surely the crew would understand. Now that he was this close, Redmond almost felt sorry for him. A great career wrecked by unchecked passion.

He reached the second to last airlock. Trembling, he rechecked his gun. Tranquilizer dart ready. Safety off.

As he pressed the button, he glanced up. The status light above the door was out. Time slowed. *Not* out. A piece of tape covered it, one edge curling. He didn't have to pull it off to know the light glowed red. There was no air in the chamber beyond. Time nearly stopped; he turned, ran, each stride taking minutes to finish, the door at the other end impossibly far away. He thought, how long do I have to cover fifty feet? Did I take two seconds to start running, or five? How thoroughly did Grant subvert the computer? Enough to lure him down the corridor. Enough to hide the vacuum in that segment. Enough to create a subtle bait in an elevated carbon dioxide count in the chamber.

A klaxon screamed an alert. Two steps from the airlock, one step. He was through. Hit the button to close the door, which started its lumberous trip. Grabbed an access panel handle. How many seconds?

Wind, then a roar, tearing at him, *sucking* him back. Feet off the floor. Mouth open to equalize the pressure.

Very slow time. Hours in his head until the door closed behind him. Blood flowing from one ear, trickling into the corner of his mouth. Air cascading through the vents to replace the loss. Emergency lights pulsing in the ceiling. More klaxons, a virtual chorus shouting around him.

Then time caught up. Redmond let go of the handle, slid to the floor. Told the computer to shut down the alarms. He couldn't move his left arm. Carefully he felt his shoulder; it wasn't shaped right, a dislocation.

Grant hadn't been in the segment at all. It was a trap.

On Redmond's visor, numbers and reports scrolled past, the ship reacting to the segment's emergency. Attitude jets fired, nudging the *Atonement* back on course. External repair bots activated and rushed to seal whatever hole Grant had created. How Grant had fooled the computer into ignoring the damage at first was a puzzle. Redmond flicked from system to system. Nearly every part of the ship responded to the damage. Medcentral kicked into high alert, poised to warm a crew if needed. Every bot on board looked to be on the move. He couldn't track the commands being issued, and through the blizzard of numbers, he searched for Grant. It all came down to Grant who hated Redmond so much he'd risked the integrity of the entire ship to get him. How could he know that blowing that segment wouldn't have collapsed the entire corridor? Every door behind Redmond had been open. If he hadn't closed the airlock that saved his life, half the *Atonement* could have explosively decompressed. This was beyond any feud.

Redmond dragged himself upright. As soon as the computer ferreted out Grant's meddling, he'd find him and deal with him. Briefly he considered waking the crew himself. With forty-eight extra helpers, they'd neutralize Grant in a hurry.

No. That wouldn't be good. In their lifetime of battle, the only rule that couldn't be broken was that it remained private. Only Redmond could hurt Grant, and only Grant could hurt Redmond. When they were eighteen and playing football, Grant took on a linebacker who was going to blindside Redmond. Strained all the ligaments in Grant's left knee. Redmond had watched the video later, seen how Grant had broke his pattern to save him. Grant took an injury rather than letting someone else hurt Redmond. On the next play, Redmond went purposely low on a block and snapped the linebacker's ankle.

No, he wanted to see Grant himself, to look him in the face before he pulled the trigger. There would be no outside help. Redmond's arm hung awkwardly at his side as he walked toward the sleepbay. The gun he carried loosely in the other hand.

Two Deaf Policemen Heard the Noise

At first Redmond didn't hear the whispering voice. He had turned his earplug down low to tune out the computer's constant yammering.

"The doors are locked, you bastard."

Redmond paused. It was Grant, his raspy breathing filling Redmond's ear.

"You almost killed everyone with that stunt," said Redmond, forcing himself to speak calmly.

"If you wouldn't have screwed with the computers, the doors behind you would have closed. Nobody was at risk."

The computer beeped. "Program done," it announced. A report popped up, showing the changes Grant had made to the system. Redmond reactivated Grant as a crew member, and the computer showed his location in the living quarters lounge, directly behind the south sleepbay. Another adjustment, and the vid showed the true image. Grant stood in the middle of the lounge, his hands on his hips. So he'd only been one door away when Redmond had awakened. He swallowed. Had Grant got there just before Redmond had dogged the door, or had he been in the sleepbay before Redmond revived?

"What the hell did you do to the bots?" said Grant.

Redmond ran a dozen scenarios through his head. With the decompression as evidence, immobilizing Grant would look like an act of good will. The crew would give him a medal. Redmond could leave a record of the events and wake with the rest of the crew, a hero.

In the vid, Grant moved sideways through the room, his eyes intent on one wall. He didn't look seventy-three years older than when Redmond had seen him last. His hair was dark, still messy from the long sleep, and his face still baby-like, which belied his biological age of twenty-nine. He carried himself gracefully, like a spider, Redmond thought. One of those garden spiders with long legs that moved from thread to thread with perfect certainty.

"What's wrong with the bots?" Grant said again.

"What do you mean?" said Redmond. Grant's ghostly image floated in the air before him. Redmond cut through the gymnasium's bare space—all the equipment was stored—and into the hallway that would bring him to the lounge's back door. If he jammed it like he'd done the one into the sleeproom, Grant wouldn't be able to get out, even if he talked the ship into cooperating.

"Damn it! A bot's hunting me!" yelled Grant, an unusual tenor in his voice. He was frightened.

Something moved at the bottom of the display. In the middle of the empty gym, Redmond stopped walking so he could concentrate on the image. Grant maneuvered himself behind a couch, his posture wary. A bot slid through one corner of the picture, almost out of view. Redmond sent a command, and the vid went wide angle.

"What's it holding?" said Redmond. A multi-limbed extension had unfolded from the bot's round shell, and it gripped an odd tool. Grant held himself taut, ready to spring away, and his normally graceful movements became panicked. The bot rolled a couple feet to its left, then rotated so the tool pointed at Grant, but the vid resolution wasn't good enough for Redmond to see what it was. Hands on the couch's top, Grant sidled away, apprehension on his face. Redmond flicked through ship data until he ran into a block. Puzzled, he tried another query. Blank. All information on the bots was locked up. It wouldn't access. This wasn't his work; it wasn't Grant's either. Redmond tried a data runaround. Nothing. A backdoor he'd built into the programming was closed too. Tension rose in his throat. The bot skittered around a chair, keeping the tool aimed.

Redmond said, "Stay low. Stay away from it." He pressed the earplug hard against his head so he could hear better. Grant's quick breathing rasped.

A pop.

"Damn it!" Grant clutched his chest. "It shot me." He took a shaky step toward the door, then fell. The bot withdrew the extension before heading for a tunnel.

"Grant! Grant!" Redmond ran toward the lounge, Grant's vital signs displayed in the air in front of him. Breathing and pulse slowed. Only his hands and the top of his head were visible; the couch hid the rest. One hand clenched. Then he spasmed for a couple seconds.

And Came and Killed the Two Dead Boys

The airlock swung ponderously closed before Redmond could get to it. He pounded on it, his hardest blows failing to elicit more than dull slaps. Even as he punched the button to open it, he knew it was useless. The heads-up display revealed more and more of the ship's control locking out. None of them responded.

Across the gym, the door he'd come in was closed too.

Almost weeping, he watched Grant's vitals retreating to straight lines. How had this happened? Who else had tinkered with the computers? He could have sworn that only he and Grant were capable of this kind of work.

When the bot tunnel door squeaked open, though, he knew. It was the ship. Grant alerted a deep self-preservation program when he blew open the corridor segment. The Blind Man was awake; the ship was protecting itself. As the bot rolled toward him, tool arm extended, grasping the same weapon that shot Grant, Redmond looked at Grant's vital signs one more time. Were they flat, or was there the tiniest twitch in all of them? Would the ship kill them, or was it only putting them to sleep for the rest of the crew to deal with?

He didn't try to dodge, but even as he surrendered he couldn't help shuddering. The beetle-backed bot, its tiny vid eyes shining, seemed nearly alive. And it paused. Why did it pause if it wasn't to savor the moment?

Redmond stared at it, and it stared back. Only the sentient gloat.

The bot fired.

And if you don't believe this lie is true,
Ask the blind man, he saw it, too.

WHERE AND WHEN

THE TWO SCIENTISTS SURVEYED THE CABIN'S INTERIOR FROM THEIR POSI-tions behind the crowd at the windows. Jake flicked the command that turned his recorders on, his eyes and ears sending the signal to the computer buried in his jawbone, while Martin stepped to a table and retrieved what turned out to be a menu. He held the pages like they were holy script.

"After all these years," Jake exulted while turning slowly for the recorder's sake. A silk wallpaper imprinted with a map of the world covered the wall beside him. Rich contrasting carpet. Recessed ceiling lights. The transition had been without effect. No sound or dizziness. No flash of light or sensation of falling. Just a blink. "What did we do differently?"

"The math never came out even, but it should have always worked. Maybe there are more opportune moments." Martin carefully opened the thin document. "A thousand failed attempts. Wouldn't Brownson be proud."

Jake grimaced. "If he had survived." For an instant, he thought he saw Brownson among the people at the window. Broad shoulders. One arm. Gray hair. But the light shifted, and Jake could see he was wrong. Two arms. Blonde hair. A stranger. The project had been Brownson's from the beginning. All the theoretical work, most of the construction, only letting them help when he needed two hands. Spending long nights bouncing his ideas off them. Arguing with them about paradoxes. His faith buoyed them when they were ready to quit. His determination to succeed drove them on. His obsession. He should be here, Jake thought. This day belongs to him.

A soft thrumming filled the air, and both men compensated slightly as the floor moved beneath their feet.

Jake's breathing came hard. It *had* been a thousand attempts. They'd poured over Brownson's papers until their vision had blurred. Constructed and reconstructed the device dozens of times. Was it a math problem? Was there a flaw in the underlying theories? Were the old saws about paradox and the impossibilities true, the ones that worried Brownson incessantly? "We must be able to get around it," he'd said. If only the old man had confided in them more before he'd died in the explosion, alone in the lab. "I'm going to try something," he'd said. The investigators concluded later that a bomb destroyed the building. They found chemical traces and a melted timing mechanism. Rival government? Terrorists? Jake and Martin had labored from then on in paranoid secrecy.

"Where and when are we?" Jake said to himself. We're here! he thought, wherever here is. And we're now, whenever that is. He panned around the long room, across the backs of the people at the windows, and over metal-framed chairs pushed up to the tables. He lingered his focus on a yellow piano in the room's center. A wine glass and crystal carafe poised above the keyboard tossed bright glisters from the ceiling lights. The room smelled of cologne and perfume and roast beef. His fingers glided coolly on the silk wall. Jake smiled. What style were the clothes the people wore? 1920s? 1930s? If he queried the computer, it might tell him, but it was more fun to guess. None turned to look at them.

At the window, a middle-aged woman with a cane hooked over her arm said, "Finally. The family has been waiting for hours." Reading glasses hung from a silver cord around her neck.

Ahh, English, thought Jake. He spoke French, German, Italian, Spanish and a smattering of Mandarin. Martin knew Portuguese, Arabic and Russian. If needed, their computer implanted in his jaw could translate, but that was an awkward way to talk. Jake hoped the recorder caught what the people said. Voices from the past. Real ones. The linguists would salivate over the subtleties of vowel shifts, the nuances and shading of pronunciations from hundreds of years in the past. Not radio recordings or movie voices, but real people talking among themselves. The social historians would write treatises on the ways of the era based on his recordings. Whole new areas of study would be opened up. They'd succeeded! They'd jumped the unjumpable chasm.

"The Germans build a marvelous ship, but they can't control the rain and wind," an older man with dark muttonchops and a gray smoking jacket replied. "Not yet, anyway." From the way the woman with the cane and the muttonchopped man stood together, their arms almost touching, their chins at the same angle as they looked out the window, Jake guessed they were husband and wife.

Jake moved to an unoccupied length of window. By putting his face next to the glass that leaned out from the top, he could see that three hundred feet below a grassy airfield waited. He strained to see what was to the right and left beyond the cabin: long stretches of silver-gray fabric, and above them a bulging gray fabric shelf that blocked part of the sky. No wings, he thought. We're in a blimp.

Cars the size of matchboxes covered the ground on one side of a long wooden building. People ran beneath them. He hoped the glass wouldn't mess up the recorder's images.

The muttonchopped man said, "We're tail heavy. If those folks don't watch out below, they'll get a good soaking."

"How so, dear?" asked his wife. She smiled at him, a brief look, then she gazed out again.

"Water ballast."

A nearly subsonic, mechanical thump bumped the room, then the people who'd been running scattered, their hands covering their heads as water streamed down from somewhere aft of the cabin. The muttonchopped man laughed.

Martin sidled up beside Jake. "Look at this," Martin whispered, holding the menu he'd retrieved from the table.

Jake scanned the German text. "Nice wine list. Do you want the beef broth with marrow dumplings or the cold Rhine salmon with spiced sauce and potato salad?" He could barely keep from giggling. They had done it!

"No, not the food. Look at the name." He stabbed a finger at the top of the page.

Trying to settle his heart, trying to keep the grin off his face, Jake read the heading.

"We're going to Hindenburg? Is that where this airfield is?" Were the people he'd listened to American or English tourists on holiday in Germany?

Martin shook his head. "No, no. We're *on* the *Hindenburg*. The zeppelin. The *Hindenburg*."

Jake's computer squeaked for attention with a bone-induction message only he could hear: *The Hindenburg, first commercial flights in 1936. Final flight, May 6, 1937. Gas volume of 7,062,000 cubic feet. Gross lift of 242.2 tons. Originally designed for helium, the ship . . ."* Jake flicked the voice off.

Ahead and to the left of the ship, a solid-looking tower of crossbeams and heavy struts awaited them. The zeppelin turned ponderously toward it.

The tower slid slowly toward the front of the ship. The grass below had given way to cement and tarmac, dark with long puddles of standing water. Fragments of the ship's reflection shown back at them.

"*When* are we on the *Hindenburg*?" said Jake. A crew member opened one of the windows so the passengers could see better. A refreshing, rain-scented breeze filled the cabin.

Martin tapped his finger against the top of the menu impatiently. "What does it matter? We're on the *Hindenburg*. The go-down-in-flames-oh-the-humanity Hindenburg."

"It *does* matter. The *Hindenburg* flew for a year before it blew up. If it's 1936, we're in great shape. Can you imagine? 1936! Franklin Roosevelt is president. The Berlin Olympics. The Spanish Civil War. Picasso is alive, and so is Errol Flynn and Ginger Rogers. We can go to Hollywood! What are the odds of all the places and times in the world that we'd end up on the *Hindenburg* in 1937 when it goes down?"

"Why are we in an airship at all?" Martin looked out the window at the ground. "Brownson said temporal and physical destinations were random. No guessing where we'd end up, but this seems precise. If we'd arrived ten feet that way," he waved beyond the cabin, "our visit here would have been short."

Long cables dropped from the front of the ship. Men on the ground ran to catch them. The hum that pervaded the background shifted, and the cabin shuddered. Jake braced a hand against the slick metal window sill to compensate for the change in speed.

Martin shook his head. He stepped around Jake. "Excuse me, sir," he said to the man with muttonchops. "My friend here is a little confused. Would you tell him what year it is?"

Before the man could answer, Jake heard a soft pop from outside the window, like a gas burner being turned on. The woman with the cane over her arm leaned out the open window, looking up. "What is that, dear?" She reached behind her without turning her head and grabbed the muttonchopped man's wrist. "It's like a sunrise."

A pink and yellow glow brightened the zeppelin's fabric toward the tail. Jake leaned out too to record the image, but the soft glimmer turned into flames racing toward them, furiously fast.

Jake pushed away from the window.

"It's on fire!" someone screamed. The floor began to sink beneath their feet.

Martin faced Jake, his expression serious. "1937."

They reached for their panic switches under their shirts at the same time. Before the world blinked away, the muttonchopped man and the woman with the cane threw themselves out the window. We're still 300 feet above the ground, Jake thought before it all flickered and they were back in the laboratory.

Collapsed in a chair, Jake still breathed in interrupted hitches, his heart pounding in his throat. His hand fluttered as he reached for the coffee cup. Martin, though, bustled from his workbook full of figures, to the computer, and back again.

"*Nothing* in Brownson's notes said we could end up in a zeppelin."

Jake closed his hand on the cup. Gripped hard to stop the shaking. "Not *any* zeppelin. The *Hindenburg*." He shut his eyes for a second, but he could see the mooring mast looming in front of him, beams and struts reflecting a hard, blazing light. In his vision, the woman, her cane still carefully tucked over her arm, tumbled out the window after her husband.

Martin ran his finger down a line of notes, turned the page, kept reading. "A hundred to four hundred years in the past, Brownson said. Location variable. But the math kept us on the ground I thought. Of course, the damn math never made any sense in the first place. Equations never balanced equally. Nothing reduced perfectly. Nothing was absolute."

Jake shivered as he pushed away from the chair, glad for the coffee's heat. From their lab's single window, he could see the tar paper and gravel roof running to a low, brick border. Beyond that, a few clouds rested on the horizon. Their lab perched on the roof of the industrial park's highest building. If he opened the door and walked to the edge, a handful of equally nondescript structures with equally bland roofs would lay out before him, like a bleak checkerboard. They were far from Brownson's destroyed lab and whoever bombed it. He remembered the last time they'd seen Brownson, his only hand protectively over the top of the device, the place for the sleeve for his other arm sewn shut at the shoulder. No sleeve dangled. "Don't want it catching in the equipment," he'd said. Brownson, now, was gone, in explosion and fire, like the passengers on the *Hindenburg*.

"Those people are all dead."

Martin looked up from the notebook. "You're being sentimental. They've been dead for two hundred and fifty years. Their children are dead too, and their children. But if you're talking about the people on the *Hindenburg* we saw, that's not true. Only thirty-three died because of the crash. Sixty-two lived."

The flames had come down so fast. "Only thirty-three?" Jake's mouth was dry. Every swallow hurt.

After a moment, Martin, his voice distracted and preoccupied, said, "Yes, and two dogs. The rest got out when the ship was low enough. Didn't your computer tell you all this?"

"I turned it off."

Jake could still feel the radiant heat. The people screaming, all of them at once. The floor slipping away toward the ship's tail. Glassware tumbling from the tables, and chairs falling toward the back wall. He had kept pressing the panic switch. How long would the device take to snatch them back? What if it wouldn't?

"I behaved badly," said Jake. "I . . ." His gaze roamed the room. Electronic equipment piled on the work table. Security video displayed on four monitors. No one would plant a bomb in their lab! The table, the monitors, the lab on a building's roof were so far away from the collapsing ship, from old people jumping from windows. "I didn't help anyone."

Martin turned the computer off. He shut the notebook. "Jake, those people were dead before we got there. They'd been dead for a quarter of a millennium. You couldn't help them. You couldn't harm them. You couldn't change their fate." He sat on the table's edge and smiled. "I know it's a shock. I'm still quivering myself." He held his hand out, but if it was trembling, Jake couldn't see it. "We traveled in time, Jake, and we returned. All that nonsense about causality loops and killing your grandfather so you won't be born, and a dead butterfly changing human history, it's wrong. Brownson's fears were wrong. We can travel in time. Think about how wonderful you felt when you realized what we'd done."

Surprisingly, the coffee tasted good. Jake took another sip. "That's true. When we arrived. Yes, it was great." He brightened. "We've made history."

Martin laughed. "That's the spirit." He checked the clock on the wall. "It's early, still. You know what we need to do, don't you?"

Jake sat up, put the coffee cup on the table, straightened his shoulders, ran a quick diagnostic on his implanted computer. "Yes, I do."

"That's right," said Martin. "We have to go again."

He pressed the button that activated their synchronized devices.

"See, we're on the ground," said Martin.

They stood on a narrow brick-paved road between a line of two-story shops, neatly-swept concrete stairways leading to their doors, arched stone lintels over the windows. The signs were in French. *Tobacco and Supplies. Fresh bread every morning at 10:00.* Overhead, low, dark clouds grayed the sky, but the sun on the horizon cut under them, casting shadows on the buildings across the street.

A newspaper hung inside the bakery's window. "*Les Colonies*, 'Voice of the French Peoples Everywhere,'" said Jake. His computer said, *There are 785 unique matches to newspapers entitled Les Colonies.* Then it pinged off. Jake needed more information for it to give him a useful analysis. He wiped a thin layer of dust from the glass, then read from the top story. "It says the governor and his wife are in town and not to worry." He struggled with the translation. "The commission, it says, declares that the crisis is past. It doesn't say what the crisis is. Lots of news about an upcoming election."

"So, where and when in the French speaking countries are we?" Martin walked part way down the street, peering into the windows. "Everything seems closed."

Jake scanned the rest of the paper he could see. "Religious holiday. Ascension day. Early morning services at *Notre-Dame de l' Assomption.*" The computer chirped to define Ascension Day.

Martin looked back at him, eyebrows raised.

"Catholic holy day in May. Everyone goes to mass. No date on the paper, though. No city name."

Ladies' hats rested on red velvet stands at the next shop. Martin sniffed. "Do you smell that? It's the ocean."

Jake joined Martin walking up the street which curved slowly to the left. Their shoes kicked up puffs of dust, and when Jake turned, he saw their footprints buffed the bricks clean as if they had just missed a momentary snow storm, but the air was warm. A pile of wooden baskets were turned upside down beside one shop door, shreds of lettuce clinging to the slats.

"Ah, there you go," said Martin. A gap between two buildings revealed a bay to their left only a couple blocks away. A handful of single and double-masted boats, their sails furled, rested quietly on the smooth water, where sea gulls perched on the docks' pilings or skimmed the surface between the ships.

Appearing from around the street's curve, a family walked toward them. The man wore a jacket with wide lapels, and he carried a walking stick. Beside him, the woman held the front of her long dress up to keep the hem from trailing in the dust. A pair of ten-year-old boys walked primly behind them, both hugging a book to their chests. When they passed, Jake offered a "Bonjour."

The man stopped, tipped his hat, revealing dark hair slicked to his skull and parted in the middle. "Bonjour. You are scientists?" the man said in a French Jake barely understood. Some kind of creole? The woman stood beside him, and the children hid behind, but they peeked around her skirt.

"We are visitors," Jake said, confused. Why would the man call them scientists? It would only be more startling if he'd called them time travelers. "Yes, scientists, I suppose. Why do you ask?"

"Your clothes, monsieur. The fashion on the continent, I suppose. We don't get important visitors on the island often."

"We are safe?" said the woman. Her voice was surprisingly deep. "There is noise at night, and the dust. The children worry." She waved her hand at the air.

One of the children shook his head. Jake put his hand to his mouth to hide a smile.

"Of course we're safe," said the man. "The governor's family, after all. Would they be within a hundred miles of here if we were not? Come, we will be late. Au voir."

The man set off at a brisk pace. The woman gathered a child's hand in each hand, and followed.

"What did you find out?" said Martin. "Did you get a date?"

"No. We're on an island, though. Not France. And he said something about the continent. A French colony then. And they're worried about something. He thought we were scientists."

Martin looked at the road. "There's no room for an automobile here. No radio or television antennas. Sailing ships in the harbor. We could be in the 1800s." He laughed. "It worked again, Jake. We've slipped time's surly bonds."

Unease kept Jake from joining Martin's joy. The memory lingered too strongly of the growing roar, the flames reaching around the zeppelin's side. How could they have arrived then and there? A change in the light caught Jake's attention. Where the sun cut a sharp shadow on the buildings now all was a uniform shade, as if dusk was falling. Rolling like a slow ocean at storm, the clouds squirmed overhead. The two-story buildings standing so close together under a ceiling of black clouds suddenly seemed imprisoning. Jake ran ahead. What hid on the other side? Why were the clouds so strange? He passed an old man in his Sunday best, walking with a heavy limp. A young girl, leading a dog on leash, watched wide-eyed as Jake dashed by.

"What are you doing?" yelled Martin.

Jake reached a junction. Across the street, a small park held cast-iron benches with brightly painted red seats. In a small white gazebo, surrounded by yellow flower beds, a man in military uniform leaned on the railing, smoking a pipe. He tipped his hat at Jake, but Jake's attention was beyond the gazebo, up and up. Martin joined him. "We should stay together. This is an unfamiliar time, and . . ."

Beyond the park, beyond and above the rows of houses that made the rest of the city, a mountain rose against the sky, pouring black clouds from its peak. No gentle oozing of clouds either. They catapulted from the shrouded mountain, ascended, caught in a high wind that didn't reach the ground, and flattened over the town.

Jake strode across the street, into the park, his gaze trapped by the silent display. The mountain was close, no more than five miles. Houses in rows lapped against the sloping flank of it. How quiet the town was. None of the seabirds called out. Water in the bay made no sound under the docks. Only his muffled footfalls in the dusty grass. His own breathing.

On the gazebo, the soldier watched Jake's approach.

"Where are we?" Jake demanded. He gripped the gazebo's railing as if to vault himself beside the soldier, a teenager, by his unlined face, so new to his uniform that he looked uncomfortable in it.

"Martinique," said the man with a rise in his voice, like he had asked a question.

Nervelessly, Jake's hand fell away from the painted wood. All the horizon held was the mountain and its billowing performance. "What town is this?" he nearly whispered. Martin walked to the gazebo's side, staring at the volcano.

Puzzled, the young man said, "It is St. Pierre. My company is here to proctor the election."

"Oh, no," said Jake. "We've done it again."

Martin turned back to him. "What?"

"I know the mountain."

From somewhere in the town behind them, a church bell rang out, breaking the silence with its somber tolling.

The soldier laughed nervously. "The Angelus bells. I must be going, monsieur."

"That's Mount Pelee, isn't it?" said Jake in English. "C'est Mont Pelee?" He grabbed the soldier's arm as he went down the steps. Under the heavy flannel uniform, the man's arm felt slender. He's just a boy, thought Jake.

"Yes, Pelee. I must go to the cathedral," said the young man. "I'm already late."

Jake's computer said, *Mt. Pelee exploded in . . .* A thunderous clap of sound overwhelmed the rest of the message.

On the mountain, a cloud wall boiled down the slope, its folds and wrinkles glowing like veins on fire. Trees vanished behind it. Within seconds, the upper half of the prominence became all cloud, rolling down, swallowing land, obscuring what before had been clear. Martin said, "Should we be worried about that? What is it?"

The soldier wrenched free from Jake's grasp, glanced over his shoulder at the mountain, then ran down the street, away from the engulfing cloud. In its squeaky voice, the computer recited a litany of facts.

Jake didn't move. Didn't even twitch. His thoughts slowed down and felt cold to him. Emotionless. "Pyroclastic flow." Another explosion ripped the hidden mountain top.

Martin took a step back. "Will it reach us?"

"In about two minutes." Near the peak, the smoke radiated an incandescent orange, and a series of smaller detonations like cannon fire rattled the park. Jake's insides had emptied. Had the family with the two little boys reached the church yet? If they were lucky, they had time for a short prayer. The computer talked to him. Twenty-nine thousand people would die in the next few minutes: the governor and his wife, in town to calm the population, the scientists who pronounced the volcano safe, the farmers who had fled fields where crops had died in the weeks of ash fall, the people who'd abandoned villages close to the mountain for the safety of St. Pierre, all of them would be gone. Only a prisoner in a basement cell would survive. Rescuers would find him days later, horribly burned, crying weakly from beneath the jail's rubble. "Geologists call it nuee ardente, the glowing cloud. Super-heated air and volcanic ash traveling a hundred miles an hour. Strong enough to knock down buildings. So hot that breathing it boils the lungs."

"How did we get here?" shouted Martin above the growing roar. Furious, he glared at the cloud that reached the town's edge, hiding homes and shops and factories. "This is not random at all!" He touched the button inside his shirt, vanished.

Jake could feel the fear around him. If he turned, citizens would be on the street, drawn by the noise. The cathedral would empty. Hymn books in hand, they'd be waiting. Children, grandparents, craftsmen, soldiers, wives. Trash in the street beyond the park stirred. Now, all was dark. As if it contained a thousand freight trains rumbling headlong down their doomed tracks, the mountain bellowed.

Before the heat. Before the flesh-stripping wind. Jake pressed the button within his shirt.

*

Without taking his hand off the monitor input, Jake flicked from one image to the next, grainy black and white photographs of buildings without roofs, all the windows gone, bricks scattered in the street, and everywhere, bodies burned black. "They had plenty of warning, you know," he said. "The mountain had been misbehaving for weeks. People had already died. There were mud avalanches and a tidal wave and ash falls, but they didn't leave. How can you keep your children with you when there are . . . signs . . . portents?" He sighed and turned off the monitor. "When there are evil omens in the sky?"

"Damn it, Jake. What's important here is the impossibility of us showing up at two disasters. History is mostly boring, repetitious, day after day existence where people go about their ordinary lives. Historic events are rare. How could we possibly be present for two of them in a row?"

"I don't know what the science is, here. Brownson's math looks more like chants and incantations to me than physics anyway. We built a machine that we don't understand. I wonder if Brownson even knew. If only we could ask him."

Martin swore and slapped his notebook closed. "The one-armed bastard. Maybe if he hadn't been so cryptic with us, we'd have a better chance of figuring it out." He paced around the lab, head down. "We've been time travelers for all of what, ten minutes total? Both times we've been scared. We're not thinking straight." He paused, looked at Jake. "We need rationality. *We* were never in danger. We could come back to the lab anytime." He paced again, circling their work table, passing behind Jake at the monitor. "Here's the problem: we only have two points on the graph. We can't reach a conclusion without more information. I say we try again."

The blank screen looked back at Jake, but he could still picture the old images from centuries past. He'd never thought of the people who'd lived before as people, really. Those lives were abstractions. Nothing to do with him. But he could see them now, the living, beating, desperately intense faces from the past, trying to avoid their fates, staring down the rushing pyroclastic cloud burning toward them at a hundred miles an hour, or on the *Hindenburg*, waiting for the ground to come close enough so they could jump, not knowing if the raging hydrogen and diesel-fueled fire would reach them first.

"I don't want to visit the dead anymore," he said.

Martin put his hands on the back of Jake's chair. He could see Martin's reflection in the monitor overlaying the ghost images of a destroyed town. "I told you already, they were dead before we started. *We're* dead, Jake, to someone in our future, but you're thinking about it all wrong. They're alive too. Everything they've ever done is still being done. Nothing is in the past now. It's all redoable. Replayable."

He checked the equipment strapped across his chest under his shirt. "We have to go again, and we need to do it now. I can't tell from Brownson's figures why it's working. So much of his calculations are about the paradoxes, and they're a waste. 'Solve the paradox!' he said. 'Solve the paradox!' There's no paradox. We've traveled, but we can't guarantee we can keep doing it. Maybe the Earth has to be in the right place in its orbit. Maybe the atmospheric conditions have to be just perfect. If we don't go now, we might not be able to go again."

For a moment, Jake didn't stir. It was like the weight of Mount Pelee coming toward him and nothing mattered. He pushed away from the monitor and faced Martin. Finally, he nodded. Martin was right, he was dead any way he figured it.

At first Jake thought he'd gone blind until he saw the nearly full moon through thin clouds. A cold wind pushed against his face. He took a step, kicked something yielding, and a sleepy voice said, "Watch it, goll darn ya. Can't a soldier get a decent sleep anywhere on this boat?"

Standing still, Jake listened until his eyes adapted to the pale light. Water sloshed heavily to both sides. A substantial pounding vibrated the floor beneath his feet, and before the first faint lights grew visible on the shore a couple hundred yards away, he'd already decided they were on a steamboat near the bow. He turned his back to the wind. Moonlight revealed twin gray smokestacks belching smoke and sparks above a pilot's cabin, and dark forms that covered the deck like a lumpy landscape. He looked down. The man he'd kicked had rolled onto his side, pulling a thin blanket over him. The bundles were men sleeping on nearly every inch of exposed surface. Walking without stepping on someone would be hard.

"When and where are we?" said Martin.

"Someplace that's going to sink soon, or catch fire, or be attacked," Jake said.

Martin grunted. "I should have brought a coat."

"Go back and get one." On the shore, ghostly trees touched their branches to the water. A lone cabin, a dim light flickering in its window, peeked out from the woods. On the boat's other side, the river reflected the moon like a long, undulating silver plate until it vanished in a low fog that hovered just off the surface. The air smelled cool, wet and muddy.

"Big river. Steamboat. English spoken here. The Mississippi." Martin strode over a silent shape, careful not to step on it. Jake followed. Gingerly they moved toward the shore-side railing. Men sat up there, some leaning their heads on the shoulders of others. Some talked among themselves.

"He's dead, the bastards," said one. No one replied. "A coward's shot, I tell ya. A yella deed, it was."

Jake took a place at the rail. Below, the river flowed past slowly. The ship's headway was gradual. The cabin on shore crept astern.

"You'll feel better when we hit Cairo and head home," said another voice.

"Vicksburg, Memphis, Cairo, Evansville. What's it matter? Dead is dead."

Farther down the boat, the paddle wheel churned, digging into the water with quick, ponderous movement.

"You didn't even vote for him."

"I would've."

Dampness on the rail chilled Jake's arms. The only warmth was Martin standing beside him, blocking the wind.

"Who is dead?" said Martin.

A log with one crooked branch sticking out like a bony, broken bone drifted by only thirty feet away. At the end opposite the branch, a pair of birds, their beaks tucked under wing, huddled side by side. "The president, ya cracker. Ain't ya talked to anyone? Some southern dog of an actor they say done it."

Jake leaned back, but the men were swathed in shadow. He couldn't see who spoke.

"Lincoln?" said Martin. "Are you talking about the assassination of Lincoln?"

Someone snorted in disbelief. "Twarn't Jefferson Davis."

Jake's computer squeaked to life. Before he muted the citation, it said, *Abraham Lincoln died on April 14, 1865. John Wilkes Booth fired on the president during a performance . . .*

"How long ago?" said Jake. He couldn't remember much about the Civil War beyond the obvious. If Lincoln was already dead, then the war was over. Antietam and Gettysburg and Chancellorsville were in the past. Certainly nothing to fear, like the destruction of the *Hindenburg* or Mt. Pelee erupting. The shooting had ended.

"Don't know what today is," said the voice. "Ten days, maybe. Two weeks."

Jake activated a search for the dates with attention on disasters. A second later, the computer said, *At approximately 2:00 a.m., April 27, 1865, the massively overloaded steamboat, Sultana, exploded. At the time it carried approximately 2,100 repatriated Yankee soldiers, most from the Andersonville prison camp. Between 1,700 and 1,900 men died.* The voice carried on. Facts, figures.

Jake swallowed hard. "This is the *Sultana*, isn't it?"

"Yep."

"Would you know what time it is?"

"Don't know that neither."

Jake whispered to Martin. "The boat is going to blow up."

Martin's head dropped to his arms. "That doesn't make sense. The figures . . . the math . . . random times, Brownson said."

Closer to the pilot's cabin, another man slouched on the rail. Jake's gaze lingered on him. The moon's light burnished him like a bleached shadow. Was this also a soldier who would never make it home? His posture seemed familiar and out of place.

"We should leave, Jake. An explosion won't give us time to escape. I need to get to the lab and redo the calculations. I've missed something."

Jake straightened, moved toward the pilot house. A rift in the cloud cover brightened the light for a moment, showing the man's shirt sewed shut at the shoulder. No arm. Jake thought, these are Civil War veterans; many of them have lost a limb. As he looked at the landscape of sleeping men, he saw a half dozen crutches resting across blankets. Still, Jake's neck tingled. No empty sleeve dangled from the one-armed man. It was gone, sewn up, as if there had never been an arm for that space.

Martin sounded panicked. "I'm going."

Jake's back grew cold. Wind brushed against him, and the air felt empty. Without looking, Jake knew that Martin had gone. He approached the man at the rail, stepping over outstretched legs, until he stood next to him.

"You were fools to come. It's not worth it," said Brownson. The old man stared into the water, the side of his face a chalky reflection of moon and river air. "How much time did you give yourself?"

"I don't know, but it can't be long." Jake imagined the boilers deep in the ship's bowels, leaking steam, overpressured, fighting the current and the crowded deck, maybe seconds from ripping at the seams. He put his hand next to Brownson's, and behind his eyes he felt a sudden pressure. His voice caught in his throat. "Your lab . . . they've bombed it. You can't go back."

"They?" Brownson sounded tired. His voice was flat.

"Yes. Someone. Maybe another government. They might have found out what we were doing and became scared. Maybe they thought you could solve the paradox. But there was a bomb. You sent us away that day, or we would have gone up too."

"So, how did you get here? How did you arrange it?" said Brownson.

Jake could feel his brow wrinkling. "What do you mean? Your machine, of course. Your design worked. There's no paradox."

Brownson turned to face him. Moon shadows under his eyes made him look a hundred years old. "I didn't solve the paradox—I worked around it, and so did you, or you wouldn't be here."

No answer worked. What did he mean? "We just activated the device. We didn't solve anything."

Closing his eyes, the old man sighed as if he never wanted to breathe again. "The information paradox stops time travel, as I argued. Information that would change people's actions can't go forward or back. The timeline is immutable."

If it wasn't for the beating of the paddle wheel and the soaking Mississippi breeze, Jake could almost feel back home in the lab. This was the direction of a hundred arguments. It was where the math piled up, making no sense. "But we're here."

"Yes, we are, and we can go anywhere the information we carry doesn't matter. We go to time's dead ends, like this sad ship."

Jake's thinking felt sluggish. So much had happened in the last hour. Too much to comprehend. "I don't understand."

How close were the boilers to letting go? Jake's hand crept up to the panic button under his shirt.

Brownson said, "We can't bring information from the future to the past, but we can't bring it forward either. Not if we could tell other people what we found. I planted the bomb."

Overhead, the moon vanished within the clouds, and darkness covered the steamboat. Brownson's voice came out of the black. "It was sealed. Undefusable. When I set it, when I couldn't get away, I made the first trip. I've proven that you can travel in time, but no one will ever know."

"How much time?" Jake's hand caressed the switch.

"How much time did you give yourself?"

"We didn't do anything."

"You didn't? Then it must be something else. Something unexpected." Brownson faced away from the river, looking over the sleeping forms. The two soldiers Jake had talked to earlier were still conversing. "Lincoln's dead, the cowards. Lincoln's dead," spoke one, his voice without feeling. Brownson said, "You poor boy. These men didn't do anything either, but their stories are over. The unexpected is on its way for them, the inevitable, as it is for me, here or in my lab or somewhere else." He paused for a raspy breath. "Just as it is for you. Your lab won't be there long."

Before he could hear another word, before the boilers could let loose to fling hundreds of men into the frigid Mississippi, before the bitter soldier talking in the cloud-veiled night could say again that Lincoln was dead, Jake pressed the button and disappeared.

Martin sat at the worktable, his hands wrapped around the back of his head, his forehead pressed against the scarred work surface. He didn't look at Jake when he appeared in the room, but he talked anyway. Perhaps he'd been talking the whole time. "Our destinations weren't random. The physics of the paradox tossed us where we couldn't matter."

"I know."

"The math says that Pelee is here, right here in the room with us, and so is the *Sultana* and the *Hindenburg* and everything else. The end is on its way." He began weeping.

"What did you say about Brownson's math?" said Jake.

"Tornado. Earthquake. Meteor strike. Nuclear bomb. Fire. Flood. Famine . . . quick famine. It's on the way. That's how the equations balance."

Jake ripped open his shirt. Double checked the equipment. Power was good. "You told me something about the math once, about the equations." He looked out the window. Was the sky turning dark? Was there a rumble in the building's basement. The unexpected was surely on its way. "Brownson told us that information couldn't travel in time. That's the paradox at work, but you said the math never solved perfectly. The numbers were always a little unbalanced."

"I don't get you," said Martin. "The numbers don't matter now."

"Only thirty-three people died on the *Hindenburg*. One man survived Mount Pelee. Five hundred or so lived through the Sultana." Jake spoke fast. What had happened began to make sense, if he had enough time. If he could get to where he needed to go before the time ran out. "If information is prevented from traveling backwards and forwards *perfectly*, if the equations add up *perfectly*, then we should only have been able to travel where there were no survivors. There could be no chance for escape, but if I get to the right place I might have a chance."

He pressed the button and found himself on a steel deck, slick with ice. The ship's name, *Halifax*, was printed across a lifeboat.

He pressed the button. Martin flinched when he reappeared.

Jake pressed again. Another mountain rose up before him. Its top too was smoke-covered.

He pressed the button. Martin said, "Where are you going?"

The button gave way. A cityscape. People streamed by, many on bicycles. Street signs were in Japanese. Without looking, he knew a lone bomber flew over the city.

"Tell me where and when," shouted Martin.

Jake paused, ready to go again. How much time did he have? None to be wasted, for sure, but the numbers didn't lie. Their imperfections held all the hope he needed. Maybe *most* of information could not go from the future to the past. All he could believe was that in the fractions that didn't add up, he could slip away.

"The *Hindenburg*," he said. "If I wait long enough. If I jump from the window not so high that I'll die, not so low that the ship will crush me, then I'll survive. Sixty-two people lived. I can be the uncounted sixty-third."

There's no point in not trying, he thought, and he pressed the button.

A WOW FINISH

EARLE WOKE UP LAST, ON THE FLOOR UNDER A SHEET. DURANCE STOOD AT the window, watching the rain, while Hoffman, achingly beautiful sat on the end of the bed, elbow on knee, chin in hand. They were already dressed.

Of all the field trips to all the times in all the world, she had to choose mine, Earle thought, conscious that he was naked beneath the thin covering. He wondered which of them had put the sheet over him.

"It's a pity we always arrive in a storm," said Durance. He tugged at his dark tie. "And the outfits are uncomfortable." He wore a beige double-breasted suit with matching pants creased so sharply Earle thought he could cut paper with them.

"Allergens," said Hoffman without moving. "The air's cleaner on a rainy day. God knows what you'd react to here. Street dust. Pollutants. Pigeons. It's safer on wet days. Cowardly, perhaps, but safer." She smiled at Earle. "You going to lay there all evening?"

Earle rolled to his side. His clothes were neatly piled beside him. He pulled them under the sheet and dressed there, aware that Hoffman only had to shift her gaze a foot to be looking right at him. It was a struggle to get into the shoes. The stiff leather bit into his ankles, but they had a nice shine to them, and putting them on made him feel more there. More real. Somewhere distant a bell rang. He realized he'd been hearing it for a while. Beyond that a steady rumble quivered just on the edge of his perceptions.

"Look at this phone," said Durance, picking it up. At first Earle thought that it was tied to the table. Durance said, "Wires *and* a dial. How do you work it?"

Hoffman stood from the bed, smoothing the front of her skirt with the edge of her hands. She'd cut her hair short for the trip and given it a curl. "Honestly, it's like you've never been in the field before."

"Nothing before 2020. My master's was on post-rock pop, but I got interested in the roots of neuro big band. Earle has been in the Twentieth Century, though. I sampled that thing you did on the *Hindenburg*. Nice work."

Earle struggled with the shirt's buttons. "Beginner's luck. I was a last minute replacement."

Durance shrugged, then put the phone back on the table. "Hard to believe the trouble I'm going through to put in an extra footnote. Tiny Hill and his orchestra are in the Green Room here in the Edison. Harry James is uptown at the Astor, and Benny Goodman opens there tomorrow. Cab Calloway plays the Park Central."

"Pretty good lineup," said Earle.

"I tried talking Hoffman into going with me. A live band has to be better than a dusty old movie. So why go?" Durance laughed and put his hand on Hoffman's shoulder. She leaned into him. Earle turned away, concentrated on tying his shoe.

"Ask Earle. It's *Casablanca*," she said. "Opening week. I don't get it either. The *Hindenburg*, now that was important, but a film? Well, for a me a theater's as good a place as any."

Durance sniffed. "I read up on the movie. Who can watch this stuff? Ancient black and white that you can't edit while you watch, and bad piano bar music on top of that. Dooley Wilson didn't even play the piano. He was a drummer. Then there's a bunch of Germans singing an off-tune version of 'Die Wacht am Rhein' instead of 'Deutschland uber Alles,' which would have made more sense. I wouldn't get anything useful. Hard to believe people would get worked up over it. Twentieth Century sentimentalism."

"I've never seen it," said Hoffman. "Studied the background, though. Vichy France. The German advances. The resistance movement. Bogart. Bergman. I'm ready."

Earle paused in straightening his jacket. He didn't know that she had never seen the film. There might be hope yet. He dropped the sheet on the bed as he walked to the window. Traffic flowed below, rumbling. "Broadway," he said. "The Great White Way. 1942. Three and a half weeks until Christmas, and an entire world that hasn't seen *Casablanca*." He could feel the cars passing through his fingertips resting on the window sill. "Bogart said, 'When it's December 1941 in Casablanca, what time is it in New York?'"

Durance shrugged. "That's 47th. Broadway is around the corner. It's just an old movie. You could have stayed home and watched it on video."

"And you could listen to big band recordings whenever you want. Why'd *you* make the trip?" said Earle.

Durance glanced at Hoffman. He said, "Experiential research. I'm nanoed to the gills. Download the lot uptime, and I'll have a couple years' work worth of data in my twenty-four hours. No paper's complete anymore without actual field hours," but his glance said it all.

"Me too. Serves me right for asking a direct question," said Earle.

Hoffman slipped her arms into a coat, then flipped the white blouse's collars over the blue wool, as if she's always worn the style. She pulled on a pair of white gloves. Earle could hear Bogart's dialogue in his head: "I remember every detail. The Germans wore gray. You wore blue."

"We'd better get going, Earle. It's a four-block walk, and I want good seats."

Durance said, "I've got a half hour before the band starts here. Last chance at some decent music, Hoffman."

She shook her head at him as she headed for the door.

In the hallway, a sign read, WHEN IN DOUBT, PUT IT OUT.

She ran her fingers along the sign. Earle knew she was calling for info out of habit, but they weren't tied in here. No instant details about whatever they wanted. No augmentation at all. They had to fit in. "Cigarettes?" said Hoffman. She buttoned her coat. "I didn't think the anti-smoking trend came along for another fifty years." She sniffed. "It doesn't smell like it's working either."

Earle adjusted his hat, a dark snap-brim with a black silk band above the brim. "It's a light-dimming measure. They were afraid German submarines might cruise up the Hudson River to shell the Rockefeller Center or something. They never really turned the lights out on Broadway, though."

Hoffman laughed, "That's funny. For a second there I tried to edit out the smell. It's weird to be stuck with one version of the world."

"Nope. Can't change a thing. Just like the natives. No VR ghosts. No info on demand. It's a single-track existence. Besides, you'd stick out wearing your regular headgear."

Earle looked down the long hall, doors opening on each side, a serving tray on the floor next to the nearest room, on the tray a partly eaten sandwich on a plate beside an empty cup. That's exactly it, he thought, that makes this so good. One reality. Of course, even in the editable world, Hoffman had left him.

A bell chimed, and the elevator arrived. Earle started in recognition. That was the bell he'd been hearing. The doors opened to reveal a mirrored back wall. His coat looked good next to hers. Wide lapels. Plain epaulets on the shoulders. Buckled cinch bands at the wrists. He turned his collar up.

"You look like Bogart," Hoffman said.

"In a raincoat and hat, everyone looks like Bogart." He tried not to consider her face in the mirror. "Why'd you choose this trip? There were others to this era."

"I wouldn't have come if I had known that you were here. I'm still research assistant for Dr. Monroe. She's doing that monograph on women's social development in the mid-twentieth. This slot was open. Besides, she wanted me to see how contemporary women react to Ingrid Bergman saying"—she pulled a notecard from her pocket and read—"'I don't know what's right any longer. You have to think for both of us.'"

"You'll love Capitaine Renault then. His hobby is preying on pretty girls who need exit visas but don't have any money."

Hoffman raised her eyebrows. "And this is the classic film you argued was 'the cultural pivot point in American consciousness?'"

If that bothered her, Earle thought, he couldn't wait to see her response to Renault saying, "How extravagant you are, throwing away women like that. Someday they may be scarce."

The elevator opened onto the lobby level.

Hoffman stepped out first. "Heavens. If you love art deco, this is the place."

Gold-rimmed half-dome chandeliers hung from gold chains above the gold and brown carpet. Overstuffed chairs nestled up to tiny tables where a handful of people sipped from china cups.

A pair of sailors in dress whites walked by. "We could catch *The Skin of Our Teeth* if you wanted to see a show," said one.

"I hate Thornton Wilder," said the other. "We've only got two days. I'm going to spend the time snuggling up to that hat check girl or someone just like her."

Hoffman took a step after them, then turned to Earle. "That's the kind of material I need. They're so primitive."

"I don't know. You'd get the same talk in the grad dorms on a Friday night."

"Really?" Hoffman looked offended.

She took a complimentary umbrella from the doorman. Earle waved off the offer. He wanted to feel the rain tapping against his hat, to get more into the moment of time that was *this* time. He needed to submerge in 1942 so that it would be visceral. He couldn't just watch the video because the video wasn't theater. Experiential research meant that there was no substitute for being there. Like Durance, his system practically leaked nanos. They recorded everything he sensed. They made a duplicate of the experience he could return to again and again for study. Better than eyewitness reporting. So, no umbrella. Connect to the moment, walking in the rain with Hoffman, like Paris, where Bogart waited in the rain for Bergman at the train station. "Where is she? Have you seen her?" Bogart asked. The storm poured down. "No, Mr. Richard," said Sam. "I can't find her." Sam handed Bogart a note. It read in part, "Richard, I cannot go with you or ever see you again." The ink ran in the rain.

They stepped through the doors onto the sidewalk. Earle held his hand out. Droplets pelted his palm. He could imagine the note in it, the ink leaking off the page. A car passed, splashing water onto their shoes.

Hoffman said, "I thought it would be louder. You know, all the gasoline engines."

Rain hissed off the street, drummed steadily against the buildings. Tires whined on the pavement. Lights glistened on the wet surfaces. Two couples, huddled under their umbrellas, hurried into the Edison's doors. This is New York at war, thought

Earle. You couldn't tell. Despite gasoline rationing, traffic was heavy. A restaurant sign advertised a variety of steaks. Other than the sailors in the lobby, he hadn't seen military personnel or equipment. Were there anti-aircraft guns on the roofs?

He wanted to ask her about Durance. Hoffman hadn't seen the film. He could say Bogart's line without a hint of irony, "Tell me, who was it you left me for? Was it Durance, or were there others in between?"

Hoffman said, "It's breezy wearing a dress. These nylons aren't insulating at all. What did women do when it snowed?"

"They toughed it out, but they suffered. They took jobs in the factories and raised kids on their own, and waited for terrible telegrams to tell them their husbands weren't coming home." Cars eased by, dripping water from their fenders. Earle strained to see the people within. God, it's 1942, he thought. Soldiers are dying by the thousands. Northern Africa, southern France. Drowning next to the flames of their burning freighters. Broken airplanes tumbling. Many, many more are yet to die.

Hoffman shivered.

They crossed 48th. Low-hanging clouds hid the buildings' tops. The few pedestrians walked briskly under their umbrellas.

"It's amazing how every place in the past feels just like home," Hoffman said. "I mean, the air smells different–all those hydrocarbons–and the architecture's dated, but *I'm* the same. I could have been born here just as easily as any other time. Of course, half of my brain feels like it's turned off, but other than that . . ." She stepped around a puddle.

She doesn't see it, thought Earle. There's *nothing* here that's like home. Life here was both straightforward and mysterious. Everything was what it appeared to be, but nothing provided answers. The buildings, the sidewalks, the stores, the people, unaugmented and uneditedable, but all mute, their histories hidden. All of it's different. How could he explain that to her so that she'd know? "If you want to see sights unique to the era, we could cross over a few blocks. St. Patrick's Cathedral and the Waldorf-Astoria are that way." He pointed east, across Broadway.

"The cars are huge!"

A yellow Nash coup cruised by, rain water running off its long hood, the silhouette of a couple, visible for just a moment in the front seat. Packards, Olds, Mercurys, Studebakers, Plymouths, De Sotos, Grahams, Fords, and others he couldn't identify splashed through the shallow pools. A car twice as long as any he'd ever driven in glided on broad whitewalls, a covered spare tire mounted on the running board behind the front wheel. A Cadillac, probably, or a Rio. He whistled in appreciation.

Hoffman walked several steps ahead, hidden beneath her umbrella. What I need, thought Earle, is something she wants. I need a Ugarte to give me letters of transit. A passport to her heart. Ugarte, Peter Lorre in a beautifully done small part, said the letters were "signed by General DeGaull. Cannot be rescinded. Not even questioned." Ugarte killed a pair of German couriers to get them.

Earle shook his head. How did Bogart get Bergman back? He practically called her a whore, but she still loved him. *Casablanca* started as a story of a jilted lover's bitterness. Bogart wanted to punish Bergman for leaving him, but the vengeance went awry. Instead of hurting her, he drew her in. Bergman said, "I can't fight it anymore. I ran away from you once. I can't do it again."

"Tell me about the movie," Hoffman said.

Earle sped up so that he walked beside her.

"*Casablanca* is a pivot point for Americans' attitudes about themselves and the war. They didn't think that at the time. It was just another movie, but when cultural historians look back now, they see it. It's a slice of the times. Go in with an open mind; maybe you'll get more out of it than you believe. If you keep your eyes open, you'll see all sorts of gender attitudes."

Hoffman peeked from under the umbrella. "These gloves aren't very warm either. December in New York is cold," Hoffman said. She jammed her free hand under her armpit. "So what should I be looking for?"

He smiled. "Start with Yvonne. It's implied that she and Bogart have a relationship, but he dumps her in an early scene. She says, 'Where were you last night?' and he says, 'That's so long ago I can't remember.' It's a classic demonstration of Bogart indifference. The really interesting moment is with a Bulgarian girl later in the film. She wants Bogart's advice on love and sacrifice. I don't want to spoil it, but her quandary reflects on what's going on between Bogart, Bergman and Henreid."

"Henreid?"

"Victor Laszlo in the film, Bergman's husband."

"Right. Sorry. I got him mixed up with Greenstreet."

"He owns the Blue Parrot. Another big actor doing a nice turn in a small role."

Hoffman lifted the umbrella so she could look at him. Her eyes caught the oncoming car lights. "Just how many times have you seen this film? You never talked about it a year ago."

"Maybe a hundred."

"Heavens! So you've been a *Casablanca* fan your whole life?"

They crossed 49th. "No, not really. I saw it the first time in January." He blushed. "Well . . . um . . . I was doing a lot of other things too. Have to keep busy, you know."

"It's just hard to believe that a piece of film could be worth the trip." She kept glancing at the traffic to her side, but didn't say anything else as they approached the theater. Her silence was disconcerting. A hundred times, he thought. She'll think I've spent all my days watching romances. How pathetic. But he did watch it a hundred times, reclining in his academic's cubical, the film playing on the ceiling.

Sometimes, while walking on campus, he had edited the world into black and white, and Sam playing "As Time Goes By." University noir, he had thought.

The line into the theater was short. Earle fingered the unfamiliar paper cash in his pocket. Seventy-five cents each for admission. For a moment he panicked when he couldn't remember if dollars were more than cents as he handed the woman at the ticket window a five. She smiled and pushed back a pair of quarters and three dollars.

In the lobby, Hoffman folded the umbrella, after fumbling with the mechanism for a moment, then looked at the change. "Is this any way to run an economy? It's so clumsy, passing around metal and paper. How many people do you think *touched* this? Yuck."

"You sound like Durance," he said.

She laughed. "Sorry. He can be a bit overwhelming. Infectious cynicism. Most of the time I edit him down. I'm going to mingle a bit before the show. See what I can learn."

Earle moved to the edge of the room so he could survey the area. Like the Edison, the lobby was opulent, more like a museum than a theater. He laughed to himself. Experiential research always affected him this way, and it was hard to shake the idea that the world he was walking through was virtual and augmented instead of being actual. This was the *real* world. 1942. A paranoid world at war, although, as someone once told him, it isn't paranoia if they're really out to get you. All kinds of history happened in '42. The Japanese captured Manila, Bataan fell, Roosevelt interned Japanese-Americans, MacArthur left the Phillipines, an oil refinery in California was shelled by a Japanese sub, the civilian draft began. The war hit close to New York too. In June, the FBI arrested four German saboteurs after a U-boat landed them on Long Island.

The people waiting to see *Casablanca* didn't look nervous. They chatted in the low murmur people use when in public. He wondered if the first audiences for *Romeo and Juliet* were the same way. No idea what awaited them inside. It is just another play, they would have been thinking. An idle way to spend a few hours. But the world was different afterwards. Those first audiences were there at the beginning, like people standing in a mountain meadow, unaware that the tiny stream at their feet was the progenitor of the Mississippi.

A handful stood near the coatroom. A couple leaned close together under a BUY WAR BONDS poster. Others entered a door into the theater.

"Shall we?" said Hoffman.

They took seats near the front. The room smelled of plush and colognes, and the wet street on people's shoes. Earle eyed the curtain at the front of the room apprehensively. It stretched nearly the length of the stage. "We could be too close. The image might not hold up when you're near the screen."

"They wouldn't have chairs here if it wasn't good." Hoffman sat, then squirmed a bit. "You wouldn't believe what I'm wearing *under* this," she said. "It's all seams and scratchy cloth."

Earle surveyed the theater. *Casablanca* had its opening night three days earlier. Now, fewer than half the seats were filled, almost all folks in their twenties or older. He breathed deeply. His record of the experience would be clearer if he stayed focused and calm. Hormonal imbalances could throw it off. He tried to forget that Hoffman was sitting next to him, her arm against his on the armrest. Slow breaths. Calmness.

The house lights dimmed, and the ceiling to floor curtains drew aside, revealing the screen.

"Very dramatic," said Hoffman. She settled deeper into her seat.

Behind them, a ratchety noise clicked into being, then a beam of light cut through the air to illuminate the screen. Earle turned. Through a small window high on the wall at the back of the theater, the projector glowed as the first film rolled. He nodded. The clicking would be the film pulling through the sprockets and the shutter flicking in front of each frame to give the illusion of movement. *That's* what I'm here for, he thought. All the reading about *Casablanca* had never told him how loud the projection equipment could be. He faced the screen. Movie Tone News, the title said. Reading hadn't told him that the floor would be sticky, or that watching a film in a huge room in the company of strangers felt so . . . well . . . so theatrical. No wonder people went to movies by the millions. This was the era before television, before computers and home theaters and specvids or tactiles or any of the entertainments he was used to. Black and white images of battleships at sea filled the screen.

The narrator's voice boomed through the theater. "Brave sailors on the USS Dakota shot down a record thirty-two enemy planes in a valiant effort in support of the South Pacific campaign." A shadowy plane raced across a gray sky, chased by tracers.

A woman a few seats to his left sat with her hands up to her mouth. Did she know someone in the navy? She might have been twenty, hair curled below her ears, a crucifix dangling from her throat, and she wore a long white skirt covered with a floral pattern, her coat folded on her lap. She appeared to be alone.

In the row in front of them there were three couples, all with the man's arm around the woman's shoulder. More than half the people in the theater were coupled up. It's a *social* occasion, Earle realized. Going to the movies wasn't just about seeing the story, it was, oddly enough, in the darkness of the theater and the noise of the movie, a way to be with someone. Granted, the communication was nonverbal, but the people must have come together to be together.

Hoffman sat beside him. He could put his arm around her. How would she respond? Her hands lightly gripped the armrests. Her legs were uncrossed. Nothing about her body language gave him a clue one way or another about what she was thinking. If he just raised his own arm, he could reach around her. Would she move in close? Her violet perfume filled his nose. From the corner of his eye, in the flickering light of the Movie Tone News, he could see the curve of her cheek, the reflected shine in her eye.

Earle's arm twitched. It would be so easy to make the motion to hold her. He could tell her that it was part of the experience of seeing a movie in 1942. He leaned to the left so he could raise his arm.

Something bumped the back of his chair. Earle turned. It was Durance, his forearms resting on their chair tops. "I figured I could catch Tiny Hill's Orchestra's late show. Thought I'd better see what this *Casablanca* fuss was all about. I had a tough time finding you in the dark!"

A sibilant "Shh!" hissed from a row back.

"It's not etiquette to talk in a theater," whispered Hoffman. She didn't appear happy to see him.

"Why not?" Durance said, his voice still too loud. "It's not a live performance."

"Shh," said Earle.

The Warner Bother's theme trumpets and drums theme filled the auditorium, and the film began.

Earle slid down in the chair until his head rested against the plush. The opening credits played over a map of Africa. He trembled. An arrow traced its way from Paris, across France, through the Mediterranean to end in Casablanca where all refugees without exit visas "wait and wait and wait."

He'd seen the picture a hundred times before. The rhythm of it was familiar—the report of the dead couriers and the stolen letters of transit, the roundup of suspects, the English couple talking to the pickpocket—but he'd never seen the movie like this, in a huge theater, and the atmosphere was different. The people sitting all around him had no idea that they were in the presence of greatness. Earle felt the same way he had at the *Hindenburg*. 1937. The ship was ridiculously large, only eighty-seven feet shorter than the *Titanic*. Earle had stood with a crowd to watch the docking. The people oohed and ahhed at her girth. They didn't know. They didn't know, but Earle did. To the unprepared, great moments felt like common ones until they were over.

On the screen, a model airplane flew over a crowded, Morrocan street. The people stared hopefully. Hoffman leaned into him. "That's not a very realistic looking airplane."

"Production costs," he whispered back. "Almost everything you see was done in the studio or back lots. No computer help."

She wrinkled her brow. "It's distracting."

"The story is not about the plane."

Scenes flicked by: Germans stepped onto the runway where Renault waited. Bogart played chess by himself at Rick's. Ugarte bragged to Bogart about selling exit Visas cheap. "I don't mind a parasite," said Bogart. "I object to a cut rate one."

Earle craned his neck to see other patrons in the theater. What were they feeling? How did the movie effect them? The woman in the floral print dress leaned forward, but he could see nothing in her or the rest of the audience's attentive faces. For a second, Durance met Earle's gaze, but he looked back to the screen.

Earle turned around. Within minutes, Bergman entered, saw Sam. She had to know right then, Earle thought. Rick was back in her life. The bar was called Rick's Café Americain and Sam was Rick's best friend. Sam knew too the heartache she brought. Earle could see it in Sam's face. Sam must have been thinking, run boss! Later he would beg Rick to leave. "Please, boss, let's go. There ain't nothing but trouble for you here. We'll take the car and drive all night. We'll get drunk. We'll go fishing and stay away until she's gone."

But Rick waited for a woman. He made Sam play "As Time Goes By."

Earle's hands rested on his knees. Hoffman had taken the armrest. She stared at the screen, the changing light brightening then shadowing her features.

Bergman walked into Rick's. "Can I tell you a story?" she asked Rick.

"Does it got a wow finish?" he said.

"I don't know the finish yet."

I don't know the finish either, thought Earle. He felt Bogart's pain in his loss of expression. Despite his tough-guy posturing, it was all there beneath. And the film played on, uneditable, inevitable, like history. He wondered what the script of the evening held for him. Was there a preordained crash coming? Was his *Hindenburg* moving toward the docking tower, with him on board instead of those poor, doomed people? But, gradually, as the film clicked on, he forgot about Hoffman sitting next to him and Durance behind. He forgot about the other people in the theater. They were all in Casablanca, holding letters of transit close to their hearts, bargaining with bitterness for love. Ignoring the Nazi Major Strasser and his arrogance. Ignoring the pain in the world around them, until the passion became too much. Laszlo lead the café's band in "La Marseillaise," overwhelming the Germans' singing of "Die Wacht am Rhein." Even Yvonne, Bogart's spurned lover who came to the bar with a German officer on her arm joined in, tears on her cheeks. Bergman looked at her driven husband across the room, who was not thinking of himself or her or of love, but of his occupied France and the German heel in its back. It was an instant where Earle often paused the film to look at Bergman's eyes. The world was in them, filled with respect for Laszlo's courage, with admiration. Anyone would give a lifetime to earn the look that Bergman considered him with, and Laszlo didn't know. He sang the song to its end, the expatriates in the café on their feet, for a moment joined in emotion.

But Earle couldn't pause the film. It rolled on. "Viva la France!" they roared. "Viva La France!"

Like he had a hundred times before, Renault closed the café under Strasser's orders. Bogart said, "How can they close me up? On what grounds?" Renault said, "I'm shocked, shocked to find that gambling is going on here." Just then the croupier handed Renault a handful of cash. "Your winnings sir." The audience laughed, which woke Earle to his mission. He broke his gaze from the screen. The woman in the floral dress didn't laugh. Her posture was tense. Earle could see she was mesmerized. What's going to happen next? she must be thinking. Her life was involved now, like the audience to any worthwhile story. What's going to happen?

In a few minutes, Bergman would wait for Bogart in his apartment. She'd plead for the letters. Finally, she'd pull a gun on him. "Go ahead and shoot," he'd say. "You'll be doing me a favor." She will put the gun down. "Richard, I tried to stay away. I thought I would never see you again, that you were out of my life." She'll weep. "The day you left Paris, if you knew what I went through. If you knew how much I loved you, how much I still love you." They'd kiss.

Why didn't Bogart see what she was doing? Earle thought. The Bulgarian girl not ten minutes earlier in the film had said, "If someone loved you very much so that your happiness was the only thing she wanted in the world, and she did a bad thing to make certain of it, could you forgive her?"

But that was the beauty. Bogart didn't. He couldn't replay the Bulgarian girl's words. He couldn't edit what Bergman said to him, nor could he tinker with his own heart. Maybe by the end of the film he figured it out, but right then, Bogart went with his own emotions. He forgot his anger and held her, Bergman, with her luminous eyes and high cheekbones and smile like a sunrise.

Hoffman whispered. "You didn't tell me the film had a sense of humor."

Earle felt her breath in his ear, her hand on his arm. "It has irony," he whispered back, keenly aware that Durance sat behind them. Did Bogart send Bergman off with Henreid at the end of the film because he knew she didn't love him? Was he that keen-sighted? And how did he know?

What was Hoffman thinking? Did she care for him in the least?

Earle forced himself to look away from the screen again. He was here to experience *Casablanca* in a world where it hadn't existed before. He had a job to do.

The woman in the floral dress held a handkerchief to her cheek, not moving. Her face was wet with tears. Henreid asked Bergman about the time she thought he was dead. "Were you lonely in Paris?" he asked. "I know how it is to be lonely," he said. Was Henreid forgiving Bergman for the affair with Bogart without even knowing about it? The woman in the floral dress sobbed silently. What was her story? Was her husband at war? Did she believe him to be dead? Even now, was there a lover?

Earle watched, awed. How seldom had he been able to feel the world through someone else. The bend of her wrist. The handkerchief's dangling end. The quiet, wracking sobs that shook her sides. How privileged he felt to be a part of her moment. What a moment of trespass on his part. Everything he hoped for in coming to see *Casablanca* was encompassed by this scene. This would be bigger than his *Hindenburg* experience.

He looked away, blinking against a momentary sting. It didn't take much to see that his problems didn't amount to—he sought for a comparison, then smiled—a hill of beans. It was Bogart's line. Whatever the woman in the floral dress was going through, his own anxieties couldn't measure up. Earle couldn't know Hoffman's mind any more than Bogart knew Bergman's, and in this time he couldn't edit in messages from her or create pictures of the two of them at romantic vacation stops, or even replay their times together. He was a time traveler stuck in the ever-present and always receding now with the people around him an enigma, like the woman in the floral dress.

On the screen, Bergman slipped away from her motel room to meet Bogart, to tell him of her life after she married Laszlo, how she thought Laszlo was dead when she'd met Bogart in Paris. Earle slid his arm out from under Hoffman's hand, then walked to the rear of the theater. From the back, he could see all the still heads. Earlier in the film he'd heard conversation, but now there was nothing but Bogart and Bergman's voices. Bergman buried her head in Bogart's shoulder. She said the line: "I ran away from you once, I can't do it again."

Earle nodded. He'd seen this moment over and over. It seemed to him that Bergman was exactly torn. She loved her husband, but she also loved Bogart. It was a perfect scene, balancing the two men she loved against the sureness that she would have to leave one behind. Maybe she believed that Laszlo really lived for his work and could go on without her, or maybe she knew that no matter what happened, if she demonstrated her love for Laszlo by deserting him for another man that she had done the right thing. There was no way to tell. Regardless, she chose Bogart and set him in motion for the end of the film.

Who was the audience rooting for? Laszlo seemed a bit of a cold fish, but he was absolutely blameless in his love for his wife and devotion to his anti-Nazism. Bogart was flawed and scarred, but his passion for Bergman redeemed him. And now, in the time the audience watched, France was still occupied. The Vichy government still danced to Germany's pipes. Soldiers were dying over what song the people would sing, "Die Wacht Am Rhine" or "La Marseillaise."

Earle moved to where he could see more of the audience. He imagined how the sequence would replay when he downloaded the nanotech recordings. The noisy projector clicking away in the background. The feel of plush beneath his hands. The hint of rain held in wet coats dripping onto the floor.

Now came the plan, the thinking that Bogart did for Bergman. Bergman believed she was leaving Casablanca with Bogart. They went to the airport. Bogart told Renault to fill out the letters of transit with Laszlo and Bergman's name. Bergman was confused. Bogart explained, the time travelers lament, that if she didn't leave she would regret it, "Maybe not today, maybe not tomorrow, but soon and for the rest of your life." The plane took off. Major Strasser was shot. Bogart and Renault walk into the fog together.

Earle closed his eyes and leaned against the wall. The soundtrack boomed out "La Marseillaise." People clapped. He opened his eyes. Some of the audience was standing, applauding the screen as the curtains closed and the lights came up. They kept clapping. Even though there were no live performers to appreciate their reaction, they applauded. Finally, they turned, gathered their umbrellas and coats to head toward the exits.

"I loved that," said a woman to her companion as they passed Earle on the way out. "Who would have believed Bogart could play a romantic lead?" said another.

Hoffman walked up the aisle, the houselights catching the shimmer in her hair. "You were right to come here. I had no idea," she said, her hand brushing his as she passed. "I'll see you in the lobby." She nodded back into the nearly empty theater.

Only Durance and the woman in the floral dress remained. Durance stood next to her, leaning down over where she was seated, speaking earnestly.

Earle glanced to the exit. Hoffman was already gone. He walked down the aisle toward Durance and the woman. It wasn't until Earle was close enough to touch them that Durance looked up.

"She seemed upset," said Durance.

"I'm better now, really," said the woman. She'd dried her face, but her mascara had smudged. "I don't know what came over me."

"I understand," said Durance. "Look," he said to Earle. "You were right." He fumbled for words, "I didn't think a film . . . it wasn't sentimental." He inhaled deeply, and in the exhalation was a hint of an emotional quiver. "They're doing the show again, aren't they, in a half hour?"

Earle nodded.

"And it will be exactly the same, won't it? They can't change it?" said Durance. The woman looked at him quizzically.

Earle understood. The film would always play out the same way. Like the *Hin-*

denburg. Like all of history, unrolling in its immutable way. That was its charm. "Yes," he said. "Of course."

Durance took a seat next to the woman. "We thought we'd see it again." He gestured toward the exits. "Could you pay for our tickets?" Durance and the woman faced the screen, waiting for the lights to go down and the curtain to open.

In the lobby, Hoffman stood by the door. They stepped onto the sidewalk without speaking, where the rain had slowed to a gentle patter, hinting of snow. A block later, while they waited to cross the street, Hoffman said, "It was a good story."

She was looking into the distance. Not at him.

"Yes," he said.

"It had a good finish."

"Yes."

As they crossed, Hoffman took his arm. He realized she hadn't brought her umbrella. Water ran off the edges of her hat. She said, "What should we do now?"

When they reached the sidewalk, she still held his arm.

Earle thought of Bogart walking into the fog with Renault. It *was* a good ending, a wow finish. Earle said, "I hear that Cab Calloway is playing at the Park Central."

Hoffman smiled in a lingering way that seemed very much like Ingrid Bergman. "Do you know how to dance?"

A passing car splashed water on their legs. Earle didn't care. They had another twenty hours or so in New York, in the city that never sleeps. Meanwhile, in *Casablanca*, Sam sang at his piano, the old song, Bogart's and Bergman's song. Everybody's song.

It's true, Earle thought as the rain came down, as the water gurgled in the gutters, as the undersides of clouds glowing in New York's evening lights twisted slowly above. Sam was right: it's still the same old story, and it would always be, as time goes by.

THE INN AT MOUNT EITHER

AFTER A MINUTE SPENT WEIGHING A FEAR OF APPEARING FOOLISH AGAINST his anxiety, Dorian approached the concierge. Behind the glassy mahogany of the concierge's booth, through the floor to ceiling windows, the afternoon clouds swept toward them across the neighboring peaks. As always, the view was spectacular. The sun cast long shadows through the valleys while the racing clouds caressed the mountain tops before swallowing them in gray, whale-like immensity, and when the clouds parted, the mountains would be the same but different, just a little, changed by their time in the clouds. That's why people always looked. Are the mountains the same, they seemed to say, or have they changed?

If Dorian stood at the window, he could peer down the mountain at the long, railed walkways that connected one section of the inn to the next. Curved glass covered some of the walkways so the guests could pass in comfort from the casinos to the restaurants, or from the workout facilities to the spas, or from the tennis courts to the pools, but others were open and guests could walk in the unencumbered mountain air, their hands sliding along guard rails with nothing but the thought of distance between them and the rocks in the sightless haze below.

Dorian cleared his throat. "I can't find my wife, Stephanie Wallace." His fingers rested on the polished wood.

Without raising his head from the clipboard he'd been studying, the concierge looked at him. "It's a big inn, sir. When did you see her last?" The man's eyebrows had a distinctively rakish look to them, turning up at the ends like a handlebar moustache, and his hair was silvery-gray.

"We were supposed to meet for lunch, but she didn't show up." Dorian glanced into the lobby, hoping that she might appear. Behind him, the room towered fifty feet to skylights. Opposite the window, the mountain's rocky side made another wall. Exotic plants that would never grow outside of the inn's protection filled every nook, spilling vegetation over the deep-toned stone.

The concierge put the clipboard on the booth. "Perhaps her plans changed, sir. There's much to do here at Mount Either."

Dorian gritted his teeth. "*Yesterday's* lunch! I've been looking for her since last night. Stephanie's not *late*. She's *gone*."

"It won't help for you to be short with me, sir. What is your room number?"

"4128."

The concierge tapped at a personal digital assistant that nestled in his palm. "This is your wife, sir?" A picture of a smiling blonde woman, glasses slid part way down her nose, peered back at Dorian from the screen.

"Yes." She'd worn her glasses on the airplane. Once they checked in, she switched to contacts.

"I show that she's still a guest."

Resisting an urge to throttle the man, Dorian said, "I know that. What I want is some help in finding her. Can't you ask the other employees to keep an eye out?"

"Of course, sir. But, as I said before, this is a big inn. Maybe she wants some privacy. Perhaps she's admiring one of our many gardens. She wouldn't be the first guest to spend a few uncounted hours sitting on a meditation vista. In fact, getting lost at the inn is a selling point. We advertise it. 'Lose yourself in the experience.'"

"It's not supposed to be literal!" snapped Dorian.

The concierge picked up the clipboard again. "I will alert the staff. You don't suppose she went through a transitionway unaccompanied, do you?"

Dorian felt himself blanching. "No, of course not." But he remembered how she'd lingered yesterday morning in the Polynesian hallway.

"Guests are to be escorted through the shift zones."

"I'm sure she wouldn't do that."

The concierge sniffed. "We're very specific in our agreement when you signed in. The management will respond strongly to guests who ignore the rules."

Dorian turned away from the concierge. A new tramload of tourists had arrived, pulling their suitcases behind them. Most were couples. Newlyweds, by the look, or retired folk. A pack of bellboys scurried to meet them, while a mellow-voiced recording intoned, "Welcome to the Inn at Mount Either. You are standing in the new lobby, two hundred and fifty feet above the historical first lobby built on the site of where Mount Either's special properties were discovered. If you are interested in a guided visit to the old lobby, dial 19 on your room phone."

"If she did go . . ." said Dorian. A hand seemed to be grasping his throat. It was all he could do to croak out, ". . . unescorted?"

The concierge said, "It's a *big* inn, sir. We will do all we can to help, but we don't really count a guest as missing until forty-eight hours have passed."

Dorian didn't know what to say. He drummed his fingers on the counter. Some of the new arrivals were at the window, looking down. The glass leaned away from the mountain, and the lobby itself protruded like a shelf, so they had an unimpeded view of the two thousand foot drop and the rest of the inn on this side of the peak, clinging to the sheer face.

"I can't wait that long. I'm going to look for her myself."

"That is your privilege, sir," said the concierge. "I'm sure she's just around the corner. Nothing stays lost here forever."

The elevator to the Polynesian transition they had visited yesterday was out of order. Dorian looked both ways down the long, curving hall, but there wasn't another elevator. The inn's maps were almost impossible to read since the inn itself was aggressively three-dimensional, riddled with elevators, stairs, ramps, sloping halls, ladders, bridges and multilevel rooms. They'd followed a guide to the Polynesian transition, but none were in sight now. Dorian went left, around the curved hall.

Finally, he reached a stairwell that spiraled down for fifty steps. He didn't recognize the hall it emptied into, but a distinctive arrow in blue and yellow pointed toward a transition. Yesterday, as they approached the zone, the wallpaper had changed from the art deco they'd grown used to, to a palm and beach motif. Following the guide, he'd held Stephanie's hand until they stepped through the transition's door and into a Polynesian mountainscape.

"You're lucky, today, folks," said the guide. "I don't think I've ever seen it looking this good."

The sun pouring through the open veranda spread heat like a warm flush on their skin. Stephanie's hand drifted from his own, and she walked to the platform's edge as if in a dream.

"Oh, Dorian," she'd said. Instead of the snow-capped mountains of the Inn at Mount Either, a series of rounded hills rose in front of them, covered with forest so thick that it was hard to imagine ground beneath it. A flock of long-necked birds wheeled below, skimming the treetops and crying out to one another. She'd stared into the distance, entranced, her blonde hair just brushing her shoulders, and for a moment he saw the young woman he'd married twenty years earlier, the jaunty athleticism in her posture, the grace in her wrists and hands.

A waiter in a flowered shirt offered them drinks off a platter.

"Can you smell it?" Stephanie said, delighted. "It's the ocean."

And Dorian could smell salt and sand under the rich vegetable forest. Stephanie loved the ocean and all that was associated with it, the seals and birds and spiny creatures crawling in tidal pools, and the way the waves slid underneath her bare toes. Her passions were intense. She'd spend hours studying art or collecting children's literature or working with other people's kids. Once she'd gotten hypothermia in a mountain stream while sorting through rocks on her hands and knees. "I thought there might be quartz crystals," she'd said through the shivers. She laughed often.

Stephanie hadn't wanted to leave the overlook. The hotel guide finally had to insist. "My shift ended twenty minutes ago, ma'am. Perhaps you can come back another day if it's still here." Then he took them back through the hallway and into the inn they had left. "This was one of the original shift zones," he'd said as they walked back to the main lobby. "They found it third."

"How marvelous it must have been," Stephanie said. "I can imagine them climbing the mountain. Squeezing through a crevice, and there they were." She looked behind them.

Dorian rushed down the corridor. He remembered fewer doors in the hallway yesterday, and the carpet had been a different color. Closing his eyes for a second, he tried to picture the inn's structure. The elevator had only gone down a couple of floors, which was about the same distance the spiral stairs had taken him, but nothing looked the same. Maybe he was in a parallel passage. He passed another blue and yellow arrow. The decor changed from dark-polished woods and brass fixtures to natural pine siding. A long mural of a desert canyon rimmed with cactus covered one wall. Then the hall ended at a door, a rough-hewn, heavy-planked structure marked by a solid iron handle to open it instead of a doorknob.

It was a transition way, but not the one from yesterday. Still, it was close. Maybe Stephanie had come down this path. The elevator might have been out of order for her too. Dorian took a deep breath and opened the door.

On the other side, a wooden bridge reached an open platform. Drooping ropes hung from thick posts that lined the bridge's side, serving as protection from the drop into the depths below. Dorian leaned on the rope at the platform's edge. The general shape of the mountains was the same, but no snow covered the peaks. The sun glared, radiating off slick-rock, dark with streaks of desert varnish. He shaded his eyes to look up the mountain. Wood structures covered most of the slope, all light-colored pine. For a moment nothing looked familiar, then he spotted the main lobby buttressed by tree-thick pylons jutting from the mountain.

A man wearing a cowboy hat and a leather fringed shirt joined him at the edge. "First time to Mount Either?" he said.

"Yes," said Dorian, confused. "How could you tell?"

"Your duds. Not quite in the motif, pard." He smiled, a gold tooth flashing in the sun, then glanced at his watch, a large-faced instrument ringed with turquoise. "You going to the barbeque? I'm going to find my wife and head that way. Gosh, I love the grub you get here." His leather boots clacked against the wood flooring as he headed to the stairs.

Dorian was alone on the platform again. "I'm looking for my wife too," he said. Overhead a lone bird circled. He thought, is that a buzzard?

A tram like a large ore cart glided past the platform, heading down. Cowboy-hatted tourists sat at one end, while a pile of saddles and bridles filled the other. At the bottom of the ravine where the tram's cable ended at a tiny building, a dozen horses no larger than grains of rice milled about in a corral.

The set of stairs that gold-tooth had ascended looked like they led to the main lobby. Dorian took the steps two at a time. If Stephanie had come this way, she hadn't returned. Would she have realized right away that she was lost? Would she have gone to the lobby for directions? She could be there even now, maybe sipping a cool drink at one of the many, nearby cafes.

But at the top of the stairs were three passages, and none of them looked like they headed up. Dorian paused. If he chose the wrong way, he could become lost himself. A bellboy in flannel shirt tucked into jeans, carrying a tray of dirty dishes on one hand above his shoulder, came out of one hallway.

"How do I get to the lobby?" said Dorian.

The bellboy transferred the heavy tray with practiced ease. His suntanned face crinkled into a weathered smile. "Right hallway until you come to the elevator. The button is marked."

Dorian nodded, then started forward.

"My right," said the bellboy as he descended the stairs.

In the lobby, Dorian took a moment to orient himself. It wasn't that this sage-scented lobby was completely different; it was the similarities that threw him off. The same tall window gazing out on the desery-looking mountains, the same exposed rock making one wall, a familiar reception desk dominating the room's center, but all the materials were different: hand-hewed timbers replaced the slick chrome support beams, big-looped throw rugs covered the plank floor where before he'd walked on expensive carpet, but what was most disorienting was the concierge, whose distinctive upward-flaring eyebrows and silver-gray hair waited for him at the reception desk as Dorian crossed the room.

"Thank goodness," said Dorian. "I wanted to find the Polynesian transition, but I ended up here instead."

"Excuse me, sir?" said the concierge. His expression was completely bland. No recognition at all.

"It's me, Dorian Wallace. I told you ten minutes ago that I was looking for my wife, Stephanie."

"I'm sorry, sir. You have me at a disadvantage."

"We talked. You said nothing stays lost forever."

The concierge shook his head. "Maybe I was thinking about something else when we chatted. What room did you say you were in?"

The situation was ludicrous. In the window behind the concierge, the sun blasted the peaks. No snow. No smoothly curved walkways stretching from wing to wing. Just heavy rope and solid wood and thick iron cable strapping the structures to the mountain. It was like an 1860 version of Dodge City turned vertical. "I'm from the real Inn at Mount Either. I'm in one of its rooms."

The concierge's forehead wrinkled. "This is the real Inn at Mount Either, sir."

Dorian stepped back. The man looked similar, but the business suit Dorian remembered had been replaced with a leather jacket, and where the silk tie had hung before, a silver clasp held a black bolo. Something about his face was different too. More wrinkles maybe? More silver in the hair? Suddenly Dorian was sure that they would have no record of his registration, and he realized he'd gone through a transition without a guide. What had the first concierge told him about management "responding strongly" to guests who ignored the rules?

Keeping the panic out of his voice, Dorian said, "My fault. I mistook you for someone else." He forced a smile. "There's so many employees here."

Nodding, the concierge turned his attention to a stack of papers on the desk. "This is a big inn, sir. Perfectly understandable."

On the way out of the lobby, Dorian paused. Had he come up a short flight of stairs to enter, or had the hallway been on the same level? At the foot of the stairs a mineral gift shop offered its wares on wooden trays inside its door. He vaguely remembered passing something like that, but he'd been in a hurry. Had he?

On an impulse, he entered the shop. Rocks and crystals of all kinds filled the shelves. "I'm looking for my wife," he said to the man behind the counter. "She might have been in here yesterday." Dorian showed him a photo from his wallet.

The man hooked his thumbs in the top of his overalls and leaned to look at the picture. "Yep, Stephanie, I know her. She liked the amethyst. I figure she spent an hour hunting for a good specimen."

Dorian caught the edge of the counter to keep from falling. His legs had no strength. He looked at the crate overflowing with purple crystals.

"Didn't buy anything, though. I offered her iron pyrite, fool's gold. She said if she couldn't have the real thing, she couldn't be happy." The man smiled. "Besides, she said her husband sometimes buys her gifts, and she didn't want to spoil his fun."

"Which way did she go?"

"Didn't really notice. Down the hallway, I reckon."

Dorian dashed to the door, then looked the way the man had indicated, as if there might be a chance to see her still. But the hall was empty. He glanced up the stairs into the lobby. The concierge was talking to a couple of men wearing six-shooters and badges. Security? The concierge pointed toward Dorian.

"Thanks," he called to the mineral shop man.

"Nice lady. I hope you find her."

The elevator at the end of the hall was not the same one he'd ridden up, but he didn't want to talk to security, so he rode it down to the transition level he'd come from. When he stepped out, the doors closed, and the elevator returned to the lobby.

Were they really after him?

After a couple confusing turns down hallways that didn't look the least bit familiar, Dorian stepped onto an open-air bridge that ended at a platform overlooking the canyon. He breathed easier. A quick dash down the transitionway, and he'd be home, but the long cables that carried the tram he'd seen earlier to the ravine's bottom were next to a platform a hundred yards farther away. An updraft ruffled his hair and dried the sweat on his face instantly. Wrong platform. The problem was how to get from the platform he was on to the one that he'd come from without retracing his steps?

He crossed the bridge back to the mountain where three choices waited: the hallway he'd exited from, a short ramp to another hallway, and a set of stairs that at least headed toward the other platform. At the top of the stairs, a blue and yellow arrow pointed in the right direction.

But the hallway's transition theme was heavy stone work, like castle fortifications, and on the door's other side, towering spires and crenelated restraining walls lined the paths. He'd missed the transition back to where he'd started. A dozen flights of stairs, two ramps and an elevator ride took him to another transition, clearly not the right one, but he needed to get back to the Inn at Mount Either he'd come from. Passing through transitions without a guide, he thought ruefully. I'm probably racking up room charges of astronomical proportions.

The next transition felt vaguely Arabic. He ran into a fellow in a rush going through the door in the opposite direction.

"Sorry, my fault," said Dorian at the same time the other man said the same thing. He only had a moment to notice the fellow was wearing the same kind of pants and shirt he wore before they dashed their separate ways.

The next had a rainforest look, but he recognized none of the birds that flew past the walkways. A blue and yellow arrow pointed down a hallway lined with jungle plants and short vines that dangled from the ceiling. He hurried past the closed doors until the hallway curved and the decor on the wall changed from matted vegetation to slick aluminum and recessed light fixtures. He pulled the door at the end of the transition zone open with relief.

The door closed behind him.

The lights were out.

He took a few steps into the darkness, then waited for his eyes to adjust. Slowly, the scene became clear. He choked back a gasp. Nothing separated him from the two-thousand-foot drop to the bottom of the canyon. For a heart-stopping moment, he felt suspended, as if at any second he would drop to the rocks in an unstoppable plunge, but he didn't fall. His hands out, he shuffled forward. The floor wasn't perfectly invisible. He could see now that a walkway leapt to an opaque platform before him, and to each side, no more than an arm reach away, nearly transparent walls and ceiling enclosed him. It reminded him of an aquarium he'd visited once, where the visitors could walk in a glass tunnel right through the water. Sharks and rays swam above and below, and the illusion of being underwater was nearly perfect. Except the illusion here was that he floated in space. Dorian looked up. Stars glinted back at him with unblinking brilliance. He'd never seen a night sky so clean-edged. On the horizon, a quarter moon cast a clear, cold light on the mountain peaks in the distance, and its silver hue glinted off the Inn at Mount Either's structures that wrapped tight around the mountain above him, but it wasn't the Mount Either he'd left. Glass and metal flowed smoothly around the contours, seamlessly leading from wall to window to walkway to elevator, and the dim light of the glass told him of the inn's life behind.

Afraid for his balance, Dorian moved back to the door like a man on ice. He tugged, but the handle didn't stir. A lighted sign in red appeared above: SORRY, TEMPORARILY OUT OF SERVICE.

After tight-roping his way across the glass walkway, Dorian found himself in a vista room. A line of comfortably padded couches faced the window and the star-studded night outside. Illuminated by the partial moon, people sat in most of the couches, staring silently at the view. He looked out. Moonlight bathed the nearest mountain in grays and blues. Shadows, like black swaths of velvet, outlined ridges and rocks and filled crevices. Dorian took an empty couch and settled in its deep embrace. Yesterday, when Stephanie missed lunch, he'd sat in the restaurant for an extra hour, and he knew something was wrong. He told himself that she must have forgotten, but that wasn't like her. Using the inn's maps as best he could—the inn's structure was complicated—he'd searched the gyms and shops, the salons and museums, hour by hour, panic building.

He realized that this was the first time he'd rested in the last twenty-four hours. Dorian closed his eyes, just for a minute, he thought.

He dreamed of Stephanie. They were in a boat crossing a broad lake. Behind them he could make out a line of trees and a distant dock, but the other shore was lost in mist. Water slapped at the bow, and the air smelled of fish and wet wood. "You're so far away," she said. Dorian wanted to weep. "I know," he said. "I know, but I'm trying to find you." He was dreaming, and he could feel the couch he was sitting in, and he could imagine the people sitting around him, staring at the night-lit mountain, but he also felt the hard wooden bench and the boat's gentle motion. "Where are you, Stephanie?" In the dream, she laughed the way she always laughed, an honest burst of humor that animated her face and eyes. She said, "No, I mean you're so far away in the boat." Dorian braced himself, lifted his feet over the seat in between them, then slid forward. Their knees touched. Stephanie placed her hands palms up on her knees. Leaning, Dorian covered them with his own.

"Your hands are so warm," she said.

Dorian kept still, his fingers resting on her wrists, her pulse beating beneath them.

Stephanie looked upon the water, the long line of ripples moving past them, breathing quietly. She said, "I could float here forever. I don't have to be going anywhere." The boat rocked, and it was like the lake stroking them. She met his gaze. "If you are with me."

A voice said, "It's beginning."

Dorian opened his eyes, and Stephanie disappeared. For a moment, he imagined the couch moved, as if the floor was the surface of a black lake, but that feeling faded, leaving him with the memory so vivid of her pulse in his fingertips and the way her lips parted when she laughed that he wondered for a second if she'd actually been there before him.

"It's beginning," an elderly woman in the couch next to him said again. Her arms looked frail, but her voice was firm.

"What?" said Dorian.

"Shhh!" she said, and hunched forward, all her attention directed out the window.

At first Dorian thought the mountain was catching fire. A flicker of red glinted from the middle of a cliff. Then it spread over the length of the rock, a brilliant, deep red like an electric ruby.

"My God," someone said. Someone else sighed.

The red spread to neighboring cliffs, but now the center glimmered with yellow, and a few seconds later almost all the red had been replaced by the yellow glow.

Leaning toward the woman next to him, Dorian said, "What is that?"

"Just spectacular," she said.

"No, what is it?"

She didn't look at him. "Refracted moonlight on the crystals. It's only this good a couple times a year, and only from this spot. No other mountain in the world does this, and if this room were any other place, we wouldn't see it. The moon has to be in the right phase."

Now the yellow light enveloped the entire mountain, except at the bottom, which had acquired a purple tint that crawled up the cliffs until the yellow vanished. Purple was Stephanie's color, the color of amethyst.

"There were clouds in the spring. We missed it," the old woman said, then she started crying.

Dorian sat with his hands in his lap, unsure of what to do.

"My husband was with me then. We'd never been here before." She wiped her tears before looking at him for the first time. Her eyes reflected the purple from the mountain. "It's just a superstition, I know, but they say if you see the lights with someone you love, they will be with you forever."

Gradually the purple vanished. The edges of a few of the larger rock faces glinted green for a moment. Finally, the mountain looked like it had when he entered the room. People rose from the couches and headed for the exits. Many were couples holding hands. The old woman didn't move. She'd wrapped her arms across her chest, as if she were hugging herself. Her knuckles were large and arthritic. She said, "I hope you come back when it isn't cloudy. I hope you come back with someone you love."

A chill swept the back of Dorian's head. "I'm looking for her."

She shrank a little deeper into her chair. "Not me. I'm waiting."

At the other end of the room, a bellboy bent to talk to a young couple still sitting. They smiled back at him, then each showed him a small piece of plastic. In the room, lit only by reflected moonlight, Dorian couldn't tell what the plastic was. The bellboy moved to the next lodger, who also showed him a plastic card. There were only a few people between Dorian and the bellboy when Dorian recognized that they were displaying their room keys. His own key didn't look like the ones they showed.

"What's the problem?" said a woman as she put her key back in her pocket.

"Nothing of concern, ma'am. A security issue, misplaced guest."

Dorian slipped out of the room and into a passageway. Half of the wall was transparent, like the entrance bridge near the transition, except the ceiling glowed to provide dim light. He followed the gentle curve and had walked for several minutes when an acetylene-bright brilliance flushed the hall into overexposed surfaces and shadows. He blinked against the glare before shading his eyes. From the mountain's base, the light grew more intense, until, soundlessly, a rocket, balanced on a flaming pillar, rose past him and streaked into the night.

He heard the people in the hall before he saw them, but short of turning back the way he came, there was no way to avoid them. They laughed and joked loudly. At first Dorian thought they must be going to a masquerade. All wore bulky suits and carried helmets under their arms.

"I've never been outside," said a young man with glasses and a moustache.

"Just don't sit on something sharp," said his motherly-looking companion. "And be sure to listen to the safety procedures. Depressurization is nothing to fool around with."

They were too preoccupied to acknowledge Dorian as they clumped past.

When they vanished around the curve, Dorian stopped, put his hand on the glass wall, and looked out again. The stars never had seemed so sharp and unblinking, and, he noticed, there was no vegetation he could see. None at all. The landscape was as desolate and bare as the—he paused as he made the comparison—as the moon, but there was the moon, nearly resting on the horizon. He shivered. Every transition at Mount Either took the guests to an exotic location, but it had never occurred to him to wonder *how* exotic. This is Earth, he thought, isn't it? Clearly Earth! But what happened to it?

The mountains weren't just dead. They were swept clean and bare, like a planet's skeleton, solid, smooth, dry and with no ability to shrug themselves into life. He pressed his forehead against the glass and shut his eyes. Where was Stephanie? She'd be taking pictures. She'd be stopping at every new view, her head cocked a little to the side, as if she were measuring the world for a painting. She'd tell him about what she'd found, and if he was quiet for too long, she'd say, "What are you thinking?" and genuinely want to know.

Dorian pushed away from the glass and continued walking, slowly at first, but soon with a purposeful stride. At a junction he chose the hallway whose stairs led toward the lobby. An elevator took him up, and when the doors opened, a bellboy stood on the other side. The bellboy, wearing a silk vest that sported a shiny name tag that read, NED, CAN I HELP?, held a personal digital assistant in one hand with Dorian's face on the screen.

"I'm Dorian Wallace."

The bellboy checked the image in his hand. "Heavens, you *are* Dorian Wallace! Thank goodness, sir. Your wife has been worried sick. Everyone has been looking for you."

Dorian's hand flew to his heart, and he clenched his shirt in a fist. "You know where Stephanie is?"

Two short hallways later, they were in the lobby; the same long window that seemed so familiar looked out on the moonlit mountains. Dorian's pulse pounded and his face felt hot. The same cliff face covered with plants made the back wall, and, Dorian thought, the same concierge, his handlebar eyebrows pointing upwards, waited at the reception desk. But he wasn't the same. Similar, but not the same. Shorter, perhaps? A little broader in the shoulders?

Stephanie stepped out from behind the concierge.

Wordlessly they embraced. Dorian held her tightly, his cheek pressing against the side of her head. She trembled in his arms. For a moment, all centered on her, on the feel of her breathing against him, of her fingers on his back. The smell of her skin. The texture of her blouse.

For a moment, all was perfect.

But she stiffened——he could feel it in her muscles—and she pushed away.

Stephanie looked at him, her hands still holding his. Dorian studied her. Where

Stephanie's hair had been curled, it now hung straight. Where her eyes had been blue with tiny white spokes, they were now blue with tinges of green.

"Who are you?" the woman asked.

"I'm Dorian. Who are you?" He released her hands, and they hung in place where he'd left them. She took a single step back.

"Oh, no," said the concierge. "This is distressing."

"Where's my husband?" the woman said. "Where's my Dorian?"

The concierge took a position between them. "The inn is not at fault here. It doesn't happen this way. If you'll come with me, sir." He took Dorian by the elbow and walked away from the reception desk. "How many transitions did you go through?" he whispered harshly.

"I . . . maybe . . ."

"You went through at least two, didn't you?"

Dorian stopped, pulled his arm away from the concierge. "The damn inn is so confusing that anybody can get lost. Give me a guide, and I'll be happy to go back to where I belong."

"It's a *big* inn. How many?" The concierge wasn't smiling, and he didn't look friendly in the least.

"What does it matter? Five or six, I think."

The concierge blanched. "You don't understand, sir. There are nine transition zones."

"So?"

"When you go through one, you come out at different Inns at Mount Either. Each inn has nine transition zones too. Nine different ones. When you go through two transitions, there are eighty-one different inns you might have come from. If you went through five . . ." He paused, closing his eyes for a second. They popped open. "You could have come from any one of 59,049 realities. If you went through six, we'd have over a half million possibilities." He grabbed Dorian's elbow again with urgency. "Where did you come from to get here?"

Dorian winced and found himself half walking and half trotting. "A jungle, I think. Ouch! What's the hurry?"

They reached an elevator. The concierge punched the button. Then he punched it again. "Zone drift. When you go through a zone, the door you came from is the way back for two or three hours, but if you wait too long, the place you came from isn't there anymore. It'll be another version of the inn. It might even be a really, really close version of the one you came from, but it won't be the same one. If you didn't dawdle in any of the zones, though, you should be okay."

Dorian glanced at his watch. When had he gone through the first transition?

The elevator door opened. "Jungle?" asked the concierge.

Dorian nodded. "Another version? Like a parallel world?"

The concierge grunted as the elevator started down. "Um, sort of. We prefer to call them non-convergent. There's a lot of variation."

"But the door to the jungle is out of order. I would have gone back through it on my own."

"We locked all the doors when we realized a guest was making unguided transitions."

Dorian followed the concierge, who made turns down hallways and chose stairwells with practiced confidence. They crossed the transparent bridge, but now the door was lit and they passed into the rainforest transition Dorian remembered.

"Okay, how did you get here?" The concierge reached behind a curtain of vines hanging next to the wall, and pulled a phone from a hatch behind.

"From a kind of a desert world, I think."

The concierge's forehead furrowed in frustration.

"I'm sure it was desert, like the Arabian Nights."

He said something into the phone, then listened to the reply.

They hurried around a hallway's long curve. Dorian hadn't looked at the scenery the first time through, but now he noticed solid vegetable weaves that made the walls, and the sweaty smell of wet wood and dripping leaves.

"How come you are here? I mean, you're just like the concierge from the inn that I came from."

They trotted up a flight of stairs, crossed a dizzying walkway over a ravine and entered a small court circled with open booths. Guests sat on stools drinking from tall bamboo cups or coconuts with straws stuck in them. An elevator rendition of jungle music played softly in the background.

"I'm everywhere," said the concierge. "So's your wife. So are you. That's the problem. You are lost, and so are about a zillion non-convergent versions of you wandering about the inn where they don't belong. Of course, there are a lot of you who didn't get lost either. The worlds aren't parallel. At least your wife had the wit to come back through the same doors she exited."

"She has a pretty good sense of direction." Dorian shook his head. "I didn't come this way. I don't remember this."

"Short cuts. Your clock is ticking. With any luck, another version of me is hustling another version of you, the right one, back to my lobby where that woman you met is waiting. How long has it been since you went through the first transition?"

"I'm sure it hasn't been two hours yet." When had he started looking?

"Good. We should make it without any trouble."

Finally they entered a transition with a western theme, rough textured pine walls and the smell of cactus.

"This is the first zone I entered."

The concierge sighed and smiled for the first time since Dorian talked to him in the lobby. "Fifteen minutes back for me. Piece of cake. From here, all I need is your room key."

Looking at the key, the concierge plucked another phone from a hidden niche. He read a string of numbers into the mouthpiece.

Minutes later, they stood at the transition back to the inn Dorian had come from. The concierge put out his hand. "I'm glad that I could help you, sir. A bellboy on the other side will escort you to the lobby, where I'm sure your wife will be glad to see you." He paused. "We've always said that a guest should lose himself in the experience."

Dorian grimaced. "I didn't think that was funny the first time I heard it."

When he entered the lobby, he spotted Stephanie right away. Her back was to him, but her blonde hair, lightly curled at the end, barely touching her shoulders, caught a ray of sun through the window and practically glowed. He remembered that once he'd told her that he liked looking for her in crowded places. "I just tell myself that I'm looking for the prettiest woman in the building, and when I find you, I'm done."

She turned, but her smile was tentative.

"Dorian? The real Dorian?"

He tried to speak. Nothing came out, and his eyes blurred.

She was in his arms. Dorian held her tightly, afraid to let go. She buried her face in his neck, and he could feel her tears on his skin. He thought about the first time he'd held her, a night when they'd parked on a cliff's edge with the city's lights spread out in the valley below, when he knew that they would be together forever. Her breathing had synchronized with his. Her shoulder fit under his arm as if the two of them had been sculpted at the same time to go together. Dorian shook with sobs, and she held him. Her crying matched his own.

A long time later, it seemed, when they'd dried their faces, made their apologies to the concierge, who just seemed happy that they were where they belonged again, and all thoughts of further repercussions for going through transitions were forgotten, they walked toward their room. Stephanie's arm wrapped around Dorian's waist, and he kept a hand on her shoulder, as if afraid that she might slip away again.

"Where were you at lunch?" Dorian asked. "I waited for an hour."

Stephanie's inhalation still sounded shaky. "I was in the wrong restaurant. When you didn't show up, I went back to the room. But you didn't come, so I started looking for you. That's when I went through the transitions. Dorian, it was all so beautiful. I lost track of time." She frowned. "They brought a man who looked like you, but he wasn't you. I've never been so frightened before."

"I know."

Dorian pulled her even tighter. It didn't matter why they'd been apart, as long as they were no longer lost. He loved the feel of her walking beside him. He loved that he could match strides with her so they wouldn't jar each other. Twenty years of marriage, and he loved that she still surprised him with her laugh.

They reached the room. Dorian slid his plastic key into the lock, but it didn't work.

"Let me," Stephanie said. The door recognized her key and let them in. "I'm so tired, I could sleep for a week." She leaned against the wall, looking at him.

"Me too. I haven't slept since yesterday."

She headed for the bed, and Dorian was glad because she couldn't see the change in expression on his face. He hadn't slept since yesterday, he'd said, but that wasn't true. He'd slept in the moon room, where he'd dreamed of Stephanie. "You're so far away," she'd said in the dream.

How long had he slept?

Stephanie pulled back the sheets. Dorian watched. Was that *exactly* the way Stephanie unmade the bed? Didn't she always wash her face first?

She walked past him into the bathroom. Her fingers touched his as she rounded the corner. "You look like you swallowed something gross."

The sink turned on. Water splashed. Dorian backed up to the edge of the bed, but he didn't sit down. Stephanie had left the door open. She always closed the bathroom door, even to brush her teeth, even to blow her nose. Her shadow moved on the carpet in the light of the open door.

How long had he slept?

Much, much later that night, long after the woman had fallen asleep, Dorian lay with his eyes wide open, listening. Straining. What did his wife sound like when she breathed? Could this possibly be her beside him, and what if it wasn't? How long would it be before she noticed? A year? Ten years? Never?

Or could she wake up right now and know? Would she lever herself up on one elbow and look at him in the dark? "You're not Dorian," she'd say. Her breath wouldn't smell like Stephanie's. Her voice wouldn't be Stephanie's. Not quite. Not exact. Not real.

She stirred slightly. Every muscle in Dorian's body tensed, but she didn't wake up.

Not then.

THE SMALL ASTRAL
OBJECT GENIUS

USTIN SET THE PEEK-A-BOO ON HIS DESK NEXT TO THE COMPUTER. THE softball-sized metal sphere rolled an inch before clicking against the keyboard, the only sound in the silent house. The house was almost always quiet now, noiseless as an empty kitchen with its cabinets neatly shut, the plates and dishes gradually collecting dust. Where to send it? Maybe this time something incredible would happen, if he just kept trying.

His computer listed options, starting with large objects or small ones. After he'd first bought the Peek-a-boo, he spent weeks sending it to the large ones: galaxies, nebulas, the gaseous remains of supernovas, star clusters. He'd double check the batteries, make sure the lens was clean, then choose one of the preprogrammed destinations. Sometimes he'd balance the device on his palm, hoping to feel the microsecond that it vanished in its dash across the light years before returning to his hand, but he never did. Not even a tingle. It sat against his skin, cool and hard and heavy, its absence too brief to sense.

An instant later, his computer pinged and the "picture taken" icon blinked red and green. Immediately would follow a confirmation from the Peek-a-boo Project website. "Thank you for participating," the message would say, or, if he was really lucky, "New object! You have contributed to man's knowledge of the universe," and his face would tingle with joy.

He'd heard rumors among his friends that there were other messages, but he'd never seen them himself.

Lots of times, of course, the monitor showed nothing, just a black screen with maybe a wink of a star here or there, but every once in a while, the Peek-a-boo appeared in the distant space oriented perfectly and captured a spectacular image. He used to like nebulas best. Several DVDs full of pictures rested on the shelf above the computer. He'd devoted an entire disk to the Rosette Nebula, taking pictures from all the angles over the course of two weeks, its vermillion gasses thrown out in parsecs wide petals, but lately he'd turned his attention to small objects: individual stars, planets, and moons.

On the monitor, the computer gave him hundreds of preprogrammed selections.

He carefully entered instead the coordinates for a planet circling Bellatrix, a giant star about 240 light years away on Orion's right shoulder, then sent the Peek-a-boo. "Picture taken," winked the message. The image began forming on the screen. Dustin leaned back in his chair, his hands resting one on the other on his chest.

Behind him, the door to his bedroom opened. He knew by the click of the door-knob, the distance the door swung into the room, a hint of lavender in the air, that it was his mother. She stood behind him without speaking for a moment, then sighed.

"Yes?" Dustin said.

She sighed again.

He turned his chair. Her hand cupped the doorknob with fingers so delicate that he wondered how she could pick up anything heavier than a pen or a book.

"Are you coming to dinner?" Her lips were colorless and thin, like her voice, but dark circles marked her eyes. He couldn't remember when Mom looked like she'd had a good night's sleep.

"Now?"

She blinked, as if his question was cruel.

"Unless you want to eat later. Your father is eating later."

"I'm not hungry." Almost half the image had appeared on the screen. Already he could see the planet's curve. This could be a good one, he thought. He forced his eyes away from the picture. If he phrased the question just right, he could make a difference. "I don't think I'll have anything. Could we wait?"

She shook her head, and then slowly backed away, pulling the door with her. "I'll put a plate in the refrigerator for you in case," she said as the door closed.

Dustin shivered for a second in the room's silence. She was like a ghost in her own house, drifting from room to room. He couldn't remember the last time she'd touched him. Maybe she wasn't even capable of it anymore. If he tried to hug her, would his arms pass through?

The planet on the monitor finished forming, a violet sphere with darker bands, like Jupiter, the arc of the terminator hiding a third of the surface. "Thank you for participating" popped over the image. He shook his head as he cleared the message. He hadn't "contributed to man's knowledge of the universe." Other people had taken this picture and added it to the database. No rings on the planet that he could see. No moons. Still, how rare, he thought. Perfect trade material. The smaller the object, the less chance his friends would have it. Space wasn't just mostly empty; it was depressingly, hugely empty. If all space was the size of his bedroom, the total mass of every galaxy and star and planet wouldn't fill a thimble. Getting a picture of an object as small as a planet 240 light years away boggled the mind. He tweaked the coordinates and sent the Peek-a-boo again for a closer look, but the image came back black. The unit might have appeared closer to the planet but with its lens pointed the wrong way, or a number in the coordinates so far down the decimal line that he couldn't imagine it ticked up or down one time too many, and the Peak-a-boo wasn't in the planet's range.

He sent it again. Black screen.

Again. Black screen.

Again.

His door opened. Dad said, "Dustin, I'm eating dinner in forty minutes. The dining room should be free then."

"I'm not hungry, Dad. I'm working on something."

Dustin could almost hear his Dad grimace. "You didn't eat already, did you?" He stepped next to Dustin's chair. Dustin looked at Dad's feet, which were bare. The toenails were trimmed neatly, although they'd grown longer than he was used to seeing. "You didn't eat with her, did you?" Dad said.

"No, really, I'm working on my computer . . ." Dustin drew in a shaky breath. ". . . but I'll go down now, if you want." Dustin tapped in an adjustment before sending the Peek-a-boo again.

Dad leaned in toward the screen, his hand on the chair's back behind Dustin's shoulder. "It's a hoax, you know. That toy doesn't go anywhere. It generates random images. Everyone knows you can't travel faster than light, and certainly not with a half pound of plastic and a couple AA batteries."

The computer indicated that the coordinates were ready. Dustin pressed the send command. "It's aluminum, not plastic, and it's not a hoax. Didn't you read that stuff I gave you about Peek-a-boo theory? Interstellar distance is a mathematical conception or something like that. Wrinkly space, they call it. Just a little push the right way, and the Peek-a-boo bounces across the wrinkle and back."

"It's Crackerjack physics, son. Nobody believes it."

"Scientists do. Every time I take a photograph, it downloads into NASA's database. We're expanding the knowledge of the universe! People all over the world are part of it! Amateurs have always been a big part of astronomy."

Dad humphed. "You know what the scam is? Sporadic reinforcement. Every once in a while you get a pat on the back, and you keep trying. It's why fishermen fish. You wouldn't believe how many Pokemon packs I bought when I was a kid, just hoping for a first edition holographic rare. Hundreds of dollars lost, I'll bet."

"The pictures are real, Dad," he said as a new image formed on the screen. At the very bottom a hint of violet curve filled in. "See, it's the same planet. I've been peppering these coordinates for a couple days." The image looked so authentic. Dustin thought, no way this is fake. No way!

Dad shrugged his shoulders. "I'm heating a pizza later. Come down if you want any."

"Not tonight. Sorry." Dustin punched the send button again. Maybe he could get a full globe shot for trade tomorrow.

Through Dustin's open shades, the stars above the western horizon flickered behind the maple's waving branches. Slowly, the nearly full moon slid through the last of the November leaves, then past each branch, lower and lower. Before it touched the top of his neighbor's house, Mars joined the gradual descent. The planet and the moon appeared close in the sky, but he knew it was an illusion. Even if their edges touched, they were really millions of miles apart. Still, he liked seeing them so close. If only he could send the Peek-a-boo there! What wonders he might see, but wrinkly space didn't wrinkle at that distance. The closest he could send the Peek-a-boo was about one hundred light years.

One by one, Pisces's last stars disappeared, and Aries, its twinkling lights wrapped around the war god, followed the creeping parade.

The clock next to the bed flicked to 4:00 a.m. Dustin listened intently. Not a living sound in the house. His parents' bedroom was directly below his. A year ago, he could hear them talking. No words, but a comforting, conversational rise and fall. Sometimes, even, laughter. Then, six months ago, it had been arguments. Shouting, to weeping, to nothing. Mother slept there still. If her shades were open like his, the moonlight would flood her space, but Dustin hadn't seen her windows open for months. In the middle of the day, she'd be in bed in the darkened room, or she'd vacuum by the tiny vacuum cleaner's light, like a dim-eyed Cyclops rolling along the carpet.

Dad slept in his study by the garage.

Dustin pushed his covers aside, crept down to the kitchen, and ate a piece of cold pizza. The milk tasted sour, and the label said it had passed its expiration by six days, so he washed it down with orange juice.

"I'll trade you a shot from the interior of the Horse Head Nebula looking toward Earth for that planetgraph you have there," said Slade. He'd dyed his Mohawk blue the week before but hadn't touched it up since, so it had turned a coppery green. A spread of pictures covered the desk before him, and his CD carrier, filled with thousands of other images he'd either taken himself or traded for sat in the black case next to the prints. "Come on, it's a good deal. All the UV bands are expressed. You could hang it in a museum." In the hallway beyond the classroom door, voices rose and fell, the busy traffic of the middle school at lunch.

Dustin handled the print, a really lovely image marked by delicate curtains of pink and vermillion. A series of numbers printed at the bottom told him how many pictures Slade had taken, and how rare the current image was. The higher the number at the bottom combined with the rarity of the image and the prestige of the photographer determined its tradability. *Peek-a-boo Monthly* printed profiles of individuals who captured the most spectacular and rare shots. Both Slade and Dustin had been listed in the "honorable mentions" in past issues, which made all their prints more valuable. He put it down. "Nice picture, but it's common. Peek-a-boo defaults to the nebulas. My grandmother could get it."

"Yeah, but not this quality."

Three other boys had gathered at their table in the empty classroom, their lunches in their laps. Each had a folder with their own pictures and their own CDs filled with images. "I'll trade for it," said one. He wore a T-shirt that read, IF I WERE AN ALIEN, I WOULDN'T TALK TO US EITHER.

Slade hardly looked at him. Dustin knew that Slade had already taken every image of interest from the boy already. The only other person in the school with anything that might appeal to Slade was Dustin.

"I've never taken a close up of an object smaller than a star. You're like a small astral object genius. How are you finding them?"

Dustin thought about the hours of punching the send command, the boxes of batteries, the long stretches of useless images that made him wonder if his monitor still worked, the quiet creak of the door behind him that told him either Mom or Dad was checking up. He would hunch closer to the screen and pretend he hadn't heard. Dad had told him once, when he was much younger, "Accept the things you can't change and change the things you can." He couldn't get them to talk, but he could take pictures of the stars, so he pressed the send button again and again.

"I keep trying," he said.

"Where's this one from?" Slade put his finger on the violet planet from last night.

"Bellatrix. I like the named objects. Tonight I thought I'd go for stars in Pisces. Maybe Torcularis Septentrionali."

"Too small. Too far away."

Dustin put the planet's image back into his stack. "I got this one, didn't I? Persistence pays."

A dark-haired girl with hair hanging over her eyes opened the door into the classroom, filling it with hallway sound. Another girl stood behind her, her eyes just as hidden. "Oh," dark-haired said, "I thought this room was empty at lunch." Dustin turned in his chair so he could see her better, his images in hand. She said, "Ewww, it's the star geeks. Weren't you guys doing role-playing games last year?"

The two girls laughed as the door shut.

*

After school Dustin reluctantly put aside the romantically named stars he'd concentrated on for the last months: Dubhe, Alphard, Shedir and others (Their names made him think of an old Sunday school tale about Shadrach, Meshach and Abednego. The idea of their names and stars and fiery furnaces had mixed in his head ever since.), and instead turned to G, F and K class stars, all which possibly could support life if they had planets the proper distance away. Numbers and letters labeled them. Sunlight through the window warmed his desktop, and he thought about drawing the curtain, but the heat felt good on his hands and arms.

The Peek-a-boo database contained over two million celestial objects. He picked a G-class star randomly, set the coordinates and punched the send button. The Peek-a-boo rested on its display base by his keyboard, a bit of dust marking its smooth curve. It didn't twitch, but within seconds a few pinpricks of light showed on the monitor. "Thank you for participating," said the popup message. He sent the Peek-a-boo again. A completely empty image this time. He rested his chin on his forearm, pressed the send button over and over. Eventually the sun slipped below the horizon, and for a while the maple tree stood as a shadow against the sunset sky. But the tree faded away, and only the early evening stars were visible. Vega and Altair shone brightly high on the window.

He thought about the Earth's orbit. If an Earth-like planet circled this star (which he hadn't even seen yet—it was possible the Peek-a-boo was missing it by dozens of light years), then it was like trying to find a dime on a high school track in the dark. He pressed the send again.

Downstairs, the front door opened. Dustin didn't stir. It would be his mother. She came home first. Her keys clattered into the bowl on the table by the coat closet. Her steps creaked on the squeaky third and seventh stair. Without looking, he knew when she stopped in the hallway behind him.

"Hi, Mom. You're home late."

"Did your father call to check on you?"

"No."

"It was his turn."

Dustin turned in his chair. Mom's hand rested on the door's frame. Everything about her, her hair, her makeup, the tidy lines of her blue pantsuit, was realtor neat. Her matching blue purse dangled from the crook of her elbow.

"Did you sell a house?"

"*He's* supposed to check up on you today. That's the agreement."

"It's no big deal." Dustin squeezed the back of his chair. His knuckles ached. "Maybe he did call, and I missed it. I've been on the computer."

The rumble of Dad's engine filled the driveway. Then, the click of his car opening and closing. Mom looked panicked for a moment, before coming into the room. She sat on the edge of Dustin's bed, her purse in her lap.

"What are you working on?" She glanced at the door.

"It's a new star," said Dustin. "I haven't tried to find it before." On the screen, the popup said, "New object! You have contributed to man's knowledge of the universe." Heart thumping, he cleared the message, and behind it, dead center, glowed a white disk the size of a silver dollar. "I got it," he said.

"That's a star?" She sounded doubtful.

"A new one, or at least I've taken a picture that no one else has. That's what the message meant. Look, I can manipulate it." He clicked on the "effects" choice in the toolbar and chose "eclipse." The disk blinked out, but the star's corona remained, a bright ring of light marked by a small flare on the lower right side. "This star is a lot like the sun."

"It probably is the sun," said Dad.

Mom flinched.

"I hope your grades aren't suffering because of this game." He walked past Mom without looking at her, then said to Dustin, "I brought Chinese if you're hungry."

Dustin saved the image, nudged the coordinates and sent the Peek-a-boo out again.

Dad picked up the Peek-a-boo, and flipped it from one hand to the other. "There's a guy in my office who brought one of these to work." Dustin rose partway from the chair, then forced himself back.

"They're a little fragile."

"They caught the guy playing with it during work hours." Dad tossed the sphere to Dustin. He caught it with both hands, cushioning it, before putting it back on its stand. Dad said, "They fired him. Good career shot because of a kid's toy, but I figured he wouldn't last anyways. Talked about *Star Trek* episodes like they were Shakespeare. Idiot."

Mom said, "I'll fix something for myself later, if you want to eat, Dustin." Dad closed his eyes for a second. She stood, then walked stiffly out of the room. Dustin wanted to ask her to stay, but he didn't speak. The two of them together were like split-screen videos: both animate and responding, although not to each other.

"You're not sending these Peek-a-boo people any money, are you?"

"Dad, there's just the connect charge, and I pay for that."

"With allowance money I give you. No one can prove the images you are taking are of anything, son. There's an article in today's *Newsweek* that shows it's a fake. Why don't you just get involved in online games like a normal kid?"

Dustin watched his computer's monitor. Three stars appeared in the upper left corner, but the screen was otherwise dark. He rested his fingertips on the keyboard. "Can I ask Mom to eat with us?"

"You can't take a picture of what's not there." Dad stepped toward the door, loosening his tie. He paused, one finger caught in the silk, the knot half undone. "She hates Chinese."

For the rest of the night, Dustin sent the Peek-a-boo out, over and over. He changed batteries at 2:00, when he realized twenty black screens in a row and no "Thank you for participating" messages meant the device hadn't moved. The challenge was that not only did Dustin not know if the star had planets circling it, but he didn't know what their orbital plane was. He could send the Peek-a-boo the right distance from the star and miss because the planet could be anywhere in the sphere of distance that far away. Plus, the Peek-a-boo could appear pointing in the wrong direction. All he could do was to keep trying.

He did get several more good shots of the star, though. He spent an hour running the best ones through the effects: corona analysis, blue-light shift, red-light shift, x-ray rendered, radio rendered, various luminosity lines emphasized, all the filters. In every way, it came out within a few percentage points of the sun. Twice more he received, "New object! You have contributed to man's knowledge of the universe."

Slade looked glum. "Have you ever lost a Peek-a-boo?" He hadn't opened his portfolio or his lunch. It didn't look like a trading day.

"No," said Dustin. His eyes felt heavy, like they were filled with syrup. When he'd finally fallen asleep, the sun had risen. "Did you leave it somewhere?"

"Not misplaced. I mean *lost* the whole fricking thing? I sent it out, and it didn't come back. One second it's there, and the next it's gone."

Dustin sat up. "Gone? Like gone, gone?"

"Yeah, bang, loud noise-hurt-my-ears gone, and get this: a message from the Peek-a-boo Project pops up and says, 'An unexpected anomaly occurred during transmission. You must replace your unit. Thank you for participating.' It gave me a 10% off coupon for my next purchase. What a ripoff!"

"So, what did you do?"

"I called Peek-a-boo, of course! Twenty-four hour service, my ass. It's a recorded message and a gazillion choices. So, I work my way down the menu, and you know what they said? 'Although very rare, an unexpected anomaly could include your Peek-a-boo unit occupying simultaneous space with a solid object, such as a star.' My aunt told me the whole thing is a con to get kids to buy more Peek-aboos. That they really aren't taking pictures at all."

Dustin looked at Slade's folder. He did have beautiful images. "Are you going to quit?"

Slade pushed away from his table. He touched his hand to the side of his Mohawk to make sure it was still straight. "Even if they're fake, I like the pictures. I'll talk my step mom out of the money when she's in a good mood." He smirked, "Besides, my grades in science have never been better."

None of the other kids who traded at lunch were in the room. Dustin's own folder, with the new star pictures, unshown inside, rested under his hand. A thought occurred to him. "Did you pick up the pieces?"

"What?" Slade pushed his portfolio under his arm so he could open his lunch bag.

"The pieces from your Peek-a-boo, when it exploded?"

Slade laughed. "There weren't any pieces! There wasn't even any smoke. It exploded into nothing. Total whack job."

When Dustin was alone, and the only sounds were kids yelling to each other in the hallways, he smiled.

Mom sat on the edge of the bed, just as she had the night before, except this pantsuit matched her beige purse. "We may need to make some changes soon, Dustin."

Warily, Dustin watched her. "Like what?"

She toyed with her purse's clasp. "School, maybe. Probably a different house. A condo, perhaps. I know of some nice ones below market price nearer my office." She glanced up, dry-eyed, just for an instant. "At least for part of the time."

Dustin felt his lungs constricting. It took effort for him to say, "This is temporary, right? It's just til things patch together?"

She slumped. "If it makes you feel better to believe that, sure."

In the empty time after she left, Dustin pushed the send button repeatedly, not really looking at the monitor, even when he got a good shot of the new star. He saved the image mechanically. No planet. Send. Send. Send.

A half hour later, Dad delivered almost the same speech, except it was an apartment with a great view of the mountains.

Dustin had lined the AA batteries on his desk like bullets. Every couple hours he popped two used ones out of the Peek-a-boo. Spent casings, he thought. They dropped to the carpet.

His hands trembled on the keyboard. He swallowed dryly. Somewhere around this star, maybe, circled a planet the same distance as Earth. He'd found the system's Jupiter about 11:00. So many systems had a Jupiter, an oversized lump of a planet, always about the same distance from the center. Star system evolution turned out to be remarkably similar, time after time. Many stars formed planets, and they formed them in about the same way, and it was because of their Jupiters that the inner planets were shielded. Jupiters inhaled planet-busting comets and shepherded the loose debris into tidy orbits that would otherwise career about unchecked. But the inner planets were so much smaller. The giant planets protected, but they also overwhelmed with their size and strength. They distracted.

Where was the tiny glimmer of the inner planets? Dustin fine tuned the coordinates, kicking the Peek-a-boo from one side of the star to the other, always taking a half-dozen pictures from one coordinate before shifting again. Even at the same coordinates, though, the unit might appear millions of miles from the last spot. A three-dimensional graph of the appearances would eventually surround a location, but there was no fine control. He could only keep trying.

At 3:00 in the morning, the Peek-a-boo felt slick and cool under his fingers. A twitch on the keyboard sent it out again. Stars appeared on the monitor. "Thank you for participating." He sent it out again. The Peek-a-boo never failed him. It always came back (but Slade's hadn't!). Graveyard silence filled the house. Out the window, clouds covered the night sky, so all he saw was his own shimmery image, like he was someone else: a small boy's spirit, his elbows planted on his ghost desk in a ghost world looking at his ghost computer. Dustin almost waved, but something stirred behind him in the reflection. He was too tired to be startled. Standing at the door, illuminated by the monitor's faint light, his Dad in pajamas looked in. His face had no color, no life, and two shadowed pits marked where his eyes should have been. Dad leaned against the doorjamb, watching Dustin, or he might have been looking beyond him, or his eyes could have been closed. The pose held for a marble moment.

Dustin blinked, and the apparition was gone. Had he really seen him? A few seconds later, the stairs creaked; Dad going down.

For a hundred heartbeats, Dustin stared at his reflection, and then through the ghost boy to the maple tree he couldn't see, and beyond that to the clouds that covered the stars, and through them to the stars themselves, trying to understand. Dad had appeared and disappeared without a sound except the squeak on the stair. Everything done in silence. No noise that Dustin didn't make himself in the perpetually quiet house. He pressed the send button again, and the key's cricket click seemed big in the muffling stillness.

The image of himself in the glass and the wavery memory of his dad behind him defined Dustin's universe. Nothing else existed. Then a new image began forming on his monitor from the top down. Not black. Yellow from side to side, like candle flame. Not a starscape. Not even a distant planet hovering in the velvet abyss. On the screen's left side, a corner of something red appeared. A straight line built toward the screen's bottom, and then an orange sphere formed on the screen's right side. The computer pinged three times. A new popup message flashed across the image: "DO NOT TOUCH YOUR PEEK-A-BOO OR TURN OFF YOUR COMPUTER!" At the same time, his phone rang. A second later, his cell phone, recharging on the nightstand chimed for attention.

Dustin jerked back. Who could be calling at 3:00 in the morning? They'd wake his parents! He picked up the phone. A recorded announcement said, "This is a Peek-a-boo priority communication. Information from your Peek-a-boo unit indicates a unique contact. Please do not attempt to send your Peek-a-boo device out again or switch programs on your computer. Representatives from Peek-a-boo will communicate with you immediately. . . . This is a Peek-a-boo priority communication. . . ."

Dad's voice interrupted. "What have you done, Dustin? Do you know what time it is?"

Mom said sleepily over the phone, "What is going on? What is going on?"

The image finished forming on the monitor behind the popup message. Dustin hesitated, the phone still to his ear. "Please do not attempt to send your Peek-a-boo device out again or switch programs on your computer," repeated the voice. Dustin closed the popup window; the screen glowed yellow, orange and red in crisp lines and shapes.

"I didn't do anything," he said. "I don't know."

"I'm coming up," said Dad.

The stairs creaked beneath his mom's slippered feet.

Mom arrived first, then Dad. They gathered behind his chair.

Dad said, "Why are they calling you in the middle of the night?"

"I don't know, Dad. Something about this." He gestured toward the monitor.

Mom said, "Is that a screensaver?"

In the distance, a police car siren sounded, coming closer.

Dustin's face flushed, the phone still in his hand, repeating the message over and over. "No, my Peek-a-boo took it."

"What is it?" Dad leaned over Dustin's shoulder. The upper half of the monitor showed colored shapes in sharp geometry. A mottled gray and yellow texture filled the bottom half, but all the angles were skewed so the image seemed to be sliding off the screen's left side.

The siren turned onto Dustin's street, its flashing blue and red lights reflecting off the neighborhood trees until the car parked in his driveway. The siren wailed to silence, and a few seconds later, a heavy knocking came from the front door.

His parents looked at Dustin first, and then toward the pounding downstairs. "Don't touch your computer, son," said Dad.

Another car without a siren or flashing lights pulled into the driveway. Doors opened. Voices jumbled together outside.

Minutes later, his room full of strangers, Dustin sat on his bed's edge and said, "I just kept sending it out." An earnest older man whose shirt was tucked in on only one side wrote Dustin's comment in a notebook.

"Had you seen a planet on that coordinate earlier?" he asked. Dustin shook his head. At Dustin's desk, two women, one in a bathrobe, and the other in a nice pant-suit, whispered vehemently back and forth about the image. "We'll need his hard drive. It could be a fake," Pantsuit said. "I don't see how," replied Bathrobe.

A man in uniform, but definitely not a policeman, carefully rolled Dustin's Peek-a-boo into a plastic bag that zipped closed when the unit plopped to the bottom.

From the hallway, Mom's voice said, "He's always been a determined boy."

Dad said, "So, you think he really found something, do you?" His tone was skeptical.

Someone in the hallway said, "He'll be famous."

"Look at this," said Bathrobe. She moved the cursor to the menu bar at the top of the screen. A few clicks later, the image reoriented itself. Now the gray and yellow texture moved to the top and became sky. Dustin blinked, then blinked again. What had seemed abstract before suddenly made sense. "Is that . . ." he said, and swallowed. "Is that a building?"

Pantsuit pointed to what had been a red blob before, "Yes, and that looks like a tree to me. . ." she bent close to the screen, ". . . with a park bench under it. A yellow one with brown arm rests."

"I don't believe it," said Bathrobe, in a voice that was clear she did.

The older man sitting on the bed with Dustin said to himself, "It's such a big universe. What are the odds a Peek-a-boo would appear close enough to a planet's surface, oriented just the right way, to take a picture of a park bench?"

Bathrobe said, "A park bench 380 million light years from Earth."

Dustin lay in his bed. The clouds had cleared, and early dawn lightened the sky enough through his window to dissolve the stars and show the blank area on his desk where his computer had sat earlier that night. Now, though, only a clean square outlined by a fine dust film showed that anything had been there at all.

"We'll replace this computer," Bathrobe had said as she left with the CPU. Pantsuit added, "And a new Peek-a-boo, even better than your old one. Later today, there will be a news conference."

The older man patted Dustin on the head as he left. "There will be a lot of news conferences, I'd say, now that you showed us where to look."

After all the bustle, after the doors slammed below and the cars departed, Dustin finally climbed into bed, but he couldn't sleep. For the longest time he stared out the window, his sheets pulled to his chin, hands locked behind his head. A few days ago, the moon had preceded Mars to the horizon, but now the red planet set first, while the moon followed, dragging Pleiades like star babies close behind. He thought about the stars passing by his window as if they were friends: Hamal, of course, and Menkar, and the sprinkling of tau stars, omi Tau, xi Tau and f Tau, then Aldebaran and Algol, and Betelgeuse, who faded last in the lightening sky. They all seemed so comforting that he didn't notice at first that the house had changed. For the longest time he tried to place the difference. Not just the missing computer. Not just the strangeness of the night's events. Something else.

He gasped in surprise, then silenced his breathing so he could hear. Below him, in his parent's room, he heard voices: his mom and dad, talking. The conversation rose and fell. It had been going on since they'd left his room. Once, he could swear, he heard laughter. Long after the morning sky had brightened to blue and the maple tree cast its shadow on the fence and their neighbor's house, Dustin listened, and not once, that morning, did his parents quit talking. Not even when they moved into the kitchen. Not even when they began fixing breakfast. Their voices broke the long silence, and Dustin knew he wasn't alone in the house.

He wasn't alone, and it was time to eat.

HOW MUSIC BEGINS

H ANDS RAISED, READY FOR THE DOWNBEAT, COWDREY BROUGHT THE BAND to attention. He took a good inhalation for them to see, thinking, "The band that breathes together, plays together." Players watched over their music stands as he tapped out a barely perceptible four beats, then, he dropped into the opening notes of "The King's Feast," a simple piece a 9th grade band might play at the season's first concert, but Elise Morgan, his best student, had composed variations for flutes and clarinets, added an oboe solo, and changed the arrangement for the cornets and trombones, so now new tonal qualities arose. Her neatly handwritten revisions crowded his score, a black and white representation of the opening chords, the musical lines blending effortlessly. Everyone on beat. Everyone on tune. At the state competition, they would sweep the awards, but this wasn't state, and they weren't really a junior high band anymore.

Eyes closed, he counted through the bars. "The King's Feast" recreated a night at Henry VIII's court. Suitably serious. A heavy drum background carrying the load. Not quite a march, but upbeat in a dignified way. Someone in the French horn section sounded a bit pitchy. Was it Thomas? Cowdrey cocked his head to isolate it, but the individual sound faded, lost in the transition to the second movement.

He lived for this moment, when the sections threaded together, when the percussion didn't overwhelm or the brass blow out the woodwinds. He smiled as he directed them through the tricky exit from the solo. His eyes open now, their eyes on him, young faces, raggedy-cut hair, shirts and blouses too small, everyone's pants inches short above their bare feet, he led them to the conclusion, slowing the saxophones down—they wanted to rush to the end—then he brought the flutes up.

Rhythm and harmony tumbled over the pomp and circumstance in Henry's court. The ladies' elegant dress. The courtiers waiting in the wings. The king himself, presiding from the throne, all painted in music. Cowdrey imagined brocade, heavy skirts, royal colors, swirling in the dance.

The last notes trembled, and he held them in hand, not letting them end until his fist's final clasp cut them off. He was the director.

Aching silence. Someone in the drum section coughed. Cowdrey waited for the lights to flicker. They had flickered after the band's first performance here, and they'd flickered again after a near perfect "Prelude and Fugue in B Flat" six months ago. Tonight though, the lights stayed steady. Behind the band, the long curved wall and the window that circled the room holding back the brown smoke on the other side were the only audience. "The King's Feast" concluded the night's performance. Cowdrey signaled the players to their feet. Instruments clanked. Sheet music rustled. He turned from the band to face the other side's enigmatic window and impenetrable haze. Playing here was like playing within a fish bowl, and not just the shape either. He bowed, and the band bowed behind him. Whatever watched, if anything, remained hidden in the roiling cloud.

"Good performance, Cougars. Leave your music on the stands for the section leaders to pick up, then you may go to dinner. Don't forget, breathing practice before breakfast with your ensembles."

Chatting, the kids headed toward the storage lockers to replace their instruments.

A clarinet player waved as she left the room. "Good night, Mr. Cowdrey."

He nodded in her direction.

"'Night, sir," said a percussionist. "See you in the morning. Good performance."

The room cleared until Elise Morgan remained, jotting post-concert notes on her clipboard. Her straight black hair reached the bottom of her ears, and her glasses, missing one ear piece, sat crookedly on her nose. As always, dark smudges sagged under her eyes. She slept little. More often than not, late at night, she'd still be working on the music. "One of the French horns came in late again. I think it's Thomas. He's waiting until the trombones start, and it throws him a half beat off."

"I didn't notice." Cowdrey sat beside her. The light metal chair creaked under his weight. Several chairs had broken in the last few months. Just two spares remained. He wondered what would happen when players had to stand for their performances. "The band sounded smooth tonight. Very confident."

Elise nodded toward the window. "They're tuning the room. Maybe they're getting it ready for Friday's concert."

Cowdrey raised his eyebrows.

Elise pointed to the domed ceiling. "See there and there. New baffles. We've lost the echo-chamber effect you mentioned last week, and check out my flute." She handed it to him. "At first, they just repadded them. Normal maintenance, but they've done other stuff too. It's a better instrument."

He held the flute, then tried a few fingerings. The keys sank smoothly. No stickiness, and the flute weighed heavy.

"Play a note," she said.

He brought the instrument to his lip, but even before he blew, he knew it was extraordinary.

"During the sixth grade, after I won state solos the second time, my parents took me to the New York Philharmonic. I met their first chair, and he let me play his flute. Custom made. Insured for $50,000." She took the instrument back from Cowdrey and rested it on her lap. "It wasn't as good as this one is now. Maybe the Perfectionists are right."

Cowdrey frowned. Misguided students with wacky theories about how they could get home shouldn't be taken seriously.

"How's that?" Cowdrey shook the irritation from his head. He thought he would check the lockers after he finished with Elise. Were the other instruments being upgraded too?

"Maybe what they want is a perfect performance, then they'll let us go. Maybe Friday will be it." She looked up at the nearest window. A brown smokey wave swirled behind it, cutting sight to no more than a yard or so beyond the glass.

Cowdrey felt fatherly. She sounded so wistful when she said, "they'll let us go." He almost reached out to touch her arm, to offer comfort, but he held himself still. No sense in sending mixed signals. "I don't know why we're here. No one knows. They shouldn't get their hopes up. After all, what's a perfect performance?"

"Any sunset is perfect. Any pebble is perfect." She scuffed her bare foot on the immaculate floor. "Weeds are perfect, and so is a parking lot at the mall when the cars are gone and you can ride your bike in all directions without hitting anything." She sighed. "And open meadows where the grass is never cut."

Cowdrey nodded, not sure how to respond. She often reminisced about meadows.

Elise closed her eyes dreamily. "I found a pebble in my band jacket. Sometimes I hold it and think about playgrounds."

"Really?"

She looked up at him, then dug into her pocket. On her open palm, a bit of shiny feldspar the size of a pencil eraser caught the ceiling light. As quick as it came out, it vanished back in her pocket. She made another note on her clipboard. "The Perfectionists are getting pretty fanatical. Others heard Thomas come in late."

"The band will maintain discipline. If anyone has a problem, they'll talk to me. That's why I'm here."

Elise looked uncomfortable. "Are you sure? With Ms. Rhodes gone . . ."

Cowdrey glanced away from her to the empty chairs and music stands. "Ms. Rhodes will be missed, but the band can continue without an assistant director."

"I'm just saying . . . it's a lot for a single adult to handle."

He composed his face to meet her eyes. "The less we think of Ms. Rhodes, the better."

Elise shrugged. "If you want it that way."

"We have the section leaders. They have taken the responsibility." He smiled.

"Half the time I think the band doesn't even need me. You all have become such strong musicians."

She wrote a last comment on her clipboard, then slipped it under her arm. "Not strong enough. Nowhere near. Today is Monday. If we don't clean things up by Friday, the Perfectionists could get scary."

"It's late." Without the rest of the band in the room, his voice sounded too loud and harsh. Truly, he could hear a pin drop with these acoustics. "I'll see you tomorrow, Elise."

"Have you thought any more about the wedding?"

"No. We're not discussing it."

Her lips pursed, as if she wanted to say something, but she put her finger to the bridge of her glasses to hold them in place, then stood. "I'll direct breathing practice for the woodwinds in the morning, if you'll take the brass. At least I can help that much."

Cowdrey nodded. In the beginning, after the first week's chaos settled down, Ms. Rhodes had led the woodwinds through their exercises. Rhodes, a somber thirty-year-old who wore padded-shoulder jackets and seldom smiled, would meet Cowdrey outside the practice rooms. He'd hand her the routine he'd written up the night before. She'd study it briefly, then follow the players. In the last few months, she'd spoken about band-related issues, but nothing else. Conversation stopped. He didn't know how to broach another subject. The last time he'd tried, he had said, "How are you holding up?" She'd looked about like a wild bird for a second, as if she heard something frightful, but her face smoothed over and she said, "To improve rhythms, hone intonation, and create dynamic phrasing, we must improve breathing. All music begins with a good breath." Red circled her exhausted eyes.

Lockers lined the hallway outside the performance hall. A cornet rested in its shaped space in the first one. Cowdrey took it out. It, too, had been improved. No longer an inexpensive junior high band instrument, the keys sank with ease; the horn glowed under the hallway's indirect lighting, the metal as warm as flesh beneath his fingers.

He returned the horn to its place before closing the door. Thoughtfully, he walked to the T-intersection. To his left, the student's rooms, their doors shut. To his right, the practice rooms, the cafeteria, and his own room. He trailed his knuckle against the wall, but as he turned to enter he noticed Ms. Rhodes's door across the hall was gone as if it had never existed in the unmarked wall. When did that happen? he thought.

As always, dinner and a water bottle waited in a box on his bed. For weeks after the band had arrived, the students had tried to catch the deliveries, but they never did. If students stayed in the room, the meals wouldn't come, so if they wanted to eat, they had to leave to practice or to perform.

Passable bread. Something that looked like bologna in the middle, but it tasted more like cheese. He washed it down with a couple of swallows. Only the water from the bottles was potable. The stuff from the showers smelled like vinegar and tasted bitter. He wondered about the pets he'd kept as a child, a lizard and two hamsters. Did the food ever taste right to them? Had he ever fed them what they needed or wanted? He rested the sandwich on his lap. Later, he looked down. His fingers had sunk into the bread, and the edges had grown crispy. He glanced at his watch. An hour had passed. Room check! He walked the long hall past the kids' doors. At first he'd insisted on making sure the right students went to the right rooms, as if they were on an overnight for weekend competition, as if they stayed at a Holiday Inn, but so often he woke kids who had already gone to sleep that now he just listened at each door. Were they quiet or crying? The first week there had been a lot of crying, and they had come close to not making it. Being a band saved them.

That week was his toughest trial. Fright. Fighting. Despair. To end it, he took the only step he knew: he called for a practice, and they became a band again.

Cowdrey trod softly from door to door, pausing, listening, and moving on.

He stopped for an extra long time outside Taylor Beau's room. Was Liz Waters in there with him? Were they in Liz's room? Cowdrey rested his hand on the doorknob. No way they could be serious about a marriage. They were children, junior high students, not adults; under astonishing circumstances, to be sure, but band standards and school regulations glued them together. For all his years as director, Cowdrey lived by one rule: would he be comfortable with the band's activities if parents or school board members watched? This marriage talk did not fit.

No sound beyond the closed door. His hand tightened on the knob; he didn't turn it. Did he want to know?

Next he paused outside Elise's door. She wouldn't be asleep. She'd be looking over the day's notes, rewriting. Cowdrey shivered thinking about her brilliance. What must it have been like for Mozart's father when a three-year-old Amadeus picked out thirds and sixths on the harpsichord, when the father realized the son had surpassed him and would continue to grow beyond his comprehension and hope? But did Mozart eat and breathe music like Elise? Did he ever believe that music would take him home? Cowdrey didn't think so. Maybe at the end of Mozart's life, when the brain fevers wracked him, and he could feel death's hand on his neck. Maybe then he wrote with equal intensity.

Not many teachers ever had the chance to work with an Elise. If they did, they prayed they wouldn't ruin her vision, that they wouldn't poison her ear.

When he reached the hall's end, he turned and repeated the process back to his door. At first, he and Ms. Rhodes had done the room check together, then stood guard in the hall until the children quieted. After a few weeks, they had traded nights.

Now, he patrolled alone. Perhaps Elise was right. Maybe it was too much for him to handle.

He sighed. The silent hall stretched before him. He felt his pulse in his arm where he leaned against the wall. Soon, his chin headed for his chest. Cowdrey jerked himself awake, walked the hallway's length two more times before admitting he had to go to bed. In wakefulness' last few seconds, head resting on the pillow, he imagined he heard doors opening, the stealthy pad of bare feet, and the hush of doors gently closing on clandestine liaisons. Could Taylor and Liz be a single case, or had he lost control? A tear crept down his cheek as consciousness flitted away.

In the morning, Elise met him in the hallway. "Here are the variations I told you about for the Beatles medley. Mostly I need the saxophones' sheets, but I also syncopated the drums for 'Eleanor Rigby,' and reworked the trombone bridge into 'Yellow Submarine,' so I'll need their music too."

Cowdrey nodded as he took the scores. "Did you sleep?"

Elise made a checkmark on her clipboard. She moved to her next item. "I thought if we told the sections to treat their breathing exercises this morning like they were all preparing for a solo, we might get better sound from them. Remember, you told us once we should breathe from the diaphragm, and if we missed it, to miss big. I think about that a lot." She smiled, made another check, then frowned. "Also, you need to drop in on Thomas. I heard a rumor." Her pencil scratched paper firmly. "Look, Mr. Cowdrey, the band is on edge. All they think about is music and getting out. To some, Thomas is a handicap. They need something else. A distraction." She made another check on her list, then, without waiting for an answer, snapped the clipboard under her arm, before striding toward the practice rooms, a girl on a mission.

"Good morning to you, too, Elise."

Soon the hallway filled with sleepy kids. Cowdrey greeted them each in turn as they passed. Most smiled. He glanced at their eyes. The red-rimmed ones would be a worry, but they had been fewer and fewer as the weeks since their arrival turned into months. At first there had been nightmares, a reliving of the night they'd been taken. He'd had a few himself: the bus's wheels humming through the night, *Junior High Band Management* open on his lap, and then the growing brightness out the bus windows, the high screech that seemed to emanate in the middle of his head before the short soft shock of waking on the fishbowl auditorium's floor with their equipment and everything else from the bus scattered about. (No bus driver, though!) Those dreams had tapered off through the months. He thought, kids are resilient. If they have a structure, that is.

Thomas came by last. A short boy who played in the band because his parents told him it would look good on a college application, he'd never been an inspired musician, but he was competent enough. Thomas kept his head down as he passed. "Good morning," he mumbled.

"Can I speak to you a moment?" Cowdrey moved away from the wall to block his path.

"Sir." The boy didn't meet Cowdrey's gaze, but even his head held low couldn't hide the bruise that glowered on his cheek.

"How'd that happen?"

Thomas glanced up, frightened for an instant, then his expression went bland and unassuming. "I fell in the shower. Slipped."

The instruments tuning up in the practice rooms filled the silence between them.

Finally, Thomas said, "Look, I want to get away from here as much as the next person. If playing on pitch, on tune and to the beat is what it's going to take, then I'll do that."

Cowdrey heard the Perfectionists echo in Thomas's speech. "There is no such thing as a perfect performance, Thomas." He thought about Elise's perfect pebble. Perfect because there were no pebbles here, nor weeds or malls or bicycles. No families. Nothing but each other and that day's playing.

Thomas shrugged. "Yeah, well maybe not, but I can be better. I don't want it to be my fault the lights don't flicker."

"We don't even know what that means, son. Flickering lights may not be their applause."

The boy's eyes revealed nothing, and for a moment he didn't appear seventeen at all. He looked adult and tired and cursed with a terrible burden.

"Thomas, if someone is threatening you or hurting you, I need to know about it. That's my job. You don't have to play solo."

Thomas studied the hallway beyond Cowdrey's shoulder. A few steps past them, the hallway branched to the auditorium with its enigmatic windows. "My mom told me once that the world is a big place, and I could become anything I wanted to, but it's not. It's no bigger than the people you know and the places you go. It's a small world here, Mr. Cowdrey, and I don't have any place to hide in it, so I'm going to go the practice room to see if I can't get my act together a little better." He pushed past the director.

The director threw himself into the morning's work. Teaching is time management, he thought, and staying on task. He moved from student to student, checking intonation and technique. "It's not all about the notes," he said to a clarinet player. "Once you know the music, it's about feeling the sound from your own instrument and your section. The song becomes more about heart than head." The player nodded and replayed the piece.

For a time, mid-morning, Cowdrey sat in the practice room with the brass section. The leaders paced the group through their pieces, focusing on problems from yesterday's session. Each had Elise Morgan's suggestions to consult. Cowdrey watched Taylor Beau and Liz Waters, the numbers three and four chairs among the cornets. The couple wore matching silver crosses on chains around their necks. He wondered if they had given them to each other. Liz kept her red hair in a pony tail, and when she finished a long run of notes, her skin flushed, chasing her freckles to the surface. Taylor often played with his eyes closed, the music consigned to memory well before the other players. Although he wasn't first chair, the section elected him for solos frequently, which he played with lighthearted enthusiasm. The director thought about Elise's question on the marriage, and he remembered the duet Taylor and Liz worked up for the state competition. They played "Ode to Joy," and when they finished, they hugged. Now that he thought about it, he should have seen the budding relationship in the hug. You can't rehearse so often with the same person that you don't start having feelings about how they play. The breathing. The fingerings. The careful attention to each other's rhythm and tone. Harmonizing. Cowdrey shivered, thinking about music's sensuous nature.

The trombone section leader gave instruction. Cowdrey half listened while thinking about his first year in college, when he'd added the teaching certification program to his music major. Just for something to fall back on, he'd thought at the time. But when graduation came around, he'd found he liked teaching as much as he liked music, so moving into the schools didn't feel like settling for less. The kids in the room laughed, breaking Cowdrey from his reverie. The section leader was part way through an old band joke that Cowdrey couldn't remember the punchline for. The leader said, "So she dated a tuba player next, and her girlfriend asks how the date went. She says his embouchure was big and sloppy. It was like kissing a jellyfish." Most laughed, even the tuba player. "So, she says she went out with a French horn player next. How'd the date go? asks her friend, and the girl says he barely could kiss at all, his lips were so close together, but she liked the way he held her." A couple kids reacted right away, and ten seconds later, almost all laughed. Some looked embarrassed. "I hope that wasn't inappropriate, Mr. Cowdrey," said the section leader.

Cowdrey smiled. "Maybe you could go through those opening notes again. If you don't come in crisply, the back half flounders." He noticed Taylor and Liz held hands. Thomas, however, wasn't laughing. He clutched his horn close to his chest, his arms crossed over it like a shield. No one seemed to be paying special attention to Thomas. Whoever the Perfectionists were, they hid well. Thomas thought about Elise's suggestion that the band needed a distraction, something else to think about besides a perfect performance. Could that be a way to protect Thomas?

The section leader directed the brass back to the first movement. Pages turned.

Instruments came up, and the group launched into the beginning measures. Cowdrey stepped back to watch and listen. They didn't look so young to him anymore. Beneath their long hair or ragged haircuts, their faces had lost the babyish look he associated with fifteen-year-olds. Just two years difference, but he could see they'd changed. Their clothes strained to contain them. Their hands had grown so that no one stretched anymore to reach their instruments' keys. Their breath control had improved since they'd arrived, the improvement that came with maturity. A ninth grader couldn't hold a note like an older musician could. A fifteen-year-old couldn't hit the high parts with the same confidence as these kids could.

How long would they stay here?

Cowdrey walked behind the players. The wall cooled his back when he rested against it. What existed on the other side? Rooms filled with the brown smoke that eddied beyond the windows in the performance hall? He tried to imagine what creatures lurked in the brown smoke. Tentacles? Claws? Amorphous blobs? Or did he lean against a metal shell, inches from interstellar space? Maybe they had arrived on the creatures' home world and an entirely alien landscape waited beyond. Maybe, even, they had never left Earth, a few steps from home, hidden for their captors' amusement (what did they want?).

But the question remained, how long would they stay? What if they would never leave?

Cowdrey frowned. A veteran teacher had told him, "When you teach, your life becomes the kids and the classroom. If there's anything else distracting you, then you're not doing the job." Of course, another teacher, equally experienced, countered, "Teaching is what you do. Life is why you do it."

He left the practice room. Pulsing sound greeted him when he opened the door into the percussionist's area. Their eyes didn't leave their music, and at the place where the bass drums kicked in, with the snares beating out a complicated counter-rhythm, he could feel his heart's pounding change to match it. Watching their hands blur to follow the music, seeing the vibrations from the instruments' side, he noticed for the first time how thick-wristed the drummers had become, like tennis pros who gained an overdeveloped forearm on their racket side, except for them both arms bulged. When Cowdrey had been in college, he went out to dinner with a long-time drummer. On a bet, the fellow had grabbed one table edge with his fingertips, and lifted it, drinks and dinner plates and all by the strength of his hands and wrists. "Years and years working a drum set, and look what it got me, a party trick." The drummer laughed.

Once again, Cowdrey saw that the kids weren't ninth graders any more. When it ended, the section leader turned to him. "I thought these changes in the backbeat Elise wrote were wonky when I saw them on the page, but once we got going on them, wow!" Others in the section nodded.

The morning unfolded. Session after session, the kids' growth struck him. They weren't in any real sense a school band anymore. They had evolved into something that had never existed in humanity before, because where before in human history had these conditions existed?

But it wasn't until he stood outside his room before lunch that he made up his mind. Elise turned the corner with her clipboard in hand, her notes for the day covering the top sheet. Instead of showing them to him, she stopped to look at the blank wall where Miss Rhodes's door once had been. Clearly she hadn't noticed the disparity in the hallway. Elise touched the wall. For a second, Cowdrey worried she pictured what he had seen when he raised the nerve to go into Rhodes's room uninvited: the sheet twisted into a rope, the cloth cutting into her neck, the pathetic letters home she'd been writing since the first day they'd arrived.

Elise placed her palm flat on the wall where the door used to be. "It's adapt or die all the time, isn't it?"

Her crooked glasses made her look childish, but the top of her head stood almost level with his chin. He remembered when she'd been just a tiny 7th grader who handled her flute with an older musician's authority, but whose feet didn't reach the ground when she sat to play. Cowdrey knew then that Elise had become the band's heart. She drew the thread that kept them together so far, not his efforts, but hers. She held the late-night meetings with the section leaders to go over changes in music. She organized the informal ensembles. She had the energy others could draw on, including himself.

"Yes, it is." He took a deep breath. Cowdrey could feel the shift in his thinking happen. Suddenly, he wasn't a junior high band director. He was an older adult trapped with fifty competent young adults, if he could let them be that. If he could adapt to change. "Let's get them ready for the practice this evening, shall we?"

Elise raised her eyebrows.

That evening, Cowdrey took the podium. Under his hands, he held the music for the practice and his baton. Paper-clipped to the top sheet were his notes for areas to emphasize along with Elise's comments. The group fidgeted and chattered as they always did before practice. Cowdrey liked standing before the full band, when the day's work came together and he could measure the progress, and even though he hated the circumstances, he had to admit he'd never had a better performance facility. The light. The sound. The way the space flowed around them. Only the smokey windows and the hidden audience jarred.

He picked up the baton. They looked at him expectantly. "Breathing first, Cougars. I'll count off the seconds. Inhale." He tapped eight seconds with the baton while they filled their lungs. "Hold." With metronomic regularity he tapped out twenty-four more beats. They exhaled for eight, relaxed for ten, and then repeated twice more. At the end, the percussionists finished their set up and the band waited. Breathing exercises calmed them, put them into the right mind. In his classroom at the junior high, which he could barely picture now, he'd hung a banner at the front: ALL MUSIC BEGINS WITH A GOOD BREATH (AND DIES WITH A LACK THEREOF).

Now they were ready. "An issue has come up that I think needs to be addressed. As most of you know, Taylor Beau and Liz Waters have asked my permission to marry." Whatever whispering that might have been going on when he started the speech lapsed into silence. For an instance, Cowdrey pictured the school board and all the parents sitting in the back. What would they say at this announcement? Would they understand? He brushed aside the image, then plunged ahead. "I have thought about the request for a long time. Considering our situation and Taylor and Liz's character, I think they would make a fine married couple."

Before the last syllable had time to fade, the band erupted into cheers and gleeful laughter. The attention at first focused on Liz and Taylor, who cried and hugged awkwardly from their chairs, their cornets still in hand, but soon Cowdrey saw a good number had surrounded Elise, shaking her hand and clapping her on the back. Cowdrey's jaw dropped. He had, in every sense, been orchestrated. Finally, in the midst, Elise caught his eye and mouthed, "Thank you." He touched his forehead in rueful respect.

Thomas put his French horn on his chair, waiting his chance to congratulate the happy couple. A trombone player stood beside him, and they smiled as they chatted. It seemed as if it had been weeks since Cowdrey could remember Thomas looking relaxed. Cowdrey thought, a good decision and a distraction in one move. He smiled too.

Elise worked her way over to him. "We'll need a wedding march."

"I think Mendelssohn's is in my books. That would be traditional. Besides, it would be appropriate. He was seventeen when he wrote it." Cowdrey reached past her to high five a couple flute players who had joined a conga line.

Elise shook her head. "That's a myth, I think. He wrote it later. Anyway, I have something I've been working on. Something of my own." Her eyes lowered.

"Why am I not surprised?"

It took the band a half hour to settle down. They cut the practice early after just two run throughs of the Beatles medley.

For the first time in two years, Cowdrey didn't walk the halls before going to bed. We are adults here, he thought. The paradigm has shifted. He sighed as he lay down, believing when he went to sleep his dreams would be undisturbed and packed with beautifully played music, but after an hour trying to convince himself he'd changed, he rose, dressed, and walked the hall, listening at each door. Satisfied at last, he went back to his room, and his dreams played undisturbed with flawless performances.

In the morning, he found a note pushed under his door. "A wedding will not get us home. They want a perfect performance! Get us home!" Cowdrey snorted in disgust. Nobody could know what they wanted. They might not want anything. He folded the note in half and put it inside his band management book. Even the Perfectionists couldn't bother him today, and they wouldn't, at least until after the wedding. And who knows, he thought, sometimes the best way to a long term goal is to focus on a short term one.

Elise distributed the new march to the section leaders, who organized a music-transcribing session. For over an hour, the band met in the auditorium to make their copies. "You'd think if aliens could snatch us up to play concerts, they could at least provide a decent photocopier," grumbled the oboist, who had several dozen bars of sixteenths and two key changes to write for herself.

A clarinet player finished, then studied the music. "This is cool. If I knew half as much as Elise does, I'd count myself a genius."

Cowdrey waited for someone to laugh. It wasn't the kind of comment kids made about each other. Someone else said, "Really!"

The rest continued to write. Cowdrey said, loud enough for everyone to hear, "Maybe what they want is a well-played *new* piece. Soon as we finish here, break into your sections and work on this."

For the next three days leading to the Friday concert and wedding, practice went better than Cowdrey could have imagined, and not just on the new piece either. They ascended to new heights during "March of the Irish Dragoons," and they suddenly mastered the eighth-note quintuplets and the bi-tonal passages in "Ascensions" they'd fumbled before. Elise popped up everywhere, tweaking the music, erasing notes and rewriting passages, so every time Cowdrey rehearsed a section she had changed his pages.

On concert day, Cowdrey went to the auditorium early. He'd already realigned the chairs and moved the sections about to get the best sound balance for the new arrangements. The director's platform could accommodate Taylor and Liz when they exchanged vows. He put his hands behind his back and circled the room. Even shoes clicking on the floor sounded beautiful in the auditorium's acoustics. He paused at the window, which cast no reflection. Behind it, the auditorium light penetrated a couple feet into the swirling brown cloud. Cowdrey cupped his hands around his eyes and leaned against the window to peer out. At first he'd been afraid to get against the glass. What if something horrible stepped forward, resolving itself from the smoke? He couldn't imagine an event more startling, but over the years the band had played in this room, no one had ever seen anything. Now the sinuous smoke's motion soothed him, as if he looked into ocean waves. It was meditative.

Elise cleared her throat when she entered. She wore her marching uniform, the most formal outfit anyone in the band had. Soon, the other members filtered in, filled with anticipation, gaily bedecked in their uniforms. A grinning Taylor and bashful Liz came in last, music tucked under their arms.

As he had a thousand times before, the director brought the band to attention, hands raised, ready for the downbeat. He inhaled deeply. A good breath, he thought. Let's all start on a good breath. Soon, they were deep into the Beatles medley. Elise had changed the music so radically the original tune vanished at times, then resurfaced later in unexpected ways. The clarinets swelled with the "Yellow Submarine" bridge as the trombones's improvisational bars ended. Later, out of a melodious but unrecognizable tune, the xylophone led them into "Hey Jude."

They moved through song after song. Never had the band's sound been so tight. Every solo hit right. Even the tricky transitions flew until they reached "The King's Feast," the second to last piece. He wiped sweat from his forehead before leading them into the opening bars, and it wasn't until he neared the end that he realized the French horns had played their part exactly on beat. Thomas had hit his entrance on cue. Cowdrey almost laughed in relief as he brought them to the conclusion. Thomas was safe.

Cowdrey put the baton on the podium and nodded to Elise who had already stored her flute on the stand next to her chair. She came forward solemnly, climbed the platform, then picked up the baton. Shuffling their papers, the band switched to her wedding march music. The baton's tip pointed up. She took her own deep breath. The march began, a lingering intro that sounded nothing like a march or wedding music, but soon the drums rose from behind—Cowdrey hadn't realized they were playing at all. He'd been paying attention to the odd harmonics in the flute and clarinet section—but there the drums were, dancing rhythms that made him shift his look to them. Then the brass opened, and the tune bounced from side to side, all in a few bars, all too quick before fading for the ceremony. Cowdrey closed his eyes. "What was that?" he thought. He almost asked her to play it again.

He stood to the side on the floor a foot below the director's platform, Taylor and Liz's wedding vows ready to read. On cue, the two held hands and came forward. Music swelled around them as they made their way toward the front. The musicians played with part attention on Elise and part on the young couple.

Cowdrey read a preamble, his heart in his throat, Elise's wedding march still in his ears. Taylor and Liz exchanged vows. They kissed. As they exited, arms around each other, two drummers threw confetti, and the band played the wedding march's coda, seeming to pick up without losing a beat. Nothing Cowdrey had ever heard sounded like this. Clarity of notes. Surprising shifts in scale. A moment where a single cornet carried the music before the band swallowed it whole, repeating the notes but changing them round so what was bright became dark, and the dark exploded like fireworks. The music filled Cowdrey's chest, pressed cold compresses of notes to his fevered head, made him sway in fear that it would end or the band would break, but they didn't. The music ascended and swooped and pressed outward and in. At the end, the sound flooded the room, as if to push the windows open to free the band from captivity and give them the grassy pastures Elise talked about so often, rushing toward the triumphant climax they'd been practicing for the last three days. Cowdrey heard wind caressing the tips of uncut grass. He smelled the meadow awash with summer heat. The music painted Earth and home so fully he nearly wept from it, but then it ended. Elise held them on the last note, her face lit with concentration and triumph. Her fist closed, cutting the band off, leaving the memory of her composition lingering in the air. Cowdrey could still hear it, ringing. The lights began to flicker. They loved it, he thought. He turned to salute Elise, the ringing emanating from the middle of his head.

Then, he recognized the sound in the strobe-effect lighting. It built until he thought it would burst him open, and he fell.

A short soft shock of waking.

His cheek rested against cool metal. A weight pressed against his other side. Groggily, Cowdrey sat up. He was in a bus parked in the dark. The student leaning against him groaned, rubbed her eyes, then sat up too. Other bodies stirred in front and behind them. Outside the window, a streetlight showed a long chain link fence and a sign, POLICE EVIDENCE YARD.

"My God," said someone in a voice filled with disbelief. "We're home."

Someone started crying. Their voices mixed. Some whooped and yelled. Some laughed, all at once, voices and sounds mixing.

They poured from the bus into the parking lot, still in uniform, holding on to each other. A boy rattled the gate locked by a large chain and a hefty padlock. A head poked up in the lit window of the building beyond. A few seconds later two policeman carrying flashlights ran out the back door. Cowdrey started counting heads, but someone noticed before he did.

"Where's Elise?"

For a second, the happy noise continued.

"Where's Elise?"

Cowdrey stood on the step into the bus, looking over the crowd. One by one, they stopped talking. They didn't appear so old now, the streetlight casting dark shadows on their faces. He stepped down, walked through them, checking each expression. No crooked glasses. No clipboard tucked under the arm.

Cowdrey pictured her alone in the empty auditorium. Were the lights still flickering? She, the one who wanted to go home the most, stood now, among the silent folding chairs, staring back at the swirling smoke behind windows. What had they wanted from us? What had they wanted?

The band looked at each other, then down at their feet, unable to meet each others' gaze. They looked down, and Cowdrey couldn't breathe.

He moved through the darkness surrounding the band, turning the ones toward him who faced away, searching their faces, but he already had accepted it. He'd lost her. Elise was gone.

As the cops unlocked the gates, shouting their questions, Cowdrey could see the days coming: the interviews, the articles in magazines, the disbelief, the changes in his life. One day, though, after the story had passed, he'd stand in front of another junior high band. He'd raise arms high before the first note, encouraging the players to take that first good breath, but Cowdrey could already feel in his chest the tightness, the constriction, and he knew he'd never be able to make the music good again.

He wouldn't be able to breathe.

ROCK HOUSE

FROM THE HIGHWAY WHERE I PARKED MY CAR, TO THE DOOR OF RICK'S HOUSE, my school-years friend, I climbed a mile of twisting, scrub oak-lined, tree-shrouded path that looked more and more to my satisfaction like an animal track the farther from the highway I traveled. Every foot into the late spring woods was a foot farther from everything else. When the sound of the last diesel truck faded in the leafy rustle, it was as if I had stepped back in time. Tree bark grew rougher, with gaps wide enough to slide my hand into. Roots crossed the trail like great, vegetable veins, and when I stopped the third time to recheck his instructions in the letter I'd received the week earlier, something large and ponderous crushed through the underbrush just out of sight. I stood, my heart paralyzed, his letter fluttering in my fingers, until the heavy snap of branches vanished in the distance and an unafraid mountain jay lighted on a rock near the trail to look me over.

Despite everything, I almost turned around then, but I'd lugged my suitcase so far already.

Rick's eccentricities drove him to excess when he was young. He'd been a bookish, washed-out shadow in college. So had his sister, Lynn, but I'd been a reader too, and we'd found camaraderie in our novels, swapping books, discussing imaginary lives between classes. They were trust fund kids, unbound by finances, and their worries were not the world's worries. By my junior year, I'd fallen in love a little bit with them both, but we didn't have any classes together my senior year. Lynn grew increasingly quiet and absent in the way pale girls can, and Rick started haunting used bookstores for rare editions, expensive leather-bound volumes with cut edges and sewn in bookmarks. I remember the second to last time we talked. He put an old book with an indecipherable title on the table beside him, which, in idleness, I picked up. He snatched it from my hands, his cheeks suddenly red, like blood under the snow, and I saw in his eyes a rage that frightened me. The next day, he tried to apologize, but all I saw was the rage. His skin became a furnace with it, baking me. We never spoke again, but I passed him or Lynn on the quad every once in a while, and I mourned the darkness in their eyes, the burnished silk of their hair. Few people know books. Few like to talk about them.

So we drifted fifteen years apart, until his letter importuning me to visit, to see the "strange edifice of my rock house home," as he put it, to "salve his maladies and afflictions." As misfortune would have it then, time lay heavy on my hands, and my office found me useless. Three weeks vacation and "more if you need it" became my prescription. A week in the mountains with my old friend, Rick, seemed like the best of the bad options. If there was a way to arrange it, I wouldn't go back. Nothing in the world seemed worth the effort.

Two turns more up the tree-shrouded track, then I came to a small clearing in the woods, thigh-high with alpine grass and spring flowers. After the aged forest's overhanging gloom, the sudden space should have lightened my spirits, but instead I felt a twinge of agoraphobia, as if the overwhelming branches held me to the Earth, and their disappearance marked the opening of a gate between me and a gray abyss. My stomach rose. I staggered a step before shaking the impression away. His letter said the clearing was his front porch, but it seemed like any other undisturbed forest space. Certainly nothing manmade marked the scene at first. I looked for a minute to find it. The mountain's shoulder swelled at the clearing's other side into a black limestone cliff shot through with bright mineral lines. At its base, cut into the stone, stood an entrance, tall and pointed like a medieval cathedral's, and when I drew close, the grass tips brushing against my fingertips, I saw that the door was stone too with a stone knocker in the center. Grotesque carvings lined the recessed archway, hideous heads no bigger than my fist, all caught in mid grimace, tiny mouths filled with cat teeth and sharp tongues. Human faces, just barely. I smiled at the sight. Rick lived on a better Earth, a literary one, and where I'd failed in my bookish dreams, he'd clearly pressed on.

I used the knocker, the sound no louder than a pebble tapped against a boulder, but a few seconds later, the door drew back.

"Allan, welcome to Rock House," said Rick, shading his eyes against the clouded sky. "I didn't realize it was day." He laughed. "I didn't realize it was spring."

He'd become even more slender since school, still as pale, but his face had developed middle-aged character. Distinct lines crossed his forehead. A patrician patina surrounded his mouth. His hand rested on the door's edge, and he opened it more to let me in as a waft of cool air brushed my face, smelling of dark stone and deep places. Awkwardly, I stepped across the threshold and into the gloom. The door closed behind me.

My eyes adjusted slowly. Thankfully, I put my suitcase down. "That's a long way to carry groceries." Two hefty lamps at either end of a dark couch provided the only light. The ceiling was high, maybe twelve feet. Later I would notice the engravings that marked its surface, but now it only seemed black except for a foot-wide crystal vein that meandered diagonally across the room.

"Backpacks are the secret." Rick gestured toward the couch.

No carpet covered the floor. The same black stone, polished to a glassy sheen, absorbed the light, and although it looked slick enough to reflect an image, I could see nothing of myself within it, not even a shadow. Glad to be done with the uphill climb, I sat. Rick stood beside the couch, his arms crossed, a scattering of nearly white hair falling across his forehead and over his eyes.

"Your house is spectacular." I turned in my seat. The walls bowed around the room, a rounded square, maybe twenty-five feet from side to side. Tapestries alternated with bare stone. A log smoldered in a niche cut into the wall. "It must have cost a fortune."

"I had it built." He leaned against the couch, partly sitting on the arm. For a moment he gazed around the room, perhaps trying to see it as I saw it. "It took time to find the right location."

"But the effort! How long would something like this take?" I imagined craftsmen dynamiting the cliff face, burrowing into the mountain, and then widening their shaft into this chamber. The floor alone would have taken hundreds of hours to turn from raw rock into a slick black plane. Slowly, out of the darkness, two other doors took shape. It wasn't just a single room. How big was Rick's house?

"A project like this never stops. It takes a life of its own." His voice sounded wan, like his complexion. "Remember, we used to talk about living in stone?" He rested his hand on his knee. "Beautiful, gothic palaces. Wuthering Heights. Prince Prospero's castle. Gormenghast." He sighed. "Khazad-dum."

"So, a nice brick bungalow in the suburbs wouldn't be enough for you?"

He smiled. "No, not for me. Not for Lynn either."

I didn't have time to reply. The shadow that marked the door on the left shifted, and a ghost filled it. I started half from my seat, but then the ghost said in Lynn's voice, "It's been a long time, Allan. The sun must be abroad." I'd almost forgotten how low she spoke. How she drew that contralto note from such a narrow reed, I never knew, but it recalled the nights in her brother's dorm, the three of us sprawled across his bed on our backs; Rick at one end, listening; Lynn at the other, propped by a pillow, a book in her hand reading out loud. My back against the wall, I crossed the two in the middle, our legs intertwined. I could almost feel Rick's bare foot braced against my thigh; how Lynn's leg draped over mine so that when she reached a climactic moment in the story her calf muscle tensed, pulling me closer to her; her voice soothing us both, like a steady wash of waves against a rocky beach. Now, her face and hair reflected the table light perfectly, but from a distance, a far moon behind thin clouds, and her white dress hung from her shoulders to her feet in an unbroken line.

She walked a step closer, and the lunar glow grew stronger. Where Rick had aged, Lynn had improved to lustrousness. She smiled and pushed her hair away from her ears. "Do you want to see the rest?"

The door on the right led to a kitchen and storage room. The chrome surfaces seemed out of place in the stone chamber.

Rick opened a cabinet beside the stove, revealing a large tank. "Propane for cooking and heat, although I prefer the fireplaces. There's solar panels outside and battery storage for electricity. We have to budget our use, I'm afraid." He turned off the lights. "We've grown used to darkness or candles. Books by candlelight, ah, that is the way they were meant to be read."

I sighed with content. The empty years after college already were fading. Books, a comfortable chair, and people to talk to about them.

Lynn excused herself when we entered the other hallway. Her fingers grazed my cheek. "It's really good to see you again, Allan." She entered the first room before closing a door behind her.

Rick grimaced, his emotions hard to discern in the hallway's dim ceiling light. "She's not totally . . . healthy. She tires, I'm afraid. We both do."

I touched my cheek. The year after college I'd taken up with a goth girl who looked somewhat like Lynn, except with black lipstick and multiple piercings. The same slenderness. A passing resemblance in her eyes and hair, but the relationship was a failure. She didn't read beyond Anne Rice. She felt lovemaking was too earthy, too mundane, below her ideas about death, decay and her fascination with vampires. I tried, but I couldn't picture Lynn when I was with her. The few times she consented, it was an act of quid pro quo, a straight exchange of services. She liked me to drive to a cemetery where I could go down on her in the car's backseat, the windows open so the cut grass and freshly turned dirt smells would fill her nose. She longed to couple on a fresh grave or in a tomb, but I was too squeamish. Her voice was wrong. She was not Lynn.

Rick opened a second door. Beyond him, the light didn't show more of the hallway than a few feet.

"Your letter said that you weren't doing well. Something about 'afflictions?'"

"Yes." A switch clicked on. "This is the guest bedroom. I hope it's comfortable enough for you." A bedside light on a small stand showed a bed, a bureau and a chair. Like the front room, tapestries hung from the ceiling to cover the walls. "Afflicted, did I say that? I suppose I am."

"You said maladies, too." I shivered. Away from the fireplace, the air bit with cave cold. I wondered if I had packed a sweater. A thick, folded quilt covered the foot end of the bed.

Two other doors opened into bedrooms. The next revealed a bathroom, where both the toilet and the sink had been shaped directly from rock. A black curtain covered the shower. I didn't realize the bathroom had a mirror until I stepped in front of the sink, where my own face startled me.

"How many square feet?" I still couldn't see the hallway's end.

"Two thousand, originally." He sounded ironic. "Now, I've lost track."

The heart of Rick's house came at the last door. Another peaked cathedral arch like the front entrance waited, but this was unadorned, and our footsteps echoed when we entered. Rick turned on a single lamp on a reading table flanked by two soft-looking chairs. Its weak rays barely reached the walls, twenty feet away, and what they illuminated were books on shelves all the way around the room. A ladder attached to a rail fifteen feet above and mounted on wheels below provided access to the higher volumes. My breath caught in my throat. Books filled every space, all leather-bound, and rarities, no doubt. Their smell filled the air, parchment and ink and binding glues.

"My library." Rick waved his hand. "It and this house have been my life's work."

The books' spines felt cool across my palm. They were solidly packed from end to end. I saw no place to add a new acquisition.

Rick stood beside me. "Here's an oddity." He took a book from a shelf above his head. "Look at this one."

Its brown cover had no title. I moved to the light, but when I tried to open it, the pages stuck at the bottom as if glued. "It's damaged." I held it out to him.

"No, not really. Look at the edge."

I turned the book on end. The bottom pages didn't look like paper at all. The surface was slick, and it clicked against my fingernail.

"Fossilization takes centuries, they say. Water carries dissolved minerals, and the minerals displace the organic material, cell by cell, so thousands of years later we can find complete trunks from ancient trees. Perfectly duplicated leaves in stone." He took the book back. "We find the dinosaurs, even, revealed in rock's slow triumph. Stone echoes."

"But it is, as you say, a gradual process. You can't be implying that your book is turning into a fossil."

"It has been on that shelf for fourteen months. Some of the titles have become . . . permanent, a part of the wall and shelf. The shelves themselves." He shrugged. "I'm not sad about it. There's a poetry here. If the trend continues, my library will always exist. I only read the same one or two of them anymore anyway." His tone became wistful. "Mostly I like to come in here and sit with the books around me."

I shivered again, but not from the cold.

"You must see this, though, at the back of the library."

He led me to a narrow exit surrounded by shelves, but it didn't look like the other doors in the house, although its top led to a point too. The edges were rolled and smooth, more like flesh than stone, and a damp seep glistened on the surface. Rick handed me a flashlight. "The electrical lines don't go this far."

I had to rotate my shoulders to squeeze through the door, and the wet stone moistened my shirt. The flashlight cut a clear shaft in the darkness to reveal the library floor's perfect plane broken into gentle corrugations, and instead of walls, long, natural stone columns connecting the floor to the ceiling. Tan stone replaced the black. "You broke into a cave?"

"I don't think so. I only discovered this a few weeks ago. It wasn't as large then."

"What do you mean?" The light played across the ceiling, catching water drops in brilliant flashes dangling from stalactite teeth.

"I mean, this room is new. It didn't exist when I finished the house."

When I turned, the flashlight changed his face into a landscape of bright whites and shadows. "I don't understand."

He walked into the strange room, dragging his hands across the stone on either side, past me so that he stood near the middle. "This is the affliction I wrote you about. My malady. My evolving rock house."

"Jesus, Rick." A water drop released from the ceiling, caught the flashlight's beam for a glittering instant, then plinked loudly like a glass bell into a shallow pool. "What can I do? Why did you ask me to come?"

He looked at me intently. "We ended on some awkwardness, I remember. I've always been sorry for that. It was my jealous soul."

I couldn't think of an adequate reply. A straightforward apology left me uncomfortable. "Are there bats, too?"

Rick shook his head.

He pointed his flashlight at his feet. The pool picked up the glare. It was if he stood on a radiant platform. "You have the imagination for it. I would have thought of you, eventually, but it was Lynn's idea. She asked me to write."

After much conversation, I grew too tired to talk. Most of the time he sat on his library chair, a book unopened in his lap. He'd lit a candle and turned out the lamp. I sat with him next to that flickering flame, reminiscing about the books we'd read in college. It made me happy to talk with him again, like those times when all that mattered were our thoughts and interpretations, when we considered ourselves a part of the literary elite, polishing off volume after volume, washing them down with wine and talk and long passing nights listening to Lynn read. I thought again of her leg draped over mine and the small contractions in her calf as her speech bathed us, of the intensity in her gaze moving from word to word. She kissed me goodnight the last time we read together, at the door of Rick's room. It was the only time. The next day was when Rick grew so angry about the antique book.

Lynn had asked for me!

When I couldn't hold my eyes open any longer, I excused myself to my room. It wasn't until I was in bed that I looked at my watch. It was only 6:30 p.m. I turned the light out.

The darkness descended. Nothing else describes it. Lying in bed, the quilt pulled to my chin, the utter blackness of a cave enveloped me. My eyes strained to see anything, vainly, waited to adjust to the darkness, but there was nothing to adjust to, and for the first time since I had entered Rick's rock house, the weight of the mountain above me made its presence known. The quiet, too, was utter. No click of a clock. No whisper of air conditioning. No refrigerator buzz. Nothing except the rush of my own pulse in my ears, and soon I couldn't hear that. I held my breath in the silence. Finally, I felt on the table beside the bed for my watch. The tiny green light exploded behind the time: 6:43. It winked out. I pressed it again just to see the hopeful green planet swimming in the unlit space. But when I pressed a third time, the light shone dimmer, and on the last press, the light barely came on before fading to nothing. My battery had died. Sadly, I put the watch back on the table. It felt cowardly to turn the table light on, and Rick had said they budgeted the electricity.

Once, when I was a child, I'd gone on a cave tour with my father. The guide stopped us in a curved hallway, and then he turned out the lights. He said, "This is what a blind man sees every day of his life." Delighted at first, I wiggled my fingers in front of my face, but the guide kept the lights off for too long. I pressed against the wall, trying to grow small, too afraid to reach for my father. My heart stuttered. Then, something touched the back of my neck.

Later, they told me I had had a seizure.

I don't know. I don't remember that part, but it seemed to me, in the instant before all memory fled, something whispered in my ear, its talon on my neck, sharp nail against my skin, teeth clicking together, an airy whisper saying things I didn't want to understand.

Now, in the room's darkness, I lay still for a minute, an hour, a night. Who could guess how long? It seemed, bizarrely, as if the bed were slowly spinning. I tried counting breaths, and wondered if I would be able to tell the difference between being awake in the lightless room or asleep in a lightless dream.

Then, I did hear a noise, a slippery creep that could have been nothing, the sound of a single hair in my ear brushing against another, or the near undetectable rush of a lone drop of water running down the wall, but it repeated. Something was in my room. I became a child again as the steps approached my bed, singular, each, and loud now that came toward me, until they must be at my bed's side. Then, a touch against the quilt. A silky swish of something brushing toward my face.

My heart, my chest, the muscles of my neck, tensed so I thought I would burst.

My back arched slightly as my body clenched. I couldn't scream or voluntarily move. Maybe I whimpered. I'm not proud of it, but the darkness like that, and the sound in the black. Then, a warm caress on my face, a warm breath of air against my lips. Lips on my lips. It took me a second to react, to realize the tongue seeking mine was real and human. I reached out from under the quilt to find an arm, and my fingers moved up to wrap in long hair. The lips pulled away. Cloth rustled. Soft clothes dropped to the floor. The quilt lifted to let in a cool draft, and the bed rocked. Knees bumped knees. The kiss again. I caressed her, slid down to the hip's fine curve and pulled her toward me.

In that total dark, only the baby seal feel of her skin on mine existed. Only her exhalations, warm and explosive against my neck. Only the taste of her mouth, the sweat on her face. Only her fertile smell. We could have been floating above a desert or marooned at sea or on an arena's wide-open floor.

Some time later, her leg still draped over my stomach, her head on my shoulder and my hand on the small of her back, my breath at last slowed to normal. I broke the peace. "After all these years, why now?"

She kissed the underside of my chin, then moved her hand between her thigh and my stomach, down until she held me again, and soon, much sooner than I would have believed possible, I stirred. She levered herself back into position, supple as an eel, but this time my senses expanded beyond the languid cavort beneath the quilt, beyond my hands gliding from sweat-slick shoulder blades to curving back, beyond our consuming mouths, to the room's stone walls, as if our gasping breath served as a bat's sonar, sending signals back to me. I sensed the room and the halls and the moisture trapped in the rocks, and a liquid, mineral sentience around us, listening and urging, greedily absorbing, until, behind that, I felt a brooding overwhelming possessiveness. The walls of Rick's rock house became quiveringly alive, dampness flushed, as if the mountain was reaching into the room, guiding us, huge limestone fingers holding us together, connecting us so firmly and deeply and singly that I thought we had become just one orgasmic being. For an instant I tried to slide out from under Lynn, from under the mountain, but the feeling was too strong, too good, too frightening, and the second time with her it was if my skull emptied out along with everything else.

When it ended, Lynn stroked my chest. Her damp hair stuck to the side of my face. She spoke. "You ask why now?" I listened to the empty room, just as sightless, but the mountain had retreated, and I felt we were alone. She said, "Nostalgia, maybe." Her palm lay still on my heart. "I needed a change." As quietly as she had entered, she left, navigating from the black room by feel or memory.

She'd said, "nostalgia," but we'd never been lovers before. Nostalgia for what? I wondered. But I didn't think about it long; I could still feel her skin against my hand, the touch of her lips under my chin. The sheets were clingy with our sweat.

I don't know how long I was awake after that sleep before I realized it. What I noticed was a swelling of passing candlelight under my door, spreading long yellow fingers that crept across the floor before vanishing, and I felt as if I had slept for some time. I didn't stir at first. The stately wash of light crossing the stone produced a strong déjà vu, like this wasn't the first passing of the light, as if this was a routine for me.

Turning the light on, I got out of bed. Goosebumps prickled my legs as I pulled on my socks, but even with them, a cool draft I hadn't noticed the night before crossed my ankles. Fully dressed, wearing both my sweatshirts, I followed the draft to one of the tapestries. The heavy fabric pulled aside reluctantly, the bottom edge of the cloth no longer cloth at all, but solid rock. At the base of the wall, a ragged hole a foot across blew a steady breeze. The room light didn't reveal anything past the first foot, but the small tunnel sloped down from the floor. Roomy for a rat; too small for a person.

My watch truly had died. I wondered about the time.

Rick sat in the kitchen with a candle next to his plate. "Nothing tastes good to me anymore." He pushed a spoonful of eggs from one side to the other. "But I'm never hungry, anyway." I took a chair on the other side. He looked at me for a long time. "My tastes have grown too sensitive, perhaps. All my senses feel acute."

I asked him about the hole in my room, but he shrugged his shoulders once, as if to say there was nothing he could do about it.

He dropped his fork onto the table. "Do you remember how we used to talk about living in castles?"

I nodded. "Great stories in castles."

"It's the stone. The people are impermanent, but the stone lasts. That's why they were given names. There were other features too."

"Drafts."

"People hiding behind the arras."

I thought about the tapestries hanging in my room. With the lights out, a voyeur wouldn't need to hide behind them. He could stand right beside my bed. "Poor Polonius," I ventured, uncertainly.

"Noises, too. No conspiracy would be safe in a castle. The quietest breath around a corner, down the hall, behind a closed door, might echo to the king's ears. The acoustics can be unpredictable."

Maybe he had a point he was trying to make with this conversation, but with the memory of my and Lynn's throaty gasps so fresh in my ear, I didn't want to know. I left the table and opened a cupboard beside the sink. "Do you have any bread?"

"It's gone bad. Canned goods or the refrigerator are all I have to offer."

Lynn drifted into the kitchen, her white dress brushing against the floor. In the candlelight, I couldn't tell if she looked at me or not as she sat. Rick took her hand, kissed her knuckles, "You're wasting."

"Aren't we all?" She took a pinch of Rick's eggs from his plate and put it in her mouth.

An orange in the bottom refrigerator drawer would do for a breakfast. "I'm chilled. I think I'll eat by the fireplace."

"We'll join you." Rick stood, still holding Lynn's hand.

The fire had died, but soon a couple good sized logs were blazing, warming my shins and face. Ruddy light illuminated the room better than the table lamps. Medieval images decorated the tapestries: knights, castles, banquets, stylized dragons, horses, grain tied in vertical bundles, and the images continued onto the ceiling, etched deeply, but they were black on black, so only the contrast of the fire-lit surfaces to the unlit grooves revealed them at all.

Rick and Lynn took seats farther away. I wondered if the fire's heat reached them. Lynn seemed paler than yesterday, if that were possible. Dark circles underscored her eyes. "Man's relationship to stone goes way back."

Rick nodded, as if this were a continued conversation. "I like Lot's wife. That was a fitting reward."

I ventured, "Didn't she turn into a salt pillar?"

Lynn sniffed. "Too bad about that. The first rain must have dissolved her into a puddle. Tokien's stone trolls. Rain and wind wouldn't touch them."

"Ah, yes, and Ozmandias, King of kings. Time consumed his kingdom, but his statue remained."

Lynn closed her eyes. "The Easter Island heads. I love a good megalith."

"They're everywhere." Rick pushed his chair closer to Lynn so he could put his arm around her shoulders. She leaned into him, and his fingers wrapped around her upper arm. It was not a brotherly embrace. "Stonehenge, Carnac, over 50,000 megaliths in Europe alone."

A log popped loudly, shooting a spark onto the floor. It pulsed a deep heart red for a minute before winking out, and it made me sad. "What time is it?"

Rick laughed, as if I'd finally asked the right question. "It's our time, of course."

Lynn nodded. "Our time, yes. The stone age."

With the firelight on their white faces, on Lynn's white dress, they looked more like statuary than people.

"No, I mean time of day."

Lynn sighed in disappointment. "Oh, I thought you meant . . ." She disentangled Rick's arm from her shoulder. "We don't open the door. Sun, moon, stars and clocks don't matter anymore. That's the beauty of Rock House. That and the books. I don't know what season it is." She yawned. "I woke too soon. I'm going back to bed."

"It's late spring." Suddenly it occurred to me that I couldn't remember if I'd slept only once in their house, of if I'd slept several times. It was disorienting. "Do you know now long I've been here?"

Lynn looked at me from the doorway, her face a pale wisp in the shadow. "You have always been here in a way."

Rick stared into the fire until the top log burned through and fell in two pieces, scattering a dozen glowing coals across the stone. He started, as if out of deep thought. "Let's go look at the tunnel you discovered."

He picked up a flashlight in the kitchen and soon crouched on the floor behind my room's tapestry. "I never visit in here. Really, with the way things are, I should inspect every day."

"What do you think *is* happening?"

He shined the light down the hole. "A thing of beauty, surely."

I fell to my knees beside him. The light didn't reach the tunnel's end.

"I thought you said it was too small to go through." Rick scrunched his shoulders together and squeezed part of his body into the hole. "I'll bet I could skinny down this."

My hand fit in the gap between his back and the top of the hole. "It was smaller earlier."

He wiggled out, then turned so he rested against the wall. "I'll stay here for a while. If I sit quietly long enough, I hear things. Maybe I'll hear the mountain changing." He smiled. "I'm feeling a bit tired anyway."

Rick placed his hands flat on the cool floor and leaned his head back. I realized he wore the thinnest of shirts, the collar open to mid-chest. How could he not be cold? His eyes were shut, and he looked nearly asleep already.

"I'll peruse your library for a bit."

Rick nodded.

I took a candle with me down the hall and through the library's arched door. After some searching, I found a copy of an old favorite, *Lud in the Mist*. The chairs were as comfortable as they looked. The candle cast a bright light from the table. Soon I was deep into the book, reading each page by yellow glow, holding my finger under the next, ready to turn. From the other chamber, the gentle chime of water dripping into the pool provided a jeweled rhythm, steady and clean. From time to time, I caught myself nodding before reading on.

When the candle burnt down to the nub, I lit another, and after what seemed like no time at all, another one. Page after page turned weightlessly, and it seemed as if I'd been reading *Lud in the Mist* all my life, as if I'd reached the last page just to flip back to the beginning again. Somewhere in there, I slept, then woke to the library's total blackness, but the weight of the book was comforting on my lap, and water dripping from stone onto stone didn't sound intimidating at all. When I lit the next candle, I saw many stubs on the table top, their burnt wicks caught in the last smears of wax. I brought my hand before my face. My fingernails were longer than I ever remembered seeing them.

I put the book aside. My back cracked a dozen times when I stood, and both knees popped on their first steps. The candle cast a globe around me, wavering in Rock House's drafts. A few clicks of the hallway switch on the moisture-coated wall were futile. A drip fell on my wrist. I held the candle high. On the ceiling above the light switch, a stalactite several inches long glistened; beyond that, droplets clung to the ceiling as far as the light reached. The floor felt as if it had a slight tilt to the left, and the corners that had looked so square and keenly hewed from the rock in my memory seemed rougher. The hallway didn't look as much like a hallway now as it looked like a passageway.

The light switch in my room was no good either.

The tough parts of walking with a bare candle for illumination are that every little breath threatens to puff it out, and that the light shines directly back into the eyes. I cupped my free hand behind the flame to protect it and to shield myself. A breeze flowed from the hole in my wall, where the tapestry had flopped back into position, although the air pressure held it away from the wall. Rick's legs stuck out from under it.

I tried to speak, but my voice croaked like a rusty pipe instead. I coughed, then tried again. "Have you heard the mountain changing?" The question didn't have the feel of a joke.

Rick didn't answer, and when I crouched beside him, my candle nearly guttered out. I put my hand on his leg. The hard surface cooled my hand. Already mourning, I pulled the tapestry away. Rick's eyes were closed. His skin had taken on the same shade as the stone in his new library room, which meant, if anything, he had gained color. Reluctantly, I touched his face. As hard as the rock it had become, an incredibly detailed and expression-filled rendering of my old friend, his head leaning back, tilted just a touch to the side, as if he'd fallen asleep while sitting there. The wall behind him held him tight, and his legs had melded to the stone floor.

"Ah, Rick." Suddenly exhausted, I sat at his feet, the heavy tapestry resting against my back. Soon, water drips soaked my sweatshirts. I could almost feel the hungry minerals looking for a way into my skin, to begin the molecule-by-molecule replacement. All I needed was to sit and let it happen. The thought of it was attractive, to sit, to gain respite, to put all things aside. This was the first of three temptations.

Beside him, the hole in the wall had widened to almost my height, peaked at the top like the library door. The tunnel sloped just as steeply, but now the candle illuminated a set of steps leading away. Rousing myself, I stood on the top stair. I had never felt an invitation more clearly. "Come down," it said, and it would be so easy to slip from one step to the next, easing ever deeper into the earth, until the entrance behind would be long forgotten, and the journey in became all that there was. The voice called within me. I even took another step down, so that it seemed the rock trembled, while the limestone stairs became more slippery. In that sedimentary air, I smelled the fecundness of an ocean, the hidden underside of the bowl that held the sea, filled with seaweed and fish flesh. What waited at the bottom of that long descent? What lay at the root of the world? But I turned away from this second temptation to flee the room. The last I saw of Rick were his feet poking out from under the solid tapestry, never to move again.

Which brought me to Lynn's room. I should have been thinking of how she would respond to her brother's fate, but I wasn't sound anymore. Rock House felt like a drowsy hallucination with all the logic of a daydream. I thought of warm afternoons on the summer porch, drifting to sleep with bees in the background, where my imagination lifted anchor and anything could happen, except here was no sun other than the tiny one balanced on my candle's wick, and no warmth to relax into. Instead, I was eager to see her so I could share her thoughts on stone that changed and on a brother who had joined it. Only Lynn and Lynn's voice offered a counter to the mountain's offer. She, who walked undaunted in the perpetual night, might help me to understand.

And she waited for me, awake on her bed, lying on her back, a nearly translucent sheet covering her. She didn't blink against the light. "I hoped you would come, Allan." Her low voice lingered in the air. "I knew you would be on time."

"What time, Lynn? In time for what?"

"To make it complete. Immortality is possible, but loneliness would be certain if you were not here."

Confused, I moved next to her on the bed. Candlelight penetrated her sheet, revealing her without uncovering. Here, too, the ceiling dripped. A drop hit the sheet, soaked in. Her skin, where it touched the wet fabric, showed through.

"Be with me," she said, "and I will stay unafraid." Other than her eyes and mouth, she hadn't moved. "Did I ever tell you who my favorite characters in all of literature are?"

I put my hand on her arm. It was reassuringly soft. "Aren't you cold?"

"This is my temperature, now. I have . . . grown accustomed to it."

Her lips were colorless with chill. I wrapped my palm around the side of her face. Her jaw moved under my hand. Her gaze shifted to meet mine. I smiled. "No, you never told me your favorite characters."

Then I noticed her hair. The candlelight revealed so little, but when I shifted to caress her face, the light fell on her hair spread across her pillow. They were one. The bed, the pillow, her hair had turned to stone. The side of her face, where my fingers rested, shifted. Skin grew solid. Below the syncopated patter of water dripping everywhere, I could hear her body changing, like ice crackling in a cup.

"Medusa and her two sisters. The Gorgons were misunderstood." Her breath grew short. "It's not too late, Allan. Embrace me now. Be with me, and we will be eternal."

The third temptation: a single move, and the intervening sheet would be gone. I could cover her, and my hardness would meet hers, forever. No more fleshy disappointments. No blind stumbling among the blind who didn't recognize the world they lived in. No reading books that none understood or talked of or cared about. It could be all Lynn and stone and our glittering underground world. I could see it now: we'd become the castle walls that stand long after the defenders have left the ramparts, the darkling cave that held dragons, the tall rocks at Stonehenge, all everlasting. I could be like that too with Lynn, an unseen monument to literature and love. Might someone stumble upon us in a far future? What would they make of the lovers' statue?

I could choose to be immortal and unchanging, or I could stay among the flawed, the human.

Stone crept across the side or her mouth. "Quick," she whispered. Then an eye glazed over, and what once was liquid and living stilled. I tried to squeeze her hand, to communicate what I couldn't say and what she couldn't hear, now, but her hands had already gone rigid. My heart froze. I might as well have turned to stone for the little I did in Lynn's last moments with me. At the end, her sheet crystallized. With a touch, it shattered, leaving Lynn on her bed, waiting for me to join her for all time. The empress of limestone.

Finally, the grief drove me out of her room and out of Rock House. The front door gave way stiffly, reluctantly. Outside, a hard winter sun glared off an unbroken snow field. My eyes burned and watered. I covered them for minutes before I could look upon the sunlit world. Across the snow, trees' bare limbs rattled in the wind. Late spring had become winter.

I waded into the snow.

A year later, I looked for Rock House again. Underbrush choked the trail so I made a dozen bad turns, but when I came to the clearing, there was no door. Just rough stone, cool even on a hot, summer day. I rested my face against the hard surface. The rock wall would last as long as time, as long as Rick and Lynn.

In silence, the mountain neither praised nor condemned. It only stood, like those great immortal books that Rick and Lynn and I read late at night, night after night, intertwined on his bed. All those marvelous authors whose works became human monuments. They would survive forever. So, with my fragile flesh pressed against the unmoving stone, I couldn't help feeling that hesitation stole my choice. My chance to last had passed.

Behind me, the sun heated the waving grass. Trees creaked and leaves brushed against one another in an unceasing whisper. All living, living until winter came and stilled them, living until new grass and leaves and trees replaced them, temporary, fleshy and weak. Pretty in the sad way a soap bubble buoyed in the wind is pretty, catching the light until it pops.

I trudged away from Rock House, deeper and deeper into the living land, empty of all hope.

If you can, some time, rest your hand on a castle wall. Touch a statue. Pick up a round rock from a river and put it in your pocket.

Only stone goes on.

OF LATE I'VE DREAMT OF VENUS

L IKE A SHINY PIE PLATE, VENUS HUNG HIGH IN THE OBSERVATION ALCOVE'S window, a full globe afire with sunlight. Elizabeth Audrey contemplated its placid surface. Many would say it was gorgeous. Alexander Pope called the bright light "the torch of Venus," and some ancient astronomer, besotted with the winkless glimmer, named the planet after the goddess of love and beauty. At this distance, clouded bands swirled across the shimmering lamp, illuminating the dark room. She held her hands behind her back, feet apart, watching the flowing weather patterns. Henry Harrison, her young assistant, sat at a console to the window's side.

"Soon," he said.

"Shhh." She sniffed. The air smelled of cold machinery and air scrubbers, a tainted chemical breath with no organic trace about it.

Beyond Venus's wet light, a mantle of stars shown with measured steadiness. One slipped behind the planet's fully lit edge. Elizabeth could measure their orbit's progress by the swallowing and spitting out of stars.

Elizabeth said, "Did you talk to the surgeon about your scar?"

Henry touched the side of his face, tracing a line from the corner of his eye to his ear.

"No. It didn't seem important."

"You don't need to live with it. A little surgery. You heal in deep sleep. Two hundred years from now when we wake, you'll be . . . improved." She lifted her foot from the floor with a magnetic click and then snapped down hard a few inches away. "I hate free fall. How long?"

"Final countdown. We'll be back in the carousel soon and you can have your weight again."

The scene from the window cast a mellow light. Silent. Grand. A poet would write about it if one were here.

"Ahh," said Elizabeth. A red pustule rose in the planet's swirling atmosphere. She leaned forward, put her palms against the window. Orange light boiled in the clouds, spreading away from the bloody center, disrupting the bands. "It's begun."

Henry read data on his screens. Input numbers. Checked other monitors. Tapped keys quickly. "A clean hit, on target." He didn't look at the actual show beyond, but watched his sensitive devices instead. "Beta should strike . . . now."

A second convulsion colored the disk, this one a brilliant white at its center which settled into a deep red, overlapping the first burst's color. A third flash, duller, erupted on the globe.

"Was that . . .?"

"Perfect as your money could buy."

In the next ten minutes, four more hits. Elizabeth stood at the window while red and orange storms pulsed in Venus's disk. Henry joined her, mirroring her stance. He pursed his lips. "You can see the dust. If this had been Earth, the dinosaurs would have died seven times."

The planet's silver sheen faded somewhat, and lightning flashes flickered in the roiling confusion.

"No dinosaurs ever walked there, Henry."

He sighed. "Venus has its own charms, or it did."

Elizabeth looked at him. The reflected light from the window caught in his dark eyes. They were the best part of him, the way they looked at her when he didn't think she noticed. Sometimes she wished she could just fall in love with his eyes, but then she saw the scar, and he really was too short and so young, ten years shy of her forty, practically a child, although a brilliant and efficient one. She'd ask the surgeon on her own. Henry would hardly object to a few cosmetic changes while he slept. What else was there to do during the down time anyway except to improve? She had been considering thinning her waist a bit, toning her back muscles.

Henry clopped back to his station, then studied figures on a screen she couldn't see. "There are seismic irregularities, as predicted, making the final calculations more difficult, but the planet is spinning slightly faster now, just a bit. We've also pushed it out of its orbit a bit. The next series will bump it back. You're one step closer to your new Earth."

She turned from him, irritated. "If Venus only becomes another Earth, I failed. We can make it better. A planet to be truly proud of. How are things on Earth, anyway?"

His fingers flicked over the controls. "In the twenty-seven years we slept, your corporation in the asteroid belt has tripled in size, improving the ability to redirect asteroids above projections. We're two years ahead of schedule there. The Kuiper Belt initiative is also ahead of schedule." He reread a section. "We're having trouble with the comet deflection plan. Lots of support for redirecting the Earth-crossing asteroids, but opposition to the comets. Some groups contest our aiming them all at Venus. There's a lobby defending Halley's Comet for its 'historical and traditional values,' as well as several groups who argue that 'comets possess a lasting mythic and aesthetic relation with the people of Earth.' The political wing of the advertising and public relations departments are working the problem, but they have requested budget increases."

Elizabeth snorted derisively. "Give them Halley's Comet. It doesn't have as much water as it used to anyway."

"Noted." Henry sent the order. "Your investments and companies are sound."

"How is the United Nation's terraforming project on Mars going?"

"Badly. They've lost momentum."

"Too big of a project to run by democracies and committees. Too long." She sighed. "If nothing needs my attention, then I suppose it's time for bed."

Henry shut his monitors off, powered down the equipment. A metal curtain slid across the view window, separating them from Venus's tortured atmosphere. "Two hundred years hardly seems like going to bed. Everyone I know will be dead when we awake."

Elizabeth shrugged. "They're all twenty-seven years older than when you talked with them last. As far as they're concerned, you're the dead one."

A door opened in the center of the floor. Elizabeth looked down the ladder that connected the alcove with the rest of the habitat. The ladder rotated beneath her. She timed her step to land on the top rung, then moved down so she held the ladder, leaving her head and shoulders at floor level. The room turned slowly around her. "No second thoughts, Henry. You knew the cost going in."

He nodded at her. She saw in his eyes the yearning. The dream of a terraformed Venus hadn't brought him onto the project, made him say goodbye to everyone he'd ever known, committed him to a project on a time scale never attempted.

No, he came for her.

The rotation turned her so she didn't have to see his gaze. She continued down the ladder. Mostly she thought about the project and the long line of asteroids on their way to add their inertia to Venus's spin, but below those thoughts ran a thread about Henry. She thought, as long as he remains a reliable assistant, what does it matter why he signed up? Henry Harrison isn't the first man who worked for me because he wanted me.

Two hundred years of suspended life, trembling on death's edge, metabolism so slow that only the most sensitive instruments detected it. Busy nanomechs coursing through the veins, correcting flaws, patching breakdowns, keeping the protein machine whole and ready to function. Automatic devices moving the still limbs through a range of motion every day, maintaining joint flexibility, stretching muscles, reminding the body that it was alive because really, really, Elizabeth Audrey, the richest human being who ever lived, whose wealth purchased and sold nations, whose power now stretched over generations, was mostly dead. A whisper could end it.

Maybe in her dreams she heard that deadly voice caressing her, and she would hear it for sure if she were a weaker woman, but if she did hear, she ignored it. Instead she dreamed of Venus transformed. A vision big enough for her ambition. A Venus fit for her feet. A planet done right, not like old Earth, sputtering in its wastes. A Venus fit for a queen.

Elizabeth walked spinward in the carousel; the silky robe she donned after the doctors revived her flapped against her bare legs. Two hundred years didn't feel bad, and the slimming in her waist gave her a limberness she didn't remember from before. The air smelled fresher too, less metal-washed. It should, she thought. Much of her money was devoted to research and development.

Henry joined her in the dining room for breakfast.

"What's the progress?" she asked. Bacon and egg scents seeped from the kitchen.

He smiled. "How did you sleep? How are you feeling? Good to see you. It's only been two centuries."

Elizabeth waved the questions away. "Are we on schedule?"

Henry shrugged. "As we projected, the plans evolved. There have been breakthroughs that make the job easier. We've shaded the planet with a combination of solar shields, aluminum dust rail-gunned from the moon, and both manned and unmanned reflective aerostat structures in the upper atmosphere, cooling it considerably, although we have a long way to go. An unforeseen benefit has been dry ice harvesting, which we've been selling to the U.N's Mars project. Venus's frozen greenhouse gasses are heating Mars. Of course, the bombardment of asteroids and comets has been continuous."

A young man, carrying a tray of covered plates, walked toward them from the kitchen. He wore his dark hair short, and his loose, pale shirt was buttoned all the way to his neck. He nodded at Henry as he put the tray in front of them, but he seemed to avoid looking at Elizabeth. Without waiting for thanks, he backed away.

"Who was that?" Elizabeth uncovered a steaming omelet.

"Shawcroft. He's a bio-ecopoiesis engineer. Good man. He helped design an algae that grows on the underside of the aerostats for oxygen production. The surface is still too warm for biologicals."

Elizabeth tasted the omelet. The food made her stomach uneasy, and didn't look as appetizing as she hoped. "What's he doing serving me breakfast then?"

Henry laughed. "To see you, of course. You're the Elizabeth Audrey, asleep for two hundred years, but still pulling the strings. His career exists because of your investments. He won a lottery among the crew to bring out the tray."

"What about you? He acted like he knew you."

Uncovering his plate, Henry revealed a pancake under a layer of strawberries. "I've been awake for four years. He and I play handball almost every day."

Elizabeth chewed a small bite thoughtfully. Henry's face did look older.

"What did you think of my gift?"

Henry touched the side of his face between his eye and ear. Without smiling he said, "For a couple of years I was mad as hell. I'm sorry you reminded me." His fork separated a strawberry and chunk of pancake from the rest.

Elizabeth tried to meet his eyes. He couldn't be seriously angry. Without the scar, he looked much better.

He put the fork down, the bite uneaten. "Are you ready for a visit to Laputa? You can check the facilities, and they would be honored if you came down."

"Laputa?" She relaxed in the remembering, not realizing until then that she'd been tense. After two hundred years, so much could have changed. When she let the doctor hook her to the complicated devices, she had thought about unstable governments, about unplanned celestial events, about changes in corporate policy. Who could guarantee that she'd wake up in the world she'd designed? This was the great leap of faith she'd made when she started the project. The plan for her to see it to the end would be to outlive everyone around her, and the way to do that was to be the test subject for the long sleep. Henry, for obvious reasons, accompanied her. "You really named the workstation that?"

"A city now. Much more than a station. The name was in your notes. I don't think Jonathan Swift imagined it this way, though." He pushed his plate away. "It's quite a bit bigger than the initial designs. The more functions we built in, the more cubic feet of air we needed to keep from sinking into the hotter regions of the atmosphere. It's the largest completely man-made structure in the solar system. Tourist traffic alone makes it profitable."

The trip from the carousel to Laputa took a little more than an hour under constant acceleration or deceleration except for a stomach lurching moment midway when the craft turned. Out the porthole beside her seat, she could see Venus's changed face. Where the sun hit, it was much darker, but the sun itself was darker too, fuzzy and red, partly blocked by the dust umbrella protecting the planet from the heat, cooling it from its initial 900 degrees Fahrenheit. Henry offered a glass of wine. She sipped it, enjoying its crisp edge. Wine swirled in the bottom of the glass. She sipped again, held the taste in her mouth for a few seconds before swallowing. "I don't recognize this."

He sat across from her. The wine bottle rested in a secure holder in the table's center. "It's an eighty-year-old Chateau Laputa. One of the original bottles of Venusian aperitif. Bit of a gamble. Some of this vintage didn't age well, but it turns out being 30 percent closer to the sun makes for excellent grapes. They grew them in soil from the surface, heavily treated, of course." The ferry shuddered. "Upper edges of the atmosphere. We'll be there soon."

Through the porthole, Laputa appeared first as a bright red glimmer on Venus's broad horizon, and as they grew closer, revealing details. Elizabeth realized the glow was the sun's reflected light. And then she saw Laputa truly was huge; it felt like flying low over the San Gabriels into the Los Angeles basin, when the city opened beneath her. But Laputa dwarfed that. They continued to travel, bumping hard through turbulence until the floating city's boundaries disappeared to the left and right, and then they were over the structure, their shadow racing across the mirrored surface.

Inside she toured the engineering facilities where they built floating atmosphere converters to work on the carbon dioxide gasses that trapped so much heat. She met dozens of project managers and spoke briefly to a room full of chief technicians. They didn't ask questions. They didn't act like the groups of upper management she was used to working with. There was no jockeying for position, none of the push and pull of internal politics that made corporate board rooms so interestingly tense. None of the high stakes adrenaline she was so used to. They listened. They took notes. They answered her questions, but they were quiet, attentive. Worshipful, almost.

Henry drove her in a compact electric cart to the physics labs that controlled the steady rain of Kuiper Belt objects bringing water to the planet, even though it still boiled into vapor on the scalding surface. In a large presentation room, dominated by a map of the solar system alive with lights, each representing a ship or a station, the chief geologist finished his speech. A long line of dots representing asteroids and Kuiper Belt objects in transit traced a curved path through the system ending at Venus. "Fifteen years from now, liquid water will exist at the poles. We should have northern and southern hemisphere lakes by the time you inspect again, perhaps the beginning of an ocean if the weather patterns develop according to the models." He bowed when he finished and kept his eyes lowered.

Everywhere they went, and everyone they talked to treated her with the same deference. Only Henry would meet her gaze. "You are the Elizabeth Audrey," he said again when she complained. "Maker of worlds. Come with me. I think you'll enjoy this. We have transport waiting."

They walked out of a physics lab, leaving behind obsequious scientists and engineers. Henry led, and Elizabeth noticed as she had before that he was a short man. If he were only six or seven inches taller, he might earn more respect. Their next sleep was scheduled for four hundred years. If she talked to the doctors, they could do the work and Henry would not need to be bothered with the decision himself. After all, if he was going to be her sole representative in the future where no one knew her except as the ultimate absentee boss, then he should look the part.

"This is it," he said as the car sped from between two buildings. He stopped and sat beside her while she took it in. A wall of structures a mile away loomed over a plain, a part of the huge circle that enclosed the space. High overhead, Laputa's roof arced to the far horizons. The sun glowed sullenly, a red bright spot in the dark sky. Away from the city's artificial light, red tinted her arms, the metal edges on the car, Henry's face. She turned her hands over. Even her palms took on a red shade.

"What is this place?"

"Blister Park. Come on."

As soon as they stepped out of the car, Elizabeth saw. The floor was clear. Beneath their feet swirled the clouds of Venus, almost black in Laputa's shadow, but far away the city stopped and sunlight came down, illuminating a smoky show of reds and oranges and browns. They moved farther from the car, away from the building, and soon the illusion that they were walking on air seemed almost complete.

Below, in the shadow, bright red and yellow lights twinkled.

"Volcanoes," said Henry. "Venus was volcanically active before, but our asteroid and comet bombardment to spin the planet provoked eruptions. The atmospheric technicians tell me this is good, though. They use the new chemicals in the air to catalyze out what they don't want and to create what they do. There will be a breathable atmosphere before they are done."

"Keeping in mind the improvements in technology, how long until I can walk on the ground unprotected?"

"Still another thousand years or so. If we engineer ourselves instead, it would be much quicker. We need heat tolerance, and a system that uses less oxygen."

"For the workers, yes. The ones that prepare the way, but Venus will not be complete until it is the planet that Earth should have been." She could picture it, a surface rich with forests, and an ecosystem in balance, humanity appropriately humble in the face of a world done right.

"But this has a beauty of its own." Henry moved beside her. The light from below cast shadows on his face.

"It was ugly when we started, Henry. Almost no rotation. Hundreds of degrees too hot. Too much carbon dioxide. Pressure at the surface equivalent to being a kilometer underwater. No life. Nothing. The least attractive spot in the solar system, and it's still ugly now. It will be beautiful, though, when I'm done. When I've reshaped it."

Elizabeth walked toward the middle of Blister Park. She held her hands away from her sides, palms down, like a tightrope walker. If she didn't look up, all she saw beyond her feet were clouds and the volcanoes' dim pulsing. Surprisingly, she felt no vertigo. She moved on the invisible surface as if she'd been born to it. "I'm a god," she said.

*

In a four hundred year long dream, knowing she was dreaming, Elizabeth ran down a long hill with her brother. She hadn't known her brother. He died at child-birth, one of the thousands who didn't make it through the still birth plagues where children were so warped in gestation they couldn't draw breath on their own. It became simpler and more merciful to let them die, death after death. Science took just a few years to find the cause of the plague that killed her brother, the first of the toxic-Earth plagues, but it was too late for him.

In the dream, though, he ran beside her toward the stream that flowed through cool grasses. At the edge, they stopped. No frogs today. No crawdads hiding under rocks. She didn't know why she'd expected frogs and crawdads; they were never in the dream, never, but still the same disappointment washed through her. A boggy flat stretched from both sides, and the reeds that poked up through the smelly muck were brown and broken. A mass of cardboard stuck out of the water, covered with a noxious-looking slime.

Elizabeth held her brother's hand as they walked downstream, careful to keep their feet dry. Around the corner the stream ducked under a fence and into a park. They pushed open a gate. Here, closely clipped lawn painted the hill to a cement curb lining the stream, which now flowed through an open culvert. Signs warned them to stay out of the water, but her brother lay on his chest, reaching down to touch the ripples. In the dream, Elizabeth tried to shout, but her throat constricted. His fingers brushed the water, and then he turned to look at her, his eyes serious and dark (where had she seen those eyes before?). A scar marked the side of his face. She wanted to rub it away, but when she dropped to her knees to touch him, his skin had grown cold, like a statue. And then he was a statue, a bronze of a boy lying on his side by a stream, his clothes a solid metal, a patina of corrosion in the places that were not buffed smooth.

Elizabeth sat beside him, beside the contained stream. In the sky, no clouds, but a dozen contrails crisscrossed each other, like a giant tic tac toe game. The air smelled of city and too many people piled on one another, story on story in high rises beyond the park. A clatter of metal against metal clanged in the distance. More construction. On the stream's other side, flowers in unnaturally neat rows filled a garden held behind a plastic border. She looked back beyond the fence where trash filled the water. Neither was right. She knew neither was right, but it was too late to shout. Her brother was dead, and she had no breath behind her scream. The statue couldn't hold her hand.

*

Elizabeth couldn't breathe. She choked and then coughed, an unproductive spasm that didn't give her a chance to inhale before she coughed again. Her chest hurt. People bustled around her, but she hadn't opened her eyes yet. She was suffocating. Someone held her hand. A mask went over her face, and pressure built up within it, pushing against her eyeballs.

"Relax, Eliza. Let the machine help you."

She opened her mouth, allowing the pressure's force to open her throat, filling her lungs. The air tasted sweet! She could feel tears pooling where the mask wrapped her cheeks. The pressure relented and she exhaled on her own before it built again, respirating her at its own pace.

She took slow breaths, each one quivering on the trigger of another spasm, but breath by breath the urge to cough subsided until her lungs moved easily. "I don't need this," she tried to say, but the mask muffled her. She tapped the hard surface with her finger. The mask came off. She was in the awakening room. A doctor stood to one side, the mask clasped, ready to put it back if her breathing struggled. Beside him, a technician bent over what looked like a small clipboard. When he turned, she saw information flashing across the surface. Her information, she assumed. Henry sat on the edge of the bed, holding her hand.

For a minute she inhaled and exhaled carefully, testing each movement. Then she looked at him. "Did you call me Eliza?" Her voice cracked and felt dry in her throat.

He let go of her hand. "Sorry. Emotional moment."

"Don't let it happen again." She shut her eyes. "Where are we?"

"Laputa, but we've anchored. The floating city's era has passed. Not enough pressure in the atmosphere."

Later, Elizabeth and Henry walked a hallway in the infirmary. Her steps were unsteady. When they turned a corner, she almost fell. Henry grabbed her arm to hold her upright. They had dressed her in a white robe with stiff, exaggerated collar and cuffs. Change of fashion she guessed.

"It was harder this time."

"We're into new territory in long sleep. Others have been packed, but it's just until cures for their diseases are found or they outlive their enemies or they want a one-way trip to the future. If they've got the money, they can buy the bed. The arc ships heading to the Zeta Reticula system use long sleep too. It's a 4,000 year trip, but they're waking up every one hundred years for equipment maintenance. Only you and I have slept so long uninterrupted."

Elizabeth shook her head, trying to clear the fuzziness. "Am I damaged?" She took longer steps as if she could force strength upon herself.

"I hope not, or I'm damaged too. They're still testing me, and I've been up for six years. I told them I was okay after a week." They turned another corner in the hall. Henry held her arm again, making Elizabeth feel like an old woman, which she was, now that she thought about it. "We're walking to an auditorium now. There will be a ceremony. The people want to see you."

"Public relations never goes away."

Henry looked diplomatic. The extra years he had been awake gave his face more character than Elizabeth remembered. A map of tiny wrinkles sprung from the corners of his dark eyes. "Well, the situation's a bit more complicated than that. We should have foreseen."

Elizabeth moved steadily forward, already more confident, eager to see how much closer they were to her goal. "Complicated how?"

"Lots of changes. Governments have risen and fallen. Politics went through several evolutions. The business environment metamorphed during the time."

"They didn't nationalize me, did they?" Elizabeth stopped. The idea that she might have lost control frightened her. Her stomach knotted. The companies, the investments, the foreboding weight of her multi-industrial empire might have fled her grasp in the years she slept. Anything could have happened while she slumbered. "They haven't taken my assets?"

Henry gazed down at her solemnly. Elizabeth realized the doctors had done their work. He was now at least two or three inches taller than she. His hair matched his eyes, still black. Some gray there would give him more distinction. She made a note to herself to order the change for him, maybe a deeper timbre to his voice to give him authority.

"We should have known that a corporation couldn't last for hundreds of years, Elizabeth. Even a dozen decades would be asking for a lot, but your CEOs, multiple generations of them, made decisions to preserve your initiative. We're still on schedule."

"I can talk to heads of state. Solidify our position." She pictured the crowded board rooms, the private conversations over expensive dinners at exclusive restaurants, the phone calls and e-mails, all with her at the center, pulling threads, massaging egos, handing down favors with imperial aplomb.

"You won't need to." He led her to a set of double doors. Inside, two lines of exquisitely dressed men and women gave them a hallway to walk through. Many of the people bowed as Elizabeth and Henry passed. Elizabeth still didn't feel completely focused. A surreal air hovered about the scene. "Madam Audrey," one man said as he touched the back of his hand to his forehead and bent at the waist. No one else spoke. At the hallway's end, an ornate set of doors that reached to the high ceiling swung open. Elizabeth slowed. She couldn't see the other side of the dark room beyond, but it seemed huge, and there was movement in the dark. Lights flooded a stage that she and Henry stepped onto. She shaded her eyes, and the roar began, hundreds of thousands of voices, cheering, cheering, cheering, and they were cheering for her.

Henry leaned in, cupped his hand around her ear. "They arranged for you to become a religion. It's the only organization that would last long enough to see it to the end."

The next morning, Elizabeth joined Henry in a vehicle garage where a heavily insulated truck waited for them. "First," said Henry, "I want to point out that we are going to exit through those doors and into a Venus morning. Thirteen hours from now, the sun will set. Your original plan was for a twenty-four hour day/night cycle, but after four hundred years of asteroid and comet bombardment, the terraformers saw that we were getting diminishing returns. At some point, each collision produced more problems for them to undo than they were solving, so they decided to stop and leave Venus with a longer day."

Elizabeth frowned. "I don't like compromise." She did feel steadier on her feet than she had yesterday, and climbed into the car before Henry could give her assistance. "What's second?"

"Best I show you." He pulled the truck into an airlock. When the outside doors opened, a red, dusty light flooded the bay. Elizabeth slid close to the window. A graded road led into a series of low hills that faded in the hazy red air. The car pulled out of the garage, and for the first time, Elizabeth could see first hand what her efforts had produced. A brisk breeze whipped dust off the road ahead of them.

"Still warm, still too much carbon dioxide, still too much surface pressure, but we're very close, Elizabeth." The truck climbed the first hill, and from the top, as far as the dusty air allowed, similar hills reached all around. "The final changes go the slowest."

In front of them, the morning sun glared red and unbelievably large. The truck lurched through a turn as it ascended a second hill.

"I thought there would be more evidence of the meteor strikes."

Henry laughed. "Oh, heavens, there is, but it's all on the equator. We have created a badlands like nothing this solar system has ever seen. Some of the strikes broke the tectonic plates, bringing up rock from thousands of feet below the surface, liquefying, vaporizing, shattering. Venus' equator regions are already legendary. Anything could get lost there or hide there. It truly is untamable. See this?" He held out his wrist. A shiny black bracelet set with green and yellow stones caught the sun light. "The metal is carbon nanotubes. If you need it made out of carbon, Venus can make it. Every spaceship hull in the solar system is manufactured here. The jewels were mined in the badlands. Ah, we're here."

He stopped the truck on the hilltop. Before them, a lake rippled in the wind, filling the valleys so that what she had thought were other hills earlier she could see were islands.

Elizabeth gasped. "Liquid water."

"Do you want to go fishing?"

"Really?"

Henry rested his forearms on the steering wheel and looked out onto the lake. "Kind of a joke. No, not this time. There are thermophilic shrimp, though, and adapted corals, engineered crabs, modified algaes, mutated anemones, evolved sponges, and dozens of other heat-happy organisms who like water just short of boiling. About the biggest thing out there that we know of is a heat tolerant eel that grows to a foot or so. I've been boating at night. Almost all the species we introduced bioluminescence. It makes them easier to keep track of. Blues, yellows, greens. The boat's wake is a trail of fire." He sounded meditative. His fingers dangled, nearly touching the dashboard. Elizabeth had never noticed before how strong his hands looked. Calluses marked the fingertips. A line of dark grit was under his fingernails. "On land, we've introduce lichens, soil bacterias, nothing complicated. They do best near the lakes. Rain is undependable."

"How long did you say you were awake before you woke me up?"

He didn't turn his head. "Six years. I wanted to make sure everything was ready for you."

She looked at the lake again. A film of black dust piled at the corner of the window like a soot snow drift. The wind picked up, tearing froth off the tops of waves, and it moaned, passing over the truck. Elizabeth couldn't imagine finding anything attractive in the desolate landscape. Dry, toxic, inhospitable except for the most primitive of life. She pictured its surface in six hundred years, when she awoke. Brush would cover the hills and heather would fill the valleys. Willows would line the bank of this heated lake. What did Henry see in it now?

Henry said, "The doctors are worried about putting you to sleep for so long. Your system didn't respond the way they would like."

Outside a bank of clouds moved across the sun, casting the lake and hills into a weird, maroon twilight. Dust devils twirled off the road before beating themselves into nothingness in the rocks higher on the hills. If the wind uncovered a bizarre version of a cow's skull, dry and leering, by the road, Elizabeth would not have been surprised. Nothing was right about the planet yet. Nothing was done.

"I can't stay here, Henry. I have to see it to the end."

Henry nodded, but before he put the truck in gear to take them back to Laputa, he faced her. "Do not try to change me again as we sleep. Do not, ever, be so impertinent again."

For a second, Elizabeth thought she saw hatred there, just a glimpse that flashed in the back of his dark eyes, and she respected it.

But two weeks later, when it came time to sleep, she met with the doctors. She gave orders. Just a touch, a tweak, a fine tuning. Henry wouldn't mind, she thought, if he loved her like she knew he did, he wouldn't mind at all.

In the six-century dream, Elizabeth, watched the rain from comets covering Venus. The water ice started beyond Neptune's orbit, like ghostly icebergs drifting in space so distant that the sun was merely a bright star among other stars. Gently nudged, they began their long journeys inward, finally, catastrophically for them, exploding into Venus's atmosphere, contributing water to a planet long without.

Rain fell. It fell in spurts, in squalls, in flurries, in long sizzling sheets that worked their way into cracks beneath the surface, nourishing the alien life planted there, until there came a time when the rain didn't just fall on rock. Plants grew, their leaves upturned, catching the water as it fell, spreading it to roots.

The rain eroded. Cut through stone. Carried silt. Formed rivulets, creeks, streams, rivers. Gathered in pools, ponds, lakes, seas. Evaporated, formed clouds, fell again.

And then, finally, in the highest of high places, appeared the first snow.

Elizabeth saw herself standing in Venus's snow, the perfect crystals falling on her bare arms, one by one pausing for a moment as petite sculptures before melting. Snow cleared the dust and smelled crisp as a fresh apple. She ran through the white blanket, splashing her legs as she ran, looking for her brother. Where was he? This was water he could play in. This water wouldn't harm him. She'd made it safe in her dream. At a lake's edge, she stopped, looking both directions as far as she could, but he wasn't there, just the silent snow falling onto the red-tinted water. Each snowflake, when it met the lake, glowed for a second, until the water's surface itself provided the only light in the dream. Plenty of light to see him if he was there, but he wasn't.

She stood at the lake's edge for centuries.

"She's awake."

Soft light fell all around, like snow. Time passed. Darkness. Light again. I'm under the snow, she thought. Darkness.

"She's awake."

Her arms were moved. Light was provided. A question was asked. A tube was pulled from her throat. She was hurt. All very passive. Darkness.

"She's awake."

Elizabeth forced her eyes open. An older man sat on the bed beside her, holding her hand. Beside him stood a medical technician in a lab coat. The man holding her hand had a haggard face. Worry lines across his forehead. A little baggy in the jowls. It wasn't until she blinked her vision clear that she could see his eyes.

"Henry?"

He mouthed a silent, "Yes."

"How long?"

He patted the top of her hand. "Six hundred years."

She tried to sit up. Before she was halfway, though, her calves cramped.

"Probably easier to lay still right now," Henry said. "The doctors here have some wonderful treatments. Since you've made it this far, you should be up soon."

Breathing softly, Elizabeth considered what he said for a moment. "There was a doubt?"

"Big one for a long time."

The ache in her legs dwindled to a dim reminder, no worse than the one she felt in her neck and back and chest. She squeezed his hand. "Henry, I'm glad you're here."

"You can take care of her now," he said to the lab-coated man.

For the next two days, doctors came and went. They wheeled her from one examining room to the next. Most of the time she couldn't tell what they were doing. Strange instruments. Peculiar instructions. Doctors nodding to each other over results that didn't make sense to her. Even their conversation confused her, speaking with a dialect too thick for her to decipher. Although she did have one moment of relief when one asked her to stick out her tongue and say, "Ahh." The tongue depressor even appeared to be made from wood.

They weren't subservient, however. Brisk, efficient and friendly, but not servile. When she saw Henry again, she asked him about it. He met her in a sitting room where other patients sat reading or visiting quietly. The medical techs insisted she stay in a wheelchair, although she walked quite well in a physical therapy session earlier in the day.

"All that I've learned from our strange journey, Elizabeth, is that time changes everything. You're not a religion anymore. Actually, now you're kind of a curiosity. I expect someone from the history guild will want to talk with you. Marvelous opportunity, you know, to actually chat face to face with the Elizabeth Audrey."

Something in the way he said it caught her ear. "What about my holdings? What about the corporations?"

Henry covered her hand with his own. "Gone, I'm afraid. Long, long gone now."

The tears came unbidden. She thought of herself as a strong person. Finally, she shook the tremors off and dried her face. "We need to get to work then to get it back. How close are we to finishing the project?"

Henry smiled. She'd always liked his eyes, but now the years in his expression set them off beautifully. "I'll let you judge for yourself."

When he stood, a medical tech who had been waiting a few seats away, rushed over to help.

"That's okay. I'll take her," Henry said.

"Thank you, sir," said the tech. "I'll be close if you need me."

Elizabeth looked from the tech to Henry and back again. She recognized a power order when she saw one. "How old are you Henry? How long have you been awake this time?"

He turned her chair toward the exit and began rolling her toward the door. "Twenty-two years. I'm sixty-two now."

The door opened into a wide space. A ceiling a hundred feet above enclosed the multiple levels and balconies she saw on the other side. Pedestrians walked purposefully to and fro.

"What is this, a mall?"

"More like a business park, but you've got the right idea."

A pair of woman dressed in dark, functional leather longcoats walked past them. One laughed at something the other said. Pale clean circles surrounded their eyes in faces that were uniformly filthy.

"Prospectors do a lot of trading here," said Henry, as way of explanation.

He wheeled her to a garage a level lower and helped her into a car. This one didn't appear nearly as heavy as the truck she'd ridden in with him what seemed like a lifetime ago.

"It's time for you to see Venus in its glory," said Henry.

A half hour later he parked the car on what might have been the same hill he'd taken her to before, but now the burgundy sun rested low on the opposite horizon, and where before the landscape was marked by wind, rock and water, plants grew everywhere. Thick-stemmed vines clung to the rocks beside the road. Low bushes dotted the slope to the water's edge. Here and there, short pine-looking trees poked from the soil, their trunks all leaning the same way and their branches pointing away from the lake. And there was color everywhere. Not only were there the gray and black rocks she remembered, but also tans and browns and yellows. Across the face of the hill to their left, a copper sheen caught the sun, and on the hill to their right, the mossy clumps growing between the rough stones were a vibrant blue.

But no heather covered the hills. Where she imagined a world with waterfalls, there was only sharp-edged stone. Where she hoped for soft yellow light on fields of flowers, there was a red sun, bloat as a toad on the horizon. She saw a rough land.

A figure dressed in a leather longcoat, goggles covering the eyes, walked past their car, saw Henry, and tipped his leather hat as he continued on toward the lake where a small complex of buildings serviced two long docks and a dozen moored boats.

Elizabeth tried to contain her disappointment. "This is not even close to what I worked so hard for. I wanted a world that was what Earth should have been, what it could have been if we hadn't ruined it. Venus could have been paradise!" The outburst left her short of breath. In the car's confines, her breathing sounded loud and harsh. "I had a brother . . ."

"You were an only child." Henry sounded quizzical.

"No, I . . ." Panic rose in Elizabeth's throat. She did have a brother, didn't she? It took a second for her to sort it out for herself. A thousand years of dreaming could feel more convincing than a few decades of reality.

"We have to get out of here. Take me back."

"Wait," said Henry. He reclined his seat a little before folding his hands across his chest. He watched the sun setting on the lake's other side. Elizabeth leaned back in her chair, her heart thudding hard.

The sun slipped deeper into the hills behind the lake. Elizabeth relaxed. Could she get the money back again? She knew no one. The game was surely different now. A wind scurried across the water, rocked the boats, and then rushed up the road to toss sand against the car. Shadows lengthened. She felt so tired, so truly, truly old.

"You know," Harry said, "I talked to the doctors before I went to sleep the last time. It took considerable persuasion on my part, but I discovered you'd told them to work on me again. For a while, I thought the best action would be to go to your bed and kick out the plug. It was tempting."

Henry didn't move while he spoke. His hands stayed still as he watched the setting sun.

Elizabeth floundered for a moment, unsure of how to reply. When they'd started this project a month ago ("No, a thousand years ago," she thought), he would have never spoken to her like this, and she would have had no trouble telling him what she thought, but this wasn't the same Henry, not by any measure. "I'm sorry, Henry. I didn't think you would mind, really. They were changes for your own good."

"I loved you once, but you have a mean sense of perfection, Eliza."

The sun's last glimmer dropped out of sight. "Watch now," he said. The horizon glowed like a campfire coal, then, as sudden as a sunset can be sudden, low clouds that had been invisible until now picked up red edges, their middles pulsating cherry gold, and the air from the horizon line all the way to nearly directly overhead turned a deep purple with scarlet streaks, changing shades even as she realized they were there.

A half hour later, still in silence, they watched. Stars appeared in the moonless sky. A boat left the quay, trailing a bioluminescent streak behind it.

Elizabeth found she was crying again. "My, God, it's beautiful, Henry, but it's not what I was trying to make. It's not better than Earth."

"It's Venus," he said. "It doesn't have to be better."

By now, night had completely fallen. There were no board room meetings to attend. No calls to make. No projects to shepherd to success. Elizabeth felt very small sitting in the car with Henry. Her muscles ached. She suspected she would never be physically as capable as she once was. A thousand years of long sleep had taken their toll.

"What about you, Henry. You said you loved me once. Will you stay with me?"

She couldn't tell in the dark if he turned to look at her or not.

"You couldn't shape me into what you wanted either."

He started the car, which turned on the dashboard controls, but made no noise. The light revealed his hands on the wheel.

"My days of shaping are done, Henry."

He drove them the long way home, over hills and around the lake. They didn't speak. Neither knew what to say to the other, yet.

JUST BEFORE RECESS

PARKER KEPT A SUN IN HIS DESK. HE FED IT GRAVEL AND TWIGS, AND ONCE his gum when it lost its flavor. The warm varnished desktop felt good against his forearms, and the desk's toasty metal bottom kept the chill off his legs.

Today Mr. Earl was grading papers at the front of the class, every once in a while glancing up at the 3rd graders to make sure none of them were talking or passing notes or looking out the window. Parker would quickly shift his gaze down to his textbook so Mr. Earl wouldn't give him the glare, a sure sign that Parker's name would soon go up on the board with the other kids who had lost their lunch privileges for the day. He could feel Mr. Earl's attention pass over him like a search light.

Slipping a pebble out of his pocket, Parker carefully lifted his desktop a quarter of an inch and slipped the rock in. It made a tiny clink when it dropped to the bottom. He leaned the desk away from him until he heard the pebble roll toward the sun, followed by the tiny hiss that meant the rock had vanished into it.

Two days ago he'd opened his desk to put his lunch in, but instead of the pencil box and tissue box and books he expected to see, a cloud swirled in the space, at its center, a dull, pulsing red glow. He shut the desk and looked around to see if anyone else had noticed. An hour later, the dusty swirl in his desk had contracted to a bright spot in the middle. He cautiously moved his hand toward it. At first he felt only the heat, but when he got within a few inches, the skin on his palm began to sting, like the flesh was pulling away. He snatched his hand back, then tried a pencil. When the point moved close enough, the pencil tugged toward the sun, then snapped out of his fingers into the tiny light, brightening it slightly in the process.

Now the sun was as large as a golf ball. When Parker rolled a marble across his desk, its path would curve toward the sun within, sometimes circling several times before resting exactly above it.

"Parker," Mr. Earl said, "your reading group is waiting for you."

In the back of the class, his three reading partners sat on the mats, their books on their laps. Parker pushed away from his desk and joined them.

"Where's your book?" Mr. Earl said, his eyebrows contracting into a single line above his eyes.

Parker shrugged. Mr. Earl growled. "You need to be more responsible, young man. Go get your book."

The other students looked on, relieved that Mr. Earl's attention was on Parker and not on them.

"I don't have it, sir," said Parker. It had disappeared into the sun along with everything else.

Mr. Earl's hands clenched slightly. Parker cringed as his teacher pushed away from his desk. Mr. Earl almost never left his desk. Students came to him. He didn't go to students unless the infraction was terribly, terribly bad.

"You, young man, are irresponsible. Remember our talk about responsibility on the first day of school?" He looked at each of his students who nodded in turn. "Isn't your book in your desk where it belongs?"

"No, sir," said Parker. How could he explain about the swirling dust, the pulsing red glow, the sun's pinpoint of light?

"Of course it is. That is where your books should always be. Everything in its place. A place for everything. Isn't that right?" His question sounded like an accusation.

Parker nodded. "But my book isn't there, Mr. Earl."

The teacher took two long strides and stood beside Parker's desk. Before the boy could speak, Mr. Earl threw the desktop open. For a second, he stared into it. A white glow reflected off his face. "What is this?" he said, as he reached toward the brightness.

"Careful, Mr. Earl," Parker started to say, but it was too late.

The teacher screeched before lurching against the desk. He went down quickly, his feet vanishing into the desk last.

A long silence filled the room. Parker stood, walked back to his desk. The sun within had grown, its heat baking like a tiny oven. He closed the top, which snapped down hard on its own at the last moment.

The other students hadn't moved. Parker looked at them. They looked at him. Over the intercom, a bell softly chimed.

"Recess," said Parker, and they all ran outside to play.

THE RADIO MAGICIAN

IN THE EVENING CLARENCE SPRAWLED ON THE RAGGED HOOK RUG, FACING the cathedral front of the burnished wood Edison, a pillow tucked beneath his chin, a blanket wrapped around his shoulders, and his useless legs encased in casts, sticking behind him. Eyes shut, he listened to KLZ, the Reynolds Radio Company, and then slowly rotated the dial through the other Denver stations. Sometimes late at night he'd pick up WDAF out of Kansas City or WAAF in Chicago. Everywhere he turned he found wavering voices, scratchy baseball games, foreign speech and strange music. News from overseas. Poland invaded. President Roosevelt. Big bands. The slightest twist of the wooden knob brought new sounds, all so far, far away from his tiny bedroom and the ragged hook rug. He wished he could crawl in among the glowing tubes with their tiny suns suspended in glass cages. They warmed his chilled hands. He'd listen as hard as he could so that he wouldn't hear his own breathing, so he wouldn't even *think* about his breathing. Did that breath hurt? What about the next one? Did the muscles in his chest tighten up just a little that time?

Mom had said, "You're luckier than some, son. It's only your legs."

So far, thought Clarence. So far. No, he didn't want to think about breathing.

So, he listened to *The Shadow, Bobby Benson and the B-Bar-B Riders, The Tom Mix Ralston Straight Shooters*, and he loved Charlie Chan stories from *Five Star Theater*, but mostly he listened for *Professor Gilded's Glorious Magical Extravaganza*. On the table by the window, the clock ticked to the hour, just as the announcer said, "Now, for your listening pleasure, Denver's very own radio magician." Clarence shivered in delight, and waited impatiently through a Pepsodent commercial.

"We return today to disappearance and transference," said Professor Gilded. "Last session, we talked of coins that moved from one hand to the next, from your hand to a pocket, from a pocket to a purse, or coins that vanished all together."

Clarence scooted closer to the radio, holding his own coin tight, a gold quarter eagle that felt warm and smooth. Tonight he barely had a headache, so the show was more enjoyable.

"You see, I put a coin in my left hand. I show it to the audience. The coin is there, I assure you. Its edges press against my skin. Everyone has seen it go into my left hand. That is the secret. Everyone must see."

Clarence pictured Professor Gilded on his tiny radio stage. Once *The Denver Post* had printed a picture of the professor's broadcast. Beside him, his top hat rested on a spindly legged table. The audience of ten who were there by the luck of having their names drawn from letters they'd sent the show, leaned forward. Every week Clarence wrote Professor Gilded a letter, but his name had never been drawn.

Last week, Father had patted Clarence's head. "How would we get you there, Clarence boy? You won't be going on that journey while you are sick. But write your letters. It's good your mind is so active." Then Father drew a long breath through his pipe, and held it in his lungs before releasing a steady gray stream.

Professor Gilded continued, "The coin does not know the trick. That is the trick. The coin does not know. So when the magic happens, the coin has jumped from my left hand to wherever I want it to go." He paused. A quiet drum rolled in the background as it did before the magic occurred. "Where do you think the coin has appeared this time? It is not in my left hand as you can see." The audience oohed and then clapped. Clarence squirmed in contentment. He *could* see Professor Gilded's empty hand. "Young lady with the fancy hat sitting in the back row. Yes, you. Would you check inside that beautiful red ribbon on the hat?"

A surprised squeal burst from the background. The audience buzzed with startled conversation.

The announcer said, "Ma'am could you describe what happened for our listeners?"

"The coin was inside my hat! Professor Gilded never moved from the stage!" She giggled suddenly. "I'm going to keep this forever."

Clarence squeezed the quarter eagle, a birthday present. "A ten-year-old deserves real money," Mother had said as she gave it to him. "It's a lucky coin, minted the year your father and I were born." She put her finger on the date, 1910. "You can't spend it. It's not legal money anymore." She leaned close, like a conspirator. "We were supposed to turn all the gold over to the government in 1933, but I held this one for you." The secret made the coin worth even more. Sometimes he thought of what the two and a half dollars could buy, and it made him feel rich.

Clarence pressed the small coin's bumpy edges against his skin, clenched it in his fist, turned the hand over, willed the coin to vanish. He scrunched his forehead, focused, tried to believe the quarter eagle was no longer in his grasp. But it was no good, just like wishing he could move his legs was no good. Even getting around on crutches would be better than his plaster jail. New crutches rested against the closet door. Beneath them in a box waited leg braces with long metal bars, heavy leather straps and black buckles. Someday, his mother promised, he would walk in them. The casts, though, were too heavy, and he couldn't swing his legs to keep himself moving forward. A week ago he'd tried, only to fall face first onto the hardwood floor.

Professor Gilded's voice broke in. "We do not dabble in the supernatural here. Charlatans claim their magic is real. The coin's disappearance is an illusion, a trick of perception only, but our perceptions make reality for us all. If you perceive you are cowardly, then illusion becomes the world. If you perceive you are ill, then illness becomes you."

Clarence's eyes popped open. He turned the sound up, his own attempts at the trick forgotten. Beneath his casts, his legs ached. He remembered running home down the long muddy lane beside the field, its corn already harvested, the broken stalks lying across each other. He'd run on the weeds beside the lane to keep his shoes dry. Then he stumbled. For a second, he thought he'd stepped in the mud, but he could see the shoe was clean. His right leg dragged again. He slowed to a heavy limp, massaging his thigh through his jeans. What was wrong with his leg? The house had never looked so far away. Too far to call for help. He leaned on the fence and felt his strength fading.

Just as he reached the gate an hour later, Mom came out on the porch to look for him. She ran to him as he fell, her face wet with fear. By morning, the left leg had gone weak too. How far would it stretch? As the doctor poked at him later that day, Clarence made a fist, then unmade it, over and over. Would the paralysis spread? Fist. No fist. Fist. No fist.

Professor Gilded said, "The world's illusions cloud perceptions. Most fail to recognize reality before them. They believe they are poor, or ugly, or life's horizons are short. If my assistant will allow me to demonstrate, observe the reality of my four-legged friend."

The sound of clopping came from the speakers before the announcer said, "Professor Gilded's beautiful assistant, Sonia, is leading a horse into the studio, a strawberry roan, courtesy of the Phipps Ranch. I have to tell you folks, livestock in a radio studio is not what you see every day." Chairs scraped across a wooden floor. Someone said, "Give him a bit of room."

The announcer whispered, "The studio is not large, my friends. Our audience has moved to the back wall. The horse, a gentle one, chosen especially for this demonstration, stands no more than five feet from them. Professor Gilded's stage gives him a height advantage. He's removing a large, blue blanket from the chest behind him."

Clarence turned the sound up again. The big trick always ended the show. First, the small demonstrations. Cards that reordered themselves. Balls that multiplied. Flowers that changed colors. Handkerchiefs that metamorphosed into birds. All the while Professor Gilded lectured on magic, on the magic he was doing and the magic in the world, as he built to the finale, something so impressive that his audience clapped and clapped and clapped until the sound faded and the show ended. But he'd never worked with a horse! He couldn't possibly make a horse vanish from a small studio in front of an attentive audience. Not even Houdini could accomplish such a feat. For a moment, Clarence didn't think about his legs.

"A beautiful animal, the horse. Much more intelligent than humanity imagines. Please, people, run your hands along the horse's side. Don't be shy. Feel his beating heart. Ahh, a true horse fancier, are you? Yes, check his hooves. This is a hale and healthy representative of his breed. Assure yourselves of his reality, for, I promise you, in a moment you will doubt your memories and senses, and, perhaps, you will wonder what other illusions you harbor about the world."

Outside Clarence's window, a trolley car rattled by. Every fifteen minutes the trolley clattered, reminding him that his parents had moved from the farm so they were close to Broadway and Denver General Hospital. "We can't risk him, Thomas," Mom said. "The doctors warned about the disease migrating into his lungs. We might need Dr. Drinker's respirator until Clarence becomes strong again." Father had only nodded, and soon he completed negotiations with their neighbor to lease the land. Within weeks, both parents had found part-time work, which was remarkable. Jobs were hard to come by. Mom cleaned houses while Dad sorted mail. Clarence envisioned the virus like a horrible mold. Its name sounded like a mold, poliomyelitis. The doctors put his legs in casts. Itching during the day was intolerable, but Clarence could force a pencil, or a ruler, or a straightened coat hanger only so far under the plaster. Maybe the virus really reassembled a mold, growing out of sight in the cast's moist darkness. If the casts came off now, would his legs look human anymore? And that wasn't the worst. In his blood, he pictured the virus marching toward his lungs, filling them with cauliflower-like lumps of gray and green mold until he couldn't inhale. Mom called the machine they would put him in "Dr. Drinker's respirator," an iron lung, and Porter's hospital only had one. Iron lung. Iron lung. Nothing sounded more frightening. It made him think of iron crosses and invasions, a German army charging up his arteries' roads, a blitzkrieg to the heart. But that wasn't the worst. Close as they lived now, the iron lung would do no good if someone else filled the machine. Clarence was not the only sick child in Denver. An eleven-year-old from Broomfield lay in the machine now. The *Post* put his picture in the paper yesterday. The caption read, "Young Sean Garrison, completely paralyzed from the neck down, battles for his life against all odds." But he didn't look like he was battling in the picture. He looked like he'd lost, and all the weight of that loss, and all the grief, were written in his face.

Professor Gilded said, "Could you hold the edge of the blanket, Sonia? There, stand on the stool so you may reach high enough. Ah, it is a good horse, longing for its stable perhaps, for a fresh pile of hay and a rub down for the evening."

The announcer's lowered voice barely leaked from the speakers. "I and the audience cannot see the roan, but we see the blanket's ends. There is no place to lead the horse. I can hardly describe the tension as we wait for Professor Gilded's wonder. I'm afraid he has set himself too daunting a task tonight."

A drum rumbled in the background.

Professor Gilded asked, "Do you believe the horse is still behind the blanket? If I have planted doubt thoroughly enough, then the horse may both be there and not be there. You have no way of telling, unless, of course, you walk around my blanket." He paused. The drum rolled louder. "Or, I can pull the blanket away."

A clatter, a scream, then voices in tumult. Another scream.

"I cannot believe what I am witnessing," gasped the announcer. "Too much. Too much." A hard click, as if the microphone hit something. "Oh, be glad you cannot see."

Someone sobbed.

"Professor Gilded holds his blanket over his arm, like a cape. Sonia stands beside him. The horse, the beautiful roan that walked into the studio is gone, but . . . the bones . . . a pile of bones sits on the floor. Horse bones, dry and clean, piled as if flesh and fur disappeared. No muscle. Oh, please, can we have a commercial now?" Another click.

Professor Gilded's soothing voice said, "An illusion, I assure you. A trick of light and distraction, as all the best magic is."

"Sonia takes the blanket," said the announcer's shaky voice. "He picks up the skull."

"Alas, Horatio, I knew him well." Professor Gilded laughed, a long satisfying chuckle. "The magic show is theater in the best tradition. Shakespeare wove illusions too. The bard said, 'I'll cross it, though it blast me. Stay, illusion! If thou hast any sound, or use of voice, speak to me, if there be any good thing to be done.' As you leave the studio you will find the lovely roan on the street, awaiting your inspection."

The show's closing musical notes played. Clarence realized he had pressed himself off the floor with his hands so his head was closer to the speaker. His arms trembled with the effort.

The announcer appeared to have recovered composure. "Tonight's show was brought to you by the kind attention of our sponsors. Be sure to shop for products that support the continued broadcast of *Professor Gilded's Glorious Magical Extravaganza.*" The music rose, but Clarence heard the announcer say to someone in the background, so muffled that Clarence wondered if he heard it at all, "What the hell was that?"

Clarence's bedroom door opened. He twisted to his side to see his mother holding a basin, several towels, and a filled bucket heavy enough to make her lean.

"Show over, son?" She put the towels, bucket and basin next to him on the rug.

"Yes, it was a good one." He shivered with the thought of bones. Professor Gilded *said* the horse was outside the studio and that the show was a trick, but how could he fool that many people who stood so close? A horse is not a coin to be hidden in a sleeve or to be gripped by the back of the hand while the audience sees an empty palm. Clarence knew coin tricks and the names of tricks: the gangster spin, the backspin bounce, the knuckle roll, the horizontal waterfall. He could flick a coin into a hidden pocket, make a coin between two cards vanish, pull a coin out of someone's hair, but they were practiced techniques, not magic. Making a coin disappear just involved making the audience's eye go to the wrong place. When he did the tricks for his friends, he watched their eyes, and when they looked away from the coin, he had them.

Clarence turned his hand over. Where was his quarter eagle? A red circle showed where he'd held it so tight for so long, but where was it?

"I'm going to need you on your back, Clarence. Help me here."

She knelt beside him and lifted his right leg over his left as he rolled. Still, despite her care, his casted foot thumped when it hit the floor. "I'm tired of waiting this disease out," she said. She sat back on her heels. "Are you tired of just waiting?"

Clarence nodded. On his back, he looked for the coin. Perhaps it rolled under the radio. She'd tied her hair into a bun behind her ears, but strays escaped from all sides, touching her cheeks with black threads and sticking to the sweat of her forehead. He rested on his elbows so he could see the casts, smudged now with weeks of dragging around. "What are you thinking?"

Mom took a heavy pair of scissors from the basin, then filled the basin from the bucket. Steam eddied off the surface. "There's a nurse in Australia who claims that putting children in casts is exactly the wrong thing to do." She snipped the scissors open and shut a few times. "Your muscles are paralyzed, but they're not dead, so we're going to remind them what it feels like to be active." As she talked, she worked her way down the cast, using both hands to clip through the plaster-stiffened cloth. Clarence wanted to shrink away from the blade as Mom cut past the knee and down the shin. "President Roosevelt himself recovered from polio, and look how far he's gotten. There." She pulled the cast apart like a long clam. Clarence's leg, marked with grime at the thigh and ankle, lay as pale as a fish in the middle. No mold! But it smelled like the root cellar. Clarence wrinkled his nose.

Mom moved to the next one. When she finished, she dipped a towel in the basin, then cupped her hand under his knee and gently lifted. A ripple of pain flashed from his knee to the back of his thigh. Clarence gasped.

"Sorry," said Mom. She draped the hot towel over his leg. Water pooled in the cast. "The Aussie nurse says that the muscles will respond to stimulation. I'm going to rub the muscles, but I also have to move your leg, son. It might be uncomfortable." She put one hand under his knee again and the other on the foot. Her serious eyes stared into his. Clarence nodded. Mom pressed the foot toward him while pulling the knee up.

Clarence had read that polio is the cruelest of diseases: it paralyzes but feeling remains. Liquid fire poured down his leg, like the skin would turn inside out. He scrunched his eyes tight. Thigh muscles stretched, moved, tore apart, melted, screamed a thousand tiny voices of death and torment, remade themselves into agony battalions, fought bloody battles, crushed each other with stones, ground salt into their wounds, flailed their backs with rose stems, broke their bones, pulled their fingernails off, stuck each other with rusty pitchforks, then twisted them deeper and deeper.

"There," said Mom. "That's one. Four more on this leg before we go to the next."

In the middle of the night, Clarence lay on his back in bed, his legs' memory a throbbing reminder of the session Mom said they would go through again in the morning. The clock ticked loudly in the hallway, forever holding tonight's pain and the inescapable progress to tomorrow's session.

From the bedroom next door, Mom and Dad argued. "How could an Australian nurse know more than our own doctor?" Dad talked calmly, his voice a steady rumble. "If her system was good, don't you think doctors here, American doctors, would prescribe it?"

"Sister Kenny has shown results. I don't have faith in that 'convalescent serum.' It doesn't make sense to pump blood in him from people who have recovered from the disease. That doesn't work for other diseases."

Like all of their arguments, they were reasonable with each other, but Clarence still rolled over carefully, helping his left leg to go over his right, biting his lower lip until it stopped moving, then buried his head under the pillow. The sheets smelled of the menthol and petroleum jelly Mom had rubbed into his skin.

A little while later, their voices quieted, then their bedroom door clicked open. Steps creaked in the hallway before his own door opened. Mom padded into the room. Peeking under the pillow, Clarence saw her bare legs beneath her short robe and the thick wool socks she wore as slippers. She rubbed his back gently.

"I'm awake," Clarence said, sliding the pillow aside.

Mom's hand stopped. "You should be asleep. Sleep heals." She kneaded the muscles under his shoulder blade. The motion felt comforting. Clarence sighed. He remembered today's broadcast. He had wanted to tell Mom about it earlier, but hadn't had a chance. "Do you think Professor Gilded can really make a horse disappear?"

Mom laughed. "I saw a magic show once. The magician sawed a woman in half, and then he put her back together. He made a table float, so I suppose, but, Clarence, it's a *radio* show. He could tell you he was making the state capitol vanish and you wouldn't know any different."

"There were people there, ten of them. They saw Professor Gilded turn a real horse into a pile of bones, and then the horse was whole again, outside the studio."

Mom moved to the other shoulder blade. "They *said* ten people were there. They could be actors." She scooted farther up on the bed so she could rub his shoulders. "But maybe it is true, son. Marvelous things happen all the time, miracles, even."

"Do you think Professor Gilded makes miracles?"

She stopped rubbing again. "You have to believe in miracles. Miracles and hard work. That's a powerful combination."

"Does Dad believe in miracles?"

"Well, that's a good question. He told me once that he believes in Jesus, but he doesn't believe someone who says he's talked to him lately."

Clarence giggled.

She patted his head. "Now, you go to sleep. In the morning we'll try a little of the hard work and see if we can't help our miracle along. How do your legs feel?"

"They hurt. They didn't hurt as much in the casts."

"I think they'll feel better soon. Remember, they haven't moved in a month." She pushed herself up from the bed. "Oh, I found your birthday quarter eagle in my sock when I put it on." The coin clicked when she placed it on his nightstand. "I have no idea how it got there, but you better hold onto it. Remember, it's for luck." She tucked the covers in so they pulled snug against his chest. "Don't forget, tomorrow your dad and I will both be at work. Mrs. Bentley from next door will come by to see if you need anything."

Clarence nodded. In all the times Mom and Dad had been gone together, Mrs. Bentley never dropped in, which was okay because Clarence could listen to the radio as long as he wanted.

After she left, Clarence pulled himself close enough to the nightstand to reach the coin. New aches broke out as his legs shifted, but he gritted his teeth until his fingers found its mellow, round shape. From the light coming in off the street, he examined its soft gold. It fitted neatly into his palm, then vanished into his fist. "Now you see it," he said in the empty room. "Now you don't." He opened the hand where the quarter eagle still sat, but he imagined what it would be like to make it go away. When his hand hid it, the coin was both there and not there. He only had to choose the reality where it wasn't, and the hand would be empty. How did the coin get into Mom's sock? What had he been thinking about the coin during Professor Gilded's show?

He fell asleep thinking about coins appearing out of a lady's hat, and long red velvet lined black robes, and then, finally, as he slid into the deep darkness, he dreamed of a horse galloping across a field of spring hay, a divine roan with a long tail whipping behind, until it staggered on suddenly weakened legs, trying so hard to stay upright and running. It buckled, whinnying in terror as only a horse can, its eyes wide, its nostrils snorting, before the fur and flesh disappeared. Pathetically, it took one skeletal step, then clattered into a pile of crisp white bones. Green hay poked up between its ribs as the skull rolled a few feet more, the last of its momentum used up. In the dream, Clarence cried until he saw a gold glimmer reflected in the horse's jaw. It was his quarter eagle clenched between the teeth, catching the sun.

Then, he slept.

In the morning, the massage hurt even worse. Mom bit her lips in as she pushed her thumbs deep into Clarence's thigh muscles, and she rubbed and bent and twisted and grinded and pinched for weeks until Clarence couldn't hold his breath any longer. He released his pain in short gasps, concentrating on the radio as she dug her thumbs deep into the back of his thighs. The news reported Britain, France, Australia and New Zealand declared war on Germany. Then a commentator argued America should stay out of the conflict.

"There. Not so bad, was it. Just ten minutes this time," said Mom. She used the back of her wrists to wipe her eyes. "We'll have you walking before Christmas."

When she left, Clarence lay on his back, staring at the ceiling. Polio, he realized, had made him a little kid again. He couldn't see the tops of tables without someone lifting him. He couldn't reach the upper drawers on the dresser. All he saw when looking up at the window were clouds and the leafy branches. With the casts, he could at least slide himself around the room and even get to the bathroom without help, although it took a gymnastic maneuver that left his arms quivering to get himself onto the toilet.

From the higher vantage point of the bed, he could see most of the tree. Someone yelled to someone else, and their feet pounded on the sidewalk as they ran by. Maybe they were playing tag. Maybe they were throwing a ball back and forth. Clarence couldn't see enough to tell. Then the trolley rattled down the middle of the street. The trolley stopped at the end of the block and ran all the way to downtown Denver, passing the radio station with its soundstage. Even now, Professor Gilded could be preparing for today's show.

Clarence rolled onto his side. The crutches and leg braces rested in the shadow next to the window. Professor Gilded's show began in two hours. By trolley, he could be there in fifteen minutes, if only he could get to the trolley's stop at the corner.

It took most of an hour to get into his pants. The pant legs folded over and kept twisting, so he had to inch them up his legs. He looked up every time the house creaked, afraid Mrs. Bentley would choose this moment to check on him, sitting on the floor in his underwear. His feet wouldn't cooperate, and when his toes caught the

cloth, sharp pains raced up the back of his legs. By the time he buttoned the top button, perspiration ran into his eyes and dripped from his chin. Getting into the braces
took less time, but the leather was stiff and fastening the heavy buckles hurt his
fingers. When he finished, he rested on his back. Placing the crutches under his arms
while maintaining his balance seemed an impossible task, but there was only fifty
minutes until the show started, and his legs felt so much lighter and flexible without
the casts that he was sure he could get to the trolley on time.

He clumped through the hallway to the front door. In his left pocket nestled the
quarter eagle; in the right, five dimes. He had no idea what the trolley cost. At the
door, he rested his hands on the doorknob. For a month he'd been lying or sitting.
His head hadn't been this much higher than his feet for weeks. Every muscle from
the hips down tingled and ached. Clarence bit the inside of his mouth and opened
the door, clenching the crutches tight under his arms. When he stepped outside, he
realized he hadn't felt the sun on his face since he'd gotten sick.

The trolley man took a dime for the ride after lifting Clarence to a seat. "You
hurt your legs, son? Where you going?" He smelled of garlic and cigarettes.

"The KLZ radio studio." Clarence tried to keep the tremor out of his voice. The
half block walk to the trolley stop had been the longest sustained effort of his life.
Every crack in the sidewalk, every pebble, every movement threatened to pitch him
over. In the house, he'd used a footstool and chair to get himself upright enough for
the crutches. There was no way to help himself in the open. He would just have to
lay there until someone saved him.

The woman on the seat next to him, holding a basket full of knitting, nodded and smiled. "You'll need to get off at 15th street. I listen to KLZ all the time."
She glanced at his leg braces. "Must be hard getting around in school. I hope your
schoolmates are kind."

Clarence leaned the crutches against the trolley's wall, careful to keep them
from falling. The trolley lurched into motion, clacking over the tracks toward downtown Denver. Even the jiggling hurt. He focused on the shops passing by the windows and smiled through the pain. The radio station was only fifteen minutes away,
now. He fingered the quarter eagle. It's here and it's not here, he thought. Only
thinking makes it so.

A few minutes later, the trolley passed the hospital. A pair of marble lions, their
jaws open, flanked the double door entrance at the top of a flight of stairs. To the left,
a wheelchair ramp rose along the side of the building for the crippled. The building's
severe white face rose six stories into the sky punctuated by rows of dark windows.
Clarence's breathing tightened just looking at it. Somewhere inside, Sean Garrison
stared at the ceiling, the iron lung squeezing his chest to expel the air, then reversing
the pressure so he could inhale. Clarence could almost hear the wheezing sounds. He

wondered, how does he itch his nose? He couldn't move a muscle below his neck. What does he think about? Clarence was glad when they left the hospital behind.

KLZ wasn't directly on Broadway, it turned out. The conductor lowered Clarence to the sidewalk, clamping his arms to his crutches so he hit the cement ready to go. "The station's a block that way, son," he said, pointing. "Watch your step."

Clarence's legs quivered beneath him as the trolley rumbled away. The radio station's sign looked awfully far. He gritted his teeth and leaned forward.

Ten minutes later his arms ached with the effort to keep him upright, but he stood before KLZ's front door, a heavy metal and glass barrier. In the shadow of the room behind the door, he saw a secretary looking at him, a prim blonde with dark-framed glasses, like a librarian. Before he could brace himself to pull the door open, she was holding it for him.

"My word, child, what are doing here by yourself? Where are your parents?"

"They're at work. Do you mind if I sit down?" Clarence lowered himself gingerly onto one of the two worn leather chairs in the lobby. He sighed, his eyes closed, as the weight fell from his arms and legs. A ceiling fan creaked through slow revolutions and stirred the smell of furniture polish and old magazines. Across the small receiving area, in the other chair, a balding man wearing a blue bow tie and a white shirt studied a newspaper. He glanced at Clarence, briefly meeting his eyes, then turned a page and returned to his reading. Behind the secretary's desk, three doors, marked STUDIO 1, STUDIO 2, and SOUND ENGINEER, were closed. Drooping wires high on the wall connected to a bare speaker, playing KLZ's afternoon news softly, a litany of political reaction to the events in Europe. Polish soldiers were in retreat. British bombers attacked German war ships.

"You look like you could use a glass of water." The secretary disappeared through the sound stage door.

Sweat soaked the sides of Clarence's shirt. His legs throbbed from the arch of his feet, where the braces' metal bar clamped against his shoes, to the grinding spots where the leather upper straps dug into his hips. Even his fingers hurt from squeezing the crutches, and he doubted he could make the one block trip back to the trolley stop, but he was here. He had arrived! He couldn't keep a smile off his face.

The secretary returned with the water. Clarence rolled the cool glass against his forehead before drinking half of it in one long swallow.

"Is Professor Gilded here?" he asked. "I'd like to meet him."

"That old fraud?" said the man in the bow tie, putting his newspaper down. He winked at the secretary. "He's a bore."

Clarence's jaw tightened up until he realized the man was teasing. At least he was pretty sure he wasn't serious.

"Do you know him?" Clarence pulled the quarter eagle out of his pocket. "I've been practicing magic." He did a quick knuckle roll back and forth with the coin.

The bow-tied man put his paper aside. "Can you do a pass under and around?"

Clarence rolled the coin between his fourth and little finger, tucked it under, caught it on his thumb, then brought it around from underneath. "Sure. I learned that one first."

The man produced a half dollar from a vest pocket, then walked it from finger to finger on his right hand. "Okay, we'll race. First one to get the coin around their hand ten times wins. It's a little unfair. My hands are bigger and the coin has farther to go."

They counted out loud. Clarence was at eight when the man reached ten, flipped the coin into the air, and then watched solemnly as the white feather it had turned into drifted to the floor.

"You're pretty good for a kid. Can you do a sleeve flick? How about a coin cascade?"

Clarence nodded.

The secretary, who had returned to her desk, laughed. "Don't get him going. He'll talk your ear off about magic." She looked at the clock. "Bob will be here in a couple minutes. You'd better get into the studio."

The bow-tied man dismissed her comment with a wave. He leaned toward Clarence, his elbows on his knees. "So, why do you want to see Professor Gilded?"

Clarence tried to recall the picture of Gilded from *The Denver Post*. His hair had been thick and black, almost touching his shoulders, and a moustache hid most of his mouth. Was it possible that the bald, bow-tied man was Professor Gilded? But where was the accent? Clarence imagined Gilded as tall, like a black-cloaked Abraham Lincoln. Who was this guy?

As if reading his mind, the bow-tied man said, "I'm John Albenice, his understudy. You can tell me."

A couple dressed in their Sunday best pushed through the door. The woman in a floral print dress with her hair pinned up, whose pinched cheeks and pointed chin made her look a little like Clarence's fourth grade teacher, walked straight to the secretary and said, "We're here for Professor Gilded's afternoon performance. We have an invitation." She put an envelope on the desk. Her husband stood behind her, his hands pushed into his pockets, as if he really didn't want to be there.

"Of course, studio two, please." The secretary opened the door for them. Clarence glimpsed a short hallway.

"Will Professor Gilded be here soon?" He raised himself out of the chair to get a last look before the door closed. "He said perception is reality. He said if I perceive that I'm sick, that I am. I wanted to ask him what he meant by that."

John leaned back in his chair. He idly pulled his bow tie. "Professor Gilded says a lot of things on the air you probably shouldn't listen to, kid. He's paid to talk, you know. He's an entertainer."

The secretary cleared her throat and looked purposefully at the clock.

"Look, I've got to get ready for the show. He just meant that magic happens in your head." He stood up and started for the studio. "Are you as proficient with cards as you are with coins?"

"I can do a pretty good fan and a table spread, but my hands are too small for a one-hand shuffle. I'll have to grow into lots of tricks." He held up his hand like a starfish.

"Huh," John said. "Have you tried cutting down a deck? Smaller cards might do it." He tapped his chin thoughtfully. "I hadn't considered that before. I'll bet small cards might get a lot of kids interested in sleight of hand."

"Oh, no," said the secretary.

The door opened. A gray-headed man carrying a briefcase walked partway into the foyer, and then froze when he saw John.

"I told you to stay the gawd damned hell away from me, freak," said the man, bringing the briefcase to his chest like a shield.

The secretary stiffened. "Bob, there's a child in the room."

Clarence recognized the man's voice. He introduced and narrated *Professor Gilded's Glorious Magical Extravaganza*. He said "hell" on the air at the end of the last show.

John straightened. His voice deepened. "I'm not responsible for your irrational fears. If you can't separate a trick from reality, then you have the problem, not me." It was Professor Gilded's voice, without the accent. He stood in between the two chairs, only a yard from Clarence, and he didn't look like he was going to move.

Keeping his briefcase between them, the other man scooted along the front windows until he reached the sound engineer's door. He found the knob without looking away from John. "I'll announce the show, but I don't want to have anything to do with you. Keep your distance. There's nothing natural about you." The door slammed behind him.

John shrugged. He looked at Clarence. "Sorry you had to see that. He had difficulty with the horse trick. It . . . disturbed him."

"Did you . . . I mean, did the professor really make a horse turn into bones?" Clarence's heart thumped in his throat.

"If you think so, then he did. That's the perception trick. An audience thought he did. And Bob there . . . well," he moved toward the studio door. "He believes."

He stopped at the secretary's desk. "The only thing I really know about magic, kid, is that if there isn't some of it in the world, then we live in a dark, dark place. If you've got any, you have to share it."

The secretary reached into her hair. "Hey, what's this?"

John plucked the object off her palm. He looked at it, genuinely puzzled. "1910 quarter eagle. Isn't this yours?" He walked back to Clarence, the coin between his fingers. "Nice trick."

The coin dropped into Clarence's hand. He hadn't even realized that John had taken it.

"Nice trick yourself."

John paused. "I didn't do anything. How'd you pull it off? Pass it when she gave you the water? No, don't tell me. A magician never tells. But I like it. Effective illusion. Okay, gotta go. There will be a whole audience here soon, and the stage isn't ready." He shook Clarence's hand. "Somebody's got to amaze them all." He laughed, and Clarence thought he'd heard a hint of a European accent in it.

Then, he was gone. Clarence tossed the gold piece from one hand to the other.

The secretary looked at him pityingly. "If there were room in the studio, kid, he'd let you in, but we're booked for weeks."

When Clarence stood on the sidewalk outside the radio station, his arms felt completely without strength. Had he used up everything he had to get to the station? He stepped forward, letting most of his weight rest on the crutches, his breath ripping in short gasps against his aching legs. No hike could have ever been longer. He thought about soldiers marching to far off fronts, their courage flitting about them, not knowing if they would make it back, but he kept pushing forward, his braces clicking against the cement. The metal creaked at the knees, and he went steps at a time with his eyes closed.

By the time he reached the trolley stop, he could hardly inhale, and his heart flurried like a trapped bird. Was this the beginning of a new paralysis? He whimpered. Cars passed on Broadway in the afternoon sun, and only after agonizing minutes the trolley trundled into sight.

"Please," gasped Clarence as the same driver from his ride downtown lifted him into the car, "can you take me to the hospital?"

Every bump jarred his legs. He held the back of his thighs to try to keep them from bouncing, but he couldn't anticipate the next jolt. His cheek rested against the wooden sill under the window, and tears leaked between his closed eyelids. Finally the trolley stopped.

"Hospital, young man," said the driver, concern in his voice.

Clarence struggled to get his crutches under his arms.

"No need. I've sent someone in to get you a wheelchair." He placed his hand on Clarence's shoulder. "You don't look good."

A nurse appeared at the trolley door and helped Clarence into the wheelchair.

"I'll take him to emergency," said the nurse. "We can evaluate him there."

"No," said Clarence. The trolley driver wrung his hands. Passengers crowded at the windows. A little girl holding a book waved at him through the glass. Clarence waved back weakly. "I need to go to the polio ward. I need to get to the iron lung."

The nurse started pushing him up the sidewalk toward the ramp. "You have polio? Are you experiencing breathing difficulty?" She sounded businesslike.

Clarence relaxed his head against the back of the wheelchair. He rested his hand on the quarter eagle in his pants pocket, its shape a solid comfort. "I'm not sick. I'm visiting. I want to see it."

"You look sick." The nurse walked beside him as they rose up the ramp and into the hospital's entrance way.

"Honest, I'm okay. I think I probably tried to do too much today. My legs hurt a little," he lied, "but I really want to see the polio ward."

He rolled into an elevator.

"There's someone in the iron lung already," she said.

Lights flicked beside each floor as the elevator went up. Clarence had never been in an elevator before. "I know. Sean Garrison. He was in the paper. How is he doing?"

"You're really not sick?" She looked down at him doubtfully. "If you're not, you're the sorriest looking healthy boy I've ever seen."

"I walked to the trolley all by myself."

"Hmmm." The elevator stopped and the doors opened. "I hope you don't mind if I have a doctor check you anyway, and we need to talk to your parents."

Forty beds separated by light green curtains filled the polio ward. At some, family members sat by the wan children. Antiseptic smells filled the air.

She wheeled him into a broad hallway, and then into a room where a large steel canister dominated the middle. A compressor whirred under the device, stopped, shifted, then whirred again with a lighter tone. Clarence knew the machine was switching back and forth between exhaling and inhaling. A dark-haired boy lay face up, only his head outside of the iron lung, looking at him blankly through a mirror positioned above his face. Grief lines marked his face. His eyes were bloodshot and red-rimmed. Clarence had never seen anyone so sad. A long window in the metal showed his arms and chest, while another showed his legs. Two rubber-lined holes permitted doctors to reach in to rearrange the patient if necessary, but the only way to actually touch him would be to undo the heavy clasps that locked the head end to the rest of the machine.

Clarence pushed the top of the wheels to move closer. "Hi, I'm Clarence."

In the background, the motor clicked. "I'm sick," whispered the boy, and Clarence knew that he could only whisper because the power to speak came from the machine compression. He could talk when the iron lung made him exhale. Putting his hand on his own chest, Clarence tried to imagine being inside the canister.

The motor cycled several times. Clarence looked at Sean's reflection in the mirror. Sean looked back.

"Would you like to see a magic trick?" said Clarence.

The motor whirred.

Sean's voice was a falling leaf. "No."

"I'll show you anyway." The 1910 quarter eagle came out of Clarence's pocket. In the sterile hospital light, its gold glowed. He did knuckle rolls for Sean. He did false drops and sleight of hand passes, showing the coin and then vanishing it. He stacked the gold coin with the three dimes he had left, hid them under a tissue, then asked Sean where the coin was, top, bottom or middle. Wherever Sean said it was, when Clarence uncovered the coins, there it was.

Two more nurses came into the room, watching Clarence go through his repertoire. They clapped when the coins reappeared in unexpected places.

"Magic is about perception," said Clarence, leaning close to Sean. Sitting in his wheelchair, his head was on the same level. "What we perceive is our reality. If you think you are hungry, then you find food. If you think you are cold, you shiver." Clarence paused. He thought about Professor Gilded on his stage talking to an audience. What happened that night when the horse turned into bones? How did Gilded perceive it? Did the animal shimmer before the flesh dissolved? Clarence flourished the quarter eagle. Sean watched, his eyes dark and intent.

"Now I'll show you a trick that will amaze you. I don't even know if I can do it, but I'll try. Are you ready?"

Sean nodded, mostly with his eyes.

The nurses leaned in.

Clarence clasped the coin in his right hand hard enough that he could feel the ribbed edge marking his palm. He let his thoughts drift from it, so that he was both holding the coin and not holding it. Forced distraction, but to himself, not his audience. He thought about war news and Pepsodent and *Bobby Benson and the B-Bar-B Riders*. Instead of the coin, he imagined the Edison's polished wood tuning knob in his fingers as he slowly turned from station to station, of how delicious the sound tasted late at night when his parents had gone to bed and the search for voices made the time flee. Clarence thought about magic. He thought about "take a card, any card" and "abracadabra" and "there's nothing up my sleeve." There were illusions and tricks, and then there was magic. There was a horse that was there and not there. Perception made it real. Perception ruled.

When he opened his hand, the coin was gone.

One of the nurses sighed, disappointed. After all the other tricks Clarence had done, this one must have seemed anticlimactic.

Clarence smiled. He said to Sean, "The coin is gone. Do you know where it is?"

Sean waited until the machine reversed so he could speak. "Is it . . ." The motor clicked. He inhaled. It flipped into the exhalation cycle. " . . . in my hand?"

"What?" said a nurse. She stepped to the side of the iron lung to look through the window. "Oh, my gosh." The other two nurses crowded around her. "He's got it in his hand! How did the coin get in there?"

Clarence touched Sean's forehead. "A friend of mine told me the world is a dark, dark place, if we see it that way, and if we've got any magic, we should share it."

Sean waited for the machine to give him the air. "Okay."

"You need to get better. Someone else might need that iron lung."

"I will."

Clarence shifted in his wheelchair. One of the braces clanked against the chair's metal frame, and he realized his legs didn't hurt as badly as they had on the trolley. He'd barely thought of them while he did the magic. The thought made him happy.

The nurses were still marveling about the coin. Clarence could see it through the window in the paralyzed boy's hand.

Slowly, Sean's fingers closed over it.

WHERE DID YOU COME FROM, WHERE DID YOU GO

MONDAY STARTED BIZARRE. AT THE BUS STOP, THE SUN ROSE LIKE A DIS-eased orange, dark and ruddy at the bottom and a sick yellow at the top. "It's the fires in California," said someone as we shivered in the October cold, but it looked like an omen to me. I shouldn't have worn a skirt.

The bus arrived late. A little girl who'd missed her ride to the elementary school sat in my seat. I asked her to move. She said, "Who do you think you are?" I had to sit on the other side and watch houses slide by I'd never watched before. At the high school, scraps of paper and an empty milk carton littered the hallway by my locker. The janitors must have taken the weekend off. My locker combination didn't work the first three times, and then it did. In the meantime, kids walked back and forth behind me, headed to their rooms. I didn't catch what anyone said, and what I did hear sounded foreign.

My stomach hurt.

And to top it off, Ms. Benda didn't show up for English. A stranger stood at the door, wearing a substitute teacher badge, checking off names as we entered the room. There was a line. He looked up when I stepped behind Carmen Tripp, and then did a double take, before looking away. He didn't meet my eyes when he asked, "Do you know who you are?"

I said, "Olivia Langdon."

"Of course." He studied the clipboard and made a mark.

He wrote his name on the board before the bell, Mr. Herbert. Thirtyish. Bad complexion. Black tie. Shirt untucked in back. One gray sock and one blue one peeking out from pants an inch too short. He carefully put his briefcase on the desk, patted it twice, like it was a pet dog, then stepped behind the podium. The school district scrapes the bottom of the barrel for subs. Latasha texted me before the bell rang. "wrdo." I sent back, "no kdng."

To open class, he said, "You're all dead." He glanced at his briefcase. "But two of you will be famous. Hey, nonny, nonny."

This is going to be interesting, I thought. Ms. Benda had spent the last week discussing symbolism in Steinbeck's *The Pearl*, a book that had taken me all of a half hour to finish. Her idea of an entertaining class was to move onto a grammar lesson after fifteen minutes of spirited defense of Steinbeck's contribution to American literature. The week before she'd done the same routine, except the author was Sherwood Anderson. She practically collapsed with joy while reading "I'm a Fool" out loud.

Mr. Herbert said, "In the future, I mean, you're dead. A hundred years from now, high school students will be reading the classics, maybe some of the same books you are studying today, but you will be long gone, so how are you going to spend your days now?"

Latasha, sitting near the front, said, "Doing college applications." A couple of kids laughed.

"Thank you, Latasha." He didn't consult the seating chart, but stared at her intensely. I wondered if he'd memorized everyone's name at the door. My phone buzzed. Latasha texted, "& drnkng beer."

"Of course, maybe they will be reading what one of you has written. Mark Twain was your age once, you know, and so was Sylvia Plath and Ernest Hemingway. I wonder if they knew they would be literary legends when they were seventeen. If they could feel it." He paced slowly from the podium to the desk, looking out at us. "I wonder what the rest of the class would think if they had known they were in the presence of greatness."

Latasha texted, "17 yr old Hmngwy on a date—yum."

I sent back, "perv."

Tyler what's-his-name, from the golf team, raised his hand, and then said before Mr. Herbert could call on him, "We're studying *The Pearl*. Are we going to have a quiz on yesterday's reading?"

Somebody groaned. Depend on Tyler to bring up the quiz. I texted to Latasha, "a-hole."

She snickered. Like me, she palmed her phone in her lap, out of sight. She typed with her thumb without looking. Beneath the desks where the teacher couldn't see, a whole other conversation was taking place. I'll bet half the kids were texting at any time. I once had an argument with my boyfriend, broke up with him, made up and broke up again before the end of a lesson on Emily Dickinson's "Twas Just This Time, Last Year, When I Died."

Mr. Herbert touched a pile of papers on Ms. Benda's desk. Undoubtedly the quizzes. "Nobody reads Steinbeck anymore." He looked mournful. When I think back on the incident, this is where I started creeping out. I thought for a moment he was going to cry in that way a street person will just start crying for no reason, or have an argument with himself.

"What do you mean?" said Tyler. "We started on Monday. It was *The Pearl* or *The Red Pony*. We got to vote."

Mr. Herbert gathered himself and shrugged. "Literary reputations wax and wane. How many of you read Rudyard Kipling now?"

Nobody raised their hand. I looked around. The class was sitting up, watching Herbert warily. They caught the same vibe I did.

He moved up and down the rows, then stopped at my desk. "How about you, Olivia? Have you read 'The Man Who Would be King'? How about *The Story of the Gadsbys*?"

"You mean *The Great Gatsby*?"

He leaned too close too me, and his hands were on my desk. The little hairs on his knuckles caught the light. Definite boundary issues. Hospital breath. "No, that was Fitzgerald, another fading star."

I wanted to bolt.

Somebody whispered to someone else on the other side of the room. Their heads bent together in my peripheral vision, but I couldn't look away. Mr. Herbert's face moved a half foot from my own. "Even you might be famous in the future." His shoulders scrunched up, and his tongue clicked against the back of his teeth twice. Then he straightened. My heart pounded in relief as he moved away.

"Wouldn't that be something, to teach in the class where a young William Shakespeare listened to your words, where you could observe the child on his way to becoming . . . a shaper of culture?"

Latasha texted, "bghs ntfk," which translated as "bughouse nutfuck."

What Latasha said out loud was, "If I had a time machine, I wouldn't want to teach Sylvia Plath. I'd go back and kill Hitler when he was in high school."

Mr. Herbert jumped like he'd been shocked. "Interesting example, Latasha. Almost prescient. But how would you know him? Hitler, I mean. When he was seventeen, he wanted to be an artist."

He sidled to the front of the class. I'd never actually seen anyone "sidle" before. Peculiar looking.

The class watched, all of them. Something wasn't right with his voice; it quivered, and when he reached the desk and actually stroked his briefcase, I could almost hear the goosebumps rising on the other kids' skin.

Latasha seemed unperturbed, but that's the way she has always been, utterly confident. She called it detachment. She'd told me once that you had to be able to step back from what was going on or you couldn't judge it. When she burned her leg so badly on a motorcycle exhaust pipe last summer (who hops on a motorcycle with a guy she just met while wearing a short skirt anyway?), she said that she smelled the burning skin before she felt it, and it was like it was happening to someone else.

"I'd have a picture of him, of course. Even Hitler didn't know he was Hitler at seventeen."

"Yes." Mr. Herbert laughed, and by then everyone had to have been convinced he was not right. "Hitler didn't know. Mark Twain didn't know. Twain thought he would be a riverboat captain."

He toyed with his briefcase's latch. Suddenly, I pictured a gun in it, or a bomb.

"Now here's an interesting thought." His finger popped the latch, then he pressed it closed with a click. "What if Adolf Hitler and Sylvia Plath were in the same high school class? Wouldn't that be an incredible coincidence? Don't you think a historian would love to see their interactions, if he could?" The latch popped open again. He snapped it shut.

Mr. Herbert looked out at us, waiting for an answer. Finally, Taylor said in a shaky voice, "They couldn't be classmates, could they? He was in Germany, and she was American?"

I texted Latasha, "911?"

"Did you know that Plath's epitaph on her tombstone reads, 'Even amidst fierce flames the golden lotus can be planted.' If she and Hitler had been classmates, wouldn't that have been an appropriate message? He would have destroyed and she would have created. But Plath isn't influential enough. No, imagine William Shakespeare and Adolf Hitler in the same class. The bright and dark, side by side, maybe drinking buddies when they were young." He glanced at his watch. "I don't have much time. Hey, nonny."

No one said anything to that. I wondered if I could text the main office to send help. Maybe I was crazy, and Mr. Herbert was just an eccentric, or he was setting us up for an amazing lesson on John Steinbeck. I was in a classroom once where the teacher staged an argument with a principal. The principal came in and began yelling at her, but it was nonsense, like, "We don't flatter pancakes when they are stuffed with raisins." Then Ms. Benda took an umbrella from her desk, put it in the corner of the room, while he pulled an apple, a bouquet of flowers and a flashlight out of a red backpack he carried, dropping them one by one into the trashcan. She walked to the black board and started writing, all the time they were still yelling. This went on for a minute, before she said, "Thank you," and he left. She told us to write down everything that happened in detail in our notebooks. It turned out the whole façade was an exercise in observation and description.

What if Mr. Herbert were doing something like that to us?

Mr. Herbert opened the briefcase. I took a deep breath.

He said, "The real question is what would you do if you met Shakespeare and Hitler in the same room. Would it be better to save the literature at the cost of the lives, or should the lives be spent? What if that was your only choice because you couldn't come back in time with a weapon, not even a knife—your companions would know—but you could make a bomb?" When his hand came out of the briefcase, it held a switch. His thumb rested on the button.

My fingers quivered above my phone. It wasn't his words, so much, but the posture of his back, how his head jutted forward to scan us, like a vulture. And, of course, the button.

He said, "The first row is dismissed. Take your books." They filed out, sweat on their brows. One girl whimpered. I knew I didn't need to text anyone. They'd get help. Mr. Herbert dismissed the fourth and fifth row. That left my row and Latasha's. I sat in the back seat. She sat in a front seat, near the door. He walked toward me. "Everyone from here forward can leave."

In a minute it was just Latasha, Mr. Herbert and me. I said, "Why would you kill Shakespeare too?" Under my desk I thumbed a message, "I wll dstract & u run." I hit send. The way Mr. Herbert was turned, he couldn't see her. She shook her head.

He sat on a student desk, his feet on the chair. His pants pulled above his socks, revealing a strip of pale skin. "What if a writer was only great because she wrote out of great suffering? What if she wrote about war and loss so well that she destroyed war forever after that? She'd have no destiny without Hitler. Better she write nothing at all than less than her best."

My phone hummed with a new text, but I couldn't look down.

Latasha said, "You can get help."

When he turned to look at her, I checked the message. "Rscue in t/hall."

"I don't need help. I'm saving the world."

A sharp buzzing filled the room. Mr. Herbert's button hand glowed blue and sprayed a shower of sparks. He howled as two men ran in. One tackled him, knocking over seats and desks. The other bent over the briefcase. I found myself standing, backed into a corner. I don't remember getting out of my chair or stepping back.

Latasha hadn't moved. "You boys from the future too?"

They looked at her. For a moment the scene seemed ludicrous. Mr. Herbert wasn't moving. Maybe he was unconscious. The man who had tackled him put a device in his pocket that looked a bit like a toy gun, while the other man held up a box that he'd yanked from the briefcase. It dangled a couple of wires.

"Uh . . . no. We're . . . um . . . the police."

The one at the briefcase had two buttons in the middle of his shirt that were undone, and I'd never seen a police uniform that looked like his. Kind of cheesy, like one that you'd get at a costume shop. But I didn't have much time to look because they both picked up Mr. Herbert and hustled him and the briefcase out the door.

Latasha and I faced each other, then dashed into the hallway. At the end toward the main office, a crowd of kids and the assistant principal stood. Mr. Herbert and the two policemen were gone.

Much later, after we'd been interviewed and debriefed, after our parents came to pick us up, after we stayed up to watch the evening news, I lay in bed staring at the ceiling. My heart had long since settled into a calm rhythm, and my hands had quit shaking, but every time I closed my eyes I could see Mr. Herbert's face six inches from my own, breathing his antiseptic breath in my face.

My phone buzzed beside my head on the nightstand. I picked it up, opened to the screen. The text message from Latasha glowed in the dark. "Whch 1 R U?"

I closed the phone. My counselor at school told me once that most kids change their minds four times about what they are going to be while in college, and very few students end up as they imagined themselves. I pictured a young Adolf Hitler lying in his bed at night, his future stretching out before him like a canvas. Did he know, deep down? Could he sense his destiny?

I thought about how I would text it. How would I send the message? It would be a question I'd send to myself, "Whch 1 M I?"

But I didn't know the answer.

SOLACE

THE WALL DISPLAY DIDN'T LAST TWO SLEEP CYCLES. WHEN MEGHAN WOKE the first time, one hundred years into the 4,000 years long journey to Zeta Reticula, she waved her hand at the sensor, and the steel wall morphed into a long view of the Crystal River. On the left side, aspen leaves trembled in a breeze she couldn't feel. The river itself cut across the image, appearing between trees, tumbling over rocks, chuckling and hissing through the speakers before draining onto the floor at the bottom of the image. On the river's right bank, the generator house, a remnant of 19th Century mining, clung to a gray granite outcrop. A tall water chute dropped from the building's bottom, down the short cliff to a pool below. She'd taken the picture on her last hike before reporting for flight training. Every crewmember's room had a display. Only hers showed the same scene continuously. She joined the crew for their fourteen-day work period, and then returned to the long-sleep bed.

But when she awoke the second time, two hundred years after they left Earth orbit, the metal wall remained grimly blank. She sat on her bunk's edge, empty, knowing the lead in her limbs was the result of a hundred years of sleep but believing that sadness caused it. No mountain. No river. No rustic generator house standing against the aspen. She called for crew chief Teague.

While she waited, she opened the box under her bed where she kept a souvenir from Earth, a miner's iron candle stick holder, a long spike at one end, a brass handle on the other, and a metal loop in the middle to hold the candle. She'd found it in a pit beside the generator house after she'd taken the picture. It had a nice heft to it, balanced in her hand. She had cleaned the rust off so the metal shined, but pits marred what must have at one time been a smooth surface. She liked the roughness under her fingers.

After checking the circuits, crew chief Teague said, "Everything about this expedition is an experiment." He punched at the manual overrides for the display behind a cover plate in Meghan's room. "There's no way to test the effects of time on technology except to watch it over time, and that's what we're doing." He clicked the plate shut. "All that matters is keeping life support, guidance, and propulsion running for the whole trip. You make sure hydroponics continue to function. I work in mechanical repair. Teams service the power plant. One of the four crews is awake every twenty-five years, but we don't have time to repair a luxury like your display wall. We're janitors." He ran his hand down the blank surface. "It's already an old ship, and we have a long, long way to go."

"*We* have to keep running too. The people."

"Yes, there is that." He rubbed his chin while looking at the candle stick holder in her lap. "Interesting piece. Does the handle unscrew?"

She twisted it. "Seems stuck."

"We could open in the machine shop."

She shook her head.

After Teague left, Meghan tried to remember how the river looked and sounded. With the wall display working, she could imagine an aspen breeze on her face, the rushing water's pebbly smell. She could remember uneven ground, slickness of spray-splashed rocks, stirred leaves' sweetness. With eyes closed, she tried to evoke the memory. Hadn't the ground been a little slippery with gravel? Hadn't there been a crow circling overhead? When she was a little girl, her mother died. A month later Meghan could not remember Mom's face. Only after digging into a scrapbook did the sense of her mother come back to her. Now, it was just as bad, but what she couldn't remember was Earth. The metal walls, the synthetic cushioning on the floor, the ventilation's constant hiss seemed like they had been a part of her forever, and the Earth slipped away, piece by piece.

She placed the flat of her hand on the blank wall. It's only two years, she thought. In two years I'll be out of the ship, if the planet around Zeta Reticula is habitable. But she shivered. Only two subjective years. She'd spend most of the trip in the long-sleep cocoon. If the technology worked, she would leave the ship in 4,000 real years.

Teague was right, though, about untested technology. Nearly every element of the expedition was a prototype. Could a human-manufactured device continue to function after 4,000 years, even with constant maintenance? The Egyptian pyramids were 4,500 years old, and they still stood, but they were merely rocks in a pile, not a sophisticated space vehicle. After 4,000 years, the pyramids weren't expected to enter an orbit around a distant planet while maintaining a sustainable environment against the deadliness of space.

And what of the people on board? The only test of the technology that kept a person alive for 4,000 years and preserved the seeds and fertilized ova would take 4,000 years. Dr. Arnold, who knew all their medical charts by heart, told her that what she felt was homesickness. Like Meghan and the rest of the crew, he was in his twenties, but he spoke with maturity. Meghan trusted him. "Look for these symptoms," he said, "episodic or constant crying, nausea, difficulty sleeping, disrupted menstrual cycle." He consulted his notes. "Of course, those symptoms may also be induced by long sleep." His assistant, Dr. Singh, nodded in agreement.

"Doctor Arnold, I'm two hundred years late on my last period."

Already she felt old. Already, with the sun no more than a bright star in their wake, she felt creaky and removed, a part of the dead. I shouldn't be able to sense Earth's pull from here, she thought. I shouldn't have come. They should have known that a hydroponics officer wouldn't do well away from Earth, away from forests and long stretches of mountain grass. Even when we arrive, if everything works, if the planet is hospitable, it will take years and years to grow Earth trees to sit beneath. I'll never see an aspen again.

I won't make it.

Isaac scooted his stool closer to the tiny woodstove. If he sat close enough, long enough, the warmth crept through his mittens and the arms of his coat. His knees, only a few inches from the stove, nearly blistered, but the cold pressed against his back. It slipped around the sides of his hood. He eyed the tiny pile of wood by the stove, the remains of the table he'd broken into pieces the day before. All the cabin's goods sat on the floor since he'd burned the shelves earlier. Beside the remains of the table, the only other wood was a small box of kindling in case the fire went out, and the chair he sat on. Outside, snow covered the ground so deeply that there was no hope of finding deadfall. Besides, every tree within a mile had either been cut down for mine timbers or had its low branches cut off for firewood. He'd hauled the wood he'd been burning for the last ten days from a site four miles upstream, but that was long before the storm moved in, cutting visibility to a few feet.

In the room below, machinery thumped steadily. Water poured through a sluice to turn a wheel connected to a squat generator. Cables ran up the mountain to the mines' compressors, clearing dead air from the tunnels and powering the drills, but Isaac couldn't tell if the miners were still working. They probably were hunkered down like he was, in their bunk houses near the digging, or they were stuck in the town of Crystal. If they were working, the compressors needed to run.

He looked out the window. Thick frost coated the inside of the glass and snow piled half way up outside dimmed what light the dark afternoon offered. The window in his tiny, second story maintenance room was at least fifteen feet above the ground. Two weeks of non-stop snow had nearly buried the building. Ten days ago, when the supplies clerk dropped off a bag full of dried meat and two loaves of bread, he'd said, "First winter in the mountains, boy? It'll get so cold your piss will freeze before it splashes your boots."

Isaac hadn't been able to open the outside door for the last three days. Heavy snow blocked it. He rubbed his mittens together, trying to distribute the heat. A steady wind moaned outside. Trees creaked. Something snapped sharply overhead. He glanced at the thick timbers supporting the roof. How much weight could they hold? How much crushing snow lay above him?

He sighed, unwilling to leave the stove's meager heat, but he had a job to do. Checking for candles in his coat pocket, he walked down to the darkness of the generator room, a "Tommie Sticker" in hand to hold the light. It was a fancy one, with a brass match holder and a screw-on cap to keep the matches dry serving as the handle. Ice covered the stairs, and the air smelled wet and cold. He jammed the spike end of the Tommie Sticker into the plank wall, then carefully lit the candle, using both hands to hold the match steady against his shivering. Oil for the lamp had run out two days ago. The wavering candle revealed water pounding through the sluice against the horizontal wheel, turning it ponderously counter-clockwise.

Isaac used a two-pound hammer and chisel to clear ice from the water's entrance and exit points. If the machinery stopped, miners would be without ventilation or power. Ice blocks as big as his head broke free from the structure and clattered to the unlevel floor, where they slid to the far wall. Despite the cold, he soon built up a sweat. He pulled his hood back and unfastened the coat's top. When he finished, he would strip his coat and layers of shirts, replacing the damp undershirt with a dry one. If he didn't, he'd be too cold to sleep later.

The work wasn't unlike living in the monastery, he thought, complete with a vow of silence and constant labor to keep his hands busy. He thought about God and God's plan. He never felt as close to heaven as he did when he worked alone, cut off from human conversation and the daily distractions. In a way, he hoped the storm would hold. As long as the weather cut him off, he could replicate life in the monastery. He had loved his room there. The rough-hewn bed and the blanket thrown over a thin mattress. He'd read by candlelight there, too. Yes, the generator house reminded him of the monastery. The wooden building felt like a cradle of the miraculous, a miracle that never occurred when he had been an initiate.

It hadn't been this cold, though. No, not nearly so cold at all.

Meghan came awake slowly and in pain. Dr. Arnold had decided four cycles ago that the powerful painkillers they used to soften the shift from the long sleep's near death to full wakefulness were damaging, so they didn't flood her system with them before they woke her. Lying as still as she could in the cocoon, her elbows and knees ached, as did her ankles and wrists. Even her knuckles hurt. A tear squeezed out of each eye and raced into her ears as she thought about clenching her fists for the first time on her own in a hundred years. Every move would hurt, at first, even though the mechanical manipulators flexed her joints daily.

When she'd gone to sleep last, Crew Chief Teague had refused. She'd shaken his hand before heading to her cocoon. "I'll be okay," he said. "I'll have a rich and long life, working in the ship. In twenty-five years I'll greet the next work crew."

"I'll never see you again," said Meghan.

"Maybe you will. I'll be old though." He didn't meet her eyes. "I can't face the dark."

Meghan could say nothing to that because she understood. Each time, climbing into the cocoon seemed like entering death. A one-hundred-year-long instant later she woke to pain. Even her skin hurt, the now active cells firing neurons back and forth, renewing contacts that had laid moribund for so long, but as she lay in the cocoon this time, she thought about Teague wandering through the ship, all the crews sleeping, and he would wander for years and years and years, twenty-five of them completely alone until the next crew woke, and what could he say to them? He'd have a quarter of a century of experience that none of them could share. For them, Earth was only a couple months in their wake. They were still young in all ways except years. Teague would greet them. "Hi," he might say. "I'm what you will be someday." In him, they'd watch their mortality.

Then, he'd wait twenty-five more years, alone, if he lived, and as an elderly man, he would welcome the next crew to their two weeks of busy wakefulness.

It was unlikely he would meet a third crew. He would be ninety-seven years old, and despite what he said, he certainly would not be alive when she awoke.

She had closed her eyes as the cocoon's lid came down. Her muscles tightened. In a blink, the pain would come, the one-hundred-year blink.

And it did.

It took several hours before she could shuffle to the infirmary. Waking was worse this time. Doctor Arnold said, "We haven't gone a fifth of the way, yet." He massaged her hands, lighting them with a million wincing tingles. "Some of the medical staff may stay awake longer than the two weeks for research." Even though he was young, like her, tiny creases that would become worry lines were evident on his forehead.

She thought his eyes were kind, though. He flinched when she flinched. "Sorry," he said. "I'm trying to be gentle."

When Meghan reached her room, she pulled the protective plastic off her bed and found a fragile note folded on her pillow from Crew Chief Teague, who wrote, "Try the wall now." He had signed and dated it twenty years earlier. An old man wrote this, she thought.

She waved her hand at the sensor, provoking a cascade of pain down her side. The wall flickered. The speakers whispered. Then the Crystal River winked into existence. Water burbled over rocks. Leaves rasped against each other. A long cloud in the distance slid slowly across a mountain top.

How long had Teague worked on the wall? A present for a young girl he would never see again.

The speakers popped twice, like a computer chip crunching somewhere and the sound turned off, then the image brightened and washed into a pure white. Meghan shaded her eyes before it too vanished. His repair lasted for ten seconds. How long had he worked on it? She tried to open the service panel, but it remained stubbornly closed. Frustrated, she slapped her hand against it, then grabbed the iron candle stick holder from under the bed. Its sharp end pried the small hatch open. Looking at the circuit board underneath revealed nothing, though. Circuit boards were not her area of expertise. The hatch wouldn't reclose.

Meghan stared at the blank wall for a long time before seeking out Dr. Arnold and his soft, kind hands.

"What is that?" he asked, pointing to the candleholder.

Meghan turned the artifact over in her fingers. She hadn't realized that she still carried it. "It's all I have from Earth. It's a miner's light."

She slept with him for the rest of the two weeks until they returned to the cocoons again. The first time, as she pulled his shirt over his head, he said, "You're going to have to quit calling me Dr. Arnold. My name's Sean."

Once, she woke up, still unfamiliar with Sean's shape, and listened to his breathing in the dark room. If she tried hard, it reminded her of wind through the leaves.

Isaac considered the various forms of meditation. He'd learned to plant a question in his mind, then to spend the day or days or weeks contemplating its implications and meaning. While pondering the question, he would read from the Bible or the many studies in the monastery's library. Meditation was best during his vows of silence. At length, the question would glow in his head, like campfire coals. Now, lying on his bed, squeezing his arms close to his body, trying not to shiver, he considered why God allowed cold. Genesis told him that cold was one of the ways God showed man that the Earth would continue. It said, "While the earth remaineth, seedtime and harvest, and cold and heat, and summer and winter, and day and night shall not cease."

Twice in the night, the roof creaked loudly, the second time dumping a pile of snow onto the floor. Holding the Tommy Sticker high, he could see where a board had broken. He wondered how he could get outside of the generator house to knock snow off the roof, but the wind roared and the window showed no outside light at all now. He wasn't sure if it was day or night. Was such a storm normal? He had no mountain experience. The monastery had been challenging, but it didn't teach him how survive here. If it had *snowed* for forty days and forty nights for Noah, instead of raining, it could hardly be worse than this.

The Bible wasn't clear on snow. Mostly it appeared in the comparison "white as snow" in a dozen passages. He remembered somewhere the prophets linked it to leprosy. By candle he found the verse in Numbers. Turning the pages with his mittens was impossible, so he shucked them off and put them between his legs to keep them warm. The passage said, "And the cloud departed from off the tabernacle; and, behold, Miriam became leprous, white as snow: and Aaron looked upon Miriam, and, behold, she was leprous." In Exodus he came across Moses turning a rod into a snake and back into a rod again. Then God said to Moses, "Put now thine hand into thy bosom. And he put his hand into his bosom: and when he took it out, behold, his hand was leprous as snow."

Even God didn't like snow.

The roof creaked again, sending another icy spill to the growing pile.

The door wouldn't move. Forcing the weight that rested against was impossible, so he tried the window and pushed it up. A solid white wall stood revealed. He jabbed a shovel into it, dumped snow on the floor, dug in again. A half hour later, he'd cleared a tunnel to the surface, about a foot above the window. He pushed the snow shoes out the hole and, then climbed after them. The wind slammed into his face when he rolled to the surface, and his arm sank to his arm pit when he tried to right himself. Strapping on the broad snow shoes took longer than he wished. Snow worked its way into the top of his shoes, froze into little balls on his gloves and fell down his collar. He couldn't see even to the trees that stood twenty yards away from the generator house. His eyes watered, and his cheeks stung. The air's gray luminosity revealed that it was day, but he could barely tell, nor did it matter.

He had imagined by the height of the snow on the generator house that the river valley would be twenty feet under, but he could see now that a huge drift covered the house. Standing on the show shoes, his chest was as high as the roof's eave, but the snow on the roof was piled higher than his head. Isaac realized that knocking the weight off could be dangerous. If it all came off the steep roof at the same time, it could easily bury him, so he tentatively dug into the overhang, stretching as far as he could with the shovel. A slab dropped off, revealing the wood shingles beneath. Another jab broke free a coffin-sized slab that made a thud he felt through his feet. A crack opened up in the bank of snow that remained on the roof. Isaac backed away as fast as he could as the gap widened, and two thirds of the mass slid ponderously off, leaving only a thin sliver at the ridge.

Snow covered the hole he'd just climbed from, blocking his way back.

"Crackers," he said, the strongest explicative he used. Breath froze on his chin.

Before he could get back into the house, though, he needed to sweep the other side. Lifting knees high to clear the snow shoes, he moved around the building.

As he waded through the drift, he thought about the book of Amos, which said, "And I will smite the winter house with the summer house; and the houses of ivory shall perish, and the great houses shall have an end, saith the Lord."

What Isaac needed here was a little smiting.

By the time he'd finished, dug his way back into the generator house and closed the window, he was exhausted, but, more dangerously, he was freezing. The fire in the stove had gone out, and without a buffering layer of snow on the roof, a draft blew through the room. The water wheel had picked up an ominous screech, so instead of trying to light the fire, he put a candle into the Tommie Sticker and walked down the stairs. Ice had formed in the trough where the stream entered the generator wheel, and now water poured onto the floor, deflected by the blockage. The wheel turned half as slow as it should. Water poured onto the floor, some of it freezing against the wood, but most flowing down the slant to the far wall.

Too tired even for a well earned, "Crackers!" he swung the two-pound hammer against the blockage. It barely chipped, and he lost his footing, sprawling beneath the water wheel. Icy water drenched him. Isaac scrambled away, slipping on the slick floor. If he didn't clear the trough soon, the wheel would freeze solid. It could become unusable until spring, and only then after extensive repair.

Carefully, this time, keep his weight distributed on both feet, he sidled toward the trough, hammer in hand. He thought of Lamech, Noah's father, who the Bible said of, "And he called his name Noah, saying, This same shall comfort us concerning our work and toil of our hands, because of the ground which the LORD hath cursed."

The ice was the curse, the hammer the work. So cold he could hardly hold the heavy tool, Isaac swung it against the obstruction.

When she woke again, an elderly man leaned over the cocoon. "Don't move, Meghan. You shouldn't feel pain, but you're likely to be nauseous for a few minutes."

She closed her eyes. I'm five hundred and twenty years old now, she thought. Over thirty-five hundred years to go.

When she opened her eyes, the old man still leaned in, looking concerned. His hand reached over the edge to cup her upper arm. "Are you okay?"

Tentatively, she nodded, then waited to see if the movement would bother her. Her stomach twisted, but the discomfort passed. "I think so." Her joints didn't ache, but her thinking felt fuzzy. She looked at him closely. "Crew Chief Teague?" He shook his head. "No, he's dead." She squinted. "Dr. Arnold?"

He nodded. "I'm still Sean. It took years to figure out what was wrong with the long sleep."

"How many?"

"Almost forty."

She remembered Sean's smooth skin. How he felt when she woke but he still slept. How he'd held her when she talked about Earth and her fears.

"I'm dying," she had said, their last night together. "We will never get to where we are going, and we will never go back."

The night before, a hundred years earlier, Sean had rocked her gently, holding her head to his chest. "We're not dead yet."

Now, Meghan didn't recognize his eyes. He held out a hand to help her from the cocoon, but she didn't take it. He was a stranger. She sat up on her own, felt sick again. When it passed, and she climbed out, Sean stood back, looking at her sadly. "I missed you," he said.

"It's only been a few minutes for me."

"That's true."

She stood awkwardly for a minute, unsure of what to say.

Finally, she offered, "I have work to do."

"Of course. Me too." Lights flickered on the other cocoons, and she realized he'd woken her first.

For the first week, she only saw him at meals, but she sat on the other side of the cafeteria. She tried not to think about the blank wall and her candle holder keepsake. With effort, she avoided pulling the box from under the bed. She thought, maybe if I don't look at it, I won't long for it. I won't miss it. Meghan concentrated on the hydroponic tanks. Every connection needed to be refitted. She retooled valves, serviced pumps, recalibrated the chemical testing equipment, met with the horticulturists who talked about genetic drift, mutations and evolution. Over the course of five hundred years, the plants adapted to the artificial environment. The most efficient at extracting nutrients from the fluids flourished. The more aggressive that grew faster or taller crowded out their weaker cousins.

She couldn't sleep during her rest hours, so she wandered back to the hydroponics rooms. All the plants were low growers, flourishing under lights hanging from the ceiling. Tomatoes, strawberries, cucumbers, ferns of various sorts, beets, peppers and numerous others. Nothing that grew tall. Tree seeds were held in storage for planet fall when they reached Zeta Reticula, although there was a question if they would germinate. No one had ever planted a 4,000-year-old seed before. She walked down the long row, letting the palm of her hand brush the plant tops while imagining the aspen the ship carried. Would there be an aspen grove one day on the planet orbiting Zeta Reticula? Aspen preferred to spread from their roots. If just one seed germinated, she could grow a forest. Would Earth trees flourish so far from their native sun?

The fear gathered in her chest like a tightness, so she rubbed her fist between her breasts as she walked, trying to work through the tension. At the end of the row of vegetation, she looked up one of the ship's long spokes, a huge hollow chamber that reached the ship's core, the center they revolved around to produce the illusion of gravity. She'd grown used to the effect that had disoriented her at first, moving from the claustrophobic pressure of the growing room to the shocking reach of empty space. She crossed the fifty-foot diameter of the spoke to get to the next row of plants.

At the end of the final work day before entering the cocoon again, she walked through the plants one last time. They smelled wet and vaguely chemical, but not green, not natural at all, so she kept going until she reached Sean's room and raised her hand to knock. She paused. It seemed that only two weeks ago she had kissed a young man goodbye. She couldn't picture the ship without him. Every day she expected to see him turn a corner, to join her in the hydroponic labs. He never did. Instead, an old man looked at her mournfully when she passed by. He sacrificed forty years to save her and the rest. She almost left.

When he opened the door, Meghan said, "I missed you too."

Sean let her in, the age spots on his hand were prominent in the harsh, hallway light. "I have something for you." He opened a drawer and removed the metal candle holder. "I know how much it meant. I thought about having them open it for you. We could find out if there's anything inside."

She traced her finger along the loop where the candle would have been placed. Rubbed the rough brass cap at one end. If held the wrong way, it looked like a weapon, the five-inch long, narrow spike that would hold the antique in a mine wall or stuck into wood could also hurt someone. "I'd forgotten about it," she lied.

As the talked quietly in his room, she started to see the man she used to know. Beneath the thinning hair, behind the wrinkles and tiredness, she recognized him.

When they slipped under the sheets later, Sean said, "I don't have as much to offer as I did before. I'm not . . . young."

"Just hold me, then, and let's sleep."

But after hours of listening to his soft breathing and thinking that he still sounded a little like wind through aspens, he woke up, and Meghan found he had more life in him than he thought.

Isaac stood next to the cold stove. His clothes no longer dripped. They crackled when he moved. Next to his skin, though, they were soaked, and he could feel them sucking away the little heat that remained. One ceiling board had broken completely while he'd knocked the snow off the roof, and the supplies directly underneath were covered, including the boxes of matches. He scooped snow off the floor in double handfuls until he found them, but the boxes were squashed and the matches ruined. The match heads smeared against the striker when he tried to light them.

Dully, his head feeling sluggish and slow, he knelt on the pile of snow for a minute. Flakes came down through the hole in the room, swirling in a breeze that hadn't been there before. Without matches, he'd never light the fire. Maybe he could get the snowshoes back on and make his way to the miners' cabins, but he knew the steep trail, completely hidden in the storm, would be almost impossible to hike, even if his clothes weren't already wet and he wasn't exhausted. He couldn't feel his knees against the snow, and the cold crept up his legs. He thought about just staying still. His chin drifted to his chest. Resting sounded good. In a few minutes, he would get up, but for now, a little sleep was all he needed. The vibration and steady thumping of the generator below annoyed him though, then, frightened, he stood. If he slept, the generator would surely freeze, and so would he. If he didn't have duties, he could rest, but the others depended on him.

Isaac waved his arms to restore circulation, slapping his hands against his arms, then staggered toward the stairs. With renewed vigor, the wind shook the house. No light came from the depths. His candle had gone out, so he swept his hand against the wood, careful to not fall again on the slick floor, until he hit the Tommie Sticker. Water gurgled against the power wheel behind him. With a yank, he pulled the candle holder from the wood, forced himself to climb the stairs, before sitting by the stove. It took a dozen tries to unscrew the brass cap holding the matches. There were only three. Carefully, he lit one, but before he touched the candle, the breeze blew it out. He nearly wept. With the new hole in the roof, there was no place he could guarantee the next match would stay lit long enough to start the fire.

He opened the stove door, pushed his hands inside, out of the wind, to light the second match. It flicked to life, but the draw up the chimney immediately snuffed it out.

Isaac took a deep breath, closed the stove flue to stop the wind, and mumbled a prayer before lighting the last match. The water in his shoes felt like it was freezing. He couldn't feel his feet at all. The match caught, held steady. Carefully, he pushed the candle wick into the flame. It flared into life. He jammed the candle between two charcoaled logs in the stove before feeding kindling to the flame. Soon, smoke flowed from the open stove. Isaac coughed, and his eyes teared, as he kicked the stool apart for bigger pieces of wood, the last fuel in the house, but he didn't open the flue until a healthy flame filled the iron stove. Heat baked off the sides. His gloves steamed on top the stove as he warmed his hands. Piece by piece, he removed his clothes to hang around the stove before wrapping his blanket around his shivering shoulders. Water dripped from his coat and pants. Heat rolled off the stove, tingling his cheeks, sending stabbing sparks through his toes and feet. He grimaced and moved closer.

The wood walls of the house rattled in a torrent of wind, whipping the fire in the little stove into a tiny inferno. At its peak, when surely the house would have to shatter, the wind stopped, and for the first time in ten days, the house fell silent except for the river's heart beating through the generator below.

The storm had broken.

In the cabin's sudden quiet, Isaac reached for his bible, opened it randomly to read the first verse his eye fell upon. Surely the storm's cessation was a miracle. Surely a message would be at hand. He wrote the verse on a slip of paper, rolled it into a tube, then sealed it inside the Tommy Sticker. By the time he finished, his face felt warm and his toes stopped aching.

Sean didn't wake up after the seventh long sleep.

Dr. Singh said, "He knew the dangers when he let himself age. The sleep process is hard. I'm sorry." She consulted her notes. "Dr. Arnold was a great man. His work on long sleep cellular degradation and preservation was groundbreaking. If we were still on Earth, he surely would receive a Nobel Prize. We should all make it to Zeta Reticula because of him." Singh shook her head sympathetically. "I understand you were close."

Meghan gripped the edge of the examination table. "I saw him yesterday . . . before the last sleep I mean. I just saw him." She felt every minute of her seven hundred and twenty-two years.

"Me too," said Singh. "If you need them, I can prescribe anti-depressants, but I'd rather not. Drug interaction is difficult to predict."

Meghan walked the long hall from the infirmary to Sean's apartment. The plastic sheets covered his bed and the desk, coated by a thin layer of dust. Despite automated cleaning mechanisms, dust still fell on surfaces they couldn't reach. She pulled the plastic off his desk and let it fall to the floor. He'd left a notebook and her candle holder in the middle. She turned the cover back carefully. The paper that started the trip seven hundred years ago, even though it was acid free and specially milled to last, had become brittle. Any hand-written notes that were expected to be permanent were written on plastic paper, but Sean had enjoyed the feel of real pages better.

He had written "To Meghan" inside the cover; the rest of the pages were blank.

When she sat on the edge of the bed, the plastic crackled. The candle holder rested on her lap. She wondered, did everyone feel so empty, and what could she do about it? Her fingers pressed against the cool metal. Although remembering the aspen shaking in the valley of her wall display escaped her, she felt connected through the hard shape. How often had this candle holder stuck in a mine wall to light a few feet of rock? Who else had held it? Had it ever been more than just a tool to them? Her fingers traveled from the pointed end, past the coil that held the candle, to the burnished brass tube. For the first time, Meghan really examined the antique as a practical object instead of art. Was that a cap on the end of what she had thought was the handle? She twisted it hard. Nothing. Maybe the antique did have something in it, another connection to Earth. Both Teague and Sean had wondered, now she wanted to know.

A few minutes later she asked the machine shop chief, a stout woman whose name Meghan had never known, "Do you have a way to open it?"

The chief turned it over. She said, "It's brass, I think. From the 19th Century, you say? I can cut it apart, but it will cause damage."

"Go ahead."

The chief handled the cutting tool delicately, sending tiny sparks flurrying as she sliced through the candle holder's end. A coin-sized piece of metal dropped to the floor. Meghan leaned over her shoulder as the chief used a pair of tweezers to pull the rolled-up slip of paper from the cavity.

Meghan shivered. "It's almost a thousand years old!"

"There's writing."

"A message." Meghan feared the paper would crumble before she could discover what it said.

"What does it mean?" asked the shop chief after they'd carefully unrolled it.

"It's a Bible verse, I think. I think I know."

Meghan left the puzzled shop chief behind and headed toward hydroponics, already planning new pipes and grow lights. She would have to leave explanations and instructions for the next shift's hydroponic officers.

Isaac climbed through the window and up to the surface again, the last of the chair burning in the stove behind him. The air bit just as cruelly, but without the wind behind it, and the clouds clearing, he didn't feel as cold, although dampness squished in his temporarily warm clothes. If he couldn't find more wood soon, though, the fire would wink out again, and storm or no storm, he would freeze. Holding a short-handled axe, he girded himself for the long hike up the canyon where he might be able to find firewood.

For a moment, he tried to orient himself. Snow transformed the valley, hiding all that had been familiar. The hundreds of tree trunks that marked the land before were deeply covered so the vista before him was smooth, clean and hypnotic. The Crystal River had almost entirely vanished, revealed only by a narrow crack in the snow from where the water's glassy voice arose.

What surprised him most, though, were the trees that remained. Two weeks earlier, their lowest branches were twenty feet above the ground, the easy to reach ones having been chopped off for wood. Now, though, where the snow drifted, their needles brushed the crystalline surface. He would have no trouble finding fuel. He thought, why that tree there carries enough dead limbs to keep me warm for a month. It felt like a miracle.

He thought about the Bible verse he'd written on the slip of paper. He wasn't sure what it meant, but it had filled him with hope: "Come, let us take our fill of love until the morning: let us solace ourselves with loves. For the goodman is not at home, he is gone a long journey." A bit from Proverbs.

When spring came, he would take the Tommie Sticker with its message and bury it by the pump house. Somewhere, someone might read it, and it would help. He was sure of it.

Meghan kept her eyes closed for a long time after she awoke until, finally, Dr. Singh's familiar voice said, "I know you can hear me. Your vitals don't lie."

"I'm eight hundred and twenty-two years old today." She hadn't moved even a finger yet, but she didn't feel tired like she had the last time. She only felt hopeful.

She waited through Dr. Singh's tests impatiently. "I have to get to work," Meghan said.

Rushing through the hallways, she barely acknowledged other crew members' greetings. They, too, had work to do. So much of the trip waited before them. So much more space had to be traversed before they could come to a rest.

The first hydroponics lab looked much like she had left it, although she noted the tanks that held the plants steady would need rebuilding on her shift. She passed under one of the spokes, the cathedral-like height earning not a glance. Did her experiment work, she thought. Did the other hydroponics officers follow her direction? She couldn't see far in front of her. The ceiling's downward bulge cut off her view until she was almost there, and then, she saw.

At the end of the row, where normally the plants stopped, her jury-rigged piping led to the new plant tanks. A thick trunk rose from the tank, and as she entered the space below the next spoke, her gaze traveled up the tree's long stretch. Guy wires attached to the vertical space's sides held the tree steady. At the top, new grow fixtures hung suspended from other wires, bathing the aspen in light.

Meghan held her breath. An aspen, under the right conditions, can grow to eighty feet. This one was easily that tall. She walked around the tree. New piping and tanks connected to her original work. Three other trees grew from them. The closest tank came from her co-worker twenty-five years down the line, and the tree from that tank nearly matched her own. A smaller tree, only fifty years old, grew from the next tank, and the last tank held the smallest tree, still over thirty feet to its top. The history attached to it showed it had been built twenty-five years ago. Each officer had added a tree to the grove.

Meghan sat on the floor so she could look up with less strain. Each tree's branches touched the next. The room smelled of aspen, a light leafy odor that reminded her of mountains and streams, and an old generator house perched on the edge of a short cliff.

After she'd sat for a while, she realized that air currents in the ship flowed up the spoke. What she heard, finally, was not the ubiquitous mechanical hiss from the ventilation vents. What she heard was the gentle rustle of leaves touching leaves, a sound that she thought she'd long left behind and would never hear again.

LATE HOMEWORK

"**M**ISS LINDERMAN," SAID THE VOICE—IT SOUNDED LIKE THE PRINCIPAL'S secretary—"there's been an accident. Two of our students were killed driving home from a haunted house. Cathy Jackson and Melinda Cranford."

Miss Linderman held the phone tight in the dark room. On the dresser, her clock's red letters glowed 2:59.

"If you think you'll need a substitute, I can arrange one for you."

"No, I'll go in. It will be easier on the kids if I'm there. They were in my afternoon Literature and Composition class."

She hung up but didn't fall asleep. She watched the clock instead until it was time to get up for school.

When fifth hour came, kids filed in almost solemnly. Pushing was half-hearted. Laughter sounded too shrill and cut off early. Quietly, students walked around Cathy and Melinda's empty desks a bit wider than would be normal, and when the bell rang, they lapsed into silence.

Miss Linderman busied herself marking role. Nothing in education classes prepared her for students' deaths, but in her twelve years they had happened like the tolling of a relentless bell that rang every other year.

This year took two. Cathy and Melinda made the death class roster a total of seven. Seven young spirits snuffed out. Seven memorials in the yearbooks. "We will miss you, Harper." "The class of '02 celebrates Gracie's irrepressible spirit." Two years ago the message read, "Trey is gone but not forgotten." Miss Linderman could see the white doves released at graduations they never attended.

She didn't want to look up at her class. Today was Halloween. She was afraid she'd see familiar faces, like she did every Halloween. The faces that expected her to lead them, to teach them, perhaps even to save them, but all she had to offer was grammar, literature, and an encouragement to write better. On Halloween especially, on a holiday about death, she wished to give them more.

The Halloween day was never like any other day for Miss Linderman. Twelve years ago, also on Halloween, she lost her first student; the first of seven, and it hit her just as hard today.

"I know you have heard what happened last night," she said. "The counseling department asked me to remind you their doors are open for anyone who would like to talk. They also suggested I let you share your feelings before we start if you would like."

No one spoke. Cathy and Melinda had kept mostly to themselves. They were a majority of two against the world. Their friendship held them together and kept them secure.

Finally, to break the silence, Miss Linderman said, "If you'd get out your homework, make sure your name is on it, then pass it to the front."

Papers rustled and made their way from student to student until they were piled on her desk.

What would she say to them now? Would "Let's review gerunds," be appropriate? How about, "Turn to the chapter on Emily Dickenson"?

What could she say to the students in the last row who always seemed so far away?

The door at the back of the room opened. Miss Linderman glanced up. Melinda and Cathy walked in, their books clasped to their chests, looking lost. They took their seats. No one else acknowledged them.

"Perhaps it would be best if we did a reading assignment today," she said. "We can work at our own pace."

Miss Linderman's hands shook as she wrote on the board. Students opened their books. Read to themselves. Wrote responses to the questions at the end of the chapter. They handed them in when the bell rang. The class filed out. All but Cathy and Melinda, and five other students sitting in the back row.

Cathy and Melinda stood. They approached her, apologetically, holding out papers to turn in. She could see it was their homework.

Before she could accept it, though, even before she reached out her hand, the papers faded to mist and were gone. Where the girls stood a moment before, dust motes stirred and then were still.

The five students in the back looked at her as they had last Halloween. Two years ago, there had been only four, and then Trey walked through the door, tried to turn in his late homework, but he dissolved.

The remaining students dimmed into nothingness. Miss Linderman was alone in the room.

In thirty years, she thought, I will retire. At this rate, my Halloween class will be twenty-five students.

I'll wait, after I retire, for the end. Maybe then I'll join my absent students.

Maybe then I'll take their homework, and I can teach and they can learn, and none of us will fade away.

CLASSROOM OF THE LIVING DEAD

THEY CAME FOR ME ON A MONDAY MORNING WHEN I WAS TOO EXHAUSTED to hear the back door caving in. Only when their hands were on me did I realize that all was lost, but the dead didn't consume me. They dragged me out of the house, shambled the three blocks to the school, holding me tight in their rotted hands, shuffling in that loose-limbed, broken way that they had, until they'd pulled me up the stairs, through the front doors with their glass knocked out, down the hall strewn with books and abandoned backpacks, until we came to my room.

Here, too, windows were broken, and the Venetian blinds hung askew. Morning sun slanted through the uneven slats. They pushed me toward my podium. I clung to the top, sick with fear. When would they kill me? Would I become like them?

They stumbled against the desks, former students, all of them: Daniel, who used to play his guitar at lunch; Lisa, with her pierced lip and blue-dyed hair; Landon, who read manga and drew big-breasted girls in the back of his notebooks, all my students. They bumped into the chairs, moaning low in their throats, until they were sitting, a terrible parody of the class they once had been.

What did they want, with their white-washed eyes and bruised faces? They looked at me, blank-faced, but ravenous, expectant, somehow. Hands gripped the sides of their desks. A breeze stirred a loose paper on the windowsill.

Finally, Joselyn, a girl who used to look like she ran a brush through her long, brunette hair a thousand strokes before she came to class, raised her hand, her hair a knotted mess, now, her blouse, torn and stained. She raised her hand and waited.

"Yes, Joselyn," I squeaked.

She opened her mouth, and for a while nothing came except a strangled gasping, until she forced the word: "Braaaiiins." Her hand dropped with a thud. "Braaaiiins."

"That's what you want?"

She nodded. They all nodded.

Was this what remained, after they died, after they reanimated? A desire to continue, to be a little bit of what they once were? Was it all habit? Would the athletes head to the gym after school to make layups? Would the marching band tramp across the field, their tuneless instruments dead in their grips?

Joselyn said, "Braaaiiins," a third time.

I found a marker in the desk. What could be more surreal, but who was I after all? The world had ended. The apocalypse had arrived. Still, I was who I was. They were what they had become.

I turned to the board. "Today, I will show you how to diagram sentences." I wrote on the white surface. I drew lines and made connections and spoke the arcane language of grammar. When I faced the class again, they were silent and attentive.

"Braaaiiins," someone in the back groaned.

By the time the sun had traveled to the horizon, I'd filled the board and erased it a dozen times. It didn't matter what I talked about. They didn't answer questions. They didn't move.

But they let me live.

Tomorrow I think I'll teach literature. Some Dickenson, some Poe. Tomorrow I'll teach to the dead and for the moment pretend that the world will go on.

Tomorrow they won't have to drag me to school.

MRS. HATCHER'S EVALUATION

YESTERDAY'S CONVERSATION WITH PRINCIPAL WAHR KEPT VICE PRINCIPAL Salas awake all night. "We need to cut the dead weight, Salas. Those teachers who aren't on board with the new curriculum will be moved out, and I want them moved out immediately." Wahr, a skinny man with just the barest wisps of white hair on an otherwise bald head, kept one hand on his keyboard and the other on his phone. As he talked, he studied his computer screen which Salas couldn't see. "Hatcher's the worst. She ignores the lesson plan template we instituted last year. She doesn't write her objectives on the board for the students to see, and I've sat in her class. Lecture from the tardy bell to the dismissal bell. She's a dinosaur. I'm adding her to your evaluations. Vice Principal Leanny has ignored Hatcher's performance forever. We need fresh eyes on her."

"I haven't heard anything bad about Hatcher," said Salas. "She earned teacher of the year two years ago."

"Popular student vote. Doesn't mean squat." Wahr leaned forward. "Here's how I know she needs to go. My son is going to be a freshman next year, and I don't want him in her class. Best practice, Salas. We're a 'best practice' school, and all the studies say lecture doesn't work in social studies." Wahr turned his attention back to the computer screen, then tapped a couple keys. "Watch her. I've got to eliminate a teaching position, and now that the state has removed tenure protection, she's the best candidate. Here's two other possibilities. You're doing their evaluations now." Wahr dropped file folders on the desk between them. "Evaluate and choose. Somebody's got to go. Budget, Salas. Budget and best practice."

He knew Hatcher, a pleasant, older woman, tending toward fat, who looked like Salas's grandmother. He'd never observed her teaching, though. That night, as the moon moved a tree's shadow across his bedroom wall, Salas realized he'd have to start Hatcher's evaluation immediately. He'd get notes from Leanny, then drop in to Hatcher's last period American History class.

Vice Principal Salas organized his day by piles. The tallish one on the left contained discipline action sheets for students in trouble, many for attendance issues, but also for cell phones in the classroom, smoking, drugs, insubordination, and one for a Theodore Remmick, a freshman who'd brought a small propane torch to school in his backpack. Parent contact sheets made the middle pile. He spent most days on the phone talking to parents, often about the first stack. Teacher evaluations made up the third pile. Much of the time he avoided the third pile. He'd been vice principal at Hareton High for fourteen years, and he knew all the teachers. If they weren't sending kids for discipline (which meant they weren't good at classroom management), then he limited his contact with them to drop in visits while they were teaching. Salas evaluated the N-Z teachers. Leanny handled the other half of the alphabet.

Salas dreaded evaluations. Before he'd taken the vice principal job, he'd taught four P.E. classes and one Remedial Reading (his minor had been English), so he felt silly trying to evaluate the academic disciplines. He'd gone into P.E. because he liked sports and kids. He'd been an indifferent student himself.

"Hi, Salas. What did you need?" Vice Principal Leanny leaned into his office without stepping in, her gray-rooted dark hair pulled into a ponytail. She'd started teaching French and Spanish the same year Hatcher joined the faculty, but moved into administration after ten years. With Jack Quinn's retirement from tech ed three years ago, the two women were the longest tenured employees in the building and old friends.

"What can you tell me about Mrs. Hatcher?"

Leanny grimaced. "Wahr's after her, isn't he? It's not the first time. Best teacher we have. I don't know why Wahr wants to mix up the evaluations. I've been giving her exemplaries as long as I can remember."

"No one gets exemplaries!" Wahr had directed them not to give teachers the highest rating. He had said, "Everyone can get better. Besides, if we give a teacher the highest rating, it's hard to fire him."

"I know. Wahr has a fit."

Salas said, "I heard she ignores the curriculum and just lectures. That doesn't sound good."

"You haven't observed her, have you? Don't do a drive by. Give her a half hour."

"Can you send me your notes on her for this year? I need to get up to speed."

"Sure. Check your e-mail later." Leanny rubbed her forehead, as if she had a headache. "Theodore Remmick is waiting outside. Is he for you? His family lives on my street. They're a piece of work."

Salas sighed. "Yeah, send him in."

"By the way, I heard you're Wahr's hit man now."

"What?" He glanced guiltily at the folders the principal had given him.

"Wahr hands that duty off. He's never fired anyone. The last time the school lost teachers, he gave it to the head counselor. Sorry it's you. The counselor quit the next year. He worried he'd be asked to do it again."

Salas shrugged. "What are you going to do? Send Remmick in, would you?"

Theodore Remmick has to be the smallest boy in the freshman class, thought Salas. The boy's feet hovered above the floor as he sat in the chair by the round table where Salas talked to the discipline problems. Remmick's nose was narrow, and his hair hung over his eyes as he looked down.

"Why a propane torch?" said Salas. "What were you going to do with it?"

Remmick said, "Did you know a cow didn't kick over a lantern in the O'Leary's barn to start the Chicago fire in 1871? Some newspaper guy invented the story to sell papers." Remmick smiled without looking up. "Like a fire that killed 300 people needed a fabrication to be more interesting."

Salas paused. Sometimes a kid would deny the accusation. Sometimes he rationalized or defended, or he wouldn't speak at all. Talking nonsense introduced a new tactic.

"You know, a propane torch is a safety issue."

"The fire burned so hot the roofs blocks away caught fire before the flames reached them. The fire jumped the Chicago River. That's a big river. And it kept going. Started on Sunday morning and didn't stop until Monday evening when the wind died and it rained."

"What does this have to do with a propane torch? Were you going to burn something?"

Remmick brushed the hair off his forehead. His eyes were brown and clear. "From Lake Michigan's shore, the sky above the city turned orange. Thousands of people fled to the lake. I saw flame tornadoes rising through the smoke, and it roared like a train." He closed his eyes as if feeling heat on his face.

"Son, why'd you bring a propane torch to school?" Salas put the torch on his desk. It was tiny, a hobbiest's tool, not much larger than a cigarette lighter.

"Project for class. Can I go now? I'm missing band." He squirmed in his seat.

Salas looked at the boy thoughtfully. "They don't have torches in the shop?"

"I'm not in shop. History. It's a group assignment. I volunteered it."

The discipline guide for the district didn't list a propane torch in any category, so Salas decided to lump it under "item inappropriate for a school setting" on the action sheet. "A week lunch detention, and any project in the future that involves flame or explosions, assume you can't do it."

Remmick hopped from the chair, and then offered Salas his hand. "Thank you, Mr. Salas. I'll keep it in mind."

When the boy left, Salas shook his head. I could write a book, he thought for the umpteenth time in his education career.

*

The History department head, Mr. Young, really was young. The wall posters still hadn't yellowed, and he flinched when he saw Salas at the door: a classic, inexperienced reaction. He had become the department head by arriving late at the meeting last spring, when the history teachers voted on who would attend the extra meetings and take charge of the departmental paperwork.

"According to the district pacing guidelines, the American History classes should be looking at the causes of WWI. If she's only to 1871, she's almost a half century behind." Young ran his finger down the teaching objectives for the class. "They should know mutual defense alliances, nationalism, militarism and imperialism, and from the unit they will be able to discuss America's emergence as a military and industrial power. They only get a week. We have to be to the Cold War by April's end or the first week in May." He thumbed open a section in the notebook. "We have two required benchmarks for the unit: a multiple choice test and a short essay question. I have the rubric for the essay if you'd like to see it."

Salas tried to look interested. He remembered being 15 himself and his own tour through American History. He recalled biplanes from WWI, but nothing else, which made him think about Snoopy vs. the Red Baron. Of the classes he'd hated, history bored him the most. If it weren't for sports eligibility, he'd never be motivated to pass.

Salas almost asked Young what he thought of Mrs. Hatcher, but he didn't want to start rumors.

From the back, Hatcher's classroom looked like most social studies rooms. She'd covered one wall in maps. Presidents and historical scenes covered the other wall. A long whiteboard stretched across the front. Book-filled cabinets stood behind him. He smelled dry erase markers and carpet cleaner as he leveraged himself into a student desk the right size for a 6th grader, maybe, but not comfortable for an adult.

Mrs. Hatcher stood beside her desk at the front, straightening papers—she'd waved when he walked in. Salas filled in the preliminary observations on the evaluation check list. Although Hatcher did have writing on her white board, Salas didn't understand it. In one column were names: "DeKoven, Meagher, Catherine, Barber." Then some presidents: "Harrison, Jackson, Adams, Monroe" Then some states: "Michigan, Illinois, Indiana, Ohio, Ontario." Salas was pretty sure Ontario was in Canada. She'd written one sentence on the board: "It ends at Fullerton Ave."

What Hatcher had not written were the class learning targets, which were required. Somewhere she should have posted what teaching standards the students were addressing for the day, and what they should be expected to do when the lesson ended. Salas had the WWI standards Young had given him, including, "I will be able to explain why America became involved in the First World War."

Students trickled into the room, taking desks around Salas. Theodore Remmick came in, nodded in Salas's direction, then found his place. A dark-haired girl who clearly didn't know the dress code, dressed showing too much skin, sat in the desk in front of him. "You look pretty mature to be a freshman," she said.

"Just a visit," said Salas.

The tardy bell rang. Salas waited for tardy students so he could record Hatcher's procedure with them, but students filled all the desks, and there were no tardies. Conversation buzzed in the room.

Hatcher started speaking without asking for the students to quit talking. Salas gave her a low mark in the "Commands student attention before beginning instruction" category.

"We've moved the Chicago Fire project to Saturday." By the time she said "Saturday," the room had grown quiet. "Can somebody bring a big box fan? I'll provide the extension cord."

A boy sitting underneath the covered wagons poster raised his hand.

"Thank you, Sean. Remember it's at 10:00 in the back parking lot." She stepped behind her podium. "We're going to jump four years to 1876 today and talk about the Battle of the Greasy Grass, which some might recognize as the Indian name for the battle better known as Custer's Last Stand."

Salas flicked through the required social studies scope and sequence guide for American History. He couldn't find the Chicago Fire, and the class should have covered Custer's Last Stand a month earlier, and only in passing. The district's guidelines emphasized teaching the industrial revolution into the 1870s, and to be "cautious" in discussing "controversial" topics, which included the "resettlement of indigenous natives."

"Five years after Chicago's devastating fire, the city was rebuilding and recovering to become one of America's busiest commerce centers. Meanwhile, 1,200 miles away, in the Montana wilds, General George Armstrong Custer led the 7th Calvary in an attempt to return Cheyenne and Lakota Indians to their reservations."

Most students were not taking notes, and although they weren't talking, they didn't seem to be paying attention to Hatcher, either. Her soft, almost melodious voice lulled him, and within a few minutes, he lost track. The dress code violation slumped into her desk so her shoulders lowered to the chair's top. He wrote a comment on the evaluation sheet, "Straightforward lecture. No attempt to engage students' attention." He also noted she hadn't given the students a task, like taking notes, nor had she handed out any aids to guide their thinking, like a graphical organizer or an outline template.

Hatcher droned on and on. Salas looked up at the clock. Only ten minutes into the class. He thought about leaving and then returning to watch what she did in the last five minutes, but the room's warmth relaxed him. Several students had closed their eyes. Besides, the waiting papers in his office weren't going anywhere.

His thoughts drifted to what he knew about The Battle of the Little Big Horn: almost nothing. He'd seen a movie with Dustin Hoffman in it years before, *Little Big Man*, that had the battle in it.

Hatcher's voice rose and fell in the background, like a breeze. Salas listened, and he found himself imagining the sun setting behind the low Montana hills. He pictured sitting on a horse blanket, back from the cooking fire. It had been too hot during the day for him to want to sit closer. He leaned against his bedding, his mind drifting. They'd been told not to set up tents, which meant they'd do a night march, another long, stumbling trek in the dark, walking from one desolate spot to the next.

Salas twitched, then looked around the room. Had any students noticed he'd almost gone to sleep? None appeared to be looking at him, though. Some were in the exaggerated slump mode like the girl sitting in front of him. A couple rested their heads on their arms. Some propped their elbows on their desks and cupped their chins.

Still, Hatcher continued talking. "Single-shot Springfield carbines jammed when overheated," she said, and then went on to horses used as breastworks. Twenty minutes passed. Salas closed his eyes. The pencil in his hand grew heavy, reminding him of a gun stock, how it would feel, its solidity. He propped the gun across his knees, sitting on the ground. In the distance, gunfire, the heavy pop of Springfields filled the afternoon air. Custer's forces, he thought. Custer would drive the enemy back and join them. There were so many hostiles! Even their women were in the battle, waving blankets, scaring the horses away. Did Reno and Benteen know what they were doing?

He took a long, warm drink from his canteen. Other soldiers sat around him, exhausted, frightened. They smelled of dust and horse sweat and days of travel. More gunfire to the north, but the sounds didn't appear to be getting closer. A horsefly landed on his neck. Bit him. He slapped at it, too tired to care.

Behind the muffled battle sounds and the tired horses' breathing, he heard a bell. He cocked his head. Who would be ringing a bell on the battlefield, in the sun and dirt and waving grass? He regripped the rifle, and it became a pencil, and the dismissal bell rang, ending class.

"Tomorrow we will cover the aftermath," said Hatcher. "Sitting Bull, Crazy Horse and the others make for an interesting story."

Salas looked around, confused. Some students appeared dazed too, but they shook it off before heading into the hallway.

*

Before going home that afternoon, Salas stopped in the school library to pick up a book on Custer's Last Stand, but the books were gone. The librarian said, "It was a massacre. Every source checked out before the first bus left the parking lot. Kids were on the computers doing searches like crazy until we closed."

That night it took a long time to fall asleep. What had happened in Hatcher's class? The experience unnerved him a bit. Had he suffered a fugue or a blackout? He scratched at the spot on his neck where the horsefly had bit him. The insect must have been in Hatcher's room, and he incorporated it into the Custer hallucination, because it left a distinct welt on his skin. When he did fall asleep, screams and gunfire and arrows haunted his dreams.

At the day's beginning, Leanny leaned into his office the same way she'd done the day before. "Did you watch her yesterday? What did you think?"

Salas nodded. When he'd gone over his observation sheet from the day before, he had a hard time remembering what he'd seen in Hatcher's class. If he'd drifted off while evaluating her, it wouldn't be fair to the teacher.

"I'm not sure." He swallowed. "I'm not sure what I learned."

Leanny nodded knowingly. "But you learned, didn't you? Did you know that more Hatcher kids go into education than any other teacher in the building? Talk to counseling. They'll tell you. I'll bet half the history teachers in the district are Hatcher's former students. You want to know something else interesting? Look up Theodore Remmick's grades for this year. He hasn't had a mark above 'D' since sixth grade." She laughed. "I saw him in the lunch detention room yesterday after you talked to him, reading."

Salas checked his to-do list. He needed to observe the other two teachers Wahr had added to his evaluations, plus handle today's parent contacts. He hoped he wouldn't have a schedule buster, but he ended up spending the morning talking to a junior who had started (and ended) a fight in the locker room. Fighting drew an automatic suspension, but the other student's parents also wanted to press assault charges, so the campus police officer visited his office several times, as did the district's lawyer, both boys' parents, the teacher, and witnesses who couldn't agree on even the most basic details.

At one point, the parents who wanted to press charges started yelling at Coach Persigo for not supervising the locker room "in a professional manner." They said they wanted to sue him and the school district.

It took Salas a half hour afterwards with Persigo to convince him the parents weren't going to sue. "I've been in the district too long to put up with this shit," said Persigo. "We got a real chance to make the playoffs this year. I don't need the distraction. I can't teach classes, coach baseball and worry about lawsuits at the same time. No respect. There's no respect. "

A false fire alarm cleared the building ten minutes before lunch, which took forty-five minutes for the fire department to respond to, so Salas spent almost an hour wandering around the practice football and baseball fields with the students and their teachers, waiting for the okay to reenter the school.

Leanny caught up to him as he followed the students back into the building. She walked beside him for a minute without talking. Finally, she said, "Do you have an opinion about the new evaluation forms?"

"They're clear. Fill in the rubric. Add up the score. Teachers know what's expected. Evaluators know what to look for."

"Did you notice there's no measurement like 'Instills a love of learning in students'? It doesn't say, 'Changes students' attitude about the subject' or 'Enriches students' lives' or 'Provides a meaningful adult role model' or "Creates an environment for student self discovery'?"

Salas put his hands behind his back. Most students were entering the building through the gym doors. They'd piled up to squeeze through the bottle neck, and they weren't in a hurry to get back to class. He and Leanny stopped behind the milling heads. "You can't evaluate those areas. They're subjective."

"Exactly," said Leanny. "How much do you remember from high school? I mean, if you had to take a subject test in any class you took, how would you do?"

Leanny smiled at him, which made Salas think she was leading him to a trap. "Not well, probably. I haven't studied for the tests."

"Exactly, so if you don't remember much, and you can't pass the tests, what was high school's point? Did you get a measurable experience from it?"

Mostly Salas remembered being on the baseball team during high school. He remembered sitting in Algebra, keeping one eye on the clock and one on the cloud cover out the window. If it rained, they'd go to the gym to throw, which he didn't like. In the winter, he did weight room work and he ran. By late February, he started marking the calendar, tracking the days left until spring training. He loved it when the coaches trotted with them out to the field, wearing their sweats and ball jackets. He loved wheeling the trashcan full of bats into the dugout. He remembered stepping onto the freshly swept infield and how satisfying a grounder thumping into the glove's pocket felt.

"I decided to major in P.E. in high school."

"So other subjects for four years were worth it. You discovered what you loved!"

The crowd shuffled forward. In a few minutes he would be back at his desk, trying to do a full day's work in the half day he had left.

"I don't know. Where are you going with this?"

"Just saying the evaluations aren't the whole picture. Maybe high school is more than observable, measurable achievement."

Wahr waited for Salas in his office. "We need to move up the schedule on these evaluations. The superintendent wants preliminary staffing done by next week. I'm putting out a note to teachers who are quitting, transferring or retiring. We still have to cut a position, though. How's Hatcher's evaluation? Did you watch her?"

Salas didn't know where to go in his own office. Wahr partially sat on the desk, so Salas didn't feel like he could sit in the desk chair. He felt like an intruder. "She looks bad on paper. She lectured for the whole period."

"Just like I said. You need to do at least two more observations. We can't move on a teacher without three full observations. Collect her lesson plans and check her students' benchmark test scores to complete the packet."

Salas thought about the class he'd watched. He could still smell the horses at Greasy Grass. "She gave an . . . interesting presentation. Being in her room felt . . . different."

"I don't care if she delivered the Sermon on the Mount. You can't talk to fifteen-year-olds for that long and be effective. She's an expensive, entrenched fossil who's teaching like it's 1950. I can replace her with a first year teacher whose salary would be half as much and who would know the latest trends in education."

"She might not be our best choice to cut."

Wahr snorted, pushed himself up from the desk, and said, "I need a name by next week. It ought to be Hatcher, but somehow we've got to trim a position. Make a choice."

Hatcher started the afternoon class with Sitting Bull, but by the end had somehow moved into the Alaskan gold rush. Afterwards, when he looked at his observation sheet, he had written "last American frontier," "Jack London," and "Klondike." He hadn't written how she began class, whether the students' learning objectives were on the board, or if she had varied her teaching technique.

As he walked away from her room, though, he rubbed his wrists. They ached and his hands were icy cold as if he had been holding a heavy gold pan in the frigid river's rolling water, swirling and swirling and swirling the nondescript sand at the pan's bottom, hoping for telltale color, hoping for a nugget to make the weeks in the wilderness worthwhile. Moving through the hallway, jostled by students going to class, he thought he could still hear the mosquitoes' incessant buzz, and smell the wind coming down from the frozen mountain tops, still snow-capped in the summer's middle.

After school, the librarian said, "Sorry. We had a rush on gold mining books. You missed out again."

*

Coach Persigo called Salas that evening, just after Salas had settled in front of the television with a sandwich and a beer. The public broadcast station scheduled an interesting sounding documentary on the Alaskan Gold Rush.

"That kid's parents hired a lawyer. He called me to schedule a deposition. Thirty-five years teaching school, and my techniques are called into question because one immature kid can't settle an argument without hitting another immature kid. Is that my fault? Kids get into it some time. Is that my fault?"

Salas gripped the phone tightly. He never knew what to say to a teacher in full rant mode.

"I've got grandkids, Salas, and I don't see them enough. My gutters need painting. I don't have time to waste on a stupid lawsuit."

Salas gave him the school district's lawyer's number. "I'm sure it will come to nothing, Coach. The parents don't have a case. You know how folks can get. A week from now we'll be laughing about this."

Persigo didn't speak. Salas could hear him breathing. The television showed a snow-covered mountain range, and then zoomed until it focused on a lone man leading a burro up a rude trail. A pick and shovel were strapped to the animal's back. Salas longed to turn up the sound.

"You'd better be right," said Persigo. "Life's too short."

Salas met with Mrs. Hatcher at lunch to go over his observations, a mandated step in the evaluation process. She dropped her lesson plan book on his conference table and sat in the same chair students who were in trouble used. Even her hands are plump, Salas thought. She personified softness, like a teacher-shaped pillow, but she gazed at him sharply, and when she smiled her face broke into laugh lines.

"Your lecture interested me," said Salas. "You clearly know your subject area." ("Subject Area Knowledge" was another area on the evaluation, but he wasn't sure how to evaluate her there. Did she *really* know her subject area? He'd fallen into the weird daydream both days, and he didn't know what she'd said.)

"I love history. I think what I've learned most as a teacher in all these years is a passion for my subject." Her voice was just as gentle in person as in the classroom, and she smelled of lavender.

"Yes, that's clear." Salas took a deep breath. He ran his finger down the check-sheet identifying her shortcomings, which were many. But he couldn't force himself to make a criticism. He had thought this conference would be perfunctory. He'd point out that she ignored the district's guidelines and policies, allow her to say whatever she wanted in her defense, and then be able to say later they had had a meeting, which the union required. He'd done numerous evaluation meetings in the past with other teachers that were no more substantial.

The truth, he thought, is I don't have any idea what's going on in any teacher's classroom. I'm in them such a small percentage of the time. He remembered his first assistant coaching position. The head coach had sent him to the practice field with the freshmen boys who wanted to play infield. He was supposed to show them technique and evaluate who could start for the first freshmen game coming up in a week. Ambition and idealism filled him. *Any* boy can learn to play better, he'd thought. They just needed time and the right instruction. He worked with the group for two hours, but just before the practice ended, the head coach stopped by to watch. He said to Salas as he left, "Bad technique. It'll be a miracle if they win a game this year."

Salas had been dumbfounded. He thought, But you should see how far they've come! You should have seen them two hours ago!

"Can I see your lesson plans?" Salas asked.

Mrs. Hatcher pushed them toward him. She'd written little in individual days. This week, for example, included the Chicago Fire, the Battle of the Little Big Horn, and the Alaska Gold Rush. Hatcher had written "1850-1900" and drawn an arrow through the week.

"Not very detailed," said Salas.

Mrs. Hatcher laughed. "Detail's in the head, Mr. Salas. I know what to cover."

"But I don't see your learning objectives. You haven't written the standards you're teaching. You don't write them on the board either. I'm supposed to be able to ask any student in your class the learning objective for the day's lesson, and they should be able to tell me. That's best practice."

"Did you ask them this week?"

"Uh, no, but you never stated an objective. They wouldn't know it."

Mrs. Hatcher picked up her lesson plan book. "The goal is always the same, Mr. Salas. When they leave my room, they know a little more history than when they came in, and they want to find out more."

"It's hardly measurable." Salas felt miserable. This wasn't how he'd planned this meeting. He was on the defensive, while Mrs. Hatcher seemed confident and self assured.

"Come in tomorrow. Ask the kids at the beginning and the end. You might find it interesting."

"What's the lesson?"

"It's a good one. The wizard of Menlo Park. Did you know, at the same time Custer made his fatal pursuit at Bighorn, Thomas Edison was working on the idea that would become the phonograph? History is seeing connections. Little Big Horn occurs in 1876, the same year H.G. Wells, the guy who wrote *The Time Machine* turned ten. H. G. Wells dies in 1946, the year after the atomic bomb. Albert Einstein will be born in 1879. So, three years after Custer's men have to use their single-shot carbines as clubs because they can't clear jams from their guns fast enough, the man who gives us the math for the nuclear age comes into the world. Einstein died in 1955. I was a year old in 1955. Einstein, a man who lived when I lived could have talked to people who remembered Little Big Horn. History's a big story, Mr. Salas, but it's not incoherent. Everything touches everything. That's the lesson."

Salas checked on the lunch detention kids after Mrs. Hatcher left his office. Theodore Remmick had taken a seat in the back, where he read quietly. He had propped the book up on the desk. At first, Salas thought it was a Japanese anime so many kids liked. A bright cartoon image splashed across the book's cover, but when Salas took another step closer, he could see the title: *The Great Chicago Fire of 1871*. The illustration showed a fireman handling a fire hose. He looked panicked.

Principal Wahr met Salas in the hallway outside the detention room. His words echoed in the empty hallway. "Persigo's in your half of the alphabet, right?"

"Yes, I meant to talk to you about him."

"No need. He turned in his resignation. Some nonsense: lawyers, kids fighting in the locker room, and no respect. He's going to finish the year, but he's done. One less evaluation on your plate. Phys Ed averages 54 kids a class. We'll replace him, but we still need to eliminate a position. Put your action plan on my desk Monday. I don't want to be messing with staffing while graduation is coming up. Here are the forms you'll need." He handed Salas a multi-page packet. "Have you observed the other teachers I suggested?"

"This afternoon, if I'm not interrupted."

But the drama teacher reported someone had stolen her purse from her desk, so Salas spent the time going over surveillance footage with the campus police officer. After two hours, they noticed the teacher didn't have her purse when she came into the building from the parking lot.

He only had time to get to Hatcher's class as the bell rang. Students left her room more slowly than they did most classes, and they had the somewhat dazed expression he now recognized.

"I'm going to the library," said a boy wearing a rock band sweat shirt. "What else did Edison do?"

"Had you ever heard of Tesla?" said his friend. He rubbed his hand through his hair as if to quell static electricity. "Or Henry Ford?"

They both blinked at the lights in the ceiling like they'd never seen them before.

At home that afternoon, Salas studied the teacher release form packet. Since the state had eliminated teacher tenure several years earlier, all he needed to remove a teacher was documented malfeasance, which he'd compiled during the week. He'd complete his third observation tomorrow, during the class's weekend meeting.

According to the evaluation sheet, he'd written damning truths. By observable standards, her teaching failed. She didn't provide learning outcomes. She didn't follow departmental or district procedures. She ignored "best practice," and lectured instead. Wahr had been right.

Salas tapped his pen against the papers, then looked out the window, a little sick to his stomach. The afternoon sun slanted across his front yard. He recognized the 5:00 light, the last light Custer and his men saw. Their heavy fighting started maybe an hour earlier, and as the sun beat down, the men were overrun. He remembered Custer, unhorsed, among the remaining soldiers atop a low rise. No cover. No place to run.

Salas couldn't remember Hatcher talking. He remembered the battle itself. He'd been there. He remembered holding an empty revolver, and he remembered a terrible sadness as men fell, but he wasn't scared. The world grew peaceful at the end, beneath the shouts and gunfire and screaming horses. He became calm when he realized the long fight was over and he didn't need to be scared anymore.

And he remembered, too, riding away, back to the village, triumphant. A warrior among thousands, a warrior to make his ancestors and sons proud.

On Saturday, Salas walked across the parking lot toward the students. They'd parked their cars near the school, and were now in the graveled overflow parking, far from the building. He heard someone laugh, and they chattered among themselves.

Mrs. Hatcher and Mrs. Leanny, both wearing overalls, were helping the students arrange display boards on the ground. When he reached the crowd's edge, he could see the boards laid out in grids, like city streets, complete with small structures glued to their surface.

"Hi, Mr. Salas," said Theodore Remmick. He wore a ballcap backwards, clearing all the hair from his face. "I'm not going to bring it into the school." He held up the propane torch from earlier in the week. "I'm the fire marshall."

"What's the project?" Salas said.

"We need your equipment at the south end, Sean," said Mrs. Hatcher. "When we're ready, start the generator and fan. Theodore will tell you when. Careful you don't step on West 18th."

"I saw so little," said the girl Salas had sat behind his first day in Hatcher's class. Today she wore a bikini top and cutoff jeans. "So much smoke. It choked me." She rubbed her throat unconsciously. "I didn't picture the scope . . ." She waved at the miniature city.

She stepped to the side, and now Salas could see the entire display.

Mrs. Leanny joined him. "Each board represents a half mile, so it's 12 boards long and 3 boards wide. There's 34 kids in the class. Two boards short. Hatcher and I got to do one too."

Theodore Remmick crouched at the south end, then fired up his torch. A couple kids pointed cell phone cameras. "It's near 9:00 a.m., Sunday, October 10 in a city of 335,000 people. In two days, 100,00 will be homeless. The fire starts in the O'Leary's barn." He let the flame wash over a tiny building, which caught fire immediately. Several students gasped.

"I saw the fire coming," said a boy holding a camera, but he stopped filming. His hand fell to his side, and his focus drifted. "I was walking home from church with my daughter. At Beach and DeKoven, I smelled burning wood. Smoke rushed up the street. We ran and ran to the Polk Street Bridge to cross the river."

Tiny flames blackened the board's end, crisping the miniscule buildings. The students had labeled the streets. Salas recognized them from the lists in Hatcher's classroom: DeKoven, Meagher, Catherine, Barber. The Chicago River, a blue ribbon, meandered the diorama's length. He saw the bridge at Polk Street.

"Turn on the fan," said Theodore Remmick.

Salas stepped back. The students leaned forward intensely. Talk ceased. Someone sobbed. The box fan pushed the fire across the display. In a few minutes, six scale miles caught fire and burned. Stores, offices, warehouses, homes, bridges, schools and hospitals. When the fire reached the far end, Theodore intoned, "On Monday evening, the winds died. Cut the wind, Sean." The fan rattled to a stop. "And it began to rain."

Students pulled out squirt guns. They were silent at first, and the water streams hissed when they hit the board, but soon they laughed as they put out the fire, squirting each other just as often as soaking the burned city.

"I want to know more about fire fighting," said a girl. "What did they learn from this?"

"Did they change the fire codes?" said another.

"How long did it take them to rebuild?"

"Did the mayor get blamed?"

"Did other cities have fires?"

"How much did it cost?"

When Salas left, they were still talking, asking questions, eager to learn. Eager to share what they knew.

Mrs. Hatcher didn't give a lecture. She hardly spoke, Salas thought in wonder. She never taught at all, but it was the best lesson he'd ever seen.

On Monday, Salas handed his recommendations to Principal Wahr. The bald-headed man studied the one-page report silently. Salas let his gaze wander around the room. Organizational charts covered the walls: arrows pointing to boxes, boxes containing names, names associated to duties. It all seemed impersonal. Standards. Goals. Wahr had framed the school's mission: "To lead all students to reach their individual potential by rigorously pursuing and evaluating achievement of high academic and ethical standards in a disciplined, nurturing environment."

Wahr cleared his throat. "This plan cuts your position. You cut your own job."

Salas took a deep breath. "Coach Persigo turned in his retirement papers. Leanny is willing to do the extra work to save a teaching slot, and I think it's time I went back to the classroom. P.E. is where I belong."

Wahr looked baffled. "What about Hatcher? What are your recommendations?"

"You said your son will be going to school here next year, didn't you?"

"Yes. I need to keep an eye on him. Hates school right now."

Salas tried to picture Principal Wahr's boy. Maybe Wahr's son resembled Salas when he was in school. Maybe he acted indifferent and lazy, just as Salas had.

"Put him in Hatcher's U.S. History class."

"Really." The disbelief reverberated in Wahr's voice. "She'll lecture him into a coma."

"I don't think so."

Salas remembered the day's end at Greasy Grass. A desperate people, for a moment, triumphed, but it was a "last stand" for both sides, a proof you fight even when the campaign looks lost. He closed his eyes to see an image that had returned to him since he'd sat in Hatcher's room. The sun set on a swell in the land they would later call Custer Hill. A growing dusk, filled with velvety shade covered the grass and brush until the details disappeared. No bodies visible now. No dead horses. No broken lances. No battle remnants. Just the stars and the rolling hills and a treeless horizon. The wind pressed his back. A coyote yipped in the distance, and the village dogs yapped in return.

He had lost friends, warriors all, but the enemy had lost many more. They would sing songs about today. They would tell stories to the childrens' childrens' children so no one would forget. The victory at Greasy Grass would join the great tales told back to back, the unbroken voice of people speaking.

It had become history.

What happened in Hatcher's room? Hypnotism, magic, time travel?

Salas rubbed the goosebumps off his arms and faced Principal Wahr.

"You won't be sorry your son is in Hatcher's class," he said. "She's exemplary."

THE HARETON K-12 COUNTY SCHOOL AND ADULT EXTENSION

THE NEW BUILDING PERCHED ON A ROCKY HILL WEST OF TOWN ON LAND no farmer could tease a crop from, so the town donated the property to the school district. Local contractors volunteered their laborers to construct the school, and that first September, when the school threw wide its doors, children had to climb four sets of stairs, fifty-five steps each, from the student drop-off area at the foot of the hill.

On opening day, some children jumped from horse-drawn buggies. Some came in shiny Model-T Fords, but most walked from town, their empty book bags in one hand, and heavy lunch buckets in the other.

Inside the school, inside the ten freshly-painted classrooms, by the lovingly buffed wooden desks with storage space beneath their as yet unmarked surfaces, waited the new teachers, all recent graduates from teaching colleges, although at the time they called them "normal" schools. The school board had decided the new teachers should be unburdened with previous experience. Only the principal, Theodore Hareton, was a veteran educator. He greeted each child at the door, shook each hand solemnly, from the tiniest five-year-old to the hulking eighteen-year-old farmers' sons who would already be tired from their morning chores, whose fingers were work-roughened and who when they wrote gripped their pencils with unfamiliarity.

Theodore Hareton signaled his secretary to ring the bell to start the first day after the last child paused at the door, a little breathless. A third grader, thought Hareton, or a small fourth grader. The girl's short brown pigtails stuck almost horizontally from her head, and her brand new pink ribbons sheened in the sun.

"Welcome to school," said Hareton. "Listen to your teachers."

"Thank you, sir."

When she went inside, Hareton looked out over the town below his feet. Two rabbits hopped out from under a bush beside the stairs, wiggled their noses at him, and vanished beneath the bushes on the other side.

Hareton took a full breath, put his hands together behind his back, and entered the building.

*

Thirty-two years passed before Theodore Hareton retired. They renamed the school after him. The community college used the classrooms in the evening to accommodate soldiers using the G.I. Bill after returning from the war.

The community had grown too. The school no longer sat at the edge of town. New neighborhoods had sprung up on all sides. The school district passed a bond issue to fund a long auto ramp on the hill's least steep side so busses and cars could now park right beside the school and its new entrance, although children who walked still climbed the cracked cement stairs to what had once been the front doors.

New wings with classrooms and a larger gymnasium had been added. Bleachers were improved next to the football field. School Hill, as the locals called it, was broad, a wide expanse of grass, scrub oak, and crumbling limestone elbows and knees punctuated the surface, but they made additions to the building as if they had no room to spread out. They excavated space for new classrooms below the ground, and they added stories to the old school. Reluctantly, it seemed, were new wings added. Construction always burrowed first, then piled on later. New structures cannibalized old; new blueprints overlaid the original ones; hundreds of contractors over the years refurbished, built on, redesigned, and modified the building until it became a stylistic hodgepodge where hallways led into hallways that emptied out into enclosed courtyards or administrative offices or storage areas even long-time students didn't recognize. Eventually they added a new wing, and then another and another and another, but always they dug first so basements rested atop subbasements, and second stories existed below third and fourth floor.

Principal Pesto, who stayed in the position for two years, famously grumbled, "They should have hired an architect when they designed this monstrosity." He also suggested the best way to improve the school would be to burn it down, but his was a minority opinion. Teachers within the county clambered to be transferred to the Hareton school, and most teachers who took a position there stayed until they retired. Many teachers were alumni.

Principal Millhauser took over from Pesto and oversaw the school's most ambitious expansion. He had been assistant curator at the famous Barnum Museum before moving to Hareton, and it was Millhouser who approved many of the school's most radical features, including the minarets, the flying buttresses, the covered walkways, fanciful bridges, the hanging garden, the numerous spiral staircases, the functional follies connected to the school via tunnels and served as isolated reading rooms, the butterfly pavilion, and other expansions too varied to mention.

As the school grew, its uses became shared between several organizations. The hospital donated a walk-in clinic because the school end of town was too far from medical facilities. The recreation district paid for a pool, the first handball courts and weight rooms rather than build a separate recreation center. The arts council raised funds for a community theater for plays and concerts. The police department added an annex for public service, as did the motor venicle department. Social Services equipped a day care for the unfortunate students who became parents before graduation, but it also took the faculty's children.

Always, earth moving equipment, fenced off construction areas, and men with hardhats were a part of the campus.

During the time of fear after the second world war, the civil service added underground living quarters and bomb shelters, thick-walled rooms with cots and shelves stacked with water and canned goods. When the fear faded, janitors used the bomb shelters to store cleaning equipment. They played music on the old radios to entertain themselves when they took breaks.

Coach DeMarco was the first teacher to live on campus. His wife left him for their stock broker, but she kept the house. DeMarco finished his math classes each day, ran afternoon practice for football in the fall, basketball in the winter and baseball in the spring. Each evening, after he'd checked the locker rooms, gathered wet towels to put in the canvas bin, he'd walk through the empty building to the cafeteria where the cooks would have left him something. He'd carry the meal with him to the small room he'd taken that once had been considered as a refuge from the outside world, contemplate his lesson plans for the next day while eating, and then would go to sleep deep within the school's bowels.

Like all schools, Hareton could be a safe island away from the outside. A Bosnian Serb assassinated an Austrian duke and his wife on a Sunday. On Monday, the Ladies Quilters Society held their weekly meeting in the home ec room the way they had the Monday before, and the way they would until they disbanded nine years later because Madeline Shattner thought Betsy Habler had stolen her diamond center Amish pattern variation.

When the stock market collapsed on Black Monday, 4th grade math classes struggled with multiplication tables. Coach Persigo tested his classes on the rope climbs the P.E. department recently installed, and the cheerleaders worked on a new cheer one girl had seen at Boston College where she'd been visiting her aunt (at the time, they referred to themselves as "yell leaders").

On another Monday, after a Japanese surprise attack on the American navy at Pearl Harbor, Mr. Carr introduced his biology class to the frogs they would be dissecting on Tuesday. Senior class vice president, Cynthia Taddler swore she would never touch the dead, nasty thing, but her twin sister, Donna looked forward to the experience and spent Monday evening carefully cutting open apples so she could make a clean incision the next day.

During the Afghan Virus Crisis, when Europe lost 1.4 million, the county cleared the cleaning equipment and stored desks from the old bomb shelters, and for two weeks in that fearful May, hundreds of citizens waited for news the plague had reached their shores. But even then, Mrs. Cross met with her ninth graders to discuss *Something Wicked This Way Comes* and Mrs. Freeman showed her videos of her summer trip to north Africa to her World Geography class.

On any given day, students may have suffered disasters at home: illnesses, beatings, broken marriages, poor food (or none), or a host of other possibilities, but when they came to class the expectation was their homework was done and they would pay close attention to their lessons.

From the very beginning, school separated itself from the "real" world, whatever that was. School might be artificial, but failures can always be made up. Falling short was expected. Professionals worked to raise people up. School is about first and second and third chances. If you are not the champion, you can be the most improved. If you are not the hardest worker, you are still a snowflake, unique and valued.

Unlike the real world, safety nets fill the school. It doesn't always work this way, but the bullies are the villains, not the victors, and the teachers are not bosses who are trying to fail you. In theory, and frequently in practice, everyone is loved. Everyone is supported, and the goal is that everyone succeeds.

The town accorded Hareton graduates a kind of status. Some took to calling it "the academy." On many doctors' walls and plumbers' and gardeners' and the mortician's a Hareton K-12 diploma proudly hung. Hareton graduates were more likely to do business with other Hareton graduates. Old timers wore their Hareton letter jackets—with the letter removed, although no matter how old and faded the jacket, the slightly darker purple where the "H" had resided showed through.

Even though the 12th graders burst with eagerness to start their lives after they finished at Hareton, and they often left town for far away colleges, they joked the "Hareton curse" would bring them back to the school for homecoming. The local superstition maintained the way to break the curse was to take a jar of dirt from the football field and sprinkle it around their house in the new town.

From its first days, Hareton became the town's center. When the wrestling team went to state, which it did year after year, a caravan followed the team bus to the state capitol, where they held the tournament. Stores would close, and hand-lettered signs in the windows said, "Gone to State." Everyone understood.

Later, when television and computers and video games took hold, and more kids worked after school jobs, the caravans grew much smaller. Still, the packed football stadium turned away fans for important home games, and basketball crowds stamped their feet so hard in enthusiasm that the stands had to be reinforced.

No matter where one stood in town, on the library steps, in front of Jake's Auto Repair, in the little park with the pink gazebo by the bicycle shop, in the alley where Christy Archer shot her mother on the day before V.E. Day, from any spot in the Catholic Cemetery (and the Odd Fellows one too), one could see Hareton on top the hill.

In the most deeply buried janitor's closet, hidden away by baffling turns and easy to forget stairwells, existed the blueprint room. In it, two huge cabinets with wide shallow drawers, held the school's schematics. Electricians, plumbers, computer technicians, structural engineers and building inspectors visited the room. They would spread plans on the single banquet table in the room's middle and try to decipher the maze.

Eventually, contractors learned any change they attempted had to be made by mapping on their own. Only long-time veterans of the building were allowed to make repairs after a new air-conditioning serviceman climbed into an air duct in the west band room and lost his way for two days.

He said he'd become turned around early, and when he thought he was going back the way he'd come he was actually going deeper into the building. He told his supervisor he peeked into classroom after classroom through the ceiling vents, but never recognizing a landmark that would orient him. His supervisor reported the man said, "Some of those students didn't look normal! Not like any kids I ever seen," but when they pressed him to explain, he quit talking, and the next day he quit his job.

The plans themselves, if laid one atop the other, and if they could somehow be made transparent, would become like an encyclopedia entry of the human body. The top plan revealed the skin, but underneath ran veins and nerves, and the next layer showed the muscles, and muscles covered organs, while organs hid the skeleton, except the transparent man that was Hareton was dozens of pages thick, and the illustrations would have to be peeled back horizontally and vertically.

An old city planner claimed the blueprints were fluid. If you looked at them long enough, the dimensions would change. A room that existed on one diagram might be in a different place when you went back to check its dimensions, or it might not be there at all.

Stories that if you put your palms on the blueprints, your skin would tingle and become warm, were just a myth. The plans were old and poorly filed. Over the years, dust had leaked into the drawers, obscuring the fine details, and time had faded the oldest diagrams. Finding the schematic was difficult, and the architects weren't careful with how accurately their plans were drawn.

All schools have a certain timelessness about them. The world moves on, but the classrooms wait, unchanged, and the teachers who stand before the students unwind time in September, their early-June triumphs now a memory, and the students who face them, looking so much like the students who had just left, that the teachers sometimes feel their efforts hadn't begun, even the long-time teachers entered September renewed.

"It's the first day of school!" the youngest students would whisper to each other. "It's the first day of school!"

Outside, peace succeeded war until peace unveiled a war again. Elections shuffled politicians from one job to another. Cars replaced horses. Better cars replaced older cars. Televisions appeared where radios once sat. Black and white images became color. Color became 3D, and then 4D, and then the televisions interfaced with the brain so there was no visible device to see.

Explorers reached both the south and north pole. They plumbed the ocean depths. They walked on the moon and on Mars, and then froze themselves for journeys that left the sun so far behind it could not be picked from the billion other stars.

Still, it's the first day of school at Hareton again. Students become unstuck from the world because the classroom is a world, a thousand tiny worlds connected by hallways. Each day in these tiny worlds behind classroom doors creations take place. Edens for the innocents, where knowledge hangs unplucked.

"Could I have your attention?" the teacher says, and everything beyond the school drops away.

What year are we in? What is the planet like outside? Is it dangerous? Do people love or hate there?

How long has my teacher been standing in front of the room? We can never know.

Once, as an homage to a retiring teacher, the senior class assembled the teacher's yearbook photos into a flip book, each photo with the teacher smiling earnestly at the camera. Four decades of teaching. The teacher sat at the retirement party when he had a moment to himself. He ruffled the pages with his thumb. If he let the pages snap by in one direction, he aged. His hair grew gray and the wrinkles deepened.

But if he flipped the other way, the years dropped. His eyes brightened. His skin smoothed. At the end, he faced the camera a young man. Bring me my students, he seemed to say. It's the first day of school.

The teacher smiled at himself, and next year his old room would have a new teacher. Next year, as if no time had passed at all, the lessons began again.

Any sufficiently sized public building houses a miniature ecosystem. Certainly at the microscopic level, flora and fauna are nearly limitless. Every surface teems with organisms striving to duplicate themselves. Desktops, door handles, banisters, drinking fountains, pens and pencils (which all too often go into students' mouths), chairs, books and lunch trays swarm with the unseen.

Mrs. Fenimore, a 6th through 8th grade mathematics teacher, starting the year after the Soviet Union exploded their first nuclear weapon, wiped down her desks each morning with a mix of water, alcohol and lemon oil she had concocted herself. Students sometimes complained their books slid off their desks too easily, but she countered that an antiseptic environment was a healthy environment. The room smelled like a citrus grove, and for all her years in the room, through all the equations and formulas she wrote in her neat hand on the board, all the papers she collected and graded, she never suffered a cold or flu. In twenty-seven years, she didn't miss a single day.

Above the microscopic menagerie, the larger denizens walk, fly, ooze and crawl. Cockroaches, various beetles, millipedes and centipedes, slugs in the damp ooze of seldom-visited access spaces, many shaped and sizes spiders, flies, moths, ants, mites, fleas and others. Occasionally, too, insects that don't flourish inside are trapped: grasshoppers, wasps, praying mantises, katydids, butterflies, and such.

Vertebrates find their niche too. Mice, naturally, but deeper in the school's hidden niches, rats with phone-cord thick tales, and tucked away in the higher places bats, some no bigger than a child's thumb, who cling to the walls and ceiling during the day and flit through cracks to hunt outside at night.

On occasion, birds are found in the building. A pigeon built a nest in the gym's high rafters and shed feathers and tiny bits of string onto the polished floor for weeks before a janitor captured it.

One year a chemistry teacher opened her classroom in the early morning, and a fox dashed out the door and down the hallway. How it got into the building and where it went were never discovered.

Inexplicably, and unique to Hareton, a student walking between classes will occasionally see a rabbit. It will hop around a corner, and when the excited student runs around to see it again, it has disappeared. Unlike the fox in the chemistry classroom or the bird in the gym, rabbits are spotted often enough that the students believe they are a special breed of indoor rabbits who thrive on bits of food students drop during the day.

It's considered good luck to see a rabbit in the school.

*

The janitorial staff at Hareton is both nameless and huge. Or better it is to say their names are forgettable. Bob. Sal. Tad. Joan. Jim. Tish. Ken. Kat.

Halls need to be swept. Boards filled with the days' lessons wait to be wiped down after the students have gone home. In the chalkboard era, a damp rag turned many times would clean away the marks so the board looked new again in the morning, and the learning started on a fresh field. In the dry-erase marker era, a chemical spritz from a bottle hung from the belt was enough to melt away words' shadows so the white board sparkled as clean as a Kansas field after a spring snow.

Even when most teachers switched to digital displays and pull down screens, the janitors dusted lenses and wiped monitors and vacuumed keyboards.

Beyond their cleaning, they open stuck lockers, repair broken equipment, haul folding chairs and tables from event to event, lubricate moving parts, repaint scratches, remove old posters from the wall, direct lost visitors to the office, work as campus security, and become friends to the students who acknowledge them (or who are assigned to clean up chores as punishment).

Whether they know it or not, their hero is John Kapelos, an actor who played Carl, a janitor, in *The Breakfast Club*. "I am the eyes and ears of this institution, my friends!" Carl said, and it is true.

The janitors know about liquor bottles in the trash cans. They read the notes dropped on the floor. They catch couples who have snuck into the wardrobe storage area behind the stage. They find paper to roll joints. They comfort kids who have hidden themselves to cry. They see teachers grading late at night.

Frank, a janitor who couldn't find a job after his dishonorable army discharge (he refused an order from an insane sergeant to open fire on an enemy he couldn't see in a sleeping village in the blackness), heard Mr. Timmons talking to himself in his room evening after evening. Timmons' wife was ill. They'd never had their own children. The medical bills were too high.

Frank knew about a bottle of pills in Timmons' desk, barbiturates prescribed to Timmons' wife. So Frank stayed close to Timmons' room, sweeping the hallway slowly, quietly. Timmons sobbed at his desk.

When Timmons opened the medicine and a fifth of bourbon from his briefcase, Frank entered the room.

"I just need to clean up a bit here, Mr. Timmons."

Timmons looked up at him, his eyes red-rimmed, surprised. In his misery, he'd come to believe no one else in the world existed.

"I'll take a sip of that joy juice, if you're offering," said Frank.

Timmons glanced at the bottle, as if he didn't know it was there.

Frank found a couple paper cups. They drank until almost midnight. When Timmons took a bathroom break, Frank slipped the pills into his pocket.

Timmons' wife recovered, while the seniors voted him teacher of the year six years later. Frank and Timmons never talked about that night where they toasted to each other with paper cups, although they passed each other in the hallways many times.

On Frank's last day in the school, fifteen years from when he'd spent an evening drinking with that very sad man, after he'd turned in his retirement papers, he found a small, wrapped box on his desk, sitting beside his clipboard filled with instructions for the day. In the box glistened a gold-rimmed shot glass. The note read, "For when paper cups aren't good enough."

Eventually, it seemed, the janitors became indistinguishable from the building. Their coveralls had the same unpainted brick, faded gray-blue tint. Morning, evening, summer and winter, they roamed Harton's convoluted hallways. Teachers who arrived very early to start planning their days sometimes ran into janitors coming up the stairs from the school's lowest levels. It seemed they never left. One wondered, if one were a wondering person, if the janitors lived in the building, or if the building generated them spontaneously.

They were pale, pale, pale, and always sweeping.

Not everyone supports the Hareton School. At various times forces have allied themselves to close the facility. It is too large, goes one argument. Focusing so many students in one place encourages depersonalization. A single, large academic facility destroys innovation and initiative.

Another group said Hareton had become a dinosaur. Old plumbing, old electrical systems, tired color schemes, and aging infrastructure needed replacing, not upgrades.

Most opposition came from fear, from not understanding. What happens in that huge, impenetrable structure on the hill? Students sometimes could not tell their parents about their day.

"What did you learn?"

"Dunno."

But the child smiled, and the parents knew their young one was holding back information. The parents who attended themselves could hardly relate what a day at Hareton could be like. There were classes, certainly, and lessons to be learned, but the former students had unfocussed memories of history classes that seemed more like dreams of history than lectures and notes.

"Do you remember the Civil War in Mrs. Hatcher's class," one alumni asked an old classmate at a twenty-year reunion.

The other nodded, holding a beer in one hand, and rubbing his shoulder with the other, as if feeling an old wound. They both cocked their heads in thoughtfulness and memory, recalling a Springfield rifle's flat crack, the high whine of a mini-ball passing overhead, the smell from the horses and themselves, the splintery fence rail pressed against their chests as they took aim and fired.

"I remember Gettysburg."

"Cemetery Ridge."

They drank, leaning their elbows on the tabletop, lost in images that rose like fish in their memories, like old soldiers returned from battle.

Not every bond issue in the county passes. Sometimes property values fall, and the school's budget shrinks, but there always seems to be money for the latest expansions: a therapy pool in the hospital annex, three handball/racquet ball courts to be shared by the recreation district and the school, solar panels for the south facing roofs, a new trough for the trout farm, elliptical machines in the shared community center, smart boards for the science department, and laptop carts for the library.

When the cement plant closed north of town, there was talk that the county couldn't afford Hareton's expense, a school that big. Money could be saved, the argument went, if students walked to smaller, neighborhood schools instead of boarding busses to Hareton. But the arguments failed. In a year, new businesses moved in. Hiring went up, and closing the school discussions faded.

Once, though, the county commissioners met for the sole purposes of making cuts to the budget for Hareton. They debated far into the morning hours. At three in the morning, at the time when men's souls turn to their mortality and dreams cut loose from day to day thoughts, they passed two plans for school improvement: a parking lot resurfacing, and landscaping for the unimproved land next to the tennis courts. When the board members woke the next morning, they couldn't recreate the discussion that went from their resolution to save money to the decision to spend it.

Assistant Principal Weber moved up to administration after seven years teaching 8th grade band. He put away the sheet music and band fund raising catalogs, replacing them with weekly discipline reports and teacher evaluations. He packed his clarinet that he had used to demonstrate new music to the band, and he never played it again.

When he'd been a teacher, he dreaded the assistant principal's visits to his room. They were watching him! he thought. They're judging me!

But when he started making his own visits, he felt like a collaborator, a friendly uncle who loved his teachers and wanted them to succeed. If he saw the teacher could make a change, maybe wait a bit longer before answering a question to the class he had asked, or writing instructions more clearly on the board, then he would write a sticky note to put in the teacher's box. After a while, the staff talked about the Weber-gram they'd received.

"Never met a metaphor he couldn't butcher," said Miss McToom, a third-year English teacher who worked for an hour and a half every night on a novel she would still be writing fourteen years later when she and Assistant Principal Weber married. She showed her latest in the lounge: "Keep your eye on the ball," it read. She'd received a note from him the week before. "Stay on your toes on the line."

Laughing, she said, "What does that even mean?" but she kept the notes in her desk.

Assistant Principal Weber found a journal Assistant Principal Schmidt had kept sixty years earlier. Schmidt had tucked the leather-bound volume behind files in a wooden cabinet drawer in Weber's office.

In Schmidt's neat hand, Weber read about kids who were suspended for chewing gum, for kids whose parents were called when the kid was caught smoking. Schmidt had a plan to prevent alcohol from "contaminating" football games. He copied his own memos to teachers into the journal. The mandate for chaperones to make kids dance at least a hand's width apart to "leave room for God" particularly amused Weber. At this year's homecoming, Weber had advised the chaperones to not watch the kids too closely on the dance floor. "It's not like when you were kids," he'd said to the teachers, some in their mid twenties. "As long as they're not taking off each other's clothes, leave them alone."

Late at night, when Weber walked the halls for his final inspection, before he'd drive home, he imagined he could hear dance music coming from the gym, old, big band music. When he opened the doors to the darkened gym, the music faded away, but for a second, Weber thought he saw high school girls in long dresses swirling around with their partners, their bellies and pelvises at least a hands width apart.

At his career's end, when Weber chaperoned his last dance, the former Miss Mc-Toom stood beside him, holding his hand, two old lovers who were ready to step aside and let the youngsters take over. Lights strobed psychedelically. Techno music pounded. The lyrics, when he could make them out, were obscene, and the kids danced so tightly together that Weber figured there would be no premarital sex afterwards. They'd all be spent on the dance floor.

But as the students gyrated, as the music crashed down around him, he thought he could see the dancers' stately figures from years gone by, mixing with their modern counterparts. He heard the band behind the band, the old bands and the gone bands, still echoing in the gym. In the old music a single clarinet took up the tune. Weber recognized the solo. He'd played it himself when he was young.

He squeezed his wife's hand. There's always room for God, he thought, no matter how close they dance. There's always room for God when the kids dance.

Through the years, the art classes took on different parts of Hareton as community art projects. Built into nooks in the hallways, sculptures gazed out on passing students, classical figures, naturally: Einstein and Newton and Mendel in the science wing, and Beethoven and Bach and Mozart near the band rooms, but also Dylan and Hendrix and Malcolm X and Hawkings.

In other nooks were more . . . interpretive pieces: a bronze whale with a baby's face, a marble hand where a mouth filled with needle teeth opened at each finger's end, a hulking piece in granite—the largest sculpture in the school—a shambling figure draped in tentacles and inhuman eyes peeking from deep, folded slits. No student lingered near the tentacled statue, and looking at it too long provoked a deep unease, nausea even, and for some children, when they had nightmares, the unnamed sculpture came alive to follow them wherever they ran.

Murals covered the largest walls. The westward expansion stretched eighty feet wide above the lockers in the oldest hallway, covered wagons and trains and telegraph lines marched from the cities on one side to canyons and prairies and gold fields on the other.

Another mural traced the history of music, starting with cellos, violins, flutes and trumpets on one end, and then tracing a long wavy musical notes line, minstrel singers and blues musicians and rock and rollers mixed with gramophones and juke boxes and phonographs and portable music players.

A sports mural covered a gym wall.

A giant solar system loomed over the entrance to the science classes.

Smaller art projects surprised even long-time teachers: Theodore Hareton's portrait tucked behind a door to the attendance office, a bench that looked as if it had been assembled from human leg bones in a remote corner of the school's wildlife observation area, a mobile of ceramic heads, each one grimacing in pain, hanging in the back of the wood shop. A hand tooled toilet in the bathroom next to the agriculture classroom.

The German teacher and French teacher met for lunch each day in the French teacher's room. They called their daily meetings the "Maginot Meal." They'd eaten in the room together for eleven years.

"When did you put that painting up?" asked the German teacher. He gestured toward the door with his sandwich.

"Which painting?" The French teacher dug listlessly into his salad. He'd been trying to lower his cholesterol for months, but all he wanted to eat were hamburgers dripping with fat and French fries drenched in mayonnaise. He looked where the German teacher pointed.

A simple painting of a mountain meadow hung in the shadows above the door. Slanting sunlight in a green bar cut through the trees, illuminating two rabbits crouched side by side next to a lilac bush. The lilac bloomed in the angled light.

The French teacher looked at the image for a long time. It seemed as if the light in the painting gradually changed, as if the sun was going down. The image grew darker. "Isn't that remarkable," he said. "I've never seen it before."

After that, they both studied the painting for a moment or two during their lunches, but they didn't comment on it again. Some days there were two rabbits. Some days, three or four. Occasionally the light came from the other direction. The lilac bush became a rose bush, and then an azalea. The seasons changed. Neither man ever touched the painting, but once, late at night when the French teacher had been grading at his desk, long past dinner, he pulled a chair to the wall where he could stand on it. He looked at the picture's frame. Dust covered it, but it looked like metal, like burnished gold.

As schools changed, so did Hareton. Life turned away from the school. Where seniors had once lived or died on the teams' fate, and tears were shed over who became the homecoming queen and king, the kids took afterschool jobs. Some took classes on line, and some tried the new neural curriculum that tied them to machines and downloaded course information directly, although the results were never consistent. A student might be able to speak Spanish who had never spoken it before, but he could have forgotten where he lived.

More students lived in the resident halls as semi-permanent boarders, while almost all the teachers took rooms for the faculty.

The school met their needs. The world outside could fall apart and did, but Hareton's on-campus mall remained a place to buy goods, to seek entertainment, and to meet with friends. The clinics serviced health problems, and the chapels catered to the souls. Classes for every knowledge were offered from preschool to retirees. In one hour students could be in a traditional class, like Sophomore English, while down the hall elderly women could be studying the Teachings of Zoroaster. Five-year-olds might be reciting the alphabet in a room next to college-aged students practicing cranio-sacral therapy.

Hareton became all things to all people, and eventually there was no reason to leave her.

*

And I don't leave. In the morning, feet rustling in the hallway outside my dorm awaken me. In the cafeteria, dozens of breakfast foods await, and then I go to class. Today, I spent the morning at the aquarium studying cephalopod life cycles. My art instructor encouraged me to draw what interested me, so I've filled my notebooks with waving arms and octopus eyes.

In the afternoon, my calculus class follows composition, where my semester project is a short novel (that I'm also illustrating), and in the evening I'm taking the laboratory section for the human sexuality class I started last semester. My study partner, Elizabeth, who is finishing a complicated bridge in her engineering class, has decided I should help her with a paper she's writing on the less practiced positions in the Kama Sutra.

We have discussed taking a two-person dorm or moving into a domed collective.

Urgency isn't driving us, however. Our choices are many, and the curriculum is broad. I have decided, though, that I would like to teach. Our teachers seem so confident and curious and passionate. I see them in the cafes, heads close together, swapping classroom stories, discussing students, sharing learning like generous royalty, following knowledge like eager hounds. I've seen their honor wall and the names, the many, many names of the teachers who have served in Hareton through the centuries, and I think I would like to see my name among them.

Now, I sit in the cafeteria again, contemplating dinner. I lean back in my chair and gaze at the skylight that stretches the room's length. Beyond it, the stars shine without winking. Beyond the skylight is the world outside, but no one goes there anymore. Was it war that drove us inside? Was it plague or famine or pestilence? I don't know. There is a rumor that Hareton encompasses the entire Earth, and for all I know, it could be true. There's another rumor that says there never was an Earth, and that Hareton has always been and will always be, that we cannot exist beyond Hareton.

I do know that I have looked through the windows in my classroom to what lies beyond and seen nothing that tempts me.

In the hallway, on the way to my room, a rabbit jumped from a doorway, twitched its nose twice in my direction, then hopped past. I stepped aside so that it wouldn't shy away, and I wondered what mission drove it, and what kind of life it lead, and I knew that tomorrow I would be lucky and fulfilled, and classes would be interesting.

At Hareton K-12 County School and Adult Extension, in the halls of the school eternal, that's the way life goes, the way it ought to go, and all that passes in its compass is holy.

MY FATHER AND THE
MOON MAIDS FROM MARS

W HEN I WAS SIX, DAD SHOWED ME THE UFO DETECTOR HE'D BUILT IN his closet.

"UFOs generate powerful magnetic fields," he said. Hanging from the inside wall, out of sight, he'd suspended a four-foot long, slender metal rod. It swung freely from a pivot at the top, and at the other end, a small magnet quivered between two electrical contacts. He gave the rod a light touch, moving the magnet against a contact. A buzzer, mounted beside the device hummed abruptly. I covered my ears.

"When a UFO moves within range, the magnet will complete the circuit and alert me."

I looked at the simple arrangement and loved my father even more. My dad knew that UFOs existed and that they might visit us at any time.

He looked at me seriously. "Don't mention this to anyone."

I imagined he thought one of our neighbors might be an alien, or that there could be an alien agent in my first grade class. Later, when I'd begun to question if he was right about anything, I decided it was because he thought people might think he was crazy.

He did become crazy, fifty years later, surrendering to Alzheimer's in the assisted living center.

He'd been there almost six months when I made one of my periodic visits. I wished I could see him more often, but I lived on the other side of the state. The knowledge that my sisters lived in town and dropped in almost daily made me feel only a little better.

"The clowns handed out candy," Dad said, "at the parade."

He slumped back in his chair, a bit of today's lunch clinging to his shirt.

"What parade, Dad?" In the hallway, a nurse walked by, her heels clicking against the tile.

"They played music," he said, looking at me and then away, like he suddenly wasn't sure.

My sister, sitting next to him on the bed, shrugged her shoulders.

He scratched behind his ear, something he'd been doing more and more over the last year. "Yesterday, maybe the day before."

Or it could have been eighty years ago, when he was six.

"We went on a plane ride after, a green biplane." He laughed to himself. "The biplane aces became barnstormers."

"Sure, Dad," I said. "Do you want more applesauce?"

"I wore goggles." He made circles with his thumb and finger on each hand and held them over his eyes, peering at me. "My house was so small."

Dad took me to see *The Blue Max* when I was twelve. Most of the time we watched science fiction or horror movies on television. When I was younger, he'd let me stay up for the 10:30 start of SciFiFlix on Friday night or Creature Features on Saturday. Great films when you're eight or nine: *The Creature from the Black Lagoon, Forbidden Planet, The Incredible Shrinking Man, Dracula, The Mummy,* and the Godzilla films. It seemed like we could always find Godzilla.

Every once in a while, a true special occasion, we'd go to the drive-in or a "sit down" theater.

I loved science fiction, but I found romance in WWI planes.

Dad's arm pressed against mine on the chair's plush armrest. He held an open box of Milkduds loosely in his fingers. I could smell them on his breath as he chewed silently. Popcorn smells too, and spilled pop. The soles of my shoes snapped free from the stickiness when I moved.

On the screen, a biplane waggled its wings. A cloud wisp passed beneath its wheels. Below, so far that details vanished, the ground turned into big squares, like patchwork.

I lived movies. When the plane turned, I leaned with it, thinking about the model planes hanging from my bedroom's ceiling. I didn't have this biplane, the one on the screen. It was German, maybe the Albatros D, a squat, efficient speed demon the Germans introduced at the end of the war. I had Fokker biplanes, some Nieuports and Sopwith Camels, but not this one.

My glasses became goggles. Gloves covered my hands. Against the wind, I checked my guns' trigger again. Somewhere, there were British fighters, but for now I flew alone, the engine's roar pillowing me.

Clouds swallow the sky for a second, surrendering the world to whiteness. Water drops stream from the wires and struts, then I am out again, into the clear. All air. All clouds. All sky, open and mine. Clouds like white islands float around, and I weave between them, the enemy forgotten.

I glimpse him, then lose him, a red flash against the blue. My heart pounds. I've been reading WWI aviation history for months. The knights of the sky. I have my heroes, Rickenbacker, Bishop, McCudden, Fonck. I lay on my bed, hands laced behind my head, studying my model planes. Sometimes I turn off the lights and sweep my flashlight across them like a lonely search light. I think about their canvas and wood construction, and how they caught fire in the air, tumbling toward the ground. Tracers cutting curved paths. Anti-aircraft explosions. The smell of oil and gas.

And always, above it all, beyond the heroes and ground's pitiful limitations, flew von Richthofen. I dreamed von Rhichtofen, and labored for days assembling his complicated plane, trying to keep the wings even, to not smudge his beautiful red craft with glue, to hang him in a place of honor in the room.

I see it again, a red plane that vanishes behind a cloud. Could it be? Is it possible? I will the plane to fly around the cloud, and it turns as I command. Where is it? Did I see it? My heart thumps hard. I grip the velvet armrest, leaning forward.

Was he there?

Then, above me, clear as an angel and more holy, the red triplane flies against the blue sky.

"The Red Baron!" I gasp, loud enough that people sitting in front of me turn to look. Someone in the theater laughs, but I don't care. It's the Red Baron.

Dad's hand is on my arm, pressing gently down. I think, was I too loud? Is he warning me to be quiet?

But he's not looking at me. He's leaning forward too, watching the screen.

The Red Baron looks over the cockpit's edge, spots us. His fingers touch his leather flight helmet.

He saluted us, the Red Baron, and then he banks away, impossibly aloft in his beautiful killing machine.

Mom died four days after she checked into the physical therapy center, a separate facility where she was supposed to recover from the back surgery. We had arranged for Dad to be in the room with her during her rehab. He couldn't really take care of himself, and whenever Mom was out of the room, he would become anxious and start looking for her. She couldn't even go to the bathroom that he would be outside her door, calling for her. She was eighty-four, weak from previous illnesses, and she'd never responded well to anesthetics. After two days on a ventilator, we agreed with the doctors that there was no hope, so they disconnected her. Thirty-five minutes later she passed on. Dad sat in a chair by her bed, holding her hand, but he wasn't focused. I'm not sure that he knew what was happening. I hoped he didn't.

We moved Dad to the assisted care center that week. He went straight from the physical therapy facility to the care center without going back to the house. We reasoned that going home would be too hard on him. He wouldn't want to leave, and he couldn't stay.

Within the month, my sisters began cleaning the house, clearing it out, and making it ready for sale. Since I lived almost three hundred miles away, they did all the work. They'd call me to talk about where furniture was going, to ask me what I wanted to keep.

Cinderella City, the Denver area's first shopping mall, opened when I was in junior high. It sported a fountain in its central plaza, a huge spray reaching toward the ceiling, falling short, then falling back in a misty clatter.

Dad walked beside me the weekend of the grand opening, taking in the stores, smelling meats and spices grilled in the food court, working our way through the crowds. He was forty, dark-haired, confident.

Girls, hired by the mall, in matching costumes of red blouses and short, silver skirts, reflective as mirrors, mixed with the crowd, handing out promotional flyers from some of the businesses. They'd all dyed their hair an unlikely blue. Background music filled the air.

"They're moon maids," Dad said.

"What?" I said. Lately I'd begun to find girls interesting in a way I never had. One stopped before us, handed Dad a green flyer for Penney's.

"Twenty percent off just this weekend," she said, all smiles and long, tanned legs. She looked at me, and I could feel the blush. She winked with a beautiful brown eye, and, astonished, I watched as she turned away to hand the next shopper an advertisement.

Dad laughed. "See, I told you, a moon maid."

Embarrassed, I shrugged. "She's not so special."

"That's where you're wrong." He dropped the Penney's flyer in a trash can. "She's a Martian moon maid, a much rarer creature. There are women, who are wonderful just as they are, moon maids, and then Martian moon maids. You are lucky to see one, and if you play your cards right, you might even talk to one and become her friend. They're like unicorns: you have to be worthy and noble. Martian moon maids have standards, after all."

"So, what is Mom?"

We turned into another broad walkway lined with stores. The color scheme changed from the light pastels we'd been walking through to darker, richer hues, and incense smells replaced the grilled meat.

"Your mom is the Martian moon maid queen, son." He spotted a cart between two stores. "Come on. I'll buy you a pretzel. Have you ever had one with mustard?"

I shook my head doubtfully. A pretzel with mustard?

I've never had a pretzel that good since. And, as far as I can tell, that was the only time he talked to me about women.

That was my sex talk from Dad.

I wandered through the transformed home. Some of the furniture had gone to the care center with Dad. Books sat in boxes in the middle of the floor. Kitchen cupboards were bare, the refrigerator empty. Their bed was gone, so their room seemed strangely large, but I could smell them in it: Dad's Chapstick and cologne. Mom's lotions. And the oddly old smell that people leave when they've grown too old to take care of hygiene like they used to.

I opened Dad's nightstand drawer. He'd built sections into it so the items were neatly organized—fingernail clipper, pencils, television remote, cough drops—all partitioned. In the back cubby, he'd put a pocket notebook. Inside were the dates for rotating the bed's mattress that showed if he'd simply flipped it over, or also swapped the foot for the head. An entry for every four months since he'd bought the mattress in 2005. The book showed the life of the previous mattresses too, and he'd created spaces for flipping the mattress for the next eight years, with places to put a check mark when he'd made the rotation.

Dad loved keeping records. In the glove compartment of the car was a notebook with every gas and oil change (complete with mileage on that tank of gas) from when he'd bought the car. I found books for cars he'd owned back to 1946 in his desk. In his workshop, he kept records for paintbrushes: purchase date, projects completed, color of paint. Next to his golf clubs he kept a tally of every game he'd played: course yardage, total score, total putts. Taped to the wall beside his flying saucer detector in the closet, I found a list of dates. I guessed they were for when he changed the battery.

When I was eight, Dad took me into his office to show me a chart he'd made. It noted bank deposits from the day I was born and continuing until I was twenty-one, more than twice my current lifetime in the future. "See, here," he said. "Your freshman year of college will be completely paid for. Your sophomore year we'll pay 80%, and junior year 50%. You'll need to start saving money now to pay the missing percent and your senior year. We will give you a weekly allowance." He brought out another chart. "If you save 50% each week, and then get a job during the summer once you turn twelve, you will have college paid for."

I was eight. All I could think about was the 50% of that allowance I could spend. In two months I might be able to buy a model plane.

*

Dad exercised on his own most of his adult life. He had a copy of the Canadian Air Force's exercise manual, and started his day with pushups, sit-ups, jumping jacks, and stretches. He liked to walk; for years and years he walked to church. Although Mom gained weight, Dad stayed slim. Age reshaped him, though, loosening the skin, redistributing weight. I have a black and white picture of him lying on a boat dock at an Indiana lake when he was twenty. He was built like a bantam boxer.

Now, at eighty-six, it can take him fifteen minutes to walk the 150 feet to the care center's cafeteria. He gets distracted. Forgets he has a destination. Refuses to be rushed. When he has a walker, he'll just pick it up and carry it. Often it appears that he's forgotten how to use it. Several times now the interns at the care center have found him on the floor in the middle of the night, where he has fallen.

Watching him walk is a bit of a nightmare. He's always on the edge of toppling. He shuffles. A stray thread in the carpet might be enough to trip him.

I'm frightened by the rate of change. Six months ago, when Mom had her back surgery, the event that precipitated their move into the care center, Dad and I parked the car in a hospital garage a quarter mile from Mom's room. He walked stairs, sidewalks and corridors without help. He chatted about Mom's progress and my kids.

A friend of mine has terminal cancer. He asked his oncologist how long he had to live. The doctor said, "Your system is compromised. An organ could fail, or an opportunistic infection could set in, like pneumonia. I can't predict catastrophe, but if nothing like that happens, I look at how fast your health is changing. If the change is observable over years, than you have years. If we're seeing change over months, than that is what you have. If the change is observable over days, you have days."

It's only been six months since he walked unaided to see Mom.

Three in the morning. I've been reading *John Carter of Mars* since midnight by the light from my open closet. If I hear footsteps overhead, I'll have time to turn off the light and feign sleep before Mom or Dad realize I'm flaunting my bedtime. I'm eleven years old.

The ceiling creaks. I look up from the book. On my dresser and desk, my aquariums bubble gently. I've been trying to breed fancy guppies. Even though the parent's tails are long, flowing and beautiful, all the babies look ordinary. This has been a disappointment.

The back door rattles. That would be Dad. He's obsessive about security. He'd equipped the house with heavy storm doors with two locks on them, and the inner doors also had two locks. He'd check them a couple of times a night. Years later, when he bought a car with a remote lock/unlock key fob, he'd open the front door, unlock the car with the remote, and then relock. A couple of hours later, he'd do it again.

He unlocks the back door. I hear the metallic rattling of keys. He's not coming downstairs, so I return to the book. A half hour later, I realize he hasn't come back in. What is Dad doing outdoors at 3:30 in the morning?

The third and fifth stair from the bottom creak, so I step long and high over them.

Dad built a telescope before I was born, a ten-inch reflector with a four-foot long barrel. He ground the mirror himself. Mom told me that it had taken months. During the school year, he would schedule a night for my class to come to our house to look at the sky. Last year, my fifth grade class saw Saturn's rings and Jupiter's moons. Mom made hot chocolate in a huge pot on the stove. Kids went out our backdoor into the yard, steaming mugs of hot chocolate in hand to wait their turn.

There's enough of the moon that I can see Dad standing by his telescope. He's not looking through it. His head is cocked back. He's staring up. I watch him for fifteen minutes before I'm too tired and bored. Back in bed, I open my book. Continue reading.

I think I must have fallen asleep before he came in.

My sisters made a box for me at my parents' house, filled with bits of Mom and Dad's life that they thought I would want. I haven't gone through it yet. On top of the stack is a huge, brass telescope that looks like it would be at home on a pirate ship. It's dinged, but the brass feels warm and smooth under my hand. When fully extended, it's longer than my arm.

Underneath the telescope sat a magazine with a familiar cover, the September 1963 *Magazine of Fantasy and Science Fiction* with part three of Robert Heinlein's "Glory Road." It was the first "adult" science fiction I'd read. I had been nine. The paper had long ago yellowed, but it smelled like Dad's books.

I'm glad they put the box aside for me. I think I'll make a display for the telescope to hang on my wall at home. Underneath, I'll have a sign made. "Dad. Watcher of the Skies."

Dad picks at the skin behind his ear. He's sitting on the chair by the door into his care center apartment. His focus is on the carpet a couple of feet in front of him. His fingers move slowly, rubbing the skin, pulling gently at his hair. I wonder what he's thinking about, or if he's thinking at all.

I have a theory about Alzheimer's: the brain is traveling, but it's not making a trail. Maybe he's remembering a conversation he had thirty years ago. Maybe he's thinking about orbital mechanics from when he worked for Martin-Marietta. It doesn't matter, really, because he won't connect the next thought with the last one.

Of course, he might not be thinking at all. Maybe his brain is idling, stuck in neutral. I can't tell, and that's frightening. His eyes move sometimes, and he blinks. His lips separate slightly, then press together.

Six months ago, the last time we had a real conversation, he said, "The thing about getting old is that people talk to you, but you can't follow what they're saying."

When I leave the care center now, I always tell Dad that I love him. I don't remember telling him that when I was a kid. I hug him—his shoulders are frail, like bird wings. His breath has gone bad. I wonder if he's brushing regularly.

Sometime in my early forties, I noticed that Dad and I never said "I love you" to each other. It might have been around the time his mother died that it occurred to me. I talked to him on the phone. He'd gone back to Indiana for the service. I wanted to offer some comfort, but I didn't know what to say to him. He sounded business-like on the phone. "I'll be home in two days," he said, no hint of loss in his voice.

"I'm sorry about grandma," I said. "I love you."

"She was gone for a long time before she died," he said. It had been a decade since she'd recognized him last.

"I'm sorry," I said again.

"Well," he said, "it wasn't unexpected."

After he hung up, I realized he hadn't said that he loved me. For a long times after, I made it a point to say, "I love you" when I talked to him on the phone, but he didn't say it back for years.

When I was fourteen, Dad and I created a UFO sighting. We didn't mean to. For a couple of months, we'd been experimenting with hot air balloons. Dad had found a pattern for them in *Mechanics Illustrated*, and I did the assembling. We cut the panels from a roll of tissue paper, then glued the edges together to create increasingly larger balloons. Dad made a launching station out of a three-foot section of aluminum air duct one foot in diameter that he mounted on a stand. For the bottom, he shaped a pad from fiberglass ceiling insulation that he soaked in oil and gasoline. We launched several balloons this way that would fill with the hot smoke and rise fifty feet. The balloons didn't last long. Anything would rip them, and the heat source sometimes threw sparks that set the balloon afire before it cleared the launch pad, but we persevered.

Finally, our largest balloon was ready: a nine-foot-tall monster that had taken me two weekends to assemble. We waited for the breezes to calm as they frequently did near sunset, filled the balloon, and then let it go. It wafted noiselessly upward, out of our back yard, over the house, and continued to rise. We'd never done a balloon this large! A wind current we couldn't feel carried it away, and it occurred to us that a balloon this large might be a hazard. What if it came down on someone's windshield!

We rushed to the car, but the wind carried the balloon across blocks. By the time we backed out of the driveway, it was already several streets away, and it was difficult to see from the car. We lost it, and all we could hope for is that it came down harmlessly somewhere, or was stuck in a tree. We joked that we had discovered a new way to toilet paper someone's house.

The next day, though, the local paper reported a series of UFO sightings. Numerous people reported a large object hovering over the town at sunset. We looked for where the witnesses lived, and they were all east of us. They'd seen our balloon, lit by the setting sun behind it, glowing in an orange light, numinous and stately, and, evidently, otherworldly.

"We don't believe he's a flight risk," said Shelly, the care center's director, "but we have found him wandering at night a couple of times."

My sisters and I look at each other around the round table tucked in the corner of Shelly's office. We're having a status check meeting. The care center takes notes about the resident's needs and behaviors, and the family brings any concerns they have. It's humane and gentle, but it's hard to think about making decisions for Dad because he can't make them for himself.

I smiled at the phrase, "flight risk." At the pace he walked now, I could spot him thirty minutes and he wouldn't be out of sight.

I'd talked to him before the meeting. It had been a good morning for him. More connected, although "connected" now meant that he would stay on script longer.

"How are you doing?" he'd say. He rested one hand on top the other, his skin so frail I thought I should be able to see the nerves and veins beneath.

"Just fine, Dad."

"And your boys?"

"Fine too."

"Pretty good weather we've been having."

"Yes, I think so too."

But if I wandered off the script, like asking him about the food, or if he'd made friends at the center, he'd say, "I don't know. Guess I haven't thought about it."

Shelly said, "Last night, he made it to the doors to the Memory Support Center. They're locked, of course, so he couldn't have gone in, but he had to pass several people to get there. None of them saw him." She laughed. Shelly's a slender woman, dark hair, dressed in a brown pant suit. When we'd met, she'd told me that before she took the job in the center, she'd been a middle school English teacher. We talked shop for a little bit, but like all English teachers, we ended up discussing how time consuming grading was. "I don't miss that," she'd said. "The residents don't write papers."

"What about the outside doors?" I said. I had a vision of him pushing through them, into the night, wandering down the street.

"Locked and alarmed. A receptionist mans the front desk by the doors twenty-four hours a day. We are very conscious of resident safety."

I think it's interesting that none of the employees in the care center call their wards "patients," which is how I think of them. The first day I'd visited the center, I passed a very old woman tucked in a couch. She was almost on her back, her chin pressed to her chest. She said so silently I nearly missed it, "Help me."

I told an intern, and within seconds three of them were bending over her.

I wondered what was wrong. How long had she been like that, unable to speak loud enough for anyone to hear?

Near the front doors of the center is a beautifully burnished maple dresser. Fresh flowers in a vase grace the top. On either side of the flowers stand a framed photograph of a care center resident. Old, very old, but well-dressed and smiling for the camera. I'd been to the center several times before I realized each was a photograph of the latest person to die. "With fondest thoughts, we celebrate Elizabeth Donner," read the brass plaque on the frame's bottom. "1928-2014."

I can't remember seeing the same photograph twice, and there are only ever two portraits. I suppose on a bad day, someone's memorial might be on the dresser for an hour or two before the next one replaces it.

The life care center is a way station, a train platform with nice bedrooms and compassionate attendants. I know the whole circle of life narrative. I'm not denying death, but underneath the friendly wallpaper and shiny dining area furniture and spotless glass I feel the cold fingers waiting to reach out. My dad is here.

"Many of our Alzheimer's patients are nomadic," said Shelly. "Sometimes they'll sleep twenty hours a day, but we don't know which twenty."

"Dad never slept through the night," said one of my sisters.

I thought about Dad at the telescope. Naturally, he wouldn't sleep at night. There were stars to see.

Someone said, I don't know who, "Maybe he's looking for Mom."

A breath caught in my throat, and I realized I was almost crying.

We talked for another half hour. Since I was in town, I could be more helpful. I would take Dad to his doctor's appointment the next day instead of one of my sisters.

*

Dad needed help into the car. I'd been maneuvering him from his room in the care center to the passenger pick up and drop off area for twenty minutes. He paused for a long time at the front doors, as if he didn't know what to make of the sunlight. I hadn't been able to get him to use the walker, so I'd gripped his pipe-stem thin arm the whole way.

He fastened the seat belt on the third try. "'39 Ford," he said. "Great car but it didn't have a rumble seat."

I wasn't sure what he was talking about. My mind was on other matters, though. I would take Dad to and from his appointment, then I'd drive home, but I'd forgotten the box with the telescope my sisters left for me. Dad's house was not on my way home. We'd have time to swing by the house before the appointment, but it would be the first time he'd been home since before Mom died. Most of the furniture was gone. Bookshelves were empty. Would he recognize it?

Fifteen minutes later, we pulled into the old driveway of the house my Mom and Dad spent sixty years of their marriage in. I'd grown up in this house. In a month or two, if our plans went well, it would be sold, and another family would be living there.

I tried not to think of that.

"I need to grab something, Dad. Will you be okay?"

He unbuckled his belt. I had assumed he would stay in the car. That would be easier, but he already opened the door. I rushed around the front of the car to help him.

Inside, he sat on a folding chair that was the only furniture left on the living room's hardwood floor. The drapes were closed, shrouding the room in twilight. At the care center, when he wasn't sleeping, he sat. He'd never fallen while sitting, so I knew he would be okay to leave alone.

I went downstairs to get the box.

It didn't weigh much. Before I turned off the lights in the basement, I looked around. My bedroom had been down here. It looked different without my parents' photographs on the wall, without the interruption of couch and table. It was unlikely I'd ever see the basement again. Maybe some other little boy or girl would use the bedroom. Maybe they too would stay up late, reading by the closet light. For a second, I thought about leaving the old science fiction magazine. What would someone else's child think of part three of "Glory Road"?

In the background, something buzzed. At first I thought it might be the furnace, but it came from upstairs. It wasn't the doorbell or a telephone, but it was incessant and familiar. I cocked my head to the side to hear better as I walked up the stairs.

The sound came from the back of the house upstairs, from the bedrooms. Dad wasn't in the chair by the door, though. I almost dropped the box as I put it on the floor.

"Dad?"

I went down the hall, glanced in his empty office, checked the bathroom and the guest bedroom. Nothing.

His bedroom was empty too. The buzzing came from the closet and filled the room.

It was Dad's UFO detector, still in working order after all these years. I moved the magnet from the contacts, cutting off the sound.

Where was Dad?

I double checked the rooms on the way out.

"Dad?"

Out the front door. He wasn't in the car. I rushed to the street. Looked both ways. The sidewalks were empty.

In the next hour, I called the police. I called my sisters. I drove the blocks, slowly, windows down, looking at porch chairs and front yard swings. How could he get so far? Where could he be?

It's dusk now. He's been gone for four hours. I've answered a thousand questions. I've cried. I've been wracked with guilt. Now, though, for the moment, the house is quiet again. Everyone is outside, somewhere, searching.

I'm looking at Dad's UFO detector, thinking about Martian mood maids and their queen. Dad introduced me to science fiction and telescopes and the stars.

It seemed fantastic, but his UFO detector had gone off.

For just a second, a tiny instant, I wanted to believe that maybe there was an alternate explanation. He wasn't just a wandering Alzheimer's patient.

He wasn't.

AUBREY COMES TO YELLOW HIGH

YELLOW HIGH'S HALLS SMELLED LIKE DUSTY STREETS IN A TEXAS SUN, like mesquite and sand and cactus, and sometimes like a thunderstorm just below the horizon; and when the double doors at the ends of the main hall opened, a wind came off the plains, swirling a dust devil, catching paper scraps and hissing grit across the lockers, but only Aubrey noticed. She clutched books to her chest as she walked from third period English to fourth period Student Senate. Other students streamed in both directions, racing the tardy bell.

She spotted Sheriff Jane Tremble leaning on the wall next to the drinking fountain, hat pushed back on her head, left hand grazing a six shooter's smooth handle. The sheriff wore two gun belts, heavy with bullets, the guns resting on her hips. Lines marked her face, like worn leather, and she perpetually squinted as she surveyed passing kids.

The sheriff caught Aubrey's eye, and touched a finger to her hat's wide brim.

Around the corner, down the hall, Wyoming Jim and Dry Gulch stepped into view. Wyoming sported an angry, red scar that started above the left ear, traversed across his face to the corner of his mouth, before ending at his chin. A revolver stuck from his belt at an easy angle.

Dry Gulch didn't look much older than twenty, but he had an old man's hitch in his walk. A shotgun hung from his hand like a club.

They stopped when they spotted the sheriff.

"You should'a git when we told you, Sheriff," bellowed Wyoming.

No student reacted. A couple junior girls in lacrosse shirts, carrying their long sticks, walked around the two gunmen, not interrupting their animated conversation.

The sheriff pushed away from the wall. Aubrey stepped to the side, knowing what was coming next.

"You boys are breaking the law, and I've got'a duty here." Her voice cut through student conversation, a controlled contralto. Resonate, resolute, confident.

Wyoming drew first, yanking a weapon from his belt, firing before he'd fully raised it. The ricochet wanged against the brick next to Aubrey's head. She flinched down and tried to make herself small. Wyoming shot again and again, shattering the

Pepsi machine, taking out a glass door in the trophy case.

The sheriff, unhurriedly, pulled a gun, aimed, and put a shot into Wyoming's chest. He flew backwards, while his revolver spun away on the slick tile. Before she could shoot again, Dry Gulch brought the shotgun up and fired both barrels. The sheriff's hat jumped from her head, and she staggered, her shirt a tattered, red mess.

She collapsed, the gun loose in her hand.

Now, smoke filled the hall. Two students were down. The Pepsi machine fizzled while a liquid gurgled from the bottom.

Three baseball players passed, heading toward Wyoming's corpse. Aubrey lost Dry Gulch. A player said, "It's too hot to take infield. Do you think coach will just put us in the batting cages this afternoon?"

The tardy bell rang. Aubrey looked down at the sheriff's still form and shook her head. A student who'd fallen during the gun fire rose to her knees. Aubrey bent to help. There were no marks on the girl. The bullet had entered, exited, and the wound healed in a few seconds. Spilled blood evaporated, faded, leaving no stain. Even the torn blouse knitted itself whole. "I must have slipped," she said.

Aubrey handed the girl her books. "That's okay. As long as you're not hurt."

Mr. Courtright handed out the intent to run forms. "We need diverse candidates if we want productive discussion about school issues." He wore a gray sweater vest over a long-sleeve flannel shirt, but he never seemed to sweat. Aubrey thought he had expressive eyebrows that communicated an entire range of messages. When he passed her the form, he flashed a we're-both-in-on-the-joke look. She'd checked his picture in the yearbook from his first year at Yellow High, twenty-five years ago. He had the same expression then, though his hairline hadn't receded yet.

Aubrey filled in the form. Next to "Office You Will Be Seeking" she wrote "junior class president," but she didn't know what to write in the space labeled "platform."

What did she hope to do if she won?

Courtright said, "You need to shape a vision of how you see the school. I'm going to give you some exercises that will help you write your speeches. We'll start with a metaphor to guide your message. Do you see school as a bucket to be filled? Is school a tug of war? Is it an ocean and the students are fish? Take a few minutes to finish this sentence: School is a . . ."

The other students bent over their papers, some already writing. Aubrey despaired. She wanted to be involved. She wanted to make the school a better place, but she didn't know why, and she certainly didn't know how. The population overwhelmed her. A million kids, it seemed, with a million different concerns!

"Barclay," said Mr. Courtland. "What's your metaphor?"

Barclay, an athletic sophomore who Aubrey knew also planned on running for junior president, leaned back in his chair. "The school's a flock of crows. They're attracted to shiny things, and they'll follow whatever glitters." He smiled at the class, practically a jewel himself.

Courtland nodded in acknowledgement. "That's a way to look at it. Billy, what's your metaphor?"

Billy, who wore black silk shirts and black pants, and sometimes black eyeliner, didn't glance from his paper, but kept writing instead. He'd been the junior class secretary and had announced a week ago he would run for senior vice president. "The school's a cesspool. We need to clean it up. Or it's a graveyard. The dead need raising."

"The goth point of view, neatly articulated. And Emmet, how about you?"

Emmet, who never spoke in class unless called on, but served committees well, glanced toward the classroom door and the hallway beyond. "It's a circus, a big parade. There's elephants out there, and performing seals, and clowns. I smell greasepaint all the time."

Aubrey studied the boy. He oozed sincerity. She almost believed him. She wondered if she listened closely would she hear the calliope he heard? Would she taste popcorn and cotton candy?

"What's your metaphor, Aubrey? How do you see the school?"

She hadn't written anything. "I don't have a metaphor, yet, Mr. Courtland. They're just hallways."

He smiled, not unkindly. "Tough to compose a speech without a vision. Keep thinking." On the board, he wrote, POSITIVES and NEGATIVES. "Now, list what you think Student Senate has done right over the year. These are areas you want to continue doing or improve. The other column should list tasks we haven't done well or haven't even tackled. Your lists are another way for you to define yourself as a candidate. Later, we'll work on your personal strengths and weaknesses inventory."

Aubrey tried to compose a list, but the problems seemed hard to define. Apathy? Helplessness? Directionlessness? Most kids she knew thought school sucked on some level, even the ones who liked school, but what, exactly sucked about it? And what would it matter what she did? Senate had no real power in the school to make change. They didn't even aim at real issues.

In the desk in front of her, Connie Pace, who drove a BMW and spent lunches redoing her makeup, wrote a list is big letters: "Longer lunches. First period release for all seniors. Reduced graduation requirements. Preferred parking for Student Senate members." Connie crossed the last one out, then added, "Senior class trip to Cabo in the spring."

Good luck with those, thought Aubrey.

The administration scheduled the dances and made the rules. They controlled the budget. Senate debated balloon colors and what activity days they would promote during homecoming. They'd gone with pajama day, cross-dress day, superhero day, underwear on the outside day, and, of course, class colors on Friday. Only Student Senate members participated. For three days they'd argued about the DJ for the Wild West dance, before choosing based on which had the better web page. Real change defied them.

Her mother said Student Senate would look good on her resume for colleges, but surely, Aubrey thought, Senate is more than an activity. Student leadership must count for something.

HOW CAN I MAKE A DIFFERENCE? she wrote on her notebook. WHAT DO I BELIEVE?

Billy leaned across the space between their desks. "What happened to your binder?" He pointed at the blue, plastic cover. A ragged hole big enough to fit her pinky through showed the desk underneath. "It looks like you shot it." He grinned darkly. "I want to kill my books too."

The Reno boys stood inside the main entrance to the cafeteria in matching dusters that hung below their knees. Frank Reno held a revolver behind him, but Aubrey saw it when she came in. Frank's brothers rested their hands on their belts, near their guns.

Aubrey watched them warily as she filled a bowl at the salad bar. The men didn't move, even when their jacket tails swayed in the breeze from the open doors or when students passed too close. Wyoming Jim joined them, looking just as he had earlier, before the sheriff killed him.

After she picked up a milk, Aubrey chose a table as far away from the gunmen as she could, near an exit, in case things got exciting.

Kids lined up at the taco bar, empty lunch trays in hand. Others filled cups at the soup station or picked up sandwiches from the ala carte display before moving to the cash register. Students packed most tables, and chatter filled the room.

Aubrey opened a notebook. She still hadn't written anything in the platform box, and she couldn't think of a poster slogan. She tried several: "Aubrey: Your Voice in Student Senate." "Give Aubrey Your Vote." "Aubrey Will Make Yellow High Fly."

They sounded stupid, but when she looked at the cafeteria crammed with students, she knew, really knew she wanted to be junior class president. Some kids ate quietly by themselves. Some ate in groups, laughing at each others' jokes. Some studied. Some read. Some were lost in whatever soundtrack their earbuds piped to them. None paid attention to her. She didn't see any friends, but looking at classmates filled her with respect and awe. They have lives, she thought, and dreams and struggles, like me. For a moment, group empathy, an affectionate fog, surrounded her. If they knew how much I cared, they'd vote for me. If only they knew.

Barclay plopped next to her at the table. "You ought to run for secretary. Junior president is a sure thing for me." He sounded matter of fact, almost chummy. "You'd be a good secretary."

Aubrey shrugged.

"Your funeral," said Barclay. "Save some time and make your campaign speech a concession."

Some boys on the other end of the cafeteria called him. He patted her shoulder as he left.

Before Aubrey could decide if she hated Barclay, or if he was right, Sheriff Jane Tremble filled the door next to Aubrey's table. Aubrey froze. The Reno brothers straightened. Between the sheriff and the four men sat two hundred high school students.

Aubrey reached out, touched the sheriff's hand. "There's too many. You can't win."

The Sheriff didn't look down. Her gaze locked like an eagle on the men across the room. "Darlin,' you're always outgunned."

Frank Reno swung his gun into view.

When the smoke cleared, and the half dozen students who'd been shot healed, picked themselves up and headed to class. Two Reno brothers lay motionless on the cafeteria floor. A fluorescent light dangled from its fixtures, spitting sparks. And Sheriff Tremble sat, back to the blood-streaked cash register, eyes open, unfocused, unblinking and very, very dead.

Billy, late to lunch as usual, walked by Aubrey's table, a square of chocolate cake balanced on a napkin. Many students had gone now, leaving behind paper wrappers, empty cups, unreturned trays, and the three bodies.

Billy, looking funereal in black, surveyed the remaining students. "Zombies. Can't save them. Can't bash their heads in."

Aubrey, suddenly angry, yelled, "Why do you care then? Why do you want to even run for office?"

The boy stepped back, surprised. "Sheesh! It's just a metaphor. I'm running for office because Lisa Autumn promised she'd be my campaign manager."

"What does that matter?"

"Lisa Autumn is cute."

Aubrey didn't know whether to laugh or cry, but after Billy left, along with the last students, she still sat at her table, looking at the Sheriff, who hadn't dropped her guns, who'd gone down shooting.

"It's not fair," said Aubrey.

If the janitor sweeping the floor by the dead Reno brothers heard, she didn't react, but kept working, pushing litter, food scraps and empty brass shell casings.

Aubrey ditched sixth period Algebra. She never ditched, but an hour with Mr. Ketchum and unsolved X's filled her with dread. She slipped from a gymnasium exit, then walked across the brittle, brown grass until reaching the split-rail fence that marked the school's boundary. Beyond, cactus covered hills undulated to the dry mountains shimmering twenty miles away. The town of Yellow, with its saloons and churches and ranching supply stores receded as she wound between mesquite and yucca. A whip-thin lizard, brown as the sand, skittered away, stopped after ten feet to eye her warily, then sprinted from sight.

A quarter mile from school, an arroyo cut across the desert, invisible until you almost fell over its edge. Aubrey slid down the sandy slope to the gravel bottom, and followed its curves. When the angles allowed, the high walls shaded the sun, cutting the temperature by ten degrees. Finally, she came to the beach chairs kids had brought over the years. On some, nylon fabric hung in tatters from aluminum frames, while several were almost new, colors hardly faded. Cigarette butts littered the area, but it was quiet and calm and isolated. She knocked sand off a chair, shook it to make sure a scorpion wasn't clinging to the underside, and sat down.

After a while, it seemed as if the wispy clouds crossing the strip of sky stood still, and the arroyo itself moved beneath them. Dry branches rattled against each other when the wind picked up. She shifted in the seat, making the metal creak. A calm settled upon her, so when she heard the rhythmic, rocky crunch of someone walking, she turned slowly, indifferently to see.

Sheriff Jane Tremble settled in a nearby chair, rolled a cigarette from a tobacco pouch she pulled from her shirt, but didn't light it.

"Aren't you supposed to be in school, butterfly?"

In the distance, a bell rang. Aubrey checked her watch.

"School's over."

The Sheriff looked at the sky. "So it is."

For a long time, neither spoke. Aubrey heard a truck engine, and then a coach's whistle. The teams would be on the fields now. The parking lot would be empty except for the athletes' cars and the teachers who stayed late. If she went into the school, there'd be no traffic. The janitors would have cleaned up. The lights would go off. The hallways would reach from end to end and cross each other like streets in the old west. She imagined the scene at night: the Sheriff at one end, walking toward the bad guys at the other, hands twitching near her guns. Their footsteps echoed.

Tension vibrated between them. Over and over and over. Every night, a shootout, an epic battle with Jane Tremble on one side and uncountable black hats waiting.

Aubrey said, "You're playing the losing hand."

Tremble laughed, put the cigarette in her shirt pocket, then stood while adjusting her guns. "It's always high noon, daisy. It's always getting' backshot or bushwacked or waylaid. That's what you're dealt."

"So, why do you do it?"

Aubrey gripped the chair's plastic arm rests until her knuckles turned white. School faded. No English essays or Honor Society meetings. No geology lessons or P.E. fitness tests. She lost memory of the bus ride every day, and the long nights where she moved from one subject to the next. She didn't think about Robert Parker who sometimes would stop at her locker just to chat, and who always seemed on the verge of asking a question he didn't dare voice. Sometimes she would look at how he held his books, and wonder what it would feel like if they walked down the hall, hand in hand.

For this instant, only Sheriff Jane Tremble, and the eternal showdown mattered to Aubrey.

The Sheriff checked the sky again, as if she had an appointment the clouds recorded.

"It's not about winning, kitten. It's about not surrendering."

Aubrey watched as the Sherriff climbed from the arroyo and headed back to the school, sure she'd never seen someone as brave and noble, sure that the universe must be as dark as Billy saw it with cemeteries and zombies and his black wardrobe. Sheriff Jane Tremble lived in a world where the hero always died.

And this time, Aubrey did cry.

Night passed slowly. Out Aubrey's bedroom window, stars crept up the clear desert sky. She watched them appear from behind the wooden frame, slide across the glass inexorably, and then vanish. The black gave way to gray, erasing the stars, and an angry sun rose.

Not now. Not before first period, thought Aubrey. The three Reno brothers, whole again, Wyoming Jim, Dry Gulch and two shooters she didn't recognize stood with their backs to her at the sophomore hall and the long main hallway junction. By their stance, she knew the Sheriff must around the corner. Seven against one, she thought. Students filled the hall, making their way past the men, talking about their concerns, yawning, laughing, yelling.

Mr. Courtland waved. "Good morning, Aubrey. Posters today. Hope you have some slogans in mind."

"Whatever," said Aubrey, but she didn't think he heard.

"We warned ya," shouted Wyoming Jim. He already had a hand on his gun.

"You boys need to clear out," drawled the Sheriff. Aubrey could see her now, feet apart, arms relaxed, thirty feet down the hall.

Dry Gulch flicked back the triggers on the shotgun. "Fill your hand, lawdog, and we'll see who's coming and going."

Aubrey put her books on the floor, next to the lockers. Four lacrosse girls stood in a group, discussing their afternoon game.

"Can I see your stick?" Aubrey asked.

"Sure. It's a Nike. Do you play?"

Aubrey felt the equipment's heft. The netting on the basket bounced as she gauged its weight. "No, not really."

She moved her grip down, holding the stick like a long baseball bat, then walked toward the Reno brothers and their gang. Staring down the Sheriff, Wyoming Jim drew his gun, but Aubrey ignored him. He was a terrible shot. She wound up and swung the stick with all her strength, slamming the two nearest brothers across the shoulder blades.

"What . . ." cried one as he turned toward Aubrey. The second brother stumbled into the third, knocking his gun hand aside just as it fired. All the men had their guns out. Something buzzed by Aubrey's cheek, and something else tugged at her blouse as she brought the stick back again and swung, missing a Reno boy, who ducked, but catching Wyoming Jim full on the back of his hat.

Dry Gulch's shotgun exploded, although Aubrey couldn't see what he fired at. Wyoming Jim swirled to see what attacked him, when a bullet tore through his shirt, spinning him around, and he fell. The Reno brother who ducked, came up pointing his weapon at Aubrey just as his forearm jerked and spouted blood. A second shot took him out.

Gun smoke obscured the view while her ears rang painfully. She stepped forward, over a downed man to swing again when Dry Gulch planted the shotgun across her chest and pushed hard. She flew backwards, landed flat on her backside, banging her head against a locker. Dry Gulch's eyes bulged, wide and wild. He cracked the gun open, dug into his pocket and came out holding two shells. Behind him, the remaining gunmen blasted at the Sheriff who aimed and fired methodically. Dry Gulch loaded the shells into the gun while casting his head about, like a dog searching for a scent.

"What is this place?" he yelled. High school students walked by, unaware. Two teachers, a few feet from the mayhem, studied a shared textbook. Stapled flyers clung to the announcements board. The warning tone sounded, letting everyone know class started in one minute. "Where in God's cursed Hell am I?"

Aubrey realized he had been as unaware of the high school as it had been of him.

The gun snapped shut. Dry Gulch drew the weapon to his shoulder, aimed at Aubrey's face, the two barrels wide, black and bottomless.

A last shot cut through the smoky air. Dry Gulch dropped the gun, grabbed at his throat, looking confused, lost and scared, then crumpled.

For a moment, Aubrey watched the passing feet. The intercom clicked on. The principal announced, "Remember, students, Friday we will be on assembly schedule for class officer speeches."

A pair of worn boots stopped a foot from Aubrey. Sheriff Jane Tremble crouched. "This don't wash," she said, wonderment in her voice. "I've never been standing when the dance ended." She surveyed the hall, a gunfighter's move. Not all enemies showed themselves in a straight up fight. "That was bravery, girl. You got wolf in you."

She helped Aubrey to her feet. The seven gunmen were down, but vanishing, dissolving into the floor. Kids walked through their translucent shapes. The Sheriff brushed Aubrey's sleeves. "Can't have you going to class looking like you been rolling in the dirt."

"You won!"

The sheriff nodded, laugh lines crinkling around her eyes. "It's a long fight." She inspected Aubrey, pushed back a strand of hair from Aubrey's forehead with a calloused finger. "Here, I think you earned this." The Sheriff unbuckled a holster, dropped to a knee, and fastened it around Aubrey's waist.

"I can't take it," said Aubrey, aghast. "It's against school rules!"

"It's a ghost gun, Aubrey. A spirit gun. Who knows what it will do if you use it. Maybe feed the hungry. Make the lame whole. Give hope to the lost. By my reckonin', you're the best person for it."

The Sheriff gently removed Aubrey's hands from the buckle. "It's yours now."

When Aubrey went to fourth period and Student Senate, the gun had faded from sight, but its weight pressed on her hip; a steady, solid, iron reality hanging below her hand, ready to leap out.

Mr. Courtland greeted her at the door. "Nice badge, Aubrey."

Aubrey glanced down. A six-pointed star on her blouse returned the ceiling lights' glow with a silver shine. She didn't remember the Sheriff pinning it to her.

"So what will your slogan be? Vote for Aubrey. There's a new marshall in town?" He smiled. "I'll bet you could pull that off."

"Sheriff," said Aubrey. "Not marshall."

Barclay laughed from the back of the room where three students helped him create campaign posters. "Aubrey a marshall? Not a chance. My campaign speech is a killer." His gang looked at her. She could almost see their dusters and weapons.

"The shootout's Friday," she said, "at noon."

The class quieted. Barclay colored his poster with broad strokes. "Yep."

"High noon." There will be dust in the gym, she thought. When the doors open, the dust will swirl, outside the sun will beat down, and she and Barclay would go face to face with everyone watching.

I don't have to win, she thought. A Sheriff doesn't think about winning or losing; she is elected to serve. I don't fix the school—it can't be fixed, not permanently. It's about the fight and who knew what the fight would be until it came to her? Her posters would be the Sheriff's badge. Underneath she'd print, AUBREY'S COME TO YELLOW HIGH.

She would never surrender.

Her eyes narrowed, not blinking, meeting Barclay's sardonic grin. For a handful of heartbeats, they locked stares until he looked away, just for a moment. It was enough.

"Take your best shot." She rested her hand on the invisible gun's polished grip, trigger finger itching.

EVERYTHING'S UNLIKELY

Happy and scared and thinking about odds, I turn from Forest onto Broadway, setting sun behind me, a mile from The Haggard Traveler, a sports bar where the afternoon phone crew meets for FAC.

Broadway's a miserable stretch of road between Forest and the bar: ten unsynchronized stop lights, one per block. During rush hours it's possible to sit through two or three cycles per light, waiting for traffic to clear, only to hit the next light red, but I'm not thinking about that much. It's Friday and FAC. Madison might be there. I hope she is. Two days away from phone banks and scripted calls, and rush hour is past. The street's nearly empty, stretching before me with its stop lights, all of them, green.

I grin as I pass under the first one. I've never seen them the same, a long line of keep-on-going glowing before me. What are the odds?

The next one stays green. Two down, eight to go. It's not a big deal if I hit green lights. I'm not in a rush. In fact, I'm nervous, chewing the inside of my lip, an old habit from grade school. Sometimes, you know, you gamble, you spin the dice and take a chance, playing the odds, like these lights, like love, where they turn green to let you through.

Unlikely events rule my day. The customer has to be home to answer the phone, and he has to not be one of those people who doesn't pick up an unidentified number, and then he can't hang up when he realizes I'm a telemarketer. This week it's timeshares. "How would you like to spend a week in your own condo in Tahoe?" I ask. "A timeshare is an investment in relaxation that's risk-free," I add. At the desk across from mine, Madison makes her pitch. We catch eyes sometimes. She has a beautiful phone voice, cultured, melodious, slightly British. I almost never hear her talk to anyone at work. She's reserved, maybe, or shy. Does she know I like her? Does she care?

She's been there six months, and all I've managed is an off-balanced, "Hey, how are you?" or "Nice day, don't ya' think?"

She's leaving, though, for another job. Today was her last day on the phone. It's now or never.

The lights remain green in front of me. I haven't timed them. Are they green for only thirty seconds? It seems like that when I'm in a hurry, but maybe it's a couple minutes. Maybe the timing changes in the evening when traffic is slower, but I've never hit four in a row.

The fourth one slides past.

These lights are like the steps we take with the customers (we're not supposed to call them "marks"). They have to listen to the entire spiel, and agree to let me connect them to the sales desk that will take the initial financials. Every step's a coin flip or worse. If they don't hang up when I introduce myself, do they stay through the friendly greeting? Do they beg off after I ask about their vacation plans? Do they cut me off at any time with a curt, "I don't think I'm interested"? The sales pitch can fail at a dozen points. Maybe on a good day, I get five or six customers to the sales desk. Once I got two in a row, a rare event.

Now the fifth light is behind me.

I'm a student of the unlikely because a telemarketer survives on the slim chance. What percent of my calls sells a condo? I have to depend on the nearly impossible to do the job, but I've always admired the long shot, the when-pigs-fly moment, the player who draws to the inside straight because defying the odds is how so many thing--great thing—happen. It's how they all happen.

Like now, when unreasonably, I pass through the sixth green light between The Haggard Traveler and me. It makes me think of movie love scenes; you know, the kind where the music swells and the couple makes eye contact. They've never expressed their love. Maybe, even, they've fought a lot, but the music is there and the picture goes soft-edged, and the two close the distance, like two suns caught in each other's gravity, and they kiss. What are the odds, I think, that two people who have never kissed each other before, both, at the same time, not knowing what the other thinks, take initiative, lean in, and go for the moment? It seems impossible. You'd be better off buying a lottery ticket. At least there's no need for an uncomfortable apology when the numbers you pick don't pay off.

Still, light seven and eight stay encouragingly green as I drive through, and only two are left. It can't be done! Not ten in a row. These last lights have stayed green for what, ninety seconds? Two minutes? My hands grip the steering wheel hard. Who would believe it? Would it matter to them? But it matters to me. The most unlikely alignment of random events, one after another, the odds shooting up exponentially each time.

The ninth light doesn't waver. Surely the tenth will flick to yellow. I resist the urge to step on the gas. At this point, it would be cheating. Do I trust the universe? If I made ten by speeding up or if I push a yellow, the achievement will forever have an asterisk in my head. I didn't really make ten lights in a row. All I can do is move forward and watch. My desires mean nothing to the light. My wanting it doesn't make a difference. The light will be what the light will be.

Then I'm close. Even if it turns yellow, I will make it (with an asterisk), but I will not be stopped. I push close to the windshield to watch, eyes up. Green as fresh cut grass. Green as Ireland in the spring. Avocado, leapy frog, margarita lime, polished jade green, like the green flash they say you can see when the sun rises on the ocean. That green. I tap the horn, purposefully do not look into the rearview mirror. I don't want any red lights in my head as I turn into The Haggard Traveler's parking lot.

Madison's by her car, key in the lock, and the only open spot is beside her. I pull in. She nods in recognition.

"Are you leaving?" I say as I get out.

"Yes," but she doesn't turn the key to open her door. "I've been here a while. I don't know anyone, really. I thought I'd go home."

My heart doesn't falter, not even a little. The lights were all green. In this instant, the unlikeliness of that fills my heart. They were green, green, green. You've got to ride the streak. Tonight I will be bold, make conversation, see if I can prolong the melody that is her voice.

"You know me," I say. "Or you could. Come back in. I'll let you buy me a beer." I grin, which is all I can do.

And she does.

A year later, we're sitting in The Haggard Traveler. I've found another job also in town. We're happy. A month ago she asked me to marry her on the same night I'd brought a ring to ask her to marry me.

"I almost wasn't here the night of our first date," she says, her elbows on the table, cradling her drink in her hands. "I would have been gone."

"What do you mean?"

"You know those lights on Broadway?"

I nod.

"Every single blessed one of them was red. It took forever to get here. I looked around when I got inside, decided to leave. If any of those lights were green, I'd have missed you in the parking lot."

She takes a drink, and then studies through her glass the light from the setting sun that bathes her with a soft, honey glow. I want to preserve the moment, hold it forever. She is so herself, her improbable, unique self, and she loves me at the same time I love her.

How can this be? How can this be? But couples sit at other tables too. The race goes on, defying probability, we always have. Statistics don't lie.

Flip a coin. What are the chances of heads? Fifty-fifty, right?

But what about this guess: what are the odds that at exactly this time tomorrow, a person, say an older guy—we'll predict his appearance too: he's gray-haired, has a moustache and gold-rimmed glasses—will stand on this spot, flipping a dime, and it will come up heads? What are the chances that all of that will happen? Today, if I had to guess, a zillion to one; a zillion, zillion, quintillion to one: odds so distant as to be nearly impossible, until it happens, and he's looking at the dime, heads up.

What were the odds? When it happens, 100 percent.

Everything's unlikely, even love, and it's happening all the time.

ON THE ROAD WITH THE AMERICAN DEAD

J EREMY LOWE RESTED HIS ARM ON THE OPEN WINDOW, ENJOYING VIBRATION and rushing air, solitude, and early evening cornfields. Engine and tire noise echoed from telephone poles and fence posts, whoosh, whoosh, whoosh. He smiled, tapping the steering wheel in accompaniment.

He liked solitary drives from client to client, sticking to two-lane roads when he could, half his backseat and trunk filled with sales brochures and toner cartridges and copier parts. He liked his window down, even when it grew cold in the fall. He smelled little creeks that ran through shallow gulches, of miles and miles of wild sun-flowers along the fields, and barbecue from unseen backyards. He liked stockyards and political signs, which he'd sometimes stop to photograph. This morning he'd snapped a shot of a Second Amendment billboard that said, "Turn in Your Arms: the Government will take care of you," printed over a picture of Indians in headdresses.

Driving was good. It gave him long breaks between actually doing his job. Sometimes he thought he should pull the car over and kick the boxes out and just drive. He thought about copies. What sort of career is about helping people make copies? They should have a machine that makes originals.

On the shoulder ahead, a two-foot-tall cross seemed to lean on a brown, fuzzy shape. Weeds grew around. When he went by, the shape resolved into a teddy bear, and then it was in his rearview mirror.

"That's mine," said the girl in the seat beside him.

Jeremy swerved, crossed the opposing lane, fought the steering when the tires dropped into the soft shoulder, then wrestled the car onto the asphalt. He eased it back into his lane, fingers locked on the wheel, breath wheezing in quick gasps. The girl sat with her hands in her lap, staring ahead. She wore blue dungarees over a white tee shirt. Short, dark hair spilled from the back of a Kansas City Royals base-ball cap. Freckled. Twenty years old. No makeup.

"It was Lisa's teddy bear. Mom couldn't find mine, but Lisa died when she was five. Lung cancer. Can you believe cancer in a little kid like that?"

It felt so much like a dream, that Jeremy pried his left hand off the steering wheel to pinch the skin on his right wrist.

"You really should watch the road here," the girl said, "'cause if something stupid happens, like spilling a soda, you just lose it."

The girl wore no shoes. Her toenails were painted pink.

"What are you doing in my car?" Jeremy couldn't tell if his heavy breathing came from almost wrecking or the surprise.

"This is the stretch I didn't get to drive. That's my place up there." She pointed to a dirt road that appeared from over a hill to his left, splitting the corn, and dumping onto the highway. Corn grew tall on both sides, poking through barbed wire fence, like a shadowed hallway. The western horizon glowed pink and peach in the fading light but the dirt road going east plunged into the glooming corn.

He looked at her as the road whipped by, but she faded and was gone.

Pulse pounded in his forehead, and he wondered if he was having a stroke or if he'd hallucinated. The wheel felt just as solid beneath his hands, though, and the wind whistled as it always did.

The black soldier in his back seat said, "She was a pretty thing. Sad though."

This time Jeremy didn't swerve. In the rearview mirror, he could see the man's dark hair and the sunset's glow in his eyes. The butt of a long rifle rested on the floor between his feet, canted diagonally toward the other window. He wore a brass-buttoned cloth coat that might have been blue, but dust obscured it. A leather bandolier crossed his chest.

"This thing goes darned fast," said the man. He watched the corn sliding by. He'd said the girl was sad, but Jeremy felt despair rolling off the man in waves. "I don't remember no crops. This road shouldn't be here."

Jeremy thought about what he knew of local history. There had been a Civil War fort near Baxter Springs. The town had a nice museum with a display about it. He'd stopped there several times, studying the paintings and maps while shaking off road weariness, before heading to ailing photocopiers in town. In one of the museum's corners, a cannon on two spoked wheels pointed out the window. He could imagine its weight behind a horse, pulling it over a rutted path. The metal had been cold beneath his hand and slightly pitted.

"Second Kansas Colored Infantry," the soldier said. "Got separated. There's too much prairie. It looks the same."

"Why are you here?" Jeremy said. If he pulled over, would the man get out?

"They killed the 3rd Wisconsin band too, you know," said the soldier. He turned away from the window. "Eleven men. Put swords through them. Set 'em on fire. Even the drummer boy. Not one had a chance to defend himself. He's the devil, he is. Executes those that surrender. His men too, all devils."

Jeremy's gut clenched, and despite the cool wind blowing through the car, sweat trickled down his back. "What do you want?"

What did the soldier want? To go home? Did he have a wife somewhere? Children?

The soldier looked thirty, maybe older. "A clear shot, that's all I need. Set that devil Quantrill where I can see him. I'll say, 'Remember the drummer boy?' and I'll send him to hell."

And then, like the dungaree girl, the soldier faded.

Jeremy pulled the car to the side of the road. Set the brake, and sat on the edge of the ditch that ran between him and the corn. The highway was empty in both directions. Crickets chirped. Stalks rustled. No stars were visible in the dark sky.

After eating dinner at the Baxter Springs Smokehouse, he spent the night at the Baxter Inn, a common stop for him. The rooms were clean, quiet and inexpensive, but he couldn't sleep. He sat cross-legged on his bed, laptop open, searching for Quantrill, a name he vaguely recognized. Quantrill had deserted the southern army during the Civil War, formed his own guerilla band, roamed through Missouri and eastern Kansas, waging his own battles. Most of the articles talked about a massacre he led in Lawrence, Kansas, but Jeremy tracked down the Baxter Springs incident easily. The drummer boy was named Johnny, and he'd been fifteen. One account said he'd been found pinned to the side of a wagon, hanging from a sword. Another said he'd been burned to death.

In the morning, Jeremy visited his Baxter Springs accounts, replacing worn parts in the copiers, leaving brochures for the new models the company encouraged customers to switch to. Nothing time consuming. He had plenty of time in the afternoon to shop.

In a dusty car lot, he traded his sedan for a similar one a year newer. The salesman looked at him curiously as Jeremy wrote the check for the difference.

"It seems like a good car. My mechanic likes it. Any particular reason you're switching?"

Jeremy thought for a second. "It makes funny noises."

He didn't prefer the road to Joplin, so instead of heading east into Missouri, and then south to Arkansas and Fayetteville, Jeremy took the longer two-lane Oklahoma route, deeper into the hilly Ozarks, a pleasant change from the flatlands. He'd picked up a plate of supermarket chicken and a six pack for his cooler. Before sunset he'd be at the Wolf Creek Park camping ground near the Neosho River.

The woman in a plain, long dress and worn bonnet appeared not long after Jeremy crossed the state line. He sensed her beside him before he saw her. He'd been watching the road unwind hypnotically before him, trying to adjust to the slight differences in the new car's steering and the unfamiliar way his back rested against the seat. He'd found a half dozen plastic cocktail stirrers in the glove box that the car dealer had missed. The idea that a drinker had owned the car first pleased him a little. He imagined the driver holding the cocktail in one hand while the other draped over the wheel. What was the story? The dealer had asked about his car, but more interesting was why this one had been traded in. Only fifteen thousand on the odometer. The engine sounded solid. No wear on the upholstery and no scratches on the paint. Maybe the previous owner heard noises too.

"So," said Jeremy, "what killed you?"

"I'm not dead," she said primly, "and it's rude of you to say so."

Jeremy tried to relax. It was just a conversation. It wasn't like he hadn't already talked to apparitions, although he'd hoped that changing cars would cure the problem. He thought, It's not the car; it's me.

"I'm pretty sure you are."

"I'd be at home with Jesus if I was dead," she said. "The roads would be paved with gold and there would be singing. Maybe you are the dead one."

Jeremy hadn't considered that. If he was dead, yesterday would make more sense.

"Okay, lets say you're not dead. What's the last thing you remember before you appeared in my car?" He was proud of himself for sounding calm, but he wasn't. His stomach knotted. He wondered what a ghost could do to him. Nothing, right? They don't have a solid existence. Unless they startle me into an accident (he remembered how close he'd come to swerving off the road when the dungaree-girl appeared), they're harmless. They couldn't do anything to him, but what did it mean that he was seeing them? The question wasn't what the ghosts could do, but what did they mean?

"We were putting in stakes," the woman said. "Thompson, that's my husband, carved them himself out of a slat from the wagon. 'Pound them deep,' he said to me, "so people will know the land is ours.' We snuck in a couple weeks early. Thompson told me if we waited, all the good land would be taken. 'The government doesn't have that much left for people to claim,' he said. 'The frontier is just about gone, but no one's going to notice the two of us. They'll just see us here and think we beat them to the spot. We soak the horse like it's just finished a good run, and when others come, they'll think we started the same time they did. They'll keep going. There's more land beyond the next hill.'"

She looked out the window just like the dungaree girl had done, watching the hills. "They didn't ride on, though. Two men on horses. They threw the stakes at his feet, dirt still clinging to them, then they shot him where he stood."

Jeremy felt cold. "Did they shoot you, too?"

The woman pushed hair off her forehead. "I don't remember. It wasn't shooting they wanted with me, though. No, I don't think there was any shooting. I heard other horses in the distance, and wagons crashing along, and shouting; everyone racing for a piece of land. That's what we were doing, Thompson and me, putting down our stakes. Building something."

She didn't fade. She winked out, like a candle, leaving a black smoke that swirled as the wind tore it apart.

Before he reached he campground, a four-year-old girl in a swimsuit and swim cap adorned with pink and green plastic flowers appeared next to him, but she cried for ten minutes without speaking, then dissolved into a moist steam. Twenty miles later, a one-legged man in an old-style navy uniform, the pants for the missing leg pinned neatly at mid-thigh, winked into existence, but he only had time to move his cane between his legs before he was gone. Jeremy spent the rest of the drive in a continuous flinch. Every passing shadow or flash of reflected light, forced a glance to the empty passenger seat.

He decided that he'd spend the next morning in Siloam Springs in Arkansas, a town he'd driven through without stopping. Maybe cold calls at new businesses would straighten him out.

Over the years, delivering copy machine supplies and servicing the clients in the Kansas, Missouri, Oklahoma, Arkansas area, Jeremy had made road friends: the folks he saw repeatedly, like gas station attendants, waitresses, shop managers and a handful of others. He might only see them three or four times a year for a few minutes, but he saw them every year. At the Springdale Pilot truck stop, he talked to Angie, the bottle-blonde, big-bosomed counter clerk who ran the tiny restaurant.

Only a single rig sat in the parking lot, and the restaurant was empty except for the two of them. Angie gathered up her four grandkids' pictures she'd spread on the table as she slid into the booth seat across from him.

"Truckers see ghosts all the time," she said. "It's not a big deal."

Jeremy's jaw dropped.

"No, really," she continued. "Long haul drivers are chemically enhanced. It's the truth," she continued. "They're sleep-deprived, coffee-powered junkies and they pop those vitality pacs we sell by the register like M&Ms—they're mostly caffeine you know. Might as well just take speed and be more honest about it, so ghosts and all sorts of stuff come with the job."

"They're hallucinating, you mean."

"Sometimes they are and sometimes they ain't." Angie canted her head to the side, studying him. "You want to share?"

Jeremy shook his head, then nodded.

Angie laughed. "You know, the wonder is we don't see more ghosts. The country should be packed with them, if everyone that dies becomes a ghost that is. What about Indian ghosts? Indians lived here for a thousand years before we showed up, and if you think about it, where are the Neanderthals? So, the ghosts talking to you too?"

"Yes," Jeremy croaked out. This conversation hadn't gone in the direction he would have predicted. He feared she would think he was crazy, so he'd mentioned ghosts as a joke. "I've seen some unbelievable things driving," he'd said.

She looked out at the highway. A truck flew by. "My husband died on that road, the first one, I mean. Husband number two doesn't drive much."

"Sorry to hear that, about your first husband, I mean. I didn't know."

Angie wiped her side of the table before gathering his empty plate and extricating herself from the booth. "Too much information. I blabber a bit. Talk of ghosts makes me think of him."

"No problem." Another truck passed the restaurant, kicking dust in its wake. "You sell electronics in the store, don't you?"

"Yep. Radar detectors. CB sets. Even got some of those gaming doodads the kids like."

"How about noise suppressing headphones?"

Angie crossed her arms. "You think if you can't hear them, they'll go away?"

Jeremy shrugged.

The headphones felt bulky and awkward, but they did quiet sound. Even if he didn't have them plugged into his music, when he turned on the noise cancelling function, engine, wind, even the radio muted to almost nothing, but the apparitions kept coming. First, a young farmer, wearing overalls and a red flannel shirt, then a woman in a summer dress, then a nurse, and then an old man in a business suit. Jeremy tried not to look at them. He turned up the music and focused on the road. The old man, though, was persistent. When he waved his hand in front of Jeremy's face, Jeremy pulled the headphones off.

"Can't you see that I don't want to talk? When someone's wearing headphones, they don't want to talk."

The old man said, "I thought they were funny-looking earmuffs."

Suddenly Jeremy realized ghosts weren't scary; they were annoying. "Look, when a guy is traveling alone on the road like I do, he doesn't want company. If he did, he'd pull over and pick up a hitchhiker, a living one."

The old man straightened his tie. "Do you know what the number one cause of single-driver, single-car accidents is?"

Jeremy glanced at the man. He wasn't a very good judge of fashion, and men's business suits from the '50s or '60s didn't look that different from modern ones to his eye, so how long had this guy been a ghost? What did he know about car accidents?

"Going to sleep?"

"Nope," said the old man. "That's number three. The number two cause is a stinging insect. Turns out that people freak out if there's a bee in the car. The number one cause is a ghost who is pissed off because the driver ignores him."

"What do you want? I've been asking every ghost between here and Baxter Springs what they want, and they won't say. Why are you appearing in my car?"

"Not just your car. Ghosts are everywhere, but not everyone sees them. Well, the ones who see us and crash see us, but not all of the rest."

"Why me and why now? I've been driving for twenty years ghost-free."

"Why do you think?"

That's all Jeremy had been mulling over since the barefooted girl with pink toenails warned him to watch the road. What if a person saw ghosts before he died? He wouldn't have a chance to tell many people about it before the last chance was gone, so the stories wouldn't leak out. Or what if the ghost who didn't think she was dead was right, and he was a ghost too? Maybe he'd been a haunt to Angie at the truck stop, or maybe Angie was also a ghost. If two ghosts met, would they recognize that there were both ghosts? The idea of ghosts unintentionally haunting each other made him grin.

"Glad you're enjoying yourself," said the old man.

"How does it work? Do you have a range, like a radio signal? Are you tied to the place you died?"

The old man looked at him curiously. "Someone's in your car who has crossed into the great mystery, proving there is an afterlife, and those are the questions you ask?"

But he vanished before Jeremy replied.

Jeremy pulled the car into the next rest stop. He liked Arkansas rest areas. Most were well-maintained and pleasant places for a leisurely lunch or for a quiet nap. Today, though, he didn't relax. He'd stored cases of replacement copier toner in the trunk along with his tool kits. By emptying the trunk, he was able to fill the passenger seat and the space in the back where the Civil War soldier had appeared. As he merged onto the highway, the fact that there wasn't a person-sized area left empty in the car pleased him.

But the old man started talking from within the boxes piled to Jeremy's right before he'd driven two miles. "Interesting idea, son. If you were wearing those headphones, you wouldn't know I was here at all until I did this."

A hand reached through the unbroken cardboard and covered Jeremy's eyes.

"Stop it!" yelled Jeremy. He ducked below the hand to see that the car had swerved across the center line. The other lane was empty.

"Wouldn't bother me if we crashed," said the ghost. "Kind of exciting, to tell the truth, but I don't like sitting in a box."

Five miles later, after Jeremy had stopped and thrown the boxes sloppily into the back, the ghost sat silently as Jeremy merged back onto the highway. Low hills, covered with the tired green of late summer rose away from them on either side. Finally, Jeremy said, "Look, I wasn't trying to be rude. It's just that you make me nervous, being dead and all."

The ghost considered him but didn't speak.

"I don't know the etiquette," Jeremy offered.

He steered the car through a long curve. To his left, a tree-covered slope stretched into a valley. At the bottom, silver glimpses of a stream peeked through the gaps. On the other side, limestone boulders marked the grassy hill.

The old man said, "It's about memory and mortality, and maybe about Odysseus and Gilgamesh."

"Ok," said Jeremy, "I'll bite. What's Odysseus have to do with you?"

"Pretty country out here, don't you think? Forests and stone and water. I used to hike these hills. See that little road coming up? Take it."

The two-lane highway curved right. A narrow, dirt path, barely wide enough for the car cut away from the asphalt and wound to the tree line below. Jeremy slowed, then turned onto the trail. A line of weeds in the middle brushed against the undercarriage. Once they were into the trees, undergrowth hemmed them in on both sides. He wondered if there was a spot where he would be able to turn around, or if he'd have to back out.

"Where we going?"

The ghost rolled his window down, Jeremy noted with interest. Ghosts could move physical objects! He felt like he'd discovered one of the universe's secrets.

"Of all the people in the world, Odysseus and Gilgamesh are still remembered. People tell their stories."

Jeremy nursed the vehicle through a muddy spot. Now, this far from the highway, pleasant, green forest smells flooded the car.

"Not much farther," said the ghost. "Everyone has stories, son. But for most of us, nearly every, single, blessed one, when we die, the stories fade. Not Gilgamesh, though. Not Odysseus. Ah, we're here."

The forest opened. Jeremy stopped the car. A blackened ring of rocks near the tree line showed that people had camped there, although not recently. After the forest shade, the pasture seemed to glow with color. Knee-high flowers, orange in the middle and yellow at the edge blanketed the ground. Jeremy had never seen so many.

They were common in patches on the highway's shoulder. Firewheel, he thought they were called.

"I stood here," said the ghost, looking through the windshield. "Before the highway was paved, when I was twenty. Been walking all day along that road. Not one car came by, but I didn't mind. I was young and I had food in my bindle. Strong legs then. Toward dusk, so I hiked down this trail, the end of a beautiful day, maybe the most beautiful day I'd ever seen. Reached this spot where we're sitting, sun cutting across it like God's hand. Smelled the stream, but when I stepped into this clearing, a herd of browsing deer stood here, and like a choir, like a congregation, they stopped eating, raised their heads up and looked at me. There must have been a hundred of them meeting me eye for eye. That's an image that stayed with me my whole life."

Jeremy tried the picture what the old man described, what he clearly was seeing this second in his memory, and he almost could.

"Gilgamesh isn't a ghost, son. Neither is Odysseus. They can rest as long as their stories aren't lost. But most everyone else . . ."

"You have to tell your stories?"

"Such as they are. When we're done, that's all we have. That's all you have. Everyone is a story."

"But why me?"

"It could be anyone," said the ghost. "It frequently is."

Then Jeremy sat alone in the car. A breeze stirred the Firewheel pasture into ripples like embers floating on the ocean, like shivers on the fluorescent sea of time.

Having resupplied his last customer, Jeremy drove toward company head-quarters in Atlanta. He stuck to the back roads and the smaller towns: Stuttgart, then DeWitt. He might go the long way around to catch Clarksdale. Maybe he'd stop at the Dale Bumpers White River National Wildlife Refuge, sit lakeside, watch the sunrise.

He'd watch the sunrise, the way light sheened across the water, the way it changed second by second until the sun fully spilled upon it, the way leaves whispered in the morning breeze, how he could turn his head and the sounds would change, and he would think about how important the moment was, how irreplaceable, and how no one would ever know how he'd been there after he was gone, unless the story was told and remembered.

But mostly he kept his window down and the seat beside him empty. He let the wind blow through the car, listened to the road's gentle roar, and he welcomed, whenever they came, the occasional ghost. Some told their stories. Some just sat.

And every once in a while, when Jeremy stopped to shake road weariness from his legs or to resupply his customers, he'd talk to the waitress or the stock boy or the office manager or the purchasing agent, and he'd share what he'd heard from the lonely dead, so they wouldn't disappear, so they wouldn't be forgotten.

THE LIES

BRI TOLD ME THE LIFT SHIPS TO TERRA STATION TOOK OFF TUESDAY AND Friday mornings from Campbell Field. They made the cabin look like an old-time luxury liner, like a zeppelin crossing the Atlantic, with wooden wainscoting and brass fittings. She said stewards in white jackets and white gloves served champagne in souvenir flutes engraved with your takeoff date.

The ship held five hundred colonists, chosen by an international lottery, but because separating loved ones was cruel, the lucky could choose three people to go with them. It could be family members or friends. Lottery winners had all debts paid, and if their leaving deprived a family of income, the corporation provided absentee pensions to prevent suffering.

Much of the ship's hull became transparent during the flight so passengers could see the flame that enveloped them at takeoff, and then the ground receding so fast that before they knew it, the sky grew dark and the horizon curved. What a joy, she said, to discover for yourself Earth's true size. In one way, the Earth was huge. The continents and oceans unrolled beneath you. Day became night and cities glowed like Christmas lights. The size, the grandeur, startled you and filled you with awe. At the same time, you saw Earth all at once, a blue and white marble, a falling soccer ball, a crystal sphere that shrank as the ship rose to its high orbit. That tiny planet held humanity, held within its history all that had happened to man, and if you raised your fist, you could eclipse it, the Earth was so small.

I told Bri that doctors had found cures for human suffering. While I traveled to the stars, diseases were being eliminated. Accurate genetic testing guaranteed medicines custom tailored. Cancers, of course, would vanish first, followed closely by communicable disease and inherited conditions. Finally, they would remake the deformed. The lame would walk, the deaf would hear, and the blind would paint new glories.

Bri's lungs would inhale fully and suck in flowers and mountains and summer storms. She'd stand from her wheelchair. When I returned, I'd put my hand in the small of her back and twirl with her on the dance floor. She would tell me about Earth's advances. Not in the whispery, painful way she spoke now, but with a full voice. She'd laugh and not cough. She'd learn to sing.

She held my hand and told me about Zeti Prime, the Earth-like planet orbiting Zeti Reticuli. Oceans lapped silver beaches circling tropical islands. Lizard-birds nested in the blue trees, and at dusk took off as one. She said they filled the sky, then swept low over the waves, hunting the tentacled fish. Zeti Prime enjoyed a lighter gravity. Colonists reported the spring in their step lasted for months before they grew used to it. Zeti Reticuli's light healed depression and it didn't promote carcinomas. Crops grown there contained more nutrients and vitamins. No one on Zeti Reticuli had died of old age yet. Colonies were small. Wherever you walked, in a few minutes you would be in the frontier. Rivers, mountains and lakes were yet unnamed.

Hike twenty miles, she said, throw seeds on the ground, then stand back.

Will there be a stream there?

Oh, yes. What will you call it?

The Tumbling Bri.

She smiled.

You'll go to a golden hospital on a hill, I said, where the nurses speak seven languages and have studied under the greatest doctors in the world. The medicine there is so powerful that healthy people are cured. Each doctor controls a ward where their breakthrough treatments are miraculous daily. The hospital's chaplain only leads services of praise. He never comforts the grieving; there is no grief there.

I have your ticket to Terra Station, she said.

Bri reached into her pajama pocket, the skin on the back of her hand as thin as tissue. She took two tries before she brought out the paper slip. Her bald head rested on my shoulder. Her ribs and backbone pressed against my arm. She closed her eyes.

Around us, other patients lay on cots. Some coughed. Some cried. No one comforted them. Light came through grimy windows. The air didn't move. At one end, a net still dangled from the basketball rim, but the backboard above us had been broken long ago. They told us there would be medical trucks coming every afternoon, but they didn't come yesterday or the day before. I gave Bri a sip of water.

Bri said, what is the hospital's name, the golden one on the hill?

Grace Taylor Hope.

I bent close to hear her.

That's funny, that your name is on it.

I have to go to work, I said. I'll be back when I finish.

No, today is your flight. You won the lottery.

Of course. I kissed her on the forehead. They'll move you to Grace Taylor Hope. I'll find you there.

I'll be better before then.

I walked in the middle of the street because bricks strewed the sidewalk. Trash filled the alleys. At University Blvd., a burned out bus on its side blocked the path. Inside, dogs growled as they fought over a hunk of meat. I didn't want to know what kind. The city smelled of scummy water and burning tires.

At Veteran's Park, I checked out rubber gloves from the foreman. They didn't put the bodies in bags anymore. There were too many. I took a girl wearing a yellow sweater from the back of a flatbed truck, put her in a wheelbarrow and pushed her up the ramp overlooking the pit. She rolled twenty feet before she stopped against the dead at the bottom.

Back to the truck. An old man with scabs on his face. Back to the truck. A small boy wearing a Cub Scout shirt. I was glad he didn't weigh much. Back to the truck.

The sun set. Diesel generators ran the lights. When one truck emptied, another took its place. At the pit's far end, an earth mover pushed dirt over the bodies. Tomorrow, we'd move to Denver University's practice fields.

My arms ached until finally I stopped under one of the angrily buzzing lights, and pulled the paper from my pocket. One edge was ragged. Maybe Bri tore it out of a book. Barely legible in pencil, it read TICKET FOR ONE TO ZETI PRIME.

Beyond the arcing whiteness, the city was dark. A fire burned to the west, too far away to worry about. Supply ships to Terra Station run every day, Bri had told me. They ride on flaming fingers to the stars, and sound like God clearing his throat. Look for them, she said.

But I looked for Grace Taylor Hope instead, the hospital on the hill. It's out there. They have a bed for Bri. Even now, they are picking her up. She'll ride in an ambulance on silk pillows. A steward in a white jacket with white gloves will offer her a soothing tea, and the driver will miss every bump in the road.

I put the ticket back in my pocket. Tomorrow things will be better. Tomorrow Bri will be strong. Tomorrow the world will turn around. She told me so.

I have a ticket to the stars.

THE CONTINUING SAGA OF TOM CORBETT: SPACE CADET

T OM'S NAME WAS HER CURSE. SHE STARTED WITH TOMIKO, BUT BY THE TIME she was four, everyone in her family called her Tom, and once that stuck, her grandfather made a joke: "Tom Corbett, eh? How's the Space Academy? Are you going to be in the Solar Guard this year?" Or "Have they let you drive Polaris yet? How's your buddies, Astro and Roger Manning doing?" He was relentless.

It was irritating until she turned ten, found out who this "Tom Corbett" person was, and then took her birthday money to the used bookstore where she found copies of *Stand by for Mars* and *Treachery in Outer Space*. From there, she discovered Tom Corbett videos on the Internet, Tom Corbett comics, and Tom Corbett View-Master discs, which meant that she had to buy a View-Master in the toy store. For the sixth grade Halloween party, she made her own Solar Guard uniform and wore it every day until Christmas.

Of course, the other kids started calling her "Space Cadet," which they didn't mean in a good way at all.

By the time she was a freshman in high school last year, "Space Cadet" was a label. She put the Tom Corbett books away. She took the "Space Academy" badge off her shirts, but it didn't matter. The nickname stuck. Some of the kids called her SC, which rhymed with "Jesse" without the "J." Some of the teachers too, who didn't even know where the name came from, called her that, even though she carefully printed her full name, Tomiko Corbett, on every piece of homework. For most people, she was Tom, Tom Corbett: space cadet.

She had taken the Solar Guard medallions off her shirts, but she couldn't take them out of her heart. Tom sat at her desk that faced her bedroom window. Her house topped a hill with open country on all sides. Her parents bought here when they thought a subdivision was going to spring up around them, but so far they were the only house. Outside, in the dark, with no trees or obstructing buildings, she had an unencumbered night view, straight east. Leo Minor nearly touched the horizon. The bright light by its mouth was Jupiter. She knew star names: Regulus, Algieba, Procyon, Pollux, and Alhena. She wondered what it would be like to be an astrogator, or to sit in the pilot's seat on the control deck. She'd toggle the intercom. "All stations report," she'd say. "All clear on the radar deck," a voice would answer, and then another, "All clear on the power deck."

She'd be in command, the control panels displayed in front of her, the power to take off to the stars underneath her hands. Tom looked at her own hands, resting on the keyboard at her desk. If only she could press the right buttons. Her bedroom window could be the control deck view panel. The stars would rush toward her. She would look up slightly, chin thrust forward, a picture of confidence and adventure for all who could see.

Tomika got up from her desk, cracked the bedroom door open. The hallway and living room were dark. Her parents had gone to bed. Good. Their room was on the other end of the house. They slept with their door shut and a fan going. When they were asleep, she could be as loud as she wanted. She shut the door, snapped off her lights, turned up the sound on the computer's speakers, and then clicked the icon on the screen. The rumble started in the background very low, almost subliminal. Tom leaned back in her chair, looking out the window, trying not to see the drapes hanging on each side. She just wanted stars as the rumble sound grew and grew. It was rocket engine noise, building, and there were electronic sounds in the background. Doors irising open or closed maybe? Blasters? Emergency klaxons? And then the engines cut out, and were replaced by footsteps on metal decks. Distant orders being shouted out. The ping from ranging equipment.

Tom strained to hear, but the voices were always indistinct. Occasionally, she'd make out a word, "Asteroid," "Orbit," "Translunar," but never an entire sentence. She'd set the sound clip to replay. The entire audio was almost ninety minutes long. Most nights, she'd fall asleep with it playing before the engine noise started again, but tonight, it replayed five times. The sun rose directly in her window as she watched.

She turned the sound off. The rising sun filled the room with warmth. She thought, if I close my eyes now, I can get a half hour of sleep before Mom tells me to get ready for school.

At breakfast, Mom, a slight, slender woman with long black hair, and Dad, whose hair was brown and curly, talked about real-estate values. They'd been looking at houses on the north side of town that they could buy, refurbish cheaply, and then sell for a huge profit. Dad thumbed through the obituaries in the newspaper.

"Here's one," he said. "The guy was ninety-four. It says his family lives in Chicago."

Mom nodded, a coffee cup in one hand and her tablet in the other. She swiped at her screen methodically. Tom wasn't sure what Mom was looking at. She said, "We could give 'em a lowball offer. Out-of-towners won't know the market, and they'd probably be glad to unload the house. I'll drive by this morning and put a flyer in their mailbox."

While Tom finished her cereal, her parents talked about discount carpets and how a cheap, new carpet in an old home could return the purchase price by 150 percent. "Fresh paint and new carpet covers a multitude of sins," said Dad.

They left together for work before Tom had to start her walk to the bus stop. She realized as she headed out the door that neither one had spoken a single word to her, but that was pretty normal.

At every stop, more elementary and junior high kids crowded onto the bus. Most high schoolers drove themselves or went with their friends. In high school, only losers took the bus, but Tom didn't mind. She gave up her seat to two fourth-grade girls who liked to sit together, and then walked down the aisle looking for an empty place. The only spot was next to Jacob Rose, another sophomore, who everyone called "Jacob the Hut," because he was huge, the biggest kid Tom had ever seen. If it weren't for Jacob, Tom would be the best mathematician in the tenth grade, but it didn't earn Jacob any friends. Jacob covered much of the seat. He scrunched next to the window to give Tom more room.

"Sorry," said Jacob in his deep voice. He held a book on his stomach, his finger marking a spot.

"What 'cha reading?"

"You'll think it's boring."

Tom settled into the seat. She braced her knees on the chair in front of her. "Try me."

Jacob shrugged. "Ok. It's *Atoms to Andromeda : Selected Lectures on Theoretical Physics, High-Energy Nuclear and Cosmic Ray Research, Plasma and Thermonuclear Physics, Astronomy, Astrophysics and Electronic Computing.*'"

When Jacob opened the book to continue reading, Tom could see pages filled with tiny print and math formulas. "Is there a graphic novel version?" she said.

Jacob glanced up, surprised, as if he'd already forgot she was there. The bus lurched into motion. Kids yelled back and forth. A ball of paper flew past them. It was a typical day. "Do you play *Destination Ceres*?" he asked.

Tom knew the game, a third person PC shooter set on fantastical versions of Mars, Venus and Ceres. The science in it was terrible.

"Do you?" she said.

"No, not really. But I like to wander around in the game. The worlds are beautiful." He looked at the kids on the bus. "I don't think I belong here."

Tom nodded. "I know just what you mean."

When they got to the school, Tom watched Jacob walking deliberately down the middle of the sidewalk. Kids ran around him as if he were a moving island.

She thought he had a kind of dignity in his steady pace.

Tom dreaded English. Last year, in the junior high, she'd turned in a book report on *Stand by for Mars*, the first book in the Space Cadet series. The assignment had been, "Choose an influential book that you read in elementary school, and explain its impact on you." Tom wrote how the book made her check out astronomy texts and encouraged her interest in rockets. Ms. Schneider, a second-year teacher, scheduled a private meeting with Tom after she turned it in.

"I'm concerned about your choice of reading. I don't think a young, twenty-first century woman should be interested in this sort of book," said Schneider to open their conversation. "It's terribly sexist. You could select much more appropriate literature."

Tom didn't have a chance to reply.

"Look at this quote," said Schneider. She had a faded copy marked with several sticky notes between the pages. "Here, Corbett and his friends, Astro and Roger Manning have gone to Crystal City. They are trying to book a room at the hotel, and Manning treats the clerk, who is a woman, of course, like a prize. He even says, 'What's the matter with beautiful girls? They're official equipment, like a radar scanner. You can't get along without them!' What sort of universe is this? Women are always 'cute' or 'pretty' or they get whistled at. Where are the women who are cadets or commanders?"

Schneider snorted derisively. "Terrible. Here, I think you should read this." She handed Tom a copy of *Girls Who Looked Under Rocks: The Lives of Six Pioneering Naturalists*. "I think this has much better role models for you."

Tom took the book. "Does it have rocket ships?"

"Phallic tripe," muttered Schneider.

Tom was pretty sure that the comment wasn't directed at her, but if Ms. Schneider didn't think that Tom knew what "phallic" meant, then she was underestimating her.

Tom read the book. It wasn't terrible, but the next book she read was *The Rocket Robot*, which was the third time for that title. She paid closer attention to Tom Corbett's world. Schneider was right about the story being all about the men, but that wasn't how Tom read it. In her mind, the characters weren't about being boys or girls. They were about having adventures, and anyone could have those. She wanted to read about going to space, and if she had to do it with male pronouns, so be it. When she read, she boarded the ship. She gave the commands. She looked out the port to see the curve of a new planet.

Today Ms. Schneider gave the class a fill-in-the-blank quiz. The first sentence was, "If a doctor gives you advice, you should listen to what _____ says." The second question was "If a kindergarten teacher is speaking, the class should pay attention to _____."

Most of the class filled in the first blank with "he" and the second blank with "her," which Schneider used to springboard into the unconscious sexist assumptions in the society. Tom's answers were "the professional" and "the alien in the corner." She didn't share that with Schneider.

After school, Tom didn't ride the bus. The land behind the school was undeveloped. It rose to a treeless, flat-topped hill, littered with nearly-white limestone on dark soil. Almost no vegetation. For the last month, Tom had been climbing the hill to work on her project. She dropped her backpack, picked up a pair of melon-sized stones, and then added them to the thirty-foot-tall letters she had been forming. The perspective was wrong for her to get a proper look at what she was writing, but if her plans were right, from directly above, the message read "TAKE ME WITH YOU."

Mom and Dad were at the kitchen table arguing about landscaping when Tom walked in the front door. Open Chinese takeout boxes surrounded their briefcases. Dad said, "Fewer plants and *newer* plants show better from the street. I say we rip out the hedges, lay down a nice, colored gravel, and plant a couple of roses. It cleans up the look, and the buyers will see possibilities."

Mom shook her head. "Too expensive and too much work. We get a gardening service to tidy up the bushes, and the house says 'I'm already beautiful' to buyers. No one gets into a house so they can spend their weekends putting in plants. Not in that neighborhood."

Tom put her backpack on the counter behind them, poured a glass of milk and grabbed a handful of cookies. "I'm home," she said.

Dad said, "A little extra investment at the beginning pays off big later. Curb appeal is everything."

"Looky-loos don't sign contracts. They don't even go inside the home. Mature landscaping is the right answer for this house."

"I'm thinking of starting a terrorist cell," said Tom. "We'll call ourselves The High School Freedom Front. I might get a tattoo."

Dad glanced her direction, nodded curtly, then turned to Mom. "Newness generates interest. Old bushes say worn out property. We've had this discussion before."

"Yes, we have. When you come to your senses, I'll be in the office faxing today's documents to the bank." Mom snapped her briefcase closed and stomped out of the kitchen.

Dad said, "Have you been home long?"

"Hours."

"There's some Moo Goo Gai Pan and rice in the fridge if you'd like some."

She held up the cookies. "I'm good," but he'd already turned away to study a thick sheaf of papers.

Back in her room, Tom opened her notebook that she'd titled "Ways to Get Off the Planet." She'd labeled sections: Rocket Engines, Ramjets, Ground-based Laser/ Microwave, Space Elevator, Project Orion (nuclear bombs), Alcubierre Drive (warp drive), Piggyback Jets, Rocket Sled Launch, High Altitude Blimp Launch, Verne Gun, Launch Loop, and Cavorite.

She'd also designed capsules using empty gas station storage tanks, train tanker cars, heavy culverts with end caps welded on, and a host of others. Based on her figuring, there was no practical way she could make a capsule capable of maintaining an atmosphere when there was a vacuum on the outside from wood, ceramic, plastic or concrete. Lately, she'd been collecting articles on 3D printers. If she had a large enough printer, she should be able to make a spaceship!

And, of course, nothing she'd put into her notebook could be built in the back yard.

She added the title of Jacob's book to her "To be Read" list. It was too long to remember, but she found it online from just the first three words: Atoms to Andromeda.

Tom opened her webpage that she'd been building for the last year. It was basic HTML (she did the coding herself in a plain text program). The page's title was SOLAR GUARD APPLICATION. Under that, she'd created what looked like a job application form. She modeled it on the college application forms they kept in the counselors' office. In it, she'd entered all her grades since 3rd grade (straight A), and included descriptions of what she'd learned in math and science. She had a section with the books she'd read, and her thoughts on them, several personal essays about what service in the Solar Guard would mean to her and why she should be chosen.

At the bottom, was an e-mail address that she'd set up just for the website. Although she'd never linked to the site anywhere, she received occasional e-mails. Some were fun, like "Is this for real? Can I join?" Some were mean. "Get a life," or "This is stupid." And some were creepy, like "Are you really a girl? Show me your boobies."

But how else was she going to contact the Solar Guard? She'd sent Morse code messages out her window with a huge flashlight, and tried the same trick with a home-built laser. She'd taken apart an old DVD burner for the laser diode and followed instructions from the Internet. The beam was surprisingly powerful. It could burn a hole in dark paper. The most expensive part of the project were the safety goggles. She'd also sent signals through a walkie-talkie she'd found in the garage, which only managed to piss off a nearby construction crew who were using the same wave length, and then she'd built her own radio transmitter and receiver. She picked up static, distant stations in foreign languages, police and fire calls, and at certain wavelengths, the beeps, pings and pulses from satellites. She liked those best.

She scrolled to her web page e-mail. Three new messages. One read, "I thought this site was about solar panels. LOL." The second one said, "I'd rather be an officer on the *Enterprise* in the United Federation of Planets." And the third said, "We are looking for a recruit. Watch the skies."

If only, she thought. But she stayed up until the horizon lightened in the east, watching the skies.

At breakfast, Mom said, "Your dad and I will be attending a week-long realtors convention in Atlanta, starting this afternoon. I've left $40 on the mantle, when you need to buy anything, and you can call us if there's a problem. If we don't answer, it's because we're listening to one of the presentations, so leave a message."

Dad was coming down the stairs with two huge suitcases when Tom left through the front door.

She rode the bus with her eyes closed, next to a third grader with a SpongeBob Square Pants lunch box. Kids shouting blended into a white noise background. The swaying and bumps lulled her into near sleep. She wasn't dreaming, but her imagination ran free. She stood before an entrance committee for the Solar Patrol, four officers with serious expressions. They argued among themselves.The one on the far left said, "Why take an Earthling, especially an American one? They've abandoned their manned space program. A few robot probes don't show a national commitment. We should be looking at Chinese recruits."

"Just because the country doesn't seem space-bound doesn't mean that we can't find a qualified candidate among them. Look at what this one has accomplished."

The first officer to speak said, "That's true. She has shown both aptitude and desire."

"We should test her further," said the officer on the other end.

"Yes, let's."

Something in the tenor of the background noise changed, and Tom realized she was still riding to school. Reluctantly, she watched the admissions committee fade away, and she was back in the bus, surrounded by noise.

She opened her eyes. A dozen kids sitting in front of her were looking over the backs of their seats. Tom thought at first they were looking at her, but a deep voice shouting incoherently behind her made her look back too.

Four boys were out of their seats, two in the aisle, two kneeling on a seat so they faced the bench behind them. Their open hands rose and fell, and the boys were laughing. Jacob cringed under their blows, his arms up, covering his face.

"Take it!" yelled one of the boys as his hand came down on the top of Jacob's unprotected head.

Smack. Smack. Smack. It was the laughing that infuriated Tom most. They weren't just hurting Jacob, they were mocking him. Some kids in the back of the bus chanted, "Fight! Fight! Fight!" but no one tried to stop the beating.

Tom looked to her right. The third grade girl was watching like everyone else. Tom grabbed her metal SpongeBob Square Pants lunchbox. It had a nice heft to it. Probably a thermos of milk inside beside a sandwich.

She slung it overhand at the nearest boy.

It was a lucky shot, but the results were spectacular. The box whacked solidly into the back of the head of one of the kneeling boys, popping open in an explosion of potato chips. At the same time, the bus suddenly slowed, throwing everyone forward.

"Hey!" yelled the bus driver, "what is going on back there? You kids get into your seats."

Three of the boys, still laughing, sat in nearby benches. One said, "That was a real bitch slapping. Did you video it?"

"No, doofus. How am I going to shoot it if I'm bitch slapping too?"

"Did you call me a doofus? A doofus? How old are you?" and they both laughed even louder.

The boy Tom had hit wasn't laughing. He had laced his fingers together over the back of his head, while eyeing the front of the bus balefully. Tom made sure not to catch his gaze. She was sure if he saw her grinning, he'd know that she'd thrown it.

Jacob sat with his head down. He rubbed a coat sleeve under his eyes. Tom picked up her books and sat next to him.

"Go away," he said.

Tom didn't move. "Are you all right?"

"Go away."

"No."

The bus made the turn toward the school after picking up the last kids. They were a mile from the building.

"They're just stupid bastards, you know," said Tom.

The boy sitting in front of them who'd been hit with the lunchbox, said to no one in particular, "I think I have a concussion or an infarction."

Someone nearby said, "Infarction isn't even a word. You're brain scrambled."

Jacob looked up, his cheeks bright red. At least a couple of the slaps had got through his arms. "We're surrounded by idiots."

"I'll grant you that," said Tom.

"And what kind of idiot lets idiots beat him up?" Jacob said bitterly.

"The kind of idiot who understands abstract algebra and differential equations in the 10th grade. You'll be buying and selling the likes of them before you're twenty-five. They're going to be sweeping the hallway outside your office so they can earn enough money to buy the inventions you're going to come up with."

Tom looked at him, his eyes bloodshot, his cheeks wet. "If I live that long. This is a bad place. I don't belong." He turned to the window and didn't speak for the rest of the drive. Tom wanted to do something, but even putting her hand on his shoulder felt patronizing. He was right. What kind of world did she live in where people could be so . . . horrible? If she could get away, she would, to a place where nobility was recognized, where the brave succeeded, and medals were earned. She needed to be in the Space Academy. She thought for a moment that she didn't have to go to school. Her parents were gone. She could walk home. For the rest of the day, she could reread the Tom Corbett books, do research on space flight, think about Mars and Venus and the places in deep space that had yet to be discovered. She could stay home all week if she wanted. The temptation was intense.

But when they got to the school, Tom shuffled down the aisle with the handful of high schoolers. She was taller than most.

As Tom stepped through the door, the third grader she'd been sitting beside exclaimed, "Someone stole my lunch!"

That night, Tom opened her bedroom window, turned her rocket noise clip as loud as the speakers could go without distortion. The night was particularly warm and clear, so clouds didn't reflect city lights. Every star shone like a diamond point. She pushed the desk out of the way so she could sit right at the window and see the most sky. But Tom hadn't slept much the last two nights, so she put her head back against her chair, closed her eyes, and let the ship sounds sweep over her. A subsonic rumble filled the background. She imagined the mighty engines throwing them forward, ever faster through space.

A life on a ship is one filled with purpose. Everyone has a job, and the destination is clear. Not like her life where she didn't know where she was going, where she didn't know her job. On a ship in the Solar Patrol, everyone belonged to the team. Each had a responsibility and purpose. She longed for clarity, for a mission.

Footsteps went by her on a metal corridor floor. A conversation rose and fell. Metal locks clinked open. Pneumatic pistons released pressure. Pumps engaged. She loved being on the ship. Gradually, she slipped into a dreamlike state. The Solar Guard committee sat before her again. "Tomika," said the first officer, "after much discussion, we have approved your application for admission into Space Academy. We can only take one from your planet, and you have been chosen."

Tom tried to contain her joy, but a smile spread through her anyway. "I'll do my best," she said.

The second officer said, "We know that. Your passion, your strength in math and science, and your drive to succeed won us over. We don't think you belong here. There's a place for you, if you earn it, among the stars."

She nearly leapt from her seat—she pictured herself throwing a handful of clothes in a bag, writing her parents a quick note, and then leaving, really leaving—but a thought stopped her. "You can only take one?"

"We don't have to take even that," said the first officer. "Sadly there are many years when we don't find a suitable candidate at all."

Tom swallowed hard. "I . . . shouldn't be the one, then. I know a better person. He's way stronger in math. A genius I think. His name is Jacob Rose. You should take him."

The first officer frowned, turned to the second one. The other two leaned in to the discussion. They murmured for several minutes.

The second officer addressed her. "We have Jacob Rose on our short list. His qualifications are known to us. You would give up your place and have him attend the academy instead? We won't offer this opportunity again."

She could see the stars glittering like a million promises behind them. What would it be like to be in the academy, studying with purpose, a future filled with service and adventure in front of her? What would it be like to climb the stairs to her own starship for the first time? "Up ship," she'd bark into the intercom. Deep in the ship's bowels, her power deck officer would reply, "Aye, aye," and the metal around her would come alive, quivering with the power that would send them out and out.

Tom felt the control buttons beneath her fingers. She smelled ship air. Everything, all of it, so real and only a breath away.

"Yes, you should take Jacob. He is better qualified."

The first officer shrugged with resignation. "We will consider your suggestion."

The committee faded, and when Tom opened her eyes, the rising sun sat on the horizon through her open window. She shivered in the morning breeze, and she realized her cheeks were wet.

She moved through her Tuesday listlessly. It was only a dream, she thought, but loss still weighed on her, like a real opportunity had passed. On Wednesday, a note from administration called her from her first hour class. She sat outside the vice principal's office with three other students. One by one they were called in. Tom went last. A stranger in a business suit and tie sat next to the vice principal. "This is Detective Tasker. He has some questions for you . . ." he glanced at a list on his desk, "Tomika."

The detective, a young man with a skinny, black moustache, asked her about Jacob. When did she see him last? Did he seem depressed? Had he said anything odd to her lately?

She told him about the slapping incident on the bus Monday. She didn't tell him about the lunchbox. The detective frowned as he wrote the information down. "This doesn't sound good," he said.

The vice principal looked concerned. "You should have reported this to us immediately, young lady. You know we have zero tolerance for bullying. We have other students to interview, but I will talk to you about your responsibility when the current situation blows over."

"What's the current situation?" asked Tom.

"Oh . . . I thought you knew. Jacob Rose is missing. He's been gone since some-time Monday night."

The detective gave her a card. "Call me if he contacts you, or you think of any-thing that might help us find him."

Some kids talked about Jacob during the day, but his absence didn't seem to affect anyone else. Tom, though, felt lighter. The dullness from yesterday faded some. She put her hand up in class more often. She chatted with the kids around her. Where was Jacob? The vice principal seemed to think that he had run away, or maybe hurt himself, but Tom dared to hope differently. Jacob had said, "I don't think I belong here."

She imagined Jacob waking in the middle of the night. "We have an opportunity for you," the first officer might say. And Jacob, as smart as he was, would go with them. They would take him into space because he was the best candidate.

The thought made her happy. If it was true, that is, if Jacob was gone and safe.

That night, she sat at her window again, her room silent. The stars flickered just as bright, but they seemed impossibly remote now. She thought about Santa Claus and the Easter Bunny and the Tooth Fairy, the fantasies of her childhood, and she knew that Tom Corbett and the Space Cadets would fade into her past too. For now, the thought that Jacob had joined the impossible Solar Guard buoyed her, but what if it was true? She'd never know. If it was true, she'd given away her one chance.

Maybe she would sell real-estate, like her parents. She flinched just thinking about it.

Still, for the moment, the stars were beautiful. The impossibly remote night sky spread out like myths made real, a visible reminder of possibility. No world could remain mundane when every night the universe could unfold like this before her.

And high in the sky above the Pleiades, a star unhooked itself from the back-ground. She thought at first that it might be a satellite, but it grew brighter and brighter, until it was no longer a star. It was a flame descending, and then she could hear it like a hum at first, but soon a roaring that shook the house and vibrated in her chest.

The ship landed, a needle balanced on end. A door opened in its side. A ramp extended from it to the ground. A tall figure emerged. Illuminated from the light within the ship, Tom recognized the first officer's uniform, and soon the officer stood outside her window. "Are you coming?" the officer asked.

"You said you could only take one. Didn't Jacob go with you?"

Standing on the lawn, only a few feet from her, the officer nodded. "The com-mittee talked about you, Tomika. We decided that a candidate who would sacrifice her dream to save someone else is exactly the kind of person the Solar Guard should recruit."

"Yes, of course." Tomika could hardly breathe.

A meteor streaked across the blackness. Tomika saw it as she ran toward the ship. The light left a trail that glowed like a sign, an arrow, like a long invitation. She dashed up the ramp, glad beyond hope, her heart throbbing like a rocket engine's pulse.

THE LAWN FAIRY WAR

GRACE LILY WHITE PARTED THE CURTAINS TO PEER THROUGH HER kitchen window into Ashley Tombley's yard. She squinted. Are those gargoyles? Yes, they are! It was bad enough that Ashley moved in, pulled up the grass, replaced it with black and gray gravel, and then tore down the nice, white picket fence so that she could erect a black, cast iron one, but now, gargoyles?

When Ashley repainted the house, Grace said nothing, although the house didn't need new paint. The Dearborns had freshened the property when they decided to sell. It had been a beautiful robin-egg blue with slightly darker trim, but Ashley painted it a stark, yellowed white with black trim. It looked like a daguerreotype of the house that used to stand there. Cast-iron furniture appeared on the porch. Two cast-iron benches faced each other in the black-graveled back yard. Cast iron meant a lot to Ashley, Grace decided.

No plants in Ashley's yard, just gravel, boulders and twisted hunks of drift-wood. It looked like a nuclear wasteland as far as Grace was concerned.

Grace loved, collected, and displayed lawn fairies. She also sought ceramic gnomes, leprechauns, elves, fairy bridges, fairy doors, and the occasional mobile if fairies dangled from it. Starting in February, when the snow cleared, she bundled out to her yard, digging, scraping, and rearranging the landscaping. By early spring, she planted seeds and bulbs, spread the new groundcover, and waited for when it was warm enough to relax in a lawn chair with a book, surrounded by her collection.

Grace opened a lawn ornament catalog on her kitchen table. She'd dog-eared the pages with new figurines, but she couldn't stop herself from returning her attention to Ashley's yard. It was lurid, desolate and terrible.

During the winter, she longed for summer smells, a good book's heft in her hand, the sun's caress on her shoulders, and the company of her lawn friends, peeking from under the lilacs, hidden among the daffodils, and frolicking in the periwinkle. Even now, she saw the fairy jamboree she'd arranged near the fence. Fairies danced through the Snow-in-Summer. A tiny tea party convened around a table in the purple Sedum.

For years, she added to the collection, never minding that the neighbors thought her a little batty. Once she overheard Beatrice Angelo talking to Wanda Lewis in the supermarket after Grace passed: "It could be worse; she could keep cats," said Beatrice. Of course, Grace would never keep cats, nasty things that dug into the sandy areas in her yard, hunting the little winged creatures who came to her fairyland bird bath.

The talk didn't bother her. What bothered her were little kids who'd sometimes steal her figurines, and the occasional hailstorm that broke them.

I'm fifty years old, Grace thought. I deserve to be happy.

She put on a shawl, went out her front door, down the rainbow-speckled steppingstones that lead to her fairy green with yellow shooting stars mailbox, and down the sidewalk to Ashley's front gate. She paused as she unlatched the cold metal clasp. Ashley had added a pair of stone wolves just inside the gate. They stood hip-high, made of dark granite, posed viciously with snarling expressions and shiny, black teeth.

She'd never been inside the gate since Ashley moved in. Now she saw an iron snake coiled in a waist-high rock's shadow. Against the house leaned a very convincing tombstone. In front of it, a pewter hand, buried at the wrist, reached out as if a corpse was trying to claw from the grave. Figures hid everywhere behind the boulders, invisible from the street: scorpions, spiders, a weird half-bear half-man the size of a puppy, trolls, and by the porch, a pair of pale stone lions. Ashley had even painted the sidewalk black. Grace pulled her shawl a little tighter, mounted stairs to the door, grimaced, and then seized the skull knocker.

Ashley answered, cigarette dangling from her black lipstick painted lips. She was taller than Grace, the same age, broader in the shoulders, henna-red hair that hung to the middle of her back. Her maroon Victorian riding jacket sported dull silver buttons, but ordinary blue jeans and white sneakers spoiled the effect.

"You have gargoyles in your back yard," said Grace, primly, realizing that she had nothing else to say beyond that.

Ashley flicked her cigarette into a bucket by the door. "Do you like them?"

Grace couldn't tell if the woman was being sarcastic.

"They're facing my kitchen." She could picture their stone eyes now, contemplating her house. "They're inappropriate for the neighborhood."

Ashley laughed. "Your yard looks like a unicorn threw up on it. Who is inappropriate?"

Grace suddenly felt ridiculous. The conversation had turned improper and confrontational. "Could you display them so I won't see them? I like the view out my kitchen window."

"They're seventeenth-century stonework. Genuine articles off Irish Catholic monasteries. They're art. Get used to them. Have you heard of a gargoyle garden? I'm making one."

Grace swallowed weakly. "More gargoyles?"

Ashley nodded. "It's taken me twenty-five years to afford my own house. It's going to look the way I like."

"I'm sorry, Ms. White," said City Planner Filcher. "The area you live in is not covered by restrictive covenants. Ms. Tombley's obligations as a homeowner are to keep her yard clear of weeds and the house in good repair. She's not running a business out of the home is she?"

Standing in the kitchen, Grace gripped the phone tight to her ear. Ashley, in her back yard, unpacked a set of three, dishwasher-sized boxes. Two young men helped her cut the cardboard away. Their truck sat in the alley at Ashley's back gate. "No! I told you that she's putting repellent statuary in her yard. Did you get that she's using *black* landscaping stone? It looks like the House of Usher over there."

"Let me see what else is a possibility." Grace heard paper shuffling. "Is she noisy between the hours of 10:00 p.m. and 6:00 a.m., or are there large groups of people coming and going from the property?"

"No." The cardboard had come off the first box, but bubble wrap and strapping tape hid the contents. Ashley gestured to the corner next to Grace's yard. The two men levered the wrapped mystery onto a dolly.

"Are there noxious odors, trash fires, automobiles in disrepair, abandoned appliances, piles of used tires, industrial equipment or barrels of toxic chemicals?"

"No, of course not. I told you the problem."

"I'm just reading from the city standards for home owners, ma'am."

"Come out here and look!" said Grace desperately. "Or I can send you pictures."

"Wait a minute," said the city planner. "Are you Grace *Lily* White?"

"Yes, why?"

Papers rustled. Faintly, a computer keyboard's clackety clack came through. "You live in the fairy house, don't you? I thought your address was familiar. You're in the system. Theft and vandalism complaints. Oh, and the 'she's the mistress of darkness' call from last year."

Grace felt herself blushing. "That was a misunderstanding. Selma Wall is a religious nut. She said my yard ornaments were idolatrous and not right for a Christian community. They're fairies, not the devil!"

"I believe the city backed you up on that issue. Am I right?"

The memory stung to think about. In Ashley's yard the workman peeled the bubble wrap in a long strip off the delivery, revealing a black-stone winged figure crouched on a pedestal. Under Ashley's direction, the men turned the heavy piece so that it looked right into her window.

Grace stepped back, as if it could see her. "I have another option," she said, and ended the call.

Grace knew Selma Wall from grade school. They'd both lived in the neighborhood their entire lives, but never been friends. In elementary school, Selma carried a Bible everywhere she quoted from with a particularly grating precision. Then, in high school, she went through a brief slutty period, marked mostly by sleeping with each of the three boys Grace had a crush on. She returned to the Bible years later when her marriage fell apart. Grace wouldn't have any contact with her at all except that Selma put in the complaint with the city about Grace's yard.

They had sat on opposite sides of a conference table in the mayor's office. The mayor, a retired telephone executive who ran for office on a can't-we-just-get-along platform, mediated.

"Miss Wall. Could you explain your objections to Miss White's decorating choices?"

If Grace thought that the misunderstanding could be settled amicably, Selma's opening put that hope to rest.

Selma put a manila folder filled with papers on the table. "I've been investigating. Most people think of Walt Disney and Tinkerbell when they picture fairies, but it's not well known that faeries," (she spelled it out) "or the 'fae' as some practitioners refer to them, are minions of the devil. This woman's display is an affront to our community's Christian values."

Two weeks later, after four more increasingly acrimonious meetings, where Selma accused Grace of witchcraft, and Grace called Selma a "sanctimonious twit," the mayor dismissed the complaint on religious freedom principles.

Grace said to him later, "But I don't worship fairies. This isn't religion. They're not real. I just like them. They're pretty."

The mayor said, "I know, but she can't see it any other way. Take your victory and run."

Selma lived in a tidy bungalow tucked behind a much larger house that faced the street. Grace walked up Selma's gravel driveway, staying as far away from a huge dog that followed her on the other side of the big house's fence. It didn't bark, but Grace had never heard more threatening breathing in her life.

If Selma thought Grace's yard was bad, what would she make of Ashley's? Certainly the two of them had an angry history, but she hoped to convince Selma that the enemy of her enemy was her friend. Grace imagined Selma galvanizing her church behind her. Selma wouldn't make the mistake of going to the city this time. She'd organize protest rallies in front of Ashley's house, because, after all, fairies were innocent, while gargoyles were clearly demonic. She wondered what Selma would make of Ashley's black lipstick.

Smiling, Grace knocked on Selma's door.

A wave of incense washed over her when Selma greeted her. She wore a long, orange robe with gold tassels hanging from the hems and a loose yellow sash across her chest. Selma faced her hands palm to palm, fingers up, and bowed slightly as a welcome.

"Selma?" said Grace. The last time she'd seen her, Selma dressed like an Amish matriarch.

They shared tea. The incense burned so thickly that Grace's eyes watered. Grace knew long before Selma announced somewhat redundantly, "I've become a Buddhist," that she wasn't going to find an ally here in her battle with Ashley.

When Grace left, Selma said, "Namaste."

"Whatever," said Grace.

Late that night, a spring wind came out of the north. The weather station predicted a freeze, so Grace covered her roses and the more delicate flowers. She apologized to the fairy figures that she covered also. "I know you like the outdoors," she said, "but the plants need protection."

Wind whistled through her old home's eaves, and the oak tree in back that she'd been meaning to prune brushed the siding with creepy scratching and thumping. She pulled a quilted throw off the couch to wrap herself, sat in her favorite chair with a new book, and read by the light of her Tiffany lamp. On the table beside her sat a warmed scone under a napkin and a small glass of wine.

The book had come in the mail the day before, *Reflections of the Cottingley Fairies: Frances Griffiths—in Her Own Words: With Additional Material by Her Daughter Christine*. The Cottingley fairies had been a sensation around 1920. Two sisters claimed to have photographed fairies in their garden. Sir Arthur Conan Doyle, the author of the Sherlock Holmes books, became very interested and championed their experiences.

Grace ran her fingers over the black and white photographs of the two young girls who appeared to be within inches of the delicate creatures, but even to her uncritical eye, the pictures screamed fake. How could anyone have thought them genuine? Decades later, the girls admitted the images were false, but still maintained they'd seen fairies in their garden.

Grace sighed. She didn't believe that fairies were real, but she liked the idea that she lived in a world where she could imagine them.

Still, she did her own fairy photography. A digital camera and digital editing created convincingly interesting pictures. She'd covered the walls in her library with them, and now, by the Tiffany lamp's light, they looked over her benignly.

Something whapped hard against the side of the house, rattling the photographs. Grace jumped, straining her ears. The wind had picked up, but she didn't believe it could carry anything large enough to cause what she'd heard. It was if someone had smacked her siding with a shovel.

She grabbed a flashlight and a coat, slipped the deadbolt on the back door, then cracked it open. A cold breeze pushed in. She shut the door behind her. From the back stoop, the yard became a dark symphony of movement, illuminated only by a streetlight through the wind tossed tree. Shadows danced, branches creaked, and the fairy mobiles clattered like skeleton teeth.

Her flashlight cut through the night. Torn leaves and dust dashed through the beam, peppering her face. She swept the light to her left and right, but she didn't see anything that would account for the noise. Holding her coat tight around her neck, Grace moved to the corner next to the driveway away from Ashley's house. She didn't like the idea of looking at the gargoyles in the middle of the night quite yet. But nothing seemed out of place there either. Among the tossing flowers, her fairies and gnomes seemed content. The wind had pushed over one of the larger pieces. It could wait for the wind to settle down before she would put it upright.

A shape moved just beyond the light. A dog? Grace scanned her neighbor's bushes. Other than the branches pitching left and right, nothing. Occasionally she'd seen a fox in the yards. Maybe that was the movement.

The front of the house was clear too. Her glider with canopy strained against the wind. The canvas awning snapped sharply, but she'd anchored the chair solidly against the possibility of wind (or thieves). It hadn't made the noise either.

With dread, she turned the corner toward Ashley's house. She directed the light at Ashley's yard. The new gargoyle, the huge one who'd been staring at her kitchen window, was gone. Had the wind pushed it over? She couldn't imagine the wind had been that strong, although now it plucked at her coat and blew hair across her face. A glittering in the flower bed before her caught the flashlight's beam. She had arranged a tableau of wood nymphs beside a two foot tall fairy castle in the center of the bed. Grace's breath froze in her throat. A castle parapet hung loose, dangling from the ribbons that decorated the building. Below the drawbridge, fairy wing fragments and sparkling, ceramic remnants were all that remained of her display. At her feet, a delicate leg and a whole wing, like the remains of a tiny massacre, stood out in a scattering of unidentifiable ceramic shards. No wind could have done this. Grace swept the flashlight down her garden, revealing unbroken fairies, but not where she'd placed them, a busted gnome, and a fairy mobile, jangling crazily. She picked up a whole fairy, a delicate beauty in lavenders and pink, as long as her hand. It dropped into her pocket.

A torrent whirled around her filled with twigs and sand. She shielded her face against it and turned her back.

The light revealed a dent in her siding. On the ground next to the house, black marble pieces mixed among her white stones. Most were no bigger than jagged, ugly marbles, but one piece, as large as a softball stood out. With her foot, she rolled it toward her. The pointed ears and leering mouth revealed themselves. It was from the gargoyle Ashley had installed earlier in the day.

The wind wasn't even blowing from Ashley's direction.

A mass swept by her head, tugged at her shoulder. She jerked the flash up, but whatever it was vanished. From the bed of Virginia Bluebells, though, a faint globe of light rose, and from the geraniums, another. Dust swirled, stinging her eyes, but she could have sworn that within the light's auras, fairy wings fluttered, steady in the wind. More appeared out of the black-eyed Susans and the golden rod until a dozen lights floated above her head, like an umbrella or shield. Were they protecting her?

In the storm's roar, something howled. Panicked, Grace pawed through the lenten rose and coneflowers for unbroken figurines. She couldn't leave them outside, but the howl called again, and two of the globes winked out. A shadow against the roiling clouds swept above.

Her pockets full of fairies, and others cradled in her arms, Grace closed her back door against the wind and the unnerving noise. She gasped heavily.

Carefully, she put the fairies on a shelf, only a handful of her collection, and it wasn't until she took her coat off that she discovered a long cut in the shoulder, like a razor or a talon, and a corresponding rent in her blouse. Her skin was untouched.

Grace stood at the gate, waiting for the owner of Chōzō Gardens and Lawn Art to open. A tree limb had come down across the street, blocking the sidewalk. A city crew with chainsaws and a wood chipper closed a lane of traffic.

"Ah, Miss White. Glad to see you again," said Eiji Kagome. He held a large bundle of keys in one had, and a coffee in the other. "Your regular business pays my girl's tuition."

"No time for chit chat," said Grace. "I'm on a mission." She pushed by Eiji as he opened the gate and headed for statuary at the back of the lot.

*

Ashley rested her forearms on her cast iron fence. "Quite a storm last night."

Grace surveyed her yard. Besides the shredded flowers and several small oak limbs, the damage wasn't terrible, as long as she ignored destroyed figurines. Dozens more had shattered. Some were ones she'd owned for years and had sentimental value. She moved with determination, picking up trash and dropping it into a heavy garbage bag.

"I see you lost a gargoyle." Grace tried to keep calm. She had thought about going into Ashley's yard at dawn with a hammer, smash for ten minutes, and her losses would be avenged, but she ate a breakfast of toast and oatmeal instead while waiting for Chōzō Gardens to open. Did Ashley know what happened last night? Was she responsible?

"Yeah, darnedest thing. They must have installed it poorly for wind to knock it off the pedestal."

Grace didn't think Ashley knew. She bent and straightened, bent and straightened. It would take the rest of the afternoon to get the yard where she wanted it.

A delivery truck parked in front of Grace's house. She smiled, took off her work gloves, and went to meet it.

"I'd like them at the corners," she said. The college-aged workman with a thick neck and impressive biceps, wearing a T-shirt that said, OLD GARDNERS NEVER DIE. THEY JUST THROW IN THE TROWEL, grunted as he hefted a box onto a dolly.

"Back yard too?"

"I've cleared spots for them."

A half hour later, the last box had been removed and the statues leveled. Ashley watched through the process.

"Dragons?" Ashley said. "Not really your motif."

Grace wiped down the jade-colored beauty that faced Ashley's yard. The wings, partially extended, reached three feet across, and the long head tilted slightly to the side, as if studying them. Each well-muscled, powerful creature looked poised to leap or fly. Strong faces. Unflinching eyes. Razor sharp claws and teeth.

"I think of them as heavy artillery," said Grace. The smallest dragon was half again as large as the remaining gargoyles in Ashley's yard. Much more imposing than Ashley's wolves. Dragons topped the mythological food chain, Grace thought. Nothing stronger. Nothing more intimidating, and nothing more territorial.

On the kitchen table, she spread her catalogs. The broken fairies could never be replaced. She mourned, but new ones could appear. Grace would grow to love them too. She imagined the tiny cottages nestled in the Marigolds, the fairy rings among the sunflowers, under the dragons' watchful gaze.

They'd dance, the fairies would, maybe only when the wind blew hard, but now that Grace knew, she'd come out at night with her camera. Maybe if she waited all night, perfectly still, full of the purest thoughts, they would dance for her like they had at Cottingley. Last night they protected her, and now she protected them. She'd told the mayor that she didn't believe fairies were real, just as she'd told herself that they were only pretty figurines.

What a relief to know she was wrong.

THE SILK SILVERED SKULLS
OF MILLEN MIR

NOTHING BEATS A GREAT BOOK," SAID LES BULLARD. HE WAITED BELOW Miss Rhonim as she stood on the ladder, searching the upper shelf. Remarkably fit for a librarian. Solid upper arms, well muscled legs. A statuesque Amazonian in black-framed glasses. She fit in with the library's décor, which leaned toward medieval armaments.

"You know you read the title when you were young?"

"Fifth grade or maybe sixth. I went through a long heroic fantasy phase. Tarzan and Conan and John Carter and Elric of Melniboné. The eternal champions. I wanted to be Doc Savage. God, I loved those books."

"This one, though, it wasn't part of a series?" She pulled on the shelf to move the ladder a couple feet.

"Nope. Just one, medium-sized book. Mine had a red leather cover and gold-edged pages. Nicest book I ever carried in my backpack. A maroon ribbon sewn into the binding to mark my spot."

"But you don't know the author?"

Les wrinkled his brow. "I can tell you how the book smelled. I can tell you what it was like to lay on my grandmother's freezer in her cellar during sweltering, summer Ohio days, reading the book by the light of the open door. I can tell you about starting the book after breakfast, and reading until it grew dark. I walked from the cellar up a little flight of stairs and into her back yard where fireflies winked over the vegetable patch. But I can't recall the author's name. It was three words, I think, like Jaime Fitz Mason or Robin Trait Curran. Something with that rhythm."

"I can't do a search for an author's name by rhythm."

"Maybe I'm misremembering the title." But Les was sure he wasn't. He closed his eyes and saw the book in the cellar's dimness, could feel the weight in his hand. Black letters embossed on red leather with a silver vine woven through them: *The Silk Silvered Skulls of Millen Mir*. He loved the opening line: "The swordsman's horse carried the weary warrior down a stony path."

Miss Rhonim ran her finger across the books' spines, one after another. "You came to the right place for hard to find books. The Orne Library at Miskatonic University is world-renowned."

Les looked down the long, poorly lit shelves. Small fluorescent fixtures hung from the ceiling at ten-foot intervals, but only the lights within fifteen feet of them were on. Darkness shrouded the rest. The cement floor reflected nothing. He couldn't see the wall at either end. "I heard your library had the best collection of uncataloged titles in North America. I've been looking for this book for decades."

"That's dedication. Heroic fantasy, fairly contemporary language, you said."

"I didn't have trouble reading it when I was twelve, but I read well above grade level. I finished *All Quiet on the Western Front* the next year. Most depressing book of all time. I swore off fine literature for years after that."

"So probably written in the late 1800s but no later than 1965 or so. We're in the right section, but we have thousands of titles, as you can see. It might take a bit." She glanced at her watch. "This is the restricted collection. There are irreplaceable texts stored down here. One of a kind. Patrons have to be accompanied."

Les bent to inspect the bottom row. His back creaked. "Why aren't these titles in a database? How do you find anything?"

She stiffened. "The Orne Library is the largest gathering of rare and historic texts in the northern hemisphere. In the general collection there are several million titles. Only Harvard contains more works than we do. Our Pickman Archive holds the finest examples of early Americana in the world, including settler diaries, journals and ledgers. We have letters from the original pilgrims. I think we do very well considering the complexity of our collection."

"I wasn't criticizing."

Miss Rhonim continued scanning book titles, clearly taking a few calming breaths. "Sorry to sound defensive, but you don't have to work in the Orne long before you realize the value of these books. Besides, the deeper collection is . . . difficult."

"What do you mean?"

"The books aren't always where we leave them. They . . . um . . . rearrange. Like this—" She held a black volume in her hand. "—is from 1788. It's misplaced. The faculty has learned to take a book when they find it. It might not be there again."

"So my title could be anywhere?" When they'd come down the long, stone stairway to this level, Les had thought they were going to a reading room or display area, but what greeted them at the bottom was a corridor formed by the ends of bookshelves that reached ceiling to floor. The lights must have been attached to motion sensors because they turned on as the two approached and blinked out behind them. At each junction, more neatly shelved books greeted him, row after row, until he lost count. They made several turns to reach the area they were in now, and not all were right angles. Some books stood in large circular shelves, like roundabouts, and others were stored in triangular formations, twenty feet to a side. Periodically they came upon a chair with an attached writing surface or a study table, but he hadn't seen another person. "I'm not surprised you lose books. The way this place is built, you could lose librarians."

"If your book exists, we have it. Looking is the only way to uncover anything; the loose organization down here is a feature, not a bug. The restricted collection is less about finding and more about discovering, Mr. Bullard. Our researchers and the books they need eventually cross paths." She replaced a book firmly on the shelf. "Imagine coming down here in the 1800s when you would have been holding a lantern."

The idea made him shiver.

They searched for another hour, Miss Rhonim using the ladder for the high shelves, and Les reading the low ones. He examined beautiful books, some with illustrated covers. One showed a burly savage wrestling an alligator, jaws open and stretching back, trying to kill the muscular human. Broken pillars, like a coliseum's remains stood in the misty background. He liked the style, but the artist was unfamiliar. "Can I check this out?"

Miss Rhonim nodded. "Twenty-four hours only. You have to sign a waiver and leave a deposit."

That night, Les made himself comfortable on the motel bed, turned on the reading light, then opened the book, *A Jungle Crown at Katung Pass* by Sideon Wayte. It had a faded inscription in pencil he hadn't noticed before: "To Beatrice, my jungle queen. Raymond, Christmas, 1908." So, written before Burroughs published Tarzan.

Twenty minutes into the book, Les climbed from the bed to stretch his back. When he'd retired two years ago, he'd looked forward to long periods of uninterrupted reading, a return to his youth. But now he couldn't stay in one posture more than thirty minutes before his back or neck hurt. Even holding the book made his elbows and fingers ache. He wondered if arthritis might be kicking in. And he could never find quite the right position for his bifocals. He kept adjusting his head to focus properly.

In junior high, he carried at least a couple novels in his backpack, waiting for class to begin so he could sneak one out. Mr. Crutcher, his 8th grade history teacher would turn his back to write on the board, and Les would have his book open. Then, like the snap of his fingers, class ended. For forty minutes, the teacher and his lesson faded away. When the bell rang, Les had to shake himself back to reality. He walked the halls in bewilderment because the literary world felt so much more real than the school. By the end of the day, he would have finished the book and started another. He read at night, long after he was supposed to be asleep so that he reached the new book's end.

Reading connected him to his youth. He didn't have to be able to run and jump like a fifteen-year-old if he could read like one.

Les sat on the bed's edge, reopened the book. The story wasn't bad, even if the language stumbled in places. Sideon Wayte couldn't turn a phrase, but he wrote with a cheerful, testosterone-soaked cheesiness. The villain was particularly black-hearted, the jungle animals "snarled with wild ferocity" and the women were slender, "small-handed" creatures who swooned on cue. In other words, *A Jungle Crown at Katung Pass* was a book of its time. It certainly didn't measure up to *The Silk Silvered Skulls of Millen Mir*.

If he could just find the book again! His gnawing obsession. For years he'd haunted used bookstores and antique shops, hoping he'd spot the familiar red cover. The summer at Grandma's house in Ohio, that had been his only title. He couldn't remember where he got it. Maybe he'd found it in her living room bookcase where she kept a collection of *Reader's Digest* condensed classics along with a few others. Surely his parents hadn't given it to him. They favored cheap paperbacks.

He'd always been a fast reader. Other books he finished in a day (even the fat and deeply depressing *All Quiet on the Western Front*), but he started *The Silk Silvered Skulls* when he arrived at Grandma's. He read every day for hours. He read after dinner and deep into the night, but he never finished the book. His memory of that summer was of delirious hours lost in *Millen Mir*. It seemed as if he was always in the middle, more pages to go, and he loved it. Other books passed too fast until the sad dread of knowing only a few pages remained crept up on him. The dream would soon end.

He'd turn the final page where the text didn't reach the bottom and the facing page was blank. *Lord of the Rings* lasted three days in the 9th grade. He didn't sleep. He faked a cough so he could skip school when he reached *The Return of the King*. Mom left him in his room, Mentholatum rubbed into his chest, vaporizer bubbling, buried in his blankets, deep in Middle Earth. The remaining pages grew fewer and fewer. Sweat poured from him as he lingered over the final paragraphs. The last pages wrinkled in the humid room until he finished, totally drained, sorry the book didn't go on.

But not *The Silk Silvered Skulls of Millen Mir*. How was it possible that he read just that one book all summer? Did he finish, and then lost in the book's spell, turn back to the beginning to start again?

Les put a pillow under his knees. Maybe if he could find just the right position, he would disappear into *A Jungle Crown at Katung Pass* like he did when he was young. He could capture the timelessness again, the dreamy creaminess of pages that vanished, of words that turned into worlds? But the pages remained stubbornly opaque. He tried squinting, turning the light down, relaxing breaths. How did he do it when he was a schoolboy? What was the secret?

After shifting position a dozen times, stretching his back twice, and drinking two cups of strong coffee, Les finished *A Jungle Crown at Katung Pass* after midnight. The story wasn't bad, but he didn't magically transport into it either. He rested the book on his chest and listened to cars on the highway whipping past the motel. The clock on the nightstand ticked loudly, and a through the thin walls, a couple argued.

When he slept, he dreamed of the ruins of Millen Mir, of dread creatures that rose from catacombs at night, of a magnificent barbarian king camped among the moss-covered walls, his back to the fire, holding back black spirits through strength of will.

Miss Rhonim met him at the double doors that lead into the Orne. She wore a brown blazer over a white blouse and mid-calf skirt. In the morning light that bathed the library's front, she looked more like a Valkyrie than a librarian. He wondered if she worked out. Les carried a small backpack. He thought it made him more like a student, albeit an elderly one. The doors closed behind them, shrouding the library's lobby in twilight silence. Real students sat in study carrels, reading by small lights mounted on goosenecks.

"I believe I have a lead on your book, Mr. Bullard. We searched fiction, but what if it was shelved as history or biography? We're going to different sections today."

The stairs to the deeper stacks loomed even darker than they had earlier. Miss Rhonim unlocked the gate and pushed it aside. Lights flicked on as they descended.

"This seems like more stairs than yesterday," said Les. He didn't climb as well as ten years ago, and the trip back become more intimidating the farther they walked.

"That's because it is. History is further down."

Swords in a long line hung from the wall to their right. Spears and shields on the left. Les touched a sword blade, moving the metal against the stone. It rang like a tiny bell. "Why all the armor?"

Miss Rhonim laughed. "Practicality. You never know when you might need a good sword. Besides, I thought you liked heroic fantasy. This should be a dream come true for you."

Like yesterday, the path into the books confused Les. Not only were many of the turns at odd angles, the floor sloped in places so they walked down or up book-lined hills. Lights turned on as they approached and turned off where they'd been. Darkness faced them and followed.

"How deep does the library go?"

"A long way." Miss Rhonim stopped in front of a stack of books that looked indistinguishable from the ones they'd already passed. None were marked with bar codes or labels. Some were titled on the spine, but many were not. "We're in the right place if your book is in history. Biography is a bit of a walk from here." She climbed a ladder. "You know the routine."

"I brought these." He pulled a pair of gardening kneepads from his backpack. "I have a couple water bottles too if you want one. I didn't notice drinking fountains yesterday. Are we going to the left or right?"

"To the left. If your title is here, it will be within this thirty feet."

Les put the kneepads on over his khakis. His knees wouldn't take the same beating as the day before when he'd spent too much time on the cold cement. He knelt to search the lowest row. Books without titles had to be slid off the shelf. Some didn't have titles on the cover either, so Les fell into a routine of reaching in, slipping the book out, checking the title page, then carefully returning it. He remembered summer days in his library at home when he'd been a boy, sitting on the floor before the books. If his mom didn't expect him home, he would finish one, put it back in its place and then read the next. When he finally stood, he'd realize that he'd skipped lunch, and it would be time to ride his bike home for dinner.

Methodically, Les checked each book. Miss Rhonim showed him where to stop and to start with the higher shelf. He paused with some, marveling at their illustrations, repulsed by others. Hand-written inscriptions in spidery calligraphy marked the inside covers, most dated from the early 1900s to 1940.

A metallic clank sounded from the darkness beyond, distinct, sharp and sudden. Miss Rhonim paused, a book in hand, preternaturally alert.

"What was that?"

"Hush," she said. "I'll check it out. You keep looking."

She climbed down the ladder noiselessly, took off her shoes, put them neatly under the ladder, then moved toward the sound, partly crouched, lithe as a cat. Ceiling lights turned on in front of her until she walked with an island of her own light. She turned down a row a hundred feet away, and suddenly Les felt naked and alone. If she didn't come back, he didn't know the way out, but worse than that was the darkness lurking beyond the fifteen feet of light to his left and right. He could almost see large things standing silently, studying him. Les's knees cracked when he stood.

Cautiously, he walked in the direction opposite of the one Miss Rhonim had taken. A ceiling light flicked on, not revealing monsters, but more books. He laughed to himself. The lights were the secret. They were motion activated, so creatures trying to sneak up on him would trigger a light and show themselves. They were the library's early warning system, but his self-assurances felt hollow. He looked back to where his backpack now sat on the edge of light. Another step or two, and it too would be lost in the dark.

"Miss Rhonim," he called. "Are you okay?" The sound faded without echo or answer. He turned his head to the side, quieted his breath. Somewhere, metal met metal, just on perception's edge. Was that a shout? Was that a roar? He ran past his backpack, following Miss Rhonim, but when he reached an intersection he stopped, gasping for breath and unsure where to go. His heart pounding obscured sounds. "Miss Rhonim! Miss Rhonim!"

Away in the darkness, a ceiling light flicked on. The librarian strode toward him.

"You really shouldn't wander in here," she said when she drew close. "It can be a bit of a maze."

"What was it? I thought I heard something."

"Nothing to worry about. A maintenance issue, really. Why don't we see if we can't find your book now."

She led him back to the shelves they'd been searching.

It wasn't until Miss Rhonim climbed the ladder again that Les noticed a rip in her blazer and blouse, a foot-long cut on her left side angling down from her armpit and ending below her shoulder blade. Les knelt, looking up at her. Not a rip so much as a clean cut like from a knife or sword. Her skin was untouched beneath. He was sure her clothes weren't damaged earlier. What happened to her when she left?

He tried to figure out how to ask her about it, but the next book he pulled from the shelf drove the question from him. Red cover. Black embossed title with a silver vine running through the letters.

"Oh, God," he said, and sat back. *The Silk Silvered Skulls of Millen Mir*, as beautiful as he remembered, by Danny Jan Milton.

"You found it?" Miss Rhonim sounded delighted as she climbed down the ladder. She crouched beside him. "May I?"

She hefted the book in her hand, opened it. "Ah, I see why you thought it was special. Not many like this one."

"What do you mean?"

Miss Rhonim said, "Have you ever gone into an elementary school library?"

Les nodded.

"Most have a sign somewhere, often by the entrance, or a bulletin board. It says, 'Books: Your Ticket to Adventure.'"

Les did remember exactly those words in his childhood library, accompanied with rockets and unicorns and castles. He thought it was true then just as he did now.

Miss Rhonim handed the book back. "Some books don't take you as far, but some, like yours, are infinity passes. I can tell just by holding it. This is a valuable book indeed, exceptionally rare."

Tears burned on Les's cheeks. He'd searched so long. "Can I . . . check it out?"

Miss Rhonim shook her head. Crouched beside him, her face so close, Les noticed her eyes for the first time, sword-metal gray with copper flecks. Startling at this distance, intense but not unkind.

Les pulled the book to his chest. "I can't?"

"Here's why." She held her hand out.

Reluctantly, Les gave it back.

The librarian opened the front cover and showed it to him. "I believe it's your book."

In familiar handwriting, the inscription read, "To Les, my little reader, from Grandma."

"How?"

Miss Rhonim straightened, towering over him. "I told you. Down in the Orne's deep stacks, you and the book you need eventually cross paths. It's one of our best features."

"I can keep it?" He ran his hand over the lettering. The leather felt warm, as if the book had a life of its own. He knew that when he opened it, when he read, it would be as if he was twelve again. He remembered landscapes that caressed his senses, fogs that chilled his face, forest meadows filled with pine and sweet grass scents, rivers clapping over rounded boulders, the long road and his companions waiting on rampart walls. Not just a ticket, but a key and a pass and a secret handshake into his childhood imagination.

Miss Rhonim turned her gaze from him, peered into the darkness beyond. Her posture alerted Les. He looked back, trying to see what she detected.

"Time to go," she said as she helped him to his feet with one hand and scooped up his backpack with the other.

Beyond the ceiling light's reach, a shuffling sound, a click like bone against stone, or claws.

"We'll be moving smartly here," she said, not flustered, but concentrated and competent. "Looks like I didn't quite solve the problem earlier."

She kept one hand on his elbow, guiding him through the book maze back toward the stairs to the main library.

"If something's following us, why don't the lights turn on?" Les kept checking over his shoulder. There was never more than fifteen feet illuminated behind him. Fifteen feet would only be three or four strides for someone, or something, running, and clearly they were being trailed. If a shape appeared, he would have no time to react.

The librarian turned at a junction, almost jerking him off his feet. "We're visitors. They're denizens. Visitors need light. Denizens don't."

Confused, Les was nearly running to keep up with her. "Do we need to get help? Are they trespassers?" But even as he asked, he thought the question ridiculous. Whatever was going on here didn't feel like a job for the police. It was like he'd stepped into one of his books. If he'd been by himself, he would have been scared, but Miss Rhonim pushed him differently. Not frightened at all. Not out of her element.

The next turn took them to the stairs.

"This is where I leave you," she said. "Just keep going up until you get to the gate." She handed him a large key. "Lock it behind you."

"How will you get out?"

The librarian stepped to the wall, took down a sword and swung it once as if she'd done it thousands of times before. "Oh, there's more ways out than the stairs."

She put her hand on his shoulder. "You're a kindred spirit, Les. I hope you enjoy your book. Now, off you go."

Propelled by her last push, Les climbed several steps. He stopped to watch her stride back into the library, sword tip up and at the ready. She rounded a corner out of sight, and the lights that followed her flicked off. Then, a yell of triumph, the hard clatter of sword on swords, a guttural yell.

Les fled up the stairs, thankful Miss Rhonim took up the battle behind. She felt like she'd stepped from the land of Millen Mir. He'd been in the presence of a hero.

Carefully, after the long, long climb, Les locked the gate as she'd directed. He found a study carrel by the front door, clicked on a reading light, and put the book on the wood desk. He'd read until she returned, not that he doubted she would. No, he didn't doubt that Miss Rhonim the librarian would return.

He settled into the chair, took a deep breath, opened the book to chapter one. The pages welcomed his fingers. He'd come home again. By the end of the first sentence, the letters weren't words on the page; they were a voice in his ear and a picture in his head.

"The swordsman's horse carried the weary warrior down a stony path."

MARS, APHIDS, AND YOUR CHEATING HEART

IMAGINE THAT TIME, SPACE AND MOTION ARE CONTAINED IN AN OCEAN INFInitely long, broad, and deep. And imagine further that you are God, and you know everything about your ocean. No part of it is unknown to you. The tiniest movement is known; the most minuscule detail is obvious. Beginnings and endings are equally known, and they have no difference. There is no cause and effect; there is only detail next to detail next to detail. Narrative, then, is an illusion created by ordering details in relation to each other chronologically, but the stories are illusions because they are already in the ocean. They don't "happen." They float, complete, unchanging, and within the context of the ocean's all-encompassing existence.

Imagine, then, how difficult it would be to extract an infinitesimal part of the ocean and turn it into a story. Difficult, of course, but not impossible. You are, after all, God. Telling story means separating details, ordering them, sharing them a word at a time, imperfectly, because they really should be communicated at once. A story should be a black spot on the page where every letter is typed on top of the other. A book, a series of books, time's entirety could be within the dot.

But if seeing everything at the same time is what it means to be God, then seeing the beauty in detail should be possible too.

On Mars during a summer windstorm, on the floor of Valles Marineris, a single sand grain shifts from its place at a crater's edge, falling a tenth of an inch to lodge among the others. This grain has a shiny side, like a mirror, catching the sun perfectly. That motion alone, one moving grain is lovely in its uniqueness, in its power and grandeur. It attracts your infinite attention, as does every moving sand grain. On nearby Earth, a ladybug crawling on a purple iris, eats an aphid. All things in relation. The iris grows next to a sidewalk that runs from the front door of a yellow house to the street. The thirty-two-year-old policewoman who planted the iris eight years ago when she bought the house is fighting breast cancer. She doesn't know it and never will because her body's immune system will win. The cancer will be there her entire, long life, never expressed, never exhibiting a symptom. Cancer won't kill her.

It's night at the yellow house. Hiding in the policewoman's bushes for the second night in a row, sitting on a canvas camp chair, two feet from the iris where the ladybug attacks and eats an aphid, with Mars shining bright in the sky, a man, Jaydee Janac, watches the house across the street. He has a camera with a long lens on a tripod in front of him, a coffee-filled thermos beside him, and a tattered paperback in his coat pocket that he occasionally rereads. A man named Bennett who doesn't trust his wife hired Jaydee. Bennett has a mistress in Santa Fe he visits every summer when he tells his wife he's away on a work retreat. They've met for thirteen years.

Still, the idea that his wife might be unfaithful eats at the man. Bennett doesn't see irony between his behavior and his suspicions. The idea that she might be seeing someone distracts him at work. Twice he's missed meetings thinking about it. He takes antacids to counter the burning in his stomach which he attributes to worry. Anxiety doesn't cause his symptoms. Bennett has an intestinal cancer that will kill him in seven months.

He doesn't know. You know. You are omniscient.

The aphid died not knowing that a ladybug was killing it. Aphids don't "know" things the way people understand knowing. In that sense, the ladybug didn't know what happened either. Insects aren't burdened with self awareness. This particular ladybug will live seven years, which will be a record, if ladybugs kept records. At the end, it will take off from a salvia, fly two feet and die. The death will be sudden, painless—not that ladybugs experience pain the way people think of pain.

Jaydee focuses his camera on the living room window. The wife went into the house thirty minutes ago. She's named Linda, a name that she always thought plain. No Princess Linda in fairytales. No heroines or famous artists or world leaders named Linda. As he did the night before, a man greets her at the door, a peck on the cheek and a quick hug. Jaydee clicks off pictures. Door closes. Lights behind the curtains in the living room dim but don't go off. He slips from the bushes, checks Linda's car that is unlocked. Finds candy bar wrappers in her trash. Nothing incriminating. He thinks it doesn't matter. With the pictures, he has all the husband needs, and Jaydee is convinced. People no longer impress him. He's worked this gig for too long. He's seen it all, like a terrible guilt chain connecting everyone: a wife cheating on a husband with the husband's brother, while the husband's brother's wife gambled online and lost their retirement fund to a bookie who lied to his parents for three years, telling them he was in college when he wasn't. He took the tuition money to set up a numbers game on campus. The gambler's partner, an underclassman studying botany, had dozens of hours of hard core pornography on his computer. One piece of film was a bit of revenge porn that the husband who started this chain had posted of him and his wife on their honeymoon, when they still loved each other. As far as Jaydee is concerned, everyone he investigates is dirty. Everyone has secrets.

Still, Jaydee makes two hundred and fifty a day for this assignment. If he uses a day or two more to find extra evidence, he can bill for the extra time.

He takes a risk, sneaks across the front yard, presses a stethoscope against the window. Two voices too low to make out. He guesses foreplay. When lovers meet, there can be a passionate rush. Once he followed a man to a hotel where his secretary waited. They fell on each other like cats, tearing and unbuttoning, their mouths seeking each other, and in their explosion, failing to latch the door. It drifted open on its own. Jaydee shot beautifully incriminating photos from the parking lot. He didn't even get out of his car.

Jaydee knows Bennett is not interested in the truth if that truth doesn't support his belief that his wife is seeing someone else. The husband's bad stomach drives his desire. He must know she is cheating. He already bought a gun to kill her and the unknown lover when Jaydee names him.

Jaydee doesn't know about the gun. He suspects it. When he talked on the phone with Bennett the night before, asking if Bennett knew the address that Linda was visiting, he heard the gun in Bennett's voice. A private investigator develops a sense about such things. You in your omniscience know. You know the husband doesn't aim well. The first time he took the gun to a range and pulled the trigger, it jumped from his hand, fell to the floor, and when it hit, the husband saw the barrel pointed straight at him. The range instructor assured him that his gun, dropped the way he dropped it, could never fire, but the husband couldn't close his eyes without seeing the black hole pointed at his face. He flinched when he pulled the trigger every time he shot after that. Accuracy doesn't matter to him, however. He plans on putting the gun directly against her head. Boom! he thinks, and the matter is settled. To tell the truth, the idea excites him. He imagines how killing her lover will feel, how justified he will be. He even thinks he will call the police himself. Who wouldn't support him once they knew?

By the house's front door, a brass plaque glints in the darkness, unreadable, but Jaydee sees the glint, cups his hand around his phone to shield the light, and checks it out: MARK TIGGS, TAROT READINGS, PALMISTRY, SEANCES. Jaydee wonders if Linda isn't cheating after all. Maybe she's here for a reading.

On Mars, the single sand grain provides just enough weight to destabilize the slope. Other grains break loose, sending a handful sliding toward the crater's bottom. Dust and sand a half inch to a foot deep coat the windward side, and the crater is one hundred and seven miles in diameter. The entire slope gives way at once sending thousands of tons to the bottom. No one observes the soundless avalanche. The newly exposed ground is several shades lighter than the sand that covered it. Mars itself becomes infinitesimally brighter in the sky. It would seem impossible that this tiniest of changes in Mar's luminosity would make a difference, but the repositioning of a single grain started the avalanche. All events in the ocean of movement, space and time start with almost nothing.

Inside the house, the woman rests her elbows on a small round table. Her eyes are closed, and she holds Tiggs' hands. Tiggs thinks about the information he found on the Internet before she arrived, the information he knew to look for after his initial interview with Linda the night before. He knows she lost her mother a year ago, and the mother's name, which came from the memorial announcement. He knows what the mother looked like and that she arranged flowers and volunteered at church. He knows Linda is the youngest of three children. He knows her husband's name, and what he looks like. This will help him give a more convincing séance. When Linda used his bathroom, he searched her purse, so he also knows she's an organ donor and that she uses the public library and that she likes candy bars and Starbucks. These last bits will be less helpful, but he's always pleased by how much a purse or wallet will tell him.

"You have lost someone close to you," the psychic says. He likes holding Linda's hands. She reminds him of his first wife, before their marriage went bad. He remembers their first year and how they laughed with each other.

Linda nods. She's skeptical. The reason she booked the session was that her best friend at work, concerned about her happiness, gave her Tiggs' address. "He's a wonder," the friend said. "You'll feel so much better."

She does feel poorly. Her mother's death hit hard, and Bennett has become distant. He doesn't join her for breakfast on the weekends. When they were first married, she knew that when she got ready for bed, he would drop whatever he was doing to join her. He said he couldn't sleep unless he was holding her. They held hands in public. Somehow all that drifted away. She suspected that he intentionally avoided her in the house. She wondered if he still loved her.

Linda doesn't believe the séance would connect her with her mother, but the idea glitters in her imagination like a jewel. She turned forty-two a month ago. Will she ever feel like an adult? she wonders. Needing her mother makes her feel weak. Still, she came. The psychic could be a charlatan and his business a scam, but if he is good, he could still comfort her. She is willing to play along. She thinks of it as a purposeful placebo. Accepting this as a con doesn't mean that she can't suspend disbelief. Lie to me, she thinks. I want it.

Mark Tiggs wonders if Linda will sleep with him. He knows a séance's atmosphere can be erotic if he plays it right. He's alone in the house with a grieving woman. Three candles flicker on the table. Incense burns on the fireplace mantle. A rain recording on a loop plays softly in the background. Once, he convinced a woman that the spirits would be more comfortable if she could release her tensions. He rubbed her shoulders, unbuttoned her top blouse buttons. Two hours later they'd advanced to massage lotions. Mark smiles at the memory. He starts his patter. "Say after me, spirits of the past, move among us. Be guided by the light of this world and visit upon us."

The woman sighs. She's glad that she's not paying full price for this.

Outside, Jaydee curses his cheapness. A stethoscope on the window doesn't give him anything close to the sound quality he needs. He hears voices without words, and there's background interference that sounds like rain. Is she cheating or isn't she?

He can do nothing except wait for Linda to leave. With luck he'll get a shot of a goodnight kiss or an embrace. That should be enough for the husband. Jaydee doesn't care what happens later. He doesn't think about the gun he hears in the husband's voice. If Linda is cheating on him. She's not innocent.

Jaydee didn't read much when he was young. He liked watching other kids on the playground and trying to figure out what kind of people they would grow up to be. He did read one book, though: a paperback called *A Princess of Mars* that he still carries with him. There is a moment in it that he often thinks about. John Carter, the hero, an ex-Confederate soldier, falls asleep in a cave, and when he wakes, he's paralyzed. Every time Jaydee rereads it, he guesses that Carter was dying, not falling asleep. He must have been shot and not recognized the wound. Suddenly, Carter stands naked by his own body. A literal out-of-body experience! Carter, naked, probably dead, sees Mars in the sky. He always loved the planet. So, in his need, he wishes to be there. Carter says, "My longing was beyond the power of opposition; I closed my eyes, stretched out my arms toward the god of my vocation and felt myself drawn with the suddenness of thought through the trackless immensity of space."

Jaydee thinks often about that passage. Now, with nothing to do, crouching below Mark Tiggs' living room window at night, Jaydee sees Mars low in the sky. He's never seen it brighter, and he wonders if this is one of those times when Mars is close to the Earth. He's right, it is close to Earth. It is bright, infinitesimally bright enough to keep his attention a moment longer than it would have, and it reminds him of John Carter, a Virginia soldier who became a great hero on Mars, who fell in love, rescued a princess and became a prince himself. If he could, he would wish himself there like John Carter. Sentimentality overwhelms him, and he feels like he did when he read the book the first time, wonder-filled and hopeful. What am I doing with my life, he thinks. How is this a noble thing to do? He pictures the god, Mars, striding toward him, sword in hand.

Inside, Tiggs moves deeper into his standard séance. He does voices. He triggers a mechanism that raps on the table as if in answer to questions. Curtains flutter and candles flicker on his command. "You miss a powerful female figure in your life," he says.

Skeptical as she is, Linda grips Tiggs' hands tightly. Sweat beads on her brow, runs down her back. "Yes," she whispers.

Tiggs doesn't know, but he is slightly psychic. You are omniscient and see the spirits in the room that Tiggs sometimes senses. The dead linger. Current science does not understand this. It does in a later time, not that time means anything to you, a god yourself. Linda's mother isn't in Tiggs' house, though. She is content elsewhere, but eager spirits, forceful ones, swirl about, trying to break through. They can't. They almost never do. Tiggs feels a presence just the same. A tingle runs along his arms. He closes his eyes and sees the figure of a war god, red and glorious, bare-chested, holding a sword. Tiggs' pulse races. His eyes fly open and he breathes hard. Suddenly he has no interest in seducing this woman. He wants her out of the house so he can open the Scotch he keeps above the stove.

For a moment, Tiggs bridges the gap between his mind and Jaydee's. It's Jaydee's vision he sees. No ghost. No god, but an ideal in Jaydee's head.

"We're done," Tiggs says. "The spirits are not aligned correctly." He releases Linda's hands. Tiggs returns her check. "Sometimes the dead are moody." The vision shakes his confidence, rattles him in a way he's never been before.

Confused, Linda gathers her coat, moves to the door. She does not know of the convocation of events: that Tiggs can sometimes read minds, that the mind he reads crouches outside the house, that Mars captures Jaydee's attention and causes him to think about an old novel he loves, that an infinite number of events have met to drive her from Tiggs' home.

She also doesn't know that a ladybug is flying right now toward the door she exits. The ladybug ate an aphid a moment before and had the energy to leave the iris. It could have flown any direction, but it only chose one, the one that existed in the ocean and has always existed.

Linda opens the door. The porch light comes on. At the same time, the ladybug lands on her cheek. She closes the door softly, afraid to jar it.

Jaydee hides only two feet from her behind the thinnest screen of leaves. The quickness of her exit surprises him. Linda moves her finger under the bug on her cheek. The porch light bathes her in a soft, yellow glow. Her hair, catches the light too, haloing her head in a nimbus. She is slightly twisted, one hand on the door as she turned away, the other moving on her cheek. She looks like a princess, not in her dress, but in her posture. Self possessed. At home within herself. Royal. Dignified. Jaydee sees the ladybug, red on her skin. He doesn't connect the ladybug's color with Mars, but his chest swells when he realizes she is saving it, the smallest of gestures, yet Jaydee nearly chokes on the tenderness. Linda moves her hand with the ladybug toward the bush by the door. She waits while it walks off her finger onto a leaf. Her eyes widen and lock on Jaydee only a foot deeper in the bush.

Jaydee says, "Don't go home. Your husband thinks you are having an affair. He will kill you."

"You have been watching me?" Her voice doesn't shake. The scene is too surreal to feel frightening. It is out of her experience.

"He hired me."

Linda nods. She reorders clues in her head: how Bennett talks to her, the questions he asks, his behavior. Too, she hears conviction in Jaydee's voice. She looks toward the street. Her car sits under a light. She will drive to her sister's who lives a town away.

"What will you tell him?"

"He doesn't want the truth."

"Tell him I went south."

"Are you going south?"

"Not if you tell him I am."

Jaydee nods, rises from the bushes, his stethoscope dangling from his neck. He wonders if he will curse himself for sentimentality later, although he doesn't think so. Linda walks to her car while Jaydee watches. She's not a princess, he realizes. There still is an aura about her. It's her humanity and her kind moment on the porch. It's Mars a little higher in the sky, a reddish beacon to an imaginary world where a man become a hero.

Jaydee doesn't really know why he did it. His client won't be happy. Jaydee probably won't be able to collect on the job. He's wasted several days, but he's not sad. Strangely, he's buoyant. He's almost to his car when a thought occurs to him. He returns to Mark Tiggs' porch, knocks on the door. Warns him.

It seems the right thing to do.

Jaydee hasn't done the right thing for a long time. The world's a strange place, he thinks. Who knows why anything happens?

You do, though. You know.

The ocean is vast. This story is a drop in it, almost impossible to extract from the rest of the sea since all is connected. Almost impossible, but not for you. You are God. You know that everything connects to everything somehow.

Like you know that on Pluto, a long sheet of water ice between two boulders in the stygian black cracks the entire length, shifting one boulder several inches. It changes a picture the *New Horizons* spacecraft takes of the surface. An astrophysicist notices, and later that impacts the Kentucky Derby. It stops a war. It cures a disease.

That's the way of the universe.

You are God.

You know.

ORPHANED

THE BOY SAT CROSS-LEGGED IN THE MIDDLE OF THE FLOOR, CHANTING NAMES: "Metis, Adrastea, Amalthea, Thebe . . ." He said them to calm himself. His mom told him, "Facts fight fears."

He climbed into Dad's chair by the communication console where he surveyed buttons, toggles, sliding switches, small joysticks and an array of lights. Some blinked, some were green. One was red. A countdown timer clicked off numbers methodically: "0D, 2H, 12M, 8S." The 12 became 11 while he watched.

He pressed a button. His dad always pressed buttons when he sat here. "Ethan to Dad and Mom," he said. The speaker above a small video screen that displayed nothing remained silent. Ethan tried his call again. Dad made calls too, except he said, "Captain Ramis to Relay Central" to talk to his bosses, or "Base to Mobile One" when he called Mom. She said the same thing when she sat in that seat, but she'd be calling Dad. Someone always answered when they called. Mobile One would answer on its own if Mom and Dad were in the habitat. It could explore independently. "It has a bright AI," Dad said.

But no one answered. He was sure he pressed the right button. He'd seen Mom and Dad use it a thousand times, but they also adjusted dials before making a call. He didn't know what the settings were. He murmured, "Io, Europa, Ganyemede, Calisto."

Through the tiny port beside the communication array sat Mobile One, eighty yards away on Io's uneven surface. Something happened to it: the six-wheeled car was canted to the side, lying on its single door, the top pressed to a rock, crushing the communications array. "Ethan to Mom and Dad," he said again. "Are you okay?"

Behind him, Mom had hung a "Happy Birthday" banner over the dining room table. She and Dad had been figuring out how to make a cake for him before they'd left. They'd wrapped a present that sat in the table's middle. "I'm five today," thought Ethan. "Today's my birthday." Mom would hold him close and call him her "little miracle." Dad bounced him on his knee when he sat at his workstation. He played games with him. He read to Ethan and said he was their "science project." He said, "You, my child, are a 'misappropriation of resources,'" then laughed and hugged him.

"Station, why aren't they answering?"

The station said, "The Mobile One Rover appears to be incapacitated."

"What if they're hurt?"

"My medical facility is top notch. It can print skin, major organs, eyes, and other desired replacements. It can also diagnose and treat most known illnesses."

"Call Relay Station. They'll help."

"Relay Station will not be within range for four more days. You will have to be brave."

"Shut up, Station." Ethan hated AI pep talks. It was always telling him to work hard or be happy or to "solve the problem."

Ethan went back to the port. In the distance, one of Io's numerous volcanoes spewed sulfur dioxide into the sky. Sunlight caught the flume, turning it into a sparkling fountain.

If he could call Relay Station himself, he would, even though Mom and Dad warned him to never talk to them. They sent him from the room when they called. "They don't know about you," said Mom. She told him when he went to bed about their journey to Io, about how they were to man the station for seven years before coming home. "We were too lonely," Mom said, "so you came along. You're our secret child. You're a treasure and twice as precious."

Ethan checked the countdown timer again. 0D, 2H, 7M, 49S. It was the air supply in Mobile One.

"Are they okay? How's their telemetry?" No one told Ethan that he had a strange vocabulary for a five-year-old. In fact, it wasn't unusual for someone raised the way he was. He knew words like silicate, caldera, Colchis Regio, and he knew that Io was subject to tidal heating. He could disassemble and reassemble a space suit, and he could sort and store rock samples. He could name Jupiter's sixty-three moons.

"No telemetry data is available from Mobile One."

"Is there air in the rover? Has it ruptured?" Ethan swallowed heavily. He knew about vacuums. Outside the habitat was beautiful but empty and deadly cold. Jupiter filled half the sky, white, gray and orange striped, always changing and always huge.

"No telemetry data is available from Mobile One. But your parents wear space suits when in the rover. Even if there was a loss of pressure, they could survive."

Ethan grabbed handholds and propelled himself through the living area and work area, barely touching the floor in the light gravity, past hydroponics and the power plant until he was in the garage. Mobile Two stood under the lights, a duplicate of the rover marooned outside the station. Access covers were open. Wires led to panels on the walls. "Can we fix Mobile Two?" said Ethan.

"It has no AI," said Station.

"I don't need it to be smart. Can we drive it?"

"The AI controls the complicated gearing in the wheels, adjusts life support, and is the coordinator for all mechanical operations. Without the AI, the rover cannot be operated safely."

Ethan climbed up the vehicle's side to the cabin. "We're only going to Mom and Dad."

Inside the vehicle were two rotating seats and numerous control panels. Mom and Dad took him for rides many times. They used one set of controls to drive it and another manipulated the mechanical arms on the front and back. Once, Mom let him move the arms. He stretched them out from the rover, opened their clawed hands, and drug them through the sulfur dioxide frost that covered the surface.

"Is this strong enough to set Mobile One upright?"

Station said, "Mobile Two suffered damage in a quake five years ago. It cannot maintain cabin pressure. It cannot be operated safely without the AI. You will not be able to control it efficiently to effect a rescue. This line of questioning is not brave; it is foolish."

"Tell me how to get Mobile Two ready to move."

The Station didn't answer.

"Don't be such a baby!" yelled Ethan.

Ethan tried not to imagine that he was already too late. Dad told him once while they were doing one of their regular safety inspections, "The universe doesn't forgive mistakes." They were checking the motion dampers the station rested on. If one failed, any of Io's regularly occurring, strong quakes could shake the station to pieces. "Io is like a big ball of putty," Dad said. "Jupiter's gravity and the other moons squeeze and pull on it all the time. The surface rises and falls more than a hundred yards per cycle. It's like being in an elevator."

Maybe Mom and Dad made a mistake.

"Themisto, Leda, Himalia, Lysithia." Ethan detached power cables like he'd seen his parents do before. The heavy connectors were hard for him to budge. He had to grip with both hands, brace a foot against Mobile Two and pull.

"How much time, Station?"

"One hour, twenty-one minutes. I have run diagnostics on Mobile Two. The cabin may not hold air. The heating units are off line. The vehicle has not moved on its own power for one thousand, eight hundred and twenty-five days."

Ethan ran around the rover, disconnecting wires and closing panels. "Is it strong enough to push Mobile One off its side?"

"Yes . . . probably, but, Ethan, if you lose your air and freeze, you will not have saved anyone. Your parents will not approve of you doing this."

"What I need is a spacesuit that fits."

"One does not exist."

"Can you help me drive Mobile Two?"

"I can remotely monitor rover status. I can answer questions." The speakers whispered. Station hadn't finished talking but was deciding how to phrase its thought. "If you leave, I will be lonely."

Ethan worked grimly, silently. Station sang songs to him at night, read him poems, played word games. When Mom and Dad worked, Station was his friend. It cheered him when he was sad.

Station said, "If the cabin loses pressure, the liquids in your skin will boil away, lowering your temperature precipitously. This will be painful. The garage depressurizes in sixty seconds. It repressurizes in five minutes. A human being loses consciousness in fifteen seconds in a vacuum."

"If you can't be helpful, stop talking." Ethan opened a locker, pulled out a reflective blanket and tossed it into the rover.

"Elara, Carpo, Euproie, Thelxinoe." The chanting quieted his breathing. He circled the rover. All the cables and wires were detached. The pathway to the garage door was clear. He started to climb the ladder, then jumped off and ran back to his sleeping area. In his toy box, he found the six-inch-tall astronaut his parents had printed for him. Mom called it an "action figure." The miniature stood resolutely with his feet apart, hands on his hips, looking up as if he expected to rise on his own in a moment. Ethan called him Alpha-man. Alpha-man explored new planets, he made friends with alien creatures (Mom and Dad had printed them too), and Alpha-man always knew what to do. Mom told him Alpha-man adventures before he went to bed.

Ethan put Alpha-man on the mission specialist seat in the rover, while he fastened himself into the pilot's seat. A push of a button, and the door closed with a pneumatic finality, popping his ears as the cabin established its own pressure. He threw a switch that turned the garage lights to flashing red. Air rushed from the space. At first the pumps sucking the air away sounded loud. Then the noise faded. Ethan listened intently. Was there a hiss? Of all the sounds on the habitat, leaking air was the one he feared most. Twice he'd discovered leaks after large quakes. As powerful as the motion dampers on the station were, a heavy shaking strained the structure. Doors automatically closed to isolate compromised areas. Mom and Dad sprinted to make repairs. In every room, sealant and patching material stood ready.

The panic always started with a hiss.

No hiss. Just steady fan noise. The garage doors opened outward, revealing Io's dim surface. Dad told him that the sun lit Io's surface about the same brightness as on Earth right after the sunset. Ethan had seen pictures of Earth. The sun's brightness during the day didn't look as weird to him as a sky without stars or Jupiter's looming presence.

Controls on Mobile 2 were straightforward. One joystick steered while the other changed speed. The AI adjusted power to the wheels depending on the traction. Mom told him that driving across Io was like navigating a field of concrete bubble wrap. Lava flow created the moon's surface. Gas-filled cavities and lava tubes formed beneath the elastic rock before cooling, some very thick, but some parchment thin. Broken bubbles, like cracked egg shells, scattered across the plain, monstrous gaping holes rimmed with silicate rock, iron and iron sulfate teeth.

"How much time?"

"Thirty-seven minutes."

"Euantha, Helike, Orthosie, Locaste."

Ethan slid the joystick forward. Electric wheels clicked into motion; the rover lurched and then stopped.

Station said, "You must continue to press the joystick forward or Mobile Two will halt. I'm detecting a slight air leak in the cabin. The rover will automatically compensate by pumping in more air."

Ethan felt good. He was three feet closer to rescuing his parents, seventy-nine yards to go, so he pressed the joystick, following the path Mobile one had taken.

"Why did they fall over? They've driven this way a thousand times."

"Without readings, I would guess an undetected sinkhole."

The rover cleared the garage doors, jerking forward, allowing Ethan to see more of Io than was visible from the habitat. A second volcano sprayed beyond the horizon, marking Jupiter with a silver haze.

He wrapped the blanket tightly around his shoulders. Without heating units, the air that blew into the cabin was already cold. Beyond that, the heat he carried with him quickly dissipated. His breath blew out in frost.

"Your air leak is increasing, Ethan." Station sounded desolate.

A slight whistle sounded from the door, and the blowers redoubled their efforts, but Mobile Two advanced steadily. Now, it was only twenty yards away. He saw a light from Mobile One's cabin that he hadn't been able to see before. It glowed on the rock the rover had fallen against, so it still had power. The wheels on the left side had broken through the brittle surface. What had been a level path yesterday now had a pothole large enough to tip Mobile One.

The whistle raised in volume. Ethan swallowed to clear his ears. "Praxidike, Harpalyke, Mneme, Hermippe."

Ten feet from the crippled rover, Ethan slowed Mobile Two. He gasped a little for breath, and he realized his nose was bleeding. His face and hands lost feeling. The forward arms took a minute to unship. At first, they wouldn't move. Ethan shoved the control forward that should have extended them, but they only whined. Then he remembered and threw a toggle that released them. A heavy thump from the rover's roof told him they were free.

"If you lose air pressure, you will have fifteen seconds of consciousness," said Station.

Ethan maneuvered the arms so he could scoot them under the fallen rover. "That is not helpful." He wished there was a window in back that he could see through. Were his parents okay? If he could right the vehicle, and the door wasn't jammed shut, they could walk to the habitat. Dots swam in front of his eyes. He tapped the joystick that moved Mobile Two forward. The hands slid through the yellowish frost, under the metal. He pulled the lever back. If the hands held, if Mobile One wasn't too heavy, if his parents were alive, this could work.

Servos inside whined in protest. The arms were designed for medium to light tasks, like collecting samples or moving rocks, not picking up an entire exploration vehicle.

Station said, "Oh, no. Be brave."

With a pop, an entire section of seal around the door gave way. A whirlwind stirred dust and a scrap of paper. Alpha-man flew off the mission specialist's chair. Stuck to gap in the door for a second, then fell. Twin ice picks jammed into Ethan's ears. He screamed but couldn't hear it as his lungs emptied themselves. No air came in when he inhaled. His eyes burned. Bubbles formed on the backs of his hands. Everything in him shrieked with pain, but Mobile One stirred! Ethan held the joystick back. His face, his arms, all of him seemed to swell.

Fifteen seconds is what Station said. Slowly Mobile One tipped toward upright. Time slowed. Surely fifteen seconds had passed, but he could still see what was happening. Ice crystals formed in his mouth and nasal passages. Pain. Pain. Pain. He held on. He held on.

"Thyone, Ananke, Herse . . ."

A flicker . . .

He dreamed.

Mom leaned over him.

"Aetne, Kale, Tygete . . ."

I'm awake, he thought.

A flicker . . .

Dad examined Ethan's arm. "His skin is freeze dried. Muscles ruined." Dad pulled on the skin. It flaked away. Broke off in chunks. Ethan felt nothing.

A flicker . . .

His arms were naked metal rods that ended in shiny metal skeleton hands. Ethan couldn't move.

"We'll reprint the damaged parts. We can build him again."

Mom said, "Is the AI intact? Is he still Ethan?" She looked down on him. Ethan tried to show her that he was there, but nothing moved. He couldn't even blink.

Dad thought for a moment. "I think so. A rover's AI is built for abuse. A freezing wouldn't wipe it clean."

Ethan saw Mom's hand coming down. She must be touching my head, he thought.

"So he'll still be my little boy?"

Dad smiled. "Far as I can tell. He's come a long way from being a wiped rover AI."

Station said, "He's not dead? You can make him again?"

Mom and Dad nodded.

Station sobbed.

MOTHER AZALEA'S SAD HOME FOR FORGOTTEN ADULTS

TAD ROLLED MRS. YOST TOWARD THE MOVIE HALL WHERE WE WERE SHOW-ing last year's remake of *Shane*. Her chin rested on her chest, and her white hair was so thin that freckles on her scalp showed through. She was ninety-one. Like everyone, her backstory was interesting. She'd been a mother twice, a grandmother once. Her first child died in the 2031 Estonian dustup. Mrs. Yost had been a dancer, a teacher, and a mayor. Undoubtedly, if I pursued her biography deep enough, I'd find a great narrative. Everyone had a great narrative, when I spent time with it. But she was ninety-one and her story ended years ago.

"How's her QL?" I asked. Tad, looking particularly androgynous, put his/her, whatever, fingers against the old woman's neck. His smooth features caught the sun benignly. Of course, he was designed to look benign.

"Fifteen, I'm afraid, Director Brandt," he said. "A two-point slip."

Mrs. Yost sighed. Tad's fingers had left an oily residue on the wrinkled neck. He dosed her with something. Probably an anti-depressant. Maybe some vitamins or a hormone supplement. Nothing for me to do. Watching them slide reminded me how helpless I was in the face of their decline.

I must have looked depressed myself. Tad touched my wrist before I could move, read me. "Sixty-four, Director Brandt. You've dropped. Can I give you some-thing?"

I pulled my cuff down to cover where he'd touched. "No, I'm good."

Nice weather brought many residents to the courtyard. Bev pushed Mr. Ham-mond's chair toward the fountains. Ric sat with Mr. Claussen by the rose garden. Bob walked behind Mrs. Black, holding onto the thick support belt in case the old woman couldn't control the walker. I'd seen each this morning, checking their meds, and monitoring their QLs. A little redundant, really. The resident assistants like Tad did the actual work, diagnosing and dosing, along with guiding residents through physical therapy, getting them to and from the cafeteria, preparing them for bed, gathering their laundry and cleaning their rooms. No job was too messy, and they never grew impatient. My work was talking to families when they enrolled their relatives. It's a personal service we offer at Mother Azalea's.

Meg walked beside a young man in an electric wheelchair he guided with a chin joystick. She bent, whispered in his ear, then came toward me. "Would you like to meet Rocky Rhodes? He's moving into Mrs. Franck's old room."

I'd read Rocky's application last week. Twenty years old. Presented with fast moving adolescent ALS. I'd never seen a case like his. ALS affected older people. Before he landed in the chair six months ago, his parents took him to Hawaii for his twentieth birthday, fulfilling a lifelong wish. No one expected he'd make his twenty-first. Meg said, "QL nineteen."

I whistled. QL: quality of life. Anything under fifty was miserable.

"Hi, Rocky. I'm Davis Brandt, Director of Resident Services. Most people call me Dave." He smelled like the mint we use in our massage lotions to prevent bed sores.

Rocky struggled to speak, clearing his throat several times. Dark, curly hair. Light brown eyes that were red and weepy underneath. Young features, like a fifteen-year-old. Hands set in a dead spider curl in his lap. "Nice to meet you," he said, finally. "Did you notice the cumulonimbus? It might storm this afternoon. Nothing like a good thunder buster, is there?" Once he started talking, he did pretty well. Very little slurring. "I'll bet you think my name is funny," he continued. "It's my parents' fault. They named my brother Dusty."

He smiled. Good control of facial muscles, although he'd clearly lost everything from the neck down.

"We're glad to have you here at Mother Azalea's. Can we get anything to make you more comfortable?" Which felt like a ridiculous question. With a QL of nineteen, people want morphine, or a short push over a long drop.

"Some dancers and a jazz band would be nice."

I laughed. Clouds rose up beyond Mother Azalea's, white and huge at their top, but dark below. For now, though, sunlight flooded the courtyard. I didn't laugh too often at my job.

Last night's rain washed the air clean, and long puddles darkened the sidewalk. Rocky had been right about the storm. Thunder woke me several times. I parked in my spot at the home.

Inside the main entrance to Mother Azalea's stood a long, cherry wood display table. Pearl's Flowers brought in a fresh bouquet every morning that they arranged in the middle. We reserved the rest of the table for resident art: clay sculptures, glistening pots, and ashtrays. On the wall hung paintings and drawings. The art show rotated. When a resident died, we took down his creations. It's too depressing to leave them. I picked up a heavy plate done with a gray glaze. Mrs. Yost did this piece a year ago, before she'd given up on the activity. Her fingerprints were visible on the edge. I wondered if she'd left the imperfection on purpose.

Tad joined me. "She passed last night." He held out his hand for the plate, which he put in a black plastic trash bag.

"Augmented or natural?"

"Her QL dropped below fifteen."

He reached out to touch me. It's built in, his mission to measure and diagnose. A QL number wouldn't do me any good, though. I leaned away, and he knew to leave me alone.

I moved a six-inch-tall bright purple glazed elephant to fill the space. "Make sure her charts are updated before you finalize them."

"Of course."

Tad stood perfectly still. I'd suggested a couple years ago that resident assistants be programmed to move when at rest. Even a soldier sways a little at attention. You don't think they do until you see a resident assistant who isn't moving. They're a statue or a photograph. It's creepy, like the smoothness of their skin. "I'm taking Mr. Rhodes out for some sun," he said. "We had to turn down his music last night. He likes it loud." He triggered into motion, walking toward the stairs to do his rounds.

"Oh, what did Mrs. Yost think of *Shane*?"

He looked back but kept moving. "I don't think she knew she was there."

Later, in the courtyard, Rocky drove his wheelchair from patient to patient, stopping for a bit with each. Some didn't respond, but others smiled. Mr. Glick who never talked to anyone grew animated. I couldn't hear, but Glick waved his arm as he made a point. Rocky nodded . Eventually, Rocky talked to everyone. Tad followed, implacable, unshakeable, a chronic shadow.

We don't see visitors often at Mother Azalea's. I get it. The home is out in the country and a long commute for most; plus, no one likes reminders of mortality. My first year here, I sat with a patient named Punky Chu. If you're a baseball buff, you might remember Punky. He shortstopped for a few years for the Houston Astros when they won the World Series twice in a row. He'd been fighting Hodgkin's Lymphoma for several years, but the cancer spread everywhere. His QL had hovered around seventeen for a month. Everything in his system that could go wrong went wrong except for his brain. He stayed rational right to the end. He grabbed my hand on the last day and said, "There're two kinds of people in the world. Those who come to Mother Azalea's, and those who will."

A smooth-faced RA came by, put her fingers on his neck briefly, taking a reading. She shook her head and mouthed to me, "Fourteen." By this time, Punky was too ill even for a wheelchair. I could wrap my thumb and index finger around his upper arm with room to spare.

It was the first time I saw the "mercy touch." The RA brushed her fingertips across Punky's forehead, leaving a gleaming trail that quickly absorbed into his skin. Almost all the medications are administered that way. The residents don't even know they're being dosed. They never struggle with taking their medicine. Treatments are accurate and adaptable to the patient's condition.

Punky's eyes glazed over, then he relaxed and seemed to sleep. I stayed until he passed, a half hour later.

I totally understand why we don't get visitors. They are dead when they come in. Their relatives mourn when they drop them off.

Rocky Rhodes, though, had a visitor. Her name was Kaytee Shimla. About Rocky's age with lovely straight black hair that hung to the middle of her back. "We started dating in high school," she said, "before he got sick." She kept her thin, dark features carefully composed, but she carried a handkerchief that she twisted back and forth.

"I'll take you to him."

A patch of sun shone through the window, blinding Rocky. He'd turned his head away from it. Kaytee went to him and rested her hand on his. "Hey, good looking," he said.

Embarrassed that no one had adjusted the blinds, I squeezed between the bed and the wall—the room was very small—and closed them, but Rocky cleared his throat. "Leave them open, please." He turned his head painfully toward me. "I like the warmth."

I left the two of them alone. Kaytee was crying while Rocky made consoling noises. Tad met me in the hall outside. "He's at sixteen."

I flinched and hoped Tad didn't notice. He'd try to read me again. "Really?" The QL scores are conglomerated from numerous measurements. The big four are discomfort, depression, prognosis and hope. When discomfort and depression are high, and the patient has lost hope, the QL plunges. This is why prognosis is a part of the formula. Otherwise any teenager with a stomach ache who just broke up with his sweetheart would bottom out on the scale. "He doesn't act like he's feeling poorly." To get a score under thirty, there has to be physical discomfort, but I could light my foot on fire and not drop to a sixteen.

"Readings show continuous pain from his arms, legs and back, and that's after Tramadol. He's requested that we don't administer antidepressants, even though brain scans show he's suffering profoundly. The fact that he converses is an anomaly. The course of his disease is irreversible. All indications show no reason for optimism."

Back in the room, Rocky and Kaytee held hands. He said something that made her laugh as she wiped her eyes.

Tad joined the tableau. With the light coming though the window, falling on the bedridden Rocky, Kaytee sitting beside him while leaning on the bed, and Tad standing beside, his fingers taking a reading from Rocky's neck, they all looked like models for a Dutch master.

I spent the afternoon revisiting ALS articles, Lou Gehrig's disease. Its first impact is the scariest: death of neurons. Everything beyond that is technical and meaningless because over and over the information described an unstoppable condition. Neurons die. Muscles weaken until, eventually, the lungs stop or a secondary infection kills the patient. A frightening number succumb because they can't swallow effectively and choke, or they aspirate food and develop pneumonia. No matter the end, the patient remains cruelly clear-headed. It was partly through activist ALS patients that quality of life decisions became so much a part of our routine at Mother Azalea's and centres like ours. No one argues more cogently for ending his life than the one who sees death's relentless approach.

Rocky's QL was sixteen, two points away from the end. When his number dropped, Tad would touch him as he did so often to take readings or administer treatments. It would feel like every other touch: kind, gentle and caring. Rocky would not know. He'd drift to sleep, his suffering done.

I watched the remake of *Shane* with the residents the afternoon that Kaytee visited. It featured quick cuts, a pounding score and long, lingering looks between Shane, the gunfighter, and Marian, the farmer's wife. They'd had a tete-a-tete behind the barn that turned romantic, which made me think about King Arthur, Lancelot and Guinevere. The eight-year-old son was precocious. The film wasn't that good. Being in a room full of residents all south of thirty on their QL didn't help. I've counseled patients in discomfort. It's like talking to someone wearing ear buds. They're listening to a different conversation. When it gets bad, that other conversation floods their senses.

I didn't see what the big deal about this film was until I watched the original later in my apartment. It's slow, even though Jack Palance as the bad guy is pretty good. I almost turned it off a couple times, but I hung on until the end and started crying. Shane knocks the farmer out to stop him from meeting Palance's character in a gunfight he would surely lose. Marian asks if Shane did it for her, and he says yes, and for her husband and little boy. There's gunplay. The bad guys die, but one shot hits Shane. He's bleeding at the end. The little boy calls "Shane, Shane, come back!" as the wounded fighter rides off.

I wondered what Rocky would think of it.

A week after Rocky checked in, Tad dropped by my office. A monitor that couldn't be seen from the door displayed residents' statistics. I could rotate through everything: calories, blood values, urinalysis, sleep duration, diagnosis, prognosis, medications, QL and numerous others. I'd sorted the residents by expected passing. Most didn't hit that list until they were ten days out or so. Of our eighty-two residents, twelve had a date next to their name. Rocky's QL had dropped to fifteen, and the program projected his passing tomorrow.

"How does he seem?"

"When he's awake he's . . . chipper. Still plays his music too loud." Tad held his hands folded at belt level. They were still. I remembered Kaytee's hands, wringing all she could from her handkerchief. Tad's hands, though, took measurements, dispensed medicine, and when needed, ended suffering. They never moved without purpose, and they didn't reflect emotions. He didn't have them.

"You said he's not on an anti-depressant?" I could see from Rocky's chart that he wasn't, but I had residents whose QL was in the fifties who complained more than him.

"No. He's profoundly depressed."

"As well he should be."

I flicked through screen after screen. Everything of Rocky's that we could measure, we measured. All tracked, and all bad. Yesterday, though, he passed me in the hall, a food tray on his lap. He was on a stomach tube, and hadn't eaten solids for two months. I said, "Trying to kill yourself, I see." He took a long time to speak, and clearly it was all he could do to do it. Finally, he got out, "Mrs. Thompson in the room next to mine is still hungry. I thought she'd like a sandwich."

After I watched *Shane* the second time, I looked the movie up. There's a theory that Shane is dying in the last scene. The bullet that hit him was fatal, but he doesn't say anything about it, even when the little boy discovers Shane is bleeding. Shane tells him to go home to his mother and says that everything is all right. It's a puzzling moment. Everything isn't all right if he's dying. His story is over, yet he tries to do a good deed.

Rocky's chair hummed as he churned toward Mrs. Thompson's room, a sandwich on his lap.

I brought up the housing assignments. Tad waited in his creepily non-moving mode, face completely blank.

"I'd like you to move Rocky to a suite this afternoon."

"Yes, sir," said Tad.

I made an adjustment to Rocky's billing, then picked up my phone.

At three in the morning, most residents sleep at Mother Azalea's, but old age and illness throw off lifetime rhythms. I sat in a folding chair in front of Rocky Rhode's suite. When I'd checked on him an hour ago, his breathing was phlegmy and laboured, like he breathed through wet cloth, as if he'd just been water boarded.

Mr. Hammonds thumped by with his walker while Bev followed. I checked his last QL on my tablet: twenty-seven. He'd made six circuits since I'd taken my position at midnight. I assumed he walked the four hallways, rested at his room, then started again. He had a maniacal, focused intensity and a practiced cadence. Where did he think he was going? Hammonds had been career military. Was he keeping his post? Patrolling a perimeter? Did he know that death trailed him only three paces back? Bev nodded at me as she passed. I'd reviewed Rocky's QL an hour earlier. Fourteen.

Tad turned the corner and walked the long corridor toward me. I pushed myself back so the chair rested against the door.

"Excuse me, Director," he said. "I need to check on Mr. Rhodes."

I looked at his beautifully made hands. As normal as mine. Knuckles, veins, fingernails. I couldn't take my eyes off them.

"No. We're letting him rest."

Tad hesitated. The resident assistants were strong. They had to be able to lift a patient from a bed, or help them out of the therapy pool. They were built to be quick enough to catch anyone from falling down. Sometimes the residents struck out in their dementia or frustration, and the resident assistant had to avoid the blow. Sophisticated programs controlled their actions, and we made them autonomous. A resident assistant could sit with a client and hold meaningful conversations. I'd spoken to them myself. At times it was easy to forget they were not, after all, people.

They made decisions and solved problems. I wasn't sure if I was a problem. With a touch, he could pacify me, put me to sleep, or worse.

"This is highly irregular, sir. I need to check his vitals. He's due for medications."

I swallowed dryly. My pulse throbbed in my throat. "I am taking care of Mr. Rhodes for tonight, and we are letting him rest."

"To break procedure, sir . . . is this the best course for this patient?"

"He's well tended, Tad. I'm relieving you temporarily. See to your other charges."

His eyes and expression told me nothing. Mr. Hammond continued down the hall on his inexorable route.

"As you wish, sir." Tad turned away, heading back the way he'd come.

I stayed all night. Tad could be tenacious. A bay window at the hallway's east end gradually lightened and the sun rose.

The room smelled of Rocky's sickness. Poor ventilation and a closed door for the night would account for that. He looked twisted under the sheets, as if he'd tossed and turned, which wasn't possible. His breaths were short, raspy, and a silence after one made me worry about the next.

When I opened the blinds, though, he watched. His eyes watered. The bed told me his QL had dropped to twelve. I'd never seen a twelve. The number said his discomfort, his misery were incomprehensible. In his head, he lived in another country, a hellish, inwardly turned self contemplation that should be gibbering for release, but Rocky's eyes didn't waver as I took a seat next to him and put my hand on his arm.

The trumpeter arrived first, his instrument case in hand. "Are you Davis Brandt?"

I nodded.

The sax player and cellist came together. "Did someone order a jazz band?" the sax man asked. While they unpacked their instruments, a woman pulling a hand dolly filled with drums and cymbals started unloading equipment. She assembled the high hat. "Good thing you have a big room." A man in a white zoot suit helped her hook the triangle and cowbell to the bass drum. His partner wore a blue, shoulder-padded blazer, a wide belt, and narrow split skirt that dropped to her ankles.

Tad came to the door, took a step toward Rocky. I waved him back.

"We have a play list," said the drummer. She set herself up behind the drums. "But we can take requests."

Rocky couldn't move, but his eyes turned to the band.

"Play your set."

"It'll be loud in here," the trumpet man said doubtfully.

"That's okay. He likes it."

I recognized the first tune, but I couldn't name it. Something upbeat. The couple in the Zoot suit and padded blazer danced in the open space beside the bed. Rocky's head nodded ever so slightly to the rhythm. At the door, other tenants gathered. Some in chairs. Some in walkers. The resident assistants too. All the three-lettered servants who did the work at Mother Azalea's, lending their aids to the forgotten adults. The drummer did vocals. Ella Fitzgerald tunes and Billie Holliday and Sarah Vaughan.

They played until noon, and somewhere along the way, Rocky fell asleep. His chest rose and fell as the band quietly packed their equipment. Tad stayed behind, unmoving.

I didn't move either. Maybe I fell asleep too. The room grew warm and bright as the afternoon sun reached across the floor and rested on Rocky's bed.

Shane, I thought, Shane. Come back.

Rocky passed on his own. Tad knew from the door. He came over and stood by me, his hand touching mine. I felt empty and clean, not sad. The music still rang in my ears. The beat reverberated. Tad touched my wrist, let his hand stay for a moment.

"How are you doing?" he said.

My breath caught before I answered. "I'm okay."

"I know."

I didn't ask him about my QL. The number didn't matter, but I knew it had to be high. In a world where Rocky could listen to a jazz band at the end and pass when he was ready, my number had to be good.

PIRATE READERS

KELSIE TAPPED HER DESKTOP™ RHYTHMICALLY, SWITCHING THE DIS-play's background image each time. As long as she interacted with the interface, it wouldn't flag her as being inactive. Mr. Dettis the instructional coach helped a student across the room from her, so she wasn't worried he would direct her to spend more "time on task." He moved with studied efficiency. Short, wiry, a mouth that never smiled. Close-set eyes. She checked her achievement status update: 27 percent through 8th grade social studies, 42 percent through math, the same with science, 11 percent through Spanish, 14 percent through 9th grade literacy, and only 33 percent through 7th grade P.E. It seemed like days since any of the numbers had moved.

School was *so* boring! More than that, it was claustrophobic. Almost no place to go where she wasn't watched—where she wasn't evaluated and measured. For being such a big building, it was the smallest place she knew.

Dettis followed the same route going from station to station, narrating in a monotone as he went. "Tom is working on an algebra problem. Tina has finished annotating a poem. Kipp is . . . asleep." Dettis nudged the student's shoulder. Kelsie knew she had at least six minutes before he'd check with her again. She slipped the book from her backpack, a forty-year-old paperback she'd bought online. Strictly illegal in school, of course, since her reading rate and comprehension couldn't be measured as it was when she read electronically. Also, she wouldn't keep a progress log, nor would she write chapter by chapter predictions of what would happen next in the book. In short, she was pirate reading, an offense that had cost her detention three times in the year.

She opened the old book delicately, careful with the yellowed pages, then sighed with contentment at the first sentence: "Petrified with astonishment, Richard Seaton stared after the copper steam bath upon which he had been electrolyzing his solution of 'X,' the unknown metal." She glanced at the chapter's subheading: "The Occurrence of the Impossible." That's what she wanted, the impossible, or at least a world where the impossible was a legitimate concern. At school, everything related to her "individual strengths and weaknesses," her "long term goal" and her "growth plan." All reading was mandated or chosen from the "developmentally appropriate independent reading list," mostly political non-fiction.

"What's the book?" whispered Gilbert, a tall, plump boy who wore his black hair short. He tapped his Desktop too.

"It's about space travel," she whispered back.

"Oh." Gilbert looked disappointed. "That's my alternate career track, communications satellites."

"No, not commercial applications. People going to space, like to other planets. It's an adventure with characters. It's . . . interesting."

"Why read? You can watch a movie."

"I get two recreational movie hours a week, just like you. The school suggests documentaries. That's not enough."

Gilbert glanced over Kelsie's shoulder, straightened and turned his attention to his work.

Kelsie slipped the book between her legs, and called up the multiple choice questions on the chart displayed on her desk. Question number one was "According to the graph, which month will Farmer McDonald have to increase his water requisition to save his crop?"

"Kelsie is reading a chart," Dettis announced. She sighed with relief.

At lunch, Gilbert lined up behind her. "Where do you get books like that without your parents finding out?"

Her tray popped out from the dispenser along with her nutritional goal card: I WILL CONSUME NO MORE THAN 140 GRAMS OF CARBOHYDRATES TODAY. She looked doubtfully at the main course, a pile of oily-looking brown rice with little orange cubes that might be carrots.

"Don't browse for books. That's a tip-off for sure. Search for household decor. There's a sub category for a den or study. Some people buy books for the retro look. Don't get leather-backed facsimiles. They cost a fortune and there's nothing inside them. But if you look under 'budget decorating,' you can order books with real pages. They sell them by the pound. You can also check antique stores, but they're pricey again."

"I don't know," said Gilbert wistfully. "I set up a fake name on our account at home when I was nine, and I downloaded some cool stuff. There was a graphic novel, and this great story called *Little Brother*. I don't remember who wrote it, but the school caught me. Mom and Dad were furious. 'You're derailing your education,' Dad said. If they catch me again I'll be chained to my desk."

"That's the best thing about these." She held up the book. "No trail. I've been reading in my room at night. I have a curfew, and my parents can tell when my lights are on, but my e-reader gives me enough light to see my book, and no one knows."

"Clever." Gilbert studied his tray, which held steamed vegetables and a serving of limp lettuce. "I'm cursed by a slow metabolism. If this doesn't work they're going to feed me cardboard. Do you have any extras?"

"Food?"

He blushed. "No, books."

She fished into her backpack, made sure no one was looking, and passed him her copy. "I have this title twice. Tell me what you think when you're done."

That night, Kelsie read under the covers about Dick Seaton and his rival Mark DuQuesne. She found herself smiling at the science, which was terrible, but also hopeful. Seaton built a spaceship, the *Skylark* to rescue his kidnapped fiancée and 'Peg' Spencer. There were battles and aliens and marriages. When Kelsie fell asleep, she dreamed about floating above far planets, about suns with strange light, about looking out her window and seeing possibilities.

"That was so good," said Gilbert. He had put the book in a bag to return to her, but seemed reluctant to hand it over. Kelsie didn't know the short girl with spiky red hair standing beside him. "Bernice wondered if she could borrow it. And I wanted to know if there was a sequel. I was going to look it up, but the instructional coaches notice and change my reading lists. I searched for information on sailing once, and for months, all my reading excerpts were about boats. I just wanted to know the difference between port and starboard."

Kelsie nodded. Everyone's curriculum was based on aptitude and interest. She'd started reading science fiction a year ago and used her computer to look up Connie Willis, a writer who used to be famous. After that, her reading selections at school became science fictional, which would be a good thing except that the selections were never the entire work, and reading that way wasn't fun. She remembered in particular a two paragraph section from Ursula Le Guin's "The Ones Who Walk Away from Omelas," but the questions weren't on what Kelsie felt about the story or her thoughts; they asked what rhetorical strategy Le Guin used, and then there were a bunch of questions about mood and tone. She really wanted to read the whole story, but she couldn't find the complete tale without provoking extra excerpts she would have to respond to.

She'd asked Mr. Dettis why they were never assigned novels, and he said, "You do not need a long work to learn how to analyze text. Novels take too much time."

Nothing in her life encouraged her to read less than her literacy class.

Bernice lent *The Skylark of Space* to Debra who lent it to Richard. Richard returned the book to her with rubber bands around it to keep the pages together. In the meantime, Kelsie tracked down the sequel, which was confusingly called *Skylark Three*.

She passed it to Gilbert while Mr. Dettis went through a presentation on maximizing multiple-choice test scores.

"How old do you think he is?' whispered Kelsie.

"Forty-nine. It's on the school's profile."

Dettis reminded them to start by eliminating the least likely answers, a strategy Kelsie learned her first year in school. "Why in the world would he take a job like this?"

"I saw him at the mall once with his family. He's really a pretty nice guy. He's budded, you know."

"Budded?"

"Yeah. My mom teaches in the elementary school. They give her an earbud that coaches her as she teaches. They're monitoring her performance, and feed her scripts. She says that it's the school trying to guarantee students receive the best education, but I don't think she likes it."

"Eww, that's terrible."

Both her and Gilbert's Desktops chirped a warning that they were not taking notes. She turned to her display and wrote, "Ignore bad choices."

At lunch, Gilbert, Bernice, Debra and Richard sat with her.

"I almost got caught last night," explained Richard, a pale, blond boy who chewed his fingernails when he was nervous. "I was in bed. My sister came in. I didn't even hear her. Fortunately, my back was to the door. She didn't see it."

Debra said, "My parents have books in the living room. They're all in French or something. Dad dusts them on the weekend when he cleans house. I've never seen him read one though."

"There are other authors who write this kind of stuff, right?" said Bernice. "I love the space part of the story, but the women don't do anything. I could imagine parts of it excerpted, and one of the answer choices would be, DEMONSTRATION OF SEXIST ASSUMPTIONS."

Kelsie bristled. "That's possible, but a likelier one would be, REFLECTION OF THE TIME'S CULTURAL ATTITUDES. Here, try these." She gave Bernice *The Shore of Women* by Pamela Sargent; Debra took Frederick Pohl's *Gateway*; Richard received Lois McMaster Bujold's *Dreamweaver's Dilemma*, and Gilbert got the *Skylark Three* title. "When I buy them by the boxful, I don't get to choose what's in it. I have other kinds of books. There's western, fantasy, mystery, thriller and horror. Do you want to mix it up?"

They shook their heads.

Kelsie shrugged but understood. "We'll stick with science fiction for now."

Dad met her at the door when she came home. "I found these in the basement." He pointed to paperbacks he'd stacked on the dining room table. "We have talked about this behavior before, young lady."

Kelsie tried to act casual. She laughed. "It's an industrial arts project, Dad.

Multimedia. I'm learning how to work the carving laser. Paperbacks are cheap, they carve easily, and I can assemble the whole thing with paper glue. It's way better than the aluminum structure some kids are doing."

"Did Instructional Coach Dettis assign this?"

"No, he's academic. This is vocational."

"Wouldn't paper burn?"

"Charred edges are a feature of the piece."

Dad looked carefully at her while stroking his chin. "I think you're putting one over on me."

Kelsie held her breath.

"If you can push your achievement numbers up at school, I won't tell your mom about the 'art supplies.'"

In the next month, the pirate reading group added two more members. Bratton liked Larry Niven's *Ringworld* so much that he paid her rather than returning it, while Tyra asked only for horror titles. Kelsie gave her Stephen King and Clive Barker, but when Tyra got a taste of Lovecraft, that's all she wanted.

Kelsie found Dorothy Haley at the bottom of the box under a James Patterson title (there were a lot of Patterson books). Haley wrote *Red Star Triumphant*. The cover showed a silver-blue spaceship crossing a bloodshot sun. Kelsie hadn't finished by dawn and was still reading when called for breakfast. She padded to the top of the stairs and called down. "I have a headache, Mom. I think I should stay home today." After the usual checking of her temperature and the inevitable, "Maybe I should take her to the doctor," which Kelsie assured them would not be necessary, she went to bed. Soon, both parents left for work. Kelsie opened the book, which was newer than many the company sent her. She buried her nose in it. It even smelled good. Stomach down on the bed, her chin lapped over the edge, she let the book rest on the floor. Jewell Ripkin, the *Innisfree*'s captain, had lost touch with her crew while exploring the giant derelict ship they'd discovered. Kelsie turned the pages, drifting from her bedroom. Captain Ripkin trusted her sensors that told her the air within the ship was breathable. The first lungful was a welcome change from the suit that recycled what she breathed. Now, helmet off, ship sounds were clear. Somewhere, a light ringing, like a thimble on metal caught her ear. What could be making the noise?

Kelsie read until she realized she was hungry. It was nearly 5:00. Her parents would be home soon.

At school, Gilbert leaned into her cubicle. "They caught Tyra. She's in the principal's office now."

"Is it about pirate reading?"

"I heard Dettis talking to her. She used vocabulary in her last essay they couldn't account for. He said, 'Where'd you get cyclopean, eldritch and gibbous?'"

"What was she supposed to be writing about?"

"Rhetorical strategies in George Washington's inaugural address."

"Gibbous?"

Gilbert said, "Yeah, I don't know how either."

Kelsie stiffened. Getting caught would be her fourth strike. If Tyra told who gave her the book, she'd be moved to a high supervision academy. Instead of Dettis visiting her a few times an hour to check on her progress, she'd be in a constantly monitored class. No time to call her own at all. She envied the kids who learned independently. Most didn't leave their homes except for field trips. They could read all they wanted as long as their learning objective were met.

She said, "You've got to hold my book. If they search my backpack, I'm done for."

Gilbert shook his head. "She could give us all up. Either Tyra stays quiet, or we're sunk even if we don't have books on us."

Kelsie tried to focus on her Desktop, her heart pounding. It was a history lesson. She was supposed to read three excerpted articles about Joseph McCarthy and the Cold War, watch a short video, listen to a speech, and then write an essay that synthesized the material into "an original argument." She'd done this kind of prompt numerous times. After she submitted it, her Desktop would instantly spit back the piece with all mistakes marked, questions about her thoughts ("What did you mean in paragraph two?" "Can you strengthen your third argument with another reference?" etc.), and a graph that showed where her essay scored compared to both her previous writing and to other students who had responded to similar assignments.

She couldn't remember the last time she'd written about anything that mattered to her.

But maybe if she looked really involved in the essay, Dettis wouldn't stop at her station. He wouldn't put his hand on her shoulder and say, "Can you come with me?" to ask her about the books.

Dettis didn't talk to her.

At lunch, Trya said she sat outside the principal's office for an hour. When she went in, he said that there had been a mistake and that she could return to her desk.

"Weirdest thing ever," Tyra said.

Gilbert said, "We were just lucky. We should dump the books and pretend to be normal kids."

Kelsie looked down the table at them, her little pirate reading group. Bernice, Debra, Bratton and Richard hadn't said anything. She didn't know how they felt. She thought about how much she looked forward to discussing what she read with them and hearing their reaction to books she'd shared. Gilbert was probably right. There was no way they wouldn't get caught and her role in the group exposed.

What would Captain Jewell Ripkin do?

At home she sat on the top stair into the basement. Her parents wouldn't be home for hours. Kelsie had laid the books out on the floor. Not counting the ones she would never give away (she'd found another Dorothy Haley book called *Bone Singularity*), almost 200 paperbacks stared up at her. She could shut the group down, read the books herself, even the non-science fiction ones, and never share. At least she could still be a pirate reader. She sat for a long time before packing them into the boxes and hiding them again.

Late at night, lying awake in the dark, she realized what Ripkin would do. There was only one solution.

Her backpack weighed heavy on her shoulder as she walked into school. The students who learned best early in the morning were already there. Others, whose biorhythms peaked later were yet to arrive. A couple of instructional coaches passed her in the hall. She couldn't tell if they were budded, but the coaches when they weren't in their classrooms always sounded livelier. She suspected they didn't put the earbuds in until they were in class.

Kelsie went to the girl's locker room first, a place where there were no video cameras. Lockers only locked during classes, so she picked one in the corner, where whoever used it would have more privacy, and she put a book in it. This morning she'd used a permanent marker on a blank name tag to write, IT'S AGAINST THE RULES TO READ THIS BOOK, and then drew a little skull and crossbones. The sticker went on the back to save the cover image. She put another one in a locker on the other side. The third book went into a stall in a bathroom. She looped a string through the fourth and fifth book to hang in a coat closet.

When Kelsie headed to Dettis's room, the backpack was five books lighter and she felt as if the gravity in the school had changed. She was Captain Ripkin on the bridge of the *Innisfree*, rocketing forward. Those books couldn't be traced to her. She thought of them as idea grenades she'd rolled into the building.

The feeling only lasted until she saw a book she'd brought in the trashcan. At lunch she saw another thrown out, and when she left school for the day, the janitor swept a paperback with his big push broom along with dust, dirt and paper scraps. He pushed the mess into a dustbin. The IT'S AGAINST THE RULES TO READ THIS BOOK sticker was clear just as the book tumbled from sight.

Kelsie walked home, her head hung down. Nobody read the books. They were just thrown away! But the longer she walked, the better she felt. Sure, three books were lost, but maybe the other two found homes. Maybe even now some kid was reading it, free from curriculum, reading just for fun.

She prepared five more stickers and put them on the books. If she placed five a day, it would be forty school days before she ran out.

That night, she dreamed about long space voyages and heroes, about acceleration couches and airlocks. In her dream, she stood at the spaceship door, looking out on a strange landscape and smelling a distant sea. She woke happy. By the week's end, she'd dropped twenty-five books in the school. Were people finding them? If they were, they hid it well, but she felt good while doing it.

Mr. Dettis stopped at her desk before she'd even opened the program to where she'd stopped yesterday. "I need you to come with me." He held a paperback under his arm. Kelsie didn't need to see it to know a pirate reading sticker was on it. She started to speak.

He frowned and shook his head.

Dettis lead her from the classroom toward his office. Silent, Kelsie followed, convinced that everybody they passed knew she was in trouble. Moving to the high supervision education unit would be bad enough. Only the worst kids needed that kind of instruction, but her parents would be furious. She clutched her hands in front of her. Maybe if she ran?

Mostly she felt the weight of *Bone Singularity* in her backpack. She'd just started it. If Dettis confiscated the book, she didn't know if she could get another copy. It would be like "The Ones Who Walk Away from Omelas," but a thousand times worse.

A long haired boy, looking miserable, sat in a chair outside of Dettis's office. He didn't glance up as they passed through the office door. She settled into a stiff wooden chair without a seat cushion in front of Dettis's desk,. Dettis closed the door behind her. He moved behind his desk, then carefully dug into his ear. A flesh-colored button popped out.

"Okay, now we can talk." He opened a cabinet and pulled paperback books out by the handful, stacking them in front of her. "You're not the only pirate reading group in the school, you know."

"What?"

More books joined the first ones. They weren't titles she recognized. "There's a fantasy group going pretty strong. I've identified four readers in that crowd, and another that leans toward techno-thrillers. There's three in that, but you're the only one doing guerrilla distribution." He put the book with her sticker in front of her. "What do you have to say for yourself?"

Kelsie thought about dozens of replies. Some were questions like, "Have you read books?" or "Don't you remember being a kid?" And some were defiant. "You can't control what I think" or "Nobody cares about what you have us read."

What she went with was, "How did you find out?"

"Word use in your essays, the same way I caught Tyra. I had to add words to old vocabulary lists to make it look like she had been exposed to that language before, just like I did for you." Dettis spread the rest of the books, covering his desk. "They're beautiful, aren't they?"

"Excuse me?"

"Beautiful, the books." Dettis picked up one with a hooped object floating in space called *Ringworld*. "I remember the first time I read this one."

Kelsie sagged back in her chair. "Whose side are you on? You're an instructional coach."

"Only when I'm wearing this, Kelsie." He pointed to the ear bud on the desk. "Before I got one of those, I was a teacher. Completely different job." He handed her *Ringworld*. "You might like this one."

She held the book on her lap. The edges were soft. It was a much-read copy. "I can keep bringing books to the school?"

"If you don't get caught." He returned the books to the cabinet. Four more cabinets just liked it lined the wall. Did books fill them all? "And you've got to improve your progress. Read what you want anywhere but at school."

"I don't know." Kelsie thought about *Bone Singularity*. Even now she wanted to take it from her pack to see what Dorothy Haley did on the first page. It also was all she could do to not open *Ringworld*. "That will be hard."

"There's nothing I can do. I would if I could, but I can help you with this. I can give you title suggestions. I can find authors for you. All the pirate readers can benefit if you'll be smart and work in the system."

Kelsie squeezed the book. Where would it take her? What other books could Dettis guide her to? "You're a pirate librarian!" she exclaimed.

He laughed. It was the first time she'd seen Mr. Dettis look happy. "I guess I am." He closed the cabinet and locked it. "So here's the deal. Don't read in class. Don't let anyone see you bringing in books. If you find something really good, let me know. Oh, and I've got someone I want you to meet." He opened the door to let the long-haired boy in.

"Troy," Dettis said. "This is the girl I told you about, Kelsie. Ask her the question."

Dettis picked up his earbud, but didn't put it back in. "Go to class when you're done."

He closed the door as he left. Troy looked embarrassed. His long hair covered his eyes. "Hi."

"Hi," she said.

"Mr. Dettis said you liked science fiction."

"I do."

"I . . ." He swallowed hard. "I wrote a story, actually a bunch of them, with space ships and aliens in them. On my own. Not for school. Mr. Dettis said you might read them and tell me what you think. He said you were my audience."

Kelsie was dumbstruck. If reading without the school knowing was hard, writing had to be twice as difficult. He would have to write it all by hand. No computer could check it.

Troy pulled a notebook from his back pack and held it out to her. Inside, the first page contained just a title in a tidy script, "The Jupiter Dilemma."

"You're a pirate writer," she said.

Troy blushed. "It's what's in my head."

His handwriting covered page after page. He'd even drawn illustrations. Characters in space suits. Rockets balanced on long exhaust tails. A comet streaking above an alien mountain range.

"I'm honored," said Kelsie. "Thank you for sharing your work with me."

"I have other notebooks." Troy moved the hair away from his eyes. They were deep blue.

Suddenly, the school didn't feel so small.

GRADUATION IN THE TIME
OF YOG SOTHOTH

JACKSON CLUNG GRIMLY TO HIS SEAT AS THE BUS RATTLED OVER A CORD-uroy stretch of road, tossing him against Gwynn. She held a flute case in her lap, while in the back of the bus, the rest of the flute section, seven girls and a boy, piped a discordant, screeching melody that wasn't improved by bouncing around as the bus lurched down the rough track. Gwyn wore her hair short, seldom used makeup, and he'd often seen her sitting in between classes working on a sketch pad.

"Weren't you supposed to play today?" said Jackson. The bus lurched left, pushing them the other way.

"Last week for seniors." She looked out the window. The woods that lined the road when they took the bus in kindergarten were now blasted, shattered and burnt fragments that stuck up from the ground in painful angles. "The underclassmen have to learn how to play without us."

Jackson nodded. Only five days until graduation. "Same with newspaper. The senior editors handed their duties over to the juniors the first of the month," which stung because Jackson had been the sports editor. He was sure Drew Whittier didn't have the same drive to get to the heart of a news story that he had. How would the fall preview go without Jackson's input? Did Drew have the same contacts on the football team? Did he know anything about cross-country? The section would be a mess.

It was hard to think, and even harder to be optimistic with the flutes shrieking behind him, but he wished they played louder, protecting them. Through the tinted windows, the low-hanging clouds swirled, glowing orange and red at their edges as if reflecting an unseen fire, a sure sign an Old One was about. Only flute music placated them, although that was no guarantee. Three years earlier the Forensic team didn't escape, even though they traveled with that year's state-championship flute section. Some of those kids were still in the school, in a separate room, tended by aids who pushed their wheelchairs about and fed them.

Gwyn leaned into him, "Do you have your speech ready?"

Jackson grimaced. "Everything I write sounds stupid. What do I say about our future? We might not even have a future." He'd been both proud and terrified when

Principal Akeley named him valedictorian. At the beginning of the year, Howard Durst and Emma Chen had higher grade point averages, but they found Howard in the library on Halloween, slack jawed and drooling after reading from The Book of Azathoth, which was supposedly locked up and unavailable to students, while Emma fell for a weirdly fishlike football player from cross-county rival, Dunwich High, and failed all her first semester classes except Mythology.

Gwyn said, "Write something hopeful."

The road to the high school entered Trimount Canyon where low, limestone bluffs rose on either side. Jackson relaxed. He felt safer within the stone walls. They'd be harder to notice here, but they hadn't gone a half mile before the bus slowed, then pulled onto the shoulder. Pale rock blocked the view out the windows across the aisle. Cloud-shrouded light illuminated the road through his window, though. The flute section redoubled their effort. A tremor shook the bus, then another. Dust drifted from the cliff walls as the sky darkened and grew more crimson.

"Put your heads down, kids," shouted the bus driver. "Heads down and stay down until I clear you to sit up. Just like the drills." She sounded calm, as if she did this every day. Even as Jackson pressed his chest into his knees, he marveled at how collected she was. Without the flutes, silence ruled.

The bus trembled again. Whatever Old One came their way was immensely huge and heavy. Would it step on them without even seeing them? Or would it pick them up, shake them about like pebbles in a box? Would it stare at them, sucking their minds into madness before he tossed them aside or dropped them down his terrible throat?

Gwyn grabbed his hand. They'd never held hands before. She was just a friend who'd been his classes since preschool, like many of the seniors.

She whispered, "Will you open with a joke? Last year's valedictorian told that great one about the three blind guys at a nudist colony."

An Old One had never come this close to Jackson. They left omens in the sky: blood moons, tortured clouds and foul winds; signs in the sea: unnatural tides, fish kills, strange eruptions, but never a genuine appearance. Like tornados or tigers or tsunamis: they were much talked about, often part of nightmares, but not actually real.

He knew when it passed over. The hairs on the back of his neck stood, and then a pull from above from the Old One's self-generated gravity. An icy, pure glacier abyss opened in the sky, as if the bus had turned upside down and longed to fall up. Jackson swallowed hard and clung to Gwyn's hand. A thought looped, faster and faster: If I survive . . . If I survive . . . If I survive.

Then his organs shifted. The pull released, and darkness relented.

Jackson breathed deep. "I don't know. A joke might be cheesy. I thought a shared memory like when Mrs. Peterson made hot fudge sundaes in kindergarten."

They hadn't sat up. Heads down, holding hands, Jackson felt as if they were alone somewhere, sharing a lifelong past. When the Old One eclipsed the sky, Jackson couldn't tell if he was feeling Gwyn's hand or if he was her feeling his hand. It seemed in that instant he saw the bus floor from his eyes and hers. For a blink, he sat in her mind, surrounded by her thoughts, being her, and he knew she'd become him. She hadn't been as scared as he was; she'd thought about painting the clouds— blending the orange into the red and the red into gray. That close to pure, psychic alieness, they'd joined. The power to drive a human mind mad must have degrees. They hadn't been taken over the edge, but they altered. Their skin melded; their nervous system became singular. The Old One, its mind more vast than human imagination, washed through them without bending from its alien mission and unknowable intents. Jackson had never been closer to anyone.

"Did you feel that?" Gwyn asked.

"Old One aura. Remember from the orientation?" He shivered. He couldn't feel more exposed if they sat next to each other naked. How would they look each other in the face again?

Gwyn stayed down. The bus driver hadn't freed them yet. Jackson could tell Gwynn searched for words. How would she process what they'd gone through? Would she be able to talk to him?

Finally, she cleared her throat. "I forgot about those sundaes." She squeezed his hand. "Every day was sunny then, even the rainy ones."

In the hallway, Jackson pushed past the Acolyte Club who'd set up tables against the wall with promotional flyers and pamphlets. "We're doing a chant around the flagpole after school to placate our benign overlords," said a sophomore boy Jackson knew from the newspaper. The boy had blue lines on both sides of his neck in nesting curves, imitating gills. Jackson couldn't tell if they were drawn or tattoos. Lots of kids had them, and many greased their hair and brushed it straight back from their foreheads, as if they'd risen from the ocean. Lately they sported large black buttons with yellow writing that read, Nothing Without Sacrifice.

"DBD," the kid said. "DBD, bro."

Jackson shook his head, refusing the flyer . DBD: Dead but Dreaming. Jackson thought, aren't we all.

Half the school belonged to the Acolyte Club. A group of teachers sponsored, slicking their hair back too. The rumor was that some of them encouraged the Acolyte Club to circulate the petition, asking the school board to change Kennedy High's college-oriented, liberal arts curriculum into a religious one. They listed classes they wanted to add to graduation requirements, including "Important Figures, Relics and Places from Abdul Alhazred to Zon Mezzamalech," "Sea Wisdom;" and "Intro to the Outer Mysteries."

Gwyn sat behind him in British Lit. Jackson took out his notebook with quotes he'd been collecting that he might use in the speech. She looked over his shoulder. "Is that Othello?"

Jackson turned back the pages, one by one so she could see. "Yep. Othello, Macbeth, Gilgamesh, the romantic poets and the realists, stuff from American presidents, movie quotes, song lyrics, advertising slogans, and stuff my parents say. Nothing has struck a spark yet."

He didn't want to meet her eyes, but she wasn't talking about the trip to school, which was good.

A couple girls a row over whispered to each other, looking Jackson and Gwynn's way.

Gwynn said, "The word is out about our close encounter. Everyone on our bus will be famous by lunch. What are you going to say about what happened?"

"I'm not sure I know what happened."

"Ask one of the Acolytes. They'll have an explanation."

Jackson almost laughed despite himself. "Will it involve the transmutation of souls or surrendering ourselves to the vast indifference of the universe?"

"I almost wouldn't mind the dissolution of self as long as they don't ask me to wear my hair like that."

Jackson said, "One of them told me that in madness lies sanity, and then asked if he could copy my Calculus."

"Everyone wants to copy your Calculus."

"You're not helping me with the speech."

"Do you want help?"

Jackson faced her. He hadn't ever looked at her eyes before, not with this attention. They were dark brown on the edges, fading into gold near the pupils. She's the girl with the treasure-well eyes.

During lunch, Principal Akeley looked up when Jackson entered her office. She often wore floral pantsuits. Today's ensemble leaned toward pinks and purples, as if a giant orchid had thrown up on her, but she had an unforced smile and liked to joke. Normally Jackson didn't mind talking to her, but not today. She'd want to know about the speech. Instead, she went a worse direction.

"Have you decided on a college, Jackson?" She put her hand on a short stack of brochures on the desk. "You missed the early application deadlines."

"Umm, not completely. Maybe the University of New Mexico in Albuquerque."

"Long way from home. Long way from the ocean."

"That might be the point."

"Why not Miskatonic?"

"M.I.T.?"

Akeley raised an eyebrow.

Jackson said, "Miskatonic in Town. Nobody wants to go to college that close to their parents."

Principal Akeley shook her head. "It's the same everywhere."

"Then does it matter? I was going to apply to Stanford." He regretted saying it. He didn't want to sound bitter. Paolo Alto didn't exist anymore. In its place, a four mile wide crater filled with the Pacific seethed and bubbled. Last summer, for weeks, news covered the disaster. They showed seabirds by the hundreds of thousands gathered on the shore, piping a terrible din, wheeling about in great clouds above the water, but never landing, and whatever stirred the unnatural bay didn't surface.

She hunched forward on her desk, and grew intense. "They don't care about us, Jackson. I don't believe they know we exist."

"Don't say that to the acolytes."

Akeley continued, "Today, on the bus, might never happen to you or anyone you know again. Stanford may never happen again. They could disappear as suddenly as they arrived. You can't make your decisions based on the worst case scenario."

"I know. I know. But it's harder for us, for the seniors, I think. What did you worry about in high school?"

The principal straightened her folders, then glanced at her clock, looking infinitely tired. Jackson realized she had other appointments. "The world changes. Growing up is challenge enough. How's your speech coming? You know I need to approve it first."

"I'll have something for you soon. Tomorrow after school?"

She squinted. "You haven't started it yet."

"Not the speech itself, but I've been thinking. I've gathered material."

"A lot of people depend on you to make a good show of it. Parents, alumni, the school board and all your peers. Give them something to think about."

They shook hands.

Outside her office, Jackson thought, way to take the pressure off, Akeley.

Jackson knew Gwynn was on her way before she appeared around a corner of the school a hundred yards away and walked toward the bleachers where he sat. All day he'd noticed ghost feelings: the weight of a pen in his hand when he wasn't holding anything, a necklace he wasn't wearing rubbing against his neck, an inhalation when he exhaled. They were Gwynn's experiences. He wondered if their link would fade.

She set her art portfolio and book bag on the bleacher, then settled onto the bench next to him. "Weird day, huh?"

"Indeed."

Something itched between Jackson's shoulder blades. He thought about trying to get to it, but he knew he'd look stupid stretching about.

Gwynn put her hand behind him and scratched at exactly the right spot.

"Thanks," Jackson said. They looked at the football field and clouds without speaking for a minute before he realized what she'd done. He glanced at her. She clasped her hands in her lap, sitting still. From the other side of the school, a dull, rhythmic mumble arose. He recognized the source: the chant at the flagpole. It would take a lot of acolytes to be that loud. The story of what happened with the bus had lit them up. Interruptions filled the afternoon as teachers reminded acolytes to stop whispering. Several times, Jackson caught an acolyte staring at him.

She said, "I got a C on my final art project."

"No way!" The yearbook had named Gwynn "Most Artistic," and the newspaper had written an article about her winning entry at the Massachusetts Art Institute High School Show in December. "How in the world did that happen?"

"Because of this." She pulled a small canvas from the portfolio. On it she'd painted an orange resting on a worn wooden table. A single rose lay before it. Behind both, a crystal pitcher, half full of tea, glowed warmly in sunlight from a window not in the picture. Even with his limited understanding of art, Jackson gasped. Something in the way she'd painted it made the shadows utterly real, and the orange's skin held and reflected the light.

"That's beautiful. What didn't she like about it?"

Gywnn laughed. "The assignment was a still-life, clearly, but she put on the table a dead rose, a broken pitcher, and a nasty, rotted orange. She said, 'make your painting reflect a mood.' Evidently she wasn't going for what I saw. Last week we did multi-media with mutant ceramic tuna, rubber octopuses and seaweed. The art room looked like an insane asylum fish market. Gave me nightmares."

"Does she wear her hair slicked back?"

"You know it."

On the horizon, clouds swirled and pulsed with internal light. Jackson watched them warily.

Gwynn put the painting back in the portfolio, then produced a notebook and pen. "I have an idea for your speech, but you have to answer some questions first."

"Shoot."

She made a mark on her notebook. "Good. Do you want to be funny, serious, or both."

"Both."

"Check."

"Are you giving the speech for your parents, your friends, the senior class or just yourself?"

Jackson wrinkled his brow. He hadn't considered that, plus, the chanting and roiling clouds distracted him. "I'm not sure."

"You'll have to decide."

On the school's other side, the murmur intensified. Jackson had heard the chants before, and seen bathroom graffiti featuring strange words, not in English, unpronounceable with too many consonants and lots of apostrophes. Jackson almost missed the casual racism and crude sex talk from elementary school. Yesterday, below a poorly rendered representation of what might have been a slaughtered sheep, or a dog drawn by Picasso, someone had written, **In his house at R'lyeh dead Cthulhu lies dreaming**. Underneath that, in a different hand, was a reply, **Wake him!**

"The acolytes are moving," said Gwynn. A crowd flowed around the school, heading toward them, arms in the air, repeating, "Iä Hastur cf'ayak'vulgtmm, vugt-lagln vulgtmm."

More emerged, hundreds of them, walking slowly, waving hands in the air. Jackson recognized some. Bud and Terrance from newspaper. Chuck who had played third base in junior high. Junior class president Lisa Schmaltz, her face filled with zeal, the bizarre words tumbling from her lips. Many were seniors he'd march with into the gym for graduation in a week, friends he'd known for years.

Gwynn said, "That's creepy."

"Have you seen the buttons?"

Jackson joined her. She stood. "Do you think they're literal, about sacrifice, I mean?"

Together, they started down the bleachers. Jackson said with a calm he didn't feel, "They've been eyeing me all day. I don't want to find out."

They broke into a run across the football field, away from the chanting students and didn't stop until they reached a low hill overlooking the school. The crowd filled the football field, arms still in the air, weaving back and forth, words now indistinct, but "Cthulhu R'lyeh" seemed a key component.

Jackson shivered, then moved closer to Gwynn. He was afraid to hold her hand again. Memory of the morning was too intense, but he felt safer next to her. The clouds darkened. A cutting wind swept through the trees behind them. Jackson heard it rushing through the leaves before it pressed against his back, cold and smelling of the Atlantic. On the field, the chanting rose in volume. Arms swayed, hands dancing like demented starfish. The students undulated in obscene synchronization. For a second, he was convinced that whatever monstrosity that missed them this morning was returning to finish the job, that if he looked up, a huge object would descend, a tentacled, leprous, oozing mass, the base of a huge trunk that disappeared into the clouds, a single leg of the creature whose head must reach into the stratosphere.

The image trembled in his mind as vivid as a prophetic vision.

Principal Akeley appeared at the crowd's edge carrying a megaphone, while the congregants looked to the clouds, ecstatically repeating whatever appeal they were making.

She brought the megaphone up, fumbled with it until it emitted a siren howl. The kids nearest to her looked her way.

"Students," she said. "Buses will not wait. If you miss your ride, you will have to walk home or call your parents."

Jackson imagined the acolytes falling upon her, their primitive lusts let loose and indulged, but the chant faltered. Arms fell to their sides, and they moved toward the school. A student tossed a Frisbee to another. Kids laughed. They hummed with lively chatter. Within a couple minutes, the field emptied.

"We survived," said Gwynn.

"Indeed."

Their hands moved toward each other, a mutual decision, and they touched. Nothing had changed from the morning. The connection remained. Jackson knew Gwynn and she knew him. No consummation could be more complete. They would be friends forever. More than friends.

And nothing in the future seemed bleak.

Jackson thought about the folder filled with quotes in his locker. For the first time, he imagined himself giving the speech, not what he would say, that was still a mystery, but he knew he wanted to speak of hope.

He said, "How does this sound: None of us knows our future, but we don't need to when we have each other."

Gwynn shivered. "Corny. Corny but true."

The clouds above the school folded upon themselves then flashed from internal lightning. A few seconds later, the rumble washed across them. Something incomprehensible moved above, but Jackson realized it always had. For all of time the universe had been indifferent to humanity.

We are on our own.

Graduating from high school, really graduating, meant finally realizing that truth.

ACKNOWLEDGEMENTS

M any people need to be thanked for a book that took thirty years to write. First and foremost, Patrick Swenson who published several of these stories in *Talebones*, and then believed in the worth of the rest enough to gather them in five collections, starting with *Strangers and Beggars* in 2002. His friendship and support have been irreplaceable. Thanks to every editor who has responded to my manuscripts, but particularly Shawna McCarthy, Honna Swenson, Stanley Schmidt, Gardner Dozois, John Joseph Adams, Ellen Datlow, Sheila Williams, Trevor Quachri, George Scithers, Darrell Schweitzer, Wendy S. Delmater, Jonathan Laden and Michele Barasso, Robert N. Stephenson, and Andy Cox.

Since most of my career balances on the back of the short story markets, I owe much to Ralan at Ralan.com and David Steffen at the Submission Grinder for keeping up-to-date information on the genre magazines.

In the years I've learned from numerous mentors who have been kind enough to talk about writing at length. Poets and teachers Eric "Reckless" Shaffer and Sara Backer tag teamed me at U.C. Davis, arguing convincingly that it all starts with poetry. Other powerful voices in my head came from James Patrick Kelly, Connie Willis (where is her book on writing!?), Charles Coleman Finlay, Cory Doctorow, Robert Sawyer, Kevin Anderson, John Pitts, Jay Lake, Kij Johnson, Daniel Abraham, Nancy Kress, Louise Marley, Susan Forest, Jim Hines, Ken Scholes, Joe Haldeman, Robert Silverberg, Bruce Holland Rogers, Brenda Cooper, and everyone else who said something at a writing panel or during a workshop that stuck in my head long after their name slipped away.

I've been blessed with insightful first readers who pointed out strengths and weaknesses in my work I couldn't find on my own. They provoked the "seeing again" that revision is all about. My wife

Tammy and sister Janet have read and responded to almost everything I've written. Writing groups have given the stories the kind of treatment I'd expect from thugs in a back alley, but in a good way. Of the many who have looked at my manuscripts, Carrie Vaughn (thank you also for role-modeling how a professional should behave), Brian Hiebert, Craig Jones, Mike Bateman, and Karen and Barry Fishler have done the most heavy lifting.

Most of all, I'd like to acknowledge the love and support from my immediate and extended family. They've never said, "Shouldn't you be doing lawn work?" when I've been writing, even when the weeds were clearly winning. Thank you Tammy, Dylan, Sam, Teague, Sharon, Janet, Ginger, Gary and Mike.

ABOUT THE AUTHOR

James Van Pelt, a high school English teacher, is also a full-time science fiction, fantasy and horror writer (among other things). His short stories have appeared in numerous magazines and anthologies, including *Asimov's*, *Analog*, *Talebones*, *Realms of Fantasy*, *Weird Tales* and others. His books include five short story collections and two novels.

He has been a Nebula finalist, a John W. Campbell Award finalist, and has been nominated for Pushcart prizes. His first collection was named a Best Book for Young Adults by the American Library Association, and his fourth collection won the Colorado Book Award. Many of his short stories have appeared in various Year's Best collections.

PUBLICATION HISTORY

"Parallel Highways" originally appeared in *After Shocks* (2000) | "Miss Hathaway's Spider" originally appeared in in *Talebones* (1998) | "Happy Ending" originally appeared in *Realms of Fantasy* (1998) | "Plant Life" originally appeared in *Aberrations* (1993) | "O Tannenbaum" originally appeared in *Weird Tales* (1998) | "Nor a Lender Be" originally appeared in *Analog* (1999) |"Shark Attack: a Love Story" originally appeared in *Weird Tales* (1999) | "The Diorama" originally appeared in *TransVersions* (1999) | "The Comeback" originally appeared in *Analog* (2000) | "Friday, After the Game" originally appeared in *Analog* (2000) | "The Safety of the Herd" originally appeared in *Asimov's* (2002) | "Savannah is Six" originally appeared in *Dark Terrors 5* (2000) | "Saturn Ring Blues" originally appeared in *On Spec* (2001); reprinted in *Best of the Rest 3: The Best Unknown SF and Fantasy of 2001* (2001) | "Once They Were Monarchs" originally appeared in *Alfred Hitchcock's Mystery Magazine* (2000) | "Origin of the Species" originally appeared in *Weird Tales* (2002); reprinted in *The Year's Best Fantasy 3*, David G. Hartwell, editor (2003) | "Night Sweats" originally appeared in *Realms of Fantasy* (2001) | "What Weena Knew" originally appeared in *Analog* (2001) | "The Infodict" originally appeared in *Asimov's* (2001) | "The Last Age Should Show Your Heart" originally appeared in *Bones of the World* (2001) | "Perceptual Set" originally appeared in *Analog* (2002) | "The Stars Underfoot" originally appeared in *Realms of Fantasy* (2001) | "The Yard God" originally appeared in *Talebones* (2001) | "The Last of the O-Forms" originally appeared in *Asimov's* (2002); reprinted in *The Nebula Award Showcase 2002*, Kim Stanley Robinson, editor (2005); reprinted in *Wastelands*, John Joseph Adams, editor (2008) | "Its Hour Come Round" originally appeared in *Talebones* (2002) | "The Sound of One Foot Dancing" originally appeared in *Alfred Hitchcock's Mystery Magazine* (2003) | "The Boy Behind the Gate" originally appeared in *Dark Terrors 6* (2002); reprinted in *The Mammoth Book of New Horror 16*, Stephen Jones, editor (2003) | "Do Good" originally appeared in *Polyphony*, Deborah Lane & Jay Lake, editors (2002) | "A Flock of Birds" originally appeared on *Scifi.com* (2002); reprinted in *The Year's Best Science Fiction, Twentieth Annual Collection*, Gardner Dozois, editor (2003) | "Notes From the Field" originally appeared in *3SF* (2002) | "The Long Way Home" originally appeared in *Asimov's* (2003); reprinted in *The Year's Best Science Fiction, Twenty-first Annual Collection*, Gardner Dozois, editor (2004) | "The Ice Cream Man" originally appeared in *Asimov's* (2005) | "Echoing" originally appeared in Asimov's (2004) | "The Miracle at Ramah" originally appeared in *Dragons, Knights and Angels: the Magazine of Christian Fantasy and Science Fiction* Selena Thomason, editor (2003); previously uncollected | "One Day, in the Middle of the Night" originally appeared in *Talebones* (2005) | "Where and When" originally appeared in *All-Star Zeppelin Adventure Stories*, David Moles & Jay Lake, editors (2004) | "A Wow Finish" originally appeared in *Amazing Stories* (2004) | "The Inn at Mount Either" originally appeared in *Analog* (2005); reprinted in *Year's Best: Science Fiction*, Rich Horton, editor (2006) | "The Small Astral Object Genius" originally appeared in *Asimov's* (2006); reprinted in *Trochu divne kusy 3*, Martin Šust, editor (2007) | "How Music Begins" originally appeared in *Asimov's* (2007); reprinted in *Year's Best SF 13*, David G. Hartwell and Kathryn Cramer, editors (2009) | "Rock House" originally appeared in *Talebones* (2008) | "Of Late I've Dreamt of Venus" originally appeared in *Visual Journeys*, Eric Reynolds, editor (2007); reprinted in *The Year's Best Science Fiction, Twenty-fifth Annual Collection*, Gardner Dozois, editor (2008) | "Just Before Recess" originally appeared in *Flash Fiction Online* (2008) | "The Radio Magician" originally appeared in *Realms of Fantasy* (2009) | "Where Did You Come From, Where Did You Go" originally appeared in *Cucurbital* as "Who Do You Think You Are?", Lawrence M. Schoen, editor (2009) | "Solace" originally appeared in *Analog* (2009); reprinted in *The Year's Best Science Fiction, Twenty-seventh Annual Collection*, Gardner Dozois, editor (2010); reprinted in *Clarkesworld*, Neil Clarke, editor (2015); previously uncollected | "Late Homework," originally appeared in *Daily Science Fiction* (2011); previously uncollected | "Classroom of the Living Dead" originally appeared in *Daily Science Fiction* (2011) | "Mrs. Hatcher's Evaluation" originally appeared in *Asimov's* (2012) |"The Hareton K-12 County School and Adult Extension" originally appeared in *Interzone* (2013); previously uncollected | "My Father and the Moon Maids from Mars" originally appeared in *Interzone* (2014); previously uncollected | "Aubrey Comes to Yellow High" originally appeared in *Orson Scott Card's Intergalactic Medicine Show* (2014); previously uncollected | "Everything's Unlikely" originally appeared in *Daily Science Fiction* (2015); previously uncollected | "On the Road with the American Dead" originally appeared in *Black Static* (2015); previously uncollected | "The Lies" originally appeared in *Daily Science Fiction* (2016) | "The Continuing Saga of Tom Corbett: Space Cadet" originally appeared in *Analog* (2016) | "The Lawn Fairy War" originally appeared in *Metaphysical Circus: Love and War in the Slipstream* (2016) | "The Silk Silvered Skulls of Millen Mir" originally appeared in *Triangulation: Beneath the Surface*, Jamie Lackey, editor (2016) | "Mars, Aphids and Your Cheating Heart" originally appeared in *Interzone* (2016) | "Orphaned" originally appeared in *Orson Scott Card's Intergalactic Medicine Show* (2016) | "Mother Azalea's Sad Home for Forgotten Adults" originally appeared in *The Sum of Us*, Susan Forest & Lucas K. Law, editors (2017); previously uncollected | "Pirate Readers" originally appeared in *Deep Magic* (2017); previously uncollected | "Graduation in the Time of Yog Sothoth" originally appeared in *Diabolical Plots*, David Steffen, editor (2018); previously uncollected

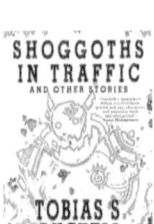